PBK

D1330115

CECILIA VALDÉS

CECILIA VALDÉS

OR

EL ANGEL HILL

CIRILO VILLAVERDE

Translated from the Spanish by
HELEN LANE

EDITED WITH AN INTRODUCTION AND NOTES
BY SIBYLLE FISCHER

OXFORD
UNIVERSITY PRESS
2005

OXFORD
UNIVERSITY PRESS

Oxford University Press, Inc., publishes works
that further Oxford University's objective of excellence
in research, scholarship, and education.

Oxford   New York
Auckland   Cape Town   Dar es Salaam   Hong Kong   Karachi
Kuala Lumpur   Madrid   Melbourne   Mexico City   Nairobi
New Delhi   Shanghai   Taipei   Toronto

With offices in
Argentina   Austria   Brazil   Chile   Czech Republic   France   Greece
Guatemala   Hungary   Italy   Japan   Poland   Portugal   Singapore
South Korea   Switzerland   Thailand   Turkey   Ukraine   Vietnam

Copyright © 2005 by Oxford University Press, Inc.

Published by Oxford University Press, Inc.
198 Madison Avenue, New York, New York 10016
www.oup.com

Oxford is a registered trademark of Oxford University Press

Library of Congress Cataloging-in-Publication Data
Villaverde, Cirilo, 1812–1894.
   [Cecilia Valdés. English]
   Cecilia Valdés or El Angel Hill / by Cirilo Villaverde;
translated from the Spanish by Helen Lane;
edited with an introduction and notes by Sibylle Fischer.
      p. cm.—(Library of Latin America)
Includes bibliographical references.

ISBN–13: 987-0-19-514394-2 (cl)
ISBN–10: 0-19-514394-9 (cl)
ISBN–13: 978-0-19-514395-9 (pbk)
ISBN–10: 0-19-514395-7 (pbk)

I. Brouwers-Fischer, Sibylle. II. Title. III. Series.
PQ7389.V55C413 2004   863'.5—dc22   2003058232

9 8 7 6 5 4 3 2 1

Printed in the United States of America
on acid-free paper

Contents

Series Editors' General Introduction
vii

Introduction
xi

About This Translation
xxxi

Cecilia Valdés
xxxiii

Dedication
xxxv

Prologue
xxxvii

Notes
493

Bibliography
499

Series Editors' General Introduction

The Library of Latin America series makes available in translation major nineteenth-century authors whose work has been neglected in the English-speaking world. The titles for the translations from the Spanish and Portuguese were suggested by an editorial committee that included Jean Franco (general editor responsible for works in Spanish), Richard Graham (series editor responsible for works in Portuguese), Tulio Halperín Donghi (at the University of California, Berkeley), Iván Jaksić (at the University of Notre Dame), Naomi Lindstrom (at the University of Texas at Austin), Francine Masiello (at the University of California, Berkeley), and Eduardo Lozano of the Library at the University of Pittsburgh. The late Antonio Cornejo Polar of the University of California, Berkeley, was also one of the founding members of the committee. The translations have been funded thanks to the generosity of the Lampadia Foundation and the Andrew W. Mellon Foundation.

During the period of national formation between 1810 and into the early years of the twentieth century, the new nations of Latin America fashioned their identities, drew up constitutions, engaged in bitter struggles over territory, and debated questions of education, government, ethnicity, and culture. This was a unique period unlike the process of nation formation in Europe and one which should be more familiar than it is to students of comparative politics, history, and literature.

The image of the nation, was envisioned by the lettered classes—a minority in countries in which indigenous, mestizo, black or mulatto peasants and slaves predominated—although there were also alternative nationalisms at the grassroots level. The cultural elite were well educated in European thought and letters, but as statesmen, journalists, poets, and academics, they confronted the problem of the racial and linguistic heterogeneity of the continent and the difficulties of integrating the population into a modern nation-state. Some of the writers whose works will be translated in the Library of Latin America series played leading roles in politics. Fray Servando Teresa de Mier, a friar who translated Rousseau's *The Social Contract* and was one of the most colorful characters of the independence period, was faced with imprisonment and expulsion from Mexico for his heterodox beliefs; on his return, after independence, he was elected to the congress. Domingo Faustino Sarmiento, exiled from his native Argentina under the dictatorship of Rosas, wrote *Facundo: Civilización y barbarie*, a stinging denunciation of that government. He returned after Rosas' overthrow and was elected president in 1868. Andrés Bello was born in Venezuela, lived in London where he published poetry during the independence period, settled in Chile where he founded the University, wrote his grammar of the Spanish language, and drew up the country's legal code.

These post-independence intelligentsia were not simply dreaming castles in the air, but vitally contributed to the founding of nations and the shaping of culture. The advantage of hindsight may make us aware of problems they themselves did not foresee, but this should not affect our assessment of their truly astonishing energies and achievements. Although there is a recent translation of Sarmiento's celebrated *Facundo*, there is no translation of his memoirs, *Recuerdos de provincia* (*Provincial Recollections*). The predominance of memoirs in the Library of Latin America Series is no accident—many of these offer entertaining insights into a vast and complex continent.

Nor have we neglected the novel. The Series includes new translations of the outstanding Brazilian writer Machado de Assis' work, including *Dom Casmurro* and *The Posthumous Memoirs of Brás Cubas*. There is no reason why other novels and writers who are not so well known outside Latin America—the Peruvian novelist Clorinda Matto de Turner's *Aves sin nido*, Nataniel Aguirre's *Juan de la Rosa*, José de Alencar's *Iracema*, Juana Manuela Gorriti's short stories—should not be read with as much interest as the political novels of Anthony Trollope.

A series on nineteenth-century Latin America cannot, however, be limited to literary genres such as the novel, the poem, and the short story. The literature of independent Latin America was eclectic and strongly influenced by the periodical press newly liberated from scrutiny by colonial authorities and the Inquisition. Newspapers were miscellanies of fiction, essays, poems, and translations from all manner of European writing. The novels written on the eve of Mexican Independence by José Joaquín Fernández de Lizardi, included disquisitions on secular education and law, and denunciations of the evils of gaming and idleness. Other works, such as a well-known poem by Andrés Bello, "Ode to Tropical Agriculture," and novels such as *Amalia* by José Mórmol and the Bolivian Nataniel Aguirre's *Juan de la Rosa*, were openly partisan. By the end of the century, sophisticated scholars were beginning to address the history of their countries, as did João Capistrano de Abreu in his *Capítulos de história colonial*.

It is often in memoirs such as those by Fray Servando Teresa de Mier or Sarmiento that we find the descriptions of everyday life that in Europe were incorporated into the realist novel. Latin American literature at this time was seen largely as a pedagogical tool, a "light" alternative to speeches, sermons, and philosophical tracts—though, in fact, especially in the early part of the century, even the readership for novels was quite small because of the high rate of illiteracy. Nevertheless the vigorous orally transmitted culture of the gaucho and the urban underclasses became the linguistic repertoire of some of the most interesting nineteenth-century writers—most notably José Hernández, author of the "gauchesque" poem "Martin Fierrio," which enjoyed an unparalleled popularity. But for many writers the task was not to appropriate popular language but to civilize, and their literary works were strongly influenced by the high style of political oratory.

The editorial committee has not attempted to limit its selection to the better-known writers such as Machado de Assis; it has also selected many works that have never appeared in translation or writers whose works have not been translated recently. The Series now makes these works available to the English-speaking public.

Because of the preferences of funding organizations, the series initially focuses on writing from Brazil, the Southern Cone, the Andean region, and Mexico. Each of our editions will have an introduction that places the work in its appropriate context and includes explanatory notes.

We owe special thanks to the late Robert Glynn of the Lampadia Foundation, whose initiative gave the project a jump-start, and to Richard Ekman and his successors at the Andrew W. Mellon Foundation, which also generously supported the project. We also thank the Rockefeller Foundation for funding the 1996 symposium, "Culture and Nation in Iberoamerica," organized by the editorial board of the Library of Latin America. The support of Edward Barry of Oxford University Press was crucial in the founding years of the project, as has been the advice and help of Ellen Chodosh and Elda Rotor of Oxford University Press. The John Carter Brown Library at Brown University in Providence, Rhode Island, has been serving since 1998 as the grant administrator of the project.

—Jean Franco
—Richard Graham

Introduction

Cecilia Valdés is the most important novel of nineteenth-century Cuba. It is a story of masters, slaves, and free people of color, of sugar plantations, torture, adultery, incest, contempt born out of racial prejudice, and murderous revenge: a vast canvas of life in a slaveholding colony, at times horrifying, at times quaint, but extraordinary nevertheless, and without equal in nineteenth-century Spanish American literature.

Written between 1839 and 1882 by the exiled Cuban writer and political activist Cirilo Villaverde (1812–1894) and published in New York in 1882, *Cecilia Valdés* soon achieved mythical status. It was celebrated, attacked and rewritten by other novelists, set to music, and, eventually, adapted for the screen.[1] The *mulata* herself became a national icon and an improbable Cuban patron saint of sorts. Asking himself why Cecilia Valdés acquired the status of a national myth, César Leante, one of Cuba's important twentieth-century writers, states that it is because "Cecilia Valdés *is* the Cuban nation": "because Villaverde's protagonist symbolizes, in her flesh and her spirit, the racial and cultural combination that determines the Cuban being."[2]

Certainly, the novel's fame is not based on the kind of linguistic lucidity and high literary sophistication we find in some of the twentieth-century texts by Cuban writers like José Lezama Lima, Alejo Carpentier, Virgilio Piñera, or Guillermo Cabrera Infante. Cuban literature was in its beginnings when Villaverde started to develop the Cecilia material in

the late 1830s. The constant meddling of the Spanish censor placed severe constraints on all writerly ambitions and publication possibilities,
and there were few examples a young author could draw on. So perhaps
it is not surprising that when Villaverde returned to the topic more than
40 years after writing the first sketches, the text ended up a little un-
wieldy. There are digressions into legal and political history, some of the
characters seem to lack consistency, and, most unsettling of all, the novel
appears to treat as a mystery a fact that most readers would have guessed
very quickly: Cecilia's supposedly unknown father is the Spanish plantation owner and slave trader Cándido Gamboa, which makes her love affair with Leonardo Gamboa incestuous.

But perhaps these complaints are beside the point, and not just because the institutional weakness of literature in nineteenth-century
Cuba would excuse certain artistic shortcomings. After all, would we expect the kind of finely articulated portrait of social totality which, according to some literary scholars, is the hallmark of the nineteenth-
century realist novel, when the protagonists live in different worlds,
separated by the abyss of color and status? Aren't we already beyond the
domain of all conceivable realisms when some fictional characters have
as much control over the lives of others as a writer has over her creations?

Cecilia Valdés has the texture of a story woven together from different
materials, affects, and aspirations. There is the representation of social
realities that most critics have praised and the melodrama most critics
dismiss; an antislavery plot, which some readers endorse but others find
wanting; less contentiously, the anticolonial sentiment; and, finally, the
nostalgia that came with the distance of exile and the forgetfulness of 40
years spent in New York City.

How should we read this unique, fascinating, contradictory novel?[3] Is
it really an antislavery novel or is it caught within the narrow limits of the
Cuban antislavery movement of the 1830s and 1840s that never went beyond the call for an end to the slave trade (but did at times include the demand for "repatriation" of the people of African descent)? Does it inau-
gurate the idea of "la Cuba mulata," the idea of a Cuban national identity
grounded in miscegenation, or does it, on the contrary, offer new justifi-
cations for racial hierarchies?[4] After all, Cuba was the last territory in the
Caribbean to outlaw slavery, in 1886, and, for reasons not unrelated to the
issue of slavery, did not gain independence until 1902. Whichever way we
might end up answering these questions, Villaverde's painstaking dissec-
tion of a society that was produced by colonialism and slavery is an invaluable inquiry into questions that provoke controversies to this day:

What constitutes Cuban national culture? How do Cuba's European and African heritage relate? What would it take for a nation that took shape under colonialism and slavery to become free? Now as then, color, social status, political persuasion, and even location—Havana, Miami, New York—inflect and complicate any possible answer to these questions.

A Story Being Written

Cirilo Villaverde wrote the first version of the Cecilia story in 1839, when he was 27 years old and had abandoned his legal career for that of a journalist, writer, and teacher. He had spent his childhood on a sugar plantation in the Western province of Pinar del Río, where his father was a physician. Eventually he moved to Havana, where he received his education in the foremost institutions of the time. Despite the growing sense of crisis in the 1830s—or perhaps because of it—there was a brief flourishing of literary activities. Journals like *La Moda o Recreo Semanal del Bello Sexo* (1829 to 1831) and the *Revista Bimestre Cubana* (1831 to 1834) became venues for articles about cultural and educational issues. There was an attempt to create a Cuban Academy of Literature, spearheaded by Domingo del Monte, one of the most influential Creole intellectuals. When that project failed because of conflicts between the planters and the cultural elite, del Monte moved his literary activities into a more private setting. From 1835 on, the liberal Creole elite met in del Monte's home in Havana where they read their manuscripts and talked about the challenges facing the colony. It was for this audience that Juan Francisco Manzano wrote his *Autobiography of a Slave*, the only Spanish American slave narrative known to this day; and it was here, too, that Villaverde presented his first brief stories.[5]

There can be no doubt that the problems these reform-minded Cuban Creoles contemplated were considerable and in many ways different from those of their counterparts on the Spanish American mainland. The Spanish colonies on the mainland had gained independence in the early nineteenth century, but Spain made it very clear that it was not willing to give up on Cuba. After the collapse of the sugar economy in the former French colony of Saint Domingue and the establishment of the independent black state of Haiti on the island of Hispaniola in 1804, Cuba had become the most important sugar producer in the Caribbean. Although in 1817 Spain had signed a treaty with England that banned the slave trade, more slaves than ever before were brought to Cuba. Within the ten years of the signing of the treaty the slave population increased from 199,000 to 287,000. By 1846, there were 324,000 slaves and 149,000 free people of color on the island (36% and 17% of the total population, respectively), and the slave population (as well as the free population of color) continued to grow into the second half of the nineteenth century.[6] There had been a few separatist conspiracies in Cuba, but none had had much success, in part because the planters and slave owners felt that the Spanish military presence in Cuba was a much needed protection against slave insurgency. With Haiti serving as a reminder of the dangers of racial warfare and the very real possibility of revolutionary antislavery, an alliance between white Cubans and people of color was unthinkable in the first half of the nineteenth century—and without it, Cuban independence remained elusive.

At first sight, the "primitive" version of the Cecilia material of 1839, titled simply "Cecilia Valdés" and published in two parts in the Cuban magazine *La Siempreviva* (not included in this edition) shows no traces of this situation. Barely 25 pages long, it is the story of a *mulata* whom the narrator claims to have known in 1826 or 1827, when she was only ten and freely roamed the streets of Havana. As she grows up, Cecilia is seduced by the promise of a life of privilege from a morally corrupt white man named Leocadio Gamboa. The story ends with Cecilia having vanished from sight, thus fullfilling, in a manner of speaking, her grandmother's cautionary tale according to which girls that run about too much fall prey to the devil. More folk tale or genre picture than social critique, the story does not mention slavery and reserves its moralizing digressions largely for an attack on sexual licentiousness.

Later that same year, upon request of a friend, Villaverde developed the Cecilia material into a lengthy text of more than two hundred pages. Like the "primitive" "Cecilia Valdés," the novelistic treatment of 1839, now with the subtitle "La Loma del Angel" ("El Angel Hill" in our translation), does not have any obvious connection to the issue of slavery. Although it is marked as Volume One of a more extensive novel, no further chapters appear after 1839.

While Villaverde put the Cecilia story aside to pursue numerous other writing projects, he also became involved in the anti-Spanish activities of General Narciso López, whose goal was the annexation of Cuba to the United States. In 1848, the so-called Conspiracy de la Rosa Cubana was uncovered and Villaverde was sentenced to prison. In 1849 he managed to escape and eventually settled in New York, where he continued to pursue the goal of Cuban liberation from Spanish rule, first in support of further annexationist plans, and later in support of Cuban independence.

Villaverde's return to the Cecilia story in 1879, forty years after he first invented the character of the *mulata*, must have been at least in part prompted by the end of the first war of independence, the so-called Ten-Year War (1868–1878), which brought about neither the abolition of the institution of slavery nor independence. To be sure, Spain offered Cuba representation in the *Cortes*, the slave trade finally stopped (the last known slave ship arrived in 1873), and the promise of (variously limited) measures of emancipation became a bargaining tool for both the insurgents and the Spanish authorities in their rush to build up their armies by enlisting free people of color and slaves. But when part of the leadership of the insurgents decided to put down arms and accept a compromise, the more radical Cuban forces, among them many blacks and mulattoes, launched what came to be known as the Guerra Chiquita, the Little War (1879–1880). The fragile alliance between white and non-white Cuban Creoles had broken down again. Clearly, things had changed, but not quite enough. Cuba was not to gain independence for another 20 years.

Writing between 1879 and 1882, Villaverde's frustration is palpable on the pages of the novel. In a departure from the original chronology of the 1839 story, he dates Cecilia's birth back to 1812, a choice clearly intended to signal the personal and historical significance of the Cecilia story. For one thing, it means that the *mulata* not only shares the initials of Villaverde's name, but also his date of birth. The year 1812 also marks an important date in Cuba's political history. It was the beginning of a brief constitutional period—which would link Cecilia to the history of colonial despotism in Cuba—and, most important, the year of the Aponte conspiracy, the most extensive and well-planned slave uprising in Cuban history.[7] For white Creoles, 1812 signified the nightmare of a slave revolution—the possibility that Cuba could turn into another Haiti where the former slaves had successfully waged war against the French colonial regime. Villaverde was by no means the only intellectual for whom 1812 was añ ominous reminder of what could happen to Cubans if they were not vigilant. Almost a hundred years later, on the eve of the declaration of the Cuban Republic, the events of the 1812 conspiracy are called up again by Francisco Calcagno, who had briefly collaborated with Villaverde in the 1850s and was certainly no advocate of slavery. His historical novel *Aponte* opens with a gory depiction of the leader's severed head, surrounded by flies and an unbearable stench: a barbaric monster with "a soul as black as his face" and savagely sharpened crocodile-teeth who had modeled himself on the Haitian generals

Dessalines and Christophe.[8] We find no more than a passing reference to radical antislavery in *Cecilia Valdés*, but no doubt 1812 casts a long shadow over the events of the novel.

The bulk of the novel takes place in 1830 and 1831, when Cecilia would have been about 18 years old, precisely the time, too, when Cuban literary life was beginning to flourish and the racial composition of the island had become a major topic of conversation among the liberal elite. *Cecilia Valdés* portrays these elite circles as well as the life of plantation slaves, but most interesting, perhaps, the novel tells us about the emerging culture of the free people of color, the class Cecilia herself belonged to.[9]

Along with the slave population, the class of free people of color had been growing at a rapid rate in the 1820s and 1830s. An economically successful petty bourgeoisie with considerable social ambitions had come into being, and probably for that very reason was submitted to increasingly rigid laws and regulations. A report by the governor of the Eastern province of Oriente on the issue of allowing marriages between people of different color in 1855, for example, argues as follows:

> There is little doubt that the dissemination of ideas of equality of the white class with the coloured race puts in jeopardy the tranquility of the Island. . . . ; it is no less true that by authorizing marriages between one and the other [race] the links of subordination of the coloured people to the white will tend to be subverted and weakened, and . . . the day would come when those encouraged by the example of unequal marriages which favour them, will aspire impetuously to acheive a rank which society denies them and as a consequence public order would be upset; it is therefore the Government's duty to prevent such a situation at all cost.[10]

Interracial marriages were not made legal in Cuba until 1881.

White Creoles were also increasingly alarmed by the fact that the free people of color were beginning to dominate certain sectors of Cuban culture. In his prize-winning "Memorandum about Idleness in Cuba" (1831), José Antonio Saco includes a section with the title: "The Arts Are in the Hands of the People of Color."

> Among the enormous evils that this [i.e. African] race has brought to our land, is that they have alienated our white population from the arts . . . [A]ll of them became the exclusive patrimony of the people of color, leaving for the whites the literary career and two or three others that were taken to be honorable . . . In this deplorable situation, no white Cuban could be expected to devote himself to the arts, because the mere fact of

embracing them was taken to mean that he renounced the privileges of his class.[11]

According to other contemporary witnesses there were people of color with "abundant wealth," who owned slaves and "who in their lifestyle, in their dress, and in their speech imitated those white gentlemen who still remained in Cuba, and among them [there was] no lack of people fond of reading serious books and even making verse."[12] Villaverde gave some of the well-known free persons of color walk-on roles in his novel: there are Claudio Brindis de Salas and Ulpiano Estrada, both of them musicians; the military official Tondá; the fashionable tailor Francisco Uribe, who apparently owned two houses and twelve slaves at the time of his death in 1844; the musician Tomás Vuelta y Flores who left behind a minor fortune; and, of course, the popular poet Gabriel de la Concepción Valdés, *alias* Plácido.

By the time Villaverde fled Cuba in 1849, the culture of the free people of color had been violently destroyed. In 1844, the Spanish authorities claimed to have uncovered a vast conspiracy of slaves and free people of color which, according to the authorities, had the goal "to exterminate all whites, and to become masters of the Island and to claim it for themselves with the help and protection of foreign powers," that is, Haiti and England.[13] The musician Brindis de Salas had been forced into exile, the tailor Uribe had committed suicide in prison, and the poet Plácido, accused of being one of the leaders, had been executed by firing squad.

Until quite recently, there was a consensus among historians that the Escalera conspiracy was a fabrication of the colonial authorities.[14] The violence in the aftermath of the supposed discovery was such that 1844 became known as "el año del cuero" [the year of the whip] in Cuban history. The class of free people of color lost its intellectual leadership and the white liberal elite suffered severe set-backs. Based on Plácido's testimony, in particular, charges were brought against Domingo del Monte and another leading intellectual figure, José de la Luz y Caballero. Both were ultimately acquitted, but the colonial slaveholding regime had fortified itself for decades to come.

Like many of his contemporaries, Villaverde thought of the so-called Escalera Conspiracy (Conspiracy of the Ladder)—named after the method of torture the authorities preferred for interrogation and punishment—as a catastrophe in Cuban history. Like the Aponte Conspiracy of 1812, the year 1844 is present in the novel as a mere shadow, a faint melancholy veil cast over the story of a culture and a set of characters that had vanished. *Cecilia Valdés* ends, ominously, in 1831 (or possibly 1832[15]), with Leonardo's death at the hands of José Dolores Pimienta, a mulatto musician. In history, it happened the other way around: 1844 was a preventive strike against the likes of Pimienta. *Cecilia Valdés* is thus a testimony to a culture that had been almost destroyed by the onslaught of colonial violence when Villaverde returned to his manuscript. But it is also a melancholy reflection of the political fears and racial anxieties of those liberal Creoles who proved unable to rid Cuba of the colonial regime and racial slavery.

Slavery, Incest, Miscegenation

In the preface to his novel, Villaverde gives the reader some fairly strong directions: *Cecilia Valdés* is, he says, a novel that aspires to realism, not a romance—Cuban reality in the 1830s simply did not allow for anything else. So we would expect an unflinching portrait of colonial despotism and the brutality of slavery, and of course, that is, in part, what we get. But what are we to make of the melodramatic aspects of the story? What moved Villaverde to place incest at the center of the novel? And having done so, why did he undercut any possible suspense by making the mystery so obvious?

As early as 1891, the mulatto writer Martín Morúa Delgado, himself the son of a black slave woman and a white father, mounted an attack against Villaverde. Far from counting *Cecilia Valdés* as an antislavery novel, Morúa Delgado saw it as a retrograde text that ultimately justifies the racial hierarchies of a bygone era.[16] He insists that because of his failure to transcend the ideological limitations of the time, Villaverde was unable to give a realistic portrait of Cuba under slavery. Why, he asks, does Cecilia generate so much racial anxiety, while no one asks any questions about Leonardo's sister Adela, who bears such a close resemblance to Cecilia that people repeatedly mistake one for the other?[17] And the plot, he says, just does not make sense: everybody around Cecilia and Leonardo knew they were siblings and would have told them so. For Morúa Delgado, the improbable romance and incest story combines with Villaverde's lingering racial prejudice in a way that irredeemably distorts the portrait of slavery and racial subordination in colonial Cuba.

Acknowledging the questions raised by *Cecilia Valdés*'s plot, Doris Sommer has recently proposed a very different, and rather more favorable, reading. She relates the incest theme and the odd handling of the mystery to racially determined differentials of power and knowledge that produce fatal discontinuities: whites will not listen to blacks, and blacks are fearful of sharing their knowledge with whites. For Sommer, "the most pointed political effort" in the novel has to do with the stuttering and stammering of the narrator who pretends to guard a secret that is a secret only for those who won't listen to slaves, and thereby frames the reader, so that we become in a sense complicit in a racially inflected practice of interpretation.[18]

But even if we agree with Sommer that what appears to be a plot problem may well be an ingenious meta-narrative device that signals the conditions and constraints of communication in a society that practices racial slavery, can we really disregard what the mystery is about: incest and miscegenation?[19] Traditionally, of course, critics have dismissed the incest theme as purely conventional: the 1839 story "Cecilia Valdés" was, like most longer narratives at the time, written to be read in installments; unsurprisingly, these so-called *folletines* tended to be somewhat sensationalist and incest was one of the more lurid topics available.[20] Nevertheless, it is striking that the issue of incest turns up with such frequency in the Cuban antislavery narratives.[21] In Félix Tanco y Bosmiel's story, titled "Petrona y Rosalía" (written in 1838 but not published until 1925), the master's son Ricardo coerces the slave girl Rosalía into having sex with him. The incest theme is introduced when it becomes clear that Rosalía is a daughter of Ricardo's father, and then is resolved by an undeveloped secondary plot, when it is revealed that Ricardo, too, is the product of an adulterous affair and not his father's biological son after all. Incest avoided, by a hair's breadth. Anselmo Suárez y Romero's brief novel *Francisco* (written in the 1830s, published posthumously in 1880) does not invoke incest in the strict sense but insists that the master's son and the slave girl Dorotea, whom he forces into a sexual relationship, were *hermanos de leche* (literally "milk siblings," i.e., suckled by the same wet-nurse). The son's actions are criminal not just because of their brutality but also because he is practically Dorotea's brother. Even Gertudis Gómez de Avellaneda's novel *Sab* (1841), which was written in Spain and has a very different plot from the narratives mentioned so far, suggests the possibility that the secret love the title hero, a mulatto slave, harbors for his mistress Carlota might be more familial than any of the characters would like to admit. Sab's mother never revealed to him who his father was; the novel leaves little doubt, however, that it was Carlota's uncle, which would make Carlota and Sab first cousins.

In this context, Villaverde's use of the incest theme becomes very interesting indeed. Contrary to what most critics say, the 1839 story already hinted at incest.[22] This may mean that the early versions already have links to the issues of slavery and racial hierarchies, albeit less obvious ones than the 1882 novel with its horrifying descriptions of conditions on the Cuban sugar plantations. Or we could argue the other way around: the fact that the 1882 novel has such a strong antislavery theme but is based on an incest story that has no obvious antislavery theme shows that there is very likely some sort of internal connection between the two themes. Either way, the presence of incest in the 1839 story could help to explain the most odd aspect of the 1882 plot: adding vast amounts of material to the story effectively meant that the secret of Cecilia's origins had to be transformed from a mere insinuation with largely allegorical or figurative significance into a major plot line. The fact that Villaverde held on to the idea, despite the significant technical challenge it posed, is further evidence that the themes of incest and of racial hierarchies and slavery must have had some peculiar affinity for Cuban writers at the time.[23]

One of the few readers of *Cecilia Valdés* to have grasped the centrality of the incestuous melodrama is the director Humberto Solás. His film *Cecilia* (1981) opens with Cecilia's grandmother telling a story about the goddess Oshun, which segues into a gothic scene, acted and shot in the dark, melodramatic style Solás had developed in his masterpiece *Lucía* (1968). This second scene is based on the tale Cecilia's grandmother tells to steer her away from Leonardo, who was already showing a devious interest in the little girl, and is at first sight not part of the main narrative.[24] But of course, there is a link: it is about evil desire, a desire that can never escape its incestuous origins. In the film, a very pale young man, draped in black cloth (played by the same actor who later represents Leonardo), beckons a little girl—presumably Cecilia—to come along with him and leads her up the tower of a mission church. The girl follows him freely at first but then panics and tries to escape by running further and further up the tower. The sequence ends, much in the manner of Hitchcock's *Vertigo*, with Cecilia in free fall from the top platform into the church yard below.[25] The main story of Solás's film, by contrast, is mostly presented like a conventional period drama. Unlike most literary critics, Solás seems to say that we get to the real story only if we go through the melodrama, not by subtracting it. On this account nothing could be more misguided than the tendency among critics to divide the novel into a (praiseworthy) realist novel, which deals with slavery, racial subordination, and colonialism, and a trashy melodrama, which deals with murder, incest, and sexual desire.

But the question still remains: What moved Villaverde and his fellow writers in the 1830s to invoke incest when their immediate concern was slavery? What *is* the connection between incest, slavery, and miscegenation? The juxtaposition of themes is after all surprising: in a society that practices racial slavery, miscegenation would presumably be linked to fears of a difference perceived as too important or too great, as opposed to incest, which would naturally be linked to fears about excessive closeness.

In an amply documented study of the theme of miscegenation and incest in the literature of the Americas, Werner Sollors has argued that the linkage of the two can serve a variety of ideological positions. Liberal authors—and Villaverde as well as the other writers mentioned would almost certainly fall into that category—linked incest and miscegenation through what Sollors calls a "realistic argument": when kinship between people of different color is denied as a matter of course, miscegenation can easily turn out to be incest.[26] The implication is that the liberal antislavery narratives view incest unequivocally as evil. We are invited to read the liberal authors as embracing the view that the incest taboo is the most universal and most rigorously enforced rule of human society and indeed what separates humans from animals. In this vision, incest signals sexual desire unbridled by societal laws and leads to a regression and brutalization of the human being. The mere hint at the possibility of incest serves, we are supposed to believe, as a condemnation of slavery.[27]

The problem with this interpretation is that it does not quite fit *Cecilia Valdés* or any of the other Cuban narratives that suggest incest. To be sure, incest is usually invoked as an act that is sinful over and above the debasement implied in involuntary or dishonest sexual relations. But nowhere does incest appear as that most horrific of all possibilities. The incest in question is not that between parents and offspring, but is of a slightly more distant sort—between half-siblings: nowhere do we find an Oedipus figure, roaming his former domain as a blind beggar and vagrant. True horror is reserved for the depiction of the mistreatment of slaves. The birth of Cecilia's incestuously conceived daughter, by contrast, is very much underplayed and not accompanied by any sense of doom or catastrophe. In many of the Cuban stories, incest has an almost fantasmagoric character, like a mere thought, which is neither asserted nor denied. Whether incest actually occurs (in the story *or* in reality) seems less significant than the fact of its overwhelming rhetorical, fantasmagoric "presence."

It is important to remember, too, that the prohibition on incest is by no means a straight-forward matter. If we believe Freud, all desire is in its origins narcissistic, that is, a desire for sameness. There would be no need for an incest taboo if incest were not unconsciously desired. And it is not the case, either, that in Western culture incestuous desires have invariably been linked to individual or familial pathologies: within the romantic revolutionary culture of the eighteenth century, for example, sibling incest often had a vaguely positive valence, possibly on the grounds that universal fraternity would lead to universal endogamy.[28] It is perhaps the Marquis de Sade who takes this argument to its most literal extreme. After listing examples from around the globe to the effect that an incestuous act tends to be at the mythical foundation of cultures, he says: "I would venture, in a word, that incest ought to be every government's law—every government whose basis is fraternity. . . . Is it not an abominable view wherein it is made to appear a crime for a man to place higher value upon the enjoyment of an object to which natural feeling draws him close?"[29] Here incest is defended on two accounts, one political and one naturalistic. First, pervasive incest is the logical consequence of de Sade's vision of fraternity, according to which true brotherhood entails the abolition of all exclusivist sexual rights and the guarantee of equal access of all men to all women (de Sade's egalitarianism apparently does not go so far as to include an inversion of this demand for equal access). Second, incest is based on the most natural attraction.

Although Villaverde and later critics of *Cecilia Valdés* certainly do not point to de Sade as their witness, there are striking echoes. For César Leante, who embraces the ideal of "la Cuba mulata," for instance, the attraction between Cecilia and Leonardo is a natural expression of the equality of the races and is thus foundational for the Cuban nation.[30] And a closer look at Villaverde's novel itself shows that the narrator vacillates between treating incest as a horrific possibility looming on the horizon and extending a rather more indulgent view. On the one hand, it is difficult not to notice that relations among the Gamboas—particularly Doña Rosa's exalted love for her son—are highly oedipal and presented to us in a decidedly critical light. And the private aspects of the infraction are compounded by political ones: incest comes about when Creole sons repeat the abusive and exploitative deeds of the Spanish fathers. We are given plenty of reasons to think that incest is an abominable sin. And yet, on the other hand, the affection between Leonardo and his sister Adela is treated as a rather endearing fact: if Leonardo and Adela had not been brother and sister by birth, the narrator says, "they would have loved each other as did the most celebrated lovers that the world has ever known" (94). So it is perfectly clear that Leonardo desires

Cecilia precisely as a representative of his sister. The fact that Cecilia turns out to *be* his sister is simply the ultimate fulfilment of his incestuous desire—but that fact does not seem to worry the narrator.

It appears, then, that on the one hand, the incest theme has a (weakly) positive valence, rooted in familial indulgence, mutual sympathy, and ideas of equality; on the other hand, it is invoked as a sign of the moral debasement of Cuban society. I suspect that it was precisely this constitutive ambiguity that made the incest theme attractive for the Cuban authors and readers of antislavery texts. In the idea of incest desire and horror are most intimately and inextricably connected. The implicit, perhaps unconscious, oscillations between incest conceived as the most natural and the most unnatural desire, as that desire which is shared by all humans and that which separates humans from animals, is what makes incest narratives such an apt vehicle for expressing universalist aspirations *and* fears about racial difference and miscegenation.

One way of looking at this affective ambiguity is simply to read it as the literary expression of deep-seated psychological conflicts surrounding differences of race or color. But we should not forget that there is a strand in the complex theme of incestuous desire that is linked to one of the central political and ideological conflicts at the time: the conflict over equality and its meaning. In a logically illegitimate, but emotionally plausible leap, the incest fantasy produces a thought of the form "if they are just like us, then sexual relations are incestuous." What under racial slavery would be the greatest difference, namely, the difference of color or race, thus turns into a troubling—and potentially excessive—closeness.

The incest story could be read then as offering a fictional scenario in which the only real alternative to the colonial slaveholding system—racial equality—remains veiled through narratives that refer us back to the horror and desire forever attached to the idea of incest. They offer a fantasy that allows the reader to deplore the abuses of a slaveholding society while eluding the necessity of recognizing the Other as an autonomous, independently constituted subject.[31] As soon as the idea of equality suggests itself, it turns into a possibly transgressive sameness. The thought that has been avoided is one that would postulate equality without requiring sameness, and which we encounter, significantly, in the Preamble to the revolutionary Constitution of 1805 of neighboring Haiti: "In the presence of the Supreme Being, before whom all mortals are equal, and who has scattered so many kinds of different beings on the surface of the globe for the sole purpose of manifesting his glory and power through the diversity of his works; Before the whole creation, whose disowned children we have so unjustly and for so long been considered; we declare. . . ."[32]

Afterlives

In the collusion of slavery/incest/miscegenation, we can trace the complicated and conflictive history of philanthropic reformism, racial panic, and counter/revolutionary ideologies in nineteenth-century Cuba. It is no surprise, then, that those who chose to rewrite *Cecilia Valdés* in some way or other all seem to focus on precisely this cluster of issues. Aware of the profound ambiguities in an account that denounces slavery through a plot that turns on incest between free people of different color, Morúa Delgado, the first Cuban author to offer his own version of the Cecilia story in his novel *Sofía*, makes some highly significant changes. The protagonist, now named Sofía, is a slave; and she is genotypically white.[33] As the daughter of the slave trader Unzúazu and a prostitute, she was declared an orphan and a *mulata* at birth and eventually became a house slave for the Unzúazu family. Like Cecilia, she bears a striking resemblance to her half-sister, one of the daughters in the Unzúazu household. Unaware of Sofía's origins, the son of the family forces her into a sexual relationship. The narrator's comments make it very clear, however, that this is not a mere coincidence. The incestuous relationship is in some sense desired as such and the coincidence lies in the desire being fulfilled without the protagonist being aware of it. Incestuous desire is a desire for sameness; it is the pursuit of racial purity that leads to the cultivation of desires for endogamy and, at the limit, incest. This desire for sameness, now clearly construed as a pathology, can be acted on under the veil of the slaveholding regime. Morúa Delgado thus gives a different reading of the internal link between miscegenation, racial slavery, and incest: it is an effect of the racial anxieties of white Cubans. The only truly human desire, in this account, is for difference and this is what is, or should be, at the foundation of the Cuban nation.

Humberto Solás may well have been influenced by Morúa Delgado when he decided to make the incestuous familial relations one of the main threads of his film *Cecilia*. Doña Rosa's sexual fixation on her son Leonardo, and Leonardo's selfish exploitation of oedipal conflicts, in particular, are at the core of Solás's version of the story. Like Morúa Delgado, Solás seems to want to clear things up: the endogamic practices of the Cuban sacarocracy are a pathological side effect of racial slavery.

The last twist in the long story of Cecilia, incest, and miscegenation in Cuba we owe to Reinaldo Arenas. His *La loma del angel*, published in 1987 and translated into English under the title "Graveyard of the Angels," is a brief savage pastiche of Villaverde's novel which subsumes its realist strand under the melodrama and recasts the whole story in a decidedly ironic voice. In his preface Arenas provocatively asserts incest as the main theme of *Cecilia Valdés* and introduces it under the heading "irreverencies." The "eternal tragedy of men" is, he claims, "their loneliness, their inability to communicate with each other, their solipsistic unease, and, therefore, their search for an ideal lover who cannot be anything but a mirror—or reflection—of our selves."[34] Contrary to what many critics have said, incestuous love and melodrama, not social realism, are at the core of *Cecilia Valdés*. The entire novel "is permeated by incessant, aptly insinuated, incestuous ramifications" that extend much beyond the relationship between Cecilia and Leonardo. And that, it seems, is a good thing.

In a turn that surely was directed against Morúa Delgado, Humberto Solás, and others, who in their rewritings and criticisms ultimately tried to straighten Villaverde's story, Arenas makes their denunciations of all desires that do not fit the heterosexual exogamic norm seem rather prudish. It is as if melodrama with its moralistic contrasts of good and evil, sensational conflicts, and deadly resolutions has finally exhausted itself. So when in Arenas's novel Cecilia's mother finally tells her daughter about her true origins, thus revealing that her lover was her half-brother, Cecilia blandly responds: "Con razón nos queríamos tanto." [That's why we loved each other so much.]

In the end, these versions and rewritings of the story show that *Cecilia Valdés* is not just the sepia-toned image of safely beloved Cubanity, but a testimony to a deeply troubled past that continues to produce dramatically different views of the good life, of justice, and of Cuba's future. Readers continue to react to *Cecilia Valdés* precisely because Villaverde does not—perhaps he could not—resolve the ideological and affective ambiguities of a national culture that took shape under slavery and colonialism. Of course, Villaverde meant the novel to be part of the struggle against both, but the goals of these struggles never were identical: liberty always had a different meaning for those who were fighting against racial subordination and those whose aims were local autonomy or sovereignty. Creole modernity took shape precisely through a negotiation of these competing claims, and it was not racial liberation that carried the day. *Cecilia Valdés* is a monument to the free people of color who bore the brunt of Spanish despotism, to the horrors of racial slavery, and to the liberal aspirations of young Creoles in the 1830s. As such it is one of the foundational texts of an emerging national culture: already in José Martí's obituary of 1894, Cirilo Villaverde is not just the first and foremost Cuban novelist, he is the wise and unassailable forefather of Cuban independence who could die with a calm conscience in his New York exile because he never did anything to support or sustain the regime that degraded his beloved Cuba.[35] But there is a more worldly if also less saintly side to *Cecilia Valdés*, and it is that side, I suspect, that continues to provoke retorts and rebuttals from writers and intellectuals: *Cecilia Valdés* recalls and reflects all those affective ambiguities and political conflicts that later discourses of national liberation and progress admit only as part of some long and happily overcome past.

NOTES

1. The novel was not published in Cuba until 1903, that is, after Independence. I have counted 14 major Cuban editions of the novel between 1903 and 1982, but there are very likely more by minor or regional publishers. To this day, the *zarzuela* (an operatic genre of Spanish origin) *Cecilia Valdés* (1932) by the Cuban composer Gonzalo Roig is frequently performed in Cuba and in the United States. Humberto Solás's 1981 six-part film *Cecilia* is an adaptation of the novel that mixes, perhaps not entirely successfully, the experimental techniques characteristic of post-1959 Cuban cinema and the conventionalism of a shot-for-television historical drama. The role of Cecilia is played by Daisy Granados, better known for her role in Gutiérrez Alea's 1968 *Memories of Underdevelopment*.

2. "Cecilia Valdés, espejo de la esclavitud" (*Casa de las Américas* 15, 89, 1975), 25. See also Reynaldo González, in *Contradanzas y Latigazos* (Havana: Letras Cubanas, 1983, 31–52) and Nancy Morejón, "'Cecilia Valdés': mito y realidad" (*Universidad de La Habana* no. 212, 1980) for an account of the mythical status of Cecilia Valdés in Cuba.

3. There is a long and excellent tradition of critical commentary on *Cecilia Valdés*. For further references of a more general nature, see the bibliography at the end of this volume. For literary criticsm of *Cecilia Valdés*, see the critical editions of *Cecilia Valdés* in Spanish.

4. The term "miscegenation" (derived from Latin *miscere* "to mix," and *genus*, which can mean anything from "sort" and "kind" to "gender," but is here intended to mean "race") was invented in 1864 in a pamphlet against Abraham Lincoln, who was at the time running for re-election (Werner Sollors, *Neither Black nor White Yet Both: Thematic Explorations of Interracial Literature* [Cambridge: Harvard University Press, 1997], 287). Applying it to Cuba in the 1830s is thus something of an anachronism. Given its etymological and semantic close-

ness to the Spanish term *mestizaje*, however, it seems permissible to use the term as a convenient short-hand here. In Cuba, various terms are commonly used to signify conceptions of racial, ethnic, and cultural mixture, from *mestizaje* and *mulatez* to Fernando Ortiz's anthropological concept of *transculturation* (*Cuban Counterpoint of Sugar and Tobacco* [1940], Durham: Duke University Press, 1995). See Juan G. Gelpí, "El discurso jerárquico en *Cecilia Valdés*," *Revista de Crítica Literaria Latinoamericana* 17, 1991, 47–61, for an analysis of racial, social, and linguistic hierarchies in *Cecilia Valdés*.

5. On del Monte and his salon, see Urbano Martínez Carmenate, *Domingo Del Monte y su tiempo* (La Habana: Ediciones Unión, 1997). Del Monte's correspondence has been published, in seven volumes, under the title *Centón epistolario de Domingo del Monte* (Havana: Imprenta "El Siglo XX," 1930) and is an invaluable source for understanding the cultural controversies of the time. For a detailed account of the development of the Cecilia material from Villaverde's early narratives to the rewritings by Morúa Delgado and Arenas, see William Luis, *Literary Bondage: Slavery in Cuban Narrative* (Austin: University of Texas Press, 1990).

6. Figures for slave populations and free people of color are notoriously unreliable. I am here giving rounded numbers, based on Verena Martínez-Alier, *Marriage, Class, and Colour in Nineteenth-Century Cuba: A Study of Racial Attitudes and Sexual Values in a Slave Society*, 2nd. ed. (Ann Arbor: University of Michigan Press, 1989) 3.

7. Aponte is mentioned a couple of times, in the novel. See endnote 23 for further details of the events.

8. Francisco Calcagno, *Aponte* (Barcelona: Tip. de Francisco Costa, 1901), 8.

9. For the culture and economy of the free people of color in Cuba at the time, see Pedro Deschamps Chapeaux's work, especially *El negro en la economía habanera del siglo XIX*. (La Habana: Instituto Cubano del Libro, 1971); for the historical figures in *Cecilia Valdés*, see his "Autenticidad de algunos negros y mulatos de *Cecilia Valdés*" (*Gaceta de Cuba* no. 81, 1970), 24–27. For the legal and customary rules that regulated social relations, especially sexual relations and marriage, between people of different color, see Martínez-Alier, *Marriage*.

10. Quoted in Martínez-Alier, *Marriage*, 46.

11. José Antonio Saco López, *Memoria sobre la vagancia en la isla de Cuba* (Santiago de Cuba: Instituto Cubano del Libro, 1974), 58–9. Note that Saco uses the term *arts* to refer to what we would call "fine arts," but also "crafts" and "trade."

12. The Spanish patrician José del Castillo quoted in Robert L. Paquette, *The Conspiracy of La Escalera and the Conflict between Empires over Slavery in Cuba* (Middletown: Wesleyan University Press, 1988), 127.

13. Quoted from contemporary accounts by Leopoldo Horrego Estuch, *Plácido, el poeta infortunado* (La Habana: Dirección General de Cultura, Ministerio Educación, 1960), 345.

14. This consensus no longer exists. As the moral and political evaluation of resistance to slavery and revolutionary antislavery even in mainstream historiography changed in the last few decades, scholars began to review the records of the Escalera Conspiracy. Most recent work tends to argue that there were conspiratorial activities, although perhaps not the vast coordinated plot the colonial authorities claimed to have uncovered. Views on what exactly happened continue to vary greatly, as do estimates of how many people fell victim to the repression. For a review of the literature on the Escalera Conspiracy, see Paquette, *Sugar Is Made with Blood,* 3–26.

15. In his preface, Villaverde claims that the novel runs from 1812 to 1831. See William Luis, *Literary Bondage* 110, for a discussion of the probably unintentional ambiguities in the novel's chronology.

16. "Las novelas del Sr. Villaverde" in *Obras Completas,* vol. 5: "Impresiones literarias y otras páginas," 17–51 (Havana: Edición de la Comisión del Centenario de Martín Morúa Delgado, 1959). Luis, by contrast, places *Cecilia Valdés* squarely within what he calls the counterdiscourse of antislavery in Cuba (*Literary Bondage*), 118–19. For an account of Villaverde's changing views on race and color, see Doris Sommer, *Proceed with Caution when Engaged by Minority Writing in the Americas* (Cambridge: Harvard University Press, 1999), 194–202. For a more critical view of Villaverde, see Vera M. Kutzinski, *Sugar's Secrets: Race and the Erotics of Cuban Nationalism* (Charlottesville and London: University Press of Virginia, 1993), 56–7 and 103. For a more general assessment of the racial politics of Cuban antislavery, see Iván Schulman, "Reflections on Cuba and Its Antislavery Literature," *SECLOLAS Annals* 7 (March 1976), 59–67, and Sibylle Fischer, *Modernity Disavowed: Haiti and the Cultures of Slavery in the Age of Revolution* (Durham: Duke University Press, 2004), 107–128.

17. "Las novelas del Sr. Villaverde," 53.

18. *Proceed with Caution,* 187–210, and *Foundational Fictions: The National Romances of Latin America* (Berkeley: University of California Press, 1991), 126–131.

19. The most detailed treatment of the incest theme in relation to slavery in *Cecilia Valdés* is Adriana Méndez-Rodenas's "Incest and Identity in *Cecilia Valdés*: Villaverde and the Origins of the Text" (*Cuban Studies,* 24 [1995], 83–104). Drawing on many of the same passages I analyze in my argument, Méndez-Rodenas applies the Lacanian concept of "the Name-of-the-Father" to the novel.

20. See for instance Reynaldo González, who discusses the issue at some length and points out that many of Villaverde's early stories were about spectacular or improbable events (*Contradanzas,* 91–104).

21. See William Luis, who reads this as a form of societal "neurosis" (*Literary Bondage* 118, 182).

22. There is a scene in the Gamboa mansion in the story of 1839 that leaves no doubt that Cecilia bears an uncanny similarity with the Gamboa children, and another scene that signals that Cecilia's grandmother knows the secret of Cecilia's birth and tries her best to keep her from having any contact with the Gamboa son ("La primitiva Cecilia Valdés" [Havana: Imprenta de 'Cuba Intelectual', 1910]).

23. Sollors (299) reads *Cecilia Valdés* in the context of U.S.-American post–Civil War discourses on race and racial mixture. While that certainly opens up interesting possibilities as far as the migration of ideological topoi is concerned, the presence of the miscegenation/incest topos in Cuba of the 1830s suggests that the influence may well have gone from the Caribbean to the United States, rather than the other way around, as Sollors seems to suggest. For a discussion of the incest theme in eighteenth-century French Caribbean discourse, see Edouard Glissant, *Poétique de la Relation* (Paris: Gallimard, 1990), and Doris Garraway's "Race, Reproduction and Family Romance in Saint-Domingue" in *The Libertine Colony: Creolization in the Early French Caribbean* (Durham: Duke University Press, forthcoming). For a discussion of incest in the literature of the Americas, see Ana Dopico, *Houses Divided: Genealogical Imaginaries and Political Visions in the Americas* (Durham: Duke University Press, forthcoming), chapters one and four.

24. This sequence is based on pages 23–25 in this translation.

25. The numerous allusions to *Vertigo*—the rush up the tower of a colonial mission church, the camera that keeps circling vertiginously as the characters approach the top platform, and so on—are not merely a skillful display of cinematic self-referentiality. Like *Cecilia Valdés*, *Vertigo* has raised questions about story-telling: Why does Hitchcock give his game away halfway through the film and thus undercut the operation of suspense? And like *Cecilia Valdés*, *Vertigo* is the story of catastrophic misrecognitions in which one woman is made to represent another, only to turn out to be that other: Madelaine *is* Judy, Cecilia *is* Leonardo's sister.

26. *Neither Black nor White*, 316–8.

27. See, for example, Luis (*Literary Bondage*, 117–8) and Vera M. Kutzinski, who explains the figure of incest as the "specter of . . . confused, and thus probably 'contaminated,' genealogies, for which women are usually held responsible" (*Sugar's Secrets*, 27). See Lévi-Strauss's *Elementary Structure of Kinship*, trans. James Harle Bell, eds. John Richard von Sturmer and Rodney Needham (Boston: Beacon Press, 1971), 3–25, for a critical review of the nineteenth- and early twentieth-century literature on this topic.

28. *Neither Black nor White*, 316–9. Gómez de Avellaneda's *Sab*—a novel very much written in the romantic tradition—with its idyllic account of Carlota and Sab growing up together, would be a case in point. Sab has the most pure and unspoiled love for the girl who in all likelihood is his first cousin. Endogamy combines with the Rousseauian notion of ideal romantic love, according to which the perfect marriage is based on the growing up together of a boy and a girl "like brother and sister." Bernadin de St. Pierre's highly influential *Paul et Virginie* (1788) is the classical example of a heterosexual union being founded on a shared childhood—indeed, a closeness that differs little from that of biological siblings. Interestingly, it seems that of all the Cuban writers of the mid-nineteenth century, Gómez de Avellaneda comes closest to proclaiming miscegenation as the foundation of Cuban national culture: the line between national endogamy, miscegenation, and incest can be very porous indeed.

29. *Philosophy in the Bedroom*, 324–5. In *The Marquis de Sade: The Complete Justine, Philosophy in the Bedroom, and Other Writings*, trans. Richard Seaver and Austryn Wainhouse, New York: Grove Press, 1965.

30. William Luis glosses Leantes as saying that "Cecilia and Leonardo had to be brother and sister because so are the two races which they represent" (*Literary Bondage*, 117). But when Leante emphatically proclaims, for example, that the novel's "tragedy does not lie in the incestuous love affair of Leonardo and Cecilia, but in the historical space—which is real and truthful—which frames the novel" ("Cecilia Valdés, espejo de la esclavitud," 20), he, like so many other readers, wants to separate the realist novel from the melodrama and pulp intrigue.

31. For a very suggestive reading of the incest theme in relation to the political and philosophical problem of recognition, see Judith Butler, *Antigone's Claim: Kinship between Life and Death* (New York: Columbia University Press, 2000), esp. 12–13.

32. Cited from Louis Joseph Janvier's edition *Les Constitutions d'Haïti (1801–1885)* (Paris: Flammarion, 1886), vol. 1.

33. For a detailed account of the similarities and differences between *Cecilia Valdés* and *Sofía*, see Luis, *Literary Bondage*, 141–48. For a detailed reading of *Sofía*, see Kutzinski, *Sugar's Secret*, 106–33.

34. *La loma del angel* (Miami: Ediciones Universal, 1995), 9; my trans.

35. "Cirilo Villaverde," *Obras Completas*, vol. 5 (Havana: Editorial Nacional de Cuba, 1963), 241–3.

About This Translation

This translation is based on the text established by Esteban Rodríguez Herrera (Havana: Lex, 1953). At several instances, the translator and I decided to accept the conjectures and corrections proposed by Jean Lamore in his edition (Madrid: Cátedra, 1992). The notes draw on the ample critical literature on *Cecilia Valdés*, nineteenth-century Cuban culture and history, and the rich documentation offered by Rodríguez Herrera and Jean Lamore in their notes to the novel.

A word about the language of *Cecilia Valdés*. One of the most remarkable features of the novel is the representation of the varieties of nonstandard Spanish spoken in Cuba at the time. There is the often archaic Spanish of uneducated or illiterate white native speakers; the faulty Spanish that results from hypercorrection often spoken by people who lack education and try to hide it; the Spanish of white non-native speakers; the language of the free people of color, where certain deviations from standard Spanish appear to have acquired systematic status; and finally, the improvised Spanish of slaves who were born and raised in Africa. Helen Lane's translation captures these variations through creative use of nonstandard English. For an attempt to systematize and categorize Villaverde's transcription of nonstandard Spanish, see the edition prepared by Olga Blondet Tudisco and Antonio Tudisco (New York: Anaya, 1971, 38–43).

I would like to thank David Sartorius, who provided valuable research assistance to Helen Lane.

Helen Lane did not live to see the publication of this translation. It was a great pleasure to have known her and an honor to have worked with her. I dedicate my Introduction to her memory.

CECILIA VALDÉS
OR
EL ANGEL HILL

To the Women of Cuba

Far from Cuba, and with no hope of ever seeing its sun, its flowers, or its palms again, to whom, save to you, dear country-women, the reflection of the most beautiful side of our homeland, could I more rightfully dedicate these sad pages?

The Author

Prologue

I brought out the first volume of this novel in an edition printed by the Imprenta Literaria of Don Lino Valdés in the middle of the year 1839. At the same time I began the composition of the second volume which was to be the conclusion of it; but I did not work on it a great deal, both because I moved to Matanzas shortly thereafter to serve as one of the teachers in the secondary school of La Empresa that had recently been founded in that city, and because once I had settled there, I began to composition of another novel, *La joven de la flecha de oro*, that I finished and had printed in one volume in the year 1841.

On my return to the capital in 1842, while continuing to teach, I joined the editorial staff of *El Faro Industrial*, to which I devoted all my literary works and novels that followed one upon the other almost without interruption until the middle of 1848. In its columns, among many other texts of diverse sorts, the following appeared in the form of serial stories: *El ciego y su perro, La excursión a Vuelta Abajo, La peineta calada, El guajiro, El misionero del Caroni, El penitente, etc.*[1]

After midnight on October 20 of this latter year, I was surprised in bed and placed under arrest by Barreda, the chief of police of the district of Monserrate, accompanied by a great crowd of soldiers and constables, and taken to the public prison, by order of the captain general of the island, Don Federico Roncaly.

Confined like a wild animal to a dark, damp cell, I remained there for six consecutive months, at the end of which, after being tried and sentenced to prison by the permanent military commission as a conspirator against the rights of the crown of Spain, I managed to escape on April 4, 1849, along with Don Vicente Fernández Blanco, a common criminal, and the turnkey of the prison, García Rey, who shortly thereafter was the cause of a serious controversy between the governments of Spain and the United States. By a strange happenstance, the three of us left the port of Havana together in a sailboat, but we remained in one another's company only as far as the estuary of Apalachicola, on the southern coast of Florida, whence I traveled overland to Savannah and New York.

Once outside of Cuba, I completely altered my way of life. I replaced my literary tastes with higher thoughts: I went from the world of illusions to the world of realities; I abandoned, at last, the frivolous occupations of the slave in a land of slaves, to take part in the undertakings of the free man in a free land. My manuscripts and books had been left behind, and even though they were sent to me a while later, I was fated not to be able to do anything with them, since first as a member of the editorial staff of *La Verdad*, a Cuban separatist newspaper, and then as General Narciso López's military secretary, I led a very active and agitated life, far removed from sedentary studies and work.

The failure of Cárdenas's expedition in 1850, the disaster of the invasion of Las Pozas, and the death of the distinguished leader of our ill-advised attempt at revolution in 1851 did not put a stop to, but on the contrary, lent new life to our plans to liberate Cuba, a hope that Cuban patriots had been cherishing since the earliest years of this century. All of them, however, like those of earlier days, ended in disasters and misfortunes in the year 1854.

In 1858 I found myself in Havana once again after a nine-year absence. My novel *Dos amores* having been reprinted at that time in Señor Próspero Massana's press, on his advice I undertook to revise, or better put, to recast the other novel, *Cecilia Valdés*, of which only the first volume existed in printed form and a small portion of the second in manuscript. I had mapped out the new plan for the novel down to its smallest details, written the foreword, and was working on the development of the plot when I was once again obliged to leave the country.

The vicissitudes that followed this second voluntary expatriation, the necessity of providing for the subsistence of my family in a foreign country, the political agitation that had begun to be felt in Cuba since 1865, and the journalistic tasks that I then took on, did not give me the energy or the leisure, especially with no expectation of any immediate monetary reward, to devote myself wholeheartedly to the long and tedious labor required to cut, expand, and completely recast the most voluminous and most complicated of my literary works.

After the renewed agitation of 1865 to 1868 came the revolution of the latter year and the bloody, decade-long war in Cuba, accompanied by the tumultuous scenes staged by Cuban emigres in all the nearby countries, especially in New York. As before, and as ever, I replaced my literary occupations with militant politics, inasmuch as the pen and the word were instruments at least as violent in the United States as the rifle and the machete in Cuba.

During most of this era of delirium and of patriotic dreams, the manuscript of the novel of course lay sleeping. What am I saying? It did not progress beyond half a dozen chapters, drafted in my spare moments, when the memory of my motherland soaked in the blood of her best sons, was there before me in all her horror and all her beauty and seemed to demand of those who loved her well and deeply the faithful portrayal of her existence from a threefold point of view—physical, moral, and social—before her death or else her elevation to the life of free peoples entirely changed the characteristic features of her former countenance.

Hence in no sense can I be said to have really devoted 40 years (the period dating from 1839 to the present) to the composition of the novel. Once I resolved to finish it, some two or three years ago, the most that I have been able to do has been to finish a chapter, with many interruptions, every two weeks, at times every month, working a few hours during the week and all day every Sunday.

Composing works of the imagination in this way, it is not easy to keep the interest of the narrative constant, or the action always lively and well plotted, or the style even and natural, or the well-tempered and sustained tone that works in the novelistic genre require. And that is one of the reasons that impel me to speak of the novel and of myself.

The other is that, in the final analysis, my painting has turned out to be so somber and so tragic that, being Cuban as I am to the very marrow, and a moral man, I would feel a sort of fear or shame were I to present it to the public without an explanatory word in my defense. I am fully aware that foreigners, that is to say, persons who are not closely acquainted with the customs or the period of the history of Cuba that I have attempted to paint will perhaps believe that I have chosen the darkest colors and overloaded the painting with shadows for the mere pleasure of creating an effect à la Rembrandt or à la Gustave Doré. Nothing was farther from my mind. I pride myself on being, before all else, a writer who is a realist, taking this word in the artistic sense attributed to it in the modern era.

For over 30 years I have not read a single novel, Walter Scott and Alessandro Manzoni being the only models that I have been able to follow on setting down the various panoramic scenes of *Cecilia Valdés*. I am aware that it would have been better for my work had I written an idyll, a pastoral romance, or even a story along the lines of *Paul and Virginia* or of *Atala and René*;[2] but although more entertaining and moral, such a narrative would not have been the portrait of any living person, or the description of the customs and passions of a flesh-and-blood people, subject to special political and civil laws, imbued with a certain order of ideas and surrounded by real and positive influences. Far from inventing or imagining characters and scenes of pure fantasy that beggars belief, I have raised realism, as I understand it, to the point of presenting the principal characters of the novel warts and all, as the vulgar saying goes, dressed in the attire that they wore in life, the majority of them with their real name and surname, speaking the very language they used in the historical scene in which they figure, copying, where appropriate, *d'après nature*, their physical and moral physiognomy, so that those who knew them by sight or through tradition may easily recognize them and at least say: the resemblance is undeniable.

I have scarcely aspired to anything else. The only thing I must add in order to unburden my conscience, in case someone is of the opinion that the painting has nothing hallowed or edifying about it, is that, on situating the action of the novel with Havana as the theater and in the era from 1812 to 1831, I did not find characters that could represent with fair to middling fidelity the role, for example, of the peasant Lorenzo, or that of the gentle Don Abundio, or of the energetic Father Cristóbal, or of the hallowed Archbishop Carlos Borromeo; at the same time there was an abundance of those who could pass, with no inconsistency, for faithful copies of the Canosos, the Tramoyas, and the Don Rodrigos, bullies, braggarts, and rakehells whom all countries and all eras seem to engender.

Nor must the author be held responsible if the painting does not enlighten, does not teach a lesson, does not instruct by delighting. The most that it has been in my power to do is to abstain from all indecent or gross painting—an error into which it is easy to fall, in view of the conditions, the character, and the passions of the majority of the figures in the novel—because I have never believed that the public writer, in the desire to appear to be a faithful and exact painter of manners and morals, should forget that the virtue and the modesty of the reader deserve his respect.

As for the rest, the work that is today first seeing the light of day in its entirety does not contain all the defects of language and of style found in the first volume printed in Havana; if there is greater decorum and truth in the portrayal of the characters, if certain scenes and sentences of scant or dubious morality have been eliminated, if the general tone of the composition is more uniform and animated, this is owed in large part to the advice of my wife, whom I have been able to consult chapter by chapter as I finished each of them.

New York, May, 1879   C. Villaverde

I

I

Such is the fruit of sin, Tello,
a harvest of sorrow.

Solís

Around dusk on a day in November of the year 1812, following the Calle de Compostela heading northward from the city was a calash drawn by a pair of mules, on one of which, as was the custom, the black calash driver was mounted. The driver's attire, the harnesses of the mules, and the solid silver ornaments made it plain to see that the person to whom such luxurious equipment belonged was rich. The curtain or cloth hood hung from studs, not only in front, but also on one side and half of the other, fastened down by a strip of calfskin. Whoever it was inside the carriage at that time, there is no denying that he or she had an interest in remaining incognito, although the precaution seemed unnecessary, inasmuch as there was not a living soul out on the streets, nor was there any light visible other than that of the stars or the artificial light from a few houses as it escaped through the wide slits in the closed doors. The mules came to a sudden halt on the corner of the Callejón de San Juan de Dios and from the calash there alighted, slowly and with considerable effort, a tall gentleman, well turned out, dressed in a black swallowtail coat buttoned to the neck showing underneath his tight-fitting waistcoat or underjacket, long trousers of woven hemp and silk, a horsehair bow tie, and a beaver hat with an enormous crown and a narrow brim. From what could be seen in the half-light from the stars, the man's most notable features were his aquiline nose, his quite vivacious eyes, his oval face, and his short beard. The shadow cast by his hat and by the towering walls of the nearby convent perhaps darkened the color of his beard and hair without making it appear to be black.

"Go on up to the Calle de lo Empedrado," the gentleman said in an imperious but low-pitched tone of voice, leaning his left hand on the saddle of the mule inside the shafts, "and wait immediately alongside the corner. In case the night patrol meets up with you, say that you belong to Don Joaquín Gómez and that you are awaiting his orders. Do you understand, Pío?"

"Yes, señor," replied the calash driver, who had been holding his hat in his hand once his master began speaking. And he went on, with the mules setting the pace, to the spot pointed out to him by the latter.

The Callejón de San Juan de Dios is only two blocks long, closed off at one end by the walls of the convent of Santa Catalina and at the other by the houses on the Calle de la Habana. The hospital of San Juan de Dios, which gives the narrow street its name, and which always allows the warm breath of its patients to escape through its tall square windows, occupies all one side of the second block, and the three other sides are occupied by little houses with red Spanish roof tiles and only one story high, the last houses in particular being above street level, with either one or two stone steps at the door. The best looking of the little dwellings were those in the first block as one entered the street by way of the Calle de Compostela. They were all more or less the same size, each with only one window and door, the latter made of cedar painted brick-red with large-headed studs and the former with mirrored glass or set in a simple molding and closed off with thick wooden balustrades. The pavement of the street was in its original and natural state, made of cobblestones and without sidewalks.

The unknown gentleman, hugging the walls beneath the projecting eaves of Spanish tiles, stopped at the door of the third little house on his right and tapped twice on it with the tips of his fingers. His arrival was no doubt expected, because it took the person who drew the bolt with which the door was barred from inside only time enough to move from the window to the door before it opened. That person was the mistress of the house; a mulatto woman about 40 years old, of average height, heavy-set although still small-waisted, with bare round shoulders, a fine head, a rather thick nose, an expressive mouth and abundant, very kinky hair. She was wearing a fine embroidered blouse with short sleeves and serge petticoats with no pleats and no trimming.

There were few pieces of furniture in the room: next to the wall on the right a mahogany table, on which a wax candle was burning inside a glass chimney or *fanal,* and several heavy cedar chairs with leather seats and backs, studded with copper tacks. In that era this was considered a luxury, especially in the case of a woman of color, who occupied that house as its mistress and not as a servant. The gentleman did not shake hands with her when he entered; he merely greeted her in a grave yet gracious and amiable way, this being unquestionably even odder, inasmuch as aside from the difference in their social status and race that in their respective ages was noticeable at first glance and there existed between them no other relation save that of more or less sincere and selfless friendship. He immediately asked, in a melancholy tone of voice and drawing as close to the woman as he could so as not to have to raise his voice, which was a little hoarse:

"And how is the sick girl?"

The mulatto shook her head with an even sadder air and answered in three monosyllables:

"Ah! Quite ill."

Somewhat more animatedly, though her face did not brighten, a moment later she added:

"Didn't I tell the señor? At any moment still, that blow will be the death of her."[3]

"How can that be?" the gentleman replied uneasily. "Didn't you tell me last night that she was better and calmer?"

"She was, yes, señor; but she was very disenquieted and agitated all morning long. She said the sheets made her feel hot, and several times she tried to get out of bed, seeking air. So it was necessary to send for the doctor. He came and prescribed a sedative: she took it, because the poor thing takes anything she's given. They all make her sleep like a log, and then she wakens up with a start. Ah, señor, her sleep is so much like death! It frightens me, it badly frightens me. I told the señor from the beginning, it was great a blow to her. That girl doesn't have the strength to bear it. Ah, my señor, this time we're going to lose her, it's happening before my eyes; my heart tells me so."

And she said no more, for emotion had stifled her voice in her throat.

"I see that you're discouraged, *Seña* Josefa,"[4] the stranger said gently and feelingly. "Haven't you tried to convince her that the separation is only for a very short time? She isn't a child . . ."

"Haven't I tried, you ask! It seems as though the señor doesn't know her, not even still. She won't listen to reason. She's the most willful and stubborn girl ever born. What's more, ever since that incident, from then thereon she hasn't been in her right mind. Didn't the señor himself try to console her and calm her on that fatal night? And what good did it do? Remember what we-all be: nothing. The señor is going to see with his own eyes that he chose the wrong time to subject her to such a test. The 40 days hadn't yet gone by when all at once she had a fever that kept going up. Yes," she concluded, deeply moved and in tears, "I've accepted the fact that she won't come out of this alive or in her right mind."

"May it be God's will, *Seña* Josefa, that such fateful prophecies don't come true," said the worried gentleman. After a few moments he added: "She is young and strong, and nature will yet win out over her sorrows and misfortunes. I place more trust in this than in the obscure science of physicians. Apart from that, you know that what has been done was for the good of everyone, that is to say. . . . Later on you will all thank me, I am certain. I could not or should not have given her my name. No, no," he repeated as though embarrassed by the echo of his own voice. "No one knows that better than you. You who are a reasonable woman will know and acknowledge that that was how it had to be. The child had to have a name, a name that she must not be ashamed of tomorrow, or another day, that of Valdés, with which perhaps she will be able to marry well.[5] There was no other way for her to be named that, save to put her in the Royal Foundling Home. This could not have been more painful for the mother, I know full well, than it was for . . . all of us. But within a few short days they will have baptized her there and then I will have her brought here by María de Regla, my black, who three months ago lost a son from the seven-day sickness and is suckling the girl in the Foundling Home by my order. She will return her, healthy, safe, and Christian, to the arms of her mother. I have arranged all this with Montes de Oca, the physician of the Royal Home, through whom I frequently have news of the child. In the beginning she cried a great deal and refused to take María de Regla's breast, and hence she lost a little weight. But all that is over now and she's plump and the picture of health, according to what Montes de Oca has told me, that is to say, for I have not seen her since the night that I put her in the turnbox. . . . My eyes followed her. How much that step cost me is indescribable . . . But to go on to something else. You know, however, that there is no misunderstanding involved."

"I know it all too well," the mulatto said, drying her tears. "There can be no misunderstanding, no. In that regard my mind is at ease, since despite her screams, which rent my soul, I drew the blue half moon on her left shoulder, as the señor ordered me to do. I don't know which one of us it probably hurt most, her or me. . . . The mother, the mother, my señor, is the one who keeps me from having a moment's peace. She can't withstand this blow. She will perforce lose her mind or her life. I repeat this once again to the señor."

Seña Josefa, as her unknown visitor addressed her, was considered an intelligent woman, even though because no one had seen to it that she was properly educated she often fell into the same linguistic errors common to the uneducated in Cuba. Despite her advanced age and her many sorrows, she continued to show the signs of a beautiful and distinguished youth, fine eyes, the amorous expression of her mouth, and her nicely rounded neck, shoulders, and arms. She had the olive color resulting from the mixture of the black female and the Indian male; but her kinky hair and her oval face did not support the probability of such an intermingling, but rather that of a black mother and a white father. When young, she had led a comfortable life, enjoyed sensual pleasures, and rubbed elbows with well-bred and well-mannered people. The sorrow that was afflicting her at the moment must have been deeply felt, to judge from the frequency of her sighs, the repeated furrowing of her brow, and the abundance of aqueous fluid bathing her large eyes, misting over their brightness. Moreover, there was more desperation than real sorrow in her attitude. In fact, as we shall soon see, she had more than enough reason for the former and not sufficient reason for the latter.

There were times when both persons were silent, each one absorbed in his or her own thoughts, which surely did not coincide at even one point, when suddenly a lament and a heartrending cry coming from inside the house were heard. The woman uttered a sorrowful exclamation, raised both hands to her head, and ran as if with clipped wings through the first room to the second. The gentleman mechanically made the same gesture with his hands and followed her footsteps in silence, albeit at a certain distance. In the second room there was no light other than the pale flicker of a little oil lamp on a table, on which there could be seen a niche or puppeteer's platform, where a full-length figure, wearing an ankle-length garment or a woman's gown, who was looking heavenward and whose breast was pierced by a sword with a hilt that appeared to be made of silver, was venerated. On the opposite side of the room was a bed with silk hangings that were the worse for wear, and at the head of it a chair upholstered in leather, from which the moment she entered the room *Seña* Josefa had banished an emaciated elderly black woman, the very image of death, whose white hair contrasted with the ebony of her long bony neck. She was holding a rosary in her right hand and wearing a number of scapulars on her bosom on top of her white blouse; encircling the waist of her burlap skirt was a long black leather belt like that of an Augustinian friar. She looked as if she were totally self-absorbed or praying with great fervor, and when *Seña* Josefa touched her on the shoulder, she suddenly raised her head, turned it toward the door of the room, saw the stranger standing in the doorway, gestured in horror or fear, and disappeared through the door at the other end of the room without a word.

Seña Josefa occupied her place. She carefully opened the curtains of the bed, and motioned to the gentleman to come closer, which he did, with what appeared to be repugnance. The eyes of both of them were riveted on the pale face of a 20-year-old girl, lying face up and seemingly dead. Because she was not moving at the time, her eyes were sunken in their sockets and her eyelids closed, the eyelashes of them so long that they cast a shadow over her cheeks. Her head was all that lay outside the sheets and was almost buried in the pillow, hidden beneath a mop of black, wavy hair spread out every which way in the greatest disorder. From somewhere in the middle of that black background there stood out the oval face, pale as wax, of the sick girl, with its sharp chin, high rectangular forehead, small mouth, thick lips, and a rather shapely nose for a woman of mixed race, as was doubtless true of the one of whom we are now speaking. The face as a whole was good-looking, feminine; but there was such an expression of anxiety and melancholy in this countenance withered by illness that it was pitiful to contemplate. Moved by this sentiment perhaps, *Seña* Josefa said in the gentleman's ear: "She's fallen asleep."

The gentleman answered by shaking his head, perhaps because at that instant he thought he noted a convulsive tremor run through the patient's entire body from head to foot. After the tremor her breast began to rise, a movement easy to perceive from above the sheet, like a wave suddenly beginning to form in a calm sea, a precursor of the sigh from the bottom of her heart that she breathed immediately thereafter, accompanied by a painful high-pitched moan. Realizing what might happen next, without being able to keep it from happening, he first averted his eyes and then little by little discreetly withdrew to the foot of the bed. Sitting up at that instant, the sick woman exclaimed with a panicked expression:

"Mama! Was that her grace?"

"My girl! What is it you want? Are you feeling better?"

"Ah! Mamita!" the girl went on with the same air of consternation. "I saw her, I just saw her. Yes, I have no doubt of it. There she is!" she added, pointing heavenward. "She's going away! They're taking her from me! She must be dead. Ay!" And another heartrending cry escaped her.

"Daughter!" her mother said to her in distress. "Waken up. You're dreaming or imagining things."

"Come here, Mamita, your grace can see for herself."

Saying this, she drew her mother to her by the arm.

"Look at her! Isn't that the Blessed Virgin inside a golden cloud, with bare feet, resting on the wings of countless angels? It's her. Look! Over this way. Over there! Look! She's rising in the air!"

"Visions, my girl. Pay no attention. Lie down and rest."

"How does your grace expect me to lie down if I see that they're taking my daughter away, my beloved daughter?"

"Who is taking her away, darling?"

"Who is taking her away? Doesn't your grace see? The Blessed Virgin. She's taking her away in her arms. She must be dead. Ah!"

"She hasn't died, don't you believe it," *Seña* Josefa said feebly, for on this point she was no more certain than the young woman who was ill. "Your little daughter is alive and you will see her soon. Those are dreams you are having."

"Dreams, dreams," the young woman repeated, distraught. "I was dreaming? Can it be only a dream? But what about my daughter? Where is she? Why have they taken her from me? And your grace is to blame for my losing her," she concluded with an angry gesture and in an angry tone of voice.

Seña Josefa did not have the courage to answer back, either so as not to irritate the sick woman further with a denial little short of useless, or because the accusation was direct and well founded. She merely turned her eyes to her right, whereupon those of the sick woman naturally fell upon the ill-defined bulk of the stranger, who was trying to hide behind the draperies of the bed.

"Who's there?" she asked, pointing with her finger. "Ah! It's him, the one who stole my daughter! My executioner! What have you come to look for here? Have you come, you basilisk, to gloat over what you've done? You've come at the right moment. Gloat however much you please. My daughter has flown up to heaven, that I know, I'm convinced of it; I will follow her very soon; but you, you, the cause of our damnation and death, you will descend . . . to hell."

"Blessed Jesus!" *Seña* Josefa exclaimed, crossing herself. "You don't know what you're saying. Be still."

And bathed in tears, she flung herself on her daughter with the twofold objective of keeping her from getting out of bed and from going on with that terrible rebuke of the unknown gentleman. Out of prudence or out of remorse, the latter said nothing and bent his head still lower. In any event, he was definitely annoyed and was struggling with himself to come to a decision. Because, foreseeing it, he had come to this sickroom to place himself within range of the apparently well-founded recriminations of this woman, who, though delirious, was throwing up to him the loss of her daughter and the ruin of her mind. But he made no attempt to defend himself. He felt, on the contrary, humiliated, highly offended, for while his intentions were altogether innocent, guided by the desire for the good of all the parties directly involved, the results were well on their way to being utterly disastrous. In the eyes of his own conscience, justification was easy; the world, however, would judge him by the facts. And he had a terrible fear of this judgment.

Meanwhile the struggle between mother and daughter went on. The latter, her eyes panic-stricken, her hair disheveled, her forehead drenched in sweat, her cheeks burning with fever, pushed her mother away with both hands and said to her over and over: "Let go of me, Mamita, let me see that face of a heretic. I want to call him to account for my daughter. He has taken her away from me, he, a man with the bowels of a wild beast." And the mother, still bathed in tears and holding her close in her arms, answered her: "For the love of God, my daughter, for the Immaculate Conception of Mary Most Holy, for your health, for that of your daughter, who is alive and well, be still, calm yourself, I beg of you, in the name of all that you love most."

But since that struggle had gone on for too long, the gentleman went over to the bed, took one of the sick woman's hands in one of his, which she did not push away, and in a solemn voice, yet one full of exquisite tenderness, said to her:

"Charo, listen to me. I promise you that tomorrow you will see your daughter. Come to your senses. Calm yourself! No more acts of madness."

Either because the long and violent struggle had drained all her strength, or because the voice of the unknown gentleman commanded respect, the sick woman, heaving a deep sigh, suddenly fell back on the pillow and lay there for a brief moment without moving. At first the mother's one thought was that she had breathed her last. For that reason she put her hand over her daughter's heart, and since, either because of the fear that had overtaken her, or because the patient's blood had frozen in her veins, for a few instants her mother could feel no heartbeat. Hence, in utter horror, she turned to the gentleman, who seemed to be impassively contemplating that silent scene, and in a voice filled with bitter recrimination, said to him:

"Does the señor see? She is dead."

These words were not enough to make the gentleman lose his natural equanimity. Far from it; with great calm and deliberation he took the girl's pulse, as a doctor would, and then said:

"Bring ether. She has fainted. This girl is very weak; she needs food."

"The doctor has forbidden her to eat," *Seña* Josefa remarked.

"The doctor has no idea what fish he's angling for. Give her broth. But hurry with the ether."

Once the volatile alkali had been fetched, they put it to her nose; but the only signs of life that the girl gave were a quivering of her eyelids, which incidentally she did not open, and a silent weeping, or with her tears falling in a steady stream as the graphic common expression has it. As this was happening at the bedside of the sick woman, the white head of the elderly black woman previously mentioned peeked in through the door standing ajar at the far end of the room; but she withdrew it all of a sudden and crossed herself as though she had seen the devil, doubtless because the unknown gentleman was still there. Finally, the latter left that place of sorrow and tribulation, bade *Seña* Josefa good-bye with a mere nod of his head, and went out onto the street murmuring in indignation:

"And I'm the only one who is to blame!"

I I

I am alone, I was born alone,
My mother had me alone,
I must make my way alone,
Like a feather in the air.

A few years before, or better put, one or two years after the fall of the second brief constitutional period,[6] in which a state of siege was declared against the island of Cuba and its Captain General, Don Francisco Dionisio Vives, a common sight in the streets of the district of El Angel was a youngster about twelve years old, who either because of her habit of wandering all about, or else because of other circumstances of which we shall speak in a moment, attracted everyone's attention.

Her face belonged to the same type as that of the virgins of the most renowned painters. For along with a high forehead, crowned with abundant naturally wavy black hair, she had very regular features, a straight nose descending from between her eyebrows and because it was rather short, raising her upper lip almost imperceptibly, baring two rows of little white teeth. Her eyebrows formed an arch and thus further shadowed her black almond eyes, which were all animation and fire. She had a small mouth and full lips, indicating voluptuousness rather than strength of character. Her plump round cheeks and a dimple in the middle of her chin formed an attractive whole, which in order to be perfect lacked only a less spiteful if not downright wicked expression.

As for her body, she was not fat but thin, short for her age rather than tall, and her torso, seen from the back, narrow at the neck and widening out at the shoulders, was in delightful harmony, even beneath her humble garments, with her supple, narrow waist, which bore comparison only with the stem of a wineglass. Her complexion could be said to be healthy, with a ruddy incarnation, speaking in the sense of flesh tint that painters attribute to this expression, although once one looked closely at it, one noticed that despite its healthy glow there was too much ocher in the color of her face, as a result of which her complexion was neither diaphanous nor free of other shadings. To what race, then, did this girl belong? It is difficult to say. However, a knowing eye could not help noticing that her red lips had a dark border or edging, and that the bright glow of her face ended in a sort of half-shadow near her hairline. Her blood was not pure and it could be stated with assurance that three or four generations back it had been mixed with Ethiopian blood.

But in any event such were her strange beauty, her happiness and vivacity, that they endowed her with a sort of magic spell, which did not allow one's mind to wander but instead only to admire her and overlook the shortcomings or excesses of her lineage. People had never seen her sad, never ill-humored or quarreling with anyone; nor could anyone come up with any answers as to where she lived or what she subsisted on.

What, then, was such a pretty youngster doing pounding the pavement day and night, like a famished stray dog? Was there no one who could look after her or control her vagabond nature?

Meanwhile the girl grew older, high-spirited and full of life, paying no heed to the inquiries and the malicious gossip of which she was the object, and never realizing that her life on the streets, which seemed quite natural to her, aroused people's suspicions and fears, apart from compassion in the case of a few old ladies; that her nascent graces and the careless and carefree life she led aroused hopes of a bastard lineage in young lads' hearts, which beat faster on seeing her cross the Plazuela del Cristo, when on the run and with the cunning of a fox she stole a black bean cake or a crackling from the black women who set up stands there to fry them after nightfall; or when she nonchalantly put her little hand into crates of raisins at food stands on the corners of the streets; or when she swiped a ripe banana, a mango, or a guava from a fruit vendor's box; or when she wound the lead of the blind man's guide dog around the cannon on the corner, or led the sightless man to San Juan de Dios if he was going to Santa Clara: all these were pranks worthy of praise in a youngster of her age and outward appearance.

Her ordinary attire, not always clean, consisted of a gingham skirt, with which she wore neither a kerchief nor any other footwear than a pair of wooden clogs, which announced her approach from afar since they clattered loudly on the stone sidewalks of the few streets that had such refinements at the time. The only adornment around her neck was a filigree chaplet, a sort of necklace, with a gold and coral cross hanging from it—a keepsake of her beloved unknown mother.

Despite the life she led and despite her attire, she seemed so pretty and so pure that a person was tempted to believe that she would never cease to be what she was, an innocent young maiden who was preparing to enter the world through a seemingly golden door, and who spent her days without even suspecting its existence. Nonetheless, the streets of the city, the squares, the public establishments, as was noted previously, were her school, and in such places, one may surmise, her tender heart, meant perhaps to harbor virtues, the loveliest of feminine charms, drank instead in torrents the poisoned waters of vice, and nourished itself from her earliest years on the lewd scenes staged each day by an indecent and depraved people. And how to free herself from such an influence? How to keep her vivacious eyes from seeing? Her ever alert ears from hearing? That soul brimming over with life and youth from precociously opening her eyes wide and pricking up her ears to pass judgment on everything that happened round about her, instead of sleeping the sleep of innocence? Very soon, in truth, the legion of passions that consume the heart and humble the proudest brows knocked on her door!

One afternoon, among others, the girl was running, as usual as fast as her legs would carry her, down a certain street whose name need not be mentioned here. Peering out from one of the tall, broad iron grilles over the windows of a house of aristocratic appearance were two girls more or less her age and a young girl of 14 or 15, who, as they saw that shooting star streak by, as one of them put it, all three of them overcome with curiosity, insistently called her over. The youngster, not waiting to be asked twice, immediately came inside through the carriage entrance and nonchalantly presented herself at the door of the drawing room, where the three girls were already waiting. They took her by the hand and led her into the presence of a rather stout lady, very neatly dressed, who was lolling in an ample rocking chair with her feet resting on a footstool.

"Ah!" the lady exclaimed once she had had a look at her from up close. "How adorable she is!" This said, she straightened up in the chair, a move that cost her considerable effort, and added:

"What is your name?"

"Cecilia," the girl replied promptly.

"And your mother?"

"I have no mother."

"Poor thing! And your father?"

"I'm a Valdés, from the Royal Foundling Home. I don't have a father."

"All the better!" the lady exclaimed, turning this information over in her mind.

"Papa, Papa," the oldest of the girls said, addressing a gentleman who was reclining on a sofa to the right of the dais. "Papa, have you ever seen such a darling girl?"

"Come, come," the father answered almost without turning his head. "Leave her in peace." But the words had barely escaped his lips when Cecilia fixed her eyes on him, and taken by surprise but laughing at the same time, said: "Ah! I know that man who is sitting over there." The latter, from beneath his hands, with which he was shading his forehead, cast a fierce glance at her that clearly showed his ill humor and annoyance. He immediately rose to his feet and left the drawing room without another word. It is strange indeed that this one man felt no liking for the pretty street urchin.

"So you have no father or mother?" the good lady asked again, somewhat perturbed by the scene that had just taken place. "And how do you live? With whom do you live? Are you a daughter of the earth or of the air?"

"Hail Mary Immaculate!" the girl exclaimed, lowering her head to her right shoulder and staring at her questioners. "For heaven's sake! What inquisitive people! I live with my grandmother, who is a very good little old lady, who loves me a great deal and lets me do anything I please. My mother died a long time ago and . . . so did my father. I don't know anything more and don't ask me any more questions."

The young girls were eager to question Cecilia further and learn other details concerning her life and her kinfolk; but, for one thing, their father had told them to leave her in peace, and for another, their mother, incapable now of getting the better of her annoyance, indicated to them by a very meaningful gesture that it was time for such an impudent youngster to leave. Showered with gifts and bidden good-bye, Cecilia finally left via the carriage entrance on her way back out onto the street, just as a young man in summer attire, that is to say, a tight-fitting waistcoat and trousers of blue and white checked cotton, was coming down from the upper floor. The moment her spied her, he recognized her and called out to her from overhead:

"Cecilia, hey, Cecilia! Listen, look!"

Without slowing her pace, but continuing to look at the one who was shouting to her, she said to him at the door leading to the street: "Nyah! Nyah." And at the same time she spread her right hand open, placed her thumb on the tip of her nose and waggled her other fingers back and forth very quickly. This is a way of making fun of someone that is often used by youngsters in our streets, as if to say: "Ha! Ha! I put one over on you! So there! I didn't get caught up in all your nonsense."

This is not the place to describe the scene that followed the girl's departure from that dwelling. It can be said that the gentleman and the lady of the house did not mention her name again. The girls, on the contrary, even when they went back to the window to see and greet their girl friends, who were passing by in their luxurious two-wheeled carriages after their afternoon outing, never left off speaking of Cecilia and repeating her name, with a helping hand from their older brother then, who knew her and frequently chanced to meet her on his way to Father Morales's Latin class, opposite the convent of Santa Teresa.

In the meantime the youngster, walking on along the street, ended up at the little square of Santa Catalina, leapt up onto its embankment, which runs all along the front of it, and then went down to the Calle del Aguacate via a stairway of dry masonry. Once there, she turned to the right, albeit with a certain caution, at the little house immediately adjacent to the corner occupied by a tavern. She did not knock or halt in front of the door, but gently pushed on the right-hand, or male, panel of the door, which was held shut by half an iron ball lying on the floor. The door had once been painted a bright red, but having been faded by many rains, the sun, and time, there was nothing left of the paint save for dark red spots around the nail heads and in the deep moldings of the door panels. The little window, which was tall and made of mirrored glass, had only three or four balustrades and had lost its original paint, leaving only a thin coat of lead. As for the interior, its appearance was even more shabby, if possible, than the exterior. It consisted of a small parlor, divided by a screen so as to form a bedroom, the door of which led straight to the street, and another bedroom on the right that led to the narrow patio no longer than the back of the little house. To the left of the entrance and three feet above the floor was a hollow in the dividing wall, a sort of niche, at the back of which there could be seen a Mater Dolorosa, portrayed full-length, though far short of full scale, with a fiery sword transpiercing her breast. This odd painting was illuminated day and night by two *mariposas*, that is to say, two button molds each with its own wick, floating in three parts of water and one of oil, inside ordinary drinking glasses. A garland of nothing but artificial flowers and pieces of cardboard painted gold and silver, crumpled, faded and dusty, adorned the devotional image. And all about, on the walls, on the screen and behind the doors and the window were a great many placards, that read for instance: Hail Mary Immaculate! May the Grace of God Be in This House! Long Live Jesus! Long Live Mary! May Grace Live and Sin Die!, and many others of the same sort that there is no need to repeat. Unframed colored prints, fastened to the walls with sealing wafers or paste, were more numerous than the placards, all of them of saints, printed by the Boloña Press on ordinary paper and received by petitioners' hands at convents in exchange for alms, or bought at the church door on feast days.

The furniture was limited to a minimum, although even its few shabby pieces could readily be recognized as having seen better days when they were new. The most covetable piece in the house was an easy chair with large arms, wobbly and much the worse for wear now. There were also three or four cedar chairs with calfskin seats and backs, of the same style, strong, sturdy, and very old. Forming a matched set with them was a corner table of the same wood, whose feet were carved in the form of a satyr's cloven hoof, with moldings and a grape leaf motif.

Despite the cramped quarters of that haven, it housed a drowsy cat, several pigeons and hens, doubtless on intimate terms with its only two human inhabitants, since they wandered all about, leapt on the backs of the chairs, mewed, billed and cooed and cackled with no consideration or fear. On one side of the bedroom was a tall, rectangular bed, which was always unoccupied, since it was of uncomfortable untanned leather, whose hardness was mitigated by a feather mattress, permanently covered with a crazyquilt or *taracea*, stitched together from a thousand and one scraps of cloth. Instead of draperies the carved columns of the bed supported images of Saint Blaise, scapulars, cardboard crosses, chunks of glass, and blessed fronds from Palm Sundays of years long past.

Properly speaking, this was not a house except insofar as it gave shelter to two persons, because outside of the two rooms mentioned, it had no comforts and no place to take one's ease save for the aforementioned patio, where the kitchen was located, or rather, the cookstove, a little wooden box full of ashes mounted on four straight legs and protected from the rain by a sort of tile overhang. We have described at such length the hovel that Cecilia entered so that the imagination of the kind reader would linger over the contrast offered by such a pretty girl, brimming over with life and youth, amid such an antiquated setting, leaving the impression that heaven had placed her there so as to keep continually whispering in her ear: Daughter, contemplate what you will become and be more sensible.

But we are certain that that was the last thought in Cecilia's head, in fact doubly certain, since her greatest concern was not to be heard entering by a certain person who, sitting in her armchair with her back turned, facing the niche, appeared to be praying or dozing. Nonetheless, no matter how carefully the little rascal set one foot down after the other, she was unable to do so quietly enough so that the old woman did not distinctly hear her or sense her presence, for she had very sharp ears and was neither praying nor sleeping, but reading, all bent over, a little prayer book bound in parchment.

"Hello there!" the old woman said to her, looking at her out of the corner of her eye above the perfectly round rims of her spectacles, sitting astride the tip of her nose, like a lad on the rump of a horse. "Hello, young lady! So you're here, are you? A good thing you are! Is this any hour to come ask for your granny's blessing? (Because the girl had drawn closer with her arms crossed.) Where have you been until now, you little minx? (The church bell for evening prayers had already rung.) How nicely dressed you are!" And she then grabbed her hand all of a sudden, whereupon her book fell to the floor, scaring the cat that often sat blinking on a chair, the doves, and the hens. "Come here, you creature possessed by the devil," she added; "butterfly without wings, sheep without a flock, lunatic fit for the stocks; come here, I must find out where you've been until such a late hour. What, have you no one to keep you in line, no Holy Father to excommunicate you? Who has ever seen the likes of you? Have you nothing else to do but run around loose on the street? Is there no one who can keep track of you? Just wait and see! This is the last straw!"

Far from being frightened or running off, Cecilia threw herself into the arms of her ill-humored and crotchety grandmother with peals of laughter, and as if to make her hold her tongue, gave her all the presents that had been showered on her by the girls in the house where she had been.

I I I

With more calculated displays of affection and shrewdness than were natural in a girl of her age, Cecilia embraced and kissed her grandmother, whom she addressed as Chepilla (a whimsical derivation of Josefa), the name most people called her. That was enough to placate her, and there is nothing surprising about that, for, as we shall see later, that woman had been so unhappy, had felt such a need to be loved by the only being in the world who genuinely concerned her, that continuing to be stern with her granddaughter would have been the same as prolonging her own martyrdom. She naturally fell silent all of a sudden and simply sat there contemplating Cecilia, just as moments before she had been contemplating, in fervent prayer, the sweet face of the Blessed Virgin.

As the girl clasped the old woman's waist with her shapely arms and rested her beautiful head on her breast, like the flower that appears on a dry tree trunk and with its leaves and its fragrance makes a show of life alongside death itself, *Seña* Josefa's figure looked odder and uglier than it really was. Her very face formed a contrast with the remainder of her body. Either because she was in the habit of wearing her hair pulled back, or because that was the countenance that nature had given her, the truth was that her forehead looked too broad, her nose large and blunt, her chin sharp, and her eye sockets sunken. This gave her face a depraved expression, not easily overlooked, at least by the wary observer. And yet her arms were soft, and her hands could be described as pretty. But her most notable facial feature was her big eyes, dark and piercing, vestiges of features that had once been attractive, rendered inharmonious now by a premature old age.

Of mulatto origin, she had copper-colored skin, and with the passage of the years and the wrinkles that they brought it had become swarthy or *achinado*, to avail ourselves of the common expression used in Cuba to designate the offspring of a mulatto man and a black woman, or vice versa. She might have been 60 years old, even though she looked older, because her hair was beginning to turn white, something that in people of color usually happens later than in those of the Caucasian race. The sufferings of the soul destroy the human face before the mortal human body. As we shall see later, only Christian resignation, the work of her faith in God, the nourishment with which in the end she sustained her spirit during long hours devoted to prayer and meditation, had doubtless kept her on her feet in the face of the onslaughts of her miserable fate. Moreover, with the sad conviction that a blink of an eye separated her past and her future, and what she should and could expect from her granddaughter, a lovely flower tossed into the middle of the public square to be trampled on by the first passerby, and now in the last third of her life, with all the remorse of the past, rather than growing angry, she realized that she had best placate the invisible wrath of her judge and find moments of calm for herself before her final hour struck.

At the hour when our narrative takes her by surprise, even if she had been past 80, she would have believed that she had lived a very short time if her last moments were approaching and she was about to leave behind in the world her forsaken young granddaughter, and it was not to be her lot to witness the denouement of a drama in which, although she was not its heroine, she had for some time played, much against her will, a very important role. Once the naturally irascible character of *Seña* Josefa had accommodated itself to the rule of conduct that has been mentioned earlier as a means of attaining forgiveness for her own sins, it is easy to understand why, even though justifiably angry at Cecilia because she had come home late, and because of her many other previous misdeeds, she felt more inclined to excuse her than to reprimand her.

Later, as Cecilia came to her with her cajolery, instead of drawing away from her, this served her as a plausible pretext for carrying out her intention. To her credit, promptly changing her tone of voice and expression, she limited herself to asking her for a second time where she had been.

"Who, me?" the girl repeated, leaning both elbows on her grandmother's knees and toying with the scapulars hanging from her neck.

"Who, me? At the home of some very pretty girls who saw me passing by and called out to me to come in. Inside was a fat woman sitting in a rocking chair, who asked me what my name was, and what my mother's name was, and who my father was, and where I lived . . ."

"Good Lord! Good Lord!" *Seña* Josefa exclaimed, crossing herself.

"Oh, my!" the girl went on, paying no attention to her grandmother. "What inquisitive people! And I haven't told your grace, have I, how one of those girls wanted to cut my hair to make a chignon for herself? Yes indeed. But I cleared out of there."

"Just look at how wicked she is and how high she climbs!" the grandmother exclaimed again, as though talking to herself.

"And had it not been for a man who was sitting on the sofa," Cecilia went on, "and who scolded the girls and told them to leave me alone and then went off to his room in a rage . . . Doesn't your grace know who that man is, Granny? I've seen him talking with your grace several times there at Paula, when we go to Mass. Yes, yes, it's him, I'm certain of it! And now I remember that he's the same man who calls me a streetwalker, a harlot, a hussy, and a good many other things every time he meets me on the street. Ah! And he says that he's going to send soldiers who'll nab me and take me to prison. And I don't know what-all else! I'm really scared of that man. He must be terribly bad-tempered!"

"Child! Child!" the old woman exclaimed as if to herself, holding her a short distance away from her breast and looking at her in a strange way, her eyes riveted on her, more annoyed than surprised. But as though a grave thought or a painful memory had occurred to her as she was half admonishing her and half counseling her, which was perhaps tantamount to enlightening her about something that she ought to remain ignorant of all her life, to her granddaughter's surprise she suddenly fell silent, as if her sad spirits were struggling in a sea of doubts. Little by little the rough sea grew calm: the dense clouds that lay piled up on that naturally dark horizon vanished; and clasping the girl in her arms once again, she added in as gentle a voice as she could muster, for it was hoarse by nature, and with all the calm in which she could cloak her face:

"Cecilia! My darling daughter, never go to that house again."

"Why, Granny?"

"Because," the grandmother answered, her mind seemingly elsewhere, "I don't really know, my beloved girl, I don't know; I wouldn't be able to tell you if I wanted to . . . but it's as plain as day, child, that those people are very wicked."

"Wicked!" Cecilia repeated, bewildered. "When they gave me so many caresses, and sweets, and satin for shoes? If you only knew how they pampered me . . . !"

"Don't set any store by them, child. You're very trusting and that's not good. For the very reason that they pampered you so much you must be doubly on the alert. They want to attract you in order to do you some sort of harm. A person can't say what people are capable of. So many things happen now that were never seen in my day . . . ! At the very least what they were trying to do was to put you off your guard so as to get a pair of scissors and snip! lop off your hair. That would be a shame, because yours is so pretty. What's more, that hair of yours doesn't belong to you, but to the Virgin, who saved you from that grave illness . . . Remember! I promised her that if you got well I'd give her your hair to adorn her statue in the church of Santa Catalina. Don't trust them, I tell you."

Saying this, she took her granddaughter's head between her two hands and spread her abundant curls out over her back and shoulders.

"Yes," Cecilia replied, clamping her lips together and raising her forehead with a scornful air: "since I'm so stupid that they could fool me just like that . . ."

"Nonetheless, daughter, the best thing to do with dice is not to play with them. I know very well that you're a docile and clever girl, but I'm certain you don't know those people. Look, pay no attention to them even if their gullet dries out calling to you, don't go inside to where they are. But now that I remember: the best thing is not to go within even a hundred leagues of where they are. Then that man that you yourself say makes a face at you wherever he happens to come across you: heaven only knows who he might be! Even though we ought not to think badly of anyone, nonetheless, seeing that he might be a saint but might just as readily be a dev . . . (And she crossed herself without finishing the word.) May the Lord be with us. What's more, Cecilia, you're very innocent, but a bit hare-brained, and in that house . . . Didn't you know? There's a witch who spirits away pretty girls. By a miracle of his divine Majesty you've escaped. You were there in the afternoon, isn't that so?"

"In the late afternoon; there were no lights on in the houses yet."

"Heaven help you if you were to go inside at night! Come, don't ever go to that house as long as you live, or ever walk along that block either."

"Hmmm! So a lad who's already a grown-up also lives there. I keep running into him at the convent of Santa Teresa, with a book under his arm. Every time he sees me he tries to catch up with me and find out what my name is . . ."

"A student, depraved like all the rest of them. At least you escaped from the clutches of the Evil One himself. But I keep seeing that you have a head as hard as a rock, that no matter how hard I try to advise you I don't get anywhere. In fact, who has ever seen a girl as pretty as you loafing about on the streets until all hours of the night, with your slippers dragging and your hair loose and unkempt? Who are you learning these bad habits from? Why won't you listen to me?"

"And doesn't Nemesia, the daughter of *Seño* Pimienta the musician, stay out on the streets till ten? Only the night before last, no less, I came across her in the Plazuela del Cristo playing *lunita* with a bunch of boys."[7]

"And you're trying to compare yourself with *Seño* Pimienta's daughter, who's a little mulatto dressed in rags, a street urchin with no upbringing? Any day now they'll be bringing that girl possessed by the devil back home on a plank with her head split in two. The leopard, my girl, never changes its spots. You're better born than she is. Your father is a white gentleman, and some day you'll be rich and ride in a carriage. Who knows? But Nemesia will never be more than what she is. She'll marry, if she marries, a mulatto like herself, because her father is more black than anything else. You, on the contrary, are almost white and can aspire to marrying a white. Why not? God gave us what we need to get ahead. And you should know that a white, even a poor one, makes a satisfactory husband; but a black or a mulatto, not a chance. . . . I'm speaking from experience. . . . Since I was married twice. . . . Let's not remember things from the past. . . . If you only knew what happened to a young girl, almost exactly your age, because she didn't heed the advice of a grandmother of hers who predicted that if she insisted on going about the streets late at night a terrible misfortune was going to befall her. . . ."

"Tell me about it, tell me about it, Chepilla," the girl repeated, as curious as anyone else would be.

"Well, then: on a night as dark as they come, with a strong wind blowing—incidentally, it was Saint Bartholomew's Night, on which, as I've already told you before, the devil goes out on the loose beginning at three in the afternoon—a girl whose name was Narcisa was sitting singing softly in the stone doorway of her house, while her grandmother prayed, sitting off by herself in a corner behind the window. . . . I remember as if it were this very day. Well, let me tell you, they had tolled the bells at Espíritu Santo to summon people to say the prayers for the dead, and since the wind had blown out the street lamps, the streets were very dark, like a wolf's maw, and silent and lonely. Then, as I was saying, the girl was singing and the old woman was saying the rosary when a violin, mind you, is heard being played on the other side of El Angel. What did that Narcisa imagine? That there was a ball going on, and without asking her grandmother's permission, without saying a word, she set off at a run and didn't stop until she'd reached El Angel Hill. So when the old woman finished praying, believing that her granddaughter was in bed, she bolted the door, as was only natural."

"And left the poor girl out in the street?" Cecilia interrupted the storyteller, showing her feelings of friendship and sympathy for the girl.

"You'll see in a minute. The little old woman, before going to bed, because it was already late and she was so sleepy she was about to drop, took a candle and went to her granddaughter's cot to see if she was asleep. Just imagine what a state she was in when she found the cot empty, for she loved her granddaughter dearly. She ran to the street door, opened it, and called out to her granddaughter: Narcisa! Narcisa! But Narcisa doesn't answer. Naturally, for how was she to answer, poor girl, if the devil had carried her off?

"How did that happen?" Cecilia asked in bewilderment.

"I'll tell you," *Seña* Chepa went on calmly, noting that her tale of tales was having the desired effect. Well, let me tell you, when Narcisa arrived at the Cinco Esquinas in El Angel, where the five streets meet, a very handsome young man appeared and asked her where she was going at that hour of the night. 'To watch a ball,' the guileless girl answered. 'I'll take you to it,' the young man answered; and taking her by one arm led her out to the wall. Although it was very dark, Narcisa noticed that as they walked along the stranger was turning dark, very dark, as black as coal; that the hair on his head was standing on end, each lock as straight as a shoemaker's awl; that when he laughed he bared teeth the size of a wild boar's; that two horns were sprouting from his forehead; that he had a hairy tail dragging on the ground behind him; that fire was coming out of his mouth as from a bakery oven. Narcisa then screamed in terror and tried to escape, but the black figure sank his nails into her throat to keep her from screaming, and picking her up bodily, climbed up to the tower of El Angel Hill, which as you may have noticed, has no cross, and from there he threw her inside a deep, deep shaft that opened and then closed again, swallowing her up in an instant. So, my girl, that's what happens to girls who don't heed the advice of their elders."

Seña Chepa ended her story there and Cecilia's stupefaction and fear began; she started to tremble from head to foot and her teeth began to chatter, although she continued to yawn, because she was more sleepy than she was frightened; and so she stumbled off to bed, which is what the clever old woman was aiming at. She told many other stories of the same sort to the vagabond girl; but we are certain that they bore no other fruit than to fill her granddaughter's head with superstitions and scare her a bit. That is to say, they didn't keep the girl from doing as she pleased, stealing out of the house through the window at times, and at others taking advantage of being sent to the tavern next door on the corner on an errand to roam from street to street and square to square: sometimes in pursuit of exciting music coming from a ball, or else chasing after the drum rolls at the changing of the guard, or following the carriages of a funeral procession, or, finally, searching out a crowd of young people vying for little silver coins flung into their midst after a baptism.

I V

They have a way of thinking
Full of obscenity, and spread it abroad
In a thousand scandalous indecencies
That pollute the wind
And broadcast far and wide what they love.

González Carvajal

Five or six years after the period to which we have confined ourselves in the two previous chapters, at the end of the month of September the convent of La Merced had begun the series of *ferias* with which until the year 1832 it was the custom in Cuba to celebrate religious holidays honoring the patron saints of churches and convents; these nine-day periods coincided at times with the cycle of the Sacrament, introduced into Cuban rites of worship as early as the first years of the century by His Reverence Bishop Espada y Landa.[8]

These *novenarios*, let it be said in passing, began nine days before the one on which that of the patron saint fell, and then went on for another nine, thereby constituting two successive novenary periods, that is to say, 18 days of public celebration, religious and secular, that were more grotesque and irreverent in nature than they were devout and edifying.

During this time High Mass was said with a sermon in the morning and the *Salve Maria* was sung at Vespers inside the church, with a procession through the streets on the saint's day.

Outside the temple there was held what was meant by a *feria* in Cuba, which amounted to the accumulation in the little plaza or in the nearby streets of innumerable mobile stands, consisting of a table or wooden panel set on a sawhorse, with a canvas awning overhead and lighted by one or more oil lamps, where there were sold, not any industrial or commercial article of the country certainly, or any product of the soil, or game or poultry or cattle, but only trifles of very little value, preserves of several sorts, pies, corn cakes, hazelnuts, sugar icings, *agualoja*, a drink made of honey, water, and spices, and milk punch. In the strict sense of the word, a *feria* was not the celebration of a religious holiday.

But this was naturally not the most notable feature of our fiestas that came round each year. In the spectacle there was something that stood out because of its vulgar and insolent nature. We now limit ourselves to the gambling games and sleight of hand tricks that were part of the *ferias* and that aroused the greed of the unwary with their deceptively promised stupendous winnings. Most of them were conducted or performed by men of color of the worst sort. Although their stratagems were crude, they nonetheless hoodwinked many who considered themselves very canny. They took place in the little plaza or in the street, in the dim light of oil lamps or paper lanterns, and people of all classes, social conditions, ages, and sexes took part in them. For those high on the social ladder, by which we mean for the whites, there was something less vulgar, the houses where dances were held, and where a Farruco, a Brito, an Illas, or a Marqués de Casa Calvo kept a gaming table or a game of monte going from dusk until past midnight throughout the 18 days of the *feria*.

Every effort was made to ensure that such a house or houses would be as close as possible to the parish church or convent where the *novenario* was being held. There was dancing in the drawing room, the orchestra played in the dining room and in the patio the game known as monte took place.

The table was long and narrow, so that the largest number of players could be seated on either side, with the dealer at one end and his assistant, called the croupier, at the other. For the protection of the players and the cards in case of rain, frequent in autumn, a canvas awning was stretched from the eaves of the house to the top of the wall dividing it from the house immediately adjoining it. Not all the cardsharps, let it be said to our shame, were of the stronger sex, already adults, or laymen, for in the eager crowd of those who were mayhap risking on the turn of a card their family's sustenance on the following day or the honor of their wife, daughter, or sister, there could be seen a lady more intent on the draw of the cards than on her own decorum, or a youth as yet still beardless, or a friar eager for money, dressed in his habit of coarse straw-colored wool, with his broad-brimmed hat pulled down over his forehead, the beads of his long rosary between the index finger and thumb of his left hand, and his right busy placing a gold or silver coin in the most promising place, invariably winning or losing in a mood as imperturbable as his face.

The banker, to call the dealer by his more respectable name, was the one who paid for renting the house, hiring the musicians, and providing the spermaceti candles with which the ballroom, the dining room, and the gaming table were illuminated. All this was done to attract gamblers. There was no entry fee, although the director of the dance, who also was paid for his services, did not allow just anyone to enter. In that era strong currency, that is to say Spanish *duros* and doubloons, circulated widely. Small silver coins were scarce, and it was something to hear the continuous heavy clinking of the *pesotes columnarios*[9] and the loud ringing of the *onzas*, which the gamblers mechanically let fall from one hand to the other or onto the table, as if to distract their thoughts and somehow break the solemn silence of the high stakes.

That nothing of what is outlined here in broad strokes was prohibited or merely tolerated by the authorities can be clearly inferred from the fact that gaming houses in Cuba paid a contribution to the government for supposedly charitable causes. What else? The overt way in which monte was played everywhere on the Island, in particular during the last years of Captain General Don Francisco Dionisio Vives's command, made it evident, beyond a doubt, that his policy or that of his administration was based on the Machiavellian principle of corrupting in order to dominate, copying that other celebrated principle of the Roman statesman: *divide et impera*. For corrupting people's spirits was tantamount to dividing them, so that they would not see their own misery and degradation.

But this digression, however necessary it may be, has diverted us somewhat from the object of the present story. Our entire attention was attracted by a lower class dance that was being held in the sector of the city that looks to the south. The house where it took place was wretched-looking, not so much because of its sagging, dirty facade as for the site where it was located, which was none other than that of the porter's lodge of San José, opposite the wall, in a sunken, stony street.

Although it had a wide door with a side wicket, it did not constitute what is meant in Cuba by a *zaguán* or carriage entrance, for it opened directly onto the drawing room. Behind this latter came the dining room with the corresponding *tinajero,* a stand for water containers, with a pyramidal framework of cedar, within which thin-slatted shutters enclosed the filtering stone, the potbellied vat of red earthenware, the jars of a sort of terracotta, and the jars of pale clay from Valencia, in Spain. The master bedroom, largely occupied by two rows of large chairs of red calfskin, a bed with draperies of white muslin and an armoire, which in Havana is called an *escaparate* or showcase, opened onto the aforementioned dining room via a side door. Other bedrooms came next, full of ordinary pieces of furniture, and parallel to them was a long narrow patio, partially obstructed by the tall rim of a well whose brackish waters were shared by the house next door, with the bedrooms and the patio leading to a sitting room running crosswise and open on all sides.

In this latter was a regular-sized table, with a tablecloth already spread over it and laid with place settings for up to ten people; some cool drinks and food: *agualoja,* lemonade, sweet wines, preserves, frosted sponge cake, ladyfingers, meringues, a ham decorated with ribbons tied in bows and confetti, and a large fish, practically swimming in a thick, highly seasoned sauce. In the drawing room were many ordinary wooden chairs lined up against the walls, and on the right as one entered from the street, a settee, with various music stands in front of it. As our story begins, it was occupied by seven black and mulatto musicians, three violinists, a bassist, a flutist, a pair of kettledrummers. The musician who was to play the clarinet was a young mulatto, well turned out and not badlooking, who despite his youth was the director of that little orchestra. He was standing at the end of the settee nearest the street. His fellow musicians, almost all of them older than he, called him Pimienta, and regardless of whether that was a nickname (for it means "pepper") or his real surname, that is what we shall henceforth call him. His distracted and even somber gaze never left the street door, as though he were waiting for something or someone at the moment of which we are now speaking.

But that door, like the window with a square sash, was being besieged by a crowd of curious onlookers of every age and social status, who scarcely allowed the women and men who had the right or the desire to enter the room to gain access to it. And we say the right or the desire, because no one presented a ticket, nor was there a director of the dance to receive them or show them around. The ball was clearly one of those that, even though we do not know the origin of the word, were called *cunas*[10] in Havana. We know only that they were held during *ferias*, that colored individuals of both sexes were freely given entrée to them, as were young whites who were in the habit of honoring them with their presence. The fact, however, that good refreshments had been set out inside, was proof that if that was a *cuna*, in the broad sense of the word, at least a certain number of those present had been sent an invitation or were expecting to be well received, as in truth they were. The mistress of the house, a rich and extravagantly openhanded mulatto named Mercedes, was celebrating her saint's day with her close friends, and opened her door so that those fond of dancing could enjoy this diversion and contribute to the greater splendor and interest of the gathering by their presence.

It must have been eight o'clock at night. Since afternoon, the first autumn downpours had been falling, and although they had stopped around dusk, after having soaked the ground, leaving the streets impassable, they had not refreshed the atmosphere. Quite to the contrary, it was still so saturated with humidity that it adhered to one's skin and boiled in one's pores. But this did not deter the curious onlookers who, as we have said earlier, besieged the door and the window in such numbers that they finally filled almost half the narrow winding street; nor did it deter those attending the dance, who as the night went on arrived in greater and greater numbers, some on foot, others in carriages. Around nine the drawing room where the dancing was to take place was a teeming throng of human heads; the women seated in the chairs around the room and the men standing in the middle, forming a compact group, all with their hats still on; hence the tallest head doubtless bumped into the crystal ball suspended from a beam by three copper chains, inside which a single spermaceti candle burned to dimly light that crowd as incongruous as it was heterogeneous.

A fairly large number of black and mulatto women had entered, most of them dressed outlandishly. The men of the same class, more numerous than the women, were dressed in no better taste, although almost all of them were wearing a wool jacket and a piqué vest, the minority a close-fitting coat of drill or blue and white checked cotton, which was the usual attire for men at the time, and a wool hat. There were also a goodly number of young Creoles from respectable, well-off families, who were unabashedly rubbing elbows with the people of color and taking part in their most characteristic diversion, some simply out of a liking for it, others impelled by motives of less innocent origin. It would appear that some of them, a small number in all truth, did not behave discreetly toward the women of their own class, if we are to judge by the lack of decorum with which they lingered in the ballroom and addressed their acquaintances or friends in the presence of those silent but knowing female spectators who were watching them from outside the window of the house.

Among the aforementioned young men, one of them, whom his companions called Leonardo, stood out, as much because of his handsome, manly face and figure as because of his jovial manner. He was wearing trousers and a coat of coarse drill with pink stripes, a white piqué waistcoat, a silk tie fastened around his neck by a gold ring and the ends left loose, a hat of palm fiber, so delicate that it appeared to be made of fine cambric, short silk flesh-colored socks and low shoes with a small gold buckle to one side. Underneath his waistcoat there could be seen an iridescent red and white ribbon, folded in two with its ends held down by another gold buckle. This served as a chain for the watch in the pocket of his trousers. There was another man present who stood out even more than Leonardo, if that is possible, although in a different way—that is to say, because of how greatly the blacks and mulattos differed from his opinion, and laughed at his coarse jokes, and because of the familiarity with which he treated the women, in particular the mistress of the house. This individual, while close to forty, hadn't the least sign of a beard, his face was white, with large eyes that had a mad look about them, a long nose, red at the tip, a sign of his intemperance, and a large but expressive mouth. He invariably carried a rattan cane under his left arm, with a gold handle and black silk tassels. He was accompanied everywhere, as a person's body is accompanied by its shadow, by a man of unremarkable appearance, notable only for the narrowness of his forehead, for his lively little blazing eyes and above all for his enormous black sideburns, that gave him more the air of a brigand than of a constable, a post he held at that time (for the other man whom he was accompanying was none other than Cantalapiedra, the commissioner of the district of El Angel),[11] which he had abandoned to follow the trail of the enticing *cuna*.

The orchestra had been playing sentimental and lively Cuban country dances for some time now, although the ball, to employ the common phrase, hadn't yet really taken off. The mistress of the house painstakingly seated her closest and most elderly friends in the chairs in the master bedroom, so that even as they remained on the sidelines, safe from all the trampling and tripping, they could enjoy the festivities while at the same time not losing sight of the individuals who were the object either of their concern or of their affections, those young people of an age to stay on in the ballroom. Pimienta, the clarinetist, remained standing at the head of the orchestra, playing his favorite instrument, almost facing the street, as though the person worthy of hearing his music had not yet come in, or as though this watchfulness were useless, since not a man or woman entered who did not have a word to say to him in passing. He invariably returned all these greetings with a nod of his head, except when it came the turn of Captain Cantalapiedra, who with his usual familiar manner, put his hand on his shoulder and said something to him in secret, whereupon Pimienta answered, removing the mouthpiece of his instrument from between his lips: "So it would seem, Captain."

It was quite evident that each time a woman who for some reason was noteworthy, the violinists, doubtless to do her honor, wielded their bows more vigorously, the flutist or fife player pierced people's eardrums with his high-pitched instrument, the drummer pounded to perfection, the bass player (later on the famous Claudio Brindis), bent down over his instrument and produced the lowest notes imaginable, and the clarinetist performed the most difficult and most melodious variations. There is no doubt about it: those men were inspired, and the Cuban country dance, their creation, even with such a small orchestra, lost not one iota of its piquant charm or its profoundly sentimental-sly nature.

V

*"Have you ever in your life seen
A more graceful woman?"*
*"No.
Nor did there ever come out to the Park
One neater and better turned out."*
Calderón, *Mañanas de Abril y Mayo*

After making the rounds of the ballroom, Cantalapiedra burst into the bedroom of the mistress of the house and put his hands over her eyes just as she was bending over the bed to place on it the shawl of one of her friends who had just come in from the street. The aforementioned mistress of the house, Mercedes Ayala, was a gay, high-spirited mulatto, despite her being a little over 30; plump, short, and not bad-looking. Caught from behind, this neither flustered nor embarrassed her; rather, she spontaneously resorted to using both hands to feel those of the person keeping her from seeing, and immediately said: "It can't be anyone else but Cantalapiedra."

"How did you recognize me, my mulatto friend?" he asked.

"Well!" she replied. "Because of the charm of certain persons."

"My charm or yours?"

"Both, señor, so as not to quarrel about it."

Whereupon the commissioner gently drew her to him by the waist with his right arm and whispered something in her ear that sent her into peals of laughter; although, pushing him away with both hands, she replied:

"Nonsense! I don't believe a word of it, you flatterer! The girl who drives men crazy is arriving. I'm in on the whole story. . . . Look."

If by those last words Mercedes was alluding to one of the two girls who at that very moment alighted from a luxurious carriage at the door of the house, an event heralded by the general movement of heads inside and outside of it, there is no doubt that she was perfectly right; there was no girl who was prettier or more capable of addling the brain of a man enamored of her. She was the taller and svelter of the two, the one who took the lead on alighting from the carriage just as she did on entering the ballroom, on the arm of a mulatto who came out to receive her as she stepped off the footboard, and the one who, both by the regularity of her features and symmetry of her bodily contours, by the narrowness of her waist, in contrast to the breadth of her bare shoulders, by the amorous tilt of her head, and her complexion with a slight bronze tinge, might well have been taken to be the Venus of the hybrid Caucasian-Ethiopian race. Over an undergown of white satin she was wearing a transparent silk tulle gown with hooped short sleeves which made them look like two little globes, a broad sash of red ribbon across her chest, long silk elbow-length gloves, three strings of bright coral around her neck and atop her head a white marabou plume together with natural flowers, which, with her hair done up in a chignon underneath a row of curls from one temple to the other in back, gave her head the look of an old-fashioned black velvet bonnet, which was what she or her coiffeur had set out to copy. Her companion was dressed and coiffed in more or less the same way, but since she was not nearly as slender and beautiful, she did not attract as much attention.

The women were all eyes, the men made way for her, made some flattering or ribald remark to her, and in an instant the muffled whisper of "The Little Bronze Virgin, The Little Bronze Virgin" ran from one end of the house to the other. Even without the orchestra, the animation and the movement on every hand were clear indications that the queen of the ball had just made her appearance. As she passed alongside the clarinetist Pimienta, she tapped him on the arm with her fan, accompanying the gesture with a smile, as a sign to the musician, who obviously was avidly awaiting that moment, to bring forth from his instrument the strangest and most heartfelt melodies, as though the muse of his platonic dreams had descended to earth and taken on the form of a woman solely to inspire him. It may be said, in short, that the touch of her fan had on the musician the effect of an electrical discharge, the sensation of which, if it is apropos to express it in such a way, could be read both in his face and in his entire body, from his head to the soles of his feet. The two of them did not exchange words, naturally, nor did words seem necessary, at least insofar as he was concerned, for the language of her eyes and of his music was the most eloquent possible for any sensitive being to employ in order to express the ardor of his amorous passion.

The companion of the so-called Little Bronze Virgin also tapped Pimienta with her fan and smiled at him; but even the least observant spectator could see that the touch of the fan and the smile of the one did not have anywhere near the same magic influence on him as those of the other. On the contrary, the other's glances were met with a calm and natural gesture, whereby it was easy to deduce that there was a mutual understanding between her and the musician, albeit the sort of understanding that stems from friendship or kinship, not love. Be that as it may, Pimienta's eyes followed the two girls, insofar as the dense crowd permitted, until they entered the first bedroom through the dining room door, whereupon he stopped playing his clarinet and the music ended.

The young white men, with Cantalapiedra at their head, had finally installed themselves in the dining room, near that door leading to the next room, so as to be on the lookout both for the women entering from the street and for those who came out of the bedroom to dance in the ballroom. The minute the young man whom they called Leonardo had noted the approach of the carriage in which the two aforementioned girls were arriving, he had elbowed his way to the street with considerable difficulty and headed straight for the driver, to whom he addressed himself in a low voice. In order to hear him, the driver leaned down from the saddle of the horse that he was riding, doffed his hat as a sign of respect, and replying "yes, señor," drove the carriage off at once, rounding the corner of the Paula Women's Hospital at breakneck speed.

As the two girls were making their way from the dining room to the bedroom, the prettier of the two asked her friend, in a tone of voice that those nearby could hear:

"Did you see him, Nene?"

"Is love making you blind?" her companion answered her by asking another question.

"It's not that, my dear little halfbreed;[12] it's just that I didn't see him. What do you expect?"

"He darted right by you as we were coming in."

At this the other girl cast a quick glance around the group of heads surrounding her and leaning over her in their eagerness to contemplate her as much as they desired and to attract her gaze. But there is no doubt that her eyes did not happen to meet those of the individual whose name neither of the two mentioned, because she frowned and gave clear signs of her displeasure. Cantalapiedra, however, on hearing her words and noting the expression on her face, said: "What! How is it possible that you don't see me? Here I am, darling!"

The young girl made a face that spoke volumes and did not utter a word in reply. Nemesia, on the contrary, who was dying to exchange words with him, answered with more cleverness than charm:

"The señor could have been here all his life. Ary a soul was inquiring after him."

"I wasn't speaking to you, you dull creature."

"Nor was there any need to, you nobody."

"What language, what language," the commissioner repeated twice.

All this happened in an instant, as meanwhile the girls did not look back or stop to converse for any longer a time than it took for the men to make way for them. Already standing at the bedroom door, Mercedes received her friends with open arms and a great show of joy and affection. And either as a compliment, or because it expressed her real feelings, she said, almost shouting: "We were waiting for you so as to get the ball really started. How is Chepilla?" she asked, going on talking with the younger of the two girls. "Didn't she come? I was beginning to think that something had happened to her."

"I very nearly didn't come myself," the girl to whom the question had been addressed answered. "Chepilla wasn't feeling well, and then she started being so insolent . . . The gig waited for us for half an hour at least."

"It's best she didn't come," Mercedes continued, "because this affair is going to go on till dawn and her strength would have given out. Hand me your shawls."

It was now time for the festivities to begin. In fact, a tall, bald mulatto rather well along in years but quite robust soon appeared in the bedroom occupied by the matrons, planted himself in front of Mercedes Ayala, and said to her in a hoarse voice with his arms upraised:

"I have come for grace and charm in person to open the ball."

"Well, brother, go to the other door, because you won't find her here," Mercedes replied, laughing heartily.

"Don't give me any excuses, señora, because I'm persistent. Besides, the honor of opening the ball belongs to no one but the mistress of the house; besides, it's your saint's day."

"That would be all well and good if at this distinguished gathering there were no pretty girls, to whom power and glory everywhere rightly belong."

"It is plain to see," the bald mulatto added, "that at such a distinguished gathering there is no lack tonight of a great number of very pretty girls, but this attribute, which the mistress of the house also shares, does not give them the right to open the ball. Today, on your saint's day, Merceditas, it is you who are the mistress of the house in which we are celebrating such a happy day, and it is you who are the world's wit and charm. Have I spoken truly?" he concluded, looking round at all those present in search of their approval.

All of them, to a greater or lesser degree, either by their words or by their gestures, indicated that they agreed, so that Mercedes was obliged to stand up and reluctantly follow her companion to the ballroom. By then the men had cleared the room, leaving a good-sized empty space in the middle. The bald man led Mercedes by the hand and stood stock still with her, facing the orchestra which he imperiously ordered to play a court minuet. This grave and elaborately formal dance had fallen into disuse in the era of which we are speaking; but because it was the custom in respectable or elite circles, people of color in Cuba always reserved it for opening their fiestas.

That old-fashioned dance was executed fairly gracefully by the woman and grotesquely by the man; the former was greeted by the spectators with thunderous applause, and then, without further ado, the real dancing began, that is to say, what is known as Cuban dance, a modification of Spanish dance so special and so unusual that its origin is scarcely discernible. One of the many men present made so bold as to invite the young girl with the white plume in her hair, whom we might call the muse of that fiesta, to dance, and without waiting to be asked twice and without the slightest qualm, she accepted the invitation without reservation. As she went from the bedroom to the ballroom to take her place in the rows of dancers, the following audible exclamation escaped one of the women:

"How lovely she is! May God bless her and keep her."

"The very picture of her mother, may she rest in peace," another woman added.

"What! That girl's mother is dead?" a third asked in great surprise.

"Well, I declare! Are you just now finding that out?" replied the one who had spoken second. "Didn't you hear that she died as a result of having lost her daughter just a few days after the baby was born?"

"I don't understand how she lost her if she's alive."

"You didn't let me esplain, *Seña* Caridad. She lost her daughter a few days after she was born because she was taken away from her when she least expected. Some people say it was her grandmother who took her, in order to put her in the Royal Foundling Home so that she could pass as white; others say that the thief wasn't the grandmother, but the baby's father, a very important gentleman who had repented of his dealings with the mother and the pledges made to her. The mother lost her mind as well as her daughter, and when they returned her daughter to her on the advice of the doctors, it was too late, because while she may have recovered her mind, despite there being those who doubt it, she didn't recover her health and died in Paula Hospital."

"You've told quite a story, *Seña* Trinidad," Mercedes said softly, smiling incredulously at the mulatto woman who had just spoken.

"My girl," Trinidad replied in a loud voice, "I told it the way it was told to me; I didn't put in or leave out anything on my own."

"Well, according to my information, which is from a reliable source," Mercedes continued, "either you or the one who told you the story added a great deal that was her own invention. I say that because it is not known for certain whether the girl's mother is alive or dead; the only thing that's proven fact is that the grandmother has kept the name of the girl's father hidden from her, though a person would have to be blind not to see or recognize who he was. At any rate he goes from one window to another to this very day, following the girl's footsteps, so as not to lose sight of her for a moment. It would appear that that ungrateful and inhuman man, having repented of his conduct toward poor Rosario Alarcón, has as yet found no other way of expiating his sin save to follow his daughter from *cuna* to *cuna* and from fiesta to fiesta, to see if he can save her from the world's dangers. Don't worry. He has his work cut out for him. Because a person has to clip the wings of a bird a little at a time once it has begun to fly."

"But may I ask," said the woman they called Caridad, "who the distinguished gentleman in question is? Because I'm someone who doesn't know who he is and has never seen him, and it doesn't seem to me that I'm either deaf or blind."

"Since I know what unsatisfied curiosity is like, *Seña* Caridad, I'm going to keep you from wondering any longer," Mercedes said, drawing closer to her. "I believe that I am speaking with a woman who can keep a secret, and so I'll tell you the whole story. To be precise, there is no need for me to keep everything to myself at this late date. I can tell you that the man is . . . ," and placing both hands on the shoulders of the inquisitive woman she whispered in her ear the name of the individual. "Do you know who he is now?" Mercedes ended up by asking.

"Of course," *Seña* Caridad answered. "I know him like I know the palm of my hand. The one I used to know best of all. Incidentally . . . But watch your tongue, Caridad."

It must have been ten at night and the ball was at its height. People were dancing in a frenzy. We say in a frenzy because we cannot find a term that captures the reality of that incessant movement of people's feet as they shifted them voluptuously back and forth along with their bodies to the rhythm of the music; turning round and round and pressing together amid the jam-packed crowd of dancers and onlookers and that rise and fall of the dance without letup or respite. Above the sound of the orchestra with its deafening kettledrums there could be heard, in perfect time to the music, the monotonous and continuous shuffling of feet; a requisite without which people of color do not believe that it is possible to keep perfect time to the music when dancing Creole-style.

In the era of which we are speaking, the latest vogue was for country dances with set figures, some of which were so difficult and complicated that it was necessary to learn them first before daring to perform them in public, since anyone who made a misstep laid himself open to ridicule; such a mistake was known as "getting lost." The man who placed himself at the head of the dancers set the figure, and the other couples had to follow it or leave the rows of dancers. At every *cuna* there was usually an expert dancer or "maestro" to whom the other dancers yielded or granted the right to "set the figure," which on taking the lead again, he changed at will. The one who set the most unusual and complicated figures enhanced his reputation as an excellent dancer and the women regarded it as an honor to be his companion or partner. As for the maestro, in addition to that distinction, which was sometimes vied for, he enjoyed the certainty of not "getting lost" or of finding himself sadly obliged to sit down without having even danced after having taken his place in the rows of dancers.

On the night in question, the maestro danced with Nemesia, the closest friend of the young girl with the white plume in her hair. He had set many figures and most unusual ones, knowingly leaving for last the most difficult and complicated one of all. The second, third, fourth, and fifth couples came through the test with flying colors, executing the figure with the same couplings, uncouplings, and poses as the maestro; but despite the space that the partner of the so-called Little Bronze Virgin had at his disposal to study the figure and learn it, since he occupied the sixth place in the rows of dancers, as his turn came he became more and more anxious and turned his face toward the musicians with a gesture of supplication, as if hoping that they would guess the fix he was in and stop the music. His anxiety was communicated to his partner, who realized that she was about to endure the shame of having to go sit down at the liveliest and most intriguing moment of the dance. Fear overcame her entirely, making her pale and nervous. What went through the minds of that couple soon became visible to the eyes of the other couples and of many of the spectators.

The mere idea that the one who had thus far been the queen of the *cuna* might be obliged to leave the rows of dancers before the end of the figure had filled the other girls with cruel and envious rejoicing, for they had been greatly mortified by the favoritism and public showers of praise of which she had been made the object by the men from the moment she first appeared at the ball. In those critical circumstances, Pimienta, who had never once lost sight of her in the midst of her capricious gyrations and the tumult of the dance, quickly realized what was happening, and without warning anyone of his intent, suddenly stopped the music. The young girl's partner breathed a sigh of relief, and she repaid that most timely aid from the orchestra conductor with a celestial smile.

V I

And from amid the indiscreet tumult
Furiously whirling around her,
No one said to her: See there,
That gentleman who adores you in secret,
Is listening and looking at you.

Ramón de Palma, *Quince de Agosto*

The discreet reader will already have realized that the Little Bronze Virgin of the preceding pages was none other than Cecilia Valdés, that same young vagabond whom we endeavored to introduce at the beginning of this true story. Hence by this time she had reached the flower of her youth and of her beauty and was beginning to collect the idolatrous tributes that a sensual and depraved people always generously offers those two deities. When the reader remembers Cecilia's careless upbringing and adds to this the indecent flirtatious advances to which men subjected her, along with the fact that she belonged to a mixed, inferior race, he or she will conceive more or less of an idea of her pride and vanity, the driving forces of her imperious temperament. And so with no shame and no misgivings, she frequently made clear her preferences for men of the superior white race, since it was from them that she could hope for distinction and pleasures, the reason she was in the habit of saying openly that the only thing mulatto-colored she wanted was her silk shawls, and the only thing black her eyes and hair.

It is easy to believe that such a frankly voiced opinion ran contrary to the aspirations of mulatto and black men, and therefore did not sit well with them, as the common expression has it. Nonetheless, either because they did not believe her to be sincere when she expressed it, or because they hoped that she would make an exception, or because, being as beautiful as she was, it was impossible to see her without loving her, the truth is that more than one mulatto was hopelessly in love with her, above all others Pimienta, the musician, as the reader will doubtless have noted. This fellow enjoyed the inestimable advantage over her other suitors of being the brother of Cecilia's intimate friend and companion since her childhood, and therefore he could see her often, be on close terms with her, make himself necessary, and perhaps win her rebellious heart by dint of devotion and perseverance. Who has not cherished in his life an even more ephemeral hope? In any event, Pimienta always kept in mind that popular song of Spanish poets that begins: "While it is not hard, water carves away/ the hardest marble," and with due respect for the truth it can be said that Cecilia distinguished him from the other men of his class who besieged her so as to extol her, although this distinction, up until now, had not gone beyond an act or two of friendship toward a man who in any case was most likable, courteous, and attentive to women.

Once the dance was over, the drawing room used for the ball filled up again and groups began to form around the women who were the favorites, thanks to their beauty, their amiability, or their flirtatiousness. But amid the apparent confusion that then reigned in that house, anyone could see that between the men of color and the white men at least, a dividing line was now in place which, tacitly and to all appearances effortlessly, both groups respected. The truth is that both devoted themselves so wholeheartedly to the enjoyment of the moment that it is not particularly surprising that they forgot their mutual jealousy and hatred for the time being. Moreover, the whites did not abandon the dining room and the main bedroom, the two gathering places of the mulatto girls with whom they were on friendly terms or had some other sort of relation or would like to have one, something neither new nor unusual, given their marked predilection for such girls. Cecilia and Nemesia, for one or another of these reasons, or on account of their close friendship with the mistress of the house, went straight to her bedroom the moment the dance ended and seated themselves behind the matrons on the side of the room next to the dining room. There, without further ado, the group of young white men congregated, for as has already been said, these two girls were the most intriguing ones at the ball. There were undoubtedly three conspicuous persons in this group: Commissioner Cantalapiedra, Diego Meneses, and his close friend, the young man known as Leonardo. This latter had rested his right hand on the corner of the back of the chair occupied by Cecilia, who, either accidentally or deliberately, squeezed his fingers as she leaned back.

"Is that the way you treat your friends?" Leonardo said to her without taking his hand away, even though his fingers smarted fairly badly.

Cecilia confined herself to looking at him disapprovingly out of the corner of her eyes and then averting them, as though the word "friend" sounded jarring coming from someone who should have known that he was treated as an enemy.

"That girl is very disdainful today," said Cantalapiedra, who had noted her gesture and her look.

"And when isn't she?" Nemesia said, without turning her head.

"Nobody asked you for your opinion," the commissioner replied.

"And who asked the señor for his?" Nemesia added, looking askance at him.

"Who, me?"—this from Leonardo.

"He meant me, Cecilia," Nemesia explained.

"Pay no attention, girl," Cecilia said to her friend.

"If it weren't for the fact that . . . I'd make you softer than a glove," Cantalapiedra added, addressing Cecilia directly.

"The man hasn't yet been born who can make me knuckle under," she replied.

"You're speaking words tonight that sound very naive," Leonardo said to her then, leaning over far enough to place his mouth next to her ear.

"You owe me and you'll pay me," she answered him swiftly in the appropriate tone of voice.

"The good payer admits his faults, my father often says."

"I wouldn't know anything about that," Cecilia replied. "All I know is that you snubbed me tonight."

"I did, my darling?"

Just then Pimienta walked in through the drawing room door, greeting his female friends to right and left, and when he came within reach of Cecilia, she grabbed his right arm with unusual familiarity and said to him, affecting a glib air and tone of voice: "Listen! A man should keep his word!"

"My girl," he answered in a solemn tone of voice, although he did not take the matter all that seriously, "José Dolores Pimienta always keeps his word."

"The truth is that the country dance you promised hasn't been played yet."

"It will be played, Little Virgin, it will be played, because you must keep in mind that grapes ripen in their own good time."

"I was expecting it when the first dance was played."

"A mistake. Country dances dedicated to someone aren't played as part of the first dance but the second, and I didn't intend to break that rule with the one I composed."

"What name did you give it?" Cecilia asked.

"The one that the girl to whom it's dedicated deserves in every way: *I sell caramels.*"

"Ah! Then I'm certainly not that girl," Cecilia said, embarrassed.

"Who can say, girl! The grapes took a long time to ripen!" Pimienta added, addressing his sister Nemesia.

"Don't say a word to me, José Dolores," she replied. "It took God and no little help to persuade Chepilla to let us come by ourselves, because in the state she's in she couldn't come with us. She agreed at the last minute because we'd be going in a gig. And even so (in order to add the next words she looked at Cecilia as though consulting the expression on her face), if we hadn't made up our minds to climb into it, we'd still be at Chepilla's . . . She flew into a rage as soon as she peeked out the door and recognized . . ."

"Chepilla didn't get mad because of that at all, girl," Cecilia vehemently interrupted her friend. "She didn't want us to come because the weather tonight was too bad for us to be going to a ball. And she was quite right, but I'd given my word. . . ."

Out of prudence or for some other reason, Pimienta walked away without awaiting any more explanations. The same was not the case with Cantalapiedra, who was an inquisitive man if ever there was one, and therefore he asked Nemesia with a wicked smile: "May I ask why Chepilla flew into a rage as soon as she recognized the gig that you were going to the ball in?"

"Since I'm not a trunk for storing anybody's secrets in," Nemesia answered promptly, "I'll tell you the truth." (Cecilia gave her a pinch, but she finished the sentence.) "Of course: because she recognized that the gig belonged to the gentleman named Leonardo."

Naturally the looks of Cantalapiedra and the others present who could hear Nemesia's words focused on the individual whom she had named, and tapping him on the shoulder Cantalapiedra said to him:

"Come, come, don't flush with embarrassment. Lending one's carriage to two royal young ladies like these on such a nasty night is no reason for anyone to suspect a gentleman of harboring bad intentions."

"That gig, like it's owner's heart, is always at the disposal of beauties," Leonardo answered, unabashed.

At that moment Pimienta came through the dining room door and distinctly heard the young white man's words, which immediately convinced him that Leonardo was the owner of the gig in which Cecilia and his sister Nemesia had come to the ball. His disillusionment wounded him to the quick; and therefore, casting a sad look at the group of young whites, he immediately went to the drawing room where, after readying his clarinet, he played a few notes so that his comrades would realize that it was time for the orchestra to reassemble. Once they had tuned their instruments, without further ado they broke out into another country dance, which after a few bars couldn't help but attract everyone's attention and give rise to a round of applause, not only because the piece was a good one, but also because the listeners were connoisseurs, an assertion that will readily be believed by those who know the natural affinity for music with which people of color are born. The applause was repeated when the title of the country dance (*Caramelo vendo*) and the person to whom it was dedicated, the Little Bronze Virgin, were announced. It may be added in passing that the fortune of that piece was the most noteworthy of all those of its kind and period, for after being played at all the holiday balls for the remainder of the year and the following winter, it became the most popular song among every class of society.

It seems superfluous to add that with a new country dance, directed by the composer himself and played with great feeling and charm, the dancers gave it their all, that is to say they kept perfect time with their bodies and their feet, whose monotonous sound to all appearances duplicated the number being played by the orchestra. The clarinet with its silvery notes said very clearly: *caramelo vendo, vendo caramelo*, as the violins and the bass viol repeated them in another register, and the kettledrums provided a deafening chorus for the melancholy voice of the vendor of this sweet. But what was there about the composer of the piece that made such a great impression? Amid the delirium of the dance, was there anyone who remembered his name? Alas, no. As the night wore on with no sign of better weather, the inquisitive people outside began to leave the door and the windows of the ball early on, and by 11 not a single white face was still peeking in through them, at least not one face of a woman. The young men of respectable families, to whom we have referred earlier, who had a certain compunction about being seen dancing with their mulatto girl friends or acquaintances, took advantage of this circumstance: Cantalapiedra chose as his partner the mistress of the house, Mercedes Ayala; Diego Meneses, Nemesia; and Leonardo, Cecilia; and partly in order to observe, insofar as possible, the line of separation, partly because of a last remaining trace of this same belated compunction decided to dance in the dining room despite its small size and its untidy state.

In such circumstances any reader can imagine the anxious state that Pimienta was in. The muse who inspired him, the woman he adored, was in the arms of a young white man, perhaps her beloved; as we know, she did not hide her feelings and surrendered herself completely to the delirium of the ball, while he, bound to the orchestra as to a rock, saw her enjoying herself and himself contributing to her pleasure without participating in it in the slightest. His agitation was not, however, great enough to impair his conducting of the orchestra, or to have an unfavorable influence on his playing of his favorite instrument. On the contrary, his perturbation and his passion appeared to find relief only by way of the stops of his clarinet; his emotions were exhaled, so to speak, by way of the strange beauty and the softness of the notes that he drew from it, spreading enchantment and animation among the dancers. As the saying goes, there was not one puppet left with its head on its shoulders, no one who escaped the spell of the music, no one not dancing, in the drawing room, in the dining room, in Mercedes's bedroom, even in the narrow open-air patio of the house. Is it not strange, then, that at that moment it did not even occur to those who were having such a good time and so greatly enjoying themselves that the composer and the moving spirit behind all that happiness and that festive mood, José Dolores Pimienta, the creator of the new country dance, was dying of love and the pangs of jealousy?

It must have been past midnight when the music stopped once again, and shortly thereafter those individuals who had good reason to consider themselves strangers to the mistress of the house began to leave, because up until then she had not raised her voice to tell the invited guests that it was time to have supper together. And to hurry them along, she grabbed two of her best friends by the arm and almost dragged them to the sitting room at the far end of the patio where we have already said that the supper table was laid out. The rest of the men and women followed after them, among the former Pimienta and Brindis, the musicians, Cantalapiedra and his inseparable constable, the one with the bushy sideburns, Leonardo and his friend Diego Meneses. The women, the only ones for whom there was room at the table, although they were few in number, seated themselves; the men remained standing, each one behind the chair of his friend or favorite. Cantalapiedra and Mercedes found themselves together at one end of the table, although we are unable to say whether this was by chance or in order to do the commissioner and his official position honor.

There is no doubt that the exercise provided by the dancing had whetted the appetite of the table companions of both sexes, for with some of the guests taking over the ham, others the fish, olives, and other delicacies, everyone tucked in and in no time had relieved the table of a good part of its weight. The necessity of sheer sustenance having been satisfied, there was time for the little acts of courtesy and affection that in all countries will bear the seal of the breeding of the persons who perform them. Those individuals in our true story whose physiognomy we are here outlining in broad brushstrokes did not even belong, generally speaking, to the middle class or to the class that receives a better upbringing in Cuba, and it may readily be believed that their little acts of courtesy and affection in no instance had anything delicate or refined about them.

"Say something, Cantalapiedra," someone remarked.

"Cantalapiedra doesn't say anything when he's eating," the man himself answered as he gnawed on a turkey leg.

"He shouldn't eat then if he's not going to say anything," another put in.

"Not on your life, because I'm going to eat until Judgment Day," the commissioner replied. "But how do you expect me to say something if I haven't even wet my whistle yet?"

"Here's my glass! And here's mine! Take this one!" at least ten voices exclaimed, and an equal number of arms stretched across the table toward the commissioner, who, grabbing one glass after another, each of them full of a different wine, downed them all, showing no sign of the effect that they were having on him except that his face turned a bit red and his eyes grew teary. Then, filling his own glass with delicious champagne, he coughed, puffed out his chest, and in a resounding but slightly hoarse voice, said:

"Silence! On my friend Merceditas Ayala's happy birthday, a *décima*."[13]

> I tell you on this night.
> Merceditas, of my eyes the light,
> That your gaze has in it thorns,
>   Too piercing to be borne.

Look with sad compassion then,
On one who for your eyes would even
Dare to embrace death,
To take his last breath,
Yet endures in delusion
This life of illusion.

After this vulgar and tasteless improvisation, *vivas* and bursts of deafening applause resounded, accompanied by loud pounding on plates with knives. And as though in recompense for his poetic labor, from one of the women he received an olive impaled on the same fork with which she had just lifted a morsel of food to her mouth, from another a slice of ham, from one sitting farther away a piece of turkey, from yet another a caramel, from her neighbor a candied egg yolk, until Mercedes put an end to the flood of offerings by rising to her feet and passing her glass, full of sherry, to Leonardo so that he too would improvise a poem as the obliging commissioner had done. The latter took advantage of this respite that had tacitly been granted him to get up from the table, head directly, though furtively, to the rim of the well, where, thrusting two fingers down his throat, he threw up everything that he had eaten and drunk, no small amount. And he then returned to the table, revived and reinvigorated. Thanks to a means that was as simple as it was swift he was able to go back to eating and drinking as though he hadn't swallowed a single mouthful or downed a drop the whole night long. Of the other men who had drunk to excess, some more, some less, and were unacquainted with Cantalapiedra's handy remedy, few managed to remain clear-headed, not excepting young Leonardo.

This regrettable state of affairs must be attributed to the fact that this young man, as refined as he was well-bred, had also been willing to improvise verses in honor of the heroine of the fiesta. He managed to do so tolerably well, being no less applauded and rewarded than the previous poetaster, although it was noticeable that, far from celebrating his poetic effort as did the others, Cecilia Valdés remained silent and visibly embarrassed. Nor did Nemesia take part in the festivities, albeit for a very different reason, namely because she was engaged in a rapid secret dialogue with her brother José Dolores Pimienta.

"Isn't the backboard of the gig unattended by a lackey?" he said to her.

"Perhaps not," she replied.

"And how do you know that?"

"The way I know a great many things. Do I need to be spoonfed with information?"

"Of course not, but you haven't explained yourself."

"Because there's no time now."

"There's more than enough, sister."

"Well then . . . the walls have ears."

"Indeed they do! Providing a person shouts."

"Come on, don't be obstinate. I'm telling you not to do it."

"I'm not letting the chance go by."

"You're going to have a bad time of it."

"What do I care if I do what I want to do?"

"I'm telling you again, José Dolores, don't make trouble for yourself. Don't be so pigheaded. Such stubbornness takes away any willingness I have to help you. I understand this whole thing better than you do, I see."

Before the sound of voices, of palms pounding the table, and of knives hammering plates had become less deafening, Leonardo said something in secret to Cecilia and went out to the street, dragging Meneses along with him by the arm, taking French leave of everyone, as Cantalapiedra remarked when he noticed that they were gone. Once outside, despite the slight drizzle, both young men, still arm in arm, walked along the Calle de la Habana toward the center of the city, and at the first corner, where it crossed San Isidro, Meneses went straight on and Leonardo turned off toward Paula Hospital.

Light clouds, in chiaroscuro, broken up by the fresh wind from the northeast, crossed, one after another in more or less orderly procession, the face of the waning moon, which had already passed the zenith and from time to time shed beams of pale white light.

The narrow, winding cross street that young Leonardo was following never stood out clearly, nor did he see his way on his right until he reached the little square of the aforementioned hospital, and then there was moonlight only on the left-hand side, for the walls of Paula church, tall and dark, cast a double shadow over the open space. He could make out his carriage next to them, however, the horses standing with lowered head and ears, anxious to avoid the rain and the wind which hit them straight on. The folding hood was down and the driver was nowhere to be seen, either in the saddle, his usual place, nor on the backboard, nor in the wide doorway of the church, which might have afforded him shelter. But on taking a second look, Leonardo realized where he was. Sitting on the floor of the gig, his legs were hanging outside, sheathed in knee-length leather boots, while his head and arms, bent halfway back, rested on the soft leather cushions. The whip, which had fallen from his hands in his sleep, lay on the ground; Leonardo picked it up immediately, raised one corner of the hood, and with all his strength gave him two or three lashes on his shoulders that were in full view.

"Señor!" the driver exclaimed, half in pain and half in fright, sliding down out of the gig.

Once on his feet, he could plainly be seen to be a young mulatto, rather husky, with a broad face and shoulders, stronger if not taller than the young man who had just whiplashed his back. He was dressed in the usual attire of those of his occupation on the island of Cuba, a dark wool jacket, trimmed with passementerie, a piqué waistcoat, a shirt with a sailor collar, linen trousers, heavy knee-high boots in lieu of leggings, and a round black hat, trimmed in gold. We must also mention, as a characteristic feature of a carriage driver's attire, the pair of silver spurs, which the mulatto of whom we are now speaking was not wearing at the time.

"Listen here!" said his master, for that in fact was what Leonardo was; "You were sleeping like a log, leaving the horses to do as they pleased. What about that? What would have happened if by chance they had bolted down these hellishly dark streets?"

"I wasn't asleeping, master," the driver dared remark.

"What do you mean, you weren't sleeping? Aponte, Aponte, you apparently don't know me or else you think I'm simple-minded. Look, mount your horse, and we'll settle accounts later. Take the gig to the *cuna*, pick up the two girls that you brought there in it and take them home. I'll wait for you at the big wall around Santa Clara, on the corner of the Calle de la Habana. Don't let anyone ride on the backboard. Do you understand?"

"Yes, señor," Aponte answered, taking off in the direction of the porter's lodge of San José. At the doorway of the house where the ball had been held, without dismounting, he said to a stranger who was just going inside: "Would you be so kind as to tell mistress Cecilia that the gig is here?"

Despite the carriage driver's addition of the word "mistress" to Cecilia's name, a term that in Cuba is used only for white girls, the stranger did not hesitate to convey the message to Cecilia just as it had been given to him. And she immediately rose from the table and went to get her shawl, followed by Nemesia and Mercedes. The latter accompanied them to the street door, where the few men who had not yet left had now congregated. There, still with her arm about Cecilia's waist as a sign of friendship and affection, she said to her:

"Don't trust men, you sweet little halfbreed, because you'll come out the loser."

"And have I ever trusted one of them heretofore, Merceditas?" Cecilia answered in surprise.

"Of course not, but that gig has an owner, and nobody does anything without expecting something in return. You can take that for granted. I think I've made myself clear."

This said, and with Cantalapiedra pretending to be weeping because of Cecilia's departure, thus occasioning a great deal of laughter, she and Nemesia climbed into the carriage with Pimienta giving them a hand, and now the gathering had definitely broken up.

It was probably about one in the morning by then. The wind had not died down nor was there yet an end to the light rain that, now and again, the scudding clouds let fall over the city, fast asleep in the dark of night. As the common expression goes, it was as dark as a wolf's maw. Nonetheless this did not cause the young musician to lose track of the carriage that was taking his sister and her friend home; rather than going by the sound of the wheels on the cobblestone pavement of the streets, he followed in its wake, at first walking on the double and then breaking into a trot, until he overtook it near the Calle de Acosta. He put his hand on the backboard, was propelled along naturally by the impetus of the carriage, and rode along mounted sidesaddle on it. The carriage driver immediately heard him and came to a halt. "Get down," Nemesia said to her brother through the window shutter. "There's no reason for him to do that," Cecilia said. "I can see the two of you as I guard you from the rear," Pimienta said. "Get down," Aponte said at that moment, having already dismounted. "Didn't I tell you?" Nemesia added, speaking to her brother. "The girls inside are my sister and my friend," the musician remarked, addressing the driver. "That may well be," the latter replied, "but I do not allow anyone to ride behind my gig. You're going to the dogs, pal," he added, noting that he was having a run-in with a mulatto like him. "Get down," Nemesia repeated insistently.

José Dolores Pimienta obeyed, quite evidently after a silent and terrible struggle with himself in which prudence won out; yet even though he gave up at that point, he did not abandon his resolve to follow the carriage. The driver climbed back onto his horse and went straight on till he came to the Calle de Luz, turning to the left there and heading for the Calle de la Habana. A man was standing near the cannon on the corner, sheltered from the wind and the fine drizzle by the towering adobe walls of the courtyard belonging to the convent of the Poor Clares. At this point Aponte stopped the carriage for the second time; the man climbed onto the backboard and then said in a low voice: "Giddyap!" Aponte took off at breakneck speed then, but not before giving the musician time to get close enough to note that the individual who had replaced him on the backboard of the carriage was the same young white, Leonardo, who had caused him so many pangs of jealousy at the *cuna*.

V I I

And what sort of man is he,
is he like muscatel,
is he shy and discreet
either bitter or sweet?

Lope de Vega, *La Buscona*

In the barrio of San Francisco and in one of its less crooked streets, with sidewalks or flagstones along one or two blocks, among other houses, there was one with a roof terrace that stood out because it had an upper floor above the arch of the front door, and a little balcony to the west. The common entrance, for the owners, servants, draft animals, and carriages, two of which were ordinarily stationed there, was, like that of almost all the houses in the country, through the *zaguán*, a sort of gatehouse or coach house that led to the dining room, the courtyard and the rooms known as studies.

These so-called studies could be seen in a row to the right after passing through the *zaguán*, the first of them occupied by a double-sized business desk, with two high wooden stools, one on each side, and underneath the desk a small square safe made of iron, which instead of a door had a lid that could be opened or closed whenever money bags were

53

placed in it or removed from it. On the opposite side of the house a row of downstairs rooms for the family could be seen, with a common entry by way of the drawing room, a door and a window giving onto the dining room and the courtyard.

This formed a quadrilateral, at the center of which there stood out the rim of blue stone of a reservoir or cistern, into which, by means of tin conduits and pipes buried in the ground, rain water from the rooftop drained. An adobe wall six feet high, with an arch at the right-hand end, separated the courtyard from the kitchen, stable, latrine, living quarters for the carriage drivers, and other outbuildings of the house.

Between the *zaguán* and the rooms called studies, a crude stone staircase, with cedar handrails and no landing or break save for the abrupt turn made by the last two steps almost at the bottom of it, went down to the dining room, supported by the dividing wall. This stairway also led to the suite upstairs, consisting of two rooms: the first of them served as an anteroom, as large as the *zaguán*; the second, even larger since it had the same dimensions as the studies over which it was built, served as a bedroom and study. In point of fact, its principal furnishings, which nearly filled it, were a bed with a mahogany frame, covered with a blue mosquito netting of a thin transparent fabric called *rengue*, a wardrobe of the same wood, a matching coat or clothes rack, a black horsehair sofa, a few straightbacked chairs with straw seats, a table that served as a desk, and an easy chair. On top of several of these pieces of furniture were a number of books, some open, others closed or with one or more pages with the upper corner turned down, Spanish-style clothbound volumes, edged in red, all of them apparently law books, as could be noted by reading the titles in gold lettering on the backs of some of them. On the sofa were nothing but two periodicals in the form of brochures: the more voluminous of the two with a very bad engraving on the cover showing a man, a woman, and a child, and the title *La Moda o Recreo Semanal*, the other entitled *El Regañón*.

Downstairs in the dining room there was a mahogany table with folding leaves that could be opened out to make room for 12 places, and as many as six chairs in two rows opposite the door, in the corner was the indispensable large water container, a furnishing sui generis in Cuba. To provide shade for the room and protect it against the sun's glare in the courtyard there were two large heavy canvas curtains that could be rolled up and down like theater curtains. On the dividing wall between the *zaguán* and the drawing room was an iron grating, and to let in light from outside into the drawing room, two bay windows, which extended from street level to the eaves along the roof. A crystal globe was suspended by chains from the main beam; on the side wall hung portraits in oil, likenesses of a lady and a gentleman in the prime of life, done by the famous Vicente Escobar.[14] Beneath them was a sofa, and perpendicular to it, in two rows, up to six armchairs with seats and backs upholstered in Morocco leather; in the four corners were mahogany sideboards, adorned with lamps with glass shades or porcelain flower vases. On the wall between the two windows was a tall table with gilt feet and above it a rectangular mirror, with a profusion of straightbacked chairs filling the empty spaces.

A notable feature was the white muslin curtain with a cotton fringe that hung from the lintels of each of the doors and windows of the rooms, so as to let in air and hide their interiors from the gaze of those passing by through the dining room and the courtyard.

In short, that house, so typical of Havana, as will have been seen from the detailed description of it that we have offered, exuded on every hand an air of cleanliness, tidiness and . . . luxury, for in fact the word is the right one if we take into consideration the country and the era of which we are speaking, the style and quality of the furnishings, the two carriages in the coach house, and the spaciousness itself of the dwelling. Did a respectable, well-educated and happy family live there? In a moment we shall see.

At the hour when our story begins, between six and seven in the morning on a day in October, one of the easy chairs in the dining room was occupied by a gentleman of about 50—tall, robust, with graying hair, a large aquiline nose, a small mouth, lively dark eyes, a ruddy complexion, a head that was round in the back, these being characteristic signs of strong passions and steadfastness of character. He wore his hair short and was clean-shaven; he was dressed in an ankle-length dressing gown of printed cotton over a long waistcoat of white piqué, drill trousers, and suede slippers. His feet were resting on a straightbacked chair with a straw seat, and he was holding up to eye level a newspaper whose masthead read *El Diario de la Habana*, printed on folio-sized Spanish rag stock.

As he was reading, a boy of about 12 entered, dressed in trousers and a pinstriped shirt; he had come from the far end of the courtyard and was carrying in his right hand a cup of coffee with milk on a plate and in his other hand a silver sugar bowl. Without straightening up in the easy chair, the gentleman took the cup, put sugar in the coffee, and began to sip and read at his ease as the servant stood before him, holding the plate and the sugar bowl. Once the gentleman had finished the cup of coffee, despite the fact that the boy was only a few steps away, he said to him in a thundering voice: "A cigar and a light!" The boy ran off to the kitchen and returned in a moment by way of the studies, bringing a large bull's bladder with several rolled cigars in the bottom and a little silver brazier with a live coal inside, half buried in a pile of ashes. The gentleman lit a cigar, and as the boy was about to take off again on the run, he shouted at him: "Tirso!"

"Señor!" the latter answered, also in a loud voice, as though he were already back in the kitchen or speaking with a deaf person.

"Have you been upstairs?" his master asked him.

"Yes, señor, as soon as the cook came back from the market square."

"And why hasn't young Leonardo come downstairs yet?"

"I beg your grace's leave to tell him that master Leonardo doesn't wish to be awakened because he's had a bad night."

"A bad night!" the gentleman repeated to himself. "Go wake him up and tell him to come downstairs," he said to the slave.

"Señor," the boy said, stammering and disconcerted. "Señor, your grace knows . . ."

"What's the trouble?" the master shouted, again in a thundering voice, noticing that the slave had not obeyed him and was still standing before him.

"Señor, I beg your grace's leave to tell him that the young master flies into a rage when he's awakened, and . . ."

"What? What's that you say? Ah! You dog! Go, and be quick about it if you don't want me to kick you upstairs."

And since the gentleman rose halfway out of his chair to carry out his threat, the youngster did not wait for the order to be repeated before obeying it. He reached the top of the stairs in four leaps and disappeared into young Leonardo's bedroom. Just as the boy was bounding upstairs, there appeared at the dining room door a rather stout, pretty lady with a kindly look about her, small features, and hair that was still black though she was past 40, dressed in white batiste and enveloped in a canary yellow crepe shawl, very neat and tidy from head to foot and her manner calm and dignified. She sat down alongside the gentleman in the dressing gown, whom she addressed by the surname of Gamboa when she asked him about the day's news. The latter answered her by muttering that the only important news reported in *El Diario* was the appearance of *morbus* cholera in Warsaw, where it was wreaking terrible havoc.

"And where is Warsaw?" the lady asked with a yawn.

"Well!" Gamboa answered. "It's a long way from here. Up near the North Pole, in Poland, mind you. Señor Cholera will have to keep rolling right along to reach us, and by that time . . . who knows where you and I will be!"

"God save us from hours of our lives on the wane, Cándido!" the lady exclaimed, with the same apathetic air as before.

At this point Tirso came down the stairs at twice the speed, if that is possible, with which he had gone up them; and had he not ducked his head in time, a book thrown at him from the top of the stairs would have hit it; as it was, it hit the door of the study so hard it fell to pieces. Don Cándido raised his head and the lady rose to her feet and went to the foot of the staircase, asking: "What was that all about?" In answer the little servant, thoroughly frightened, merely looked back to call her attention to young Leonardo, who was standing at the top of the stairs, wrapped in a bedsheet, with his fists clenched as a sign of his rage and as a threat. But the moment he spied his mother, which is who that lady was, his attitude and the expression on his face changed, and he was doubtless about to explain the incident when she stopped him by making a sign fraught with meaning, the equivalent, more or less, of telling him: "Don't say a word; your father is here." Therefore, without further ado, he turned around and went back to his room.

"Is master Leonardo coming?" Gamboa asked the slave, as if he had noticed neither his son's sudden appearance nor the way the book had hit the door of the study nor his wife's gesture.

"Yes, señor," Tirso answered.

"Did you give him my message?" Don Cándido persisted, in an even harsher and sterner tone of voice.

"I beg leave to tell your grace that . . . the young . . . the young master Leonardo didn't give me time to," the slave replied, badly upset and trembling.

The lady had sat down again and was following with great anxiety her spouse's words and the changes in his face. She saw him turn red as Tirso uttered the few phrases that he could manage to blurt out in his consternation; it even seemed to her as though her husband was about to get up out of his chair to thrash the slave boy, or to drag Leonardo downstairs by brute force; in the face of these two uncertain alternatives, in order to gain time, she let her right hand fall on the gentleman's left arm and said to him in a very quiet, musical voice:

"Cándido, Leonardito is getting dressed to come downstairs."

"And you, how do you know that?" Don Cándido replied heatedly, turning toward his wife.

"I just saw him half-dressed, at the top of the staircase," she answered calmly.

"You're always in the know as to when Leonard is going to act as he's supposed to, but you're blind to his misdeeds."

"I'm not aware that the poor lad has been guilty of any, at least recently."

"Naturally! Didn't I tell you? Blind, pitifully blind little Rosa, the way you breastfeed that boy is going to be the ruin of him. Tirso!" Don Cándido thundered.

Before Tirso came back from the kitchen, where he had taken refuge as soon as his master and mistress began the preceding very brief exchange, the mulatto carriage driver, whom our readers already know thanks to that scene in the barrio of San Isidro on the night of September 24, came in through the *zaguán*. He was now wearing only an ordinary shirt and a pair of trousers whose legs were rolled up to just below his knees, as if to allow the bottom edges of his white underpants to show, with their worn, raveled sawteeth rather than a neat hem. His shoes were of leather and very low cut, with a silver buckle on the side, and he was wearing gold rings in his earlobes, a kerchief tied around his head, and holding his straw hat in his right hand and in his left the halter of a horse that he was leading, tied by the tail to another of the same color and general appearance, both of them just out of the horse bath, for they were still dripping water or sweat, and the second of them had its tail done up in a knot. The mulatto had ridden the first one from the stable to the bath, near the pier at Luz, because it was still wearing a horse cloth instead of a saddle.

"But here's Aponte," Don Cándido said, on seeing him appear. "Aponte!"

"There's no need for you to question the servants," Doña Rosa put in.

"I want you to hear about one of your son's recent pranks," her husband insisted. "What time did you bring your master home last night?" he said, addressing Aponte.

"At two in the mornin'," Aponte replied.

"Where did your young master spend the night?" Don Cándido added.

"There's no point in his telling where," Doña Rosa interrupted. "Aponte, take those horses to the manger."

"Where did your young master spend the night?" Don Cándido repeated in a voice like thunder, seeing the carriage driver on the point of obeying his mistress's order.

"It's very hard for me, master, to tell your grace where my young master Leonardito spent the night."

"What? What do you mean by that?"

"I'm telling your grace that it's very hard to say, master," Aponte hastened to explain, noting that Don Cándido's anger was mounting, "because first off I took master Leonardito to Santa Catarina, den I took him to the pier at Luz, and den I stayed at the pier at Luz till midnight, and den I took him to Santa Catarina again, and den . . ."

"That's enough," Doña Rosa said in annoyance. "I know all I need to."

Aponte went off with the horses, passing by the dining room and the courtyard as he headed toward the stable, and Don Cándido, turning to his wife, said to her:

"What do you say to t-h-a-t? Doesn't that business last night strike you as a recent misdeed? I didn't know anything about it, I merely had my suspicions, because I know my son better than you do, and you've heard now that he was in Regla till midnight. Perhaps he wasn't alone. Do you want to hear now who he was with and how he spent half of his time in Regla? Can't you guess? Don't you suspect?"

"Supposing that I could guess the answer, that it was palpable," Doña Rosa remarked with a touch of contempt, "what good would it do me? Would it make me stop loving him the way I do?"

"But it's not a question of loving him or not loving him, Rosa," Don Cándido burst out impatiently. "It's a question of doing something about his misdeeds, which are beginning to border on serious ones."

"His misdeeds, if he in fact commits any, are no more than the sorts of follies that are part of being young."

"Follies, when they're repeated and no one puts a stop to them in time, end up becoming serious matters that cost many tears and many regrets."

"Well, your follies, as far as I know, didn't bring you any serious or grave consequences, and moreover his are mere youthful diversions compared to yours," Doña Rosa said with subtle sarcasm.

"Señora," Don Cándido replied in annoyance, despite the visible effort he was making to hide his irritation, "whatever follies I may have committed in my youth, they do not give Leonardo leave to lead the life he's leading with . . . your approval and applause."

"My approval! My applause! That's a good one! Nobody is a better witness than you to the fact that, far from approving and applauding Leonardito's follies, I am forever counseling and even reprehending him."

"Yes, of course! On the one hand you counsel him and reprehend him, and on the other you give him the gig, and the driver, and horses, and half a doubloon every evening so that he can go have a good time, make conquests, and party all over town with his friends. You don't approve of his follies or applaud them, but you provide him with the ways and means to commit them."

"That's right, I'm the one who provides the ways and means for the boy to ruin his life. Not you; you're a saint. Yes, indeed, your life has been exemplary."

"I don't know what such bitter mockery is leading up to."

"It's leading up to the fact that you're very hard on him, and to the fact that your severity would be a good thing if you were irreproachable, if you hadn't sinned . . ."

"Does he have as good an opinion of me as the one I merit from you, señora? Does he know that I've sinned?"

"Perhaps he does."

"If you haven't told him . . ."

"There's no need for me to put bad ideas in his head. I'd be an unnatural mother if I did such a thing. But he's no fool, and at the time your dealings with María de Regla gave rise to only too much gossip and scandal. Rumors of it might very well have reached his ears and prompted him to imitate you. A bad example . . ."

"Enough, señora," Don Cándido said, more uneasy than annoyed. "I believed, I had reason to hope that you had decided to forget all about the whole thing."

"You believed wrongly, because there are things that it isn't possible ever to forget."

"I can see that. What that means is that I was mistaken; it means that women, certain women, do not forget or forgive certain misdeeds that men commit. But, Rosa," he added, his tone of voice changing, "we're getting off the track, and that's not a good thing. The truth is that if I'm very hard on Leonardo, as you say, you're very easy on him, and I don't know which is worse in the end. He is wild, willful, and stubborn, and needs to be reined in even more than he needs the bread he eats. I note with sorrow, however, that with my severity in mind, you lead him, unwittingly of course, almost by the hand to his imminent perdition. In all truth, Rosa, it is time now that his follies and your weaknesses cease; it is time now to come to a decision that will free him from a prison and free us from eternal grief and disgrace."

"And what step can we take, Cándido? It's late, he's already almost a grown man."

"What step? Several. On His Majesty's warships hefty full-gown men are brought into line. I've been thinking that it wouldn't do him any harm to smell caulking tar for a short time. It so happens that my friend Acha, the commanding officer of *La Sabina*, is eager to teach him seamanship. Just yesterday he told me to make up my mind and turn him over to him, certain that he would be able to set him straighter than a topmast. Yes, that was the expression he used. In any event, I'm determined to put a stop to the lad's excesses."

Doña Rosa was moved to hear her husband utter these last words, and even more moved to note the tone of firm resolve with which he did so. Partly to hide the tears that were welling up in her eyes, and partly to change the subject of a conversation that wounded her to the quick, she rose from her chair once again and headed for the courtyard. At that very moment Leonardo came down the stairs, in street dress; and hearing his footsteps, she went back to the place she had just left at her husband's side. In a tone of humble pleading, her voice trembling with emotion, she said to him:

"For the love of that same son, Gamboa, don't say anything to him now. Your severity is making him rebellious and is killing me."

"Rosa!" Don Cándido murmured, looking at her reproachfully. "You are dooming him to perdition."

"Prudence, Cándido!" Doña Rosa replied, breathing more freely because she realized that her husband was inclined for the moment to practice that virtue. "Bear in mind that he's a man now, and yet you're treating him like a child."

"Rosa!" Don Cándido repeated with yet another reproachful look. "How long is this going to go on?"

"This will be the last time that I intercede for him," Doña Rosa hastened to say. "I promise you."

At that moment, young Gamboa had just reached the bottom stair and walked straight over to his mother, who rose to her feet to meet him, as if the better to protect him from his father's wrath. But the latter, silent and dejected, was already entering the study and did not see, or pretended not to see, his son kiss his mother on the forehead, nor the sign she made to indicate to him that he should also bid his father good morning.

Leonardo did not say a word, nor did he make a move to do as his mother had indicated. He merely smiled, shrugged his shoulders, and headed for the street, carrying underneath his left arm a Spanish-style clothbound volume, edged in red, and in his right hand a rattan cane with a gold handle in the shape of a crown.

VIII

For the good of the soul
Of the man they are about to execute!

Espronceda, *El reo de muerte*

The student looked down the Calle de San Ignacio toward the Plaza Vieja. On the corner of the Calle de Sol he spied two other students more or less his age, who to all appearances were waiting for him. One of them is not unknown to the reader, for he has been seen at the *cuna* on the Calle de San José. We are referring to Diego Meneses. The other was of less elegant and slender build, for in addition to his short stature he had a very short neck and rather hunched shoulders, between which a tiny round head was more or less buried. There was a certain disharmony about his forehead, narrower than it was tall; he had little piercing eyes, a slightly turned-up nose, a pointed beard, and a fresh, moist mouth, surely the most expressive of his unimpressive facial features, and kinky hair; in his face as well as in his body, the great slyness that animated his mischievous spirit was immediately evident. As he gave him a hard slap on the back, Leonardo addressed him by the name of Pancho Solfa. The latter, at once good humored and a bit irritated by the slap on the back, said:

"Every animal has its own language, and yours, Leonardo, is very expressive at times."

"I mistreat you because I love you, Pancho. Would you like another caress?"

"Enough of that, kid." And Pancho turned away, parrying with his left hand.

"What time is it?" Leonardo asked. "I just remembered that I didn't wind my watch last night and it's stopped."

"The Espíritu Santo clock has just struck seven," Diego answered. "We were about to go off without you, thinking that you were sleeping in."

"I almost didn't get up at all today. I went to bed late and my father sent someone to wake me up early this morning. Since he goes to bed with the chickens, he's always up at daybreak. Don't the two of you think we've time to take a little stroll up El Angel Hill?"

"I'd say no," Pancho said. "Unless, like a latter-day Joshua, you have the power to stop the sun."

"You're dying to get in a quotation, Pancho, whether or not it's apropos. Don't you know that the sun hasn't budged since Joshua ordered it to stop in its course? If you'd studied astronomy, you'd know that."

"You mean if he'd studied sacred history," Meneses said.

"The long and the short of it is that without having thoroughly studied either one, I know that the case at hand has to do with both and you're not the ones to lecture me," Pancho remarked.

"By the way, gentlemen, what's our lesson for today? I didn't attend classes on Friday, nor have I opened the book in all this time."

"Govantes assigned the third section for today; it's about the right of persons," Diego answered. "Open the book and you'll see."

"I haven't even had a quick look at that material," Leonardo added. "All I know is that according to the law of the land there are persons and there are things; that many of these latter, although they speak and think, do not have the same rights as the former. You, Pancho, for instance, since you're so fond of similes, are not a person but a thing in the eyes of the law."

"I don't see the similarity, because I'm not a slave, whom Roman law considers a *thing*."

"Right you are. You're not a slave, but one or another of your ancestors no doubt was, and that amounts to the same thing. Your kinky hair at least is suspect."

"You're lucky you have hair as straight as an Indian arrow. If we examine our respective genealogical trees, however, we'll find that those who are considered to be freeborn among us are at most sons of freedmen."[15]

"I see we've touched a sore spot, pal. Come on; it's no sin to hide family skeletons in the closet. My father is Spanish and doesn't have any skeletons to hide, and my mother is a Creole, but I wouldn't guarantee that she's pureblooded."

"The fact is that your father, just because he's Spanish, is not free of the suspicion of having mixed blood, since I take it that he's from Andalusia, and the first black slaves came to America from Seville. Nor were the Arabs, who were more predominant in Andalusia than in other parts of Spain, pure Caucasian by race, but African. Moreover, the union of whites and blacks was common there at the time, according to the testimony of Cervantes and other contemporary writers."

"That brief historical outline, Don Pancho, is worth its weight in gold. We know that the question of races has caused you a few headaches. It doesn't arrest my attention, nor do I believe that mixed blood looms large or carries much weight. What I can say is that it's perhaps because I have a little mulatto blood, I don't know, but I don't much like mulatto girls. I'm not ashamed to admit it."

"What's bred in the bone comes out in the flesh."

"That old proverb is irrelevant; but if you're citing it to declare that you don't like *cinnamon*, so much the worse for you, Pancho, because that means you like *coal*, a vastly inferior type."[16]

At this point in the conversation they entered the arcades of the Plaza Vieja, called the Rosario Arcades. These were made up of some four or five houses, belonging to rich or noble families of Havana, with wide balconies, supported by tall stone arches, the lights of which were concealed during the day by heavy canvas curtains, like the mainsails of boats. The upstairs floor of these houses was occupied by the owners or the tenants, who lived off their income; but the ground floor, with large rooms that were generally dark and poorly ventilated, was occupied by the shops of certain retail merchants, called knickknack dealers, or properly speaking, vendors of miscellaneous articles, who, without exception, were Spanish, usually highlanders. They kept their stock in trade of gewgaws inside, and outside, underneath the stone arches, they set out what goes by the name of bric-a-brac in glass showcases or portable display cases resting on a sort of sawhorse. They put the articles out early in the morning and took them in at night.

The first of the operations mentioned above ordinarily began shortly after seven in the morning. The merchants, two by two, brought out the showcases, one of them holding one end and the other the opposite end, as though they were coffins or as though they weighed too much for just one man to move.

Some of them had already been set out, and the vendors were walking back and forth in front of them, wearing nothing but a shirt and trousers despite the cold morning breeze, when our three students entered the arcades.

Leonardo and Diego were leading the way, laughing and chatting, paying no attention to the Spanish shop boys who were coming and going, busy setting out the merchandise before prospective customers came by. Their classmate Pancho was following along behind at a measured pace, his head bowed, saying nothing, and perhaps for this reason, or perhaps because his appearance displeased them, the fact is that the first vendor he came upon grabbed him by one arm and said to him: "Hey there, my fair lad! Don't you want to buy a pair of first-rate knives?" Pancho shook off this one with a disdainful gesture, and another one grabbed him and said: "Here, cousin, I'm selling excellent spectacles." Farther on, a third one barred his path to offer him suspenders, a fourth to shove in front of his eyes Basque penknives, better than English ones. Moving from one to the next, now smiling, now making an irritated gesture, the student, annoyed by this time, managed to advance a few steps farther. Finally, trying to making his way through a number of hawkers more disposed to make fun of him than to peddle their knickknacks, he stood stock-still and folded his arms. Fortunately, at that moment his classmates missed him, turned their heads, and noticed the circle that had gathered round him. Not knowing why, Leonardo, who was fearless, ran back, broke through the circle and got his friend out of the fix he was in. But once he found out what had happened, he let out a hearty laugh and said: "They took you for a Spanish highlander, Pancho. You also look like . . ."

"The way I look has nothing to do with it," Pancho interrupted him crossly. "The truth is that those Spaniards remind me more of Jews than of gentlemen."

Our students, after walking a short way along the Calle de San Ignacio, came out at the little square in front of the cathedral. When they reached the gates of the house known as Filomeno's, a large, dense crowd of people who were entering the square from the opposite side, that is to say, by way of the Calle de Mercaderes and El Boquete, drew their attention. The vanguard, made up for the most part of people of color, men, women, and children, barefoot, dirty, and dressed in rags, was making its way along, alternately walking a few steps and halting, and from time to time turning their head around as if it were activated by a spring. Between two rows of lightly equipped soldiers, dressed in a uniform consisting of a blue wool jacket, white trousers, a cartridge belt fastened to their waist in front, a round hat, and armed only with the short carbine carried by infantrymen, some 12 mulattos and blacks were walking, wearing ankle-length robes of black serge, each with a white muslin hood whose long point dangled down at the back of the wearer's head like a streamer, and each of them was carrying in his right hand a black cross with a short cross arm and a long shaft. Four of these doleful men were carrying on their shoulder, in a sedan chair, what appeared to be a human creature, whose head and body disappeared from sight beneath the folds of a black cloth (a serge mantle), falling vertically outside the entire conveyance.

On one side of this mysterious being a priest was walking, wearing a black silk cassock, with a bonnet on his head and a crucifix in either hand; on the other side was a quite young black, robust and agile. The latter was dressed in white trousers, a round hat, and a black wool jacket, carrying on his back what looked like a ladder edged in yellow silk. This indicated his occupation; he was nothing less than the executioner. He was walking at a measured pace and never once raised his eyes from the ground. Behind him came a white man dressed in short trousers, silk hose, a wool jacket, and a three-corned hat, all of them black. This was the court clerk. Marching immediately behind him was a high-ranking military officer, as indicated by the three stripes of gold braid on his jacket and his three-cornered hat trimmed with gold braid and a white ostrich feather. Closing the procession were other blacks and mulattos in the same black ankle-length robe and white hood as already described, and more people, all moving in solemn, silent procession, for not a sound was heard save the regular tread of the foot soldiers and the nasal voice of the priest reciting the prayers for the dying.

From this rapid description the reader from Havana will realize that a condemned criminal was being led to the gallows, accompanied by the Brothers of Charity and Faith, a religious institution made up exclusively of men of color who devoted themselves to aiding the sick and dying and burying the dead, in particular the corpses of executed criminals. It is well known that Spanish justice carries its brutality to the very portals of the tomb, hence the need for the aforementioned religious institution, which takes charge of recovering the dead body of the criminal and burying it, taking the place of kinfolk and friends forbidden by law or by custom to fulfill those functions.

The troops that guarded the criminal in such circumstances, in Havana at least, were a squad of the renowned Armida Detail, a sort of civil guard, established by Vives, which took on the role played elsewhere by the police; the high-ranking military officer was the mayor of the city, at the time Colonel Molina, later governor of Morro Castle, the post he held when he died, burdened with the hatred of those whom he had oppressed and exploited during the time that he occupied the first of these positions; the individual whom they were leading to the gallows in the way that we have described was not a man, but a woman, and moreover a white woman, the first of her class perhaps to be executed in Havana.

I X

. . . *This is the justice*
That the king orders done . . .
El Duque de Rivas, *D. Alvaro de Luna*

The story of the woman who was sentenced to death for her crime deserves to be told, however briefly. Married to a poor peasant, she lived on the outskirts of the little town of El Mariel; we do not know how long ago, nor is it any great importance. But though neither young nor pretty, she entered into illicit relations with an unmarried man of the same town. Either because her husband found out what was going on and threatened to take his vengeance, or because the lovers wished to free themselves of this impediment, the two of them agreed between themselves to kill him. And once they had managed to do so (it is not very hard to kill a man), they endeavored to hide the traces of their crime by quartering the corpse and throwing the bloody quarters, sewn inside a sack, into a nearby river. Such were the principal facts that came out during the trial.

Well then, what role did the woman play in this horrible drama? This was never made clear. In the presentation of his arguments in her defense, the young and brilliant attorney Anacleto Bermúdez, who had just arrived from Spain, in whose councils he had been admitted to the bar, displayed an eloquence as impartial as it was rare; this trial marked his debut as an astute criminal lawyer. The crime was horrible, however, and the woman's complicity was proved, for even if she had not struck the fatal blow with her own hand, she had played a major role in the murder and in the disposal of the corpse. Her death sentence was therefore mandatory, although she would be put to death by hanging, since only nobles were sentenced to death by garrotting, an event that took place even more rarely in Cuba than the execution of a white woman.

In the Spanish colonies, death by hanging was, if possible, more terrible that that by garrotting, which was introduced or became the practice some time after the execution to which we are referring here. Once he had tied two ropes around the criminal's neck, the hangman threw him from the top of the ladder, straddled his shoulders, and kicked him in the stomach with his heels to hasten his end; he then slid down to the ground by way of the feet of the hanged man, whose corpse, clad in an ankle-length robe, remained swaying back and forth in the air for eight hours, six feet from the ground. Such a spectacle should not have taken place in Havana with a white woman as the one put to death, however inferior her class or however horrible her crime.

In such a situation, and when recourse to a supposed pregnancy had failed, Bermúdez asked for and was granted as a special favor permission for his client to be garrotted to death. The reader will remember that seven or eight years after the execution on which we are concentrating here, the punishment of death by hanging was abolished in Cuba, and since the prison was situated in the west corner of the building known as Government House, in which the City Hall with all its subsidiary buildings, where the Captain General and his family resided, and where the offices of the notaries public were located, the condemned criminal had to travel a long and anguishing route before his life was put to an end on the Campo de la Punta, immediately adjacent to the sea. In fact, after walking down the Calle de Mercaderes he reached the little square in front of the cathedral, then turned down the Calle de San Ignacio, then down the Calle de Chacón, then down the Calle de Cuba, then immediately thereafter walked along the wall and passed under the dark arch of the gate called the Puerta de la Punta, which was equipped with a guard post and which served as an exit for the city's corpses that were being taken to the general cemetery to be buried.

On going out that gate of the plaza, which was hemmed in on all sides, the condemned man could see in the distance, opposite the reef along the shore against which the waves of the sea broke in little peaks of bright foam, the terrible machine: the gallows, garrote, or scaffold on which his life would end. For those whose spirit had been cowed, death in all its horror was a force that had shown itself to them long before it was dealt them. Fortunately, from the moment that she was put in the death house the woman of whom we are now speaking lost her strength, and with it the awareness of her terrible situation, making it necessary, as we have seen, to take her in a sedan chair to the place where she was to be executed, to carry her to the garrotting bench and seat her on it, and once she was dead, to dislocate the vertebrae in her neck so as to stifle in her breast her last breath of life.

Five or six years after the events that have just been recounted, the appearance of the Campo de la Punta had changed altogether. The desolate, dusty barren expanse, bordered on the west by the first wooden houses of the barrio of San Lázaro, on the south by the stacks of planks and beams imported from the United States of North America, on the north by the sea and the castle of La Punta, whose miniature parapets peeked out from behind the conical iron boilers of Carrón where sugar was refined, was replaced by a building consisting of three massive, quadrangular units, built by Captain General Don Miguel Tacón to serve respectively as a public prison, a prison storehouse, and an infantry barracks.

The open space situated on the north side of this building was even further obstructed by the construction of a number of wooden lean-to sheds to serve as shelter for some of the inmates of the prison, assigned to hammer large rocks into small stones, to be used to pave the streets of the city according to the method invented by John McAdam, a Scottish engineer.

But in any event the prison was now separated from Government House; the prisoners were transferred to a building which, albeit less than satisfactory in many respects, had been built expressly for their well-being and security; there was a more appropriate separation of the sexes and of the types of criminals, and in particular the *via crucis* of the unfortunate criminals condemned to death was reduced to a third of its former length, since it was barely 200 paces from the new prison to the shoreline opposite the reef where capital executions took place. Years before, it was from the prison and from the Puerta de la Punta, in the opposite direction, that the patriot and hero Montes de Oca, and young Eduardo Facciolo, General López and the Spaniard Pintó, the brave Estrampes, and in our day Medina and Léon and the innocent students of the University of Havana came out to meet their death.[17]

The three friends joined the grim procession and walked in it along the side of the cathedral to the main door of the seminary, a building that extends along the back of the cathedral and overlooks the port. The entrance to the classrooms had not yet been opened, and the hammering on it by some 200 Latin, philosophy, and law students—the flower of Cuban youth—could be heard from the stone steps of the porter's lodge to the barracks of San Telmo on one side, and on the other a long way toward the intersection of Tejadillo and San Ignacio, because of the narrowness of the street. By a spontaneous movement, the crowd of students divided into two lines, freeing a passage down the middle of the street for the strange procession of people preceded by a muffled sound, as of a swarm of bees seeking a place to alight.

The cortege halted in front of the main door of the seminary for a moment so as to allow four Brothers of Charity and Faith time to relieve those who had carried the sedan chair all the way from the prison. The figure inside it, meanwhile, did not change position or make the slightest movement; but despite the fact that the folds of the black mantle completely hid her features, her name and the story of her crime were passed along from one student to another.

"It would never occur to anyone that they're carrying a woman inside there," a Latin student said.

"That's true; it looks more like the statue of a weeping woman than a living person," another added.

"She is overcome with remorse," a third said. "That's why her head is bowed on her breast."

"Right you are," exclaimed a tall student, who looked like a mulatto. "And it's little wonder. I suppose she's horrified by her crime now."

"But has it been proved, as clear as day in the full light of noon, to cite a section of the *Siete Partidas*, that Panchita killed her husband?" asked our acquaintance Pancho.

"It's so definitively proved that she killed him that they're going to garrote her," the student who looked like a mulatto observed, with a certain disdainful smile. "To be more specific, after he was dead she cut him up in pieces, and after sewing him into a sisal sack, threw him into the river to feed the fishes."

"All that doesn't constitute an argument for the criminality of Panchita Tapia," her namesake was about to answer back when another student joined in the conversation, declaring in a ringing voice and a Spanish accent:

"The girl came within a hair's breadth of doing to her spouse what the *Partida* decrees is to be done to the parricide. All she would have had to

71

do was use a leather sack with bright red flames painted on the outside and place inside it a rooster, a viper, and a monkey, animals that know no father or mother."

"The Roman criminal code of the Twelve Tables," Pancho hastened to say, raising his voice and standing slightly on tiptoe, full of self-satisfaction at being able to correct the error of the student affecting a Spanish accent, "which was copied *pedem litterae* in the *Siete Partidas*, compiled by order of King Alfonso the Wise—does not mention a rooster, only a dog, a viper, and a monkey, and not because those animals know or do not know either father or mother, but merely in order to subject the criminal to their fury. The Alfonsine code considers even the woman who kills her husband a parricide. The practice today is to drag the criminal in a long narrow basket tied to the tail of a horse to the foot of the gallows. So if they didn't drag Panchita Tapia, accused of that horrendous crime, to the gallows in that way, the reason is that our customs do not permit it. I have spoken."

With these words, Pancho promptly withdrew from that group, thereby giving the Hispanicized student no time to reply. The latter confined himself to saying, as he saw him walk off:

"It's plain to see that the kid has done his homework."

At precisely that point someone came to open the heavy cedar panels of the door of the seminary, better known in those days as the Colegio de San Carlos. The main courtyard consisted of four wide walkways, flanked by stone columns forming a square. In the middle was a fountain, and all round it luxurious and leafy orange trees. On the side opposite the main entrance, to the left, was a stone staircase that led to the studies of the professors; to the right was a grille that separated the walkway from a dark, damp alley, which led to a filthy auditorium, longer than it was wide, off to one side, separated from the waters of the port by a garden or orchard with towering adobe walls. Overlooking it were four little windows set high up in the wall, through which the only light entered. Leaning against the front wall, in the middle of it, was a high-backed, badly made professor's chair, and on either side of it many wooden benches, rough-hewn but sturdy, placed transversely.

Philosophy was taught here; this science was first taught to Cuban youth at the Colegio de San Carlos by the distinguished Father Félix Varela,[18] who wrote a textbook for his students that represented a total departure from Aristotelianism, the only philosophy with a following in Cuba until then, ever since the founding of the University of Havana in 1774, in the monastery of Santo Domingo. When later on, in 1821, Father Varela left the country to serve as a representative in the Spanish parliament, his most outstanding disciple, José Antonio Saco,[19] occupied the same chair in his stead, and at various times in our history it was occupied by the jurist Francisco Javier de la Cruz, owing to the absence of its holder and the expatriation of its virtuous founder in the United States.

In the angle to the left there was another auditorium, with an entrance leading directly to the walkway, where Father Plumas taught Latin. Then, occupying almost all of the other side, there was the refectory for the seminarians and a number of professors who resided permanently in the same building, and to the left of the main entrance was the wide staircase that afforded access to the corridors of the upper floor. The law students who were not seminarians went up to their auditorium via this staircase, whereas the philosophy and Latin students entered their respective auditoriums, already mentioned, by way of the doors on the same level as the courtyard.

On the morning of the day whose events we are relating, when the law students placed a foot on the bottom step of the staircase, they halted en masse as they noticed a group of three individuals in animated conversation nearby, below the walkway. The one who was speaking might have been 28 to 30 years old. He was of average height, white, with a rather ruddy complexion, blue almond eyes, a large mouth with thick lips and straight though bushy brown hair. He had a certain reserved air about him and was elegantly dressed, in attire of English cut. The second of the three individuals could be said to be the reverse of the coin of the one already described, for besides being dumpy, he had a big head, a short neck, and very black kinky hair, big bulging eyes, a thick underlip baring uneven teeth, wide and badly spaced; he also had a complexion the color of a cured tobacco leaf that made his purity of blood very dubious. The third one differed in other ways from the two already mentioned, being thinner and older than they, with pale skin and a very pleasant, refined manner. This third individual was the professor of philosophy, Francisco Javier de la Cruz; the second one was José Agustín Govantes, a distinguished jurist who held the chair in Cuban law; and the first was José Antonio Saco, recently returned from the United States.

The latter's return had been preceded by the fame of his writings in the *Mensajero Semanal*, which he published in New York, with the cooperation of the beloved Father Varela, according to those who were versed in the events and the eminent personages of the revolutions of Mexico and Colombia. Above all, people in Havana had just read, with passionate enthusiasm, his critico-political polemic with the head of the botanical garden, Don Ramón de la Sagra, in defense of the poet from Matanzas, José María Heredia.[20]

As a result of this, young Cubans, who were now becoming caught up in politics, began to drop out of the botany class that La Sagra was attempting to teach, making fun of him, whereas they admired Saco, whom they regarded as a determined insurgent, with whose opinion regarding the government of the colony La Sagra, oddly enough, fully concurred.

One of the law students recognized him immediately, because he had studied philosophy with him in 1823, and murmured his name, which was enough to make Saco stop and utter an exclamation, more out of curiosity than anything else. This must have attracted Govantes's attention, for by means of gestures he ordered his students to go upstairs to the auditorium, where he would join them in a few moments.

And they headed there, in fact, in a mad rush and entered the auditorium amid a great din, talking of Saco, of Heredia, of the latter's celebrated anthem *El Desterrado* and his no less famous ode *El Niágara*, included in the collection of his poetry published in Toluca, Mexico; of La Sagra's botany lessons, and of the heroes of the revolution in Colombia, though at the time young people in Havana knew relatively little about it. When, shortly thereafter, Govantes entered the auditorium at a laggardly pace, with a book under his arm and a cheerful and animated expression on his face, the students suddenly stopped talking and total silence reigned. Govantes mounted the three or four steps leading to the chair, placed the book on the wide parapet in front of him so as always to be within his reach, and sat down in the straw-bottomed chair.

The law auditorium was not only the largest and roomiest one in the seminary, but also the one best situated in all respects. The entrance was located at one end, and it had four wide windows that opened onto the corridor, and another four that opened onto the port of Havana, letting in light and air and affording a view of the bulwarks of the citadel of La Cabaña and part of those of El Morro. Leaning against the dividing wall, between the windows in the middle, was the professor's chair; in front of it were two parallel rows of benches and on both sides many others placed transversely, so that the professor, from his lofty chair, dominated the entire class, despite its being spread out all over the vast room which probably held as many as 150 students from several academic classes.

Those who had studied the assigned lesson and believed themselves capable of explaining it more or less clearly, presented themselves and followed the professor's movements. Those who had not even opened the textbook, on the other hand, did not know where to hide their face or how to disappear from view. This was the case with our acquaintance Leonardo Gamboa, just as he himself had told his friends Meneses and Pancho Solfa. Inasmuch as his build and his character made it difficult for him to hide from sight, he never sat down in front of the professor's chair, but instead in one of the last benches on either side of the classroom. On the day whose events we are recounting he occupied the end seat in the corner, having obliged his friend Solfa to move out of it and let him have it. Once Govantes's gaze had taken in the entire class, he called on a student to his right, whom he addressed by the name of Martiartu, the one affecting the Spanish accent whom we have already described, and ordered him to explain the lesson, which he did easily and even quite clearly. Then he ordered the student who looked like a mulatto, whom he addressed as Mena, to do the same; immediately thereafter he called on another named Arredondo, who was sitting directly in front of Govantes's chair. When Arredondo had finished his explanation, following the text more or less word for word, Govantes's eyes turned to his left, passing over Leonardo—who had suddenly lowered his head on the pretext of picking his handkerchief, which he had purposely dropped, up off the floor—and allowed them to land on the young man seated at the other end of the same bench. The latter did not know the lesson and remained silent, and so, a moment later, the kindly professor said: "Next," with the same result. Govantes then immediately skipped to the fourth one, and then to the sixth, who couldn't answer either, until after skipping three or four in between, he said to Gamboa: "You." Leonardo dissembled as much as he could, pretending that he hadn't heard or understood, but his friend Pancho nudged him, and then, half annoyed, half embarrassed, he stood up and said:

"I'll be damned if I've studied the lesson."

His words made everyone laugh. Without turning a hair, he went on:

"But, because of what the students who preceded me have indicated through the medium of the spoken word, I deduce thereby that the subject being dealt with today is of extreme importance, and I believe that I shall not forget the main points should they become applicable in a case before the bar."

He then abruptly sat down, jabbing his index finger at the same time into the ribs of the long-suffering Pancho, and either because this hurt him or tickled him, the latter could not help leaping out of his seat. Because they were unexpected, Gamboa's peroration, as well as the jab in Pancho's ribs, caused a great burst of laughter, to which, despite his solemnity, Govantes himself contributed, and then without further ado he began the explanation of the text, which had to do, as has been said, with the right of persons. He first defined what was meant by person, according to Roman law; then what was meant by state, which he said was divided into two categories, the natural and the civil, and that this latter could be of three sorts, namely: the state of freedom, of nature, and of family. And he dealt in detail with what might be called the history of slavery, portraying it not in relation to ancient or modern society, but in relation to Roman law, Gothic law, and the law of the land; for even though a fair degree of academic freedom reigned in Cuba at that time, abolitionist ideas had not yet begun to be disseminated there.

On that day Govantes, as usual, was inspired, eloquent, giving proof after proof of his vast erudition, in which his recent conversation with Saco, the translator and annotator of the *Discourses of Heinecius*, used as a textbook at the Colegio de San Carlos since the previous year of 1829, had doubtless played no little part. As he rose to his feet, for the clock had struck nine, his students did likewise, bursting into deafening applause.

X

The wretch was taken in
By great beauty;
He lacked luck,
But abounded in stupidity;
Having taken the wrong path
For the one caught in love's trap
There was no way back.

Don Hurtado de Mendoza

We were saying that all the students of the law of the land imitated the example of their professor and rose to their feet. But even though presumably anxious to leave the classroom, they remained in their respective places until he had come down from his chair and made for the door, his head lowered and his textbook under his arm; they then filed out behind him in two columns, in respectful silence.

The few who accompanied him to the door of his cell, at the far end of the covered walkway, were the seminarians, students at the college, who could be distinguished by the ankle-length brown serge robe they were wearing that made them look like altar boys; it was certain, however, that none of them would pursue a career in the Church.

The other students who were not seminarians, some 150 in all, as we have said, broke up the formation they had fallen into once the professor walked out of the auditorium; they hurried down the wide stone staircase in a mad rush to the walkway below and went out to the street in the same disorder, as though the roomy porter's lodge of the Colegio de San Carlos had spewed all of them out at once.

On reaching the street, they scattered in various directions. A fairly large group went around the corner of the San Telmo barracks, at the very end of the Calle de San Ignacio, turned into Chacón, then into Cuba, and finally went down Cuarteles, heading for El Angel Hill, their destination. In this group of students, making a great commotion as they walked along, the curious reader of the preceding pages can readily make out the three fast friends: Gamboa, Meneses, and Solfa. The first of these was without doubt the leader of the others, for he was walking in front, brandishing in his right hand his rattan cane with the gold handle and a silver tip, like the baton of a drum major. As they approached the church of El Santo Angel Custodio which, as the reader from Havana knows, is situated on the plain of La Peñapobre, the street became narrow because of the slope of the hill and the press of people of both sexes and of every color and social status who were making their way along in the same direction.

The white women, at any rate those who were not going to the church, were riding along in light horse-drawn gigs, which were beginning to come into general use and to take the place of the *volantes* or the calashes that had been used since the end of the preceding century. Almost all of them were occupied by three ladies seated in the single forward-facing seat, the older ladies at either end, leaning back comfortably, the youngest in the middle, invariably sitting up very straight, for neither our gigs or our *volantes* are really built to hold more than two people. Although it was past nine in the morning, the sun was not too hot because of the lateness of the season; therefore almost all the gigs had their hood folded back, showing in full sunlight their precious cargo of women, the majority of them young, dressed in white or in light colors, wearing neither a toque nor a bonnet, their black braided hair held in place by a so-called *teja*, a large ornamental tortoise-shell Spanish comb in the form of a roof tile, and their shoulders and arms bare.

The white women who were making their way on foot along those stone-paved streets without sidewalks were surely going to church; this was evident from their black dresses and their lace mantillas. The people of color of both sexes, twice as numerous as the white people, were all on foot, some of them also heading for the church, and some out for a stroll or selling tortillas from their cedar vendor's boxes, corn tortillas being one of the traditions of the fiesta. The women vendors who had stationed themselves next to one of the walls along the street were for the most part African blacks, for the Creole blacks disdained this occupation. They sat on tiny leather chairs, with a little table in front of them and the flat terra cotta *burén* for cooking them on a brazier to one side. With a wooden spoon they would spread out on this griddle enough wet corn meal to make a tortilla weighing three or four ounces, and when it took on a golden brown color from the heat of the *burén*, they would sprinkle a little melted butter on top of it and offer it for sale, nice and hot and dripping with butter, at a price of two for a silver *medio*. Many young ladies did not think it beneath their dignity to at least stop their carriage and buy *tortillas de San Rafael*, as they were called, still hot from the Indian *burén*, for it seems that that was how they tasted best.

The occasion for all this hubbub and milling about was the fiesta of San Rafael, which falls on October 24, the celebration of which had begun, as we have already pointed out, nine days before. On each of these days a Mass was said in the early morning hours, a high Mass and sermon from ten to twelve, and a *Salve Maria* at Vespers. During the novena or nine-day round of prayer, the Blessed Sacrament was displayed throughout the day and night, and therefore the church was never empty of the faithful, who came from everywhere in the barrio to earn a plenary indulgence.

As we have said earlier, the little church of El Santo Angel Custodio was situated on the narrow plain of La Peñapobre, a sort of gravel bed extending for only a short distance, although quite high as compared to the general elevation of the city. To climb up to it and down from it, there were, and still are, two rough, dark stone staircases, both with stone-paved ramps as well: one which starts at the far end of the Calle de los Cuarteles, and the other which descends to the Calle de Compostela, this latter being the longer and steeper of the two.

On arriving at the top of the plateau, which also has a stone ramp leading up it, one is at the ground level of the church, whose one nave, on days when religious ceremonies were held, as on the feast day that we are describing, can be seen in its entirety, the main altar at the far end, with its wooden retable with two panels, beyond the two side doors, almost hidden beneath the forest of white tapers, gold- and silverplated candelabra, bouquets of artificial flowers and a great profusion of dazzling white bristol board cards. To the right and to the left were a retable with fewer adornments, midway between the main door and the two side doors, and under the cupola two other retables, in each of which a saint's image, usually a wood carving placed in a glass niche, was venerated.

The hip roof left the timbers of the framework roofed with red tiles exposed, and above the main arch, within which there was a small choir loft, there rose the square bell tower of three courses of stone of diminishing size. To the west, behind the main building of the church, was the sacristy, then immediately alongside it the house of the parish priest, and another stone staircase, less spacious than those in front, which led to the Calle del Ejido, a sort of crooked and uneven, low-lying back street running along the walls of the houses and the bulwarks that surrounded the land side of the city. At the front the church courtyard had an embankment of rubblework, much like a wall around a rooftop terrace. On this embankment, on the morning of the day to which we have been referring, the second or third of the San Rafael novena, several black carpenters were whiling away their time erecting, with pine planks painted the color of blocks of stone, something that resembled the parapets of a small castle, having already put the flagstaff in place and almost finished their main task.

The students had taken over the entire incline with its staircases and ramps; Leonardo Gamboa, standing at the very top with his rattan cane on his shoulder was directing the operation, so that no individual went up them, or passed along the street in a carriage or on foot, women in particular, without the students having something to say and even to do to such persons. The most conspicuous of the students, because of his voice, the position he had placed himself in, and his unrivaled stature, was Gamboa, lavishing to right and left, without a letup, a stream of witticisms and flirtatious remarks, especially on the pretty girls, with an excess of gallantry and a lamentable lack of good manners. The girls, however, either out of habit, having heard them since the cradle, or because being flattered is always pleasing, did not take offense and instead merely smiled; with their open fans, they made a graceful gesture to greet friends or acquaintances, and there was no lack of those who retorted to an indecent quip, certainly not behavior to be recommended.

Leonardo had grabbed a piece of tortilla from one of his comrades, and holding it in his left hand, made as if to offer it to the young lady who appealed to him most, with no intention of giving it to any of them, or of tasting it himself, until, of three young ladies who were riding in a gig, he thought he recognized the one sitting on the far side of the seat; hence, instead of making her the same feigned offering as he had the others, he suddenly lowered his hand and tried to hide behind the embankment of the plateau. The young lady had seen him and immediately recognized him; however, instead of smiling, as is natural when one spies a friend amid a multitude of strangers, she grew more serious and pale than she had been before, although she kept looking as long as she could at the student's hat and his forehead, which despite him still were visible above the edge of the rubblework embankment. As Gamboa knelt down, he grabbed his friend Meneses by an arm without meaning to and squeezed it in such a way that the latter couldn't keep from complaining and asking him:

"What's happening, Leonardo? In heaven's name, let go, you're pulling my arm off."

"Didn't you recognize her?" Leonardo replied, gradually straightening up.

"Who? What are you talking about?"

"That girl in the blue gig who was sitting on the end of the seat opposite us. It's now going past Cinco Esquinas. She's still looking this way. She's surely recognized me. And I thought she was many leagues away! Do you suppose she thinks that the *aguinaldos* that bloom at Christmas are still in flower?"

"I still don't know who you're talking about."

"About Isabel Ilincheta, pal. Didn't you recognize her? Even though you were really taken with her sister Rosa?"

"Ah, now I understand. I didn't recognize her, in fact. She looked very thin and sallow to me; at the plantation she was the prettiest girl there."

"When they're about to be left old maids all girls get thin and pale; and Isabel has reason to be both things, because she's the same age as I am and harbors no hopes of marrying soon."

"You'll still get hitched to her the day you least expect to."

"Who, me? She'll never be the hitching post I'd choose. I like the girl, I don't deny it; but I liked her better there, amid the flowers and the perfumed air, in the shade of the orange trees and the palms along those paths and in those gardens of her father's coffee plantation. And then too, she's a first-rate dancer. No less so than your Rosa."

"Leave Rosa out of this and let's get back to Isabel. She was head over heels in love with you, as the time-honored expression goes. Poor thing! According to what I hear, she doesn't know what you're really like. Because the truth of the matter is, you're the most faithless and fickle of men."

"I confess it, I regret it, but I can't help it; I have a hankering for a girl as long as she says no to me; the minute she says yes, even though she may be lovelier than the Blessed Virgin, I lose heart altogether. I haven't written her since May. What will she think of me? And the fact is that those girls brought up in the country are so wearisome when they love you . . . They imagine that all of us fellows from Havana are as sweet as honey and as pliable as beeswax."

"I wonder where she's staying?"

"With the Gámez sisters, her cousins, I'm sure, behind the convent of the Carmelite nuns."

"Are you hoping to come across Rosa? Since she wasn't in the gig with Isabel, it's a clear sign that she hasn't come in from the country. As for me, I swear to you that I both fear to meet Isabel face to face and have no desire to. She'd no doubt be a modern virago in her dealings with me. She isn't a woman that a man can offend with impunity."

"She has more than enough reason to be angry with you, and in all conscience you must try to appease her anger."

"Conscience, conscience," Leonardo repeated in a disdainful tone of voice. "Who ever had one when it came to dealing with women?"

"Man! Don't blaspheme, for you're the son of a woman."

This last observation was made by Pancho Solfa, who had been listening to the brief dialogue between the two friends. Leonardo looked down on him, not out of contempt, but because he was at least a foot and a half taller than Pancho, and said to him gravely:

"You're going to end up a Capuchin friar." Then, turning in a fury to Meneses, he added: "That girl is going to upset all my plans."

"I don't understand," Meneses said.

"You'll see," Leonardo replied, lost in thought. "Gentlemen," he went on, addressing the students who had followed him from the college, "let's go, I'm getting bored."

Leonardo had clearly worked himself into a bad mood; something was thwarting him, and he was not a man to tolerate stumbling blocks. But the moment he reached the street down below via the Calle de Compostela side and found himself once again amid the hustle and bustle of the crowd, he became his usual vivacious self again. In fact, when he reached Cinco Esquinas, he caught up with a middle-aged gentleman who was going in the same direction as the students. Leonardo pinned his arms down with his, covered his eyes with both hands, and said to him, disguising his voice: "Guess who."

The stranger tried in vain to work himself free from the student's clutches, persuaded perhaps that the object of that volence was to rob him in broad daylight and in full view of the crowd. But Leonardo, once his comrades and a crowd of onlookers had gathered round him, let go of the man; and, with his hat in his hand and his head bowed as a sign of respect and repentance, said to him: "A thousand pardons, sir. I have committed a most regrettable error, but you are the one to blame, for you look as much like my uncle Antonio as one egg looks like another."

The students guffawed, while at the same time the unknown gentleman, understanding that it was a joke, burst out into ill-humored and wrathful invective against the badly behaved and insolent young people of the day. That ridiculous scene took place in less time than we have taken to depict it, and as if to form a contrast with it, the moment Leonardo went past the Calle de Chacón, he stuck the tip of his rattan cane into a plump rolled-up corn tortilla beginning to brown in the heat of the *burén* of a black woman who was plumper still and practically naked, leaning against the wall at the corner and surrounded by pots and pans, and raised it in the air. The tortilla vendor gave an aggrieved exclamation, and as she straightened up on her miniature stool, being as obese and heavy as she was, she tipped over the little table in front of her, on which there were tortillas that were already toasted, and sent it rolling, whereupon her vexation mounted and her angry cries followed one upon the other even faster. Everyone laughed at the incident, except Meneses, who thanks to one of those noble and generous impulses of his good heart, took out of his waistcoat pocket a few *reales*, tossed them in the direction of the black woman's ample bosom, and succeeded in depositing them down her low-cut, scanty dress.

If her anger was thereby dissipated or her laments ceased, the students did not stop to verify the fact. Ahead of them, the Calle del Tejadillo cut across Compostela at right angles and then one came to the Calle del Empedrado—Cobblestone Street, given this name because it was the first one to serve as a trial of the paving system of the streets of Havana with smooth round stones and a drain down the middle. Leonardo turned into it on the right, after saying good-bye to his classmates and telling his close friends Meneses and Solfa that if they wished they could wait for him in the little square immediately adjacent to the convent of Santa Catalina, where he would join them within a quarter of an hour. But inasmuch as it was already lunch hour according to Cuban custom, they chose to go on to their respective houses and parted company with Leonardo until the night of the feast day of El Santo Angel Custodio.

Once by himself, the law student suddenly changed his pace and his manner. He grew serious and thoughtful, much more so than one would expect of someone of such a cheerful and prankish nature. The fact was that he was overly concerned about the appearance in Havana and at the fair of the young woman from Alquízar whose name he had said was Isabel Ilincheta. Though he denied it, he was in love with her, and he was concealing the fact that her sudden arrival had given rise to unpleasant revelations, in particular the discovery of his inconstancies, which no matter how perverted his sense of decency, could do him no honor or fail to drain the color from his face. Several times he stopped and struck with the tip of his cane the narrow flagstones of the sidewalk, a luxury enjoyed at that time, among only a few other streets, by the famous Calle del Empedrado. He wavered for a long time between going on and turning back the other way, for it is helpful for the reader to know that the direction he was headed in did not lead to his house. He finally gave an even harder blow with his cane than the preceding ones, slung it over his shoulder, as was his habit, and stepped up his pace, murmuring: "What the devil! What's done can't be undone." All this was intended to strengthen his resolve to follow through on the decision he had made.

After walking a short way, he found himself at the corner of the Calle del Aguacate, and hugging the towering walls of the convent of Santa Catalina, he did not stop until he was a short distance away from the corner where the Calle de O'Reilly intersects the street he was on at the time. There, he cast a sidelong glance at the small square window high up in the wall of a run-down cottage on the sidewalk opposite, immediately adjacent to the corner. We have described this cottage in minute detail at the end of Chapter II of this true story. The two wooden panels of the window were half-closed, and between the cedar balusters there could be seen the folds of a small curtain of white muslin, which was moving slighty at that moment, either because of the gentle morning breeze or because of the movements of someone standing behind it. In the same position, although in reverse, the rickety door could be seen: the half of an iron ball that we have spoken of elsewhere was keeping it from closing altogether.

There was undoubtedly a person standing between the half-closed panel of the little window and the white curtain, because Leonardo had barely crossed the street and placed his right hand in the empty space left in the window frame by a fallen baluster when the prettiest woman's face that perhaps existed at that time in Havana peeked out. At the sight of the mulatto, even though her eyes were gleaming, and not with love but with anger, Leonardo was completely enthralled, and forgot about Isabel, the balls at Alquízar, and the walks along the paths lined with palms and orange trees on the coffee plantations of that district. The reader of the first chapters of this story has before him at this moment Cecilia Valdés. She kept her burning lips tightly closed; her blood seemed about to pour forth from her round cheeks; her full breasts were barely held in within the confines of her dress. Finally she was the first to speak, saying more with her countenance than with her voice:

"Why have you come?"

"I just got out of class," Leonardo answered in a low and humble yet firm tone of voice.

Cecilia cast a sidelong glance inside the room, with her left hand spread open gestured to Leonardo to lower his voice a bit more and added vehemently:

"You were seen just a little while ago on El Angel Hill."

"That may well be; I was on my way here."

"But it took you a long time; it isn't all that far from there to here. Ah! A woman in love is doomed to perdition!"

"Nothing has been lost, Celia.[21] Here I am."

"Yes, I see. But who knows why you took so long? Perhaps a woman . . ."

"It had nothing to do with a woman, I swear."

"Don't swear to anything, because then I believe it even less. The thing is that Chepilla is already back from Paula Hospital and you turn up only now. There's no time left to talk. She's been home for some time. She was praying and dozing, I suppose because she was tired; and now she's raising her head and listening with the ear of a moralist. (She said this as she turned and looked inside the room again.) My friendship doesn't interest you, as everyone knows, and I'm a fool who goes on waiting for you. Accursed be the woman who loves as I do!"

"Your despair frightens me, my darling. I regret this mishap; we'll see each other tomorrow."

"The thing is that Chepilla doesn't go to Paula every day."

"I get up about seven. You know what time it was when we came back from Regla, around one in the morning."

"That didn't keep me from waking up at dawn. I went to bed with worries on my mind and you didn't; that makes a big difference."

"Stop using that ironic tone of voice that doesn't suit you at all. You know only too well that I idolize you."

"When it comes to love, actions speak louder than words, and the man who doesn't show up at a rendezvous . . ."

"Don't condemn me lightly. I've already told you why I was delayed. I insist, however, that I'm deeply sorry, and I'll prove it to you . . ."

"The latecomer be damned. You protest to no avail that you're fond of me. The man who is really in love is not a deceiver. Yes, you're deceiving me. You've wounded me to the quick. Be off with you. You don't speak, you thunder."

Leonardo took her hand and raised it to his lips, without her putting up the least resistance, and thus he knew that the storm's fury had passed and that the girl would allow him to visit her at the first opportunity. He then went on his way, and on entering the Calle de O'Reilly, he put his left foot on the running board of a *volante* that was coming down from the Puerta del Monserrate, swaying back and forth between the inordinately long shafts whose weight was resting on the hubs of two enormous wheels and the back of a real Rosinante, and sat down on the leather cushion. The shaking caused by the young man's sudden entrance caught the attention of the driver, who immediately turned his head to see what sort of passenger he had acquired without looking or waiting for one. As Leonardo collapsed on the seat, he thundered in a resounding and commanding voice: "Home."

"And where does the young master live?" the naturally startled driver asked.

"Ignoramus! You mean you don't know? Calle de San Ignacio, corner of Luz. Giddyap."

"Ah!" the driver exclaimed, and whiplashed the poor nag across its flanks so hard that it trembled all over inside its bony frame, nearly doubling over, either from pain, or from the weight of the carriage, the passenger, and the driver.

As the student, tossed back and forth like a ball, rides homeward in the rickety *volante*, we ask the reader to allow us a few reflections. To what was Cecilia aspiring by cultivating amorous relations with Leonardo Gamboa? He was a young white, from a rich family, related to the first families of Havana, who was studying to be an attorney, and if he should chance to marry, it certainly would not be with a lower-class girl, whose surname was enough to indicate her obscure origins, and whose mixed blood was clearly revealed by her kinky hair and her bronze complexion. Her incomparable beauty, then, was a relative quality, the only one perhaps that she could count on to win men's hearts; but it did not constitute a reliable reason for her to abandon the sphere into which she had been born and rise to the one in which the whites of a country of slaves moved. Perhaps others less pretty than she and with more mixed blood rubbed elbows in that era with the elite of Havana society, and even bore titles of nobility; but they either hid their obscure origins or else they had been born and bred amid abundance, and it is common knowledge that gold purifies the most turbid blood and covers up the worst defects, both physical and moral.

But we are certain that these reflections, however natural they may appear to be, never crossed Cecilia's mind. Love was a spontaneous sentiment of her ardent nature, and she saw in the young white man only the tender lover, superior because of many qualities to all those of his class who might aspire to win her heart and her favors. In the shadow of the white, however illicit their union might be, Cecilia believed and hoped that she would continue to rise in the world and make her way out of the humble sphere into which she had been born, and if she did not, her children would. Married to a mulatto, she would lower herself in her own esteem and in that of her equals: for such are the aberrations of all societies built on the same model as the Cuban.

The carriage driver, meanwhile, went down the Calle de O'Reilly at a trot, took the Calle de Cuba, drove diagonally across the little square of Santa Clara, then turned into the Calle de San Ignacio, and before his horse went one pace farther, he reined it in and stopped the carriage at the door of the house to which he had been directed. This was a proof that the black carriage driver did not merit the epithet of "ignoramus" that Leonardo had flung at him on entering the *volante*. He had not yet brought it to a full stop when the student leapt out onto the sidewalk and just as quickly tossed a coin in the driver's direction. The latter caught it in midair, brought it up to eye level, saw that it was a peseta bearing the emblem of two columns, crossed himself with it, put his spurs to his nag and went on his way, saying: "Good health to you, young master."

Beneath the cloudless sky of my homeland
I could not bring myself to be a slave,
or agree that everything in nature
was noble and happy, save for man.

José María Heredia, *A Emilia*

When he leapt out of the *volante* onto the sidewalk, Leonardo thought he noticed that a military officer, in full uniform, who was walking at a fast gait toward the Plaza Vieja, had moved away from the second window of his house, and that at the very same time there had come away from a shutter of that same window the familiar face of one of his sisters. He stepped up his pace and in fact, through another opening in the grating of the *zaguán*, he saw his elder sister Antonia raising the curtain so as to enter the nearest room through the door that led to the drawing room. This unexpected discovery upset him more than we can imagine because by putting two and two together he convinced himself, beyond a doubt, that while he had been wooing the mulatto girl there in the barrio of El Angel, a Spanish army captain, in the clear light of an October morning, had been courting his sister here in the barrio of San Francisco. The memory of the pleasant moment that he had enjoyed and that still lingered in his mind like a bright vision, grew clouded and then vanished altogether in the face of that scene at the window of his house that so greatly displeased him.

We must repeat that the generation we are now endeavoring to portray from the politico-moral point of view, of which Leonardo Gamboa and his classmates were an authentic sample, had acquired very superficial notions concerning the situation of their native land in the world of ideas and principles. Without mincing words, it can be said that their patriotism was Platonic in nature, inasmuch as it was not based on a sense of duty or on a knowledge of the rights that belonged to each of them as a citizen and as a free man.

The constitutional system that had ruled in Cuba, from 1808 to 1813 the first time, and from 1821 to 1823 the second, had taught the generation of 1830 nothing. For this generation, freedom of the press, the national militia, the frequent exercise of the right to vote, the popular gatherings, the agitation and the propaganda of the political hotheads, the clandestine meetings of the Masonic lodges, Father Varela's academic chairs of law and of political economy, his lectures on the Constitution had come and gone like a dream, like happenings in the next world or in another country. After each one of these two brief periods a wave of despotism from the mother country had flooded over Cuba and erased even the ideas and the principles sown with such exhausting labor by distinguished mentors and eminent patriots. The newspapers, the pamphlets, and the few books published by a free press in these two memorable eras had disappeared; if a rare copy existed, it was in the hands of a bibliographer, who was doubly careful to keep it hidden.

Subject to prior censorship, the free press all over the island had fallen silent after 1824, the mere handful of periodicals published after that date in one or another of the big towns being unworthy of that name. Martial law, to which the country was subjected after the Constitutional period, did not allow discussion of the questions that might have interested the people most. It was a serious crime to speak of politics in public and in private; the mention of the names of certain persons and even of certain subjects was strictly prohibited. Events of the past, then, both within and without Cuba, the attempts at revolution there, the results of the tremendous fight for freedom and independence on the continent, all lay buried in mystery and oblivion for the majority of Cubans. History, moreover, which gathers up everything and preserves it for the right occasion, still had not been written in the case of Cuba.

There was no lack of Cubans outside the country who engaged in the militant politics of the day, who strove to get news to their homeland of what was going on around it, and who could teach the people their rights and remind it of their duties. To that end, the virtuous Father Varela, among others, published *El Habanero* in Philadelphia from 1824 to 1826, but the Spanish government declared it to be a subversive paper and prohibited it from entering Cuba. We may therefore be certain that very few copies circulated inside the country. Later on, that is to say from 1828 to 1830, José Saco undertook, again in the United States, to publish *El Mensajero Semanal*, a scientific, political and literary weekly, which, for the same reasons as its predecessor, scarcely circulated in Havana and had no appreciable influence on political ideas. The one thing in this publication that caught the attention of young people in Havana, as has been pointed out earlier, was the heated debate that its distinguished editor carried on with the director of the Havana Botanical Garden, Don Ramón de la Sagra, over the impassioned criticism to which the latter had subjected the volume of poetry by the renowned Cuban Tirteus, José María Heredia, which saw the light of day in Toluca, Mexico, in the year 1828.

The patriotic verses of that famous poet exercised a greater and more general influence on the minds of youth, above all his ode "La Estrella de Cuba," published in October, 1823; his epistle "A Emilia," in 1824; and his sonnet to Don Tomás Boves. His "Himno del Desterrado"[22] of 1825 aroused keen enthusiasm in Havana; many learned it by heart and a goodly number repeated it whenever the occasion came their way to do so without endangering their personal freedom. But neither these periodicals nor these fiery verses, despite their brimming over with free-thinking and patriotic ideas, were enough to inspire that feeling for country and freedom which at times impels men to sacrifice their lives, which sends them off, sword in hand, to win their rights.

Memories of past conspiracies, moreover, still lingered on, confused if no longer sad. Of the one of the year 1812 all that lived on was the name of Aponte,[23] the rebel who had headed it, for whenever an occasion presented itself to portray a perverse or accursed individual, old women would exclaim: "He's more evil than Aponte!" Of the conspiracy of 1823, tradition had it that Lemus, the ringleader, was wailing his life away in a prison in Spain; that Peoli had escaped from the barracks in Belén disguised as a woman; that Ferrety, the informer, enjoyed special treatment from the government; and that Armona, the pursuer and apprehender of the principal conspirators, was still the chief of Captain General Don Francisco Dionisio Vives's only police force.

What was no more than a rumor had circulated that the government in Washington had opposed the invasion of Cuba and Puerto Rico by troops from Mexico and Colombia, and that as a consequence Sánchez and Agüero had been hanged in the vicinity of Puerto Príncipe in 1826 as emissaries of the insurgents. But oblivion and indifference had reached the point that in the very same days to which we were referring in the preceding pages, those implicated in the so-called Aguila Negra ("Black Eagle") conspiracy, many of whom were imprisoned in the barracks of the dragoons, in that of the militias of the men of color, in the fortress of La Punta and elsewhere, were tried for treason, which occasioned no signs of dissatisfaction or even of interest on the part of the people.

Moreover, the Cuban conspirators of previous unsuccessful attempts to bring down the government were either still far off in other countries or had died in exile, or else their patriotic ardor had cooled and they were living an obscure and peaceful life, devoting their efforts to the reparation of the damage to their health and fortunes brought on by time and human obstacles. It was not, therefore, nor could it have been, the task of those who had returned to their homeland to propagate opinions and political projects that had been conceived and cherished during the days of heady excitement and of blind faith in the cause of freedom.

For their part, Spaniards born in Cuba on the one hand and on the other those who had emigrated from the mother country, as though to excuse their cowardly, selfish, or backward-looking conduct in the war for independence, on their arrival in Cuba, devoted all their efforts to one end: misrepresenting the nature of what had happened, characterizing the motives of the patriotic sacrifices of the revolutionaries as unjust, perverse, and ignoble, belittling their heroic deeds, turning even their acts of justice and of mere reprisal into savagery. To these renegades the republican or patriot was an insurgent, that is to say a rebel and a traitor, an enemy of God and of the king; the corsair a pirate or a Moslem, as the people called the Algerians who infested the shores of the Mediterranean until the final years of the last century.

The reader from Havana, thoroughly familiar with the young people of that era whom we are endeavoring to describe, will readily believe us if we tell him that Leonardo Gamboa cared nothing about politics, and even though the thought occasionally occurred to him that Cuba was groaning in the bonds of slavery, it never even entered his mind at the time that he or some other Cuban ought to put the means to free it in place. As a Creole who was beginning to come into contact with distinguished people and to study jurisprudence, he did have some notion of a better state of society and of a less military and oppressive form of government for his homeland. However, since he was the son of a father who was wealthy, Spanish-born, and a businessman who preferred to drop by to visit with his countrymen rather than keep company with Creoles, he already felt hatred toward Spaniards, and much more still toward the Spanish military, on whose shoulders the complicated colonial structure of Cuba manifestly rested. Hence it was not possible for him to make light of the fact that a military officer was giving signs of making off with his beloved sister; on the contrary, the jealousy he felt was precisely as impassioned as the hatred inspired in him by this man who was both a military officer and a Spaniard was profound.

Leonardo thus entered his house in a foul mood. The table was set for lunch, and instead of going in search of his mother, as was his habit when he came home from class, he sought out no one and went straight up to his room, flung his textbook on a chair, took off his woolen dress coat, and donned a short coat of cotton twill with colored pinstripes. For a brief moment he hesitated between lying down on the bed, whose coolness and thin blue mosquito netting invited him to rest, and going out onto the balcony, which was still in the shade, when the little black, Tirso, appeared and said: "Young master, lunch is served." And Leonardo hurried downstairs, finding his mother and father already seated at the table. He discreetly sat down on his mother's side of the table, and she cast a loving glance at him from afar, looking as though she had been surprised and upset that he had not come to see her when he came home. His father did not even raise his eyes from the plateful of fried eggs with salsa that he was eating, despite the fact that strictly speaking he had not seen his son since the day before.

Leonardo's sisters immediately emerged from their bedrooms one after the other, dressed to go out, and sat down at the table, not saying a word, like nuns in their refectory. Each one occupied his or her respective place at it, that is to say Doña Rosa with her son, the apple of her eye, on one side, her three daughters on the other, and Don Cándido and the steward at the opposite ends of the table. This arrangement was not a happenstance; it was changed when there was a guest to whom the courtesy of a seat at table was owed. It was a clear indication of the intimate relationships, habits, and preferences of the family, particularly of the parents with regard to their offspring.

Doña Rosa's preferences left no room for doubt: Leonardo was her favorite in every respect. Don Cándido's, if on occasion he allowed them to show, were focused on his eldest daughter Antonia.

Don Cándido was a businessman rather than a social lion. With little or no culture, he had come to Cuba from the highlands of Ronda while still a young man, and had amassed a fortune thanks to hard work and thrifty habits, and thanks in particular to the good luck that had come his way through engaging in the risky slave trade on the coast of Africa.[24]

His principal trade in Havana, the one that had served him as a step on his way to the top of the ladder of prosperity, was in lumber and rough unfinished planking from North America, red roofing tiles, and bricks and lime from domestic sources, although from day to day he did not occupy himself with this business either exclusively or personally, since the title of *hacendado* given him by his friends sounded better to his ears, referring as it did to his ownership of the sugar plantation La Tinaja in the jurisdiction of El Mariel, the coffee plantation Las Mercedes in La Güira de Melena, and the cattle ranch or large fenced hacienda of Hoyo Colorado.

Out of habit rather than by nature, he was reserved and cold in his treatment of his family, since the nature of his earlier occupations and the desire to accumulate money that took possession of him once he married a rich Creole girl from one of the oldest noble families of Havana had often kept him away from home.

In the beginning of his new life his conduct had not been exemplary or worthy of serving Leonardo as a guide, as Doña Rosa has led us to understand at the end of Chapter VII. For some reason, perhaps because of his supine ignorance, he did not concern himself with the upbringing of his children, much less with their morals. Both duties became the responsibility of that discreet lady who, though she may have lacked formal learning, of a certainty possessed unerring instincts and the purest motherly love, the qualities most needed to properly guide the most impetuous of young people. Particularly where matters of upbringing are concerned, charity is the source and the mirror of all the virtues.

Moreover, being an ignorant and crude man, Don Cándido had a strange way of reprimanding his children. We have already seen that when Leonardo appeared in the dining room, his father did not even look him in the face. This was the infallible sign that he was still angry at him. In fact, whenever one or another of his children gave him reason for complaint, to all appearances a frequent occurrence, he chastised him or her, or believed that he had, by refusing to speak to the child for days and even months at a time. Consequently his children could almost never determine the real cause of their father's anger; in such cases, their mother always served as a means of communication or intermediary so as to maintain peace and harmony within the family.

Antonia, the living image of Doña Rosa physically, was 22 years old. Leonardo was past 20, and his younger sisters, Carmen and Adela, were about 18 and 17, respectively. The latter could pass anywhere for a perfect model of beauty. She possessed all the features required by Greek sculptors in the person whose statue was to be carved: a well-shaped head, regular features, symmetrical contours, a graceful bearing, a slim waist, a high forehead, and flashing eyes. Since she resembled the Greek Venus more closely than one of the Three Fates, she looked more like Don Cándido than like Doña Rosa. Between the daughter and the father there was something more than what is generally understood by the expression "a family resemblance"; she bore imprinted upon her countenance, upon her spirit, the seal that testified to her being his progeny.

Leonardo occupied at table the place opposite his sister Adela, and whenever their father was present, they exchanged knowing glances all through lunch or dinner, frequently smiled at each other, kept up, in short, affectionate brother-and-sister conversations with their eyes and their lips without uttering a word. It was quite evident that strong affinities linked the two of them. They were what is called each other's soul mate. Had they not been brother and sister by birth, they would have loved each other as did the most celebrated of lovers that the world has ever known. On the morning of the day to which we are referring, things did not take their usual course, however. Leonardo was angry or sad, or else a strange and profound anxiety had come over him; Adela, having sought to attract his gaze as usual but to no avail, furrowed her brow and attempted to burn his forehead with the rays of her divine eyes from across the table. Yet their eyes did not meet even once; in Leonardo's suddenly petrified face there was not a trace of affection for her. The innocent girl finally grew distressed. Had she given him reason to be angry at her without her knowing it? What was troubling her beloved brother? Why on the two or three times that she surprised him looking at her in indifferent and mute contemplation had he suddenly lowered his eyes or feigned utter inattention and indifference? Perhaps his behavior was not clear and Adela too young to understand that he was unintentionally making a comparative study of his sister's charming countenance. What thoughts were running through his mind at that moment? It is difficult to say. The only thing that can be asserted as a positive fact is that in Leonardo's contemplation there was more enthrallment than mental distraction, more delight than cold reflection, as though he had just now discovered in his sister's face something that he had not noticed before.

Lunch lasted about an hour, perfect silence reigning all during that time, for scarcely any sound other than that of the silverware was heard, or any voice other than that of someone asking that this or that far-off dish be brought by Tirso, the little black with whom our readers are already acquainted, and by a good-looking young black girl, standing like

Tirso, with her arms folded over her chest as they awaited orders, attentive to demands for their service. Tirso, however, served the men for the most part, Dolores the women. But it was worthy of note that both of them divined Don Cándido's very thoughts, placing before him the dish that he had designated simply by glancing at it, and as a consequence neither Tirso nor the maidservant Dolores ever took their eyes off him as they served the others at table. Woe to them if they did not obey an order promptly or misunderstood which plate he wanted to replace the one he had just tasted! Punishment was not long in coming: Don Cándido was in the habit of throwing at the hapless servant's head the first thing that came to hand. The abundance of the viands matched the variety of the dishes. In addition to the fried beef and pork and two kinds of stew, there was minced veal served in a cassava flour pie, roast chicken, gleaming with butter and seasoned with garlic cloves, fried eggs nearly drowned in salsa, boiled rice, ripe plantain, also fried, in long sweet slices, and a salad of watercress and lettuce. Once lunch was over, a third servant appeared, in his shirt sleeves, who from the grease stains on his clothes was apparently the cook, with a porcelain coffee pot in either hand, and began to fill everyone's cup with coffee and milk, Don Cándido's first of all and then in succession Doña Rosa's, Leonardo's, and his sisters', ending up with the steward's, although the latter was not sitting in the last place at a table with the master of the house at the head and the eldest daughter at the foot. The steward was nothing but a white servant, and no one was better at defining his position in that house than the other servants.

The family was drinking its coffee with boiling-hot milk when our acquaintance the carriage driver Aponte passed by the dining room, heading for the street. Though still in his shirt sleeves, he was wearing his knee-high riding boots with solid silver spurs. He was leading with his right hand two harnessed horses, whose tails were carefully braided and the ends tied with a length of worsted yarn to a ring in the saddletree, in the back. On entering the *zaguán*, Aponte let go of the reins of the team of horses, and without further ado, threw the big door to the street wide open, suspended the full weight of the shafts of the gig on the silver-plated rings screwed into the ends of them, and shouting "move back!" sent the gig rolling into the middle of the street and then turned it around and pushed it against the sidewalk outside the house. He immediately returned to take one of the horses by the bridle, gave it a hard slap in the belly with his left hand, and placed it almost by brute force between the shafts, which he then suspended by the rings to three double iron hooks hanging from the saddle, covered with little flaps of black leather. The other horse, the one he was about to mount, was attached to the carriage by two strong leather traces, fastened by loops to a whiffletree.

After the coffee Don Cándido took the bull's bladder full of *tabacos* (cigars) and sank his arm in it up to the elbow: that was how deep it was. On seeing him do that, Tirso flew to the kitchen in search of the little silver brazier filled with live coals. Before the master could bite off the end of the cigar, a step necessary to make it burn well, the slave, with an expression of humility mingled with fear, had already brought the brazier closer so that Don Cándido could light the cigar himself. As he drew the first mouthful of pungent bluish smoke from the cigar, he stood up, and followed by the steward, entered the study, as silent as when he had left it an hour before to sit down at the lunch table.

The disappearance of the father brought on, all by itself, a sudden and total change in the mood and behavior of the family, including the mother. The hearts of the children were relieved, apparently, of the burden that had been weighing heavily upon them, since the faces of all of them brightened as if in concert and their tongues loosened. Leonardo's high spirits in particular brought him to the point of drawing his mother to him with his left arm to give her several kisses on the cheek and saying to her:

"And what's the matter with him (meaning Don Cándido)? Is he angry?"

"He's angry at you," his mother replied succinctly.

"At me? Well, he's in for a hard time then."

In a moment or two, however, he turned serious again because, having noticed that his sister Antonia was not being as expansive as the others, he remembered the incident in the window overlooking the street.

"Mama," he added more gravely, "I fancy someone is pulling the wool over your eyes and you don't even sense it."

"Why do you say that, son?" Doña Rosa replied in the most gentle voice imaginable.

"Shall I tell her, Antonia?" he slyly asked his sister.

Instead of answering, Antonia turned more serious still and made as if to get up from the table, whereupon Leonardo quickly added:

"Too bad for you, Antonia, if you get up from the table and leave me with a mouthful of words unspoken. I won't say anything to Mama, but that's because I've made up my mind. There will be no more visits from army officers in my house."

"You talk as though you were the master of the house," Antonia replied scornfully.

"I'm not the master, that's true, but I can break a certain person's legs when he least expects it, and that's that."

"You're risking getting your own legs broken."

"We'll see about that."

"Suppose that instead of a Spanish army officer our visitor was a cadet. Would you object to that too?"

"A cadet! A cadet!" Leonardo repeated with pronounced scorn. "Nobody speaks of cadets, since, like officers of the militia, they don't amount to much. They're passé today; the last of them were buried on the beaches of Tampico, where Barradas had chanced to take them.[25] Those who survived the disastrous campaign have surely lost their enthusiasm for arms. Thank heaven we're now free of their fatuousness."

"So your grudge is against Spaniards, as though you think of your own father as having been born and raised in Havana."

"Your hatred of Spaniards is going to cost us dearly one of these days, Leonardo," Doña Rosa said.

"The fact is that I don't have a blind hatred of Spaniards, Mama, nor do I hate them collectively; the ones I hate are those in the military. They think they're the masters of the country, they treat us native Cubans with contempt, and because they wear epaulets and sabers they fancy they deserve our admiration and can do as they please. To gain entrée anywhere, they don't wait to be invited, and once inside they make off with all the best and prettiest girls. That's intolerable. Though if you look closely, it's the girls who are are to blame. It's as though they were dazzled by their gleaming epaulets."

"I for my part," Carmen remarked, "am an exception to the rule."

"And that goes for me too," Adela added. "Military officers, no matter how clean they are, smell of the barracks."

"Don't talk that way, child," her mother said to her, "because some military officers are most estimable men. Without looking any farther, my uncle Lázaro de Sandoval, who was a colonel of the standing regiment of Havana, participated in the siege of Pensacola and died covered with medals and scars."

"But we're not talking about those military officers, Mama," Leonardo said, leaping to his feet. "We're talking about the military officers who came from Spain to win Mexico back, and then having failed there came here so that we would make reparations for their ill humor over their ignominious defeat. Those are the military officers to whom I'm referring now. The worst of it isn't that they smell of the barracks, as Adela says, but that, as men, they're terrible husbands. Until they reach the rank of brigadier, they live in barracks or in forts, where they have tents for houses; rude and insolent aides for servants; beatings and gauntlets they subject their men to for entertainment; the drum sounding reveille for music. Almost never do they stay anywhere long enough to settle down, because, when they least expect it, they find themselves sent off, first to Trinidad, then to Puerto Príncipe, and after that to Santiago de Cuba, and then on to Bayamo. . . . And if they're married, their wife and children and household goods, of course, have to follow them from barracks to barracks, from fort to fort, from post to post, save in the case where, in order to save money, the wife stays behind with her parents as he marches off with his men. Since their aim is to find a rich woman to marry, they care little about the character and the antecedents of the women whom they finally take to the altar; sooner or later the wives scratch their husband's face and the husbands drag them around by the hair."

Antonia could bear no more: she left the table and went to the drawing room, silent and very upset.

"You've hurt your sister's feelings for no reason," Doña Rosa said to him. "She isn't thinking about any military officers, no matter how much she extols one or another of them."

"She isn't thinking about them, but she lets them flirt with her through the window, and that's what annoys me."

"Fortunately Antonia isn't a girl of that kind, my son."

"No? Alas, Mama! It's as if you're losing half your eyesight and your insight . . . I don't want to go on talking; the only thing I'm saying and keep saying is that some day when no one expects it I'm going to break one of those soldiers' legs."

He left the table immediately, and as though nothing had happened, or been said, to upset her, went over to where his sister Adela was sitting, clasped her by the waist and smothered her with kisses.

"Stop, stop," she said. "So you weren't angry at me? Your beard hurts my cheeks."

"Where are you going all dolled up like that?" Leonardo asked her, avoiding the subject his sister had brought up.

"We're going to the shop owned by Madame Pitaux, who is now living at number 153 on the Calle de la Habana. She arrived from Paris a short time ago, and from what I've been told, she's brought a thousand unusual things with her. We thought we'd take a stroll about El Angel Hill on the way there."

"It's quite late by this time to be going to the Hill. It's after 11. And now that I think of it, have all of you seen issue number IV of *La*

Moda o Recreo Semanal? It's been out since Saturday, and it's very interesting."

"Do you have it here?" Carmen asked. "It's odd that they didn't send us our copy since we subscribe to it."

"Where did you subscribe to it?"

"At La Cova, on the Calle de la Muralla, the bookstore that's the closest distribution point."

"Well, ask for it there. The copy I read was in the window of San Feliú's, because mine hasn't come either. The distributors aren't very punctual, to say the least."

"Have you found out who the Matilde is that *La Moda* talks about?" Adela asked her brother. "Because Carmen thinks that it's someone all of us know."

"I for my part fancy that she's an imaginary being. Perhaps Madame Pitaux knows something about her."

"Well, the thought has occurred to me," Carmen said, "that the Matilde of *La Moda* is none other than Micaelita Junco. It so happens that she's the most elegant woman in Havana; that the name of her brother, a real dandy, is Juanito; that she has a grandmother whose name is Doña Estefanía de Menocal, a surname much like Moncada, which is the one she's given in *La Moda*."

"I'm more and more inclined to think that you're right," Adela said. "I can't deny that the dress and coiffure that Micaelita Junco was showing off day before yesterday on the Paseo were identical to the fashion plate in *La Moda* two Saturdays ago. The truth is that I didn't like the so-called giraffe coiffure. The braid is too wide and the curls piled very high; so from the back one's head looks unattractive. The short puffed sleeves, with lace oversleeves, do look pretty in my opinion, however, and they're well suited to someone who has nicely rounded arms, as Micaelita does. Her brother Juanito, who said hello to us alongside the Neptune fountain—remember?—was also dressed in the latest style and looked just like the fashion plate in *La Moda*. His nankeen trousers without pleats, his white waistcoat and green wool dress coat without pocket flaps suited him. That's the fashion in England, I'm told. Did you notice his hat? The crown of it bumped into the branches of the trees along the Alameda even though Juanito Junco is a short little fellow."

"His bow tie is what doesn't appeal to me," Leonardo said. "It sits so high that there's no room for his neck. I'll never wear one. Those dog collars aren't to my liking. Neither are those dress coats that are the *dernier cri*; they look like they should be worn by undertakers. The narrow coattails come down to the backs of a man's knees and I fancy that that fashion is an attempt to imitate a swallowtail coat. So Federico has been bent on dressing us *à l'anglaise* and we're more comfortable with French fashions. Uribe has more charm, if not a more skillful pair of shears."

"Don't bring up Uribe, who's a mulatto tailor on the Calle de la Muralla and doesn't know the first thing about what's fashionable in Paris or London," Carmen said with pronounced scorn.

"Havana's upper crust doesn't think so," Leonardo promptly replied. "The Montalvos, the Romeros, the Valdés Herrera de Guanajays, the Count of La Reunión, Filomeno, the Marqués Morales, Peñalver, Fernandina . . . never take their custom to any other tailor. I prefer him to Federico. What's more, he receives fashion magazines from Paris by every packet boat from Le Havre."

This entertaining conversation between Leonardo and his sisters was interrupted by the carriage driver's appearance, with his whip wound around the wrist of his right hand and his round hat in his left, to announce that the gig was ready and waiting at the door. The two younger sisters immediately went in search of the eldest and their usual shawls, and the three of them surrounded their mother to ask for orders. The lady in question asked them to make several purchases for her in the linen shops or dress shops, and they then headed to the street by way of the *zaguán*.

The foreign reader should not be surprised to see three young ladies of what we may call the middle class going out onto the streets of Havana without a duenna, father, mother, or brother to accompany them. But as long as they were not on foot or paying a formal visit, two, and better yet three, young ladies could quite properly go all about the city, do their shopping, chat with the Spanish errand boys in the shops, and on the nights when there were band concerts in the Plaza de Armas or on the Alameda de Paula, receive the respects of their friends and the adoration of their lovers offered them from the footboard of their carriages. This was permissible, though custom required that to pay a visit in the neighborhood and go about on foot, the young Cuban lady, if not accompanied by a respectable relative, should nonetheless be escorted, if only by her own slave.

As Carmen was about to get into the gig, a young stranger happened to be passing by and gave her a hand to help her climb in, then did the same for Adela and finally for Antonia, receiving from them, as recompense for his courtly courtesy, a grateful smile.

And so the youngest and prettiest of the sisters occupied the place in the middle, the least comfortable surely, but doubtless the most conspicuous, affording the young lady a most suitable place for displaying to perfection her natural charms. The carriage driver immediately mounted the horse outside the carriage shafts, which because of its smooth pace, fine appearance, and carefully braided tail, was at once the driver's pride and his assurance of a comfortable ride, and the carriage took off at breakneck speed around the corner of the Plaza Vieja.

X I I

The child is known by his toys
And one is led to conjecture what his life's work will be.
Parables of Solomon

Finally only Doña Rosa Sandoval de Gamboa and her beloved son Leonardo were left at table.

He had not inherited his father's talent for business. Nor did he give evidence of an aptitude for the literary career that he had been encouraged to pursue, although he did write poetry and short articles for the *Diario de la Habana* and other newspapers. His mother, however, wanted him to become an attorney, with a doctorate from the University of Havana, cherishing the hope that by following this path he could one day be appointed a judge of the Royal Tribunal of Puerto Príncipe, and even a lieutenant governor, as learned judges appointed by the king were called in those days. She had good reason to believe that through money and her husband's relations at court, he might well secure for his firstborn son some special favor, honor, or title among the many that, motivated by such considerations, it is the custom of the Crown to grant.

Being a businessman, his father was of the opinion that there was no hope of the lad's ever getting any farther than municipal counselor or a deputy of the Commercial Tribunal or the Royal Consulate, posts of little importance with no honors or emoluments. Moreover, Don Cándido, truth to tell, did not insist on his son's studying and pursuing this or that literary career. Attorney? Banish the thought. He would develop a liking for lawsuits and would run through his father's fortune and that of his clients. Nor was Don Cándido familiar with letters, other than those in his second-grade primer, although that had not kept him from amassing a respectable fortune.

Now, in addition, a desire to acquire a title of nobility had come over him, and it did not strike him as a good idea for his son, at least, to exchange the account books or the yardstick of the merchant, or a learned professor's cap and gown, for a count's crown, although there had been a Santovenia who, only recently in fact, had made the last of the exchanges mentioned. Despite his ignorance, he recognized that Leonardo would not be outstanding, either as a man of letters or as a businessman, and said to himself, or to his wife in conversation about the subject:

"We must not get our hopes up. Leonardo will not make much of himself, no matter how hard we try or how much money we spend on his studies. He doesn't have a thought in his head except to fall in love and lounge about doing nothing. It's as plain as day. Does he have any need of great learning either in order to play a role in the world? Not really! Absolutely not. May God give you good fortune, that is to say money, son, for knowledge will bring you little, as the Spanish proverb has it. And you won't lack for money after I die. Then if I manage to secure the title of Count of Casa Gamboa that I'm seeking in Madrid, it will bring together money and nobility, two things with which the most uncultivated ignoramus can make it to the top of the ladder, enjoy special privileges, and sleep like a log, sure and certain that he won't be hounded for debts; instead everyone will doff their sombrero to him, carry him about in the palm of their hand, and be pleased to serve him, children and grownups, high-born men and pretty women alike. Alas! How much time has been lost! Had I received a title ten years ago, it would be a different story."

In fact, Leonardo showed even less ambition than talent. Admittedly, the hope of getting ahead by way of his knowledge, his studies, or his diligence never aroused his enthusiasm. Rather, trusting that on the death of his parents he would be quite wealthy, he made no effort to learn, nor did he worry about studying his law lessons, and laughed for all he was worth when, as a joke, it was said within the family circle that he might become a judge or a count, or that his father was having a family tree drawn up in Spain, with the aim of receiving a title in which there was not a single drop of Jewish or Moorish blood to be seen. Moreover, his inclinations at the time were as humble as his passions were strong and uncontrollable.

Enjoying himself to the utmost, in those days at least, was the supreme law of his soul. Anyone would have been led to believe that this was owing to the fact that because she loved him too much, his mother, far from curbing his headlong impulses, appeared to take pleasure in giving them free rein. What needs could a lad of his age and occupations have? An abundance of books, clothes, horses, carriages, servants, money were all his; he almost never needed even to take the trouble to ask for anything, because from the cradle he had been accustomed to see his desires and even his passing whims satisfied almost the moment he voiced them. In addition to all this, not a day went by without his mother giving him some costly present; she was in the habit, moreover, of tucking half a doubloon, sometimes a whole one, in the pocket of his waistcoat every afternoon. Naturally, this money was spent as it was received, with no awareness of its value, and the worst of it was that it never crossed this prodigal son's mind that he ought to set aside for tomorrow whatever was not necessary for today's expenses. How did our beardless young student scatter this money about? The astute reader will guess, rightly, that gaming, women, and orgies with his friends were the vortex that was swallowing up the Gamboa fortune and draining away the perfume of Leonardo's soul at the moment in his life when it was in full bloom.

Once his sisters had departed, then, he remained seated in the place that Adela had left, opposite his mother, at whom he was staring, with his elbows on the table and his head buried in his hands, and to whom he suddenly said:

"Do you know something, Mama?"

"Not unless you tell me," she answered, her mind seemingly elsewhere.

"Don't get the idea that I'm going to ask you for something. I don't want anything."

"I see," Doña Rosa said; and she smiled, for she realized from her beloved son's preamble that he wanted something.

"You're smiling? Then I won't say another word."

"Don't take offense, son; I'm smiling so you can see that I'm listening to you with pleasure."

"Well, yesterday afternoon on passing by Dubois's watch shop, in the Calle del Teniente Rey, he called to me to show me . . . Are you smiling again? You're going to believe that I'm about to ask you for something. I can tell you straight away that you're mistaken."

"Don't pay any attention to my smiles. Go on. I want to hear the end; what did Dubois show you?"

"Not anything really. Some repeaters he'd just received from Switzerland. They're the first ones to arrive in Havana, according to what he told me, straight from Geneva."

After saying this Leonardo fell silent, and his mother followed his example, although she for her part was apparently lost in thought. Finally she was the first to break the silence by saying:

"And how are the new repeaters? Did you like them, my son?"

The young man's face lit up and he exclaimed:

"A whole lot. They're magnificent . . . made in Geneva . . . , but I don't want a new watch, I'm telling you. The English one you gave me last year is still in working order; it's just not fashionable any more. I'd never seen a repeater before, much less one made in Geneva; you don't have to open the case to tell the time at any hour of the day or night. You press the button of a spring that's inside the metal ring, and a little bell inside strikes the hour and the quarter-hours. What an advantage! Isn't that so, mama?"

"Why didn't you tell me about those watches before your sisters went out? I would have had Antonia stop in at the watch shop."

"I didn't remember and didn't have the opportunity. Besides, Papa was present and then we got into a conversation . . . and I was distracted. But the girls don't know the first thing about watches."

Doña Rosa fell silent again for a short time, still with a thoughtful air, yet not showing any sign of anger or sternness. Meanwhile Leonardo pretended not to have noticed his mother's distraction, nor did he give any indication that he repented having caused her embarrassment with his capricious hints. On the contrary, as the poor lady thought the matter over and made certain calculations, he sat there rubbing his cheeks with the tips of his fingers and looking at the ceiling as though counting the beams leading out to support the porch roof.

"Did Dubois tell you the price of his new watches?" Doña Rosa finally went on.

"Yes . . . No. What do you want to know the price for? To buy me one? I've already told you that I don't need one or want one. To buy one for each of my sisters? Dubois doesn't have any for women; they're only for men."

"I see. But how much does Dubois want for his repeaters for men?"

"Not much, eighteen doubloons. They couldn't be cheaper, because they're gold ones, genuine Geneva repeaters."

"Your English watch didn't turn out to be a good one?"

"Not as good a one as I thought at first. It was Dubois himself who sold it to you, as I remember well; but it's clear that he was taken in or else he took you in, because it continually runs either fast or slow, and I've already taken it to his shop more times than the number of doubloons you paid for it. And to think that it cost you 20, more than the price he's asking for the ones from Geneva! Money down the drain, Mama. It's been proved over and over that English watches, even the ones Tobias makes, are often defective; genuine Geneva watches, on the contrary, are another story; almost all of them turn out to be good ones that keep exact time. At least that's what I was told by Dubois, who as you know understands watches and is a first-rate watchmaker. But you mustn't think about it any more, Mama; let's forget it. I'll get along without a reliable watch and that's all there is to it!"

"Don't worry about it and don't get upset, son," Doña Rosa replied, more than a little alarmed. "We'll find a way for you to have a Geneva watch if they're as good as you say and as Dubois believes. I've been intending all along to give you a Christmas present; it will be that watch that you were so taken with, even though there's many a day between now and Christmas. But there's one serious difficulty."

"What's that?" Leonardo asked fearfully, no matter how hard he tried to control himself.

"It so happens that I don't believe that there is all the money needed to buy it in my private purse just now, and I'll have a very hard time getting anything from your father's," Doña Rosa said gently.

"Well, if it depends on Papa, from this moment on I must give up all hope of getting the new watch. He's become more miserly than a Jew; at least everything that's for me strikes him as being either expensive or useless, whereas we know that his purse is always open for Antonia. I don't know what he's hoarding so much money for."

"You're being unfair to your father. To whom does the money you squander belong? Who provides the luxury you live in? Who works so that you can take your pleasure and divert yourself?"

"He works, it's true; he manages to get ahead and saves his money, there's no doubt about it, but would he have as much money now if you'd been poor when he married you? I'll wager not."

"I brought some 200,000 pesos as my dowry, which isn't even a fourth of our fortune today. The increase, that enormous increase, is owed to your father's exhausting labors and the money he's put aside, and what's more he wasn't poor when he married me either; no indeed; he had his own *reales*, and you should be the last one to criticize his behavior, which, moreover, is the offshoot of yours toward him."

"The sermon on my conduct toward Papa should end right there. He's unfeeling and hard-hearted toward me; can I be affectionate and soft-hearted toward him? Come, tell me. He never gives me a chance to show him my affection either, even though I'd like to. But let's say no more on the subject, let's turn the page and discuss something else, something different. What did Papa have when he married you?"

"He had something, he had quite a bit, yes indeed. He had a workshop that made building supplies such as shingles out of wood from the United States, bricks, lime . . . , there in the Alameda or Paseo, near La Punta. The land that it was on also belonged to him, although it wasn't worth much because it was low-lying and very swampy. Down there, where the school building of the Colegio de Buena Vista stands today, he also had a slave cabin. Incidentally, of the pure-blooded blacks that had been branded with the letters G and B there are still a few at the sugar plantation of La Tinaja, which I inherited from my father. Cándido, in partnership with Don Pedro Blanco, still deals in black slaves from Africa.[26] But the English prey on the slave trade to the point that many more shipments of slaves are lost than are saved."

"Imagine, Mama," Leonardo said, laughing for all he was worth, though he lowered his voice, "a plagiarist of men who was made Count . . . of the Slave Quarters, for example. What a fine title! Don't you think so, Mama?"

"What do you mean by that inane remark?" Doña Rosa asked, as greatly annoyed as she was surprised.

"Oh, Mama! You don't know that according to the Roman law code all those who kidnapped men to sell them were called plagiarists?"

"I see. In that case your father is not the real plagiarist, as you call him, but rather Don Pedro Blanco, who from his factorage in Gallinas, on the coast of Guinea, as is common knowledge (I have heard those names so many times that they are engraved on my memory) trades blacks for trinkets and other articles and sends shiploads of them to this Island. Your father takes the ones he needs for his properties and sells the rest to the plantation owners because until recently he's been acting as Blanco's consignee and before that as his partner when the slave trade from Africa was not considered as contraband or was tolerated. On his own at least, he's sent out only a few ships. He's expecting the return of his brig *Veloz* any moment now. May it be God's will not to let it fall into the clutches of the English!"

"You're unintentionally pleading in my favor. I said what I did as a joke, but it's clear, Mama, that according to a legal principle the one who holds a cow's legs down commits as great a crime as the one who kills it."

"Don't hand me any of your principles, your end results, or your Roman laws. People may say whatever you like, but the truth is that there's a vast difference between your father's conduct and Don Pedro Blanco's. The latter is over there, in the land of those savages; he's the one who trades for them; he's the one who takes them prisoner and sends them to be sold in this country; so if there's any crime or guilt in all that, it's his, and in any case not your father's. And if one looks at the matter closely, far from Gamboa's doing anything bad or improper, he's doing good, something to be looked upon with approval, because, if he receives and sells savages, that is to say, as the consignee, it's in order to baptize them and give them a religion, which surely they don't have in their land. So if that's why you said what you did, you now know that in case he's made a member of the nobility, something he's not thinking about for the moment, he won't lack for nice titles, and above all honorable ones. Anyway, as I was saying to you before, this time I won't be able to fulfill your desires without having recourse to your father's purse."

"Why don't you ask him to help you out?"

"Because I'd have to tell him the truth, that is to say, that I wanted the money so as to give you a present."

"Well, so what? He never denies you anything."

"That's true; but since he's so angry with you, I'm afraid he'll say no."

"When isn't he angry with me, Mama? It's an endemic disease of his, or rather, a chronic one. If I go out, why am I going out; if I don't go out, why am I staying home. Anyway, the years come and go and Papa is never satisfied with me. He has it in for me, Mama, that's the pure and simple truth. Why beat around the bush? The result is that nothing I do or don't do seems to him to be the right thing."

"Your father isn't so unjust, or so lacking in paternal love that if you behaved well he'd believe that you were behaving badly. Look, without going any farther, last night you were gallivanting about in Regla. What time did you come home?"

"From whom did he find out about that?"

"It matters little who his informant was, but he knows that he was told about it this morning down at the Caballería wharf."

"Come off it! That story won't hold water . . . Only vendors of jerked beef and men nosing around for news come down to the wharf early in the morning, because that's where they loaf about, spending the morning waiting for El Morro to signal the arrival of the packet boat from

Spain, or a ship from Santander or Montevideo bringing flour or jerked beef. Ne'er-do-wells like that don't go to balls at the Palacio in Regla. I've caught on to who the tattletale was; it couldn't have been anyone but Aponte. I assure you I'll get even with that no-good gossipmonger."

"He wasn't the one who told on you. However, even if he had been, you'd be wrong to beat him for it, because if your father asked him, I don't know how he could have hidden the truth from him."

"He could have said he didn't know, that he didn't hear the Espíritu Santo church bell, that . . . just anything, except that I came home at such and such an hour, or that I'd been at this place or that. Uncle Aponte has a very loose tongue and Papa hit on the right way to get it wagging by asking him. It's a miracle that Aponte didn't tell him . . . But do you want me to sum up in a few brief words what was I doing in Regla last night?"

"Don't tell me, I don't want to know; I presume you weren't doing anything bad. The sum and substance, Leonardo dear, is that you aren't applying yourself to your studies, that you're making no progress toward anything that's good or useful, and that you're wasting the time that you ought to be devoting to reading and thinking in frivolous party-going and forays that are as destructive as they are dangerous. This cannot please your father . . . or me either, for the very reason that I love you deeply. Your father and I want you to study more and go out less, to enjoy yourself, but without succumbing to dissipation, to keep yourself from staying up till all hours, to restrain yourself, to . . . in a word, to behave well."

The emotion that Doña Rosa felt left her unable to speak, her lovely eyes brimming over with tears.

"You wouldn't make a good preacher," Leonardo told her, perhaps with the intention of diverting her attention, "because you get too caught up in your subject."

"As for Aponte," Doña Rosa continued, once she had calmed down, "I know that he likes to gossip, but with all due respect for the truth, I must say that your father knew what time you came home from the noise made in the *zaguán* by the opening of the door, the entry of the carriage, and the hoofbeats of the horses. In the silence of the night, any noise is like a clap of thunder. He woke up, lit a cigar with his flint and tinder, looked at the clock and let out an angry expletive. I pretended to be asleep. It was two-thirty in the morning. . . . Anyone can still see from your face how little sleep you had last night."

There was another brief interval of silence between the two speakers, during which Leonardo yawned and stretched several times, and then, having risen to his feet, he said:

"I'm going to go get some sleep. . . . If you buy me the watch, fine; if not, it's of little importance."

He turned around and began climbing the stairs to his bedroom, one step at a time as if he were counting each stair or as if it were taking him a great deal of effort. Meanwhile his mother's eyes followed him, though she did not say another word or move from her chair; but as soon as she lost sight of him at the top of the stairs, she became extremely agitated and called out in a loud voice. "Reventos!"

The steward mentioned in the previous chapter hastened to answer such an urgent call. He was a man short in stature, heavyset, olive-skinned, with a round face and very kinky hair, whose appearance and manner alike showed determination and agility. Although tidily dressed, he was in his waistcoat; one could see from a league away that he was from Asturias, not a very common origin for Spaniards in Havana in those days. He was employed as steward in Don Cándido Gamboa's household, and although he did some bookkeeping he did not work in the study as much as he did at other tasks more in keeping with his job. When he appeared before Doña Rosa, his pen was tucked behind his ear, and she said to him in an authoritative tone of voice:

"Reventos, go tell Gamboa to give you 20 doubloons for me and bring them here to me."

The steward left and returned promptly with the money she had asked for, which he had taken out of the little iron strongbox underneath the desk, in which there were several sacks stuffed full of gold and silver coins.

"Put on your jacket," Doña Rosa added, spreading the doubloons out on the table to count them, "and go this minute to the Calle del Teniente Rey, to the back door of the San Agustín pharmacy to Dubois the watchmaker's and buy the best of the repeaters that he has just received from Geneva. Tell him that it is for me. Do you understand?"

"Yes, señora."

"I take it you know nothing about watches."

"I don't know much, let us say, but in Gijón, where I was born and raised, there is more than one watchmaker's shop; and an uncle of mine, my mother's brother, may he rest in peace, knew watch mechanisms like the palm of his hand, as the saying goes."

"That wasn't why I said that, Don Melitón. It was to warn you against any sort of double-dealing that Dubois might try on you, if he thought that the watch was for you or someone like you. . . . Do you follow me?"

"Yes, of course. I know what you mean."

"Listen. Make sure that Dubois understands that the watch is for me. He knows me, and must know that it will cost him dearly . . ."

"To sell you a cat when you asked for a hare," the steward interrupted, citing an old saw. "He'd take for granted that it would cost him an arm and a leg if he were to do such a thing, the scoundrel. I know that only too well and so does he."

"I don't consider him a scoundrel, as you call him; nonetheless it's best to be forewarned . . ."

"Because forewarned is forearmed," the steward interrupted her again, interpreting in his own way his mistress's thought.

"Oh, another thing. Have it put in an elegant box, as though it were a gift. Do you understand?"

"Of course I do! Perfectly."

"Very well. Off with you."

"On the wing."

"Will you remember? A gold watch, a repeater, Swiss, or rather, Genevan, one of the ones just received from Geneva by Dubois the watchmaker, who lives in the Calle del Teniente Rey, in the back of the San Agustín pharmacy."

"Yes, yes, Señora Doña Rosa. I'll remember all that and will keep it well in mind. And in a jiffy . . ."

"Listen! Eighteen doubloons isn't my limit. I want the best genuine Geneva repeater, no matter how much it costs. If it takes more money, come back for it."

"Señora Doña Rosa's orders will be followed to the letter."

"Ah! Reventos! Reventos! Come here. I forgot the most important thing. Have this inscription engraved inside the case: L. G. S. Oct. 24, 1830. Don't forget."

In fact, in a little more than an hour the steward was back and placed in Doña Rosa's hands a small square box of maroon leather with gold fillets. Doubtless the aforementioned señora had been impatiently awaiting him, for taking the box, opening it, contemplating the watch for a brief moment with a sort of childish happiness, rising to her feet and going upstairs to her room, paying no more attention to the steward, was but a single act.

No more time had passed than the few moments that we have just spent relating this comic scene.

Leonardo for his part was so certain that the sun would not set on that day without a new watch appearing to adorn the pocket of his trousers, that having laid them out on the sofa, opposite his bed, he lay down, his mind at ease, resolved to sleep and renew his strength, weakened by fatigue and his lack of sleep the night before. He was as yet only drowsing when the sound of little footsteps and the rustle of a woman's attire came to confirm his hopes. It was his mother. He pretended to be asleep and saw her walk over to the sofa almost silently, pick up his trousers, place in the small pocket in front a round object that gleamed brightly, hanging from a pink and blue silk ribbon that formed iridescent patterns, more than an inch wide and six inches long, with the ends fastened together by a gold buckle. He smiled with pleasure, and closed his eyes so that his mother would leave the room persuaded that she had arranged a surprise for him.

As Doña Rosa laid the trousers back down on the sofa, making sure that the ribbon of the watch was visible, and slipped into his waistcoat pocket the two doubloons left over from the purchase of the watch, she had the impression that her son had moved in the bed. She gave a start, as though she had been in the act of committing a crime, and then, in fact, a beam of light entered her conscience as a mother; she remembered vividly her husband's words in the conversation that had taken place early that morning and felt a sort of repentance. Something within her told her that even if she had not actually done evil, no recognized and reliable good would result from her tender and affectionate gestures toward Leonardo, since their source was not merits that had been earned by him, but rather the spontaneous and indiscreet motherly effusion of her heart.

Hesitating between taking the token of her love back so as to keep it for a more appropriate occasion and being obliged as a result to confront the distress and the displeasure of her son, she stood there motionless, as though transfixed. Although very brief, that was a supreme moment for the sad mother. Finally she cast a furtive glance toward the bed, saw Leonardo naked from the waist up, with his arms on the pillow and his handsome head resting on his palms, his bare chest rising as he inhaled and falling as he exhaled, like the wave that does not come in far enough to break, his nose dilated, his mouth half open to allow the air to pass freely, his face pale from sleep and the agitation of the day, yet healthy and strong, a feeling of pride took possession of her entire being, changing suddenly and completely the nature of her thoughts.

"Poor thing!" she exclaimed in a tone of voice that was almost audible. "Why would I deprive him of anything when he is at the age for taking his pleasure and diverting himself? Take your pleasure and enjoy yourself, then, as long as your health and youth last, for there will come for you, as they have come for all of us, days of sorrows and regrets. The Blessed Virgin, in whom I place so much trust and all my hope, will not fail to hear my pleas. May she protect you and save you from the world's dangers. May God make you a saint, my beloved son."

She pursed her lips, as if to throw him a kiss, and left the room as silently as she had come.

II

I

Tarde venientibus ossa.
(Those who arrive late at the banquet
gnaw the bones.)

We must leave these characters for a short time in order to occupy ourselves with others who, though in no way inferior, play a less important role in our true story. We are referring at present to the renowned clarinet player, José Dolores Pimienta.

To see him, needle in hand, sitting crosslegged along with the other assistant tailors on a low wooden platform, basting a dark green wool dress coat, still missing its sleeves and coattails, we must go inside master tailor Uribe's shop, on the Calle de la Muralla, the first door after the corner of the Calle de Villegas, on which there stood a drygoods store called El Sol.

The first of the shop buildings consisted of a rectangular room with three entrances: the original high, wide door and the two windows, whose grilles had been removed. Opposite them, at the other end of the room, was a long, narrow table on which there could be seen a number of lengths of cloth—drill, piqué, blue and white checked cotton, a type of fine-woven heavy cotton called *coquillo*, satin, and fine wool—all of them rolled up and piled at one end. And at the opposite end, two lengths of nankeen, laid out flat, on which there had been traced out with a sliver of ash-colored soapstone a pair of men's trousers.

Behind the table or counter, standing in his shirt sleeves with a white apron tied around his waist, a pair of shears in his right hand, and a strip of paper folded in half lengthwise, with small holes at intervals, draped around his neck to serve as a tape measure was Uribe, the master tailor, the favorite of the young dandies of Havana in that era. He could not have denied, even if he had wanted to, the mixed black and white blood to which he owed his origin. He was tall, thin, long-faced, with big arms out of proportion to his body, a bulbous nose, and eyes that protruded slightly or were level with his face, a mouth so small that two rows of wide teeth with gaps between them barely fit in it, black, very thick lips, and a pale copper complexion. He wore short clerical-style sideburns, sparse and kinky like his hair, though the latter was thicker, worn in ropelike locks that stood on end, giving his head the same appearance that legend attributes to Medusa.

As the tailor who was responsible for setting the tone for the fashion of the day, Uribe wore nankeen trousers with tight-fitting legs that narrowed at the top, so that they looked like an italic *M* without serifs, with the indispensable leather strap passing underneath each foot. Instead of pumps, the usual footwear of the day, he wore thong sandals of tanned goatskin, baring feet that had nothing small or shapely about them, for besides having bunions that the sandals left only too visible, they had almost no arch. However little Uribe's appearance worked in his favor, there can be no doubt that he was the most likable of tailors, ceremoniously polite and both well paid and not paid enough for his skill with his shears. He was married to a woman who, like himself, was a mulatto, tall, heavyset, easygoing, and at home at least, fond of going about barelegged, shuffling about in her satin house slippers, just as she was fond of showing more than decency allowed of her back and her plump, gleaming shoulders.

The afternoon of one of the last days of October was beginning. A great many carriages, carts, and wagons were going up and down the narrow Calle de la Muralla, perhaps the street with the heaviest traffic in the city since it ran through its center and shops of every sort were located all along it. The noise of the wheels and of the horses' hoofs on the cobblestones resounded like a clap of thunder that reached the interior of the houses open to every passing breeze. Often the vehicles collided and stopped traffic for a long time. In such a case, the thunder of the carriages gave way to the shouts and curses of the drivers of the carts and carriages, with no consideration or respect for the ladies. If a pedestrian did not wish to be trampled by the horses or crushed against the walls of the houses by the protruding hubcaps of the wheels, he was obliged to take refuge in the shops until the street was cleared.

On the afternoon of which we are speaking now, one of those frequent collisions occurred between a gig occupied by three young ladies that was going down the Calle de la Muralla, and a cart loaded with chests of sugar that was coming up the street. The hubcaps of the two vehicles heading in opposite directions collided violently, and as a result the hubcap of the second raised the wheel of the first and penetrated its spokes, breaking one of them. The two vehicles were left almost athwart the street after the collision, the gig with its rear facing the door of Uribe's tailor shop, where the mule drawing the cart had now thrust its head. The driver of the cart, seated sideways on top of one of the chests of sugar, with a whip in his right hand, lost his balance and landed in the mud and on the cobblestones of the street with a terrible thud.

And this man, an African by birth, and the other, a mulatto from Havana, instead of hurrying back to their respective vehicles in order to disentangle them and let other conveyances by, hurled awful curses and insults at each other with savage, blind fury. It wasn't that they knew each other, had had fights before, or had previous affronts to avenge; but rather, since they were both slaves, constantly oppressed and mistreated by their masters, without ever having the time or the means to satisfy their passions, they had an instinctive mortal hatred for each other and were merely giving vent to the anger that permanently possessed them the first time a chance had come their way. The young ladies in the gig, very frightened, cried out to high heaven to no avail, and the eldest of them threatened repeatedly to severely punish their carriage driver if he did not leave off fighting and attend to the nervous horses. But the two combatants in their fury, and amid the rain of whiplashes they dealt each other, did not hear a word she said. Then the Spanish shop owners and the journeymen tailors in Uribe's shop, all of them peering out the doors in their shirt sleeves, added to the din and the confusion with their shouting and their boisterous laughter, sure signs of the joy with which they were witnessing the fight.

At this juncture, a mean-looking fellow came in through one of the entrances to the tailor shop, as if to get out of the way of the wheels of the carriage, and after leaving by way of another, stretched his arm out over the folded hood of the carriage, removed the ornamental Spanish comb adorning the head of the youngest of the señoritas, whereupon her thick long braid unwound and then came undone altogether, covering her shoulder with its waves as silken and shiny as the wings of a *totí*.[27] She cried out and lifted both hands to her head; at this moment José Dolores Pimienta, like the others a mere spectator up until that moment, uttered an exclamation of astonishment, murmured the words "Little Bronze Virgin," flung himself upon the thief, or rather upon the latter's booty, as he was bearing it off in triumph. Pimienta managed to get his hands on it; but since it was made of fragile tortoise shell and was adorned, moreover, with exquisite openwork, it fell to pieces in his hand: these being the only thing he was able to return to the distressed and frightened owner of the comb. Thanks to the confusion that reined, the thief managed to escape, yet no one but the master tailor had pondered the implications of that incident. Pimienta's exclamation, however, and his generous deed when the majority of the spectators were thinking only of how entertaining they found the spectacle, had attracted Uribe's attention, and he suddenly turned and said to him:

"Are you out of your mind? Did you imagine that she too was Cecilia Valdés? If so, I'd say you're seeing visions."

"No," José Dolores answered curtly. "I know why I said what I did. Those girls are the sisters of the young gentleman Leonardo Gamboa."

"Well, finally!" Uribe exclaimed in turn. "I've been waiting to meet them. They look a lot like him. They can't deny that they're his sisters. They need help. The sisters of one of my most free-spending clients! That caps the climax . . ."

In fact, the master tailor, the journeyman tailors and other spectators managed between them to separate the combatants and disentangle the wheels of the vehicles, whereupon the two conveyances were able to go on their way, the driver of the cart leaving the scene spattered with blood from the whipping he had received at the hands of the carriage driver in his blue striped shirt. The back of this latter had perhaps been protected by the wool jacket of his livery; at least it showed no visible signs of the fray.

And once order had been restored where chaos had reigned and the street had been cleared, once the master tailor had returned to the cutting table and the other tailors to their platform, the former suddenly took his watch out of his trousers pocket and said, with a look of surprise: "Three o'clock!," then immediately adding in a louder voice: "José Dolores!"

The latter appeared almost at once before master Uribe. Draped over his shoulder were two braided skeins of thread, one of white linen and the other of black silk; pinned to the suspenders of his pants were a number of short, not very fine needles, and on the middle finger of his right hand was an open-ended thimble.

The white race and the black no doubt contributed equally to the birth of José Dolores Pimienta and of Francisco de Paula Uribe, with this essential difference: José Dolores had inherited more of the blood of the first than of the second, a circumstance responsible for his less sallow yet nonetheless pale complexion, the regularity of his facial features, the breadth of his forehead, the near perfection of his hands and the smallness of his feet, which both by their shapeliness and their high arch could easily rival those of a lady of the Caucasian race. Though he did not have a delicate constitution, the cheekbones of his oval face were very prominent, and his hair was not as kinky as Uribe's. In his manners, as in his gaze, and at times even in his tone of voice, there was a pronounced air of timidity, or of melancholy, for it is not always easy to distinguish between the two, revealing either great modesty or very tender affections.

Having a strong bent toward music, he had had to go against his very nature, something that he could not lay at anyone else's doorstep, to exchange the clarinet, his favorite instrument, for the thimble or needle of a tailor, one of the fine arts despite its being a mechanical and sedentary occupation. But necessity knows no law, as the typically Spanish adage has it, and although he was the conductor of an orchestra, frequently accompanying church choirs during the day and playing at holiday balls at night, this did not easily cover his own needs and those of his sister Nemesia. Music in Cuba, like the other fine arts, did not make those who made a career of it rich, or even afford them a comfortable living. The renowned Brindis, Ulpiano, Vuelta y Flores, and others found themselves more or less in this same situation.

"How goes the dress coat that's such a dark green it's invisible?" Uribe asked José Dolores. "Is it ready to be tried on? It's three o'clock and in a little while we'll have young gentleman Gamboa here; he's like clockwork."

"Considering what a short time it's been since you turned it over to me, *Señó* Uribe, I'm quite far along with it," Pimienta answered.

"What do you mean? Didn't I give it to you two days or more ago?"

"Begging your pardon, *Señó* Uribe, but in all truth I didn't get that garment until yesterday morning. Day before yesterday I played for high Mass at El Santo Angel Custodio, at prime I played the *Salve Maria* and then I played at the Farruco ball until after midnight. So I don't know . . ."

"All right, all right," Uribe replied sternly, interrupting him. "Is it ready to be tried on or isn't it? That's the crux of the matter."

"I'll tell you: as far as trying it on goes, he can do so at once. The lapels are basted in, and so is the collar. I was about to baste in the silk linings, so as to open up the buttonholes in it. The shoulders can be basted in when the gentleman you mention comes, and the back likewise. The sleeves are being finished by *Seña* Clara, your wife, though trying on just one of them would suffice. So at eight o'clock tonight, at the latest, the dress coat will be finished and ready for the ball, which won't begin until nine."

"The thing is that he wants it long before that, and never let it be said that Pancho de Paula Uribe y Robirosa doesn't keep his word once he's given it."

"Then you'll have to assign another tailor to help me; or rather, to finish the coat, because at six I have to accompany the *Salve Maria* at El Santo Angel Custodio and then immediately thereafter play at the Brito ball. Farruco begins its balls at Soto's house tonight and I didn't want to take my orchestra all that way. Ulpiano is conducting at the Philharmonic with his violin and Brindis is committed to playing the double bass. So think it over."

"I deeply regret the situation, José Dolores, and if I'd known that you weren't going to finish that piece of work, I wouldn't have given it to you. It's what I'm thinking twice about at the moment. I'm afraid that if another tailor takes it over now the style of it is going to be lost. Young gentleman Leonardo is the most finickal of all my clients. Can't you see that he's swimming in wealth? Don't you see how he scatters money around? It doesn't matter what things cost him! And mind you, his father Don Cándido, just the other day, as people say, didn't have a cent to his name. It's as if I can still see him when he arrived from his homeland: he was wearing esparto-grass shoes (Uribe meant esparto-grass sandals), a jacket and thick flannel trousers, and a wool cap. A little while later he set up a workshop that made wood products and roof tiles, then later on he brought bunches of blacks from Africa, and then he married a girl who owned a sugar plantation, and after that the money came pouring in from all over and today he's a great gentleman on top of the heap, his daughters ride in two-horse carriages and his son spends doubloons as though they were water. And meanwhile that poor girl . . . But shut your mouth, Uribe. Anyway, as I was saying, José Dolores, young gentleman Leonardo came here last week and said to me: 'Maestro Uribe, here's that invisible green cloth I had sent me from Paris for the express purpose of having you make me me a dress coat that's perfect. But put aside all the details that are old hat now: high waistlines measured not from the shoulder but from the nape of the neck, swallow tails. I'm no undertaker decked out in formal dress, no Juanito Junco or Pepe Montalvo. Make me a dress coat like the ones being worn by people in the height of fashion, for I'm aware that when you feel like it you know how to fit them so well they look painted on a person's body.' That lad has so much money that we have to please him or burst. What's more, since he's so elegant and so good-looking, he sets the tone when it comes to fashion, and if I manage to make him a fine dress coat, I've saved my neck. Even though to tell you the truth, I don't have enough hands for all the work that's come my way. Hence it's clear that the competition from the Englishman Federico, far from doing me any harm, has been good for me. So then, my dear José Dolores, let's get down to work!"

"I've already told you, *Señó* Uribe, that I'll do what I can; but please know that I won't have time to put the finishing touches on the coat. The part that counts most, however, is done, that is to say, the lapels and the collar. You can supervise sewing on the skirts and the back, and as for the buttonholes, nobody does them better than *seña* Clara."

"Bring the dress coat here."

The tailor brought it to him, and holding it in his hands so as to raise it to eye level, Uribe walked over to a mirror on the wall between the first window and the door. José Dolores automatically followed him. When the two of them were in front of the mirror, the master tailor said to his assistant:

"Come, José Dolores, serve as a model. . . . You have exactly the same build as young gentleman Leonardo."

"Very well, *Señó* Uribe," Pimienta answered in a foul humor. "But only this once, eh?"

"You sound very naive today, my friend. What's eating you? A while ago you mistook one of the Gamboa girls for Cecilia Valdés; now you're furious because, in order to gain time, I'm trying out their brother's dress coat on you. If you're angry because that white man is walking all over you, the worst thing you can do is take it so seriously. What can you do about it, José Dolores? Pretend to overlook it, put up with it. Act the way a dog does with wasps: show your teeth to make them think you're laughing. Don't you see that *they* are the hammer and we are the anvil? The whites came first and are eating the best slices; we colored people came later and are thankful to gnaw the bones. Forget it, my halfbreed friend, because it will be our turn some day. It can't go on like this forever. Do like I do. You don't see me kiss many hands that I'd like to cut off, do you? You'll figure that deep down I'm envious. Don't you believe it, because it's sure and certain that I wouldn't want the role of a white for anything."

"What a brave principle, *Señó* Uribe!" the assistant tailor couldn't help exclaiming in a low voice, surprised rather than alarmed that Uribe should harbor such strict principles.

"Tell me," the master tailor went on, "did you imagine that just because I'm polite to everyone who enters this shop I don't know how to make distinctions and don't have my pride? You're mistaken; as a man, I don't think anyone is better than I am. Do I think any less of myself because I'm colored? Nonsense. How many counts, attorneys, and physicians are there hereabouts who'd be ashamed if their father or mother sat down beside them in their carriage or accompanied them to the ceremony to show our allegiance to the Captain General on the days honoring the King or Queen Cristina? It may be that you're not in the know the way I am because you don't rub elbows with the nobility. But think a little about it and remember. Do you know the Count's father. . . . ? Well, he was his grandmother's steward. And the Marquise's father . . . ? A harness maker from Matanzas, dirtier than the cobbler's wax he smeared on the cord he used to sew harnesses. How much do you bet that the Marquis of . . . doesn't let those who come to visit him in his mansion on the grounds of the Cathedral see his mother? And what can you tell me of the father of that doctor of such distinction . . . ? He's a butcher through and through. (Uribe was discreet enough to pronounce the names of the persons to whom he referred in the ear of his assistant, as if to keep the others from hearing.) I for my part have no reason to hide who my progenitors were. My father was a Spanish brigadier. I'm very proud of him, and my mother was no slave and no African. If the fathers of those esteemed gentlemen I mentioned had been mere tailors, they would have passed muster, for it's common knowledge that His Majesty the King has declared our art to be a noble one, as is the occupation of cigar makers, and we have the right to use Don before our name. Tondá, even though he's a mulatto, has his "Don," thanks to the King.

"I don't bother my head about such things and I don't rightly know who my father was. I only know that he wasn't a black," Pimienta again interrupted the master tailor's impetuous torrent. "What I maintain is that the way things are going neither you, nor I, nor . . . our children will get to be a hammer. And it's very hard, extremely hard, to bear, intolerable, *Señó* Uribe," José Dolores added, his eyes clouding over and his lips trembling, "that they take colored girls away from us, while we can't even look at white women."

"And who's to blame for that?" Uribe said, whispering once more in his assistant's ear so that his wife wouldn't hear him: "It's the women's fault, not the men's. You needn't have a doubt in your mind, José Dolores, that if dark women didn't have a liking for white men, it's dead certain that white men wouldn't even look at dark women."

"That may well be, *Señó* Uribe, but what I say is: don't white men have enough with their own women? Why should they come and take ours away from us? What right do they have to do that? Who gave them any such right? Nobody. Don't fool yourself, *Señó* Uribe, if white men were content with white women, dark women wouldn't even look at white men."

"You speak like a Solomon, my halfbreed friend, except that that isn't what happens, and a person has to abide by things as they are and not by the way we'd like them to be. I've come to realize this: what's the use of complaining or of hoping that everything will turn out the way a person wishes? What can I, what can you, what can anyone else do by himself to stem the world's torrent? Nothing, nothing. So let it go. When it's many against one, there's nothing anyone can do except to make sure not to see, not to hear, not to understand, and wait till his turn comes. And it will come, I assure you. Not everything has to be so hard and fast, nor does the cloth have to tear in two lengthwise forever. Meanwhile, learn from me, I take things as they come and don't try to straighten the world out. It could get me crucified. You're going to swallow many a bitter pill in days to come, I can see that right now."

"What does it matter?" the tailor said heatedly. "As long as I make others swallow them at the same time I do. . . ."

"The thing is, if you get all worked up and grab things where they burn most, you won't get others to do the same, but you yourself will get badly burned. And that's what those white scoundrels are aiming at. Mind you, I'm not telling you to allow yourself to be mistreated by anybody, for at the same time I haven't let anyone pull the wool over my eyes. What I'm telling you is not to lose your temper and instead wait for the right moment. Do you see Clara over there, so earnest, so serious? When she was young, she too had more than one would-be white seducer, and I managed to scare the whole lot of them off without too much work or too many headaches. So I say to you, José Dolores, don't worry, don't fly off the handle, because it'll put you in a losing position; you'll get your revenge and then you'll be back where you started . . . that's our lot. Let things take their course and you'll learn to live."

During this long and lively conversation, the fitting of the dress coat never stopped for a moment. Uribe now took one lapel in his right hand, shook it and pulled it toward him, as with the palm of his left hand he flattened the folds of the assistant tailor's shirt over his chest and down his side; now he smoothed out the wrinkles in the back and the shoulders of the coat toward the middle; now he traced small crosses all down the seams on the sides with the soapstone; now, finally, he placed his scissors at the edge of the neck and the cuffs of the sleeves and cut into the cloth sewn to the burlap interlining with the white basting thread. Thus the embryo of the dress coat little by little took on the shape of his assistant's body beneath Uribe's shears and his sliver of French chalk, without the master tailor being certain withal that it would fit its real wearer well; but he placed great trust in his experience and his well-known skill. Whenever he entertained the least doubt as to the size, he had recourse to the strip of paper folded in two with small holes along both sides that served him as a tape measure and corrected the dimensions.

A long half hour had gone by as the master tailor and his assistant worked together, when a hired carriage stopped at the door of the tailor shop and there alighted from it, in one leap, the intrepid young man who had served, for the most part, as the subject of their piquant conversation.

A gentleman is not the man who is born one
but the man who knows how to be one.

The sudden arrival of the young man mentioned at the end of the previous chapter, even though it was expected, surprised Uribe, all the
more so in that his assistant had been waiting for that very moment to
throw his arms back and let the garment that was ready to be tried on fall
in the master tailor's hands.

This, however, was no reason for him to fail to go out to meet
Leonardo Gamboa and receive him with many smiles and flattering
remarks.

Whether or not the young man who had just arrived noticed Pimienta's hasty retreat, or whether he realized the motive behind it is more
than can be stated with any degree of certainty. It must be said, however,
that up until then Leonardo had not been aware that the musician was a
rabid enemy of his; and that, furthermore, he considered himself too superior to concern himself with the sympathies or antipathies of a man of
lower station, and a mulatto besides. What is certain is that he did not
even suspect that he had just been the well-nigh exclusive subject of the

conversation between the master tailor and his assistant. He was coming to the shop, moreover, at the hour agreed upon and by appointment; he would remain only as long as necessary. There was, therefore, neither an opportunity nor a reason for him to devote his attention and his thoughts to anything other than the garment that master Uribe was making for him. Nor did this allow him time for rambling remarks.

As was his habit, on alighting from the carriage he took a peseta out of his waistcoat pocket and tossed it to the driver, who caught it in mid-air. Then, without further ado, he walked straight over to the master tailor, cutting him off in the middle of his obsequious gestures with the question:

"How are you doing with my coat? Is it ready?"

"Almost finished, Señor Don Leonardito."

"I was afraid of that; I was expecting it," the latter replied impatiently. "A cobbler is more a man of his word that you are, Uribe."

"But what time is it, sir?"

"It's after four; and you promised it to me for yesterday afternoon."

"Begging the gentleman's pardon, but I promised it to him for today at seven in the evening. All finished and pressed, that is to say. Because the gentleman must be aware that no garment leaves my shop without all its frills and fripperies. The gentleman must take into account that this poor tailor can call nothing his own save his reputation, since for more than ten years he has clothed the elite of Havana, and no one can rightly say that Francisco de Paula Uribe y Robirosa . . ."

"Oh! Master Uribe! Master Uribe!" the young man interrupted him yet again, even more impatiently. "Let the man who doesn't know you take you at your word. But enough talk about your word and your reputation and your seldom, if ever, doing exactly as you promised. Let us leave all this prattle for another time and get down to facts. When all is said and done, will I have the coat tonight in time for the ball or won't I? That is the important question."

"The young gentleman will have it or I will lose the name I have. With regard to the waistcoat, which is the only article that is being made outside this shop, I am expecting it to arrive any minute now. In a word, it is in the hands of a mulatto girl who is especially good at waistcoats, and she delivers them like clockwork. Since the gentleman has been good enough to honor my workshop with his presence, we shall try the coat on, although I am dead certain that the gentleman is going to admit that I have a good eye, if nothing else. I beg him not to pay any attention to its present state, for I know that for individuals who are not tailors there seems to be two days' work left to do in this case, whereas for an expert in the craft it's a matter of just two hours. If I occasionally get behind in my work, it is not my fault or that of my assistants, but is owed, rather, to the fact that a great many orders have come my way all at once. Here in the shop I have only five assistants, and as many who work at home as I care to hire, though I always prefer to have my workers where I can see them."

Standing in front of the mirror, Leonardo had removed his dress coat with the master tailor's aid and the two of them were trying the new one on him, when all at once he thought he saw reflected in the glass the image of someone who was looking at him on the sly from behind the dining room door. Although the thought went through his mind that he had seen that face somewhere before, he suddenly was unable to remember where or when. This effort of imagination left him lost in thought, completely self-absorbed for a time. During that interval, he naturally did not see what was going on, nor did he hear or his mind register Master Uribe's chatter.

Just then a colored girl entered the tailor shop, her head half covered by a shawl of dark, transparent Canton silk, of the sort worn by Persian women. She bade everyone good afternoon, and as though she hadn't noticed the work that was going on there, walked down the room toward the master tailor's living quarters, behind the cutting table. But Uribe was impatiently waiting for her and stopped her before she reached the door, asking her:

"Have you brought the waistcoat, Nene?"

"Yes, sir," she answered in a very soft, musical voice, stopping at the head of the table, on which she deposited a small bundle that she took out from under the shawl.

The girl's name, as well as her voice, brought Leonardo out of his state of self-absorption; he turned his eyes toward her and stared at her. Each of them recognized the other immediately, and they exchanged a knowing glance and an affectionate smile, signs that surely did not escape Uribe's sharp eye. I smell a rat here, he thought. Poor girl! I pity her! What clutches she's fallen into! At any rate this is the cause of Pimienta's burning resentment. . . . He's right. . . . No, it must be on account of something else besides.

Then he took the waistcoat out of the silk shawl in which it was wrapped, and handing the latter to its owner, he added, addressing Gamboa:

"Didn't I assure the gentleman? Here is the garment. The seamstress is worth her weight in gold."

The waistcoat was of black satin, dotted with bright green bees stitched into the fabric. Leonardo did not try it on, nor did the tailor think it necessary. Nor was there time for much of anything from then on, because the majority of Uribe's customers arrived, each of them by appointment. Among them were Fernando O'Reilly, the young brother of the count of that name; Filomeno's firstborn son, later the Marquis of Aguas Claras; the secretary or confidant of the Count of Peñalver; the young Marquis of Villalta; the steward of the Count of Lombillo; and someone said to be Seiso Ferino, a protégé of the wealthy Valdés Herrera family. Almost all of them had ordered attire for themselves or for their masters at Uribe's shop, and either while out for a drive in their carriages along the Paseo outside the city walls, or coming specially, entered it and remained only as long as necessary to inquire about their orders.

When the first of the individuals named above came in, he put his hand familiarly on Leonardo's shoulder, called him by his first name, and addressed him as *tú*, the second-person pronoun used between intimate friends. They had been fellow students of philosophy at the Colegio de San Carlos from 1827 to 1828; on the latter date O'Reilly had gone off to Spain to pursue his studies for a law degree, which he received, returning to his home and native land only a few months before the day we are speaking of here, having been appointed to the post of city magistrate. After his two-year absence, this was the first time that the two of them had seen each other, since Leonardo had had neither the opportunity nor the inclination to welcome him home, perhaps because even though they had once been classmates, Fernando was nonetheless still a member of the proudest family of Havana and of the highest-ranking nobility of Spain. Moreover, he had left a bachelor and returned a married man, with a bride from Madrid, yet another reason why his tastes and enthusiasms were now very different from what they had been when the two of them attended together the eloquent lessons of the amiable philosopher Francisco Javier de la Cruz.

What occasioned the gathering of the crowd of gentlemen and their servants was nothing other than the dress ball that was being held that very night on the upper floors of the mansion situated on the Calle de San Ignacio at the corner of Teniente Rey, rented for its festivities by the Philharmonic Society, in 1828. Following the carnival season, at the end of February, which coincided with the public festivities celebrating the marriage of Princess Maria Cristina of Naples and Ferdinand VII of Spain, the aforementioned society had not opened its salons again. It was doing so now to see the year 1830 out, for it is common knowledge that the elite of Havana, the only people with the right to attend its functions, went off to the country from the beginning of December on and did not return to the city until long after Epiphany. On the eve of the ball, young people of both sexes thronged to the shops with the latest fashions and accessories to have fancy new attire made and buy adornments, jewelry, and gloves. Tailor shops such as Federico's, Turla's, and Uribe's, which were the favorites; stores such as El Palo Gordo and Maravillas; jewelry stores such as Rozan's and La Llave de Oro; dressmaker's shops such as Madame Pitaux's; shoemaker's shops such as Baró's on the Calle de O'Reilly and Las Damas on the Calle de la Salud at the corner of Manrique, outside the city walls, found themselves besieged from morning to night for several days prior to the ball by those young men and ladies most noted for their elegance and their luxurious costumes. In those days shoes or pumps of white satin from China, with ribbons to fasten them at the instep, were beginning to be worn by ladies, along with openwork silk stockings to show off their legs, for rather short dresses were the fashion. Men too wore pumps, made of calfskin with a little gold buckle on the outer side, and flesh-colored silk hose.

Uribe outdid himself in politeness and affability toward the gentlemen, for he knew how to cloak himself in these attributes when it suited him; on the other hand he was curt and sparing with his demonstrations of civility toward the servants, even though they came in the name of persons in high places. Yet he was clever enough to leave everyone happy and satisfied, since it cost him nothing to lavish promises right and left, these being the imaginary coin in which the majority of debts are paid in society. Thus he was as good as his word with those who were frank and forthright with him from the beginning; the others he let down badly, without losing their patronage thereby. And once they had all left, for none of them stayed long, he went straight to work on the garments he intended to finish in time for that night. He did not forget, naturally, Gamboa's "invisible" dress coat. The latter, satisfied that he would not be disappointed by Uribe again, gave in to his friend O'Reilly's urgent pleas and accompanied him in his gig to the promenade called El Prado, after the famous one in Madrid.

It occupied, and still occupies today, the area extending from the El Monte highway to the reef of La Punta to the north, at the bottom of the sloping embankment of the moats around the city to the west. Cienfuegos lengthened the promenade from the El Monte highway southward to the Arsenal; but that section of it has never been used as part of El Prado but rather as the Calle Ancha, the name it goes by today. Among the public works to adorn the city that originated during the administration of Don Luis de las Casas was the so-called new Prado (the one of which we are now speaking). The Count of Santa Clara finished the first fountain that las Casas had left in the planning stage, and erected another one to the north: we are referring to the Neptune Fountain, in the middle of El Prado, and the Lion Fountain at the far end. Both fountains were supplied with water from the Zanja, the royal irrigation ditch that crossed the promenade (and still does today) along the front of the botanical garden, today the main railway station on the line running from Havana to Güines, and then along the edge of the moat, finally emptying its turbid waters into the far end of the harbor, alongside the Arsenal. Much later, at the southern end of the Prado, where there had originally stood the marble statue of Charles III, which Don Miguel Tacón moved in 1835 to his military promenade, the Count of Villanueva erected along the edge of the Zanja in 1837 the beautiful fountain of the Indies or of Havana.

The new Prado was approximately a mile long, passing at an almost imperceptible 80-degree angle in front of the small plaza in which the rustic Neptune Fountain stood. El Prado consisted of four rows of trees commonly found in the woodlands of Cuba, some of them so old they were big around and bulky, and all of them inappropriate for a promenade. On the avenue down the middle, the widest one, there was room for four carriages abreast; the two narrower avenues running down either side of the main one, with a few stone seats here and there, were for the use of people on foot, that is to say men only, who on gala occasions or feast days formed endless lines that stretched along the entire length of the promenade. The majority of them, particularly on Sundays, were Spanish lads employed in the city's retail shops or in government offices, and soldiers and sailors; being bachelors and working in poorly paid occupations they could not afford a carriage of their own or hire one to visit El Prado, and if a foreigner set foot on it out of ignorance of the regulation that it was the side avenues that were reserved for pedestrians or without the consent of the sergeant of the small detachment of dragoons standing guard there, he called attention to himself and aroused the public's laughter.

Cuban or Creole young people considered it beneath their dignity to go to El Prado on foot, and above all to mingle with Spaniards in the lines of Sunday gawkers. As a result only the elite took an active part in the day's promenade: the women invariably in light gigs, a number of elderly individuals in *volantes* and certain young people from rich families on horseback. No other sort of horse-drawn vehicle was used in Havana at the time, except by the bishop and the captain general, who rode in coaches. The entertainment was limited to riding around the statue of Charles III and the Neptune Fountain when the crowd was small; when it was large the promenade stretched to the Lion Fountain or to some point between the two, where the sergeant of the detachment of dragoons calculated that he ought to station one of his men so as to maintain order and see that the carriages kept their proper distance from each other. The more carriages there were, the slower the pace at which they were allowed to move; consequently, it often turned out to be a very monotonous exercise, though one that was not really a waste of time for the young ladies, whose principal diversion consisted of riding about, recognizing their friends and acquaintances among the spectators in the side avenues, and greeting them with a wave of their half-open fan, in the graceful and elegant manner that is a gift bestowed only on the women of Havana.

Fortunately, the monotony and funereal gravity of such an innocent diversion, to which the Spanish authorities gave the arbitrary name of order, lasted only as long as there were dragoons of the detachment present on the central avenue of El Prado, that is to say, from five to six in the afternoon. For it was common knowledge that, at times with the tip of their lances, and at others with blows of their staffs, they made the carriage drivers maintain the proper pace and keep in line. But after saluting the Spanish flag in the nearby fortresses, a ceremony prior to lowering it, as were the volleys from El Morro, the detachment marched off in single file along the edge of the Zanja, heading for the street and the barracks bearing its name, and immediately thereafter the races, the real activity, beauty, and novelty of the afternoon outing, began. The promenade of carriages and men on horseback along the new Prado of Havana then became, in all truth, a spectacle worth contemplating, still partially illuminated by the last golden rays of the setting sun, which on autumn and winter afternoons tone down to handfuls of silver before blending into the perfect, pure blue of heaven's vault. The expert carriage drivers eagerly took advantage of the chance offered them to show off their skill and dexterity, not only in controlling the horses, in making their gigs wheel about violently and capriciously, but also their expertise in guiding them through all the tight spots and all the confusion, and getting them out without a single collision or so much as one wheel grazing another. Even timid young ladies, at a peak of excitement from the whirlwind of horses and carriages racing and turning at breakneck speed, enraptured in their airborne shells by the horsemen's actions and at times their words, urged them on; hence both carriage drivers and horsemen did their utmost to contribute to the danger and the magnificence of the spectacle. Little by little the ethereal light of dusk faded; a fine ash-colored powder rose in whorls up as far as the lowest branches of the thick-crowned trees and covered the entire promenade, so that when the gigs with their loads of beautiful young women left the race-course one after the other to return to the city or to the neighborhoods outside its walls, the spectator caught off his guard couldn't help believing that they were descending from the clouds, or like other Venuses, emerging from the foaming ocean waves.

In those day when the mother country believed that the art of governing colonies was confined to the setting up of a few batteries of cannon, the idea of constructing walls around Havana was conceived, a project that got under way at the beginning of the seventeenth century and was not finished until almost the end of the eighteenth. These walls were part of a vast and complete fortification of the city, on the land side as well as on the sea or harbor side, including four gates leading to the surrounding countryside, smaller posterns leading to the water, drawbridges, a wide, deep moat, embankments, warehouses, palisades, embrasures, and bulwarks topped with merlons; thus the most populous city of the Island was in fact turned into an immense citadel. That was how things stood until the arrival of the memorable Miguel Tacón, who opened three more gates in the walls and replaced the drawbridges with fixed stone bridges. But in the period to which we are referring, that is to say, when only the five original gates existed, the three in the center, called the gates of Monserrate, Muralla, and Tierra, were for the use of the public in carriages, on horseback, and on foot, and those at either end, called the gates of La Punta and of La Tenaza, were intended in particular for the circulation of goods. Through them, then, sugar, coffee, and other heavy goods passed, loaded on the one form of transport at that time, namely enormous, crude carts drawn by sluggish oxen. The garrison of the fort, numbering many men in the final days, did guard duty at the gates and at the posterns, along with the customs guard set up at all of them; hence neither anyone nor anything went in or out without being subject to a double search, as was the custom in besieged fortresses.

After the carriage in which O'Reilly and Gamboa were riding had entered the inner portcullis, where the sentry box of the customs guards was located, there appeared, on the opposite side of the drawbridge, a horse so loaded down with green corn stalks and husks for fodder, commonly known as *maloja*, that all that could be seen of it was its hoofs and its head, which the animal was trying to hold as high as it could, doubtless because of the far too heavy load that it was carrying. Atop that mountain of greenery the driver, a lad from the Canary Islands wearing the same attire as a Cuban peasant, was mounted sidesaddle, or rather, leaning back on the horse's hindquarters. The Spanish sentinel, who was pacing back and forth between the two gates with his rifle over his arm, looked first toward the drawbridge and then toward the portcullis, and stood with his two feet planted in the middle of the pathway as a sign that both parties were to stop until the question of which of them was to turn back or move to one side was resolved. Stopping the horse loaded with fodder would be tantamount to obstructing the pathway, and turning it around on the narrow bridge was impossible without risking a fall; whereas it was easy for the carriage driver to guide the horses by the reins over to the guards' barracks and leave the way clear. Despite his natural slow-wittedness, the sentinel immediately saw this clearly; he therefore gestured with his hand to the driver of the cart loaded with fodder to stop and rushed over to the carriage and shouted: "Back up!"

But being proud of the nobility and authority of his master, vain about the coat of arms embroidered on his livery, as of his silver spurs, a metal with which the horse's harness was overdecorated, as was the carriage itself, the driver, instead of obeying the sentinel's order, brought the horses to a dead stop in front of the inner gate, and looked halfway round toward his master. The latter was deeply absorbed at the moment in recounting to Gamboa the risks that he had taken in his ascent of Mount Etna in Sicily, and even the sudden halt of the carriage had not caused him to notice that an obstacle had presented itself. The master's eyes naturally met those of the slave who was asking him for orders. "Get moving!" he told him, and as though nothing untoward was taking place, went on with the intimate conversation he was having with his former classmate and friend.

The horses started up again and the sentinel then repeated the words "Back up!", leveling his bayonet at their chests; on seeing this, O'Reilly, who was proud and arrogant, flushed with indignation. He stood halfway up in his seat, as if to better display the red cross of Calatrava embroidered on the lapel of his coat, and shouted: "Corporal of the guard!" And the moment he appeared, saluting with the back of his right hand to his forehead, O'Reilly added: "Have the way cleared!"

The corporal was instantly aware of what was going on, and despite the fact that he did not know the individual who had spoken to him, from his imperious tone of voice and his red cross he presumed that he was a gentleman of importance, a high civil authority or something of the sort, and answered him, with the back of his right hand still at his forehead: "The driver of the cart is unable to back up."

"What's that you say?" Fernando exclaimed at the height of his fit of rage. "Do you know to whom you are speaking? Call the officer of the guard."

"There is no need to do so," the corporal replied. "We'll find a way to settle matters. Don't disquiet yourself, Your Excellency."

"Have that horse with the load of fodder turn back. This instant."

Hearing voices shouting, the officer of the guard, who was passing the time playing cards with several of his friends, came running, and the guards on duty, who were sitting on a bench without a back at the door of the barracks waiting about for orders as the other guards inside were sleeping like a log on the wooden platforms nailed to the floor. The officer of the guard, who we must presume was better acquainted than the corporal with the concept of what is just and what is unjust, saw only that a gentleman decorated with the cross of Calatrava was unable to continue his outing in his carriage because his path was being blocked by a peasant with his horse loaded with fodder. He therefore peremptorily ordered the bridge cleared. The order was carried out in less time than it takes to tell and the mountain of green fodder ended up on top of the railing of the drawbridge, the only feasible solution that occurred to the guards in those circumstances. In fact, the carriage was thus able to get past, though it carried part of the fodder on the cart off on the hubcap of one of its wheels. All this happened both so suddenly and so unexpectedly for the lad on the horse that all he had time to do was to fling himself to the ground, not so as to withstand the shock of a collision but so as not to be thrown into the moat. He voiced his surprise by way of a few curses, and his annoyance with mute gestures; but no one paid any attention. On the contrary, fearing even greater violence, he hastened to unload part of the fodder so that the horse could stand up straight and continue on its way to the city.

On leaving the end of the bridge to go through the narrow portcullis of the stockade, it was necessary to skirt the edge of the moat for a short distance, passing above the sluice of the Zanja, part of whose waters emptied into the the latter, forming a pond with regular dimensions. On the edge of the high embankment, at the moment of which we are speaking, a group of men and boys were standing watching something that was happening down below, in the pond.

"What's going on?" O'Reilly asked.

"I don't know," his friend answered. "I suppose there are people bathing down there."

When the question was put to the carriage driver, he informed his master without stammering that it was Polanco the mulatto and Tondá the black, renowned swimmers, having a kick-fight. In fact, completely naked, like savages from Africa, they were diving, circling about underwater and trying to do damage to each other by dealing each other tremendous kicks, the way people say crocodiles do as they attack their prey. In Cuba this is called *tirar zapatazos*. It would appear that the indecent spectacle was a common occurrence, inasmuch as O'Reilly's driver immediately identified the swimmers by name and described exactly what they were doing in the water. The mulatto had attacked a shark more than once in the harbor and stabbed it to death; the black, besides being an excellent swimmer, was well known in the entire city for his heroic courage and his active role in hunting down malefactors of his own race, with special permission from the Captain General, Don Francisco Dionisio Vives himself.

The easy victory over the lad with the corn fodder won at the gate of La Muralla had emboldened the carriage driver, who wanted to join the promenade by way of the bank of the Zanja; but he was kept from doing so by a dragoon with his lance at the ready. Despite protests by O'Reilly, who invoked his status as city magistrate, the driver was obliged to go around the statue of Charles III and wait there for an opening in order to join the line. This was the first reason for the proud young man to feel humiliated; the second awaited him at the intersection of the Calle de San Rafael and El Prado. General Vives's coach with its mounted escort came riding down San Rafael into El Prado, all the horses at full gallop; meanwhile, in order to clear the way for them, the dragoons of the detachment halted the carriages in both lines on the promenade, among them O'Reilly's, as two flankers with drawn sabers stopped and turned back those who were attempting to enter or leave by way of the Monserrate gate before His Excellency the Captain General.

This proved that in Havana there was someone superior and more privileged than a second son of a count, even one who was also a grandee of Spain of the first rank. Leonardo was not a democrat in the literal sense of the word, but the assault on the peasant with the horse carrying the corn fodder had greatly displeased him and he was almost happy at the mortifications his friend had experienced on their outing, as though they had been intended to humble his pride. It seemed evident, then, that in all circumstances the country's social distinctions were useful only to enhance the authority of the military, before which nobles and plebeians alike were obliged to humble themselves.

I I I

And in cadence a thousand beauties moved
Dressed in fantastic vestments,
And appeared before my eyes like visions
Of an oriental poet.

R. Palma

That night* the theater of elegance in Havana was to be found at the Philharmonic Society. The taste and refinement of the ladies, as well as the respectable comportment of the gentlemen, shone there in all their splendor. In addition to the members and the usual invited guests, the foreign consuls, the officers of the garrison and of the royal Navy, the aides of the captain general and a number of other personages notable for their character and background, such as the son of the renowned Marshal Ney, who was touring abroad, and the Dutch consul posted to New York were also in attendance.

The tulle gowns embroidered in gold and silver over a background of

---

*We have taken the following account almost word for word from a weekly published in Havana in 1830, entitled *La Moda. Author's note.*

white satin were particularly noteworthy, because they were the latest fashion and because they were the equal of those that Madame Minette made in Paris for the reigning Queen of Spain. The sleeves of this gown, known as sleeves *à la Cristina*, were short, wide and loose-fitting, their lower edge trimmed with a very wide, band of lace. Other gowns of tulle with extremely delicate embroidery over a sky-blue background were also seen. Tulle evening dresses over white satin trimmed with point lace edged with a narrow band of lace and sleeves *à la Cristina* likewise attracted general attention. Other gowns similar to these latter, though with different trimmings, might be mentioned, leaving many more whose elegance and taste in no way compared unfavorably with those already described.

The ladies' coiffures harmonized with their gowns. Some of the ladies wore Egyptian turbans, others white plumes tucked most gracefully in their locks; the rest hair arrangements, called *girafas*, of all sizes, adorned with blue or white flowers, matching the color of their gown, and some with gold bows artfully placed. The gathering of so many and such pretty fashionable ladies produced an impressive and beautiful effect. Utter happiness reigned and there was a smile on everyone's lips. Formal dress, which was the general rule at the society's balls, was worn only by those ladies in evening gowns and those men who insisted on wearing their richly embroidered full dress uniforms of royal gentlemen-in-waiting, of generals, of brigadiers, of colonels, of high-ranking officials, with Cadaval and Lemaur flaunting their red silk sashes, while those gentlemen who possessed neither a title nor decorations had to make do by wearing the latest Paris fashion at such gatherings.

The main wall at the front of the ballroom was adorned with a magnificent canopy, in the center of which was a portrait of King Ferdinand VII. The wall panels were hung with historical paintings and from the cornices a hanging of blue damask with white banners edged with bright silk fringes was suspended, held in place by gilded decorations and ornamental studs, from which there hung gracefully braided silk cords and tassels. The ceiling of the ballroom was upholstered in damask of the same color as the hanging.

The ball began around 10 o'clock, and at 11 the main salon was completely full. During the intermissions sherbets and refreshments of all sorts were served on huge silver platters held by liveried footmen. Those ladies who chose to partake of them outside the ballroom had at their disposal for this purpose a perfectly lighted drawing room, where refreshments were set out, with servants ready to serve them; but the courtesy and the urbanity of the male members and guests spared these latter a task which for gentlemen becomes a pleasure when it involves serving ladies.

Supper began between midnight and one in the morning, and consisted of cold turkey, Westphalian ham, cheese, excellent leg of lamb, braised shredded beef, candied fruit, preserves, full-bodied wines from Spain and other countries abroad, rich chocolate, coffee, and fruits from every country that traded with the island of Cuba. And what was most noteworthy was that, with the splendor of the table rivaling its prodigal abundance, the dishes cost nothing but the effort of asking to be served them.

It can safely be stated, without fear of contradiction, that the elegance and beauty of Havana had agreed to meet that night at the Philharmonic Society. For among those present were the Marquise of Arcos, daughter of the famous Marquis Pedro Calvo, with Luisa, her elder daughter, 15 years old at the time. It was for Luisa that the poet Plácido had improvised the following conceit:[28]

> Flitting about
> In the exquisite ambiance
> Was a mosquito dying of thirst,
> Seeking nectar from flowers.
> It landed on your mouth, and taking it
> For a rose or carnation
> Made its way inside.
> Enthralled by the pleasure it found there,
> It perished in your sweet throat
> As in a glass of honey.

There as well were the Chacón sisters, whose beauty earned them a place in the great canvas painted by Vermay[29] to perpetuate the memory of the Mass celebrated at the inauguration of the Templete in the Plaza de Armas; there the Montalvos, Teutonic types, one of whom had been named beauty queen to rule over the *corrida de cañas*, a mock tournament with cane stalks for lances that had been held the year before in the old bullring on the Campo de Marte; there Pepilla Arango, who was famous for having helped the poet Heredia to flee the country, and who later married one of Captain General Ricafort's aides-de-camp; there the Aceval sisters, as shapely as the Venus de Milo, and as outstanding for their talent as they were doomed to misfortune by their passions; there the Alcázar sisters, models of perfection, thanks to the symmetry of their small features as well as to their rosy cheeks and black hair; there the young ladies of the Junco and Lamar families from Matanzas, known by the poetic appellation of "the Nymphs of the Yumurí"; there the three Gamboa sisters, whom we have already had occasion to describe; there señorita Topete, daughter of the commandant of the naval district of Havana, who later inspired Palma's immortal poem *Quince de Agosto*;[30] there the youngest of the Gámez sisters, a Venus of Belvedere, whose abundant, wavy chestnut hair she was wearing loose, dotted with gold stars; and there finally, among many others whom it would take far too long to list by name, Isabel Ilincheta, daughter of the former advisor to Captain General Someruelos, who possessed the principal traits of the stern and modest Celto-Iberian type to which she belonged by birth.

As models of masculine handsomeness among the young men attending the society's ball that night, we might mention the lieutenant colonel of the Royal Lancers, Rafael de la Torre, who a few days later was to die, the victim of his spirited horse, fatally dashed beneath the wheels of carriages on the Paseo, alongside the statue to Charles III; Bernardo Echeverría y O'Gabán, who on gala holidays was fond of wearing the uniform of a gentleman-in-waiting with entry to the royal chamber, since it enabled him to show off his sturdy and well-proportioned legs; Ramón Montalvo, in the prime of life, as handsome as an Englishman of the bluest blood; José Gastón, Cuba's true Apollo; Dionisio Mantilla, a newcomer from France, a perfect Parisian; Diego Duarte, the lucky champion of the *corridas de cañas* held the year before to celebrate the marriage of Ferdinand VII and Maria Cristina of Naples; and several officers of the Spanish army and navy in their showy uniforms more appropriate for a parade than for a private ball.

Also contributing to the splendor of the gala ball was the presence of a number of young men who were beginning to distinguish themselves as practitioners of belles-lettres, namely Ramón de Palma, who had been one of the contestants in the *corrida de cañas*; José Antonio Echeverría, employed at the Treasury, who the following year won the poetry contest sponsored by the Literature Commission to celebrate the birth of the Infanta of Castile, Isabel de Borbón; Ignacio Valdés Machuca, known as *Desval* in the republic of letters; Policarpo Valdés, whose pen name was *Polidoro*; Anacleto Bermúdez, who was in the habit of publishing poems under the name of *Delicio*; Manuel Garay y Heredia, who published his poetry in *La Aurora* of Matanzas; Ramón Vélez Herrera, the author of the Cuban ballad *Elvira de Oquendo*; *Delio*, the pseudonym adopted by Francisco Iturrondo, the bard who sang of the ruins of the Alhambra; Domingo André, a young attorney, eloquent and amiable;

Domingo del Monte, the first to write *romances cubanos*, ballads based on Cuban themes, a learned scholar in several domains and a man of very distinguished bearing.

Diego Meneses, Francisco Solfa, Leonardo Gamboa, and several others who also attended the ball—if we except the second, who devoted himself to his philosophical studies, and the third, who had already become a member of the moneyed class—were not in the way of becoming well known by virtue of their talent, although the three of them regularly wrote for literary periodicals; and the one mentioned last was, moreover, considered to be a fairly handsome, well-built, and virile-looking young man. The literati, or rather, literary enthusiasts, above all those who cultivated poetry, were beginning to have an entrée to people who could be regarded as noblemen in Cuba, or who aspired to the nobility by virtue of their wealth, and were starting to mix with them. Certain titled families of Havana were at least showing respect for them and inviting them to their parties and social gatherings, among others, for example, the Counts of Fernandina, of Casa Bayona, of Casa Peñalver, the Marquis of Montehermoso and of Arco. These fiestas and gatherings during the year-end holidays then shifted to the lovely coffee plantations of San Antonio, Alquízar, San Andrés, and La Artemisa, which belonged to wealthy people.

Our friends Gamboa, Meneses, and Solfa did not make their appearance in the salons of the Philharmonic Society until nearly 11 o'clock that night. During the earlier hours they had been dropping in at the holiday balls in the Angel, Farruco, and Brito districts, not neglecting to put in an appearance at the colored people's *cuna* on the Calle del Empedrado, between Compostela and Aguacate. At none of these places had they taken an active part in what was going on, with the exception of Gamboa, who lost in an instant in a game of monte the two doubloons that his mother had tucked in his waistcoat pocket that very afternoon. He had no notion of the value of money, nor did he gamble because he loved to win, but merely for the excitement of the moment; but it so happened that the balls held no attraction at all for him, since there wasn't a single pretty girl to be seen at any of them. It also happened that he did not manage to see Cecilia Valdés at the window of her house, or at the *cuna*, all of these being a turn of events that conspired to put him in a most foul mood. To top off all his misfortunes, having lost his doubloons and feeling glum, when he went back with his friends to get his gig, which he had left at a hitching post on the Calle del Aguacate in the shelter of the towering walls of the convent of Santa Catalina, he discovered that it wasn't there, and only after searching for half an hour was he able to find it at a spot a good way away, and on the opposite side of the street.

Moreover, when he questioned his driver as to what had made him disobey a definite order from his young master, Aponte gave him evasive answers at first, and finally, when hard pressed, said that a stranger, his face half covered with a kerchief, had forced him, through the use of terrible threats, to give up his place and pretend that he was returning home. His story seemed to lack all credibility; Leonardo was nonetheless obliged to accept it as a true and faithful account; this put him in an even worse mood if such a thing were possible, for if Aponte's story was true, who could that individual have been, or of what interest could it have been to him to have Leonardo's carriage wait at one corner of the street instead of another? Why had he used threats? What authority did he have to do so? Aponte could not say whether the stranger was a soldier or a peasant, a district police inspector or a magistrate, white or colored. Perhaps he was an unexpected and unknown rival who by such tactics was readying himself to vie with him for the affections of Cecilia Valdés.

Such a disagreeable suspicion was corroborated by the fact that neither she nor her friend Nemesia had appeared at any of the festivities in El Angel. Moreover, the fact that she had not opened her window, even when Leonardo gave the signal that they had agreed on, poking the tip of his cane through the few balusters still left intact outside it, left almost no doubt in his mind that something extraordinary had happened in her humble, obscure home.

Be that as it might, and there being no time at present to prove or disprove his conjecture, Leonardo Gamboa was worried and altogether out of sorts as he entered the ball at the Philharmonic Society. The ball, however, had been planned to take place in the more than spacious main salon and drawing room of the palace, where as the poet says:[31]

> One night finally; between mirrors
> The light was reflected back and forth in the salons
> And the sounds of the tropical dance
> Inflamed the blood;

hence our hero was unable to escape its entrancing influence. The orchestra, conducted by the renowned violinist Ulpiano, occupied the broad corridor to the left as one mounts the regal staircase of dark stone. Then to the right was the door of the salon, opposite another that opened onto the vast balconies that formed the entryway known as El

Rosario. Having handed over their hats and canes to a black lackey, at the door of a room on the mezzanine that gave onto the landing of the staircase with two flight of stairs, the view from above opening out onto the magnificent main salon, large enough to accommodate "the run of a racehorse from start to finish," if we may be permitted that exaggeration, the students discovered that vivacious couples filled it from one end to the other. As they awaited their turn to dance a waltz, the men caught from behind, and the women in their faces, the cool midnight breeze coming in through the doors and windows thrown wide open.

As we have said previously, the *crème de la crème* of Cuban young people of both sexes was gathered there, devoted body and soul, for the moment at least, to their favorite diversion. And in the dazzling light of the crystal chandeliers, amid waves of a music as plaintive as it was voluptuous, since it came from the heart of an enslaved people, seen through the diaphanous cloud of fine dust raised by the dancers' feet, the women looked more beautiful, the men more courtly. Was it possible, then, for the spirits of the young people present to give themselves over to pastimes other than those suggested to them by the pleasing objects before them? No, it was impossible.

Gamboa immediately set out to find a partner so as to take part in the ball, although he was not particularly fond of dancing; but Meneses, who rarely danced, and Solfa who never danced, remained spectators, standing in the middle of the ballroom, observing it with a bitter smile, for as those mad young people enjoyed the pleasures of the moment to the fullest, the most stupid and brutal of kings of Spain seemed to be contemplating them with an air of deep disdain from the gilded canopy beneath which his odious likeness was displayed.

Making his way with considerable effort among the jam-packed lines of spectators and dancers, Gamboa came upon the youngest of the Gámez sisters, whose portrait we have hastily sketched earlier, in the heat of the dance. As her only greeting, without ceasing her whirling about, like a sylph, in the arms of her partner, she said to him, with her eyes rather than with her tongue: "Isabel is over there."

"Dancing?" the young man asked.

"What do you mean dancing! She's waiting for you."

"For me? What a good rest she might well have had. Because I very nearly decided not to come to the ball tonight."

In fact, to all appearances the aforementioned young lady found herself at the moment a wallflower, as the common expression has it in Cuba, that is to say, sitting on the left near the door of the drawing room between a middle-aged matron and the cultivated attorney Domingo

André, with whom she was having an animated conversation. Despite his natural nonchalance, Gamboa felt a fit of jealousy coming on that it was impossible for him to hold in check, not because he was truly in love, but because the gentleman in whose company he found her was extremely handsome and a master of the art of ingratiating himself with discreet women. We must say in passing, however, that the polestar toward which André's courtly advances were aimed in those days was another beauty quite different from Isabel Ilincheta, the same young lady whom he lost by being timid and whom the Dominican man of letters Domingo del Monte won by being bold, if we are not badly mistaken, on the very night of which we are speaking. As for Isabel, she greeted Leonardo with an adorable smile, which, far from calming him down, contributed to upsetting him even further. Once the usual greetings had been exchanged, for her companion, the mother of the Gámez sisters, was a friend of the young student, as well as of André, Isabel, as proof that she was neither the flirtatious sort nor vengeful, said with a most friendly smile:

"I was saying to this gentleman just a moment or so ago that I had promised this dance to someone, and he refuses to believe me."

"That's because you haven't danced even once yet, as far as I know," André replied.

"Of course there have been only two dances thus far," Isabel retorted, not at all flustered, "but up until now, when the third one is beginning, no one has come to invite me."

"Which means, in essence," André continued, "that I've come too late. So much the worse for me!"

"This young lady is telling the truth," Leonard put in, having recovered now from his pangs of jealousy. "As she has previously promised, at any ball where we meet she saves the third dance for me. I see, then, that I couldn't have arrived at a better time. As the saying goes, turning up at just the right moment beats hanging about for a year."

"Of course," the young attorney exclaimed, "but the thing is that when it comes to good-looking girls few of us turn up at just the right moment."

André took his leave and went off to join the two daughters of Aldama the tycoon, the younger of whom, whose name was Lola, would have relinquished the coveted laurels for beauty to very few of the young ladies present that night. Meanwhile Leonardo and Isabel, holding hands, joined the two lines of dancers, not far from the head of the line, thanks to the favor done them by mutual friends, who, although the two of them had turned up late, kept them from having to go to the end of the queue, as was the rule. Cuban dance was doubtless invented to give lovers a chance to court each other. In itself it is a simple style of dancing, the movements comfortable and easy, their primary object being to bring the two sexes closer together, in a country where Moorish customs tend to separate them: in a word, the communion of souls. For the gentleman almost always holds the lady as if suspended in midair, since as his right arm encircles her waist, his left hand gently squeezes hers. That is not dancing, inasmuch as their bodies merely follow the rhythm of the music; it is being rocked back and forth as in dreams, to the sound of a plaintive and voluptuous music; it is an intimate conversation between two beloveds; it is two mutually attracted persons caressing each other when time, space, social status and custom have kept them apart. Style is the man, someone has rightly said; dancing is a people, we say, and there is no one who can paint the character, the habits, the social and political status of Cubans more vividly than dance, and nothing that is more in harmony with the climate of the Island.

On the night in question, Isabel Ilincheta displayed marvelously well the natural charms with which heaven had endowed her. She was tall, shapely, svelte, and elegantly dressed, and therefore, since she was most modest and amiable it was a foregone conclusion that she would attract the attention of cultivated people. Even the subdued paleness of her face, the languid expression of her clear eyes and delicate lips contributed to the attractiveness of a young lady who, on the other hand, was in no way a beauty. Her charm lay in her words and her manners. She had just been entering puberty when she lost her mother, and in order to educate her, as well as to keep her safe from worldly dangers, her father had placed her in the care of the Ursuline nuns who had come from New Orleans and been established in their convent at the Puerta de Tierra since the early years of this century. After a stay of more than four years there as a boarding student, during which time she received an education that was more religious than scholarly and thorough, she withdrew to the country, to her father's coffee plantation, near the town of Alquízar, along with her younger sister Rosa and an aunt, the widow of a naval surgeon named Bohorques. This individual had made several voyages to the coast of Africa with expeditions sent out by the joint partnership of Gamboa and Blanco. He consequently contracted a terrible disease, died at sea, and was thrown overboard, like many of the hapless savages whom he had helped to kidnap from their native soil. For this reason, on many occasions his widow was the object of Don Cándido Gamboa's munificence. Leonardo visited her at the coffee plantation near Alquízar and could not help falling in love with her niece, whose modesty and charms enhanced her obvious intelligence and discerning discretion.

Isabel had not a trace of feminine softness, or, naturally, of voluptuousness in her bodily contours, as we have already indicated. And the reason was obvious: horseback riding, her favorite diversion in the country; frequent swimming in the river of San Andrés and of San Juan de Contreras, near which she spent the bathing season each year; walks almost every day on her father's plantation and on those of their neighbors; her frequent exposures to the elements for pleasure and as a consequence of her active life had strengthened and developed her physique to the point of causing her to lose the softly rounded contours of a young lady of her age and station. To complete the description of the virile and resolute air of her person, we must add that a shadow was cast upon her expressive mouth by the dark and silky down on her upper lip, which needed only frequent trimming to become a black and bushy mustache. Behind that mouth small, even white teeth could sometimes be glimpsed, and they were what constituted the magic of Isabel's smile.

It should not come as a surprise that even though Leonardo was something of a cynic and unaffectionate by nature, he should feel a passion for a young lady such as the one who has just been described. He was at the threshold of the golden gates of life. Despite his relationships and his wealth, he had not been on intimate terms with the young ladies of his milieu and upbringing, nor had he yet begun to seek in them his future life's companion. His harshness was merely external; it lay in his brusque manners, for in his heart of hearts, as there will be occasion to see, he had an inexhaustible abundance of generosity and tenderness. Fortunately God had not denied him the ability to love; it was simply that the women whom he had thus far chanced to come across had surrendered either to the ardor of his feelings, to his youthful boldness, or to the influence of his shower of gold. None of these motives could exert their power over the mind and heart of a wealthy, well-educated, modest and virtuous young lady such as Isabel Ilincheta. Leonardo, attracted at first by her physical attributes, then later on captivated by her excellent moral endowments, realized immediately that in order to win her affection it was necessary to touch her heart, to speak to her understanding. Moreover, that woman who now appeared before Leonardo's eyes in a new guise had lived in the perfect likeness of an earthly paradise when he had seen her for the first time.

If we can leave aside the slave and his sufferings, which are more bearable, notwithstanding, on coffee plantations, it will be conceded that Isabel, her sister Rosa, her aunt Doña Juana, her father and servants lived a life of peace and quiet, far from the hustle and bustle of the city, surrounded by fragrant flowers, by the coffee and orange trees green the year round, by the graceful palms, by the classic banana tree, and enthralled by the perennial song of birds and the melancholy whispering of the breeze in the countryside of Cuba. Even the season of Christmas carols and orange blossoms when Leonardo first met Isabel played a part in surrounding her with an air of enchantment in his eyes and in awakening in his breast something that he had never before felt in his 21 years of life: love.

I V

Princess: "Your name at least."
King: "Never, never, never."

Sueños de Amor y Ambición

The narrow street of La Bomba, like that of San Juan de Dios, which appears to be its continuation, is two blocks long. It is, if possible, narrower, more low-lying, and damper, even though its houses are in general more spacious. In one of the latter, at the corner of the Calle del Aguacate, Nemesia Pimienta lived with her brother José Dolores, the two of them occupying adjoining rooms, whose furnishings consisted of nothing except a couple of chairs, a rocker, a little pine table, and a folding cot, which was opened at night and closed during the day so as to leave more space.

Night had already fallen when Nemesia left Uribe's tailor shop and slowly made her way to the district of El Angel. She preferred to take the Calle del Aguacate, because even though it was darker and more deserted since there were no public establishments along it, it led straight to two places where she could stop to rest. When she reached the four corners formed by the Calle de O'Reilly and the street that crossed it, she stopped for a short time, lost in thought and hesitant. She looked first behind her, then to her right, then in front of her, her eyes riveted on the little window of the shabby little house adjoining the tavern on the left, although because it was on a line parallel to her, the only thing she could make out was the moldings of the balusters that projected slightly from the surface of the wall. It was difficult, therefore, to know whether there was someone peering out of the window or the door. As a consequence, the young mulatto crossed over to the corner down the street and gave a peculiar, high-pitched whistle, forcing her breath to pass between the teeth in the middle of her upper jaw.

A few seconds later she saw a corner of the white curtain appear through the balusters outside the window, but as she hastened to obey the signal to come ahead, she noticed that a gentleman was walking down the embankment of the convent in long strides, heading straight for the spot on which her eyes were focused. He was there to observe what was going on. Who could that individual be? Who was waiting for him in that house? He was wearing a dark tailcoat, light-colored trousers, and a hat with a narrow brim and a disproportionately broad crown that jutted out over the back of the stiff white collar of his shirt. He was neither young nor old, but middle-aged. Despite the darkness Nemesia was able to take note of all that because he was such a short distance away, no more than 30 paces. His bearing, his slow, steady movements, could be mistaken neither for those of a stripling nor for those of an elderly man.

He headed, however, with apparent caution to the place from which the corner of the white curtain could be seen; he held a brief conversation with the person hidden behind its folds, and then he walked off in long strides in the shelter of the towering walls of the convent and rounded the corner of La Punta. Nemesia soon lost sight of him in the darkness, but she had no doubt that a carriage was waiting for him in the middle of the block, for she distinctly heard the sound of wheels on the paving stones of the street, one that led away from where she was standing and favored the stranger's rapid departure.

Her curiosity aroused, the girl whistled once again, in the same way as before; an answer came from the little window in the form of a movement of the white curtain, and she hurried over to it; but instead of her dear friend Cecilia, she found only Cecilia's grandmother. Which of the two women had received the gentleman in the dark tailcoat and the hat with a bulky crown and spoken with him?—something that further aroused her curiosity and left her more bewildered than before.

"Ah! Is that you, Chepilla?" Nemesia exclaimed.

"Come in," the grandmother said, coming to the door and pushing aside with the tip of her foot the half of a cannon ball holding it shut.

The girl did not wait to be asked twice. The grandmother seemed solemn and ill at ease; and her granddaughter, sitting in one corner in a loose-fitting dress, looking dirty and disheveled, her head bent double on her bosom, her arms dangling and her fingers intertwined in her lap, was the living image of dejection and despair.

"Come in, my girl. You're most welcome here," Chepilla repeated. "Come in and sit down; do please sit down," she added, noting that the girl remained standing, bewildered and confused.

"It's late and I'm in a hurry," the latter replied, mechanically collapsing in the leather armchair in front of the niche in which a statue of Our Lady of Sorrows was venerated.

Chepilla was about to repeat her request, but since the visitor sat down without further ado, she remained standing between her and her granddaughter.

"As I was saying," Nemesia added in a moment, "it's late and I'm in a hurry. I was on my way home after taking some sewing to *Señó* Uribe's tailor shop and it got dark on me before I knew it—because it so happens that his wife Clarita is a real chatterbox, and what's more she wanted me to help her finish the skirt of a dress she's making for the night of the feast of the Immaculate Conception. José Dolores must be waiting for me. He left the tailor shop a long time before I did, because he had to accompany the *Salve Maria* at El Santo Angel Custodio. I'm sure there were lots of bigwigs at the tailor shop tonight, all of them waiting for their costumes for a ball at the Philharmonic and for the year-end holidays. *Señó* Uribe's customers have to place their orders well ahead of time. The work keeps pouring in though. Everybody says he's making a pile of money, but he spends it as fast as he makes it. . . . But now that I think of it, what's going on around here? The two of you seem very distressed," Nemesia said, noting that neither of them was listening to her.

Cecilia merely sighed and her grandmother said:

"What's happening isn't anything serious; it's just that this girl (indicating her granddaughter with a movement of her lips) seems possessed . . . God help us! (and she crossed herself): I was about to say something foolish. I want you to be the judge and the counselor-at-law in this case, even though you're more of an age to be the daughter of my daughter. That's why I asked you in. Come, tell me, my girl, what would you do if your protector, your constant friend, your only help in the world, your own father, so to speak, truly a father to us two poor, destitute women, with no other refuge under heaven, what would you do if he advised you, or let's say, if he forbade you to do something? Tell me, what would you do? Would you disobey him?"

"Granny," Cecilia said, leaping to her feet, unable to contain herself, "your grace hasn't pictured the situation as it really is."

"Hold your tongue," the grandmother replied imperiously. "Let Nemesia answer."

"But your grace is basing her argument on a false premise, and Nene can't answer correctly, even if she were willing to; your grace says that our friend, our protector, our help and refuge and I don't know what else besides, has asked and has forbidden that certain things be done and not done. And in the first place, I don't believe that that person your grace is referring to is anything that your grace says he is to us, at least not to me. In the second place, no matter how much I rack my brain, I don't see what reason or what right he has to meddle in my affairs and check to see if I go out or come in, if I laugh or cry . . ." ("I'm about to finish," Cecilia suddenly added, noticing that her grandmother was on the point of cutting her short.) "Above all, your grace has no reason to have torn my tulle gown and broken my Spanish comb, just to please an old man who has a grudge against me, and is jealous because I don't love him and never will love him, so . . ."

"Don't believe a word of what that girl says," the old woman interrupted her.

"Well, didn't your grace tear my gown and break my comb? Whose fault was it? Wasn't it the fault of that old man with the big nose that God . . . ?"

"Hold your tongue, hold your tongue," the grandmother interrupted her. "Don't blaspheme after having ranted and raved, because you'll make me think that you're in a state of mortal sin. If the ruffle of your gown got torn, wasn't it because you intended to wear it against my express wishes? Whose fault was it that the comb fell and got broken? It was your fault and nobody else's, because if you hadn't committed those acts of proud arrogance, none of that would have happened. Yes, yes, you must confess, you must do penance, repent your sins and mend your ways. You're in a state of mortal sin, and if you go on like that you're going to come to a bad end. This must be promptly remedied."

"You're outdoing yourself!" Cecilia went on despite the glaring looks her grandmother was casting her way. "I've never heard that it was a sin not to love someone you didn't like."

"And who's telling you to love him, you mad thing possessed by the devil?" Chepilla exclaimed vehemently. "Is he courting you? The sin lies in your not being thankful for the favors done us and in biting the hand that caresses us."

"Let's see, what are the favors that your grace is speaking of? The monthly stipend he sends our way? The gifts he gives me on feast days from Corpus Christi to San Juan? Only he and God know what his motive is. Isn't it odd, really odd, that he, a rich white man who has no ties to your grace, or to me either, is so generous to us two poor women of color?"

"Not again, Cecilia! Don't go on reeling off more foolishness. Only the Evil One could inspire in you ideas that are so contrary to Christian humility and charity. How can a woman who isn't grateful for favors and doesn't pay back generous deeds be a good daughter, a good wife, a good mother, or a good friend? However small the favors done us by the gentleman we're speaking of may be (and they aren't small), it is our duty to be thankful for them, since we're in no position to do anything more than that. It is a grave sin not to pay back the good done us. Your backbiting and ingratitude are going to cost us dearly."

"I don't know what your grace takes my behavior toward him to be. I scarcely know him. I neither give to him nor take from him; what I don't want is for him to order me around and meddle in my affairs."

"It would appear that you don't understand him. If he wishes you not to do this or that, is it for his own good or for yours? If he approves or disapproves of something that you say or do, what better proof can there be of his affection for you, and of his goodheartedness? Imagine, Nemesia, the individual we are speaking of (it is only right that you should know this) is as caring as a lady, and his generosity to us as great as it is disinterested, and he must feel very hurt . . ."

"Disinterested?" Cecilia repeated. "That is what I can't . . ."

"Don't interrupt me, child; I'm speaking to Nemesia. He gives us whatever we need and many things we covet. The moment I point out to him that this girl desires this or that he immediately hastens to please her. I dare you to say that that's not so, Cecilia. If you deny it you must not have a conscience."

"I don't deny it. All that is quite true, but why does he do it?"

"The best part of all," Chepilla went on, "is that he asks nothing of me, and expects from you nothing but affection, gratitude and . . . respect."

"That's the part that kills me," Cecilia again burst out vehemently. "Do you know of anyone, Nene, who gives anything without expecting something in return? I don't know any such person. The fact that he asks nothing of Granny is understandable; but that he should expect from me only affection, gratitude, and respect, as she puts it, I'll leave it to fools to believe. You know who it is that we're speaking of. Isn't that so? Well, the gentleman in question can't, strictly speaking, be considered to be an old man. He has piles of money and according to what Granny says he's been a womanizer and a lover with few equals all his life. Up until yesterday, so to speak, according to what Granny has told me, despite his being a married man with a family, he kept mistresses, preferably colored ones. He's lost more girls than he has hairs on his head; and Granny seems determined to make me believe that his generosity to me is innocent and disinterested. Let whoever doesn't know him believe it."

"You're talking just to be talking, child," the grandmother said at the end of a long interval of reflection and silence. "Everything you've said is beside the point and has nothing to do with the real matter at hand. The real matter at hand is that you do nothing to please him, nor do you feel any liking for a person who is so good to you, and all you do is deprive him of ensuring you of the good that may come your way from your doing or not doing certain things. For instance: why were you determined to go out tonight if he didn't want you to? When he was opposed to it, he had a reason. His reason could not have been anything except your good." Then she added in a gentler tone of voice: "Just think, Nene: shortly before you arrived here that good man . . . he didn't come in. Of course not! He never does. The first thing he did was to ask after Cecilia. He always does, and is very concerned about her, in a disinterested way of course: what I mean is with no other aim besides knowing how her health is. You know that, Nemesia; at least you've heard me say as much many times . . . he was at the window . . . for just a moment. As soon as he asked after Cecilia's health, as I've told you, with a great deal of interest, with the interest of a . . . as soon as I told him that she was getting ready to go to the *cuna* in El Angel, he said to me, very upset, yes, very upset, I could tell, because even his voice trembled: 'Don't let her go, *Seña* Chepa, don't let her go, keep her from going; that youngster is seeking her damnation . . . ' (That is his usual manner of speaking.) 'Don't let her go, keep her from going; at another time I'll explain what's happening.' Then he left, hugging the wall as though afraid of being seen. As he left he put a doubloon in my hand for shoes for Cecilia. Can there be greater generosity or nobility of soul? Can a person who always acts in that manner be in love? Come. Tell me. Do you see in such behavior cunning self-interest, worldly jealousy, love? Is that the way men of his age court women nowadays? Well, what do you think, Nemesia? What's your opinion?"

"To tell you the truth," Nemesia answered, her eyes searching her friend's face, "I don't know what to say, nor do I dare offer a frank opinion. However," she then added, with more feeling, "if I were Cecilia, I'd laugh at all this instead of getting angry. If the man was really in love, I'd laugh because he was, and if he wasn't I'd laugh to make fun of him and have him pay me back for all the bad things that others did to me. I wouldn't care one bit that someone like him was courting me and keeping a close watch on me around the clock; when he gave me money I'd pay him back with smiles. And let it not be said that I was doing wrong, or committing a sin, because all men are deceitful, feign love when they don't feel it, and have so many tricks up their sleeves that it's hard to know when they're really in love and when they're trying to deceive us poor women. Think bad thoughts and you'll be right, the proverb says. What harm can it do you, Celia, not to go to the *cuna* tonight?"

"It could do me neither any harm nor any good to go or not to go tonight, that's certain," Cecilia replied. "The thing is that the man that Granny is speaking of has tried to meddle in my affairs and keep a tight rein on me, out of sheer caprice or out of a wish to wear out my patience, and that's what I find intolerable."

"That's all very well, woman," Nemesia remarked gently; "but I don't see that he causes you any great inconvenience by interfering in your affairs."

"What do you mean?" Cecilia promptly replied. "Granny immediately sides with him, and scolds me, and fights with me, and tears my dress to make me stay home and please the old fool. Does that strike you as being of little importance?"

"I understand; I don't like nobody meddling in my affairs either. Even so, sometimes a person has to play the fool, so as to get more out of certain men. This one has taken it into his head to control you and keep watch on you; indulge him in his whim, woman; make sure you give him pleasure; don't get rid of him for good; smile at him, at least as long as he proves to be generous, and you'll enjoy yourself and live to a ripe old age."

For the moment the conversation was limited to Nemesia and her friend, since the old woman had returned to her armchair and her reflections.

"Look," Nemesia went on, "the one who fusses and frets goes to the grave. What's more, you can be sure that no old man, no matter how much he wheedles and cajoles, is any danger to a girl like you."

"No, I don't think he's dangerous, nor do I fear him one bit," Cecilia said. "I'm very independent and will never let anyone control me, much less a stranger."

"A stranger!" the grandmother repeated to herself, in a deep, hoarse voice.

The two girls looked at each other as though taken aback, both on account of the old woman's tone of voice and because both of them thought that she was completely absorbed in her melancholy thoughts.

"His son," Nemesia went on in a low voice. "You know who I mean. He's really someone to be afraid of. Young, good-looking, brimming over with charm on every hand, a smooth talker, with money to pour out as though it were water. . . . No woman with a heart can resist him. Isn't that so, dear? It's impossible to see him and hear him and not love him. I would beware of a man like him as I would beware of the devil. He's already given headaches to more than one girl. You can see who he takes after."

Chepilla continued to be self-absorbed, apparently neither hearing nor understanding what Nemesia was saying. Cecilia, on the contrary, once her friend mentioned her lover, was all ears, realizing that Nemesia intended to tell her an important piece of news.

"Anyway, as I was telling you," Nemesia added, "when I left *Señó* Uribe's shop, I started down the Calle del Aguacate, and when I was directly opposite the Gámez's house, which as you know is behind the convent of the Carmelite nuns, I heard music and men's and women's voices. I went over to one of the windows with the tall stone benches underneath. The shutters were open and the curtains drawn back. There was a large gathering in the drawing room: there was music, and people were singing and dancing. What day is today? Aha! The 27th of October. So it's the saint's day of the youngest of the Gámez sisters, Florencia! That's why she was dressed in white and was wearing her hair down; it was very kinky for a white woman's. At least . . . I grant you it was very pretty, because it's long and thick, though I'd like it better if it were darker."

Cecilia heaved a sigh and Nemesia went straight on without beating about the bush:

"I was saying that a number of young ladies and gentlemen were standing around Florencia in front of the piano. Do you know who was there too? Yes, I'm sure of it; it was her. Do you remember the tall, pale, good-looking girl that I told you passed by El Angel Hill in the Gámez's gig on the morning of the fiesta of San Rafael? It was the very same girl. She was having a conversation with Meneses, the friend of . . . you know who. His other friend was there too, the one who's always with the other two . . . What's his name? Sola, Sofa, Ah! Solfa, that's it. But their friend wasn't there, they merely mentioned his name. I'm certain they mentioned it . . ."

"Who did?" Cecilia asked anxiously.

"I couldn't tell you for sure; but if I'm not mistaken, it was during a conversation between Meneses and the pale girl. The two of them were talking about him. As I understood it, they were all going to the grand ball that's being held tonight at the Philharmonic."

"I was afraid of that," Cecilia said.

"Oh!" Nemesia exclaimed. "I realize now who the silk waistcoat I had to make in such a rush was for. Oh! If I'd realized it before I wouldn't have been in such a hurry to finish it on time. I sewed till far into the night, because it was given to me late yesterday afternoon and they wanted it for today at three. Whoever would have guessed it! If I had, he wouldn't have gone to the white people's ball in a waistcoat made by me. I say this because of you, darling, because it's all the same to me. He doesn't belong to me; I'm only interested because of you, because you're fond of him . . . Watch your step: men are ingrates! But it's best to say no more and not add fuel to the fire."

What had been said, in fact, was more than enough to infuriate even a young woman less fiery-tempered than Cecilia. As her friend was setting forth her thoughts on the matter, for Nemesia had surely given thought to the news that she had passed on and even to the way in which she would do so, Cecilia grew more and more angry and upset. What to do in such circumstances, if there was still time, to stop the individual who Nemesia had said was going to the Philharmonic to meet the young lady whose identity was unknown? What she felt was jealousy, rage, desperation. There wasn't room enough for her in the chair near the window. She rose to her feet several times and made as if to enter the other room, no doubt to change her clothes and go out, only to return each time to the chair. Her gorge rose, almost to the point of suffocating her.

Meanwhile the grandmother was seemingly still absorbed in devout prayer; with her eyes shut she appeared to be kneading, one after the other, between the thumb and index finger of her right hand the black beads of the rosary she was holding in her lap. Nemesia cast a sidelong glance at her friend, observing, as if through a crystal-clear pane of glass, the fierce battle being waged within her breast, and every so often Cecilia smiled almost imperceptibly, as though she had foreseen everything that was happening, or else had no fear that it would have an unhappy ending. Finally she collapsed into the chair, breathed a deep sigh, and murmured:

"Better not to: I know what I must do. I'll not be deceived by any man. It almost makes me happy. . . . I'm not going out anywhere."

Chepilla raised her eyes then and looked at her granddaughter with a certain happiness mingled with compassion. Nemesia, for her part, to all appearances pleased, or rather, let us say, proud that her coming had had precisely the desired effect, went on her way, bidding her friends a fond farewell.

V

It seems as if I am still looking at you . . .
Your terrible angry face,
Your wild eyes,
Your vile lash whistling.

J. Padrínez

Nemesia reached the door of her house just as her beloved brother José Dolores was leaving it, with his clarinet in its case underneath his arm and a roll of music scores in his hand. As was his habit, he was walking along with his head down, lost in thought. For this reason and because the street was very dark, with no light inside the house either, their paths almost crossed without either of them recognizing the other, despite their proximity. Just like that, she recognized him first, barred his way, and asked him a question by repeating a few words of a song that at the time was as popular as it was a bit risqué:

"'Where are you going with that cat on such a dark night?'"

"What!" José Dolores exclaimed in surprise. "Ah! Is that you? I got tired of waiting for you."

"You're leaving for the ball this early?"

"What time is it anyway?"

"The bell at Santa Catarina[32] was just ringing for Vespers as I went past the convent."

"You're mistaken; it must be later than you think."

"Maybe so, because my head feels like a gourd, and I don't know what's the matter with me."

"I see. I don't want to keep you too long. Nonetheless, I imagine you've time to have a bite with me . . . a cup of coffee."

"I've already gone that route. I had some coffee with milk and some bread and cheese. That will do me till midnight, when I'll try to eat some minced meat stew or something like that. You had something to tell me?"

"In the little house next to the tavern on the corner of the Calle de O'Reilly, you know where I mean, there was a real row tonight."

"How come? And how come you look as though you're happy about it?"

"It's a long story. I'll tell you. I was passing by that way . . . *Seña* Clara kept me at the shop later than usual. Anyway, I was passing by that way, even though it was quite late, because I'd made plans with Cecilia to take a stroll around in El Angel after the *Salve Maria*. She suspected that the individual who was at the shop this afternoon to pick up his new costume was going to the ball in Farruco to meet the girl from the country that he was with on the feast day of San Rafael, and she intended to catch him in the act. The calculations of a jealous woman. Just as I reached the corner I saw a man go up to the window of the little house and speak with someone who was behind the curtain. That made me even more curious, and so as soon as the man moved away I went up to the window. . . . And who do you think I came across there? Chepilla. She asked me in. There had just been a fight there with no holds barred. It seems that Cecilia had dressed up to go out with me; and her grandmother, in the tussle to keep her from leaving the house, tore her gown and broke her Spanish comb. It all happened in no time."

"Poor girl!" the musician exclaimed sympathetically.

"Cecilia is as stubborn as a mule. When she has her mind set on doing something, that's that; so her grandmother saw a way out the minute I showed up. She can't cope with her granddaughter any more. So anyway, she had me come in to see if between the two of us we could keep Celia from going out."

"And did you succeed?" José Dolores asked, showing signs of interest.

"Of course," Nemesia said deliberately. "I knew where to attack her and I didn't miss the mark. Her grandmother didn't want Cecilia to go out; I didn't want her to either, and it so happened that that man from the San Francisco district who supports the two of them had forbidden

158

it. He was the one, as I found out later, who had been standing talking with Chepilla at the window before I came across her there."

"How are he and Cecilia related? I'd like to know."

"I really don't know. Sometimes it seems to me that he shows a great deal of concern for her if he's only courting her . . ."

"What if he's her father! *Seño* Uribe firmly believes that he is and maintains that her mother is still alive. Who knows? Who has ever seen her?"

"That's what I say too."

"There you are! The way I see it, both the father and the son are in love with Celia down to the end of every last hair on her head."

"That could be, sister, because there have been lots of cases like that in the world. She probably prefers the son . . ."

"That's understandable. Who wouldn't prefer the young one to the old one?"

"In the end Celia's beauty is going to be her undoing. What can she expect to get from those two whites? The old one may give her money, luxury, and attentions, but the young one . . . ? It's not possible for him to marry her; she can be thankful if he takes her as his mistress for a time; then he'll tire of her and leave her with two or three children on her hands when she least expects it. I don't know what will become of me if something like that happens. I don't want to think about it."

"She feels affection for him, but not love. I can see that very clearly. However, if I could make her forget Leonardo the main difficulty would be overcome."

"The woman who loves truly forgets long after or never."

"There are exceptions, and since Celia is very proud, it's not impossible that precisely because she loves deeply she may forget quickly. It's no more than a flea jump from love to hate."

"That's one last hope."

"I swear to you that it's going to be very hard for him to pull the wool over her eyes and mine. I know Celia's weak point better than he does and that gives me an advantage. Just a little while ago I told her something that enraged her. She's furious with the person in question. She'll get over her fit of temper, but I'll keep at it and I'm certain I'll make her leap over the obstacles. . . . Doing everything possible to separate her from him means bringing her closer to . . ."

José Dolores didn't let her finish the sentence. He smiled sadly, and telling his sister not to wait up for him, headed for the Calle del Aguacate. Nemesia went into her room, repeating as though she were speaking to another person:

"Well, I wasn't born yesterday! I won't always have to work for somebody else. If I don't have to, neither does she. He's head over heels in love and he's very fond of mulatto girls. The thing isn't as hard as it seems to be. Let's see if I can kill two birds with one stone. She can be for José Dolores and he can be for me. It's possible, it's possible . . ."

It behooves us to return now to the gala at the Philharmonic where we left Leonardo Gamboa in the lines of dancers with Isabel Ilincheta. Knowing her partner's character very well, she expressed no complaint about his lack of punctuality in writing her, nor about his apparent coldness; she spoke to him, on the contrary, about neutral subjects: about their mutual friends in the countryside; about happenings around Alquízar; about the red rosebud that he had grafted onto the white rose bush in the garden bordering the coffee plantation; about the orange tree in whose shadow, on past Christmas holidays, they had so often eaten the sweetest oranges grown on the estate; about the elder daughter of her father's overseer, who had run away with a young peasant from the town in order to marry him, as she did, in La Ceiba del Agua.

"Aunt Juana," Isabel added, "interceded with the father and obliged him to reconcile with his daughter. So today the bride and groom are in charge of Papa's farm, on which, as you know, poultry is raised and a few animals are fattened. The bride stayed with her husband, and her father, our overseer, had to leave. I felt sorry for his wife, because she was a good woman and used to accompany us on our outings quite often. But as soon as his daughter married, the father became terribly ill-tempered: he didn't let the blacks take time out to rest, he punished them for the least little fault, always with extreme cruelty, until Papa finally dismissed him. At present we're having a rather lonely time of it, and our outings on the plantation are limited to going to the farm every afternoon and coming back home at sunset. When there's a moon . . ."

"You remember me, don't you?" Leonardo interrupted her with injudicious peevishness on noting her icy indifference.

"Naturally," she replied, apparently without noticing the feelings that her companion was experiencing. "I can't forget that on glorious afternoons, like the ones in the wintertime in the countryside, we took that walk more than once in the company of Rosa and Aunt Juana."

"I find you somewhat changed," the young man observed after a brief silence.

"Me changed? Well, that's a good one. Come, you're joking."

"You even use the formal *Usted* when you address me."

"I believe I always have."

"Not at the foot of the tree that bears those sweet oranges."

Isabel blushed, and then said:

"It has always been a habit with me to address everyone as *Usted*. Even with my own slaves, especially if they're elderly, I unthinkingly use *Usted*. The same thing often happens to Papa."

"The informal *tú* is more affectionate."

"Do you think so? *Usted* is more modest."

This sparkling dialogue was interrupted at every step, that is to say, as many times as the couple proceeding in one direction executed a figure of the dance with the couple proceeding in the other direction. Finally, they were obliged to change the subject of their conversation altogether when Meneses and Solfa, who had been going around the ballroom greeting all their lady friends, arrived at the place in the line of dancers occupied by Isabel and Leonardo. Both Meneses and Solfa had seen that young lady that very afternoon at the home of the Gámez sisters. They had little that was new to say to each other. Isabel, however, spied Meneses, and was happy to see him again.

"What's this? You don't dance?" she asked him out of curiosity.

"I almost never dance just for politeness' sake."

"Oh! If Florencia heard you say that she'd be offended."

"Florencia pleases me, I find her pretty, I like her, but if I were to dance with her now it would be merely out of courtesy. My beloved friend is far away, as you know, and it is very cruel of you to attribute to me any intention of being attentive to another lady."

"I'm beginning to be frightened by your friend Solfa, I must say," she said, suddenly turning to the latter, with the twofold aim of being attentive to everyone and of not going on joking with Meneses.

"And what have I done to arouse the fear of the fearless Isabelita?"

"Don't you realize? That's a caricature of me."

"It would be, señorita," Solfa replied promptly, "if mine were an isolated opinion, but it is not. Leonardo and Diego share it, I am certain, as do all those who know you. How, then, can I arouse fear in you?"

"Because I can see that you are implacable, that you pardon neither your enemies nor your friends."

"That too? You're making my head swim, señorita."

"Yes, go ahead and play the innocent now, someone who wouldn't hurt a fly. As if ever since you appeared at the door of the ballroom I hadn't noticed that as you made your way toward me you made slyly cutting remarks about every lady who is a real beauty. I appeal to your friend Meneses: he'll tell me whether I'm wrong or not."

Solfa and Meneses exchanged a look and a smile, with which they implicitly corroborated Isabel's keen observation, and the former said:

"That's a different matter, I grant you. I do enjoy wielding a pair of shears, but the blades of mine fell apart in my hands when I got around to you."

Just then the dance ended, and some of the various pairs of dancers, breaking up the formation, hurried to their seats in the ballroom and adjoining rooms, while others hastened out into the corridors for a breath of fresh air. The men, for the most part, divided up into groups to talk about their amorous conquests of the evening, and nearly all of them to smoke a cigar or cigarette. Leonardo took a stroll along the corridors with his amiable dance partner, who, if we may judge from her frequent smiles, didn't mind at all that their conversation went on even though the delightful music had ended.

Continuing meanwhile the tour of the fiesta that they had planned, Meneses and Solfa for their part stopped for a short time in front of the mother and sisters of their friend and classmate Leonardo Gamboa. They were sitting on the north side of the ballroom, beneath the canopy where, as we have said, the colossal portrait in oils of Bourbon King Ferdinand VII was displayed. Antonia, the oldest sister, had at her right an army captain in full dress uniform, with whom she was exchanging brief observations in a low voice; next came her mother, and to her right, her two sisters Carmen and Adela. Field Marshal Don José Cadaval was talking with the first of these three ladies; the other two were conversing with the most renowned dandies of Havana in those days: Juanito Junco and Pepe Montalvo, a cadet in the city's standing regiment. Leonardo Gamboa appeared shortly thereafter, and the Spanish captain disappeared from Antonia's side as if by magic, having received a suggestive nudge of her elbow; Cadaval went on his way, and the man-about-town and the cadet did likewise after taking their leave with a deep bow.

On spying from a distance the Spanish army officer in the company of his sister, Leonardo was reminded of the scenes that had taken place that morning, just outside the shutter of the window first, and then later on at the lunch table, feeling the same fit of jealousy and hatred come over him as the one he had previously experienced. All his desire to see and speak for a time with his mother and sisters at the ball turned cold and was dispelled instantly, and it was his respect and affection for his mother that caused him not to turned his back on them. At a gesture from him, Antonia moved over to the chair that had been left vacant by the captain, and Leonardo could thus sit down and say in Doña Rosa's ear:

"Is it possible, Mama, that you would allow that soldier to court Antonia in your presence?"

"Hold your tongue!" Doña Rosa replied sternly. "That gentleman came to bring us a message from your father, who is unable to come fetch us until one o'clock and I believe that you will thus be obliged to see us home. This eventuality makes me happy for two reasons: the first, because I can leave whenever I wish or whenever I begin to feel sleepy; the second, because you won't remain behind here and thereby cause me to spend another sleepless night."

"I must see Isabel Ilincheta and the Gámez sisters home, because their carriage has broken down and they weren't able to use it tonight."

"What! Isabel is here and hasn't come over to say hello to us?"

"Don't be surprised at that, because no doubt she was not aware that all of you had come to the ball; moreover, this has been an unusually large gathering."

"Well then, send your friends home in your gig."

"Before I do, however, all of you must see Isabel, or Isabel must come say hello to you."

"Have you fallen in love with her? You're as changeable as a weather vane. Don't even think of seducing that girl too. Bring her over and we'll see her."

"No. I thought we should have some supper and we'll all meet at the table. Everyone says that the buffet is as lavish as it is exquisite. What do you think, Adela?"

"I approve," she answered happily.

"But the thing is," Leonardo said, "that if one or another of you doesn't get me out of the fix I'm in, I won't have enough money to pay for supper."

"What about the two doubloons I put in your waistcoat this afternoon while you were napping?" Doña Rosa asked gravely.

"I didn't see any such sum, Mama. But if you put it in the pocket of the waistcoat I was wearing this morning, it's still in my room. I have barely three or four pesos in this waistcoat that I put on when I came in from my walk so as to come to the ball."

Leonardo did not offer this explanation with his usual forthrightness; he flushed and stammered several times. His mother noticed and asked him:

"Why did you appear at the ball at such a late hour? I thought you weren't coming, even though you left the house before we did. Heaven only knows where you've been."

"There was a small gathering and a pianist at the Gámez's today be-cause it's Florencia's saint's day."

"They didn't come with you, as far as I know. You're not telling the truth, Leonardo, I know that and I'm telling you in all truth that you're acting badly, very badly. I'm your best friend, son, and I'm distressed to see that with each passing day you're less frank with me. Let's go have supper," she added, quite upset. "I'll pay for everyone and here is my purse; it has some six doubloons in it."

The purse was of red silk, sewn with a knot or a loop in the middle, forming two separate compartments so as to divide the gold pieces from the silver ones and the small change. She took it out of the bosom of her gown, for ladies in that era did not have pockets in their skirts as they do today, but hung their purses from the belt or sash of their dress when they were at home. Leonardo took the money with his cheeks on fire from shame, because the humiliation of receiving twice the sum that he had lost at the gaming table was compounded by the lies with which he had endeavored to conceal his misdeed. His mother, perhaps unintentionally, and unknowingly as well, had seen into the depths of his soul as through a pane of glass. Did that serve her as a corrective? It is not yet time to examine the matter. But that incident was of grave import only for the mother and her son, though not in all its true depravity, to be sure, for the former, since it can be said that she had put her finger on the sore spot without being aware that she had. It took great effort on Leonardo's part to recover from the shock he had had; as soon as he rose to his feet and took his mother's arm to escort her to the buffet supper, he said to her:

"And where has Papa been?"

"At the home of Don Joaquín Gómez, where several plantation owners have gathered; among them Samá, Martiartu, Mañero, Suárez Argudín, Lombillo, Laza . . ."

"Does anyone know what the object of such a meeting is?"

"Captain Miranda was unable to explain it, doubtless because he himself doesn't know; but from the little that your father told me when he left the house, I gather that they're going to discuss the sending of ships to the coast of Africa. Vives is weary of Tolmé's complaints of the insolence of the judges on the accursed Mixed Commission and has sent word to Gómez in secret to have them try not to have the shipments of blacks unloaded in the vicinity of Havana. A special courier also arrived from El Mariel, with the news that a brig that looks like the *Veloz*, which they were expecting with a good load aboard, has been sighted, with an English vessel in close pursuit."

"Perhaps it captured the *Veloz*."

"In sight of the fortified tower at El Mariel? That would be too daring. Nonetheless, those Protestant Englishmen fancy that the whole world belongs to them, and it wouldn't surprise me if they had. If the shipment is lost, your father loses a huge amount of money. It's the first shipment that he's invested in with his friends from here as partners because it's such a costly venture. At least the *Veloz* is bringing five hundred blacks."

"Who gets Papa involved in such taxing affairs at the end of his days?"

"Ah, son! Would you enjoy so much luxury or so many conveniences if your father stopped working? Planks and roof tiles don't make anybody rich. What undertaking brings in more profits that the slave trade? Had those vainglorious Englishmen not taken to capturing slave ships as they're doing these days, out of sheer wickedness that is to say, since they have very few slaves and will have fewer and fewer, there would be no better or more enticing business to go into."

"Agreed, but the risks are so great that they take away any desire to take part in such a venture."

"Risks? They aren't very great compared to the profits to be made. The total cost of the *Veloz* venture, for example, was no more than 30,000 pesos, and since there are several people in on it, the quota your father put up was only a few thousand pesos. So then, if it arrives safely, how much will his share be worth? . . . Figure it out. But here's Isabel."

Doña Rosa received her with open arms; and except for Antonia, Leonardo's sisters welcomed her with sincere demonstrations of affection; Adela in particular embraced her and kissed her again and again. Adela was the youngest of the sisters, enthusiastic and forthright, and Isabel was her beloved brother's favorite. After the usual greetings and mutual complaints, all of them, and the Gámez sisters as well, with Leonardo, Meneses, and Solfa each with a lady on either arm, went into the supper room, splendidly lighted, at the far end of the mansion. There were many people and there was not enough room for them at a single table, and therefore they were obliged to occupy two, though they had been placed immediately next to each other.

The ladies and gentlemen supped on breast of turkey stew, cold slices of the same bird, and delicious Westphalian ham; some partook of rice and black beans; none of them drank wine or spirits, but all had coffee with milk to end the meal. At the usual price of such dishes ordered at similar functions, Leonardo calculated that the supper would cost at least a doubloon and a half, or twenty-five and a half *medios duros*. Eager to show off the money he had, he took the red silk purse out of his pocket and with boundless aplomb asked the young white waiter who had served both tables:

"How much do I owe?"

"Nothing," the lad answered with the same paucity of words, as he built on his left arm a porcelain tower out of the plates and cups.

"How can that be?" Leonardo asked in surprise. "Who paid in my place then?"

"Everyone knows that you're not a member of the board of directors," the waiter answered quite impertinently. "The society pays for tonight's buffet supper, and if I were like many others, I'd show you to the best seat."

"I see!" Leonardo exclaimed, deeply embarrassed and not a little mortified.

As he rose from the table he murmured:

"Those Spanish lads are sometimes too impertinent."

Whether the young waiter heard him or not is something we do not know, although from the sidelong glance he cast at Leonardo, it would appear that the words "Spaniard" and "impertinent" echoed in his ears. Florencia Gámez and Adela were eager to take part in the next dance; the latter even said as much to her brother; but he smiled absentmindedly and didn't say a word in reply.

Meanwhile Doña Rosa told the "children," as she addressed them, to go to the cloakroom to retrieve their silk shawls. At the same time the three young men went down to the mezzanine to reclaim their respective hats and canes; but here, as in the cloakroom, there were already many others ahead of them asking for their belongings, so that it took some time before our acquaintances obtained theirs. Then Leonardo went down to the entrance to tell his carriage driver to be ready to leave.

The youngest of the señoritas took advantage of this interlude to go to the places where the last dance was about to begin, reputed to be the one that the musicians accompany best. There was no lack of men to invite them to dance, and to the sound of a march they began to dance with more delight than ever, as Doña Rosa, Isabel, Antonia, Señora Gámez, and the eldest of her daughters sat down together to wait until it was time to leave.

It was past one in the morning. When Leonardo descended the stone staircase of the Philharmonic mansion, the first thing that assailed his ears was the jingle of the silver spurs of the carriage drivers on the resounding stones of the entrance, doing the heel-and-toe dance to the sound of a Cuban treble guitar. One of them played as two of them danced, one taking the part of the woman dancer; the others either clapped their hands or tapped the hard flagstones with the silver handles of their whips, never missing a beat or interjecting the slightest discordant sound. Some of them sang country ballads, thereby revealing, as they did by their dancing and guitar playing, that all of them were native Cubans.

Even here there were many who had hastened to leave the ball before the crowd; and the names of the most distinguished families of Havana were passed on from one carriage driver to another, like echoes on a staircase: "Montalvo!" a voice would shout and 20 others would repeat in succession, until it faded away in the distance or the call was answered by the approach of the Montalvo carriage; whereupon there were a number of collisions, not a few altercations between the slaves, more than one blow of the staff of his lance delivered by the dragoon who was keeping order in the street, all of this accompanied by the whistle of whips, the sound of carriage wheels, like distant claps of thunder, and the hoofbeats of the horses on the smooth cobblestones. In the midst of all that din, the carriage drivers kept shouting out the names of the families to whom they belonged: Peñalver! Cárdenas! O'Farrill! Fernandina! Arcos! Calvo! Cadaval! repeated as many times as necessary for word to reach the driver being sought, who, after all, if he wasn't at the head of the line that went all the way around the block, had to wait until his turn came to move his carriage into place if he didn't want the dragoon on duty to give him a good thrashing with the staff of his lance.

The moment the name Gamboa was shouted out, the heel-and-toe dancing stopped, because the one playing the high-pitched treble guitar was none other than our old acquaintance Aponte. The downcast slave was apparently really enjoying himself, or else he was skillfully plucking the strings of his instrument for his own distraction and that of his comrades, because two terrible threats were weighing heavily on his not at all obtuse spirit: that of his mistress in the afternoon and that of his young master at 10:30 that night; and he knew, to his great sorrow, that they did not forget or forgive the misdeeds of their slaves. But if that was his lot and there was no help for it, why get worried or upset in advance? That was the way he saw things, and more or less the way all his comrades did too, for God, in his blessed mercy, had not deprived them of a soul that could think.

Once the meeting of plantation owners was over, Don Joaquín Gómez placed his carriage at Don Cándido's disposal to return home, and he did so shortly after midnight, thus enabling him to send his carriage to the Philharmonic to take his family home when they were ready to leave. Thanks to that unexpected help, the Gámezes and their friend

Isabel were able to be driven from the ball to their residence behind the convent of Santa Teresa, and the Gamboa family back to their home immediately thereafter, all in one trip.

The carriage drivers left their respective vehicles inside the *zaguán*, took the horses to the stable in the back courtyard, placed the saddles on their sawhorses, hung up the horses' harnesses and their own livery and hats on nails in the wall in their dingy quarters; and as for Aponte, once he had finished work, with his wooden sleeping platform on his back, like Christ carrying the Cross, he returned to the *zaguán* to try to rest after the fatigue of the day, sleeping the few remaining hours until daylight. A little while before, the clock of the parish church of Espíritu Santo had struck two. The waning moon was setting behind the roof of the house on the street side; the shadow it cast had now reached the adobe wall that divided the two courtyards, so that the one in front lay in darkness, although it was not too dark to see vague shapes or recognize faces. All of a sudden a man blocked Aponte's path; the latter raised his eyes and saw that he was brandishing a whip in his right hand. Aponte halted at once, for he recognized his master, young Gamboa.

"Put the platform down," Gamboa ordered him in a voice hoarse with rage, "and then kneel down and take off your shirt."

"Master, is your grace going to punish me?" the slave said in distress, carrying out step by step what he had been ordered to do.

"Come on, hurry it up," his young master added as he dealt him the first lash to hasten matters.

"Wait, your grace, master. What did I do wrong?"

"Ah! You dog! You're asking me? Didn't I tell you that I was going to punish you because you didn't wait for me as I ordered you to, at the corner of the convent?"

"Yes, señor, young master; but it wasn't my fault."

"Well then, whose fault was it? I'll prove to you that when I order you to do something you'll do it or die."

And without further ado the whiplashes began to rain down on the bare back of the hapless slave. He writhed in pain, for a strong arm was administering the lashing, and said: "All right, my master" (meaning "enough"). "In the name of mistress Adela, master. In the name of the Señorita (as the servants called Doña Rosa Sandoval de Gamboa), my little master. If I could tell the truth, young master, your grace would see that it wasn't my fault. It's all right now, master Leonardito."

But that mouth had fallen silent, overcome by anger; that heart had turned to stone; that soul could no longer feel; that arm alone seemed animated, made of iron, tirelessly raining down blows. Tirelessly! They fell more frequently and more furiously, if not more forcefully. Don Cándido had already fallen asleep when the cracks of the whip and the moans of the carriage driver woke him with a start.

"What's that?" he asked his wife fearfully.

"Nothing; it's Leonardo punishing Aponte."

"How scandalous! Is this any time of the night to be punishing the servants? Tell that boy possessed by the devil to stay his hand, or I swear to God . . ."

"Come back to bed and go back to sleep," his wife said. "Aponte's very stubborn and needs a good lashing."

"Yes, but I'm sure that this time he hasn't done anything wrong. Look: someone has played a dirty trick on your son and now it's the poor mulatto who's paying for it."

"You don't know what he did to the girls in the Calle de la Muralla this afternoon."

"That may be, but if that boy doesn't stay his hand with Aponte I'll get up and break one of his ribs as sure as my name is Cándido. Who ever saw anything more shameless?"

Doña Rosa saw clearly that if the hiding and Aponte's screams and protests of innocence went on, Don Cándido was going to get up out of bed and do something characteristically harsh and severe, for in addition to the natural coarseness of a man with no manners he had a violent disposition. So she peeked through the shutter of the window and said: "Leonardo, that's enough."

That was sufficient. By now, moreover, the young man had either given vent to his uncontrollable anger or else his strength had given out.

After that, which of the two, the victim or the victimizer, first found rest? Or rather: What went through the soul of the master when he tumbled into bed? What through the soul of the slave when he collapsed on his hard sleeping platform? It is hard for those who have been neither victim nor victimizer to explain it, and impossible for those who have never lived in a slave country to understand it in all its power.

V I

"Greetings from the brig!"
"What say you? What's your name?"
"El Condenado."
"Where do you hail from?"
"Sarrapatán."
"What cargo are you carrying?"
"Empty sacks."
"Who's your captain?"
"Don Guindo Cerezo."

Escenas a la vista del Morro de la Habana[33]

As can be imagined, at nine o'clock on the morning of the day after the ball at the Philharmonic, everyone in the Gamboa household was sleeping, with two exceptions. We are speaking here of the world of the masters, among whose number the eight or nine servants of the family were not included, for once day had dawned they had to be up and about, fulfilling their daily tasks, no matter how they had spent the night.

Don Cándido, despite having slept only a little and despite the grave thoughts that weighed on his mind because of what had taken place at the meeting at the home of Don Joaquín Gómez, arose early and left home on foot, out of the sheer impatience characteristic of him.

A little later, nestled in one of the armchairs in the dining room, his wife was drinking coffee with milk.

It was not without a purpose that Doña Rosa sat in that spot each morning. From there it was possible to check the inside of the house and see at an early hour in the morning whether the washerwomen were preparing the bleach for the laundry or the brazier with hot coal embers for the ironing; whether the seamstresses, instead of getting to work sewing the clothes for the slaves, were wasting their time chatting with the other servants; whether the drivers were washing the carriages and greasing and cleaning the horses' harnesses; whether Aponte had come back early or late from bathing the horses, thus proving whether he had gone to the pier at Luz or the one at La Punta, farther away; whether Pío, Gamboa's elderly driver, was in the *zaguán* making women's shoes for the house servants and sometimes even for the mistresses of the house, while also serving as the doorkeeper when he didn't have to fetch the carriage and drive his master; finally, whether the cook, a black with an aristocratic manner, well-spoken and rational, as slave dealers were in the habit of saying, had gone at daybreak to the nearby market in the Plaza Vieja, to pick up the vegetables and other provisions that he had been told to buy the night before.

The cook was the one in the household who got up earliest. He had to make the fire and prepare the coffee, so that Tirso and Dolores could serve it the moment their masters awoke. The cook did not always finish the marketing at the same hour, or in a short time, even though the Plaza Vieja was only a short distance away from the Gamboas' house. On the morning that we are speaking of now, for example, he had left for the market too early. But as he headed in that direction with a little lantern in one hand, as had been required by the municipal ordinances since the days of Someruelos[34] and a large market basket in the other, the cannon shot signaling four in the morning rang out, the keeper of the keys opened the gates in the wall, and the dead silence of the city was succeeded by the tumult of the day's traffic beginning and all sorts of sounds as dissonant as they were disagreeable.

On his return from the market there was always a settling of accounts between the cook and his mistress, scoldings and threats of punishment because of the price he'd paid for the various cuts of meat, their quality, and even their weight; because instead of pullets he had brought back hens; and as for the vegetables, because he had brought back peas instead of beans, and watercress rather than lettuce, or vice versa. For being a slave means never managing to please one's masters. Doña Rosa, in short, always had some reason for complaint, and her cook often fell short of the mark out of stupidity, out of slyness, or out of carelessness.

"Dionisio, didn't I tell you to buy tender pullets?" she said, taking from the market basket the pair of birds tied tightly together by the feet. "Why have you brought me hens? Your master eats only pullets."

"They're young hens, señorita," the cook answered; the thing is that they're fat, so they look like full-grown hens. Besides, there are no pullets to be found at the market."

"I don't want to hear any tall tales like that from you, Dionisio; I'm not stupid and I wasn't born yesterday. If you know a lot, I know even more. Tell me, how much did you pay for them?"

"Two pesos, señorita. Poultry costs a good deal nowadays."

"Hail Mary Immaculate! I'll wager you bought them from that black woman who came over on the same slave ship as you, that Lucumí poultry vendor who charges more than any of the others in the Plaza. Am I right?"

"No, señorita, I bought them from a vendor from the country. Have a good look at them, your grace; their feathers still have red dirt on them."

"That's no proof, Dionisio, because your Lucumí crony could well have left the dirt on them so as to pass them off as being fresh from the country rather than ones being sold at second hand."

"Señorita, the black poultry vendor isn't my crony and I was never aboard a ship with her. She's from Africa."

"I know what I'm saying, Dionisio, and don't you correct me. If you have a law degree, I know where they straighten out doctors-at-law like you. Over at the Arsenal, and at El Vedado.* A course in law doesn't cost anything in those places. Do you understand? So watch your step,

---

*In the artillery arsenal of Havana, situated behind the headquarters of the Quartermaster Corps, there was a sort of house of correction, whose overseer, a ranking sergeant of the Corps, took charge of punishing the slave who, having committed a misdeed, was handed over to him for this purpose. He was whipped more or less severely, according to a written order, which the victim himself sometimes brought with him, always depending upon, or in exchange for, the work he could do in the Arsenal for a period of two or three weeks. He was paid by the government out of the Public Treasury, although it was not specified in the written order that this sum depended on the number of lashes received. The same thing occurred at El Vedado, land belonging to the Frías family, which because of its aridity, was used exclusively for the extraction of stones and lime for the construction of houses. There too by order of his master the slave being punished was flogged in exchange for the work he performed. *Author's note.*

Uncle Dionisio. What I don't want is for you to have yourself a feast or to give your cronies one with my money."

Silence is golden, and from painful experience gained from 30 long years of slavery, Dionisio knew very well that he shouldn't say a word from the moment that his masters began to use the formal *Usted* to address him. That was a sure sign that the tide of their wrath was rising. The storm was approaching and soon there would be bolts of lightning. Therefore the cook gathered up posthaste the poultry to be served at lunch and took refuge in his kitchen, like a good pilot who seeks temporary shelter at the first port that heaven provides.

This slave had been born and raised in Jaruco, in the mansion of the count and countess of that title. He knew how to read and write almost by intuition, acquired gifts that invested him with extraordinary merit in the eyes of his fellow slaves, in general much more ignorant than he in this regard. He was extremely fond of dancing, and was a fine minuet dancer, an art he had learned at the sumptuous feasts given by his master and mistress, for as a page, the first post he was given, he was always in contact with them; it was in that household that he met the future Countess of Merlín, a number of Captains General, the first Count of Barreto, and other notables of Cuba, as well as of Spain and other foreign countries: Louis Philippe of Orléans, for instance, who later became the King of France.

By virtue of time, industriousness, and thrift, of living among rich and generous people visited by illustrious personages, Dionisio succeeded in saving enough money to obtain his conditional manumission or *coartación*, that is to say, to fix the price at which he would be sold, if he were sold, by giving 18 doubloons, or 306 *duros*, to his master. He was put up for auction along with several other slaves, however, before the notary public Don José Salinas, following the death of the count, to help cover the great expenses occasioned by the legal proceedings to probate the latter's will and divide the inheritance he left. Dionisio's skill as a chef and a confectioner, jobs to which he had been assigned as soon as he reached manhood, gave him a higher market value than that of the other slaves who did not have a métier; consequently his *coartación* benefited him only insofar as the price for him was set at 500 pesos, instead of the 800 that his master had deemed him to be worth when he accepted the previously mentioned sum from him. In the *lote* or auction, Don Cándido bought him for less than the 500 pesos set as the price for him, although he was not the highest bidder; but he knew how to grease the palm of the notary in charge at the right time, and the higher bids went unrecorded. Dionisio suffered from two serious shortcomings, serious because of his sad condition as a black slave: the first was his fondness for women; the other, as we have said, was his fondness for dances deemed appropriate only for whites.

After the clock had struck nine that morning, Don Cándido Gamboa came in through the *zaguán* of his house. He looked dejected and tired and was drenched in sweat, not on account of the heat, which could still be felt even though it was now the end of October, but on account of his agitation during the hours before dawn that day and the thoughts that were occupying his mind. Paying no attention to his wife, who was worriedly standing waiting for him next to the dining room table, already set for lunch by the agile Tirso, he went straight from the street to the study, where the steward, Don Melitón Reventos, was sitting on top of his stool, with his pen behind his ear and his elbows leaning on the desk, reflecting on a sheet of Spanish paper in front of him, written in lines of varying length, like *arte mayor* verses.[35]

"What are you doing?" Don Cándido asked him as he came into the room without bidding him good day, perhaps because the present one had been one of the worst of his life.

"I was making the entry in the account book for the equipment that the overseer of La Tinaja is ordering for the next sugar milling, and looking to see if I'd missed anything. Sierra the slave master was here and said that he was going out to . . ."

"Never mind that, because it's not pressing, and let's get down to what really matters. Reventos, put on your jacket this minute and go as fast as your legs can carry you to Suárez Argudín's secondhand shop in the Rosario Arcade, and pick up as many striped shirts and heavy canvas trousers as he has on hand and tell him to charge them to my account. He's not likely to have as many as are needed, 400 outfits; but he can meet that number at the other secondhand shops owned by Spaniards. But if even that way all 400 can't be gotten, have him pick up 300, 250, 200 for me, as many as he can find . . . What else can we do? If we don't save that many, we'll save some."

"Some what?" Reventos asked, too curious to leave his question for later.

"Bundles, man, bundles," Don Cándido replied concisely. "Don't you know that the *Veloz* has come in?"

"It has? I swear I didn't know that."

"Well, it's arrived, or rather, they've brought it in to port. The exact number on board isn't yet known. The hatchways are nailed down, and Captain Carricarte says that, even though he took on 500, what with the long voyage and the terrible chase the English gave them, a number of them have died and had to be thrown overboard . . . lots of them, fortunately the dregs of the lot, in a word. Are you following me? Well then, take the clothes, make three or four bundles of them, depending; take them in a handcart to the Caballería pier, opposite Casa Blanca, and give them to the captain of the *Flor de Regla*, the harbor boat. You know him. Hand everything over to him, for he's already been notified and knows where all that is to be taken. Go with him, since you know the bookkeeper. So get to work! Your lunch will be kept for you if you're not back in time. In any event, the clothes must be on board before 11, you hear?"

Once the steward left, Doña Rosa entered the study at once. Her husband was nervously pacing back and forth; but on seeing her he stopped for a moment awaiting her question, which in fact she immediately asked him: "What's going on, Gamboa? Reventos has gone off at breakneck speed and here you are, all upset. Tell me, what in heaven's name is happening?"

"The same thing as usual, my girl; if we go on this way, those English rogues will be the ruin of this beautiful flower of His Catholic Majesty, our King, may God save him."

"You don't say!"

"It's just as you heard, because if the English don't allow us to import the labor that we're so very badly in need of, I don't know with what or how we're going to mill the sugar. Yes, the devil is winning, as I never tire of saying."

"That's what I keep saying too, Cándido; but let's get to the point."

"The point is this. This morning at seven El Morro signaled that there was an English vessel to leeward. Several of us were at the pier: Gómez, Azopardo, Samá, in a word all those who were at last night's meeting. Shortly thereafter El Morro signaled a captured vessel and half an hour later the English corvette *Perla** appeared at the mouth of the harbor, under the command of Lord Pege or Pegete, according to what we were told later by those who heard from La Punta the answer given by the pilot to the signal tower. What vessel do you think they'd captured?"

"The *Veloz*?"

"That's right, Rosa; with almost all the cargo aboard."

"Then the cargo was saved. What good news!"

"Saved?" don Cándido repeated bitterly. "Would to God it had been. Seeing that our fine brig is coming in as a prize . . ."

---

*His Britannic Majesty's sloop of war *Pearl*, Captain Lord Clarence Paget. *Author's note.*

"So both the brig and the cargo are lost, is that it? That would be a grave misfortune!"

"It won't be a matter of everything being lost if those of us who are interested in saving both the vessel and the cargo stay on the alert. For the moment, the steps that have been taken and will be taken later on make us harbor the hope that we can manage to wrest, if not all the bundles, at least two-thirds of them, from the clutches of the English. Can you believe, Rosa, that I sometimes image that the loss of the brig would be more painful to me than the loss of the cargo, even though it's the most valuable of all the ones that the *Veloz* has brought over from Africa, according to Captain Carricarte's bill of lading. Let there be no doubt in your mind. My brig can carry safely and in a short time not just one but several cargoes, and there aren't many like it. It's been about three years since I bought it from Didier, who's from Baltimore, and it's already made four successful voyages to Africa. This was its fifth, and it's already paid me back what it cost me. It's amazing, Rosa; it left Casa Blanca—do you remember?—in the middle of July and in less than four months it's back. That's what's called swift sailing. Who will deny now that it's the fastest vessel of all the ones that are being used on that run at present? There's Zuasnávar's *Feliz*, Abarzusa's *Vencedora*, Mártinez's *Venus*, Carballo's *Nueva Amable*, Gómez's *Veterana*, and many others that are famous. What are they by comparison to my *Veloz*? Slow, clumsy hulks. I'd deeply regret losing it; not on account of the money, though the 10,000 pesos I gave for it aren't chicken feed, but because it would be hard to build a faster ship."

"Ah, Cándido! Don't indulge in wishful thinking. You and your friends harbor hopes; I don't. When the English capture a ship, they don't let go of it, you can be sure of that. As time goes by, those Jewish Protestants seem more and more odious to me. Tell me, what makes them meddle in something that's of no concern of theirs? I rack my brains and still can't understand why England should be opposed to our bringing savages here from Guinea. Why isn't it also opposed to our bringing olive oil, raisins, and wine from Spain then? Why doesn't it consider it more humanitarian to import slaves so as to turn them into Christians and men, rather than wines and other things that only serve to satisfy people's greed and cater to their vices?"

"Rosa, the enemies of our prosperity, that is to say the English, don't understand that philosophy, nor do they want to understand it; otherwise they would have to show more consideration for us vassals of a friendly nation that earlier on was one of their allies. But I don't hold them entirely to blame; the ones I blame for the most part are those who advised our august sovereign Don Fernando VII to sign the treaty of 1817 with England.[36] That's where the evil lies. For £500,000 sterling the unwise counselors of the best of monarchs granted perfidious Albion the right to inspect our merchant ships on the high seas and to insult, as it still insults with impunity day after day, the sacred flag of the nation that not long ago was mistress of the seas and owner of two worlds. How shameful! I don't know how we tolerate . . . But to come to the point, Rosa. Since the purpose of Gómez's sudden summons of us at dusk yesterday was for us to hear the story of what had happened to the *Veloz* from Captain Carricarte himself, who reluctantly came from El Mariel to join us and see what could be done if it proved to be possible to steal a march on the English; since as you know the saying goes that the law was made to be broken. When I arrived at Gómez's, at around eight o'clock . . ."

"What's that you say?" his wife interrupted him. "You left here before seven. What took you so long? How come it took you an hour to go to Gómez's?"

"I didn't tarry anywhere along the way, I assure you," her husband replied, visibly embarrassed. "Did I say that it must have been around eight? Well, mind you that I meant to say shortly after seven, seven-fifteen, seven-thirty . . . The exact hour doesn't matter."

It didn't seem to be of any importance, but it did not fail to attract Doña Rosa's attention that it should take her husband an hour to go by carriage from the corner of the Calle de San Ignacio and Luz, where they lived, to the far end of the Calle de Cuba, to the north, where the meeting was held, when this distance can be covered in half that time on foot, even at a leisurely pace. It was only to be expected that Doña Rosa, who apparently had her doubts as to her husband's marital fidelity, should fall silent, it is true, but quite obviously she had lost her enthusiasm, and along with it her interest, in any plans that were afoot to save the captured vessel and its cargo. Noting this, Don Cándido, who knew his wife very well indeed, smote his forehead with the palm of his hand and said:

"Ah, now I remember! I took a long time because I had to go see if Madrazo, who lives across the street from Santa Catalina, was one of the men who had been notified of the meeting or not. Captain Miranda can tell you what time it was when I arrived at Gómez's. That was the only stop I made on the way. Pío can bear witness to that too. Let's get to the crux of the matter now. As I was saying, when I arrived at Gómez's house, which as you know is a long way away, opposite the city wall, I found all the men already gathered together. Madrazo was with me, and

Mañero arrived later on. Samá, Martiartu, Abrisqueta, Suárez Argudín, and La Hera, Lombillo's nephew, because his uncle had left in a rush for La Tentativa, his coffee plantation at La Puerta de la Güira, Martínez, Carballo, Azopardo were there, along with several others who, though not directly involved in the matter of the cargo aboard the *Veloz*, as large-scale importers of slaves, wanted to be thoroughly informed about what had happened in El Mariel and how we were planning to get out of the fix we were in. Carrricarte changed clothes on the mezzanine of Gómez's residence, and came downstairs as soon as all of us had arrived. We formed a regular court in the downstairs drawing room. The captain laid some papers down on the table in the middle of the room, and then, without further ado, began his account of what had happened to him from the time he left the shores of Africa until his arrival in our Island. He says that as soon as he left Gallinas, at the end of September, he sailed close to the wind and with favorable seas until he sighted Puerto Rico. There, however, a suspicious-looking sail to leeward made him change course. During the night, with the wind still fresh, he got back on course, hoping to sight the Pan de Matanzas on the afternoon of the following day. Toward nightfall, he did in fact sight it; but the same sail as before appeared in the narrowest stretch of the Bahama channel and the chase began immediately. Carricarte says that his first thought was to make port at Arcos de Canasí. It wasn't possible: the English cruiser, for that is what it turned out to be, was headed on a straight course to Cuba and was closer inshore to it; despite the fair speed of the brig, the cruiser kept right at its side, particularly as the two vessels drew even with the Tetas de Camarioca. Night fell; the *Veloz* headed for the open sea and then veered landward with the intention of putting in at Cojímar, Jaimanitas, Banes, El Mariel, Cabañas, in other words at the first harbor at which it found itself at daybreak. The wind slackened, but unfortunately the wind blowing from landward was contrary, so that when he turned to catch sight of land the sun was already up and the cruiser threatened to overtake him to windward. Carricarte then saw that he could escape only by a miracle, so he decided to gamble everything. He gave the order, then, to clear the deck, so as to make the maneuver easier and lighten the ship as much as he could, and it was no sooner said than done. In no time at all the barrels of water in reserve, a good bit of rigging and the bundles lying on deck . . ."

"The slaves from Africa, you mean? How horrible!" Doña Rosa exclaimed, raising both hands to her head.

"Well, it's obvious," Gamboa continued imperturbably. "Can't you see that by saving 80 or 100 bundles the captain would have put his own freedom at risk, as well as that of his crew, and that of the remainder of the cargo, which was three times greater in number? He proceeded according to his instructions: to save the vessel and the papers at any cost. What's more, he had to clear the deck and lighten the ship, as I've told you. There was no time to be lost. What else could he do! Carricarte himself says so, and I believe him, because he's a thoroughly honest young man, who at the time of the greatest danger put on deck only the ones who were very sick, the weakest, those who in any event would die much sooner if he sent them back down to the orlop deck just above the hull were they were packed in like sardines, because the hatches had to be battened down."

"The hatches!" Doña Rosa repeated. "That is to say the covers over the hold. So those down below at that time suffocated to death. Poor things!"

"Nonsense!" Don Cándido said with consummate scorn. "Not at all, woman. If I believe you rightly, you imagine that those sacks of coal feel and suffer as we do. That's not true at all. Come, tell me, how do they live there in their own land? In caves or swamps. And what air is there to breathe in such places? None at all, or else it's pestilential air. And do you know how they're shipped here? All thrown in together, that is to say, sitting one inside the outstretched legs of the next, in two separate rows, so as to leave a passageway down the middle for the crew to be able to hand out their food and water to them. And they don't die from that. Almost all of them have to be shackled, and a few of them have to be put in the stocks."

"What are stocks, Cándido?"

"Well! What a question to ask at lunch time! The pillory, woman."

"I just wanted to know."

"All that and a great deal more gives rise to the arbitrary harrying of us by the English. Carricarte's only regret now is that in their anxiety and their haste to clear the deck, the crew threw overboard a black 12 years old, a very amusing youngster, who could already say words in Spanish and who was handed over to him by the king of Gotto in exchange for a barrel of Vich sausages and two youngsters seven to eight years old given him by the queen of the place in exchange for a loaf of sugar and a canister of tea for her personal table."

"God's angels!" Doña Rosa exclaimed again to contain herself. And reflecting that perhaps they were not baptized, she added: "In any case, those souls . . ."

"Enough of your belief that bundles from Africa have a soul and are angels. Those are blasphemies, Rosa," her husband interrupted her abruptly. "For that's what the error of certain people stems from. . . . When the world is persuaded that blacks are animals and not men, one of the reasons that the English put forth to put a stop to the African slave trade will cease to be heard. Something similar is happening in Spain with tobacco: trade in it is forbidden, and when they find themselves closely pursued by the revenue officers the smugglers who live on it leave their contraband behind and save their skin and their horse. Do you think that tobacco has a soul? Keep in mind that there is no difference between a bale of tobacco and a black, at least when it comes to having feelings."

There was no similarity whatsoever between the two examples he had cited, nor any time for discussion, because at that moment Tirso appeared at the door of the study and said that lunch was ready. It was 10:30 in the morning, and therefore it was plain to see that Don Cándido's conversation with his wife had gone on for a long time; however, he had not told her the means he intended to use to wrest the *Veloz* and the greater part of its cargo, made up of human beings, no matter what he might call them, from the clutches of the pigheaded English.

V I I

Therefore in appropriate cases
magistrates should modify the greed of
those traders which has introduced into
Europe, and no less into these Indies,
abundant work for slaves, to such a
degree that they live off taking them
from their native lands, either by
trickery or by force, like hunters chasing
hares or partridges, and carrying them
back and forth from one port to another
like Dutch linen or jersey.

Fr. Alonso de Sandoval

Don Cándido Gamboa had been pacing back and forth in his study for quite some time after the tablecloth had been removed following lunch, when his steward, Don Melitón Reventos, came into the room, his face the color of a red-hot ember from the heat of the day, from rushing about since early that morning, and from the obvious self-satisfaction that he felt. Therefore when he noticed him, his master stopped pacing back and forth, took the cigar out of his mouth and leaned his back against the desk so as to listen at his ease to Reventos's account of the errands he had run at the secondhand stores and the port. Even Doña Rosa, whose interest in the subject was second only to her husband's, came to the study eagerly, and the following scene took place between the three persons.

Don Melitón was in no hurry to fully relieve the anxiety of his master and mistress. He believed, on the contrary, that he had just overcome a great difficulty and performed a heroic deed; and being a man of scant common sense, he assumed an air of importance that he had done nothing to deserve. After going all around the study picking up papers, straightening the goose quills in the inkwell, and opening and closing desk drawers, he turned to Don Cándido and his wife, who were watching his movements with considerable annoyance, and said:

"It's certainly hot, isn't it?"

Neither of his listeners said a word in reply, and he went on in a very satisfied tone of voice:

"Back in Gijón at this very moment a light breeze is beginning to blow, which already . . . a person must cover up, or else he'll catch cold . . . whereas this Island has a perfect climate for blacks. Don Cristóbal Colombo ought to have discovered it somewhere else where it wasn't so hot. Because, let's say for example that a lad from Castile, or from Santander, arrives here; he's robust, with cheeks that look like two cherries, in short, he's full of life, strong as a bull, and in less than six months, if he doesn't die of yellow fever, he's emaciated and dispirited for the rest of his life. What a country! Yes, this is some country, let me tell you!"

Right about then his eyes met those of Don Cándido and Doña Rosa, who were staring straight at him, and as though he had come to his senses again, he added in quite another tone of voice:

"Well, sir, it certainly seems to me that everything has turned out just as we wanted it to."

"Well, finally!" Don Cándido said, breathing hard.

"I was getting around to that," Don Melitón went on, responding to Gamboa's mounting impatience rather than to his exclamation. "I was getting around to that, but you know me, Señor Don Cándido, and you know that I'm no rapid-fire Catalan rifle."

"You don't have to tell me that twice," Don Cándido answered emphatically.

"Get to the point," Doña Rosa chimed in, in a gentle tone of voice, for she knew that an interminable argument was in the offing.

"To the point," the steward repeated, calmer now. "Well, as I was saying, the matter has turned out better than we expected. I went off—

what am I saying?—I flew like an arrow to the Rosario Arcade and burst into Don José's secondhand shop, even though the lad standing alongside the showcases outside, believing that I was going to buy out the entire shop, was tugging me by the arm, the one with my jacket . . . Those shop lads are mischievous and rather roguish little scamps, you know, who . . ."

"What I know," Don Cándido replied in annoyance, "is that you're getting to the point at a snail's pace . . ."

"Well, as I was saying," Don Melitón went on as if he hadn't heard his master, "it took me a bit of work to get rid of those rascals. 'Where is Don José?' I asked Don Liberato. 'I want to see Don José. I have an urgent message for him.' 'Shhh!' the lad said to me; 'he's much too busy now for you to see him.' 'Come here,' and he led me by the hand to the courtyard, and added: 'Look at him.' In fact, there he was, all spruced up and standing right next to the wall, absorbed in an interesting conversation, carried on through signs and half words, with a woman who could be glimpsed through the blinds of the balcony on the upstairs floor of the house. I saw only two big eyes like two burning coals and the tip of little pink fingers peeking every so often from between two green slats. 'What's the meaning of that?' I asked Don Liberato. 'Don't you understand?' he answered me. 'Our Don José is taking advantage of the absence in the countryside of his fellow Spaniard and friend to court the pretty lady.'"

Don Cándido and Doña Rosa exchanged a knowing but surprised look, and the former said:

"For the love of heaven, Don Melitón, what business of ours is a tale that has every appearance of being a slander?"

"A slander!" the steward repeated solemnly. "If only it were. It's nothing of the sort; and you'll see how much work I've done in a moment. There's no denying that he's the best fellow ever to have come from Asturias. And his golden tongue, for he's a fine orator, who once . . . It's a well-known fact that a few years ago, at the time when we had a constitutional system, he was compared to the divine Argüelles, and they once carried him in triumph right through the arcades of the Plaza Vieja. And begging Señora Doña Rosa's pardon, that sort of thing pleases women no end, and Gabriela is young and beautiful . . . you understand what I mean. Temptation, her husband's absence, courtly attentions, the devil who never sleeps . . ."

"Don Melitón," Gamboa burst out again, greatly annoyed. "Who is it you're speaking of?"

"Well! I thought you were listening to me. I'm speaking to you of

Don José, who is from my part of Spain, and of Gabriela Arenas. She's so white and pink she doesn't look as though she's from here."

Doña Rosa, who was native-born and didn't think any the less of herself for it, smiled on hearing this rude remark from her steward, who went on:

"So Señor Don José paid no attention to me; he merely said to Don Liberato in a huff: 'Deal with this fellow and don't let anyone bother me.' We immediately started to rummage through the shelves and boxes, and after a lot of hard work we managed to put together three bundles of clothes, each containing 50 pairs of shirts and trousers. Fifty weren't enough. I hurried over to Mañero's shop, where there were only 30 outfits. You know that at this time of year they're beginning the repair and rebuilding of the sugar mills, the *refacciones* as they're called here. The contractors who bring in equipment and supplies for them overland start out almost two months ahead of time. The carts take weeks to go any appreciable distance, so finished clothes for the slaves are hard to come by. Well, as I was saying, from Mañero's shop I went to the one owned by that Basque . . . the one by the name of Martiartu, where Aldama was once a shop boy. I managed to get 60 more outfits, and in order not to lose time and because I decided that the ones I had already laid my hands on would be enough, I hailed a drayman, loaded his cart with all the bundles, and we slowly, slowly made our way down to the Caballería wharf; I then made five bundles, tied them with ropes, and off we went again . . . But, mind you, as we were passing by the customs guard's sentry box, the fellow comes out and holds the mule back by the bridle. 'What does this mean? What are you doing?' I shouted at him in a rage. 'You know as well as I do,' he said to me very sarcastically, 'that if you don't have a bill of lading for these goods, I can't let them through.' 'A bill of lading?' I said to him. 'Why the devil is that required? These bundles aren't meant to be shipped anywhere. They're clothes for slaves.' 'I don't care what they are,' the man went on without letting go of the mule. 'The official bill of lading or they don't go through.' What would you have had me do in a fix like that? It was past 11. I had already heard the Customs House clock strike the hour. I searched through my pockets, found a *dobloncejo* worth two *escudos* and put it in the custom's officer's hand, saying to him: 'Here's your bill of lading, man'; and without further ado he let go of the mule's bridle. The king's face is magic."

"Indeed it is," Don Cándido said approvingly.

"That's the truth of the matter," the steward added with satisfaction. "For certain people there's no better language. But my labors didn't stop there. When we reached the pier, the boatman was there. Have you any idea how quick a man he is? In no time we unloaded the cart and then loaded the bundles onto the boat. I grabbed hold of the tiller underneath the awning, and off we went. We turn around, and in less time than it takes to tell we put in at Casa Blanca, by sail and oar. In front of us was the famous brig, riding at anchor with the prow toward Regla, looking as pleased and proud as if she had cleaved the waters of the ocean freely and hadn't been captured by those English dogs. Several marines were strolling about on deck, one of whom didn't seem to me to be one of our men; but I spied Felipillo the cook aft; he recognized me at once and gestured to me to come alongside to starboard, or if not on the port side, landward. That I did, sailing all the way around the Triscornia, and then bringing the boat round to reach the poop of the brig, beneath which we lay to, and offhandedly shoved bundle after bundle clean through a little porthole, underneath which the cook safely caught them."

"I declare!" Don Cándido exclaimed in a burst of enthusiasm, extremely rare in so serious an individual. "You really did pull off a good one. Magnificent, Don Melitón! It can be taken for granted now that at least a good part of the cargo will be saved and will bring enough to cover the expenses. Not everything has been lost. We've done it, we've done it!"

Doña Rosa would have readily shared her husband's joy and enthusiasm, but it so happened that she didn't have the slightest idea how having stealthily shoved through a little porthole at the poop of the *Veloz* the outfits of clothes bought by Don Melitón in the secondhand shops of the arcades of the Plaza Vieja could have helped save the brig's cargo. So she contented herself with looking first at one of her interlocutors and then the other, as though asking them for an explanation. That was what Gamboa took her puzzled look to mean, for he went on with the same lively enthusiasm:

"Anyone who can't see on such a clear day is blind. Rosa, don't you understand that if we dress the bundles in clean clothes they can pass for halfbreeds, who have come from . . . from Puerto Rico, from anywhere except from Africa? Do you understand now? The whole story mustn't get out. These are secrets . . . because . . . the law is made to be broken. Reventos," he added volubly, "have the servants bring you something for lunch. Rosa, have Tirso serve him lunch. He must be ravenously hungry, and what's more, he may have to go out again. I for my part must be at Gómez's at one o'clock, for he's expecting me, along with Madrazo and Mañero . . . Come on," he said, pushing his steward gently by the shoulder, "hurry up and eat your lunch."

"As fast as I can swallow," Don Melitón answered. "I don't need to be asked twice. I'm embarrassed to say that I'm so hungry that . . . Isn't it true, though, that I've been dashing from pillar to post since nine this morning? But never mind . . . It can happen to the best of men. It would be odd if I didn't feel hungry, since . . ."

Around noon Don Cándido, who had summoned the barber to come shave him, was ready to go out and the gig was waiting for him at the door. Antonia, his eldest daughter, put on his white tie with dangling embroidered ends for him, daubing him with strong-scented Macastar oil, a sort of essence of clove, in wide use at that time, and combing his hair à la Napoleon, that is to say, with the end of his hair brought so far down over his forehead that it almost touched his eyebrows and the bridge of his nose. Adela brought him his rattan cane with the gold handle and silver tip, and Tirso, who was passing by, on seeing Don Cándido spread open the big bull's bladder full of cigars, brought the little brazier over to him. Immediately thereafter, half enveloped in the bluish cloud of smoke from his exquisite havana, without a smile or a word for anyone in the family, he departed with a majestic air through the *zaguán* to the street and climbed into his carriage.

"To La Punta!" was all he said in his hoarse voice to Pío, his elderly carriage driver.

This very terse language was not an enigma to the old driver. It meant that he should drive at a trot to the home of Don Joaquín Gómez, who was living at the time in that short stretch of street so named, opposite a section of the wall between the ramparts facing the entrance to the harbor.

Awaiting him there were the master of the house, Madrazo the plantation owner, and Mañero the wholesale dealer. The latter was the most intelligent one of the four; he was in the business of importing cloth and small hardware from Europe, which he sold on credit to merchants in the plaza. That was a very slow way of making a fortune, in addition to which the vendors did not always pay the debts they had contracted promptly, the result of which was losses instead of profits. Mañero, like many of his countrymen, had therefore joined the group sending ships to the coast of Africa, thus far having better luck in that venture than in the cloth and hardware trade.

On leaving, as they did a short time later, for the palace of the Captain General, Gómez told Mañero to act as their spokesman, something agreed to most readily by Madrazo and Gamboa, realizing that they themselves were incapable of fulfilling the role of orator with even middling success. It must have been about two in the afternoon when they passed through the wide and very tall portico of that edifice which, as everyone knows, occupies the entire front of the Plaza de Armas. At that hour it was full of people who were not, certainly, the best-dressed individuals in the city, yet could not be described, in general, as belonging to the Cuban lower class. The hustle and bustle were endless and tireless. The sound of footsteps and of voices was noisy and even shrill. People came and went, and the observer could see that the most agile of them, most of them lads whose bearing and attire were not at all elegant, were carrying under their left arm, folded in half lengthwise, bundles of folio-sized documents on Spanish paper. Usually they were going in or out of different offices or tiny houses, called *accesorias* in Cuba, whose one door and perhaps a single window gave onto the portico, level with its floor paved with small smooth stones. At first glance, it was noticeable that that crowd of people had not come there merely to divert themselves or out of sheer curiosity, for they were gathered in more or less numerous groups and knots, in which everyone was speaking as loudly as possible, indeed shouting at times, their words invariably accompanied by gestures, as though they were discussing subjects of transcendent importance, or ones that greatly interested the principal actors. The reader, of course, may be certain that they were not discussing politics; this was strictly forbidden, and the right of assembly had not been exercised in Cuba since the year 1824, when the second period of the constitutional system ended. And yet to all intents and purposes that gathering was a congress.

While this was going on in the middle of the portico, next to one of the thick, solid columns was a group composed of a black woman and four children of mixed blood, the oldest of them a boy 12 years old, the youngest a little mulatto girl of seven, all clinging to the skirt of the black woman, whose head covered with a cotton shawl was bowed on her breast. In front of this sad-looking group was a black in his shirt sleeves, and at his side a white man, decently dressed, who was reading in a low voice from a bundle of papers lying open, which he was holding in both hands like a book, and the first man was repeating aloud what the other had read, ending each time with the formula:

"They are to be auctioned off; this is the last public announcement. Is there no one who will give more?"

Each one of these words seemed to pierce, as with a knife, the heart of the poor woman, for she tried to hide her head by thrusting it deeper and deeper beneath the folds of her large square shawl; she was trembling all over, and her pretty children were holding fast to her skirt. That group or scene attracted Mañero's attention; he pointed it out to

Gómez, and said in his ear: "Do you see? A farce, a farce. The auction has already been held (pointing then to one of the offices to his right). But now I understand," he added, smiting his forehead with the palm of his hand and then tapping Madrazo on the shoulder as he walked in front of him together with Gamboa. "Isn't that black woman Marzán's María de la O that you held legally in bond a while back? If I were you I'd buy her and her four children. Within a few years they'll be worth four times as much as they'd cost you now along with their mother."

"How do you know whether or not he hasn't already bought them?" Gamboa observed offhandedly.

"Does the matter interest you?" Madrazo said uneasily in answer to Gómez and Mañero.

"I'm interested on your account and on the little mulatto girl's," the latter answered with a wicked grin, giving his companion a good nudge with his elbow. "The mother of those youngsters is an excellent cook, as I know from experience, and the little girl . . . What's more, she looks a lot like her father to me."

"Like Marzán, you mean," Madrazo said.

"Yes. No. How long has it been since Marzán's lawsuit against Don Diego del Revollar and the placing of Marzán's blacks under bond on your sugar plantation in Maniman?" Mañero asked with apparent ingenuousness.

"About eight years," Gómez answered. "Marzán is from Andalusia and del Revollar from Santander like us, and the two of them have gotten along together like cats and dogs on their coffee plantations in Cuzco."

"I don't believe it was that long ago," Madrazo interrupted.

"Be that as it may," Mañero went on. "The thing is, that little girl who has a white father and a black mother is no more than seven years old and . . ."

Mañero didn't go on because at that moment Madrazo went over to a man not wearing a hat, touched him on the arm, called him by name and drew him into one of the *accesorias* that we have spoken of earlier. Holding up his open palm, Madrazo signed to his friends to wait for him, and disappeared amid the crowd of people, almost all of them standing, who filled the room.

"Didn't I tell you?" Mañero added, addressing Gómez and Gamboa. "Madrazo has bought María de la O along with her four children at auction, one of whom is, and if not may the devil take me, the spitting image of the one who bought her, and the public announcement has been nothing but a farce so as to keep up appearances and show his impartiality toward his friend Marzán. When all is said and done he has a father's goodheartedness and behaves like a good master: the family will not be sent away or broken up."

As the perspicacious reader will have realized, the *accesorias* were the offices of the notaries public of the judicial jurisdiction of Havana. They consisted of a small rectangular reception room with a door opening onto the portico and a window with an iron grill overlooking the courtyard of the palace of the Captaincy General of Cuba. There were some ten or twelve of them at the front of the building, some three more on the north side or the Calle de O'Reilly, and as many or more on the Calle de Mercaderes, among them the one that handled mortgages. The tribunal "let out," as is said here, from noon until three, and the presiding judges, along with the prosecuting attorneys, who came to take note of the proceedings in the cases assigned them, the notaries who authenticated documents, and several attorneys who had few clients and were still bachelors-at-law just beginning to practice on their own filled the notaries' offices to overflowing. Moreover, the one room was by no means a large one and was lined with desks whose tops were loaded with inkwells and papers or trial records, and behind them, next to the walls, were big tall cabinets, with wire or rope mesh for doors so that between the shelves there could be seen the numerous records bound in parchment like codices in ancient libraries.

The man not wearing a hat led Madrazo to the right side of the notary's office, in front of the first desk, somewhat larger and tidier than the others, for it had a railing and the inkwell was recognizably one made of lead, that is to say, it was not as full of ink. The individual who was sitting in a leather chair behind the desk rose most respectfully to his feet the moment he saw the plantation owner, greeted him in a friendly fashion, and in a loud voice asked for the proceedings of the case of Revollar versus Marzán. Once the individual who had read the public announcement brought the court record, opened at a sheet that was folded lengthwise, he pointed with the index finger of his left hand to a decision consisting of a few handwritten lines, and told Madrazo to sign below it. Madrazo did so, with a goose quill handed to him by the notary, and bidding him good-bye, went off immediately to join his companions.

VIII

The law is made to be broken.

Castilian proverb

Turn your eyes toward the Plaza de Armas, toward the east, that is, as everyone knows, and look at the facade of the palace of the Captaincy General of Cuba.

The entrance is vast, a sort of foyer, with rooms on both sides, whose doors open onto the foyer; the one on the left is for the officer of the guard, and the one on the right serves as quarters for the detachment of guards. The soldiers' rifles were standing in their rack, as the sentry, with his rifle across his arm, paced back and forth in front of the door.

Mañero had a manly appearance and distinguished manners, and was wearing formal dress, as though to present himself with all due dignity before the highest authority of the Island. It was not difficult, therefore, to take him at first glance to be an important personage. Moreover, having served in the national militia during the siege of Cádiz by the French army in 1823, he had acquired a military air, enhanced by the end of a red ribbon with a small gold cross which he customarily wore in the second buttonhole of his black swallowtail coat. As soon as Madrazo joined his friends again, Mañero abruptly turned around and marched at their head to the entrance of the palace.

The sentry noticed him at that moment, came to attention, presented arms and shouted:

"Guards! His Excellency the Señor Superintendent."

The soldiers on duty immediately armed themselves with their staffs of hollow rattan, the officer of the guard placed himself at the head of them, his sword unsheathed, and the drum began to sound the fall-in. The sentry's cry and the soldiers' movement drew the attention of Mañero and his friends, who, in order to clear the way, hurriedly picked up their pace; but as the soldiers presented arms and the officer gave the regulation salute, the group realized that one of their number, the one marching in front, had been mistaken for the superintendent of the treasury, Don Claudio Martínez de Pinillos, to whom, in fact, he bore a certain resemblance. The officer of the guard, however, recognized the error immediately, and in his fury, ordered the sentry to be relieved and to remain under arrest in the barracks for the remainder of the day.

Choking back their laughter so as not to further arouse the wrath of the lieutenant on duty, the four friends then began their climb up the broad staircase of the palace. Once in the spacious corridors, in single file and hat in hand, they headed for the door of the room called the Salon of the Governors. In it a respectable-looking black was sitting, who, on seeing the strangers who were approaching, rose to his feet and barred their way, as if to ask them for the day's password.

Mañero explained to him in a few words the purpose of their mission; but before the black could reply, an aide to the captain general appeared and informed them that His Excellency was not in the palace at the moment but in the courtyard of La Fuerza, trying out a pair of choice fighting cocks, or English cocks, which he had recently received as a gift from Vuelta Abajo.

"Don't hesitate to go see him there if the matter that you are bringing before him is urgent," the aide urged, noting the uncertainty of the newcomers, "because His Excellency often grants an audience amid his fighting cocks, even to the general of the marines, to foreign consuls . . ."

Although their mission was undoubtedly urgent, since the Mixed Commission was going to meet soon in order to decide whether the *Veloz* and its cargo were a legitimate prize or not, Gómez, Madrazo, and Gamboa in particular were greatly relieved, once they became convinced that the meeting with the captain general could take place a little later and in a less aristocratic and imposing setting than his palace. Between

La Fuerza and the building housing the Treasury Administration, behind the pavilions in which the office of the notary of the Treasury was set up later on, there was and still is a courtyard or plaza, annexed to the first of these two buildings, where the captain general, Don Francisco Dionisio Vives, had ordered to be constructed, in due and proper form, a *valla* or cockpit, with a floor covered with sawdust, and tiers of benches for the spectators—in short, a real *gallería*. In it up to two dozen English cocks, which are the best fighters, were cared for and trained; they came from famous broods in the Island and all of them had been gifts that private individuals had given to General Vives, his fondness for fights of that sort being common knowledge. And such fights also took place there from time to time, in particular whenever His Excellency took a notion to offer his friends and subordinates one of those spectacles, which, if not as barbaric as a bullfight, are nonetheless cruel and bloody.

The individual in charge of the care and training of the fighting cocks of the captain general of Cuba was a man with a past, as the saying has it. His name was Padrón. He had committed a perfidious murder, according to some people; one in his own defense, according to others; the truth is that, after having been arrested, tried, and sentenced to prison in Havana, thanks to the pleas and appeals of a sister of his, who was young and not bad-looking, along with the influence of the Marquis Don Pedro Calvo, who took him under his wing and protected him in view of his skill at handling fine fighting cocks, Vives got him out from behind bars and brought him to the courtyard of police headquarters where, as he put in his time supervising His Excellency's *gallería*, he was able to complete his sentence, without the bad reputation or the heavy labor of having served it out in prison. It is said that Padrón had committed other mischief in addition to the aforementioned homicide and that the relatives of the dead man had sworn eternal revenge on the murderer. But who would dare to drag him out of the courtyard of La Fuerza, the headquarters of the police force, or out from under the shelter of the captain general of the Island? Without exaggeration, Padrón, the convict Padrón, was protected there by a double force.

In the courtyard of that force of which we are now speaking, there appeared, without announcing themselves, hat in hand and bowing from the waist as a sign of profound respect, our acquaintances—the careworn slave traders, Mañero and friends. A number of persons of distinction had already made their appearance at this same site before them, among others Laborde, the naval commandant, Zurita, the fortress commander; Cadaval, the royal lieutenant; Córdoba, the colonel of the standing regiment of Havana; Molina, the warden of the fortified castle of El Morro; and a young black who was wearing a saber and gold epaulets on the shoulders of his wool jacket; the others remained a respectable distance away from Captain General Vives, who at the time was leaning against one of the wooden pillars that supported the part of the roof of the cockpit outside the tiers of seats.

The attention of this distinguished person was entirely concentrated on the swift runs and spur thrusts of a very bold copper-colored cock which Padrón was goading into a fury by allowing another fighting cock that he was holding in his left hand to peck at from time to time on its blood-red shaved head. Padrón was dressed like a Cuban peasant, that is to say in a white shirt and blue striped trousers cinched in at the waist from behind by a silver buckle which caught up the two narrow ends of the waistband. For some reason, because of a headache, as protection from the sun, or out of habit, his head was wrapped in a checkered linen bandanna, whose ends were knotted at the nape of his neck. His low-cut calfskin shoes barely covered his tiny feet with arches as high as a woman's, and he was wearing no socks. Doubtless out of respect for the captain general, he was holding his straw sombrero in his right hand, the back of which was resting against the small of his back . . . He was of average height, thin, muscular, strong, pale, with small features, and looked to be about 34 years old.

Captain General Don Francisco Dionisio Vives was only slightly taller and was dressed in a black wool tailcoat over a white piqué waistcoat, nankeen trousers, and a round beaver hat, the only insignia of the rank that he held in the Spanish army and in the politico-military government of the colony being the wide, heavy red silk sash encircling his abdomen above his waistcoat. There was nothing about his appearance or his bearing that revealed that he was a military officer. At the time of which we are speaking he was probably about 50 years old. He was of medium stature, as we have already pointed out, rather lean and spare, although with the rounded bodily contours of someone who had not led a very active life. He had a face that was almost square, longer than it was wide, regular features, blue eyes, delicate white skin, and curly hair that was still black; he did not have a mustache or a long clerical-style beard. Yes, that man had nothing of the warrior about him, and yet his king had made him commander-in-chief of the largest of his island colonies in America, at the very moment when that colony appeared to have come closest to breaking the tenuous and anomalous ties that still kept it subject to the throne of its mother country.

Although Don Agustín Ferrety's treason had placed the principal leaders of the conspiracy known as the Soles de Bolívar in Vives's hands without further difficulty in 1826, many co-conspirators of lesser note, if not of lesser courage, were able to escape to the continent and from there, through zealous emissaries, kept alive the hope of the advocates of independence on the Island and caused its authorities to live in a state of constant anxiety.

The press had fallen silent since 1824, a citizens' militia did not exist, the town councils had ceased to be popular bodies, and not so much as the shadow of freedom remained, since by the decree of 1825 the country was declared to be under martial law and the permanent military commission was established. The sudden granting of the most extensive exemptions and privileges to the most oppressive of tyrannies was too drastic a measure not to give rise to profound discontent and general uneasiness, aggravated by the fact that in the two short constitutional periods the people had become accustomed to the give-and-take of political life. Deprived of that atmosphere, it went even more eagerly than before to meetings of secret societies, many of which still existed at the end of the year 1830, the government having been unable to do away with them as easily as it had done away with constitutional guarantees. From then on conspiracy was a normal and permanent state of a good part of Cuban youth. The most intense agitation, centered in the large cities such as Havana, Matanzas, Puerto Príncipe, Bayamo, and Santiago de Cuba, grew still more intense and spread to almost all social classes.

In all cities to some degree, there were disturbances and demonstrations of resistance, because it was some time before the people bowed their neck and submitted to the yoke of colonial tyranny. Many people had been imprisoned all over the island, and all those able to elude the vigilance of the police, who at the time were slow-witted and poorly organized, escaped and headed abroad.

To counter all of this the mother country had no navy worthy of the name; it consisted of a few lumbering old sailing vessels nearly rotted away. With the exception of Havana, there were no real fortified cities. The veterans on garrison duty were few in number, and in addition insubordination had spread in their ranks. The troops on garrison duty were men who had finished their military service and soldiers from Mexico and Costa-Firme who had surrendered, and not all their highest-ranking officers were Spaniards; in the three branches of the military some were natives of the country or Creoles who were never able to earn the trust of the most suspicious of sovereigns that Spain has ever had, if Philip II is excepted.

Moreover, the combination of the disorder of the administration of the colony, the scarcity of public funds, the venality and corruption of the judges and court clerks, the lack of morality, and the general backwardness of the country presented a mortal threat to a society that was already worn out by ills of every sort brought on by many years of mis-government. During the six years of Vives's command, neither people's lives nor their property were safe, either in the towns or in the country-side. The fields were taken over by fire and sword at the hands of bands of fierce brigands. On the high seas surrounding the Island freebooters from the colonies that had just freed themselves marauded in triumph and destroyed Cuba's meager trade. On the adjacent small islands pi-rates took shelter; engaged in smuggling, they captured those ships that had escaped the freebooters and after plundering them killed the crew and set the vessels afire so as to destroy every trace of their crime.

Such was, in short, the state of things on the island of Cuba until well into the year 1828. And it is perfectly clear that without the unofficial in-tervention of the United States in 1826, the two Spanish Antilles would have been invaded by the combined forces of Mexico and Colombia, in accordance with Bolívar's plans and the wishes of the Cubans, a delega-tion of whom went to meet him with that objective in mind when he re-turned victorious from the famous battlefields of Ayacucho. Had this undertaking been carried out, it would inevitably have been the *coup de grâce* for Spanish rule in the New World. In such critical circumstances, in order to at least neutralize the machinations of the enemies of Spain within the colony, the stratagems of a diplomat rather than the sword of a warrior would have been required; a clever and duplicitous man rather than a man of action; a man of intrigue rather than one of violence; a governor human by policy rather than severe by nature; a Machiavelli rather than a Duke of Alba, and Vives was that man: chosen with great good judgment to govern Cuba by the most despotic of sovereigns that Spain has had thus far in this century.

Don Cándido Gamboa was very pleased to find an acquaintance in the group of courtiers who had come to pay their respects to the captain general in his *gallería* in the courtyard of La Fuerza. The appearance of that individual was in no way prepossessing, since besides being short in stature and rachitic, his head was hunched down between his shoulders; he had a long face and a swarthy complexion, like an extremely bilious person, and his general slovenliness was almost repugnant. In his little eyes set in deep sockets there was fire and intelligence enough, however, to redeem the shortcomings and excesses of his body and his counte-nance. When Don Cándido greeted him, he addressed him as doctor.

"How are you?" the individual answered in a shrill voice and with a laugh that could well have been called cold.

To do so he was obliged to tilt his head upward, because Don Cán-dido was a good foot taller, at least, than he.

"I'm well, except for the muddle in which I unintentionally find myself involved at present."

"And what muddle might that be?" the doctor asked, as if merely out of curiosity.

"Well! Aren't you aware that those English dogs have just captured a brig beneath the batteries of the watch tower at El Mariel, out from under our very noses, so to speak, on the pretext that it was a slave ship that had come from Guinea? But this time they've been badly disappointed: the brig hadn't come from Africa, but from Puerto Rico, and wasn't transporting blacks from Africa, but halfbreeds."

"What's that you say? I didn't know anything about it. What with taking care of all my patients I don't even have time to scratch my head, much less to inquire into news that doesn't directly affect me. Though to tell you the truth, if the exaggerated zeal of the English is detrimental to anyone, it's to me, since I'm very short of workers on my coffee plantation in El Aguacate."

"And who isn't short of them? They're what all of us plantation owners need just as much as we need our daily bread. Without workers our sugar and coffee plantations are going to rack and ruin. And it seems that that's what those English Jews, may God confound them, are out to do. Doesn't it seem to you, doctor, that the captain general shares our opinion in this regard?"

"My dear fellow! I must say that I haven't heard him express an opinion on the subject."

"Yes, but you may have heard him rail . . ."

"Against the English?" the doctor interrupted. "Most definitely. Tolmé annoys him, it's true, and he tolerates his impertinences and unruliness only with the greatest difficulty."

"Exactly, exactly," Gamboa repeated happily. "It's not for nothing that people say that you have influence with His Excellency."

"Is that so? Is that the rumor that's making the rounds?" the doctor said with signs that this piece of news gratified his vanity more than a little. "It's true that I earn tokens of His Excellency's goodwill and even his favor; but there is nothing odd about that inasmuch as I have been the personal physician of His Excellency and his family ever since they arrived from Spain, and moreover his forthrightness is well known. He singles me out for special attentions fairly often—indeed, very often."

"I know that. I hear it repeatedly from different individuals and therefore I've been thinking, or rather, it occurs to me that if you were to offer to use your influence we could still put one over on the English and leave them really frustrated. I'm certain that you would have no cause for regret either, my friend, were you to give us a hand in this fix we're in."

"I don't understand. Explain yourself, Don Cándido."

"Allow me to assume, doctor, the responsibility of informing you that the shipment captured by the English, saved in its entirety, is worth 18,000 doubloons at the very least, net, to us joint owners of it. Even if half of it is lost, that still leaves us a net profit of nine thousand, which isn't chicken feed. So you see that we can be generous to someone who helps us. You yourself could choose half a dozen young blacks from among the lot, which is made up of the best slaves that come from the coast of Gallinas, and all it would cost you would be the task of . . ."

"I still don't understand one word of what you're saying, Don Cándido."

"Well then, I'll explain further. The shipment consists of some 500 bundles, 300 of which can be passed off as mestizos imported from Puerto Rico, and this morning over 400 pairs of canvas shirts and trousers have been sent aboard. Now then, if His Excellency is of the opinion that we have need of field workers, and that the English must not be allowed to destroy our agricultural wealth, it is clear that if there is someone who will speak to him and make a good case for us, he can't help but side with us. A word from you to Señor Don Juan Montalvo, of the Mixed Commission, would be enough to have the suit decided in our favor; and you can see that it would be easy for us to be generous with . . . Furthermore, there are five or six Africans who aren't assigned to any of the parties involved, and that number won't make us joint ship owners, who number eight in all, either richer or poorer . . . Now do you understand what I have in mind?"

"Of course I do. You may count on my doing whatever is within my power, although I am greatly spurred on to do so not so much by your offer as by the wish to be of service to you and to contribute to the castigation of the ambition and the evil intentions of the English. I presume that you have come to speak with His Excellency regarding the matter."

"Yes, that is why I have come, along with my friends Gómez, Mañero and Madrazo. I believe you know them."

"I've heard of Madrazo, whose sugar plantation, Manimán, is in the same jurisdiction of Bahíahonda as my coffee plantation in El Aguacate."

"Well then, they and the other interested parties will be here and will go over everything on which I reach an agreement with you. If you believe that His Excellency will accept a small gift of a few hundred doubloons . . ."

"Leave that up to me. I know how to approach His Excellency. I will speak to him this very evening. All of you go see him first. And now that I think of it, what happened to that little girl? . . ."

"Which one? I don't know who you mean," Gamboa said, his face flushing.

"You have a poor memory, it would seem. I grant you, however, that it was some time ago, but you were interested, since you asked me repeatedly to treat the girl."

"Ah, that's another story . . . She's in Paula Hospital. . . ."

"In Paula, you say? Is she sick?"

"Worse than that, doctor. I believe that she's lost her mind and nothing can be done for her."

"What's that you're telling me? Someone that young?"

"She's not all that young."

"In her teens, I mean. Let's see. Seventeen or eighteen years ago. It was in 1812 or 1813. Yes, I'm certain. She can't be younger than that."

"You're not by any chance referring to her mother?"

"I'm asking about the child, the one I first saw in the Royal Foundling Home. She gave promise of being a handsome young woman when she grew up."

"We could talk about this from now till doomsday. The mix-up stems from the fact that I regard any girl as a child, as long as she's still in her early years, and the mother, strictly speaking, doesn't fit in that category."

"You'll remember," the doctor said, "that I didn't treat the woman you're talking about; it was Rosaín who did, although you consulted me several times about the case. I had no idea that the patient from the Callejón de San Juan de Dios had anything to do with the child at the Royal Foundling Home. I realize my error now. She was suffering from puerperal fever along with acute meningitis . . ."

At that point Gamboa ended the conversation abruptly and went back to join his friends, and Mañero asked him:

"What was that all about? A skeleton hidden in a certain person's closet?"

"No, what was in the closet was a tabby cat," Gamboa promptly shot back.

"I thought as much," Mañero said offhandedly. "You always were fond of tomcatting around. But who in the world is that annoying little man you address as 'doctor'?"

"Well, I declare! Don't you know him, my dear fellow? . . . Doctor Tomás de Montes de Oca."

"I've heard his name mentioned. I hadn't seen what he looks like though. Quite a ridiculous figure, and besides that. . . ." (The latter phrase was said in Portuguese.)

"A good physician and a skillful surgeon."

"God save me from a knife wielded by him."

"He's the doctor who treats the captain general's family."

At that point something of a stir was noted in the group of notables crowded most closely around that personage, whereupon the conversations among those farthest away ceased at once. Padrón had taken the fighting cocks back to their respective cages, and Vives was bidding Laborde, Cadaval, Zurita, Molina, and Córdoba an affectionate farewell, passing from one to the next until he reached the young black we have previously mentioned, to whom he said, without offering him his hand, much less bidding him farewell:

"Tondá, go to the secretary's office to receive your orders."

We must add a parenthesis at this point to say two words about Tondá. He was the protégé of Captain General Vives, who had taken him out of the colored militia where he held the rank of lieutenant, and after promoting him to captain, subject to the consent of His Majesty the King, authorizing him to use the title of Don and wear a saber, gave him the assignment of hunting down colored criminals in the outlying districts of the city, doubtless because a man's worst enemy is someone who shares the same origins.

And in this case, as in many others that could be cited, the tact and good judgment that Vives habitually showed in choosing his men were evident. It seems pointless to add that the protégé soon succeeded in distinguishing himself by his diligence, zeal, and cleverness in investigating crimes and chasing down criminals.

In these undertakings, as difficult as they were dangerous, his youth and strength, his self-assurance, his fairly good education, his refined manners and modest demeanor, in short, his calm courage, which at times went as far as rashness, stood him in good stead; these gifts, which incidentally earned him women's admiration, gave him magic powers in the minds of people of his race, always prone to fantasizing. And as often happens with persons who seem to have stepped straight out of a novel, the people composed songs and dances alluding to his most notable deeds and dedicated them to him; it also gave him a nickname that has so obscured, so muffled his family name, that today, after 40 years, all we can say is that people called him Tondá.

An active and loyal employee, he took only as much time to obey the order he had received as it took him to go from the courtyard of La

Fuerza to the mezzanine of the palace of the Captaincy General. At that time the office of political secretary was held by Don José M. de la Torre y Cárdenas. The latter, although he received Tondá with a smiling face, did not offer him a chair, nor did he answer his respectful greeting in kind; he merely told him that the night before, from a report by the chief of police of the district of Guadalupe, Barredo, it was known that a horrible crime had been committed in the Calle de Manrique at the corner of La Estrella, and that His Excellency wanted the matter to be promptly investigated so as to discover the identity of the perpetrator or perpetrators and be able to pursue them without a moment's respite until they were caught and handed over to the courts, because he was determined to make their punishment an exemplary one.

Immediately after the departure of the others, it was the turn of the delegation headed by Mañero, who explained their mission simply and straightforwardly, limiting himself to saying that it was not fitting and proper, either in the name of the law or of justice, that the Mixed Commission should declare the brig *Veloz*, at this very moment in Havana harbor, a fair prize, even though it was carrying a cargo of blacks, for as its papers, submitted in due and proper form, attested, it hailed from Puerto Rico and not directly from the shores of Africa; and even if trafficking in slaves with the latter was considered smuggling, trafficking with the former was not, since fortunately it still belonged, like Cuba, to the crown of His Majesty the King of Spain and the Indies, Don Ferdinand VII, may God save him.

General Vives smiled and told the petitioner to present him with a written request setting forth all the alleged arguments and facts, assuring him that he would send it on to the Mixed Commission, along with the ship's papers; he then said that he had already received news of what had happened from the English consul himself, who had appeared before him, in advance of the hour when he held audience, in the company of the commander of the privateer, Lord Clarence Paget, and added, his tone of voice and his countenance indicative of a certain sternness:

"I recognize, señores, the injustice and the damages caused us by a treaty whose terms grant England, the natural enemy of our colonies, the right to search our merchant ships; but His Majesty's ministers in their lofty wisdom saw fit to approve it, and the one thing incumbent upon us, his loyal subjects, is to respect and obey the mandate of our august monarch, may God save him. And I fancy, señores, that if you are prepared to respect the treaty, you are neither well nor ill prepared to comply with it. I turn a blind eye in vain to what all of you are doing day after day (when I speak to you in those terms, señores, I am not referring to you in particular, but to all those who are engaged in the slave trade with Africa); as things are now going, you will not stop until you have brought your shipments in to Banes, in to Cojímar, in to Los Arcos de Canasí, and even in to this very port. I have ordered in vain that the large slave stalls along the Paseo be closed and torn down, the owners of which you do not teach a lesson and instead keep bringing your black Africans into this plaza, persuaded, doubtless, that there is no better market for such merchandise. At such a time you do not remember the poor captain general, at whom the English consul aims his shots, because the minute a 'sack of coal,' as you people put it, comes in to port here, he smells it and comes to me like a man possessed to give vent to his ill humor.

"So then! I bid you farewell, and next time be more prudent. And apropos of prudence: yesterday afternoon a young clerk of a shop came to me to complain that in broad daylight in the Plaza de San Francisco he was robbed of a sack of money that was part of his capital. Is there any greater imprudence than to go around the streets showing one's money to everyone and tempting people who are out for no good? Another man complained to me that at dusk yesterday two blacks with dagger in hand stopped him near the statue of Charles III and robbed him of everything valuable that he had on him, his watch and so on. If you had been just a little more prudent, I told him, you wouldn't have risked losing your life by walking through a place as lonely as the Paseo when night was falling, an hour that evildoers choose to commit their misdeeds. Learn from my example: I don't go out on the streets at night. I say the same thing to all of you: don't fall into the clutches of the English and you'll save your shipments, and don't compromise the honor of the captain general. Prudence is the first of all the virtues in this world."

I X

I thought of you and at that moment
Nature bade me weep.

José María Heredia

In the Gamboa household its steward, Don Melitón Reventos, was a person of more importance that anyone could imagine. In the management of its general economy he had more of a say than his master, and at the same time he tried to keep up with Doña Rosa in that domain.

But where he had powerful authority was among the slaves. He was responsible for keeping both the domestic servants in Havana and those of the rural estates fed and clothed. With the former, above all, he put on the airs of a lord and master, and more than that, of a despot. The fierce steward made two exceptions in their case. In the first place, he did not like to be harsh with Aponte, the carriage driver. Not only was Aponte a stern and fearful man, but he belonged to the spoiled son of the household, who was unwilling to delegate the right to punish him to anyone.

Nor did Don Melitón treat Dolores badly, in word or deed. Far from it; he reserved for her his smiles, his tokens of esteem, and his attentions. From time to time he gave her kerchiefs and trinkets as presents, which the girl accepted without misgivings, although in order to wear them she was obliged to lie to her mistresses; for after all, she found it more than a little flattering that a white man should treat her with such courtliness.

This singling out of Dolores for Don Melitón's special favor did not stem from the fact that she was the personal maid of the young ladies of the household, and therefore treated with certain courtesies by the entire family; no, they came from a different source, the attributes of the girl as a woman: she was young, shapely and, for a black, pretty.

That day on which, because he had come back late from his errand to the *Veloz*, Don Melitón was eating his lunch at the head of the table in the dining room, with all the airs of being the master of the household, attentively served by Tirso, Dolores happened to pass by and bumped into him with her elbow just as he was raising a glass of wine to his lips. Whether it had happened by accident or was in fact deliberate, the steward took advantage of the occasion to pinch her on her bare, nicely rounded arm.

"Ay, Don Melitón!" she exclaimed without raising her voice, though she raised her hand to the place where it hurt.

"Ay, Dolores!" he mimicked her, laughing heartily.

"That hurts," the girl added.

"Not really! Take no notice. I'm still going to free you."

With her mouth Dolores made the onomatopoeic sound known as "frying an egg," as though she didn't believe the sincerity of the steward's last words for one second. Nonetheless, the word *freedom* was too sweet for the young slave girl to close her ears to the promise and her heart to the hope of seeing it fulfilled, whatever sacrifice its giver might demand of her. In any event, his eyes followed her until she disappeared through the arch leading to the courtyard and then he murmured: "That one is going to be married off to that rascal Aponte. That would be a shame!"

María de Regla, who has been mentioned at the beginning of this story, had given birth to Dolores, following her lawful marriage to Dionisio the cook, 15 years before the era we are speaking of. At the same time Doña Rosa had given birth to Adela, her youngest daughter, whom she gave to María de Regla to nurse inasmuch as at the time she did not feel up to fulfilling that sweetest of the duties of motherhood. Naturally, in order to perform such a delicate task, it became necessary for María de Regla to wean Dolores and raise her on goat's milk or cow's milk, entirely apart from her suckling her mistress's daughter.

María de Regla was expressly forbidden to divide her caresses and the treasure of her breast between the two baby girls, or even to hold them together in her arms. But despite her being a slave, fearful of the punishment with which she had been threatened, she was a mother, who loved her own daughter dearly, perhaps even more dearly because she was not being allowed to nurse her; and so whenever the other women slaves gave her the chance, late at night or out of the sight of her master and mistress, she put both babies to her breasts and suckled them with immeasurable delight. Apparently without impairment or deterioration, the wet nurse's strength provided her with ample milk for that double suckling. As they grew older, the two foster sisters were strong and healthy. María de Regla did not favor one over the other, and thus their earliest years would have gone by amid the greatest harmony had they not begun to fight for the milk that nourished them as soon as it started to dry up and to howl to high heaven, especially the white one, not being accustomed to such sharing.

Finally, her attention attracted one night by her daughter's howling, Doña Rosa caught the wet nurse sleeping between the two babies, who, with both arms outstretched, were each keeping the other from enjoying the delicious liquid. What to do in such a situation? Punish the slave on the spot for her disobedience? Change wet nurses? The one solution would be as bad as the other, Doña Rosa reflected. The first one, because the punishment would poison the slave's milk; and the second because in the eighth month of nursing, the sudden change would bring on results no less fatal to Adela's health and perhaps her very existence. Doña Rosa was so perplexed that she consulted her husband, who, a violent man if ever there was one, advised prudence and lenience until a more opportune time. Now that her first act of disobedience has been discovered, he said, it is not likely that María de Regla would repeat her misdeed. In any event, things went on in this way for a year and a half more, at the end of which time the steward unexpectedly ordered the nursemaid to be thrown out of the house and put aboard a schooner that shuttled back and forth between Havana and El Mariel, leaving her off at La Tinaja under the watchful eye of the overseer. In the year 1830 she was working in the infirmary there as a nurse, that is to say, atoning for the sin of being a loving mother that she had committed 13 years before that date.

That slavery has the power of turning topsy-turvy the notion of what is just and what is unjust in the mind of the master; that it blunts human sensibility; that it loosens the closest social ties; that it weakens the individual's feeling of dignity and even obscures people's notions of honor, is understandable; but that it closes the heart to the love of one's parents or that of brothers and sisters to the spontaneous sympathy of tender souls is something not often seen. It is not surprising, then, that María de Regla should feel in the very depths of her bosom the pain of her separation at one and the same time from her daughter, from the child's father, and from Adela herself, as well as her banishment for the rest of her days to La Tinaja.

In the unwritten code of slaveholders no measure or proportion is recognized between crime and punishment. Punishment is not dealt out to correct the slave's behavior, but to give vent to a passion of the moment; as a result the slave is punished several times for a single crime. It never rains but it pours, as the saying goes, and it was quite true in the case of María de Regla. Her banishment from Havana, the separation from her daughter and her husband, perhaps never in her life to see them again, the change of occupation from wet nurse in the city to infirmary nurse in the country, the passage from dependence on the steward's whims in the city to dependence on those of the overseer on the sugar plantation was not atonement enough, to Doña Rosa's way of thinking, for her wretched slave's sin.

Doña Rosa had never managed to find out for certain whose baby girl María de Regla had been suckling about a year and a half before giving birth to Dolores. The only information she was able to get out of Don Cándido was that Dr. Montes de Oca had engaged her to nurse the illegitimate daughter of a friend of his, whose name was not to be revealed. Month after month, through Don Cándido, Doña Rosa received, with the greatest punctuality for as long as María suckled the baby, two doubloons, the price for hiring María out. This small sum was not enough to appease her jealousy; it served, rather, to sow strong suspicions in her mind, the mystery being a constant source of complaints and quarrels between her and her husband, and indirectly, of great anxiety, which at times bordered on hatred of María de Regla.

Fortunately, these instances of injustice and cruelty occurred at a time when both children did not yet have the use of reason, and since they were growing up together and, indeed, were being nursed on the same milk, they loved each other like sisters despite their difference in status and race. When Adela was older she began attending a school for girls only a short distance away from home, along with her sister Carmen, with Dolores carrying their books to school for them, bringing them fruit and a snack at midday, and seeing them home at three in the afternoon. Carmen and Adela reached the age of puberty, as Dolores had before them, and once they left school she never left their side, by day or by night. She dressed them, combed their hair, washed their feet at bedtime; during the day she sewed alongside her mistresses, and at night she slept either on the hard floor next to Adela's bed or in the next room on a rigid sleeping platform within sight of another servant, the oldest of the female household slaves.

Dolores and Tirso were born of the same mother. Dolores, born in Havana, turned out to be black, because her father belonged to that race; Tirso, born later at La Tinaja, turned out to be a mulatto, because his father, whoever he might have been, was a white man. This was why they didn't consider themselves a real brother and sister, and why María de Regla loved Tirso, whose social status was on the rise, more than she did Dolores, who perpetuated her mother's hateful color, the principal and all too evident cause, María de Regla believed, of her unending slavery. But even in this regard she was fated to see her brightest hopes as a mother dashed. Tirso, her favorite, did not love her, but, rather, was ashamed of having been born of a black mother and the nurse on the sugar plantation to boot. Dolores, on the contrary, adored her mother. Whenever the news of the bad treatment she received at La Tinaja reached her ears, it made her weep bitter tears for her and beg Adela to bring her to Havana and get her out of that purgatory they kept her in, doing penance for such a long time now, simply because she had suckled her own daughter and the daughter of her mistress at the same time. Adela felt the power of these pitiful complaints, and despite her few years and her many distractions, hearing continually, in the dead of night, as she lay in her bed with Dolores on her knees alongside it, the sad story of María de Regla's trials and sufferings on the plantation, she was moved to tears, and between yawns promised Dolores that she would speak to Doña Rosa about the matter the very next day. That was how those two foster sisters often fell asleep, almost always with their cheeks still wet with tears.

But it so happened that on the following day Adela did not find the right moment to speak to her mother, a woman who was rather stern with her children, with the sole exception of Leonardo, the spoiled child of the household, and extremely severe with the slaves. Thus time went by. One afternoon, finally, as Adela was lying on the sofa in the drawing room because she had a slight headache, her mother came over to her, sat down at her side and began to stroke her forehead as a way of caressing her or simply because her mind was elsewhere; the young girl thereupon plucked up her courage and grabbed the opportunity by the hair, as the phrase goes:

"I would like to ask a favor of you, Mama," she said, her voice trembling with emotion or with fear.

For a brief moment Doña Rosa did not say a word in reply; she merely looked at her daughter, partly in surprise and partly lost in thought. This upset Adela even more; nonetheless she added, as fast as she could get the words out:

"You're not going to say no."

"You're ill, child," Doña Rosa said curtly. "Calm down." And she rose to her feet to leave.

"A favor, Mama. Listen a moment," Adela went on, her eyes now filled with tears, holding her mother by the skirt to keep her from leaving.

Doña Rosa sat down again, perhaps because the words, and even more the attitude of her daughter, both indicative of extraordinary agitation and anxiety, drew her attention.

"Go on, I'm listening. Tell me."

"But you won't refuse to heed my plea."

"I don't know what it is you want of me; I can scarcely say beforehand whether I will refuse you or not. I presume, however, that it's some of your usual nonsense. Out with it."

"Don't you believe, Mama, that María de Regla has atoned for her sin by now? . . ."

"Didn't I tell you?" Doña Rosa interrupted her in annoyance. "And it's for such foolishness that you hold me back and beg me to hear you out? And who told you that that black is atoning for some sin?"

"Why has she been kept on the plantation for so long a time?"

"And where would that black dog be better off?"

"In Jesus' name, Mama! It grieves me to hear you talk like that about the woman who was my wet nurse."

"I wish she'd never suckled you. You don't know how heavily the hour when I placed you in her hands has weighed on me. But God knows I did as much as I possibly could. Don't speak to me of María de Regla, I don't want to know anything about her."

"I thought you'd forgiven her."

"Forgiven! Forgiven!" Doña Rosa repeated twice, raising her voice. "Never! To me she's dead now."

"What did she do to you to be treated so harshly?"

"Who's treating her harshly?"

"Do you think work on the plantation is easy? What about the way they mistreat her?"

"As far as I know, they don't treat her any worse than she deserves."

"Well, all of them say she's mistreated."

"Who do you mean by 'all of them'?"

"I believe it was Sierra, the foreman of the field hands, who was here last week when he came for the slaves' clothes for the plantation."

"What I find surprising is that the foreman would speak to you."

"Not to me, Mama, but to someone else, and since that person knows how much I love María de Regla, what she said was passed on to me. The things that take place out there have greatly distressed me, and I would really and truly like you to do something for her and for me. She begs me to serve as her protectress and get her off the plantation . . ."

"Adela," Doña Rosa said, touched by the guilelessness and exquisite tenderness in her daughter's voice. "Adela, you don't know what a sacrifice you're demanding of me. But the year-end holidays are coming soon, all the family will be going out to the plantation and we'll see what can be done with that devilish black woman. I must warn you, however, that you shouldn't expect me to become soft-hearted all of a sudden without mature reflection. That black is a lost woman and very wary. Far from repenting and mending her ways, as I was hoping, so as to wash away the sin of disobeying my express order, she has made it worse ever since she first arrived at La Tinaja. It's going on 12 years now that I've kept her there, and they keep bringing me more complaints about her and I keep hearing more scandalous things than ever. The administrator we had out there was furious with her. And I haven't said anything to you, my girl, because the right moment didn't come my way; but it seems to me that María de Regla can no longer live with us. It would be a bad example for you, for Carmen, and even for Dolores herself. When she arrived at the plantation, she brought a civil war with her; as a result it has been necessary to change overseers, foremen, master sugar makers, carpenters, in a word, everyone with a white face, because to all appearances that accursed black woman bewitches men or else all of them easily become infatuated by anyone wearing a skirt. Tirso is a living accusation of María de Regla's morality, for his father was a Basque carpenter we had some time ago at La Tinaja . . . The lashings she's received haven't made her mend her ways. . . ."

Doña Rosa's last words made Adela tremble from head to foot, because despite Dolores's laments, she was not aware that her adored wet nurse had suffered any other punishment save for the severe one of being banished from Havana and of being separated from the persons she loved most in the world. It seemed to her that she could hear the whistle of the lash, the cries of the victim, and the rending of her flesh; horror-stricken, she covered her face with both hands, and from between her pink fingers two tears like two dew drops splashed out and were dashed to pieces on her chaste and agitated breast as she exclaimed only: "Poor thing!"

Doña Rosa realized then that she had gone too far and hurriedly added: "You see? You too are infatuated with that black. Unfortunately she suckled you and you doubtless feel a certain affection for her; I understand; nevertheless you must realize that it is very badly misplaced and later on you'll become convinced that she doesn't deserve your compassion. Wait: Christmas is not far off now. We'll find a way to do what has to be done."

In any event that was reason for hope, which Adela took only as long to share with her foster sister as it took her mother to leave her side. Dolores had only the experience of loving her young mistress, being still too young to love anyone of the opposite sex, and constantly tried to identify with her, to imitate her tone of voice, her manners, her way of walking and of dressing, her flirtatious ways; with the result that her fellow slaves, when they wanted to say something to her that would greatly please her, called her, among themselves: Miss Adela.

X

I already know what you're asking me for,
Take my heart away in it . . . here.

Ramón Mayorga

It was halfway through the month of November, 1830. The north winds had already driven onto Cuba's beaches the first migratory birds from Florida, thus proving that winter had arrived early on the continent opposite. The sea often grew swollen, and with thunderous roars broke against the reefs along the shores, strewing a long stretch of them with white foam, broken seashells, and salty sediment.

At four o'clock in the morning there was not enough light in the streets of Havana, nor could people be recognized at a distance, except for those, in all truth few in number, who were carrying a little lighted lantern swaying back and forth in their hand, as with quickened step they headed either to the markets or to the churches, in some of which there could be faintly heard the organ with which the nuns or friars accompanied the recital of matins.

It was still dark, we have said, and Don Cándido Gamboa, in his printed cotton bathrobe and nightcap, was already up, peering out from behind the shutter of the window opening onto the street, sheltered behind the white muslin curtain, awaiting his daily paper, *El Diario de la Habana*, or else trying to get a breath of air fresher than the heavy air of his bedroom.

Shortly thereafter the sound, at first muffled and then louder, of the footsteps of someone approaching from the direction of the Plaza Vieja began to be heard. Don Cándido turned his eyes that way, yet still had no idea who was approaching until the person in question was before him. She was dressed in garments made of sackcloth, consisting of a sort of shawl to cover her head and a short skirt cinched in at the waist by a long black leather belt. The matte copper color of her face, characteristic of mulattos, especially when dressed in clothes worn by old people that gave her the appearance of a woman belonging to the Indian race, further contributed to disguising her.

"Good morning, Señor Don Cándido," she said to him in a twangy voice.

"I wish you the same, *Seña* Josefa," he answered, trying to lower his voice. "You're up early."

"What does the señor expect? Worriers don't sleep."

"Well, what news do you have to offer? Let's get straight to the point."

"I've a great deal of news, and it struck me that if I delayed until daybreak I'd be in a fix and would have no way out."

"I understand. It's the order put out the other day by the Captaincy General concerning beggars and lunatics that brings *Seña* Josefa here. I was waiting for you."

"The señor has guessed rightly. I don't know how it happens that I'm still alive, nor when my troubles will end. People believed at first that they were only going to pick up the poor and the mad who are wandering about the streets. But yesterday afternoon the mother superior of Paula Hospital told me that even lunatics in private homes and in hospitals are going to be taken to San Dionisio or to an asylum they've built in the courtyard of the public welfare office. The señor can rightly reckon what state of mind I'm in after hearing this news. I haven't closed my eyes all night long. As soon as the order was publicly proclaimed my heart told me that misfortune was soon to follow."

"Perhaps there's still time to remedy it."

"May that be God's will, my señor, because if the girl is suffering there in the hospital, what won't it be like when they take her to San Dionisio, or to the new asylum over by San Lázaro? There's no one there to take care of her or see to her needs. They'll beat her. And to think that I hadn't yet lost hope of seeing her in her right mind and her health restored! Now my poor Charito will be the first to leave this world, and I'll follow along behind her. Our trials will be over . . . May it be the will of the Blessed Virgin."

"Does *Seña* Josefa believe that there is anything helpful that can be done in this situation?"

"I believe, or rather, *Seña* Soledad, the mother superior of the hospital, believes that if there is someone with influence willing to speak to the examiner, who is a most charitable and God-fearing individual, he will turn a blind eye and the order will not apply to Charito. Everything depends on him. Perhaps a doctor must be found who will give her a certificate . . . The examiner is kindness itself, and wants to help, just as *Seña* Soledad does. So then, in order that the señor will see . . ."

"I understand, I understand," Don Cándido said twice, lost in thought: "I can tell you that for the moment I have consulted Montes de Oca, who is of the opinion that they should take the patient out into the country and have salt water baths given her. We'll see what can be done."

But as footsteps were heard in the *zaguán*, he broke off the conversation and gestured to the elderly mulatto to go off as fast as her legs would carry her.

First reveille and then immediately thereafter the cannon volley from aboard the vessel *Soberano*, anchored alongside the pier of La Machina, shaking the windows of his room, awakened Leonardo Gamboa with a start. He struck a light in his box of touchwood tinder, opened the case of his watch, and saw that it was four o'clock in the morning. "Just in time," he said to himself, and hastened to get out of bed and get dressed. In order to do so, he lit a whale oil candle, using a straw with a brimstone head, for at that time matches were still unknown in Havana.

As he combed his hair in front of the mirror of the dressing table, he suddenly threw down the tortoise shell comb, consulted his watch again, and murmured:

"Four minutes after four! It's still very early and to get from here to there won't take me more than 15 minutes, even walking slowly. She told me around five o'clock. Wouldn't it be better to wait on the corner? Yes," he finally said, his mind made up. And dressed and scented, carrying his rattan cane, he left his room and started down the stone staircase.

He leaned his left hand on the cedar banister so as to tread lightly, but as soon as he reached the *zaguán*, where there was no such support and it was still pitch dark, no matter how carefully he walked, even though his pumps had no heels, he still made too much noise, that particular muffled sound that is heard when someone walks above a hollow, vaulted space below. He appeared to have suddenly awakened all the echoes of the *zaguán*, and of the adjoining drawing room, where he suspected that his father, an early bird par excellence, might be. Feeling his way along, he stumbled upon the elderly carriage driver; the latter's eyes being accustomed to the darkness, he had immediately seen the young man coming and hurried forward to meet him so as to guide him and keep him from bumping into the iron wheel band of one of the carriages.

"Pío! Is that you?" Leonardo said in a very low voice. "Open up."

"The master is looking out the window that overlooks the street," the black answered.

"Damn it! Is the wicket in the door bolted?"

"No, señor. Soon's Dionisio left for the Plaza Vieja, I unbolted it."

"Open it, very slowly."

The hinges didn't creak, but Don Cándido had heard footsteps in the *zaguán*, and leaning against the grille he thundered:

"Pío, who just left?"

"Young Lionar, master."

"Go out onto the street. Call him. Stop him. Tell him that I'm summoning him. Run, you with the lead in your feet."

Until the slave returned, Don Cándido kept pacing back and forth, greatly annoyed, between the window overlooking the street and the grille of the *zaguán*, muttering:

"Where can that scoundrel be going at this hour? He's up to no good, that's for sure. He's gone to her house. Of course, it's certain. I can see him now. And hasn't that blessed woman left anyone there to keep an eye on her? . . . Perhaps not; most likely not. Certain people can be very lazy, very careless, they don't take precautions and that brings on misfortunes . . . Only the devil could imagine a series of circumstances . . . The chance, the age, the temptation, the Evil One who never sleeps . . . I too was careless. I ought to have foreseen it, kept it from happening, yes, prevented it. But how? I should have made it my responsibility. We'll see. I'll break his neck, I'll put him on a warship as sure as my name is Cándido, and I'll have them take a lash to him to see if he won't lose some of the Creole blood he has in his veins. He's not my son, absolutely not. All this could have been avoided if I'd sent him to Spain as I thought of doing more than four years ago. His mother is to blame. I'd almost be happy if Pío didn't find him, because I could kill him. That's how angry I am at him."

Just then Pío returned, exhausted and out of breath, and said:

"No, master, the lad isn't not nowhere."

"You dolt!" Don Cándido thundered. "In which direction did you go looking for him?"

"On the rein-hand side, master."

"To the left, you mean? You two-legged animal! If he walked off to the right, how would you have come across him, you idiot? Be off with you. Get out of my sight, because if God doesn't stay me, I may just kick the stuffing out of you."

Hearing Don Cándido's earsplitting shouts, Doña Rosa appeared at the bedroom door that led to the drawing room and asked in a frightened voice:

"What's happened, Gamboa? Why are you shouting?"

"Ask your son, who's just sneaked out of here like a criminal."

"A criminal? I don't understand. Has he done something bad? Is he about to?"

"I don't know much more than you do; however, I suspect, I fear, I've got it into my head that that good-for-nothing is up to one of his tricks. A person would have to be dim-witted not to suspect that that lad wouldn't have taken to the streets at an hour when it's so dark you can't even see your own hands, carefully keeping out of my sight, so as to go to Mass or Confession."

"Perhaps he went out to get a breath of fresh air, or perhaps he was trying to please you by getting up so early in the morning. There's no reason to suspect that he's up to something bad. You at least aren't certain of that; you don't know. Why must you always think the worst of your son?"

"Because as the Spanish proverb has it: think the worst, and you'll be right. I repeat, he's up to no good. I know him better than you do, you who bore him. I know what I must do with him."

"The poor boy never manages to please you. It's as if he were your stepson. If he were, perhaps you'd be more indulgent . . ."

"Go ahead and sympathize with him. God grant that you don't have to weep for him before long."

As soon as Leonardo reached the street he noted that keeping to the sidewalk on the left a dark shape that looked like a woman was walking toward Paula Hospital. He stood there for moment, hesitating as to whether to follow the vague figure until he had made certain of who it might be and thereby heading away from his destination, but his father's voice, calling out to Pío, made him decide to walk in the opposite direction so as to reach the corner of the Calle de Santa Clara as fast as he could. He reached it in a few seconds. Because of this happenstance, the slave did not manage to catch up with him. In a few more seconds he turned into the Calle de O'Reilly and climbed up the tall embankment or terrace of the convent of Santa Catalina, crossed it from east to west, and came down again at the Calle del Aguacate by way of the stairway with three or four steps, as mentioned at the beginning of this story, proceeding straight to the little house opposite it.

Since the door of it appeared to him to be neither locked nor barred, he pushed on one panel of it with the tip of his fingers. It gave way a little, in fact; and therefore he pushed harder; the chair propped against it fell over and the door opened enough for the young man to be able to slip through its two panels and get inside without further ado. All of a sudden he could see nothing at all. The shadows inside were as dense as the damp air that filled the small room. Nonetheless, thanks to the lamp that was still burning on the stone bench to his left, he could finally make out, within reach of his hand, a pair of tame doves asleep on the back of a chair, a cat curled up in a leather armchair, and a hen underneath a table, protecting with its loving wings several chicks, whose beaks peeked out from among her feathers and they began to cheep softly again and again as they usually do with they feel afraid or cold.

He gradually shifted his gaze upward to the level of the door to the room in the back, where he saw something that seemed to him to be a woman or a vision, standing scantily dressed in a white garment and her abundant hair loose, forming a thousand curls and disheveled waves, spread out over her bosom and shoulders without managing to hide them even though it was so thick and long. Recognizing each other, running toward each other and holding each other in a close embrace amid ardent and resounding kisses was but a single act.

The women's hospital of San Francisco de Paula is simply the continuation of the church of the same name, immediately adjacent to that part of the wall that overlooks the bay. Its entrance is to the north, an opening in one of the very high adobe walls of a corridor that serves as a passageway between the church and the hospital. Leading to the entrance is a vestibule with a small roof, which looks more like the screen partition of a convent than like anything else. A sentry is posted there in order to keep the prisoners or lunatics receiving medical treatment at the hospital from escaping. Generally it is only women who are admitted in one of these two categories or the other, when their crime is not a serious one or their insanity does not make them uncontrollable.

The woman whom Leonardo had seen walking at a quick pace toward the south of the city, down the Calle de San Ignacio, did not stop until she reached the aforementioned vestibule. The horizon was abruptly beginning to grow brighter, but the sentry was already pacing, with his sword drawn, from one end of the covered vestibule to the other, and he confronted her, barring her way:

"May you have a good morning, señor soldier," said the old woman, trying to ingratiate herself with the sentry.

"We've been having them, good or bad, for some time here," the soldier answered rudely.

"It would seem that the señor soldier doesn't know me," she added in a supplicating tone of voice and attitude.

"That's not to be wondered at, because may the devil take me if I've ever had dealings with witches."

The woman crossed herself and added that she wanted to speak with *Seña* Soledad, the mother superior of the hospital.

"I don't know that old auntie either," the sentry answered, resuming his pacing. "Not a soul is stirring there inside. Go in, go in, and clear the entrance."

On crossing the threshold of the vestibule, one finds oneself in a large quadrangular courtyard, the right side of which is formed by the wall of the church and the other three sides by wide passageways, of which the one on the left leads through three wide doors to the sick ward. Several square columns made of rubblework divide it into two longitudinal naves filled with beds, the heads of which lie next to the main walls of the building, leaving the center of the ward clear. There were no other partition screens or dividing walls, so that the observer situated at any of the doors could take in all the beds at a glance. Toward the bay or the east, just as toward the south and the north, there were tall windows that let in light and gave the spacious ward healthful ventilation.

The woman in the penitential sackcloth garment had barely set foot in the patio when *Seña* Soledad, the mother superior, appeared on the side of the room next to the church, with a little lantern, and behind her a priest in a black serge cassock, without a bonnet, carrying in both hands, at chest height, a silver ciborium with a silver lid. Both were walking slowly and murmuring certain prayers, which, in the silence of the courtyard, resounded like the buzzing of so many bumblebees. They headed straight to the sick ward and crossed from one side of the room to the other. As the two of them passed alongside the old woman, the latter realized what was taking place and fell to her knees, exclaiming:

"The holy oils. May God take to His bosom the soul that is dying."

Reciting the credo with great fervor, she marshaled all her strength, her body bent almost in two, and stumbled toward the door in the middle of the ward and fell on her knees once again. She had just noticed that the priest standing alongside a bed opposite her was giving extreme unction to one of the sick women, as the mother superior, on her knees on the opposite side of the bed was holding the little lantern as high as she could so as to shed its light on that sad and desolate scene.

After accompanying the priest to the church, the mother superior returned to the ward and found the woman in the penitential garment with her head bowed, absorbed in her prayers. *Seña* Soledad touched her on the shoulder and bade her good day, whereupon the woman, in a tone of voice reduced almost to silence by anguish, said:

"So she's died?"

"She is resting in peace now," the mother superior answered briefly.

"Ah!" the old woman said and fell to the floor in a faint.

"In heaven's name! *Seña* Josefa! *Seña* Josefa!" the mother superior repeated, struggling to lift her up. "What's the matter? How much will you wager that you didn't understand me? Mind you, this has all been a misunderstanding between the two of us. I didn't understand your question and you didn't understand my answer. Charo isn't the one who has died. No indeed, it wasn't Charo, but a poor black woman who was admitted to the hospital just a few days ago. Charo is better; her breast doesn't hurt her as much. Yes, come, I want you to see the truth with your own eyes."

Little by little, with such assurances, *Seña* Josefa began to come to her senses once again. After shedding a sea of tears in silence, she felt herself to be in a frame of mind allowing her to follow the mother superior to the bedside of the sick woman who was of such interest to her. For the moment the patient was sitting up, with only a sheet covering her bent legs, which she was cradling in her bare arms, her forehead resting on her knees. Her hair was shorn almost to her scalp, as is customary with lunatics, and beneath her loose, discolored, dry skin her skeleton could be seen, all the more visible since her chemise, the only undergarment she was wearing, covered only part of her back. Her position in the bed and a feeble, hollow cough that overtook her from time to time were indications that she was alive.

"Charo, Charito," the mother superior said in a kindly voice. "Look who's here. Raise your head, my girl. Cheer up."

"My beloved daughter!" *Seña* Josefa dared to say. "Do you hear me? Do you recognize me, my darling? I'm your mother. I want to see your face. Just answer me. I bring you good news; we're going to get you out of here soon. We'll take you to the country so you'll get well and have the pleasure of meeting your daughter and holding her in your arms. Ah! If you could see her! She's so pretty. She's the picture of you when you were her age."

"See how silent she is," *Seña* Soledad said. "When she's like that she doesn't speak, she doesn't move, and we have a terrible time getting her to swallow a single mouthful. At other times she takes a notion to scream at the top of her lungs as if someone were killing her, to weep or to laugh uproariously."

But *Seña* Josefa employed to no avail means that she thought would be more effective in getting her to stir. In vain she resorted to pleas, caresses, tears; the sick woman was unresponsive to everything, she answered not a word, she failed to raise her head, she did not change position, remaining curled up in a ball. It was clear that she had not been aware of the death scene that had just taken place in one of the beds opposite hers, and of course gave no sign whatsoever of having recognized the familiar voice of *Seña* Soledad, nor the anguished voice of her despairing mother.

The day was wearing on by now and *Seña* Josefa had to hurry back home, where she had left her granddaughter by herself. She therefore hastily informed *Seña* Soledad that the gentleman who was their benefactor intended to make one last effort to cure Charo, if her illness was still curable, and that in order to accomplish that he would take her to the country, near the sea, where she could breathe a different air and go bathing regularly, under the supervision of a doctor.

"Then let's send her on her way, *Seña* Josefa, and may it do her good," the mother superior said happily. "Using only the resources we have here, it is evident that there is no cure for that poor girl. What's more, she must be taken out of here or there is no way to keep them from transferring her to the new house at the public welfare service. For days now they have been going about picking up poor people and lunatics from off the streets. Yesterday they took away Dolores Santa Cruz, such a troublemaker. And Commissioner Cantalapiedra has already notified me of the order to transfer all the madwomen whose condition allows them to be moved."

Anyone can well imagine what was in *Seña* Josefa's heart after what she had seen, heard, and felt in the hospital of San Francisco de Paula.

X I

. . . But if vice stains her purity
Filling her with its deadly cold,
Her guardian angel will raise his veil.
And God will turn his head away.

Luisa Pérez de Montes de Oca

It was bright daylight and the sun quite hot when *Seña* Josefa returned to her little house on the Calle del Aguacate. Apparently no creature there had budged, save for the hen with her chicks, who were searching about for the way out to the yard through the lintel and doorframe. The old woman's first concern was to see whether her granddaughter was asleep in the high bed; and satisfied that she was sleeping peacefully, she took off her sackcloth shawl, undid her leather belt and collapsed in the armchair, thereby dislodging the cat, which on hearing his mistress entering, was stretching, opening its mouth wide, and showing its red tongue and sharp teeth.

As she fell into the armchair she heaved a deep sigh. She was now draining the bitterest cup that human lips had ever drunk to the dregs. Her only daughter was languishing in a hospital, deprived of her mother's care, out of her mind and wasting away with consumption, without her being able to help her in any way. If she had had doubts before, on that morning *Seña* Josefa was fully convinced that her daughter would find neither a remedy nor relief from her suffering as long as she remained in that place.

Why had the grieving mother been separated for so long a time from her sick and dying daughter? That separation had lasted 16 years thus far, because as the reader will remember, María del Rosario Alarcón had lost her mind as a consequence of the emotion and shock caused her by the abduction of her newborn daughter, who had been carried off to the Royal Foundling Home. When the baby had been given back to her, well suckled and plump, it was too late: the last ray of the divine light had already been extinguished in the mother's mind. Nonetheless, if her dementia had turned out to be of a gentle and calm sort, it would have been possible to allow her to spend the remainder of her life at the side of her mother and her daughter; but at times fits of rage came over her, and when she was in that state, it was difficult to hold her down and keep her from harming herself or her dear ones.

Moreover, even though there were certain hospitals in Havana—San Francisco de Paula, for instance—that admitted a few women in that state because there was no insane asylum in the city, those demented creatures whose families were unable to keep them at home, which was true of the majority of them, wandered about the streets, becoming the laughingstock of the children and the bugbear of the timid. Among their number was Dolores Santa Cruz, to whom the mother superior of Paula Hospital had alluded.

This black woman had been a slave of the distinguished family of Jaruco, whose surname she bore. Thanks to her industriousness and thrift she had managed to buy her freedom and to put money aside. She bought a house and slaves, devoting herself to the sale at retail of meat and fruit, which at that time was a fairly lucrative business.

Though we do not know the reason, someone fought with her in court over the legal ownership of her small property. This in turn involved her in a long and costly suit which, despite her winning it without being held liable for the court costs, between lawyers, public prosecutors, notaries, officers of the court, judges, and advisors, the money that her little house and her two slaves were worth was eaten up by fees, bribes, and gratuities. The result was that one fine day the poor woman found herself literally, not figuratively, out on the street.

This must have been a hard blow for someone who greatly loved money and the satisfactions it buys. The woman who had been a slave and freed herself, who had been the owner of slaves and of several little farms, now found herself tied to the whipping post of another slavery, poverty; it was impossible for her to bear this change without becoming mentally unbalanced. Her powers of reason in fact vanished, and from then on she dressed in rags and adorned her hair with artificial flowers and bits of straw, like Ophelia, and went about the streets day and night, leaning on a long stick from which there hung a small wicker basket, shouting rowdily on street corners: "Ugh! Ugh! Here come Dolores Santa Cruz. I hasn't any money, I doesn't eat or sleep. Thieves take from me everything I has. Ugh! Ugh! Ugh!"*

Let the reader imagine the daughter of *Seña* Josefa, an ill-starred mother in her turn, publicly revealing to the people in her fits of madness the steps, the means, and perhaps the name of the person or persons through whose offices she found herself in that pitifully sad state. Such a spectacle should not have been staged, nor was it; rather, no matter how painful the sacrifice, it had to be made to the full, since the health and the happiness of the innocent child who had been the indirect cause of her mother's misfortune depended on it to a certain degree. Nor were the mother's powers of reason to grow and develop, inasmuch as she had lost them and had become an object of scorn to strangers. Nor had the time come, the grandmother believed, for mother and daughter to meet. Their separation, then, might well last forever.

The old woman's mind was occupied by such thoughts more persistently than ever when there was a knock at the front door. As though she were awakening from a heavy sleep, she got up to open the door and found herself face to face with the milk vendor, a man from the Canary Islands dressed in the usual peasant costume and carrying a milk jug underneath his arm and a little tin pitcher in his hand, who greeted her, in the peculiar intonation of his native land, with the words:

"Well, my cusomer has finely open her door this mornin'. To be trueful, this is the third time I be bringing her milk."

"I was at Mass," *Seña* Josefa answered, bringing the earthenware cooking pot for him to pour the milk into.

"So I go away thinkin' that ever' las' one of you in this house was dead."

"I just came in from the street."

After looking at the old woman in an odd way, he added:

"My cusomer ought to keep four eyes wide open, because like the proverb says, anybody who has enemies shoun't sleep."

"I don't have any enemies, thank God."

* Historical fact. *Author's note.*

221

"My cusomer may think so. But ever' las' one of us has hidden ene-mies in this world. Doesn't my cusomer have a pretty young daughter?"

"A daughter? No, señor, a granddaughter."

"Same thing. 'Cause in the pretty little face of this gran'daughter is the enemy of my cusomer's repose. There's nary a young man who woun't give his life for pretty faces. The debil take me if early this very mornin' I din't seen a good-lookin' Don Juan aroun' here. I coun't say now if he was right next to the door or the window . . . But I seen what I seen."

"The milkman is mistaken," the old woman observed, trembling and all upset. "I was away for only a short time, and my granddaughter doesn't have a young man who's chasing after her pretty little face, as the milkman puts it."

"I'm just tellin' my cusomer what I told her before, keep four eyes wide open and be on the lookout, 'cause I seen what I seen."

A new reason for concern and anxiety for the unhappy grandmother. She knew that a young white man from a wealthy family had been fol-lowing her granddaughter about like her shadow, that he gave her costly presents, that he offered her the use of his gig to attend balls on holidays, that she was definitely proud of these attentions and gifts; but she was far from believing, or even suspecting, that he might take advantage of her absence at church or at the hospital to spirit her granddaughter away, seduce her, and ruin her future.

Then it occurred to her that she had left her by herself, with the neighbor next door keeping an eye on her, and her granddaughter could well have agreed beforehand with her lover to meet right there at her house while she went off to Paula. In any event, the milkman declared that early that morning he had seen a good-looking Don Juan at the window or the door of her little house. Who knew whether he had come inside? Whose fault was it if something bad happened? Could it be pos-sible that her granddaughter would follow the same path and be led astray by almost the same means as her unfortunate mother?

"Ah!" *Seña* Josefa exclaimed, falling to her knees at the foot of the niche were the image of the Mater Dolorosa was venerated. "Blessed Virgin! What have I done to deserve such severe punishment? What grave sin have I committed? Can I have been in a state of mortal sin my whole life without knowing it? You know that I've been a good daugh-ter, a good sister, and a loving mother. I have tried to bring my children up in the holy fear of God. I have taken great care to instill in them sound principles of morality, of virtue, and of religion. I strictly obey the dictates of our Holy Mother Church. Why do you allow, Immaculate

Virgin, protectress of the weak, mother of mercy, why do you permit the Tempter in human form to lead my granddaughter, an innocent child, the Lord's tender lamb, away from the path of virtue, to drive her to sin and let her fall from divine grace as He did her wretched mother? Will you abandon me as well, most compassionate Lady, in this most difficult moment of my life?"

Although *Seña* Josefa had borrowed almost word for word the ideas and even the phrasing of books of devotion, the only ones she read, there is no doubt that the fervor of her religious faith, the thought of the new misfortune that threatened to overtake her, the awareness of the tremendous responsibility that was hers in case her suspicions turned out to be well founded, all these had inspired her, despite her lack of culture, to improvise an eloquent prayer wherein she truly expressed the feelings that had overcome her in those circumstances. Nonetheless, the fervent venting of her emotions brought her broken heart scant relief. For the warning of the man from the Canary Islands, because it was timely and well founded, had the same effect on her heart as a knife thrust into her flesh: if it moves, it lacerates; if it pierces, it kills. Nor was it easy to forget his last sententious words, not to think about them; they continued, rather, to echo in her ears: "I seen what I seen."

They also echoed in the ears of Cecilia, who had not slept since long before her grandmother came back from church; but they made a very different impression on her. They set her breast afire with anger and indignation. Who, she thought, put that man up to giving such a warning? What concern was it of his if she did or did not have a lover, if she met with him by the door or the window or not? Why his insistence that he had seen him? Accursed man! If only his tongue had run dry before he said what he said! He surely saw the young man entering or leaving as well, and if he did not say as much with the same insistence it was because her grandmother had not given him the time or the opportunity.

But she was obliged to heed her grandmother's signs of grief and emotion, which seemed extraordinary and must have had a powerful and legitimate cause. What could it be? Cecilia was unaware of what had happened at Paula Hospital. Her alarmed conscience finally deciphered the enigma. She had committed a grave fault by allowing the young white with whom she was encouraging an amorous relationship to come inside without her grandmother's knowledge and against her express order.

From that point on, the proud and independent Cecilia experienced something that she had never felt before, something that she could not explain, a revolution in her entire being. In the face of her sin she began to see herself as weak, fearful, hesitant, and to be ashamed of herself, her grandmother, and her friends. What would she look like in their eyes? The milk vendor would spread word of her misdeed all over that very same morning. At least the neighbors already knew all about it, and the minute she went out on the street they would point at her and say so loudly that she could hear: "There goes the girl who takes advantage of her grandmother's absence in church to allow the man who is known to be courting her to come inside the house."

But amid those confused ideas, Cecilia realized two things without further effort: the first, that perhaps her grandmother was not yet convinced of her sin; the second, that for the peace of mind of the two of them, since there was nothing that could be done about it now, it was best to dissimulate as much as possible until the truth had come out and her grandmother had come to a decision. In this frame of mind, she cautiously got up out of bed, threw a dress on over her chemise, and peeked out the door of the bedroom. The old woman was still on her knees and was just ending her improvised prayer. Cecilia hastened to kneel at her side, put one arm around her waist, gave her a kiss on the cheek, and asked her with exquisite tenderness: "Granny, what's the matter with your grace? Why are you so distressed?"

The old woman did not say a word in reply, went back to the armchair and burst into silent tears. There is nothing more infectious than a fit of weeping, and Cecilia was predisposed to contract the ailment. She flung herself into her grandmother's arms and mingled her tears with those of the old woman, a necessary outlet for sorrows which, however, had contrary origins. Perhaps they could have taken advantage of the emotions of that moment to arrive at an explanation that could not help but be satisfactory to both, because their mood so predisposed them; but there was another knock at the door and *Seña* Josefa hastened to open it, drying on the way her cheeks wet with tears. It was the door-to-door peddler of meat, butter and eggs, a black from Africa, with her rectangular wooden box of provisions for sale balanced on her head with a ring of rolled-up cloth underneath, and a fly-swatter made of coconut palm twigs in her right hand.

Either because of a certain tendency toward obesity, the heat, or the natural slovenliness of people of color, the peddler was dressed in a striped cotton shirt and a sort of dickey, which, when it was clean, must have been white, and which barely reached her shoulders and was even shorter in the back. Her arms bared in Greek or Roman style and her plump round cheeks shone as if, according to the custom of her homeland, she had lubricated them with lard. She was not wearing shoes, of course, but as she walked she pushed along a pair of house slippers with the tip of her toes. As soon as *Seña* Josefa opened the door, she put her box down in the doorway, and in a shrieking voice, whose volume did not match her body, said:

"Good mo'nin', buy-lady. You not buyin' anathin' from me t'day? I still not earned my first coin of de day to make de sign of de cross with."

Once the old woman had briefly answered her greeting, she helped her place her box on the floor, quickly adding that she would take a *real's* worth of pork, half a *real's* worth of eggs, and another half of butter. The peddler cut the meat by eye to exactly the right measure, and along with the rest of the order placed it on a plate that Cecilia brought. The peddler no sooner laid eyes on her than she was apparently overcome by a desire to talk her ear off.

"Habana is los', gal. Nothin' but murderin' an' stealin.' Jus' right now they fleece a fella afore my bery eyes. Dey hassle him, a 'latto wid a knife from behin' and a black in front, an' den dey tie 'im to de cannon onna co'ner of Sant Terese. In full daylight, gal, dey take he's watch an' he's money. I din't wanna look. Lotsa people passin' by. I know dat black; he de son of my hubband. Ah! I's afraid of him. I's still all atremble here inside."

Such a confused and unintelligible account greatly frightened Cecilia, because the thought went through her mind that the man who had been robbed might have been her lover, but she did her best to hide her concern and the meat vendor went on:

"Down dere by Los Sitios dey was a real free-fo-all de otha night. Tondá try to arres' de murderers ob dat grocerman on de Calle Manico and Estreya. He were in de mortary. The gobner gib orders to arres' dem. Straightaway Tondá, all by heself wid he's sword, he ketch two; Malanga, de son ob my hubban runned away tru da co'tya'd and he still hidin' out. Dat one, dat one de worses' ob all. So you see, buy-lady. Can't trus' nobody. Adios, buy-lady! Be well now."

Once the meat vendor had left, the baker came, with his basket of bread on the head of a black walking behind him, following him like his shadow. Then *Seña* Josefa remembered that she had to prepare breakfast. As we said at the beginning of this story, the stove was in the back yard, underneath an eave forming a cornice, without a chimney or anything to serve as one. The old woman made a fire in the stove using a steel, a flint, brimstone, a candle end, and a few lumps of coal, and in a short time breakfast was ready. Meanwhile Cecilia set the table and both of them took their places at it. They sat there for a long time without tasting a mouthful, without raising their eyes from their plates or saying a word. At each moment Cecilia expected her grandmother to read her sin in her face and did not dare look her in the eye, while the latter seemed very nervous and uneasy. She tried several times to say something, as was evident from the movement of her lips, and just as often her voice stuck in her throat, because instead of articulate sounds only sobs escaped her. Finally, she made one last effort and said:

"I wish I could die this very minute."

"Good heavens, Granny! Don't say that!" Cecilia exclaimed without raising her head.

"Why not, if that's the way I feel? What am I doing here in this world? What good am I? I'm a nuisance, nothing but a bother."

"I've never heard your grace talk that way."

"That may well be, but up until now I've been able to bear my troubles, despite their being grievous ones. Now, though, I'm an old woman; my strength is failing; I can bear no more. I was thinking it would be better to lie down and die."

"Doesn't your grace say that it's a sin to grumble about the trials and tribulations that God sends our way? Remember that Jesus Christ bore the Cross to Calvary."

"Woe is me! I've been doing the stations of the Cross for a very long time now, and I've reached Calvary. The only thing that has yet to take place is my crucifixion, and it seems to me to have been decreed for me by the very persons I love most in this world."

"If Granny is saying that because of me, mind you that your grace is committing a real injustice. God only knows that to relieve your grace of her burden of sorrows I would willingly give the blood in my veins."

"You don't show it; no one could ever tell. On the contrary, it seems as if you take pleasure in always doing what I don't want you to do, the very thing I forbid you to do. If you loved me as you say you do, you wouldn't do certain things . . ."

"Ah! I see what your grace is leading up to."

"I'm leading up to what I must, to what every mother who values the future of her children and her own self-respect must."

"If your grace didn't lend an ear to gossipmongers, idle prattlers, she'd save herself many a cause for grief."

"It so happens, my girl, that this time the gossip accords with what I saw with these very eyes and heard with these very ears that the earth will one day swallow up."

"What has your grace been able to see or hear that isn't mere gossip? Come, tell me."

"Cecilia, what I can see as clearly as the light of day is that despite my warnings and my advice, you are seeking your perdition as the moth seeks the candle's light."

"And if a certain person, who is the one to whom your grace is referring, marries me, showers me with riches, gives me many silk frocks, and makes me a lady and takes me to another land where nobody knows me, what would your grace say to that?"

"I would say that that is a dream that can't come true, nonsense, madness. First of all, he's white and you're colored, no matter how much your mother-of-pearl skin and your black silky hair hide that fact. Second, he's from a rich and well-known Havana family, and you are poor and of obscure origins . . . Third . . . But why wear myself out? There is yet another obstacle, even greater, weightier, insuperable. You're a scatterbrained young girl . . . a lost woman, beyond salvation. Lord God Almighty, what have I done to deserve such punishment?"

As *Seña* Josefa uttered that last exclamation, she had already risen to her feet and had her hands over her ears so as not to hear from the mouth of her granddaughter the confirmation of the unfavorable opinion she had reached regarding the latter's views of marriage. Cecilia also stood up and started to follow her grandmother, either with the intention of calming her down, or with that of justifying herself, explaining or expanding upon her idea; she halted abruptly because at that point Nemesia's familiar face appeared through the half-open front door.

X I I

. . . But place
that hand on this breast of mine.
Do you not feel, Matilde,
A volcano within it? It is my jealousy!

J. J. Milanés

"May the days be holy here," a smiling Nemesia said as she entered without knocking.

But she stood silent and motionless at the door once she saw the face and mood of her two friends. The grandmother had again collapsed into the armchair, her favorite place; the granddaughter was still standing alongside the table, on which she was leaning one hand, visibly wavering between grief and despair.

The appearance of this friend in those circumstances could not have been more timely. The old woman had said more than what prudence counseled, and the young one was afraid to delve into the innermost meaning of her grandmother's last words. What was it she knew? Why use such veiled language? Was it hiding well-founded suspicions or was it merely meant to be intimidating?

The truth is that in the argument, with the awareness of each of the two now at its keenest, if not in possession of the facts, they had both set foot on slippery ground, thus far forbidden to them, on which the first of them to enter would reap an abundant harvest of regrets and remorse. *Seña* Josefa, for her part, did not believe the moment had arrived to inform Cecilia of her real position in the world. Perhaps the milk vendor had been mistaken about the identity of the young man; perhaps the latter had merely been passing by the door of the house. If you wish to preserve a maiden's innocence, do not accuse her without proof of her having sinned. For these reasons *Seña* Josefa, though upset and filled with profound regret, in her heart of hearts joyfully greeted Nemesia's unexpected arrival.

Fortunately also, from the point of view of getting the three women out of the embarrassing situation they found themselves in, at that moment someone announced his presence at the street door by hammering on it with the door knocker, a method seldom used. *Seña* Josefa, ever prepared for such eventualities, hastened to open the door, receiving, along with a profound bow, a missive handed to her by a gray-haired black, neatly dressed in clean clothes. He had every appearance of being the carriage driver of an illustrious family. Having given her the letter, he went off, saying: "He doesn't answer."

There was, in fact, no accompanying reply, nor was the letter addressed to *Seña* Josefa, but to "Dr. Tomás de Montes de Oca. To be delivered to him personally." It was arriving at the right moment to calm the principal anxiety of *Seña* Josefa's sorely tried spirit. With the aid of her spectacles, which Cecilia brought to her, she was able to read it, muttering each line to herself:

> "My dear sir: As regards the matter we have discussed, I am sending this letter to its bearer, who will present herself to you on this very day, in order that you may explain to her what must be done regarding the aforementioned matter. I need not repeat that this will answer all concerns and that your undersigned faithful servant and friend will be eternally grateful.
>
> C. de Gamboa y Ruiz."

Having read the letter several times in order to better acquaint herself with its contents, she looked over the top of her spectacles, at her granddaughter first and then at Nemesia (who had fallen silent as she awaited the result of that wordless scene), obviously absorbed in thought, and seemingly hesitating as to what course she should take. But the words "this very day" in the letter obliged her to come to a decision, and she asked:

"What time is it?"

"It's eight o'clock," Nemesia answered promptly. "They've just changed the guards in the city. It's as if I can as yet still hear the drums."

"How happy that makes me!" *Seña* Josefa answered. "Are you in any great hurry today, my girl?" she added, addressing Nemesia.

"No, señora, not a bit. I was on my way to Uribe's tailor shop in search of sewing jobs. But as long as there's life time is long. I'll go later. It doesn't matter."

"Well then, my girl, you're going to do me a favor: stay and keep Cecilia comp'ny, and meanwhilst I'll hop over to La Merced and be back in no time. Will you stay?"

Without waiting for a reply she put her leather belt on again, threw her sackcloth shawl over her head and left the house. And no sooner had she done so than Nemesia suddenly turned to Cecilia, took both her hands in hers, and said to her:

"What did I tell you, darling? I've just run into him."

"Into who?" Cecilia asked.

"Into your beloved torment."

"And whatever do you mean by that?"

"Can that be, woman? You say that as though it wasn't of the least concern to you. When I say I ran into him it's because I believe you'll be interested to know how, when, and where I saw him. I've come to fetch you."

"I can't go out."

"In such cases daring women like you try their best."

"Granny may be back any minute and I don't want her to find me gone."

"What difference does it make? Who said anything about being afraid? And besides, it's not far. Behind Santa Teresa."

"I don't know what I'll get out of going that far."

"An eye-opener maybe."

"Well, that's why I'm not going. I don't want disillusionments so early on."

"You have to come, woman. It's in your interest, I repeat. This minute."

"I'm not dressed and my hair isn't combed."

"It doesn't matter. In no time you can put on a dress, smooth down your hair, throw your shawl over your head and ary a soul will recognize you. I'll help you."

"Nene, how can we get out of the house?"

"We'll lock the door behind us, and that'll be that. Come on, hurry up. There's no time to lose. We might get there too late, after the birds have flown."

"I'm ashamed to go out on the street in a house dress."

"Ary a soul is going to see you. Good heavens! To think that you'd miss out on the big event for a reason like that. Are you coming? It'd be a shame to disappoint us."

"What can all this be about?" Cecilia thought as she went into the bedroom to get ready, which she did, in no time.

Nemesia had succeeded in piquing her friend's curiosity and even alarming her, and was savoring beforehand the pleasure of seeing her die of jealousy.

The two girls had considerable difficulty getting the door locked. The rusted lock was fitted into the angle of the doorframe and the crossbeam on one side, the clamp of the bolt affixed to its ring in the other panel of the door and poorly fitted into the hook that served to support it; as a consequence the catch wouldn't go into the socket so that the bolt would hold fast. But finally they managed to get the door locked, with Cecilia using more skill than force; and they began slowly walking in the shadow of the tile roofs toward the south of the city.

Behind the adobe walls of the convent of Santa Teresa, opposite a house with windows that had projecting grilles and a tall stone bench beneath them, a carriage to which three matched horses were hitched had stopped, facing toward the Calle de la Muralla. The carriage driver, mounted on the left-hand horse and armed with a long machete and other equipment appertaining to his occupation, was ready to take off. On the footboard next to the sidewalk was a young man bidding a final farewell to a young lady in traveling dress, seated to the right of an elderly, respectable-looking gentleman.

The stone bench beneath one of the aforementioned windows was occupied by a gathering made up of a number of ladies and gentlemen, all acquaintances of ours; that is to say, the Gámez family, Diego Meneses and Francisco Solfa, saying goodbye to Isabel Ilincheta who, together with her father, was returning to Alquízar. All of them were calling to her from the window and she was answering them at almost the same time, poking her head out from underneath the folding top of the carriage, and meanwhile not neglecting the young man on the footboard, who was leaning one foot on it as he grasped the hand grip on his left.

At that moment the two girls arrived, walking down the street from the north. From a distance Cecilia recognized the young man acting as a footman: it was Leonardo Gamboa. And although she had not yet laid eyes on the lady in the carriage, nor had she been properly introduced to her as yet, she guessed who that person most likely was. As she walked on, she resolved to give the two of them a good scare, one that would serve to chastise them, to teach them a good lesson. To do so, she walked on ahead of her companion and gave Leonardo a hard shove, whereupon, having had no forewarning, he lost his balance, slipped, and fell into the back of the gig to one side, at the feet of the surprised lady. The latter, unaware of what was happening, or else deciding that it was only a joke, albeit a clumsy one, stuck her head out from beneath the curtain at the back window to see the aggressor, whereupon, believing that she recognized her, she exclaimed, half in fright and half laughing: "Adela!"

In fact, Cecilia, no longer in disguise since her shawl had slipped down her shoulders leaving her black hair floating loose, held down only at the level of her forehead by a red hairband, with her cheeks on fire and her eyes agleam with anger, was the very image of Leonardo Gamboa's youngest sister, though with harder and more pronounced features. But—woe unto her—Isabel realized her error almost immediately. Hardly had their eyes met when that prototype of the sweet, tender friend was transformed into a veritable harpy, hurling one word at Isabel, a single epithet, but one so indecent and filthy that it wounded her like a dart and forced her to hide her face in the corner of the carriage. The epithet was just one syllable long. Cecilia uttered it slowly, in a low voice, almost without opening her lips: "Wh . . . !"

Nemesia forcibly drew Cecilia away, Leonardo rose to his feet as best he could, Señor Ilincheta gave the order to depart, the carriage driver dug his heels into the flanks of the horse inside the shafts, at the same time allowing the tip of his whip to fall on the back of the horse outside the shafts, and the carriage left at a brisk pace, so that a few moments later it was lost from sight at the corner of the next street, down which it turned to the right toward one of the gates in the city walls, the Puerta de Tierra. The ladies and gentlemen sitting on the bench beneath the window waited in vain to see the curtain over the back window of the gig rise and a white handkerchief appear to bid them one last farewell. The curtain did not move, nor did the handkerchief appear, an indication, of course, of the disagreeable impression that the incident had produced in the minds of the invisible travelers. But even as the onlookers reflected on what had just happened, the mulatto girls had vanished, and Leonardo had disappeared along with the carriage.

On the Calle de la Merced, near the convent of the same name, as one headed for the Paula promenade, to the left was a house with a roof terrace, the only one on the block. Although the entrance was a wide one since it allowed up to two carriages to come in side by side, it was not, properly speaking, a *zaguán*. In front of the door a rickety two-wheeled carriage had halted, with a horse hitched between its shafts which, being a perfect match for the vehicle, bore a greater likeness to Don Quixote's Rosinante than to Alexander's Bucephalus. Perched astride the tall saddle, which owed its height to the many sweat cloths placed under it, the better to protect the beast's back, the black carriage driver was taking his rest, his attire, and appearance precisely as unprepossessing as the remainder of the equipment. As he waited for his master, he was either sleeping, or else had more than a little brandy coursing through his noggin, for he was having a hard time holding his head up, his forehead nodding so far at times that it touched the neck of his mount, whose immobility made it look as though it were made of stone.

Seña Josefa approached him from the side of the carriage nearest the sidewalk and addressed him a number of times, without managing to wake him up or cause him to give any signs of life. It is true that, either out of respect or natural timidity, she neither raised her voice sufficiently nor dared touch him. Nor did she know his name, but suspecting that it was José, she asked him over and over in an affectionate tone of voice: "José, José, Joseíto, is the doctor in?"

The black sat up halfway in the saddle and made horrible grimaces in an effort to open his eyes, nearly blinded by the white dust from the street, and finally said: "My name not José, my name Ciliro, an' my master de dotor be dere inside, 'les he lef.' Go in, go in."

After thanking the amiable carriage driver, the old woman went in. In the waiting room a number of people of both sexes who looked to be poor were waiting for the doctor, who at the moment was nowhere to be seen. *Seña* Josefa knew him, and immediately looked all around for him with a certain anxiety, for perhaps he had left; although the fact that the carriage was at the door and there were patients in the waiting room indicated that if he was out of the house momentarily, he had not left in order to make his usual round of house calls on his patients as he did every day after lunch. She finally managed to catch a glimpse of him in the courtyard, leaning over a man seated on a chair who every so often emitted muffled moans, more painful each time, indicating that the doctor was performing a difficult surgical operation. Montes de Oca was undoubtedly a skillful surgeon, or at least a very daring one in his wielding of the scalpel, slicing through human flesh as one slices a large loaf of bread, always, it is true, with exactly the right touch, perhaps because of the cool composure with which he performed those bloody operations.

People tell, in fact, how on a certain occasion he slit open an individual's stomach in order to remove an abscess that had formed in his liver, and the operation was a total success, for the patient did not die at his hands, but rather recovered completely, at least from that ailment. Yes indeed, he was as skillful as he was self-interested and greedy for money. He cured no one without charge; he didn't budge from his house except to make calls paid for in cold cash, or with the explicit promise that sooner or later he would be well paid for his universally recognized skill.

Seña Josefa knew immediately when the operation was over, both because the patient had stopped groaning, and because the doctor, holding up the instrument with which it had been performed, said:

"There you go! You're dismissed. Look what you had in your ear: a dry bean the size of a chickpea, since with the dampness there inside, it grew to twice its normal size."

"Thanks, doctor, a thousand thanks. May God repay you and grant you the best of health. You don't know how much that bean in my ear has tormented me. I haven't slept for over ten days, or eaten, or . . ."

"I believe it," the doctor interrupted him with a triumphant air that at the same time was more than a little mistrustful. "It took me a lot of work to extract that foreign body from your ear. That part of your ear is so delicate that if my hand had not been perfectly steady the pincers could have slipped and damaged your eardrum, leaving you deaf for the rest of your days. So, then. You will now pay me for my work, go along home and gently bathe your ear with infusions of mallows and a few drops of laudanum to soothe the irritation . . ."

"How much do I owe you, doctor?" the man asked, trembling not from the pain, but from the fear that he would be asked for a great deal of money for an operation performed in just a few moments.

"Half a doubloon," Montes de Oca answered curtly and impatiently.

The man's only recourse was to put his hand in the pocket of his trousers and take out a handkerchief that was far from clean, in one of whose corners he had tied a few coins, which surely did not amount to very much more than the sum that the surgeon had demanded for treating him. Dr. Montes de Oca then headed for the waiting room, his head down and his right shoulder hunched over as was his habit, when he unexpectedly found himself nose to nose, as the saying goes, with *Seña* Josefa, whom he asked in his twangy voice:

"What is it you want, my good woman?"

As her only answer, *Seña* Josefa handed him the letter recommending that she come see him.

"Ah!" the surgeon exclaimed after having read it. "I've already heard about this. Señor Don Cándido himself was here very early and talked to me about the matter. But I must tell you the same thing that I told him, namely, that I have not yet seen the patient, that I am not familiar with the case, and that with no knowledge of it I would have to be a clairvoyant in order to decide what should be done."

"Didn't Señor Don Cándido tell you that it's a desperate case, what I mean to say is, that there is little hope, because it's a question of life or death . . . ?" the old woman dared to remark, trembling all over.

"Yes, yes," the surgeon interrupted her. "Señor Don Cándido did mention something about that to me. The thing is that I can't take care of everything. If I were to divide myself into ten doctors I don't think I could keep up. Do you see how many people are here waiting for me? Well, many more are waiting for me elsewhere, and all of them are urgent cases. I respect Señor Don Cándido, I know that he is a generous and unselfish man and that he knows how to show his gratitude for favors done him. I desire, I am able, and it is within my power to be of service to him; I believe that if I am of service this time, he will pay me well. But you, a rational woman, will recognize that I need time, that I must examine the case for myself before venturing a diagnosis. Perhaps it is incurable, perhaps the remedy is worse than the illness. I am not a witch doctor who blindly makes a decision and thereby makes a person's sickness come out and go away. However, perhaps you can give me better information as to what Señor Don Cándido has been able to do, since, from what I understand, he knows of the case by hearsay. Who is the patient?"

"My daughter, Señor Don Tomás."

"Your daughter, you say?" About how old is she now?"

"She's going on 37."

"Well, she's not an old woman then. There's still a live body there, and it probably has some resistance. How long ago was she taken ill?"

"Oh, señor! A long time ago, a lifetime for some people, some 18 years ago now, a bit more than that rather than less."

"No, no, that isn't what I mean. How long has it been since she was admitted to Paula Hospital?"

"She was admitted shortly after she took sick. That makes it a bit less than 17 years ago, because the little one must have been about two months old when I found myself obliged to put my daughter in Paula Hospital, in accordance with the advice given me by Doctor Rosaín, because I couldn't control her at home. The señor doctor can imagine what that separation cost me. It broke my heart."

"So, then," Montes de Oca added, lost in thought, "so, then, the little girl . . ."

"My granddaughter?" *Seña* Josefa said.

"Yes, your granddaughter, the daughter of the sick woman, must be about . . ."

"She's going on 18."

"And what is she like?"

"She's a good girl, and healthy, praise be to God."

"No, that's not what I mean. I'm asking about her appearance, what the girl looks like."

"Ay, señor doctor! Her appearance and looks are what's going to be the end of me before long. Though it's wrong for me to say it, she's the prettiest thing that goes by the name of woman that this world has ever seen. Nobody would guess that she has a drop of colored blood. She looks white. Her prettiness drives me mad; I'm beside myself. I don't have a life or a moment's sleep so as to keep her safe from the young white gentlemen who go after her like flies after honey. She's left me the shadow of my former self."

"And that charming girl would be the sick woman's companion if we take her out of the hospital?"

"If the señor doctor thinks it suitable, I believe she'd be willing to be her companion."

"As far as its being suitable, I believe it would be, most suitable; but there is a difficulty. Let's see. How long has it been since the mother and the daughter have seen each other?"

"What's that? It's been a good long time. More than 17 years."

"As long as that? That's bad. But you or someone else has no doubt spoken often to the mother about the daughter and to the daughter about the mother?"

"I've indeed often spoken to the mother about her daughter, every time I've gone to see her; I've never spoken to the daughter about her mother. I'm tempted to believe she doesn't know that her mother is still alive."

"So no attempt has ever been made to allow the mother and the daughter to see each other?"

"Never."

"A bad mistake."

"I thought so too, but Señor Doctor Rosaín, who was in attendance at the delivery and was in charge of treating her afterward, advised me to separate them, and after the mother lost her mind, he told me again not to tell the daughter about it, because she would want to see her and the madwoman, in one of her fits of insanity, might easily strangle her with her own hands. Señor Doctor Don Tomás needs to know that a fit of madness came over her when her daughter said that since she had been born white she considered it beneath her to have a colored mother."

"Well, well. Rosaín was wrong. He's a good doctor, there's no denying it, except that in this case I'm of the opinion that he lost touch with the case or completely forgot about it. If the mother and the daughter see each other frequently after a long separation, perhaps a reaction will take place, and illnesses are cured with reactions or with revulsions, not with medicines, particularly those in which the nervous system appears to be affected. We are all nerves, nothing but nerves. If they are irritated, look for madness. I was thinking . . . There had been some thought of taking the patient to the country, to a farm I own near the port of Jaimanita, to see whether the revulsion being sought would be brought on with a change of air and salt water baths. But the fact is that the daughter can't go there with her mother. On that farm, on the plantation at Jaimanita, I mean, I have formed a company with the Belenitas Fathers, you see. They administer it and many of them spend fairly long periods there, during the sugar cane harvest and milling season in particular. What a scandal would break out with the appearance of a young woman as pretty as you say, in the midst of those blessed Fathers! The temptation! God save us. More than one of them would lose his senses and people would say that it was my fault. . . . But we'll see how all that can be arranged. Come back here day after tomorrow, and meanwhile I'll see the patient and tell you what must be done. I want to be of service to Señor Don Cándido, I can be of service to him, and it seems to me that that will be to the benefit of all the interested parties.

X I I I

The heart's joy keeps age in full bloom,
sadness withers the bones.

Parables of Solomon

In the era of which we have been speaking, a professional dentist was a *rara avis* in Havana. Following that Castilian saying that teaches: "If a molar hurts, have it pulled out," the occupation or art of dentistry was practiced, for the most part, by barbers in the towns, and in the country by surgeons who, armed with powerful iron forceps, did not leave a tooth or a molar alive.

There were also toothpullers who were interlopers or enthusiasts. Among them, one by the name of Fiayo had become famous for the dexterity and skill with which he painlessly yanked these appendages for mastication out by the roots and waved them in the air. His fame and popularity, however, came from the fact, first, that he used no sort of surgical instrument of any sort; and second, that he took no money for his magic dental operations.

The eldest daughter of the Gamboa family, Antonia, had been suffering for some time from an acute facial neuralgia, whose site in her upper jaw made it likely that its cause was a cavity in a molar. The doctors who were consulted, after trying the application of poultices, leeches, rinses, and compresses without apparent benefit, decided that the molar should be extracted. But the mere idea that in order to do so the dreaded forceps would have to be used made the pain-racked young lady break into sweats and fall into faints.

Around that time there arrived in Havana from the country the magical dentist Fiayo, and as usual he put up at the home of Dr. Montes de Oca.* The moment the news reached Doña Rosa's ears, she ordered horses hitched to the gig, and she and her suffering daughter headed for the Calle de la Merced. The waiting room was full of patients, some seeking advice or remedies from the doctor, and others the services of the famous toothpuller. The latter was occupying the second consulting room, the door and window of which overlooked the courtyard, and therefore had better light and was more suitable for operations on the mouth. In it was an ordinary wooden chair, in which he had the patient sit with his or her face to the east, and in no time Fiayo had pulled out by the roots the molar or the tooth pointed out to him by the interested party. It sometimes happened that he encountered greater resistance than he could overcome with nothing save the force of the thumb and index finger of his right hand, in which case he furtively put that hand in the pocket of his waistcoat, as though he were drying his hand off, armed himself with a little iron key, turned the bit into a forceps, the shaft into a lever, and his success was instantaneous and certain.

The entrance of Doña Rosa Sandoval de Gamboa with her lovely daughter Antonia occasioned no little surprise on the part of the persons present in the waiting room, Montes de Oca in particular, who even though he was the palace physician and enjoyed widespread and well-deserved fame, was not accustomed to being consulted in his own home by ladies of such distinction and such apparent wealth. This kindly condescension could not help but make a doctor of the social and material status of the one with whom we are dealing at present feel obligated; and so it was that, abandoning his patients at once, he came out to receive and attend to the newcomers. He knew Doña Rosa only by name and by sight, despite his close and long-standing ties of friendship with her husband. But in the time it took him to approach her and greet her, it crossed his mind that perhaps the unexpected appearance of that respectable lady had something to do with the patient in Paula Hospital of whom he had been speaking with old *Seña* Josefa just as Doña Rosa

* Historical fact. *Author's note.*

came into the waiting room. And once this strange thought had entered his mind, there was no way to make it go away.

"The esteemed wife of my dear friend Señor Don Cándido Gamboa y Ruiz, if I am not mistaken," Montes de Oca said.

"Your servant," Doña Rosa answered curtly.

"And I am your obedient servant. And this young lady is your daughter?"

"Yes, señor."

"That is plain to see. A lovely girl. May God keep her. Kindly come in and have a seat."

"That is not necessary," Doña Rosa said. "You are a very busy person and I came only . . ."

"I can guess why, or rather I know why, and forgive me for interrupting you," Montes de Oca said with unaccustomed officiousness. "I am pleased to see that you too are interested in the health of the patient in Paula Hospital. Such kindness and nobility of soul are most praiseworthy. I can see it, I understand perfectly; you wish to know my diagnosis concerning the state of the poor girl as soon as possible. That is most praiseworthy."

Having heard nothing about such a patient, mother and daughter looked at each other in bewilderment, a bewilderment that the doctor not only did not understand, but interpreted to be one of those feelings of astonishment mingled with gratitude that well-bred people experience when their thoughts are divined and their heartfelt desires anticipated. His vanity thus flattered, he went on, more and more pleased at his insight:

"I shall tell you, señora, with deep feeling, as I have just told the patient's elderly mother, with whom you saw me speaking a moment ago, that my diagnosis is not at all favorable. I can be even more frank with you than with the mother. There is no more strength there now, no subject, as we say; all that is left is a soul that is still alive and a body that is nothing but skin and bones, as is said of the black Africans just arrived from Guinea. Her illness stemmed from an acute case of meningitis, following a shock, which under the influence of a puerperal fever, deprived her of her powers of reason and caused a general disorder of the nervous system, a state that became chronic, and one for which to date medical science knows no remedy. During the day the most pronounced symptoms are those of a slow consumption, now in its final stage, the end of which may be more or less near, but in any case certain and fatal, unless I am badly mistaken, an end which Galen himself could not postpone one hour, one minute if he were to return to this world for that purpose alone. Patients in this category die out like candles as the tallow of which they are made is consumed. Her life will be extinguished any day, any hour now. The worst part of all, Milady Rosa, is that it is now too late to take her out of the hospital. We run the risk that she will die on us, that the candle will be snuffed out the moment it is exposed to the open air of the countryside. I deeply regret not being able to fulfill the desires of Señor Don Cándido . . ."

At that point Doña Rosa gave a start of surprise that drew the attention of the doctor, absorbed in his own thoughts, obliging him to leave his sentence unfinished. It was little wonder that she reacted to this remark as she did. A younger, less prudent woman would have uttered an exclamation, showed greater irritation and anger. The impression that Montes de Oca's last words made on her was such, however, that her face changed color, turning beet-red at first and then pale, and naturally the placid expression with which she had been listening to the unintelligible diagnosis disappeared. Although its origin was quite different, Antonia experienced the same shock of surprise. Because of her youth and naiveté, she did not understand, surely, all the slyness that might be inferred from the fact that her father wished to take a sick girl unknown to the entire family out of Paula Hospital, with the aim of having her illness treated elsewhere. But Doña Rosa's situation was not the same. What was obscure and meaningless to the daughter was a sea of light to the mother, the confirmation of her continual suspicions, the goad arousing a long-standing jealousy that was still alive. Who could that young girl be, and what sort of relations did her husband have or had he had with her to make him so determined to get her out of Paula Hospital through the influence of Dr. Montes de Oca? She must be a mulatto, since her mother was nearly coal black. She was gravely ill, the doctor had held out no hope for her recovery, by now she must be a skeleton, ugly, revolting, certain to die soon; but she had been her rival, she had enjoyed the love and the caresses of Gamboa on an equal footing with herself.

By what divine decree was she discovering in that rival's final hours a secret that she had been trying to track down for more than a decade? Vengeance was now little short of useless. Death would soon interpose itself between wife and mistress. What despair! What a tumult of passions! What a tying and untying of loose ends, hidden but not forgotten in the corners of her mind! She yearned to speak, to shout, to unburden her heavily laden heart in some way. What great relief tears would have been! As good a Christian and as circumspect as Doña Rosa was, at that moment she would doubtless have given half her life to go back in time beyond today's events to the year 1813 or 1814, when, still young, full of strength and personal charm, with less wisdom and calm, she would have found it easy, plausible to assert her rights as a wife, mother, and gentlewoman.

As she mulled all these questions over in her mind, a matter not of long minutes, but rather of seconds, and felt her blood rush to her cheeks, there passed through her mind the memory of the baby girl in the Royal Foundling Home who had been suckled by María de Regla, the slave who was now a nurse at La Tinaja; and she deduced, as a logically necessary consequence, that that episode was closely related to the sick woman in Paula Hospital. Was Gamboa trying, then, to save the life of the mother of his bastard daughter? Who could that daughter be? Was she still alive? Did she recognize him as the father who begat her? She would have to find out. Perhaps Montes de Oca knew. Making a supreme effort, she managed to control the agitation that was about to paralyze her senses and decided to drain to the dregs the cup of curiosity and jealousy. Therefore, picking up once again the thread of the conversation with Montes de Oca, who gave signs of an eagerness to show off how much he knew, she said:

"I too deeply regret that nothing can be done to help poor, uh . . ."

"Rosario Alarcón," the doctor prompted Doña Rosa, seeing that she was stammering.

"Rosario Alarcón," the latter repeated. "It was on the tip of my tongue. I have a poor memory for names. I told Gamboa that it was too late by now and I don't doubt that the disappointment will cause him real regret. And then the daughter, as soon as she learns of it . . ."

"With regard to that," Montes de Oca put in at once, "you needn't worry, Milady Rosa. The grandmother was clever enough to hide from the girl the fact that her sick mother was still alive."

"Can that possibly be?" Doña Rosa exclaimed. "It seems beyond belief . . ."

"It was as easy as could be," the doctor went on. "That is to say, I am repeating what the old woman who has just left told me, and I do not find her story absurd. I suppose that you are aware that when they put Rosario Alarcón in Paula the daughter was a very young child, without the use of reason, so that she didn't miss a mother whom she never saw again."

"So the daughter, a full-grown young woman . . ."

"And a very pretty one, no offense to present company intended," Montes de Oca said, again interrupting his interlocutor to put his own interpretation on a thought that had been merely hinted at.

"Do you mean to say that you know the girl?" Doña Rosa asked. "Perhaps she was here with her grandmother."

"No, señora, I have never seen her. I am speaking from hearsay, repeating what the grandmother told me. Or rather, I haven't seen her since the first or second month after she was born, when the Royal Foundling Home or Maternity Hospital was located on the Calle de San Luis Gonzaga, near the corner of the Calle del Campanario Viejo."

"Then that is the baby girl my slave María de Regla was hired to suckle."

"That may well be; I don't know a thing about that."

"How can that be, if it was by your order that I was paid the two doubloons a month for her hire all during the time she nursed the aforementioned baby girl?"

"By my order? I beg your pardon, Milady Rosa. I have no notion of any such hiring, nor, of course, of any such monthly payment. Might you not be mistaken?"

"Come, doctor," Doña Rosa replied. "Is it a question of a lapse of memory or sheer modesty on your part?"

"Neither one, my dear lady. I have positively no knowledge of the matter you are speaking of."

"So be it," Doña Rosa finally said, noting that the doctor was putting himself on his guard. "I understand what is going through your mind: you do not wish us to speak any further about this matter. I won't say another word about it. That does not stand in the way of my expressing my pleasure at the use you made of the services of my slave when you offered to help out a friend who found himself in a tight spot. Allow me to add, since the opportunity presents itself, that I refused to take one peso for the hire of that wet nurse, and that if I finally took the money it was because I was told that otherwise you would not accept her."

Montes de Oca remained silent. He merely bowed his head respectfully like a man who, having been caught dead to rights, with no plausible way out or any means of defense, resigns himself and awaits the verdict. But the few details he denied were precisely those that Doña Rosa must have been most certain of, namely, the hiring of the wet nurse and the wages paid for her services each month during a certain period of time. Where she was sadly mistaken was in taking for granted that Montes de Oca had been the one who supposedly arranged for the hiring of the wet nurse and paid the money for her hire. With regard to this important detail the aforementioned señora had been taken in: her husband had not told her the truth!

Now then: on seeing the doctor's stubborn denial, did Doña Rosa disabuse herself of her error? The truth is hard to prove in such cases, and therefore we shall limit ourselves to saying that once certain obscure details concerning the sick woman and the relations that her husband had had with her and her daughter had been clarified, the rest fell in place by its own momentum, was easily inferred, and informing an outsider of family secrets that perhaps he really knew nothing of was not worthy of a lady. She gave up the attack, then, and ended the conversation by begging the doctor to forgive her for having bothered him and asking him to kindly tell her whether Fiayo was available to examine her daughter Antonia's mouth. Of course he was, and the operation was performed most successfully. Then Don Tomás Montes de Oca was courteous enough to accompany the two ladies as far as the footboard of their carriage and help them climb in. And once she was seated and the ride home had begun, Doña Rosa covered her face with her hands and began to weep and sob uncontrollably and inconsolably, all this to the astonishment of her daughter, who, preoccupied by her own physical pain, had not noticed the transformation of her mother's face as soon as she was no longer in the doctor's presence.

We had best advise the reader at this point that as a consequence of a row with his father for having left the house so early in the morning, as we have already recounted, Leonardo had not returned home for three of four days, staying instead with an aunt on his mother's side. This contributed to making Doña Rosa even sadder. Not only did she refuse to sit down at the table, set for lunch, but also to give Don Cándido any explanation regarding the cause of her distress. In the midst of her tears and sighs, she uttered the name of her son and favorite several times, the reason why her daughters, presuming that the absence of their brother was the cause of her lamentation, sent Aponte out with the carriage to look for him. The young man came back home, and immediately Doña Rosa, putting her arms around him, covered his brow with kisses and tears. Meanwhile she showered him with the most affectionate epithets and said to him: "My beloved son, where were you? Why did you flee from your mother's caresses? My love, my consolation, don't leave my side. Don't you know that you are your sad mother's only help in time of trouble? You don't lie, you always tell the truth, you are the only one in this house who knows the value of a mother and a faithful wife. My life, my treasure, my faithful friend, my everything in the world, who or what will have sufficient power now to tear you from my arms? Only death."

Finally this lady, married, the mother of a family, favored by the gifts of fortune and of nature, found herself surrounded on arriving home by several persons who were very dear to her, who respected her, and who hastened to dry her tears, to offer her consolation and distraction. When all was said and done, her anguish, admittedly legitimate, was born of a disillusionment with her conjugal life from which, in the days when she fell victim to it, it was evident that her guardian angel had turned her eyes away until such time as the knowledge of it would be less painful to her. Before that time, a fit of jealousy was the only thing that had disturbed the serenity of her days, ever placid and untroubled in all other respects.

But what was there in common between the sorrow, the disillusionment, or the jealousy of Doña Rosa Sandoval de Gamboa, and the sorrow, the disillusionment, and the despair of poor *Seña* Josefa, more forsaken and lonely than before ever once she had left Dr. Montes de Oca and again crossed the threshold of her little house on the Calle del Aguacate? She had every reason then to cry out with the psalmist: "Come, heaven and earth, birds that people the air, fish that fill the waters, beasts that tread the fields, and tell me: Is there any sorrow comparable to mine?"

No one asked *Seña* Josefa why she was weeping and was plainly so distressed. Cecilia, whom she found at home on her return, was too chagrined to think of anyone else's troubles. Nemesia also kept very quiet, saying only as she bade the two of them good-bye: "I'll see you later." Even the statue of the Virgin in her niche, facing *Seña* Josefa's armchair, seemed to offer her no consolation this time. Racked with the pain of the sword piercing her breast, the Virgin's loving eyes were turned elsewhere.

And such was, after all, the timely sign that *Seña* Josefa received amid her terrible loneliness. The mother of the Savior of the world, at the very moment she lost her Son as he died nailed to a cross, clearly was teaching her through her resigned, sublime demeanor, that there are sorrows so great that there is no consolation to be found for them here below, but only there above, in heaven!

XIV

Meditating on its pain
My heart within my breast is set aflame:
Its fire cannot be contained
And passes all bounds:
And my tongue now loosened,
I spoke without restraint.

González Carvajal

The strange conduct and the ironic phrases of his beloved wife alarmed Don Cándido Gamboa. She had never used such sarcastic language. On the contrary, in her fits of jealousy she had always erred on the side of being overly frank and forthright. What new information had she discovered? Where had she been that morning to have brought about such a change in her?

It did not accord with Don Cándido's character, nor with his ideas of honor and dignity, to ask his wife for an explanation of the mystery, much less his children, with whom he seldom spoke, and less still the servants, one or another of whom knew more family secrets than was advisable for peace and happiness within the home. Worldly and astute, he believed that he could leave it to time and to the indiscretion of his wife or his children to rid him of his doubts sooner or later.

He comported himself, it is true, with greater caution. He was twice as observant as usual; and that was the one new feature of his conduct from then on toward his family. He did not have to wait very long either, for a few days later, at the lunch table, the conversation turned to Antonia's facial neuritis and to the relief she had been feeling since the extraction of her molar by Fiayo. That was all Don Cándido needed: his wife had been to the home of Montes de Oca, and it was common knowledge that it was there that Fiayo was staying and performing his dental operations.

This was a precious bit of information, except for the fact that, instead of helping him to solve the enigma, it contributed to disorienting him and up to a certain point to calming his fears inasmuch as it never entered his head that the doctor had spoken to his wife about the patient in Paula Hospital. Though he knew him to be very talkative, he couldn't imagine that his guilelessness (it was not malice) would lead him to the extreme of revealing to a woman who was a stranger to him, whom he was seeing for the first time, a matter that was of no concern or interest whatsoever to him. For what reason, moreover, would he have broached the subject? Gamboa, furthermore, took it for granted that he had spoken in confidence to the doctor about the sick woman, and even though he had not sworn him to secrecy, it was implicitly understood that he was to keep the matter entirely to himself in all circumstances.

We have already seen how fallacious all these lines of reasoning of Don Cándido's were. His reflection that *Seña* Josefa, on finding herself by chance with Doña Rosa at Montes de Oca's, had offered an explanation of the matter or spoken in her presence of the patient in Paula Hospital was equally erroneous. Persuaded, however, that this was what had taken place, he waited for *Seña* Josefa for several mornings in a row at the shutter of the window of her house.

To no avail. The doctor had been even more frank, harsher we would say, with the old woman than with Doña Rosa. He had taken away her every hope once and for all when, in everyday language, not that of science, he had convinced her that her daughter would never recover. For a woman of her advanced years, bowed down by her cares and exhausted from her labors, more and more unhappy with her granddaughter, who to all appearances was following the same path as her dying mother, that news was more than her spirit and her body could endure. To cite her own words, she had already followed the *via crucis* to its very end, she had arrived at the summit of the mount of Calvary, and the one thing that still awaited her was the crucifixion, a death that would mercifully end a life already very long in view of how greatly she had suffered, an unending fabric woven of privations and of sacrifices.

She never recovered from this blow. After fits of weeping and other demonstrations of grief, she again had recourse, with redoubled zeal, to prayer, to litanies, to almost daily confession and communion, to continual penance, falling back in the end into that state of indifference and mental and physical apathy with regard to worldly affairs that bears so great a resemblance to alienation or dementia. It was as if the mysterious fire that since the early years of her life had communicated warmth to her blood and vivified her spirit had suddenly gone out. For she ceased to be communicative, withdrew within herself, neglected her granddaughter, spent her time solely in acts of devotion that to her were second nature, an automatic reflex, and fell asleep, in a word, dreaming from that day forward the dream of life.

So great and so sudden a change could not help but attract Cecilia's attention; if in the beginning she took advantage of it to satisfy her passions and whims, later on she felt more compassion and affection for her grandmother. Knowing that even though she was suffering from no apparent illness, she would fall dead when least expected, she began to be frightened and to think more about her own future. In a word, she would be left alone in the world, with no kin, no respectable friends, no help or protection, and she redoubled her care of her grandmother, she was kinder and more helpful and obliging that she had ever been in her life. But her caresses, her loving words, her assiduous labors as a submissive and tender granddaughter met with no response worthy of the name; at times they aroused only a cold smile. . . . and a frightening one for the inexperienced girl, who thought she saw in this response a sign of premature senility, if not of mental derangement. It was not that the old woman had lost all touch with her feelings, for more than once her granddaughter found her with her cheeks wet with tears. If this was *Seña* Josefa's state immediately following her last conversation with Montes de Oca, she could hardly have approached Don Cándido to speak to him of a matter that by then had been almost completely erased from her memory.

The situation of that gentleman, to be sure, was not much more tolerable. His wife continued to treat him with unusual reserve, to the point that it bordered on coldness; while at the same time, as if out of pique, she was doubly affectionate and tender toward her son Leonardo. Each time he left the house, she accompanied him as far as the *zaguán*, and bade him good-bye there with repeated kisses and embraces. If he came home late at night, a frequent occurrence, she anxiously awaited him at the grille of the window as a woman awaits a lover, and far from remonstrating with him when he finally arrived, she kissed and embraced him once again, as though he had been gone for a long time, or had run a grave danger while he had been away. Doña Rosa couldn't do enough for her spoiled son. There is no need to add that she anticipated his every wish, divined his thoughts, and proceeded to satisfy his every whim, not as a mother, but as a lover, with eagerness and wasteful extravagance, without losing a moment's time and regardless of what it cost her. If after coming home from one of his forays he so much as hinted that he felt tired or unwell, oh heavens above!, she turned the entire household upside down, causing his sisters, the servants, the steward, every last member of the household, to concern themselves with nothing else save the relief and well-being of the indisposed young man.

Even if Don Cándido had had the calm of an ox or the patience of Job, everyone would perforce have blamed him for such things; but it made his blood boil, not so much because the mother was contributing to her sons's perversion with her inopportune pampering as because in so doing her intention was to humiliate the father. He found himself so harassed that one day he said to her:

"If you had deliberately set about ruining the boy, Rosa, it strikes me that you wouldn't have done a better job of it."

"You're not anyone to accuse me of that," she answered most emphatically.

"Nonetheless, the accusation stands."

"So I see, and I attribute it to the fact that at times men lose their . . . modesty."

"That's a harsh word, but I let it pass in deference to peace."

"You needn't let it pass, if you prefer. It makes no difference to me."

"I imagine you're forgetting that I'm as concerned about the matter as you are."

"You concerned! You as concerned as I am about the boy's good or bad conduct! A graceful way out indeed. I doubt it, I don't believe it, I deny it."

"It's no use denying it, señora; I wouldn't be his father if I said otherwise."

"Well then, I, his mother, who gave him life, who nursed him in my arms, say to you that you may exempt yourself from looking after the boy's fortunes. He has no need of a father's attentions; his mother's are quite enough."

"That doesn't keep me from worrying as I see how his mother is deliberately doing more and more to doom the lad."

"I don't believe that it matters much to his father whether he is lost or saved."

"It matters more to me than you imagine, my dear señora. If he did not bear my name . . ."

"A nice name, really, a fine one!"

"It's as good as any other. It's worth a great deal to me."

"I'd believe that that were so had I not seen that you yourself have dragged it in the mud. A nice name, as I said. You may be certain that had I known 24 years ago what I just found out today, my son would not bear the name that he does. But I am the one at fault. This wouldn't have happened to me if I had followed the advice given me by my mother, may she rest in peace."

"And what did your good mother advise you to do, may I ask?"

"I'm not embarrassed to tell you what her advice was; she told me: 'Daughter, don't marry a man whose religion or nature is different from yours.'"

"Which is tantamount to saying, it seems to me," Don Cándido added, quite hurt, "that you regret having married me. Would you have preferred a Creole who was a gambler and a fool? Of course."

"Perhaps," Doña Rosa replied in a gentler tone of voice, while her words were sharper. "But gambler or not, it's likely that a Creole, a countryman of mine, would have behaved more faithfully and more decently toward me. Surely a Creole would not have been unfaithful to me for 12 or 13 years. . . ."

"Well, you've finally come out with it!" Gamboa said, breathing more freely. "I protest against the accusation. I have never been unfaithful to you."

"And you have the nerve to deny the accusation? Who if not you assured me again and again that María de Regla was nursing the illegitimate daughter of a friend of Montes de Oca's? Who paid the two doubloons of the supposed fee for her hire as long as the infant was being suckled? No, it wasn't you. It was someone else, it was Montes de Oca's circumspect friend. The money, if so, didn't come out of your pocket; it came out of mine, or rather, you took it from me with one hand so as to give it back to me with the other."

"A thief, the work of a thief; it couldn't be clearer or cloudier," Don Cándido said, trying to make a joke of her accusation.

"You've put your finger on it exactly. And the fact that your assessment is accurate is proved by the well-known fact that my capital was much greater and clearer of encumbrances than yours when we married."

"You have no need to remind me of it."

"Of course I do!" Doña Rosa burst out determinedly. "I have still other things to remind you of. For I must tell you that under the same circumstances my husband the Creole would perhaps have gambled with his money and mine, but he certainly would not have spent a peso on love affairs with mulatto women. He certainly would not have gone to Montes de Oca to get his mistress out of Paula Hospital and see that she recovered in the countryside. He certainly wouldn't have lost his head over a young girl whose father is heaven only knows who."

"So Señora Doña Rosa Sandoval y Rojas has saved up all that for me?"

"This is my explanation," the latter continued, not disregarding her husband's mocking remark. "The hatred, yes, quite simply the hatred, that you have always professed for my son. This is the real reason behind your determination to take him from my side and send him off to eat onions and chickpeas in Spain. You were afraid that he'd discover what his mother has just discovered through sheer chance. You were afraid that he wouldn't deign to bear your name and consider it beneath him once he saw with his own eyes the mudhole through which you've dragged it. You were afraid that he'd be ashamed and indignant that his father, not a Creole gambler and a fool, but a Spanish hidalgo through and through, cheated on his mother with a dirty mulatto woman, who lies in a charity hospital atoning for her grievous faults and sins."

"I hope you'll soon be done so that . . ."

"You're hoping that I'll soon be done?" Doña Rosa interrupted him, smiling disdainfully. "I haven't set a time to finish. And why should I finish? Or what can you say, if I were to hear you out, in extenuation of your bad conduct toward the most faithful and steadfast of wives? Could you, would you dare deny the facts of which you are accused?"

"Deny them as a whole, no, explain them, yes, in such a way that you yourself would be persuaded that I am not the evildoer that your imagination makes me out to be."

"I do not care to hear any more explanations. You have deceived me with your complicated stories and tales for altogether too long a time."

"I see, then, that your intention is to vent your anger, not to give a fair hearing to reason and justice."

"What I intend, Señor Don Cándido Gamboa y Ruiz," his wife said, raising her voice and making a solemn gesture, "is to keep you from squandering either my money or my children's on paramours and on the family of your beloved. On this subject and that of mistreating my son to make him pay for your disappointments in love, my mind is made up: either you mend your ways or I'll sue for divorce."

After what had been said, Don Cándido withdrew to his study, silent and serious. And Doña Rosa greeted his withdrawal with sincere applause from the bottom of her heart. Because it is fitting and proper to apprise the reader that all during the heated dialogue recorded above, she had been making a great effort to remain in control of her emotions, in order to say everything that she had kept to herself during long years of anxieties and suspicions, before her noblest sentiments once again held sway as usual and the lesson that she had intended to teach her husband was ruined. It is fitting to say, moreover, that she had married for love, despite her mother's opposition, and perhaps for that very reason; and she did not wish to break with the father of her children and her constant companion. Then too, in their 24 years of marriage she had not had any plausible reason to regret having married, even though Don Cándido's faithfulness had never been exemplary.

The reader will also have noticed in the course of this true story that Don Cándido, before and after marrying, had been more or less a rakehell, as the vulgar saying goes. Handsome and something of a ladies' man, in his youth he had been easily infatuated or a philanderer; and this was his most glaring defect. But despite his unpolished manners and his scant culture, in the bottom of his heart there was goodness and nobility, moral qualities that to a great extent redeemed that defect. Precisely because he loved with all his heart and was a man with a conscience, when he made a commitment, however against nature it might be, he did everything in his power to fulfill it, in order to do so sometimes confronting all the difficulties that arose with a serene brow.

Eighteen or twenty years before, that is to say, four or five years after he married, the father now of two children by his lawful wife, he chanced to meet an unusually beautiful young girl. Without knowing how or when, he had a secret affair with her; a relation easy to enter into when the man is young, rich, and handsome and the woman beautiful, in her fifteenth year, and of mixed race. From this injudicious relation a baby girl was born, whom Don Cándido was bent on saving, from death first when she was an infant, and then later from poverty, obscurity, and degradation when she was a youngster. One commitment led him to another and yet another, not only concerning the little girl but her grandmother as well, for the latter was soon obliged to act as her mother, even though none of the three in that family was now in a situation, or possessed of the ability, to appreciate his favor or to recognize his costly sacrifices.

Once the years of effervescence had passed, the most propitious time for the follies of youth, the memory of his weakness began to upset him more than a little. His tremendous struggles to fulfill his obligations as lover and adulterous father without neglecting his sacred obligations as husband and upright father of a family date from that period. But Doña Rosa's jealousy, aroused to the highest degree by her pride in her race and as a married woman, by her ideas concerning a woman's virtue and the duties of the mother of a family, occupied her in such a way and blinded her to such a point that it kept her from noticing that her husband had fully repented of his previous faults, and that in order to make amends for them he was employing every means at his disposal. As the aforementioned señora, rightfully offended, threw up to him his youthful straying from the path of virtue, she failed to see that she was rending one by one his every heartstring; she failed to see that there no longer existed nor could there have existed later on the reasons for jealousy that had so badly upset her earlier; she failed to see, finally, that for some time Don Cándido, deploring the past from the depths of his soul, was simply endeavoring to avoid a great scandal, a catastrophe in the not so distant future.

X V

I lost my indifference
Along with my freedoms;
I became fond of her then,
I became fond of her, mother.
I began to love her,
She began to forget me:
May it send you into a fury, mother.
A fury that kills her.

L. de Góngora

The hours, the days, and the weeks went by and neither letters nor news of Isabel Ilincheta arrived in the city following her departure for Alquízar. It was true that communications in the capital, even with towns in the same jurisdiction, were difficult at times. But there was no shortage of private couriers, freight haulers, or itinerant peddlers who consented to take letters and parcels back and forth without charging a fee. And Isabel was in the habit of using them in order to keep up a correspondence with her cousins the Gámez girls and with Leonardo.

The latter left the house of those young ladies at dusk on the sixth or seventh of December, quite concerned, just as a young woman, her head covered with a dark shawl, was walking along the street toward the Calle de Teniente Rey. Because it seemed to him that he knew her, he quickened his pace, soon overtook her, looked at her out of the corner of his eye, and stopped her, realizing that it was Nemesia.

"Why such a hurry?" Gamboa asked her.

"Good heavens!" she exclaimed. "The gentleman should be more careful; he gave me a good scare!"

"It was because you were trying to run away from me on the sly," Leonardo said, using the language of people of color.

"It's not my nature to run away from someone on the sly or any other way, least of all from persons I respect."

"Persons you respect. Am I perchance among their number?"

"The very first among them."

"Anybody who'd believe that would believe anything."

"The gentleman doubts it?"

"What do you mean, do I doubt it? I don't believe it, because as the saying has it, love is acts, not good reasons."

"What proof does the gentleman have for saying that?"

"Many proofs. I'll give you one, the most recent of them. The day I was bidding farewell to a friend at the door of the house I had just left, who was it that brought Celia by so that she could see me and be jealous? You. Nobody but you."

"Who told you that?"

"Nobody. I suspected it at the time and now I'm convinced of it. You're worse than Aponte,[37] as my grandmother used to say."

"Don't believe it, señor," Nemesia said, a smile playing about the corners of her mouth. "The gentleman can take my word for it; it was all a mere coincidence. I was on my way to pick up some sewing jobs at *Seño* Uribe's tailor shop and Celia wanted to come with me."

"Go ahead, make me believe that you're a little saint, that butter wouldn't melt in your mouth. But be warned that you're committing a sin by declaring war on me. If you're doing so because you fancy that there's no love in my heart save for Celia, I can tell you that you're wrong. There's love in my heart for her, for my friend in the country, and still a world of affection left over for ungrateful creatures like you."

"And now I'll tell you emphatically that anyone who'd believe that would swallow anything."

"You have to believe me, because I say so and because you're the most charming mulatto girl who treads this earth."

"Flatterer! Fickle fly-by-night!" Nemesia exclaimed, obviously returning the compliment. "Men are evil, mind you. But I don't care to take off with ary a one of them or be a dish of warmed-up leftovers."

"If you're a dish, woman, it doesn't matter when you're served. Too bad for girls who are a dish that doesn't please anybody, because it's proof that they'll end up being old maids. Let's conclude a treaty; don't make war on me."

"Enough on the subject: I'm not making war on the gentleman."

"Oh yes you are. I can see it. I know the signs. Celia is angry with me on account of you. But you've chosen a bad path to lead me away from her. Don't throw fuel on the fire. In here, right in here," he added, pressing the left side of his chest with both hands, "there's room for Celia and for her most affectionate friend."

"No. For me to go inside there I'd have to be alone, all by myself. I don't want comp'ny in the heart of any man I love."

"Selfish creature!" Leonardo said to her, giving her an amorous look.

And they went their separate ways, Nemesia heading for the Calle de Villegas and her house in the Callejón de La Bomba, and Leonardo going straight on to the Calle de O'Reilly.

Nemesia had heard from the lips of the young man himself, with whom she was hopelessly in love, that there was room for her in his heart along with Cecilia. Perhaps he was simply flirting with her. What is our opinion? Leonardo's only intention was to propitiate her, flattering her feminine vanity in passing with the hope that should a certain possibility present itself, he might find his amorous desire realized. But Nemesia, reflected that were such an eventuality to come about, something she found it hard to imagine, it could easily happen that she would enter his heart accompanied by another woman and remain there all by herself, the winner of the entire field. Hence the discovery, besides causing her inexpressible joy, made her even more determined to carry out the plan that she had been working on for some time. In order to make sure that it would have the desired effect, two means offered themselves to her wicked imagination. With the knowledge that of the most pronounced traits of her friend's character, she shared with her an eminently jealous nature, together with an uncontrollable pride, Nemesia judged, and judged rightly, that if she aroused both passions to the utmost in her, even though she did not succeed in making Cecilia break with her lover, or in supplanting her in the latter's affections, she would at least cause him to abandon her friend.

Her brother José Dolores would play a principal role in the drama. She took it for granted that Cecilia would never love him. This mattered little, for once the lovers were deeply involved with each other, it would not be difficult to make Gamboa jealous, just as in her resentment toward the white man it was natural that Cecilia would be willing to flirt with the mulatto. We shall see the fateful outcome of these intrigues.

It so happened that when Leonardo Gamboa came out at the Calle de O'Reilly, a man who gave every appearance of being Nemesia's brother was just leaving the little window of Cecilia's house. That piqued his curiosity, and therefore, without warning, he approached, almost at a run, and raised the corner of the white curtain with the tip of his fingers. Behind it was Cecilia, sitting in a chair, with her elbow resting on the stone bench underneath the window and her chin on the palm of her hand. On realizing that the person who had lifted the little curtain was her lover, she gave no sign either of surprise or of joy.

Yes, he said to himself, very humiliated by what he had seen and by the indifference with which she greeted him. Yes, she's dissembling now. Who could fail to see her sitting there? She looks as if butter wouldn't melt in her mouth. "What are you doing?"

"Nothing," she answered dryly and laconically.

"Is your grandmother out?"

"Yes, señor. She's gone to Vespers, there across the street."

"Open the door, then. Let me in."

"I wouldn't dream of it."

"How long have you had such strict moral standards? I'd like to know."

"I don't know. It's up to you to say."

"What I know is that a man has just left here."

"No, señor. No one has been here since Chepilla left."

"I saw him with my own eyes."

"Your eyes deceived you. It was an illusion."

"He was about as much of an illusion as I am. I saw him, I saw him, I don't have a shadow of a doubt."

"So I'll be obliged to believe that you see visions."

"Stop speaking to me with that air of disdain, even of contempt let me say, for I find it intolerable and not at all in keeping with your character or mine. Don't dissemble either or try to persuade me that the person who has just left this window was a ghost and not a man of flesh and blood, following whose departure I find you sitting there, to all appearances perfectly calm and serene."

"Ah! That's another kettle of fish. You may have seen a man standing there where you're standing now. What I deny and will continue to deny is that you saw him leave this house, because he never set foot inside."

"In any event, he came out of here, out of this place; he was having a conversation with you and I need to know who he is and what he wanted."

"'I need,'" Cecilia repeated disdainfully. "How brave of you! Will you use force to find out? Because I'm not going to tell you."

"Be that as it may, you have to tell me, or otherwise I'll have a falling-out with you and you'll never in your life see my face again."

"That's what I'd like to see happen."

"You'll see it. In a word, will you tell me who it was?"

"No, I'm not saying."

"You seem to be trying to play games with me."

"I'm not playing; I mean every word I say."

"Very well. Open the door and let me in, because I'm ashamed to have people passing by see me. They're going to think we're having a fight."

"And they'll be right."

"Come on. Are you going to leave off being so evasive?"

"I say what I feel."

Leonardo stared at her for a moment, as if to measure the significance of her words, and then tried to take her hand, which she pulled away, and then he touched her face, with the same result. Cecilia did not seem inclined to give up one iota of the attitude that she had adopted since the beginning. Would she be capable of leaving him for another man? Was her favorite the one he had seen leaving her window? Let us sound her out a bit more, he said to himself, and immediately added aloud:

"What's really the matter with you, may I ask?"

"Who, me? Nothing."

"If you shut yourself up in that vicious circle of 'I don't know any-thing, I'm not saying a word,' I think the best thing for me to do is to clear out of here."

"As you like."

"I understand you less and less every time I see you, Celia. I suspect, however, that you're not saying what you're really feeling, and that if I were to go along with your less than sincere words and leave for good, you'd weep bitter tears. What! You're keeping silent? What do you have to say? Answer."

The position that Cecilia had taken was becoming too prolonged and too aggressive for her to maintain it much longer. She truly loved Gamboa. If she kept up her uncharacteristically severe attitude, she risked driving her lover away, not to mention the fact that she had no clear proof of his fickleness. For all these reasons, when she was forced to reply categorically, she bowed her head and burst into tears accompanied by deep sighs.

"You see?" he said to her, quite touched. "I knew your angry outbursts would lead to this. Your heart loves me even as your lips disdain me. Enough! It's all over now. Weep no more, my love, because I'll end up weeping with you. The proper thing to do now is to bury the hatchet and be as good friends as ever."

"Only on one condition would I make my peace with you," Cecilia managed to say between one sob and the next.

"Agreed. Out with that condition then."

"No. First you must promise to observe it."

"I say! That's a lot to ask. Perhaps it isn't within my capability. But who mentioned fear? Yes, I promise."

"You must promise not to go to the country for the coming Christmas holidays . . ."

"Cecilia, for heaven's sake! What strange caprices you have! What's the reason behind such a demand? You doubtless imagine that I'm leaving you forever or that I'll forget you. Think it over, and don't ask me to do the impossible."

"I've thought about it a great deal. Are you going or are you staying?"

"I'm not going nor am I staying; because an absence of two weeks in the country is neither one; it's not a permanent departure nor is it a formal staying."

"Very well," Cecilia said firmly, drying her tears. "Look. I know what I must do."

"Don't make a decision that you'll regret later. I beg you again to think things over and see my position just as it is. Do you think it would be easy for me to stay in Havana while my whole family is at La Tinaja plantation near El Mariel? Well, it wouldn't be; in the first place there won't be anyone here at home save for the steward and a few servants. In the second place, even if I were to try to stay home, my mother wouldn't allow me to, much less my father. Everyone will be leaving on the twentieth to the twenty-second and be back on the Sunday of the Lost Child. Do you understand now?"

"What I understand is that you're going to have a good time in the country with a woman I detest even though I've never met her, properly speaking, and that I cannot, will not, and do not wish to agree to your doing so."

"You're very jealous, Celia. It's your one defect. If I love you more than my life itself, more than all the women in the world, isn't that enough for you? What more do you want? Moreover, this brief absence is in the best interest of both of us; that way we'll love each other even more tenderly on my return. Then early next April, I'll receive my law degree and after that I'll have more freedom to do whatever I please. You'll see, you'll see how much we're going to enjoy ourselves. I for you, you for me."

By this time Cecilia had risen to her feet, perhaps in anticipation of her lover's departure, silent and lost in thought. Her lovely bosom, her shoulders and arms as beautifully rounded as a statue's, her extraordinarily narrow waist, so small that it could almost be encircled by a pair of hands, stood out marvelously well in the dim light of the candle inside the room, by contrast with the darkness that already reigned in the street. More enamored than ever of such beauty, Leonardo added with the greatest tenderness:

"What is needed now, darling, is for you to give me a kiss as a sign of peace and love."

Cecilia didn't say a word in reply or make the slightest movement. She appeared to be transfixed.

"Farewell!" the young man said dejectedly. "Will you not give me your hand either?"

The same silence, the same immutability. The change could not have been more complete, for if she was breathing, her round upraised breast showed no signs of it, nor of agitation or perceptible movement.

"Your grandmother will be coming at any moment," Gamboa added; "I don't want her to see me. Good-bye, then! . . . Ah! Will you tell me the name of the person who was talking with you when I arrived?"

"José Dolores Pimienta," Cecilia answered in a voice as curt as it was solemn.

Leonardo could feel all his blood rushing to his face and his cheeks burning; and as if the better to hide the shock that that name on Cecilia's lips had given him, he hurried off from that house as fast as his legs would carry him, just as the faithful emerged from the neighboring convent.

Cecilia for her part collapsed in the chair and wept bitterly.

XVI

In the life of every man guilty of a grave misdeed there comes a time when repentance is the obligatory tribute that must be paid to his alarmed conscience; yet mending his ways, since that is subject to other laws and dependent upon external circumstances, is not always within the power of human will to achieve. For guilt shares this characteristic with certain stains: the more they are washed away, the more clearly the face beneath can be seen.

Don Cándido would have truly liked to break with the past once and for all, to erase from his memory every last trace of certain facts. But without knowing how, without being able to avoid it, when he believed that he was altogether free of them, he felt in his very flesh, so to speak, the weight of the irons that bound him to the mysterious whipping post of his first sin. Its witnesses and accomplices played a large role in this. They reminded him of it unceasingly and brought him face to face with it wherever he turned his eyes.

For the enlightenment of the reader, here are some of the reasons that, as a result of his serious altercation with Doña Rosa, Don Cándido pretended to have run into Montes de Oca by chance. He did not reproach the latter for the indiscretion he had committed by talking too freely with his wife. Reproach him! On the contrary, he had never shaken his hand more effusively. The fact was that he needed him to carry out a plan that he had been mulling over in recent days. He wanted Montes de Oca, as a doctor, to certify that the sick women in Paula Hospital could not be transferred to the new insane asylum without risk to her life. This, first of all. Then, second, he wanted him to agree to act as a channel through which *Seña* Josefa, or her granddaughter in her stead, would receive a monthly pension of twenty-five and a half *duros* for an indefinite period.

Once Montes de Oca's greed had been aroused with the promise of a splendid gift, it was not difficult to get him to take care of the certificate or to accept the responsibility of seeing to the monthly pension. On Don Cándido's part, this was a way of making a thief a trustworthy accomplice; if this recourse failed, it might have proved to be a more risky matter to put the discretion of a third party to the test.

He was thereby cutting off, Gamboa believed, all future direct relations with the three accomplices of his grave sin, without going back, however, on the agreement made with them. But the worst was yet to come. How to free Cecilia Valdés of the trap that his son Leonardo was setting for her? The two of them were madly in love with each other, they saw each other frequently, and neither the recriminations she received from her grandmother nor the threats that Don Cándido brought to bear on his son through Doña Rosa sufficed to separate them. There was nothing else to do, then, save to put the young lover aboard a ship and send him out of the country, or to abduct his beloved and put her where she couldn't be seen or couldn't communicate with him. It was of no use even to contemplate the first solution: Doña Rosa would fight against it with all her strength. As for the second, it was extremely risky and was fraught with almost insuperable difficulties. Such were the thoughts that weighed most heavily on Don Cándido's mind and made him suffer the torments of hell all during the period whose events we are here recording.

So then, was it best to proceed at once to abduct the girl? There was no urgent need to do what was best at that very moment, for two principal reasons: namely, the grandmother was still alive, although ailing and in declining health; and within two weeks the family would be going off to spend the Christmas holidays at La Tinaja, and it had been agreed that Leonardo would be accompanying them.

In fact, a week before the holidays the schooner *Vencedora* was sent to El Mariel, its skipper, Francisco Sierra, entrusted with the victuals, preserves, and wines that could not be found for love nor money anywhere near the plantation, and with the personal servants of the Gamboa family, among them Tirso and Dolores. The Ilincheta sisters with their aunt, Doña Juana, would also join the family; to that end Leonardo and Diego Meneses would escort them from Alquízar.

The reason behind the coming meeting of the two families at La Tinaja was to enable the entire party to witness the first use of a steam engine to aid in the milling of the sugar cane harvest, instead of the human manpower with which up until then the original heavy sugar mill had been kept running.

Leonardo did not want to leave without first having a rendezvous with Cecilia. He obtained it easily, as much because both desired it as because at the time it appeared that *Seña* Josefa had lost all control over her granddaughter. But Leonardo's pleas, flattering words, promises of greater happiness, or threats to break off their affair were to no avail. Cecilia closed her ears to all that and held her ground, firm as a rock, with regard to her refusal to consent to her lover's leaving for the country. Her faithful heart told her that he was running off to join her fearsome rival, which was tantamount to losing him forever. Anyone else except the reckless young man would have taken into consideration the young woman's attitude and her unshakable resolve and would have admitted to admiration for her if not sympathy. But being arrogant and scatterbrained, he believed at first that he could overcome her resistance and ended up taking offense and going off feeling resentful.

This time Cecilia did not weep. Her heart rent with grief, she watched in silence as Leonardo strode off. Her lips did not part to call out after him, nor did she allow her tears, even after he had left, to reveal the anguish of her soul, since in her own estimation of herself they would be a contemptible sign of weakness. Before giving in to the harshness of fate, she decided to take noteworthy vengeance on her thankless lover. No sooner said than done; almost the moment he left her side, she hurriedly dressed, gave her grandmother a good-bye kiss, finding her buried as usual in the tiny easy chair, and left the house. But as she headed for Nemesia's house, in the Callejón de La Bomba, on reaching the corner she chanced to meet Cantalapiedra, whom she had not seen since the night of September 24. It was no use bowing her head, or drawing the folds of her crepe shawl closer to hide her face. The commissioner recognized her immediately, and like it or not, stopped her in the middle of the street, saying to her:

"Halt, in the name of the law. Surrender or it will cost you your life."

"With your permission," Cecilia replied solemnly, making as if to continue on her way.

"Give yourself up, I say, or else I shall make use of the authority vested in me by law. Respect these tassels (showing her the ones affixed to the police baton that he was carrying underneath his left arm) or I shall order Bonora (his constable, the one with the bushy sideburns, who was following him at a respectable distance) to proceed to arrest you."

"Since I haven't committed any crime, it's useless for you to show me your tassels and threaten to sic your lieutenant on me," Cecilia answered very calmly. "Let me pass, for I'm in no mood for jokes."

"Unless I see that little face outside of your shawl, don't expect me to allow you take one step more."

"Do I perchance have monkeys painted on my face?"

"My dear girl! Play games with me and you'll hear ten strike without a clock."

"I'm not playing; I'm in no mood for games. Let me go."

"Where are you going?"

"Somewhere."

"A rendezvous?"

"I never have a rendezvous with anyone; I wouldn't leave my house to meet the king of men."

"You'd fool anybody listening to you into swallowing your lies."

"How do you know whether I've lied about these things?"

"Well, we'll find out if what you say is true."

"How will you do that?"

"Easily, by following in your wake."

"Are you out of your mind, captain?"

"No, I'm quite sane. I'm the commissioner of the district and what would people say of me if I were to let a girl as pretty as you go astray, whereupon we'd be involved in court proceedings and lawsuits?"

"I'm not offended by your words because I know that you're a very fun-loving man."

"The truth is that I'm not larking around now. I don't want to offend you by even as much as the width of the black underneath a fingernail; but, I repeat, neither as the district commissioner nor as a man can I allow you to go about the streets at this hour without a valiant beau to guide you and defend you."

"Nothing will happen to me. You may be certain of that. I'm headed for somewhere very close by."

"Very well, I'm willing to believe you. May God and the Virgin guide you and keep you. But won't you let me see your little face?"

"Aren't you looking at it right now?"

"That's not how I'd like to see it. Push back those confounded folds of your shawl."

Cecilia did as she was told, perhaps so as to be free of the cheeky fellow, baring almost all of her bosom by merely letting the shawl fall down over her shoulders. At that very moment Cantalapiedra puffed hard on the cigar he was smoking, producing more light than there was round about them, since there were no street lamps in that neighborhood and the stars were too dim to see by.

"Ah!," the commissioner exclaimed excitedly. "Can there be anyone who is not dying of love for you? Accursed of God and of men be the man who does not worship you on his knees as the saints of heaven are worshiped!"

Confronted with the commissioner's comic gesture and exaggerated exclamations, Cecilia couldn't help smiling, and then she went straight on to Nemesia's house, without bothering to look back to see whether he was dogging her footsteps. Since she was thoroughly familiar with the all the ins and outs of the house, she did not knock on any of the doors but went directly from the street to her friend's room, surprising her hard at work in front of a little pine table, stitching a tailored garment in the flickering light of a tallow Flanders candle in a tin holder.

"Woman's work is never done!" Cecilia said as she came in.

"Hello there!" Nemesia exclaimed dropping her sewing and going to meet her with open arms. "How good of you to come! Ought we to draw a line in water to mark the occasion?"

"Are you alone?" Cecilia asked before sitting down in the wooden rocking chair that her friend offered her.

"Lonely at heart, rather, though José Dolores will be home soon."

"I wouldn't like him to find me here."

"Why not, dear?"

"Because men immediately fancy that you're chasing after them."

"My brother isn't one of that sort, dearie. He loves you, he adores you, he idolizes you, everybody knows that, he's forever sighing after you; but he's so bashful he wouldn't even dare remark that you have black eyes, much less fancy that you've come on his account."

"Ay, Nene!" Cecilia went on, pretending not to hear what her friend had said. "A few evenings ago Leonardo found me talking with José Dolores at the window of the house. Unfortunately. I paid dearly for it with Leonardo."

"Don't tell me!" Nemesia answered, unable to conceal altogether how happy that made her. "But the two of you have no doubt made up. Isn't that so?"

"I do hope so!" Cecilia exclaimed with a sigh. "He was furious and we had a big row. Who knows when we'll see each other again. Maybe . . . never again. He's very stubborn and I'm almost as bad."

After uttering these words, she remained silent for a moment. Her voice had stuck in her throat, and big tears appeared in her lovely eyes.

"What!" Nemesia said in surprise. "Are you really crying? Aren't you ashamed of yourself?"

"Yes," Cecilia answered with obvious feeling. "I'm crying not in pain, but in anger at myself, because I know I've been a fool."

"Indeed you have! I'm happy to hear you say that. A woman mustn't trust any man; I've told you so any number of times"

"That's not my reason for saying that, Nene. Do you call loving a man a whole lot the same thing as trusting him? Perhaps it is; and I ask you, is it in your power to love or not to love? Do you know any remedy for love and jealousy? The best thing, dear friend, would be to have no heart. That way we wouldn't feel affection for anyone."

"Well then, it looks as though you think Leonardo has deceived you."

"No, I don't feel deceived. God deliver me from that! Leonardo hasn't left me for another woman nor do I believe he will. If I even suspected such a thing I wouldn't be sitting in this chair telling you so."

"And what else do you expect, woman? I greatly fear that that fish isn't going to nibble at your baited hook again."

"What do you know that I don't?" Cecilia asked in fright.

"Nothing, nothing at all," Nemesia said. "But I can't forget the favorite saying of *Seña* Clara, Uribe's wife: "To each his own.""

"I don't understand."

"It couldn't be clearer. Doesn't *Seña* Clara have more experience than we do? Of course. She's older and has seen twice as much of the world as you and I have. But if she keeps repeating that saying, she must have a good reason. Just between the two of us, ary a soul has told me so, but I know that *Seña* Clara has always liked whites more than mulattos, and it was very hard for her to marry *Seño* Uribe. Of course, she had more disappointments and disillusionments than she has hairs on her head, and that's why she now consoles herself by repeating to girls like you and me: 'To each his own.' Do you understand now?"

"Yes, fairly well, except that I don't see how the saying applies to me."

"It fits you exactly, dearie; it catches you dead to rights. Don't you prefer whites to mulattos, just as *Seña* Clara does?"

"I don't deny it. I like whites a whole lot more that mulattos. I'd hang my head in shame if I married a mulatto and had a baby who was a throwback[38] to his father's side."

"Open your eyes, woman: goodness, love, affection, fidelity don't hold white men back at all. Leonardo isn't going to marry you in church later on either."

"Why not?" Cecilia answered vehemently. "He's promised me he would and he'll keep his word. Otherwise I wouldn't love him the way I do."

"Oh! It hurts me to hear you talk like that, but I wouldn't want to disillusion you. I'm only telling you to open your eyes, lest something bad happens when it's too late. Don't be too trusting, don't be too trusting, and always keep in mind that the ant singed its wings by venturing to fly."

"The one who dies by his own choice savors even death."

"I understand, but if a women dies unexpectedly, without pain or travail, that's all well and good; it's God's will. The thing is, dearie, that before dying a person suffers a great deal. So then, does it hurt as much when a white man leaves us for a colored woman as when he leaves us for a white one? What would you be willing to wager? That really hurts. And I imagine that that's what's happening to you now. So you hold your tongue, you don't even say 'I won't make the same mistake that so many others have made.'"

Cecilia was readying herself to deny the aptness of Nemesia's remark when José Dolores Pimienta appeared at the patio door, and while she was unable to or did not know how to say what she was thinking, he too stood mute and motionless in the doorway. He was not expecting such company, much less at that hour of the night. Once he had recovered from his surprise, he expressed in brief and carefully chosen phrases how glad he was to see her. Cecilia said that she had come only to give Nemesia a hug and a kiss, and stood up to leave.

"I have a piece of good news for you," the musician said. "It's been decided that the colored people's dress ball will be held the night before Christmas, at Soto's, on the corner of Jesús María. The señorita is of course at the top of the list of those who are invited, and it is hoped that

Nemesia, and *Seña* Clara, and Mercedita Ayala, and all our lady friends will attend. It's going to be a mighty fancy ball, an outstanding event, I assure the señorita."

"In all likelihood I won't be able to attend," Cecilia said. "Chepilla isn't feeling at all well and I'm afraid to leave her alone."

"If the señorita isn't there, you may be sure that there will be no light to illuminate the ball."

"I didn't know that you were such a flatterer," Cecilia said with a smile as she moved toward the door.

"The señorita mustn't go home by herself," José Dolores said.

"Don't worry, nobody's going to eat me. Don't trouble yourself. Good-bye!"

Despite Cecilia's objections, the musician and his sister saw Cecilia to the door of the house where she lived.

XVII

And just as he believed victory possible
He found himself run through with bright steel.

J. L. Luaces

José Dolores Pimienta had said that the colored people's ball would be held at Soto's house. It stood on the west corner of the Calle de Jesús María, where it meets the Calzada del Monte, opposite the Campo de Marte.

In front of the *zaguán* or entryway was a wide porch with a wooden railing. From it, through the very high windows thrown wide open, people who were not allowed to enter could witness the fiesta as long as they liked. Tables for the buffet supper had been set up in the square courtyard, which was covered with an awning; the orchestra played in the dining room; in the vast salon there was dancing; and in the adjoining rooms the guests rested and held intimate conversations with their friends or lovers.

The decorations of the salon consisted of nothing more than several hangings of red damask, the national color, caught up with blue ribbons to form canopies at the height of the lintels of the doors and windows. Lighting was provided by pure spermaceti candles, burning in large crystal chandeliers, with a profusion of crystal prisms that reflected the light, multiplied it, and broke it up into every color of the rainbow.

The phrase *dress ball* or *court ball* was meant to suggest one that was very formal, high toned and of a sort no longer held by whites, neither as concerned the dance music nor the unusual attire of the men and women: that of the women should and did consist of a white satin skirt, a blue sash across the bosom, and a marabou plume atop the head; that of the men, of a black wool swallowtail coat, a piqué waistcoat and a cravat of white linen, short nankeen trousers, flesh-colored silk hose, and low-cut shoes with a silver buckle, all in the style of Charles III, whose statue by Canovas stood at the end of the Prado, where today the Fountain of the Indies or of Havana is prominently displayed.

In order to enter and take part in the fiesta this special dress for the men was not all that was required; it was necessary to come provided with a ticket, which had to be presented at the entry to the committee stationed there to receive it and to assign the women places. This measure was strictly observed in the beginning; but as soon as the time came for the dancing to begin, Brindis and Pimienta, the principal committee members in charge, delegated their task to individuals who were less scrupulous and upright. It was owing to such negligence that, late at night, certain individuals who, though wearing formal dress, had no ticket and were not skilled workmen with a métier either, gained entry.

Among their number was a black of average height, somewhat stout, with a full round face and a receding hairline at both temples, whose inroads, if he lived past 40, would leave him with a completely bald pate. Although he was dressed in the required costume, his tailcoat was a little too tight-fitting, his waistcoat looked quite short on him, his stockings were so old they were faded, his shoes were missing their buckles, his shirt front was not ruffled, and his collar rode up so high that it nearly covered his ears, perhaps because he had a short, brawny neck.

Either because of these shortcomings, or excesses of which we are not well informed, the black with the receding hairline was the object of all eyes from the moment he appeared at the ball. He noticed this, for he was no fool, and in the beginning he naturally wandered about as if bewildered, avoiding the salon, which was more amply and more brightly lighted; but around 11 he tried his best to join the little groups that were forming around the pretty girls, until finally he dared to invite one of them to dance a court minuet, and displayed so much rhythm and elegance that he attracted everyone's attention. Two or three times he approached the group that was worshiping or paying court to Cecilia Valdés, the loveliest of the women at that heterogeneous gathering; he contemplated her out of the corner of his eye for a long time and then moved away with visible signs of scorn.

On one of these occasions, a journeyman tailor from Uribe's tailor shop who was observing him closely, followed him out of the salon, put his hand on his shoulder in a rather familiar way and said to him:

"What! You here?"

"What . . . what may I do for you?" the man replied as he turned around, shaking from head to foot.

"What are you doing in this part of town, kid?" the journeyman tailor asked him with even greater familiarity.

"Kindly tell me, sir," the black with the receding hairline replied in annoyance: "when and where have I been an intimate of yours?"

"Well, I declare!" the tailor answered, more than a little humiliated. "Those are insulting words."

"Insulting or not, they're the ones I use with nuisances like yourself."

"Stop playing the part of the man of mystery and master of all you survey, because I know who you are and you know who I am. Come down off the stage, pal. You might get dizzy up there, and if you fall you'll hit your head on the cookstove."

"Come on, tell me, what is it you want from me?"

"Nothing, I don't want a single thing in this world. I merely noticed that you had nothing but disdain for the prettiest girl at the ball and that piqued my curiosity."

"Does the whole complicated affair concern you?"

"To a fair degree, more than you imagine."

"And it is your intention to defend the girl, is that it?"

"I don't think you offended her. Women don't have to have the king's face and thus garner everyone's favor. There's no offense in finding someone either pleasing or displeasing."

"Well then, leave me alone."

"You're an ingrate," the tailor said to him gravely. "You're not the one who's to blame; it's my fault, for being concerned about an individual who is my inferior, a cook and . . . a slave." At that the black flew into a rage and raised his hand to give his opponent a slap in the face; but for reasons that he alone knew, he never delivered the blow. He had gained entree into that house without a ticket, he knew no one, he was an intruder, and any scandal that was caused would redound upon him. He limited himself, therefore, to threatening the tailor and telling him that they would settle accounts as soon as the ball was over, then scornfully turning his back on him. Such an exit from the scene brought the greatest possible burst of laughter from the tailor, and he said jokingly:

"Tailcoat, let go of that man."

He immediately sought out his friend José Dolores Pimienta and told him what had happened with the black with the receding hairline, the two of them had a good laugh over the incident and didn't give it another thought.

From an early hour the house was full, with people packed in like sardines, as the familiar phrase goes. The crowd of people of all colors, sexes, and social classes who had crowded together in front of both windows on the wide porch looked as lively as it did interesting and tumultuous. In the salon there wasn't even standing room, at least while there was no dancing going on; the men elbowed one another, nearly hiding altogether the women seated around the room. Cecilia, like Nemesia and *Seña* Clara, Uribe's wife, was sitting on a chair facing the street, along the stretch of wall between the dining room door and that of the master bedroom, and whenever the voices of the groups of men who came over to greet her permitted, the exclamations of admiration that her exotic beauty brought forth from the people on the porch could be heard.

At times, behind the extravagant praise of the girl's charms, voices of people of a different persuasion could be heard, since by taking her to be a young pure-blooded white, there were those who were naturally shocked to see her there and believed that anyone who consented to rub elbows so intimately with colored people was motivated by base sentiments. Meanwhile Cecilia savored to her heart's content the greatest triumph that any woman in the flower of her youth and beauty ever attained. One after another, all the men of a certain prominence who packed the ball that night, whether they knew her or not, came to greet her and render her homage, as blacks born in Cuba who have received some education and think of themselves as being refined and attentive to ladies know how to do. Among them we might mention Brindis, a musician, elegant and well-bred; Tondá, the protégé of Captain General Vives, a young black who was intelligent and as brave as a lion; Vargas and Dodge, both from Matanzas, the one a barber and the other a carpenter, who were included in the supposed conspiracy of colored people in 1844 and shot to death by a firing squad in the Paseo de Versalles of the same city; José de la Concepción Valdés, alias Plácido, the most inspired poet that Cuba has ever seen, who met the same unfortunate end as the two men just named; Tomás Vuelta y Flores, a distinguished violinist and the composer of noteworthy country dances, who perished that same year in the Conspiracy of the Ladder, so named because many of the conspirators were tied to a ladder and cruelly whipped, a torture to which they were subjected by their judges in order to extort from them a confession of their complicity in a crime whose existence has never been definitely proved; Francisco de Paula Uribe himself, a highly skilled tailor, who in order to keep himself from meeting the same fate as Vuelta y Flores, took his own life with a razor as they were shutting him up in one of the prison cells of the citadel of La Cabaña; Juan Francisco Manzano, a tender poet who had just been emancipated, thanks to the philanthropy of a number of Havana literati; and José Dolores Pimienta, a tailor and a deft clarinet player, as fair of face as his person was modest and elegant.[39]

Cecilia deigned to dance a habanera with José Dolores and Vargas, a court minuet with Brindis, and another with Dodge; she conversed amiably with Plácido, extended a graceful greeting to Tondá in return for his to her, spoke of country dances with Vuelta y Flores, and praised highly the musical talent of Ulpiano, who was conducting the orchestra for the ball.

Any average observer could note that despite the friendliness displayed by Cecilia toward all those who approached her, there was a distinct difference between her treatment of blacks and of mulattos. With the latter, for example, she danced two country dances, and with the former only elegantly formal minuets. But she gave free rein to her innate tendency toward exclusiveness when the black with the receding hairline was introduced to her and asked to be her partner for a habanera or a minuet. It is true that she did not go so far as to express her answer in the negative in the form of a harsh and curt no; she gave him as her reasons for not dancing with him the fact that she had already promised the next number to someone, that she felt very tired, and so on. The man was not satisfied, but rather, indescribably humiliated, and went off murmuring rude and threatening phrases.

Cecilia's attention was not particularly arrested by this; but a little while later, as she was strolling with Nemesia and *Seña* Clara around the buffet tables and happened on the black with the receding hairline, who appeared to be keeping a close eye on her as he stood leaning against the doorjamb of one of the side rooms, she was suddenly afraid, and gripping her friend's arm said to her in a hurried, low voice: "There he is!"

"Who?" Nemesia asked, turning her head.

"Look," Cecilia added. "Over there. That one."

At that moment the man detached himself from the doorjamb and came over and stood so close to Cecilia that his beard touched her shoulder, whereupon with no further preliminary he said to her:

"So this miss didn't think me worthy of being her dancing partner this evening?"

"What's that you're saying?" Cecilia asked, more frightened than ever.

"I'm saying," the black went on, giving Cecilia a sinister look, "I'm saying that this miss snubbed me."

"If you believe that, I offer you a thousand pardons, because I had no such intention."

"This miss told me she was tired and then immediately went out onto the ballroom floor to dance with someone else. She needn't apologize (he added in a rush, knowing that Cecilia wanted to answer back); I understand the reason why this miss snubbed me. She sees me as someone pitch-black, poorly dressed, without friends in this select gathering and has taken me for someone of no importance, someone ill-bred, someone penniless."

"You are mistaken."

"I am not mistaken. I know what I'm saying, just as I know who this miss is."

"Señor, you're mistaking me for someone else."

"I know this miss better than she imagines. I've known this miss ever since she was a suckling and crawled about on all fours. I knew her mother, I know her father like the palm of my hand, and I have many reasons to know the woman who nursed her for over a full year."

"Well, I don't know you, nor . . ."

"Nor does it matter to this miss? I understand. I must tell her however, that she holds me in contempt because she imagines she's a white because she has white skin. She isn't a white. She may fool others, but she can't fool me."

"Have you detained me to insult me?"

"No, señorita. I am not in the habit of insulting persons who wear gowns. If instead of a gown, this miss were wearing trousers, you may be sure that I wouldn't be speaking to her in this way. The pride this miss shows toward me raises my hackles all the more . . ."

"We've spoken long enough," Cecilia interrupted him, turning her back.

"As the señorita chooses," he went on, highly annoyed, "but allow me to tell her to come down off her high horse, because even though her father is white, her mother is no whiter than I am, and what's more, this miss is the reason why I've been separated from my wife for more than 12 years."

"And what do I have to do with that?"

"The señorita must have had something to do with it, because my wife was her real mother, since she nursed her from the day she was born, since the señorita's mother couldn't nurse her because she was mad . . ."

"You're the one who's mad," Cecilia exclaimed in a loud voice.

Nemesia and *Seña* Clara then surrounded their friend and tried to take her back to the ballroom. But they stopped when they spied Tondá, Uribe, his journeyman tailor, and José Dolores Pimienta himself (Cecilia's self-appointed protector), who had heard her outcry and hurried over to find out what was happening. The latter was the first to put that question to her.

"Nothing. That black," she said with sovereign contempt, "was bent on having an altercation with me . . . since he sees that I'm a woman."

"The coward!" Pimienta shouted, a modest lamb suddenly turned into a lion. And he rushed at the stranger to give him what he had coming; but the latter dodged and put himself on his guard.

José Dolores was unarmed and limited himself to adding:

"Who are you?"

"I am who I am," the other answered imperturbably.

"What is it you want here?"

"Whatever I like."

"You're to leave this house right now or I'll boot you out."

"I'd like to see you try."

"Ah, you dog! You must be a slave. Out!"

At this point Tondá, Uribe, and the journeyman tailor intervened; without their presence there would have surely been a bloody fight between the gallant musician and the stranger with the receding hairline. The aforementioned tailor called him by the name of Dionisio Gamboa, and after gradually surrounding him, they all pushed him literally out into the street on all fours. As they were throwing him out, he kept turning his head and saying, addressing Cecilia: "You imagine you're white, and you're a mulatto. Your mother is alive and she's a madwoman." Then, addressing Pimienta, he said: "Señor defender of young girls, you blood of a bedbug, the one who owes pays. There's no need to go on with this fight. We'll have this out face to face later." To the tailor, who kept saying to him: "Shut your mouth, Dionisio Gamboa, go cook in your master's kitchen, don't start shooting your mouth off, because you may get a flogging so good it'll make you lick your fingers; tailcoat, let go of that man," he replied: "My name isn't Gamboa, my name is Jaruco. And remember that you owe me too."

The behavior and in particular the words of the black with the receding hairline were of some concern to Cecilia. It so happened that everything he said about her father and mother oddly coincided with what she herself had heard and suspected before.

The mysterious language that her grandmother always used whenever she spoke of the gentleman who was their benefactor was enough to make her sometimes think that he must have a relationship to her other than merely that of a suitor, even though it never entered her mind that her father was her lover's father. Leonardo would not love her or promise her to marry her forever if he knew, as he surely must, that the two of them were so closely related. As far as her mother was concerned, Cecilia's grandmother, a better authority than the Gamboas' cook, had never assured her that she had died, yet on the other hand she had never told her that she was alive either, much less that she was insane. The sick woman whom *Seña* Josefa often visited in Paula Hospital, according to the little that had escaped her lips in moments of intense sorrow and deep sadness, was not her daughter but simply a niece of hers; perhaps the relative of a relative of a close childhood friend. The cook named Dionisio Gamboa or Jaruco was necessarily mistaken, he was repeating mere rumors, speaking from memory.

For these reasons, and taking into account Cecilia's age and happy nature, it is not surprising that, after a certain fleeting concern, she should give herself over once again to the pleasures offered her by the ball. Nonetheless, amid the whirlwind of the dance and the incense of adulation with which the men endeavored to enthrall her, the thought of the risk that the brother of her friend Nemesia was running by having defended her from the insults of a madman or an assassin made her feel uneasy from time to time.

Hence, as a grateful woman, from that point on she began to feel a sort of liking for José Dolores that she had never felt before, and in order to reduce the debt she owed him she felt no embarrassment about telling him of her fears. He laughed heartily on hearing her out, answering her, perhaps in order to calm her, that Dionisio Gamboa, Jaruco, or whatever his name was, was a wretched slave, too much the loudmouthed showoff to stop him outside the ball and have it out with him, because as the saying goes, a barking dog never bites. Cecilia remarked to him that since the black was a slave and a coward he was even more to be feared, for he would attack him treacherously rather than face to face. José Dolores's answer to this was that, indeed, he had to be on the alert and keep his eyes wide open lest he be attacked from behind; but besides that he was now armed with a knife that a friend had just lent him, and that any man who could kill him on the first try had to be as cunning as a lynx.

After the buffet supper and another habanera between twelve and one in the morning, the ball ended and everyone started home. Enjoying one another's company, *Seña* Clara, arm in arm with Uribe, her husband, Cecilia and Nemesia arm in arm with the latter's brother, walked together along the row of hovels that lined that side of the road, heading toward the gate in the wall called the Puerta de Tierra, because it was the one that was closest. As they approached the first corner of the Calle de Cienfuegos or Ancha, Cecilia noted the shadow of a man who, once he had overtaken them, turned to the right at the corner. She suspected immediately who it might be and tried to attract her companion's attention, pointing out to him the cafe named the Atenas on the opposite side of the street, dark and deserted, near the statue of Charles III, at the entrance to the promenade. But the man did not go straight on as she was hoping he would do; he took his stand on the corner and said in a loud voice: "You scoundrel, you blood of a bedbug, come on over here if you're a brave man."

It would have been necessary for José Dolores to have the blood of that insect to pretend to ignore such a challenge, delivered to him in the presence of the lady of his thoughts. He therefore made a move to loosen his two companions' hold on him, each of whom was gripping him by one arm. The two of them would have succeeded in their attempt to keep him back, had Uribe not come to his aid, saying to the young women:

"Let him take a stab at him."

That is what happened. José Dolores took out the knife, held his hat in his left hand so as to use it the way the torero works the bull with the cape, and followed his adversary's footsteps without getting too close to him.

Cecilia, Nemesia, and *Seña* Clara, clutching one another's hands and holding on to Uribe, all atremble and as anxious as can be imagined, stood near the corner awaiting the result of a fight that could not help but be a bloody one. A few moments later they heard the silvery voice of José Dolores say: "Here I am," and the hoarse voice of the black answer: "I'm here." And without further ado the horrible fight began.

The complete lack of public lighting, along with the darkness of a moonless night, kept them from seeing the movements of the combatants clearly, despite how close to them the little knot of onlookers was.

Even if Dionisio had had the serene courage of José Dolores, he did not have his agility, much less his dexterity with a knife. This was soon evident, because after a few feints and passes with his hat, a strange sound was heard first, like new cloth being ripped apart by force, and immediately thereafter the brutal thud of a heavy body hitting the ground. Cecilia and Nemesia gave a piercing scream and closed their eyes. Which of the two men had fallen? A moment of terrible anxiety!

As the one who had fallen went on dully groaning, the other appeared to be slowly approaching the road. In seconds, if not minutes, he emerged from the deep darkness that surrounded him, much deeper for the eyes of those who were waiting and could not see clearly because of the scare they had had. He was laughing as he came, as lightfooted as a fallow deer, sheathing his knife and donning his hat torn to shreds. It was José Dolores Pimienta. Cecilia was the first to welcome him, and without knowing what she was doing, out of an impulse of her generous and sensitive soul, threw her arms around his neck, asking him affectionately: "Are you hurt?" "Not a scratch!" he answered, all the more proudly inasmuch as he could feel resting on his heart the head of the woman whom he adored with no hope of her returning his adoration. On hearing his words, she wept out of sheer happiness, like a little girl who finds her doll when she thought it had been lost forever.

III

I

You deck with jasmine
The Sabean shrub
And give it the perfume that in the
gardens
Will allay Lieo's unhealthy fever.

Andrés Bello

Leonardo Gamboa left his family after lunch time at the cattle ranch or stock farm at Hoyo Colorado, and in the affable company of Diego Meneses took the turnoff to Alquízar, between Vereda Nueva and San Antonio de Los Baños, riding southwest from their point of departure.

After a few leagues they found themselves in what in those parts is called *tierra llana*, a vast level plain, at the center of which, on this side, is the town first mentioned. Its subsoil is calcareous, very porous and pure, covered with a layer of earth quite thick and loose in places, reddish or brick-colored, an indication of its high content of iron oxide, and prodigiously fertile. With a few ups and downs it extends westward to Callajabos, at the foot of the mountains of Vuelta Abajo, and eastward to the far limits of Colón, within a generally narrow latitude.

In the highest parts of this mesa, there are of course no natural springs, nor does it often rain; but the night dew is so heavy that it dampens the soil and refreshes the vegetation. Since there is no irrigation system in the region, the luxuriance of the plants that grow there and the emerald green color they display at every season of the year must be attributed to this meteorological phenomenon. The clearing of the woodlands, and the general cultivation of the mesa, particularly of that part through which our two travelers were riding, had driven away the most highly prized birds however, and the only ones to be seen were an occasional flock of *anis*, ponderous in flight and possessed of a penetrating screech, a pair of timid wild pigeons, a fleeting warbler, and little finches hidden in the nearby bushes.

The farther they journeyed from Hoyo Colorado, the more coffee plantations they went past on either side of the road, since they were the only fairly large-sized rural estates in the western part of the mesa, at least up until the year 1840. We are speaking now of the famous garden of Cuba bounded by the administrative districts of Guanajay, Güira de Melena, San Marcos, Alquízar, Ceiba del Agua, and San Antonio de Los Baños. At that time there were no properties for growing crops, in the strict sense of the word, but instead the estates were real gardens for the recreation of their sybaritic owners, as meanwhile they also served to keep the price of coffee high.

Contravening the legal system of measures observed in Cuba *ab initio*, these fine estates were divided into regular shapes, with squares prevailing, the boundaries of all of them marked by hedges of dwarf lemon trees, blackberry bushes, and more commonly by walls of dry stone or skillfully built artistic fences. These latter were covered with climbing vines or convolvulus creepers, especially the variety with little bell-shaped flowers, which came into bloom at Christmas, giving a cheery look to the countryside with their snow-white blossoms, contrasting with the intense green of the woodlands nearby, as with their exquisite and far-reaching fragrance they perfumed the air for miles and miles around.

The ostentatious and comfortable manor houses of these plantations were not located along the many streets or roads that separated the various properties from one another. Their owners sought seclusion, rather, and the deep shade offered away from the road, since that was where orange trees with their golden globes, indigenous and exotic lemon trees, different varieties of mango trees, breadfruit trees with their broad leaves, various species of cherry trees, dense-crowned tamarinds bearing fruit with acid hulls, *guanábana* trees with their heart-shaped, very sweet custard apples, and graceful palms, finally, noteworthy among the large arboreal family for their trunk as straight, cylindrical, smooth, and solid as the shaft of a Doric column, and for the lovely ring of fronds with which they are perennially crowned, all grew more luxuriantly.

Not far from the road, however, was the entrance, portal, or better yet triumphal arch, beneath whose shadow, as if through the Caudine Forks, one had to pass in order to reach the broad avenue, lined with palms and orange trees, that led to the isolated manor house hidden in the densely wooded area. Even after having proceeded well inside the property, the traveler did not always discover the whole of the group of dwellings and outbuildings on it, nor did he reach it directly, for the avenue often divided in two, forming two half circles, one leading in, the other leading out, bounded on one side by coffee trees or blackberry bushes, and on the opposite side by the flower gardens, opening out all at once before the eyes of the surprised traveler. Following along one of these half circles, he was certain to come upon the manor house and its nearby outbuildings first of all, and then the building, usually open and free-standing, that housed the sugar mill, in the center of a sort of plaza or yard, known as the *batey*, around which the floors or sheds for drying coffee beans, the storehouses or granaries, the stables, the dovecote, the henhouse, and the village made up of the straw-thatched slave cabins were located.

Leonardo Gamboa and his friend, their mounts a bit winded, and horses and riders both covered with the fine red dust of the *tierra llana*, spied the boundary markers of La Luz, the coffee plantation belonging to Don Tomás Ilincheta, located about half a league away from the town of Alquízar, after four in the afternoon of December 22, 1830. To the travelers' right, beneath a cloudless blue sky, the glorious sun of the tropics was just setting, its burning rays sending beams of light through the branches of the trees, making the shadows of the palms grow longer and longer on the green field dotted with brightly colored striped flowers, as they set afire the impalpable earthly atom blooming in the tranquil atmosphere.

The soft porous ground of the *tierra llana* echoed far into the distance with the hoofbeats of their mounts, so that long before the horsemen knocked at the entrance to the estate, the black gatekeeper was standing at the iron grille, ready to open it, having just emerged from a large, flat-roofed sentry box made of rubblework on their right. He recognized them immediately and welcomed them with the expressions of pleasure so characteristic of the people of his race and social status, saying:

"Oho! Oho! Master Leonardito, so your grace be here? Ah! Ah! and Master Dieguito also too."

"How is the family, Congo?"

"Ever'body fine, thanks be God. De girls jus' now come home wid Doña Juanita. Dey comin' from de patsure. Miracle you boys din't meet up wif dem. If your graces hurries up dey kin still catch 'em up dis side of de house."

And then he added, addressing Leonardo: "Ah! Miss Isabelita goin' be so happy! An' Miss Rosita also too!" (Then, addressing Meneses): "Don' tell me!"

The two young men smiled and went on at their tired mounts' slow gait down the middle of the magnificent tree-lined promenade, each secretly wishing, by a coincidence of feeling, that the end of their journey were still a bit farther off. It so happened that in the moments when they would first appear before their lady-loves, Leonardo was afraid that his would receive him, not as she usually did, as a friend and tender lover, but as a stern and harsh judge, because of his past weaknesses and signs of fickleness. In all truth, he felt something more like shame than happiness. Diego, for his part, about to realize his heart's most intense and intimate desire, that of seeing Rosa again in her Alquízar paradise after a year's absence, wanted to see if putting off the moment so yearned for would calm down the tumult of his blood a bit and enable him to greet her with the composure of the respectful gentleman.

But for now our friends were not given the pleasure of seeing even this caprice satisfied. For in straying from the avenue down which they had been riding, they managed to see the sisters enter the densest part of the garden, there where the Alexandria rosebushes, the Cape jasmines, and the pinks, rivals of the most beautiful ones that Turkey and Persia boasted of, may not have succeeded in entangling them in their branches but doubtless were enveloping them in their fragrance.

From the hoofbeats of the horses, the young ladies too became aware of the presence of the travelers and recognized the two of them, especially the first one to dismount, giving his horse his head; it was Leonardo. Rosa, younger and more innocent than her sister, gave an involuntary cry of joy; Isabel experienced the opposite feeling. She remembered that her leave-taking from Leonardo in Havana had been neither friendly nor cordial, and believed that before allowing the pleasure with which she ordinarily received him to enter her bosom she needed at least a satisfactory explanation from him of what had happened.

Neither Leonardo nor Diego felt capable at that moment of reading clearly in the faces of their friends what was going through their minds when the moment came to greet one another, in accordance with the stiff, cold manner dictated by Cuban custom, that is to say, without so much as a meaningful handshake. Nonetheless, the change that took place in the faces of the two sisters was a pronounced one. Isabel's turned serious and pale; Rosa's took on the color of the flower whose name she shared; and for a brief moment neither the young men nor the young ladies knew what to say or do. It was finally the more worldly wise of the two young ladies who noticed how embarrassing the situation was for all of them, and in order to put an end to it as quickly as possible, had recourse to one of the flirtatious gestures typical of her age and sex. Isabel was holding in her hand an Alexandria rose that had opened that very afternoon, and she offered it to Meneses with the words:

"Is this not your favorite flower?"

The lucky recipient's face flushed, turning redder than Rosa's had a moment before. Either seeking to hide her own blushing cheeks or to make amends for her sister's apparent slight to Gamboa, Rosa removed a carnation that she had pinned in her hair and gave it to the latter as she stammered: "Isn't this the flower that is my friend Leonardo's favorite?"

This was enough to break the spell, although throughout that afternoon and evening Isabel lavished all her attention on Meneses, failing to see the right moment for a reconciliation with Leonardo. Meanwhile the four of them together walked on to meet Doña Juana and Señor Ilincheta as they came to greet the new arrivals.

The light of day was just then fading, and the slight breeze, despite its bringing with it all the perfume of the many flowers and the pleasing fragrances that the countryside gives forth at that hour, began to be noticeably cool. The ladies, above all, were obliged to resort to their usual evening wrap, a large square silk shawl thrown over their shoulders with affected nonchalance. But as they moved inside to the main room, the melancholy tolling of the curfew bell at the neighboring coffee plantations and at La Luz, calling masters and slaves to prayer and repose, rang out. On hearing it, Doña Juana, her nieces, the two young men, and Don Tomás Ilincheta, the latter hat in hand, and the family's domestic servants, all stood with folded arms as the mistress of the house began the evening Angelus: "Hail Mary Immaculate!", to which those present answered in chorus: "Conceived without sin." "The Angel of the Lord" (Señora Juana continued) "announced to Mary that the Son of God the Father would be incarnated in her womb, for the redemption of the world. Hail Mary! Mary Most Holy received him saying: Here is the servant of the Lord. May it be done unto me according to Thy word. Hail Mary. The Son of God was made man and lived among us. Hail Mary!"

When wishes for a good night's rest had been exchanged, the two sisters first and after them the servants, kissed the hand of Doña Juana and Don Tomás, and received in answer the usual: "May God make you a saint."

Immediately thereafter a maidservant informed Isabel that the assistant overseer was waiting to see her on the other side of the porch. She took leave of her guests and went off. Speaking with the latter, her father explained the reason for her absence: "She is my steward, cashier, and bookkeeper, and believes that duty comes before devotion. She keeps the accounts of how much coffee is harvested and how much is shelled, sorted, and put in sacks, and how much is sent to Havana. When it is sold she goes over the debits and credits of the repair man; collects money and pays it out. All just the way a man would. In a word, since the death of my wife, may she rest in peace, my Isabel has taken over the house, the plantation, and all my business affairs. Heavens! I don't know what would become of me if she were taken from me too."

Who was the assistant overseer? A tall, lanky black, dark as pitch, broad-faced, with a straightforward look about him and an intelligent gaze. As soon as his mistress appeared, he knelt before her to ask her for her blessing, because he himself had just led the evening prayer of his 30 or more comrades in the middle of the *batey*, by starlight.

"Mistress," he said to her, "here be de 'count of de number of barrels we fill t'day." And did he hand her a paper? The leaf from a plant with calligraphic or arithmetical signs? Nothing like that. Even though that slave had learned by rote several prayers of the catechism taught to him so that he could be baptized, he didn't know how to write or to depict numbers. The account he spoke of consisted of just two or three short twigs from a bush in the field, with many crosswise slashes or notches, tally sticks or modern quipus to indicate the number of barrels of coffee berries harvested in eight hours' work.

When Isabel passed her fingertips across the notches of the tally sticks, she realized that the harvest had not been abundant and remarked as much to the slave.

He hastened to explain to her in his special gibberish the reason for the shortfall: "Mistress, the harvist done finish', dey no mo' coffee on de bush, no way. We finagles a lil here an' a lil dere an' we fills twenyfive barrel."

"Very well, Pedro," Isabel replied. "There's no reason to damage the coffee bushes, or to knock down green coffee berries. The harvest next year would be much smaller if that were done, Pedro; mind what I'm telling you. Set all hands to cleaning the *batey* and the main boundary paths very early tomorrow morning, till nine o'clock. We have visitors and I want everything to be nice and neat. In the afternoon some of the hands must hull and winnow the dry coffee beans and others, the women and the weakest of the lot, must sort them. We must get everything that has been hulled and winnowed ready, tomorrow if possible."

"It be done jes' as you say, mistress."

"Ah! I was forgetting the main thing," Isabel added in a sad voice. "Have Leocadio give plenty of corn and grass to the three horses with a white star on their forehead and the three bays, because they must start out on a long journey day after tomorrow."

"De mastah leave?"

"No, just Aunt Juana, Rosita, and I are leaving; we're going to spend the Christmas holidays in Vuelta Abajo."

"What! If mistress go some other where, could be dey rob de house."

"Papa is staying. We're invited to spend the Christmas holidays, as I say, with Señor Gamboa's family at La Tinaja, his coffee plantation, a long, long way from here, near El Mariel. They've put in a big steam engine to mill cane; the milling will start on Christmas Eve and they're expecting us. Master Leonardito and Master Diego Meneses, whom you know, have come to fetch us."

"So mistress go some other where?" the assistant overseer repeated pensively.

"We'll be gone only a very short time, at most only until after the Sunday of the Lost Child. I'm very sorry to leave Papa alone. But I trust to God that nothing will happen, or rather I promise myself that all of you will take good care of him."

"It be done jes' as you say, mistress."

"But if by some mischance he falls ill while we're away, I'm making you responsible, Pedro, for sending me a messenger immediately to La Tinaja, the sugar plantation near the town of Quiebrahacha. Remember those two names: Tinaja and Quiebrahacha."

"It be done jes' as you say, mistress."

"Rafael or Celedonio, either of the two will do in order to get the message to me. They know the way from here to Guanajay; from there to Quiebrahacha everybody knows that anyone who has a tongue gets to Rome."

"It be done jes' as you say, mistress."

"Very well, I trust you, Pedro. It's a great relief to us when we go away to leave the care of the house and the plantation to a man as rational and honest as you."

Even though he was given such praise, as generous as it was sincere, the black didn't use his pet phrase this time. He merely shook his head as though he were trying to dislodge a bothersome idea from it, and turned his face to one side without turning his back on his mistress, which would have signified a lack of respect.

"Listen carefully, Pedro," Isabel continued. "The white-faced horse has to be brought in from the pasture so as to take one of the two teams of three horses to Guanajay. The one who takes it, either Rafael or Celedonio, must leave at the morning Angelus or at first light day after tomorrow, dismount at the inn in Ochandarena, opposite the public square, have the horses bathed and fed well, and then wait for us, because he will have to come back with the three that we've taken from here. Will you remember all these things, Pedro?"

"I remember, mistress," the assistant overseer said sadly, and quickly added: "De poor blacks goin' to have a mighty sad Crismastide."

"Why is that?" Isabel asked with exaggerated surprise. "I'll tell Papa to let them play their drums on the two days of Christmas and on Epiphany."

"But 'cause de mistress not here, de blacks won't have a good time."

"What nonsense! None of that! Get them to dance, to have a good time so their mistress will be happy when she comes back from her journey. All right? That's all, Pedro."

The latter walked off slowly and reluctantly, and Isabel, who had been standing leaning pensively on the porch railing called him back immediately, and said: "Pedro, do you see? Because of your interruptions and all your nonsense I almost forget one of the things that was most on my mind. I have to tell you one last thing you must do. Look, Pedro, I've been trying to decide if it would be best that you keep your whip in your cabin until after Christmas. Yes, yes, that will be best, for as long as you have it in hand you'll want to use it, and I don't wish the whip to be used on anyone. Do you hear what I'm saying, Pedro? I don't want the sound of the whip to be heard while I'm away."

"De blacks goin' to dere ruin," Pedro said with a smile, "'cause mistress love 'em so."

"I don't care," Isabel replied firmly. "You know that Papa fired the overseer in April because he used his whip too much. Remember how he took it out on you. Not one lash of the whip must be heard on the plantation while I'm gone. I repeat, that's the way I want things to be; that's an order, Pedro."

Returning from her brief dialogue with the assistant overseer, Isabel found the table for supper set in the middle of the main room. It was about eight o'clock. The luxury of the silver table service, including the large solid silver candlesticks, seemed to be competing with the abundance of the food. But none of this was done out of vain show. In the first place, because the family had eaten lunch at three, a country custom in those days, their hosts presumed that the two guests were hungry and were eager to satisfy their appetites. In fact, the two sisters, their aunt, and Señor Ilincheta, who out of courtesy had all sat down on one side of the table, partook only of some chocolate or coffee with milk, with Isabel, of course, doing the honors with her characteristic charm and lack of affectation.

After supper and a pleasant conversation, Don Tomás rose from the table and retired to his room, suggesting to his daughters that they not keep the guests up too late, for they must surely be worn out and would want a night's rest after their tiring day's journey.

The manor house of La Luz was built *à la française*, that is to say, according to the layout for such residences followed by the Creoles of Guadeloupe and Martinique; for in fact an architect born in one of those two islands had drafted the plan for the house and supervised its construction. The plan was in the form of a double-armed cross, the center of which was occupied by the main room, and the two arms of it by eight bedrooms; these arms consisted of two corridors, each with a small reception room at the far end, underneath the porch roofs at the rear of the house. At the angles of the porches there were four rooms that gave on the aforementioned reception rooms on the inside, and on the gardens and the porches on the outer side. The porches, then, ran the entire length of the main room, parallel to it, and were closed off by wooden railings and heavy canvas curtains rather than venetian blinds. The main area of the house had a roof made of fronds from a variety of palm known as *cana*, or fan palm, valued for its thickness, durability, and coolness; the porches or covered passages were roofed over with flat brick tile. An admittedly generous number of doors and windows all opened to the outside, letting in, at least in the daytime, great streams of light, as well as that air always filled with the fragrance of the flowers or fruits found in such abundance round about that charming dwelling.

For reasons easy to infer, the ladies naturally did not follow the example of the master of the household. The young people felt no inclination whatsoever to separate for the remainder of the night without communicating to one another, by a word, by a look, at least a small part of everything that was effervescing in their heads. Hence, almost by instinct, they went back out onto the front porch after supper and began strolling up and down, in two groups: Isabel with her aunt and Meneses, and Rosa and Leonardo following along behind. The first time they turned around to stroll in the other direction, Leonardo asked Rosa, in a low voice, pointing to her older sister:

"What's the matter with the girl?"

This happened to be the first verse of a song that was very popular at the time; and Rosa, who was lively and mischievous, immediately answered with the second verse of the song that gave it its name:

"Measles."

"How is it treated?" Leonardo asked, quoting the third verse.

"With a knock on the head." Rosa concluded, unable to keep from laughing.

"What are you two laughing about?" Isabel asked, listening attentively to what was going on behind her.

"Don't tell her, Gamboa," Rosa said. "Don't satisfy her curiosity. She isn't with our group."

It looked as if Isabel intended to monopolize the conversation and the company of Diego Meneses for the remainder of the evening. Hence the apparent reason for Rosa's annoyance with her, as her last words revealed. Isabel could very well harbor the same suspicion, for identical reasons, regarding her younger sister, given the fact that from the beginning Rosa appropriated for herself Leonardo's attentions and company. But none of the young people was satisfied with himself or herself or with his or her companion. This was the truth of the matter; the result was that they tired of strolling back and forth sooner than might reasonably be expected, except that instead of sitting down, they leaned as if by chance against the railing, grouped, also as if by chance, the way they secretly desired: Isabel next to Leonardo, Rosa next to Meneses, and Doña Juana by herself off to one side. Doña Juana loved her nieces with a mother's love, being as she was the woman who had reared them since they were infants; she wanted to see them happily married, and since she was a matchmaker by nature, it was clear that she did not take offense at an exclusion thanks to which they were able to have the opportunity for a bit of intimate communication with their suitors.

The deepest calm reigned all around the house, the slight breeze that had arisen as the sun set having died down. The branches of the trees did not stir, nor was the light of the stars or the clear sky bright enough to be reflected in the broad leaves of the banana tree, whose fibrous trunk stood out amid the dense low-growing coffee bushes. The only sound to be heard was the distant, muffled one coming from the slaves, who, before going off for their night's rest, were preparing their frugal supper by the firelight in their cabins as they discussed the news of the night, namely, the coming absence of their mistress. But it would not be accurate to say that the chirping of the crickets hidden in the grass in greater proximity to our young people, or the flitting of the little moths passing with a fleeting whir of wings from the garden to the house, attracted by the light of the candle inside the glass shade or chimney on the table in the center of the main room, constituted any appreciable sound.

The place, then, the hour, the silence of heaven and earth, the darkness of the wide, low porch, with a limited horizon owing to the thick wooded area close by, the same struggle of the dim artificial lighting with the darkness outside all tended to lead to the arousal of the passions of the young people, their souls enraptured by the contemplation of the splendid panorama surrounding them. At such moments, even the least attractive women seem ethereal and adorable; the most timid men dare to do anything, and since they feel more deeply they express themselves with greater eloquence.

"Isabel," Leonardo said, "your conduct toward me puzzles me."

"Describe it," Isabel replied with a smile.

"I am not the proper person to describe it, for the simple reason that I am the one who has been wronged."

"That too? That's all I needed to hear."

"Does that surprise you? If not, how does our friendly farewell (on my part, that is to say) in Havana accord with your ensuing silence and indifference?"

"Without any reason that would justify the change?"

"Without any reason that would justify it. At least I have not yet been able to fathom what it might be."

"Refresh your memory with the facts."

"I fail to come up with anything, Isabel; I know of no reason."

"Really?"

"Really."

"Then I have been a madwoman, a simpleton; I have had visions."

"That's going too far, Isabel. Doesn't it occur to you that you may have interpreted wrongly an innocent act on my part or on the part of some other person with regard to me?"

"I assure you that it is not a question of interpretations, Señor Don Leonardo, but of what I saw with my own eyes."

"Let us hear then what Señora Doña Isabel saw with her own eyes."

"I saw what you saw, or rather, what happened to you on the footboard of the carriage."

"And that was sufficient reason for you to lose your affection for me and to be about to forget me?"

"It was, and indeed more than sufficient reason to humiliate and anger any woman, however blinded by passion she might be."

"I see clearly, Isabel, that everything you're saying stems from a mistake on your part, and that without meaning to you have been unfair to me."

"Explain yourself," Isabel said with apparent anxiety.

"I will tell you in a few words what happened," Leonardo went on, his face flushing, because he was about to lie intentionally. "As I was bidding you one last farewell, I naturally set one foot down on the sidewalk. One of the two mulatto girls who were passing by stumbled over me, and believing that I had deliberately tripped her, she was furious and gave me a good hard shove. You know how insolent those worthless females are when they think they've been affronted."

"Yes," Isabel said thoughtfully. After a brief pause she added: "But what reason did I give her to call me that most indecent of words that still rings in my ears?"

"Your exclamation, Isabel, and then your calling her Adela, when perhaps her name was Nicolasa or Rosario, was doubtless what made her even angrier."

"If I called her Adela, or rather, if in crying out in surprise I blurted out that name, it was because I fancied that that person was your sister. Besides taking her to be the living image of Adela, I could not and did not imagine that any other woman would play that sort of joke on you."

"I see! The thing is that it wasn't a joke on her part."

"Then she knows you and assailed you out of . . . jealousy."

"I know her by sight, I admit, and had already noticed her resemblance to my sister Adela; but I never gave her any reason to be jealous of me."

"Perhaps she's secretly in love with you."

"There wouldn't be anything special about that, except that I've never taken the least notice of her."

"I would regret doing you an injustice, Leonardo. Nonetheless, appearances are against you."

"No, Isabel, no. I am innocent. If I were deceiving you at this moment, if I weren't telling you the whole truth, if I were describing a passion for you that I didn't feel, if as a consequence I had given you a real reason to feel offended, I would be the most wicked of men."

"Very well then; let's turn over a new leaf," Isabel interrupted him, convinced now.

"Let bygones be bygones?" Leonardo asked her in an amorous tone of voice.

"Let bygones be bygones," she answered with a heavenly smile. "There would have been no happiness for me had I found myself condemned to doubt the word of the man whom I regarded as a friend and a gentleman."

"Very well," Leonardo added, his spirits lifted. "Don't you think that we should seal this sweet reconciliation?"

As he said this he furtively allowed his hand to run along the porch railing to take Isabel's, which was also resting on the railing. But by avoiding the opportunity, she avoided the danger. Her manner turned sober and she moved over next to her aunt, to whom she remarked in a loud voice that it was time to retire for the night. Leonardo's watch said 11 o'clock.

Time had flown. Diego Meneses, nonetheless, knowing that it is best to strike while the iron is hot, was able to take sufficient advantage of the occasion to make Rosa a formal declaration of his love, having found the subject or the pretext of their conversation together in the gift of the carnation which that young lady had made to Leonardo in the garden. Innocent dove of the garden of Alquízar! She who had never before heard an "I love you, Rosa," spoken intentionally and passionately. She who felt attracted to that young man as a needle is attracted to a magnet, as the little bird is to the serpent, found at hand no gesture, word, or ruse to deny that she had succumbed and that she too had loved her tempter from the first days that they had spent together on the coffee plantation of La Luz.

I I

And on the lovely coffee plantations
Everything is cool and fragrant,
Their white flowers kissed
By tropical breezes.

J. Padrine

As Cupid's sweetheart since the evening before, out of shyness fearing to meet her accomplice face to face in the clear light of day, Rosa Ilincheta delayed leaving her dressing room as long as she could. Isabel, however, had duties to fulfill and appeared very early on the south porch of her house with her parasol in her right hand, a little basket suspended by the handle from her left arm, and as her only wrap her large silk scarf embroidered with raised work.

The sun then appeared around a corner of the house, shedding light on part of the garden and projecting its shadow and that of the trees across a long stretch of the plantation's spacious *batey*. There had been a heavy morning dew. The lawn was soaked, the red dust of the roads wet down, and the leaves of the plants and the corollas of the flowers covered with tiny dewdrops, prisms breaking down the light of the life-giving sun as its rays struck them obliquely.

Isabel cast an inquisitive glance at the entire landscape spread out before her and ventured beyond the porch, for from there she had spied an Alexandria rose that had just opened in the sun's gentle warmth, in the southeast quadrant of the garden. She cut it without pricking herself or getting wet, and when she adorned her splendid braid of hair with it, she mechanically turned her eyes toward the house and it seemed to her that one of her guests was watching her from behind the shutter of the window of his room at the end of the porch, where in fact the two young men had spent the night. It was Diego Meneses, who, not having slept well, had been up since dawn and was now breathing in the pure atmosphere surrounding its striped flowers.

This incident so perturbed her that for a brief moment she hesitated between retracing her steps and continuing on, because the acts of adorning her hair and looking toward the house, although innocent and fortuitous, might be interpreted in several ways, and she shunned both frivolity and injudicious coquettishness. But she was obliged to go on and left the garden at a steady pace.

To the south, a stone fence separated the fields from the square inside which the various plantation buildings were situated. In the center was the building where coffee was milled, between the two pairs of drying floors capable of containing half the harvest at one time. Farther away, closing off the large expanse on the left, was the thick dark curb of the well with its fork and pulley for drawing water; then the dovecote, the poultry yard and several pigsties; at the back and to the right, the bell tower, or rather, the wooden column from the arm of which the bell hung suspended, covered with a small roof; the granaries or storehouses, the stables, the cowshed, and other outbuildings. The slave cabins formed an average-sized village.

The magnificent *batey* which we have been describing was not devoid of vegetation, for many trees, doubtless the most thickset ones on the whole plantation and those with the densest crowns, adorned it and shaded it. Among them were several avocado trees, along with others bearing red mammees, mangoes, and star apples; the tips of the avocado trees in particular, like the conifers in the continent to the north, seemed to be climbing to the sky. The highest and leafiest of them were the favorite nighttime perches of the guinea fowl, Cuvier's *Numidas Meneagris*, the unsociability of these exotic birds being well known. Since before sunrise the flock, which might be made up of a good hundred birds, had begun to stir and to set up the unending clamor or cackle peculiar to them, in which it seems as if one of them says *pascual* and another answers *pascual* until all of them awaken and prepare to come down from their lofty natural perches. Neither the pigeons nor the hens were giving any signs of life yet: the former because they were not early risers, and the latter because they were still shut up in their dark lofts.

Apart from this, quite a hustle and bustle could be seen everywhere in the *batey*. Of the slaves of both sexes, some were removing dry leaves and bean strings from the ground with their short hoes or grub hoes; some were clearing grass from the roads with the same tools; some were lifting with both hands the trash that had piled up and placing it in baskets that others were carrying outside the compound on their heads; some were drawing water from the deep well by hand and pouring it into an ample stone basin at the foot of the well curb for others to distribute in rustic pails made of the stems of palm fronds to the water tanks of the various sections of the plantation. Alongside the well Leocadio, the carriage driver, was watering and bathing the horses by twos or threes. Inside the mill there echoed the piercing voice of the little black, who, seated at the end of the shaft of the vertical wheel revolving in the lower millstone used to remove the outer hull of the coffee berry, was spurring on without a letup the mules that served as the motive power. Four slave women, meanwhile, were spreading out on the drying floor the coffee berries still not completely dry; meanwhile other slaves were taking the peeled or shelled beans to the winnower, whose paddles made a deafening noise and awakened echoes wherever the sound wave encountered a flexible object in its path. And once the beans were free of the least bit of hull or dust, they were taken to the storehouses, there to be sorted and classified by other slaves.

None of those who passed within range of Isabel failed to bid her good day and ask for her blessing, bending their knees as a sign of submissiveness and respect. Pedro, the assistant overseer, without the ominous symbol of his authority, proceeding from one place to another, was urging his comrades on as they went about their work and lending a hand in many cases, as if to give greater weight to his words by his acts. Isabel's appearance after climbing up onto the drying floors was the sign for the little black to raise his high-pitched silvery voice in song, a simple, unpolished one, perhaps improvised the night before, that began with this sort of verse: "Mistress goin' go away," and ended with this other, repeated in chorus by all the other blacks: "Po' slave cry." Between the first words and the refrain or chorus, the lead singer, despite the fact that he was a Creole born on the plantation, inserted phrases in pure Congolese, to which the chorus also responded with the obligatory: "Po' slave cry."

It would be fruitless to look for harmony, or even melody, in a song that was not altogether civilized nor yet completely savage; but though seemingly rather monotonous to delicate ears, it is also true that the intonation and the words were filled with melancholy. So it appeared to Isabel, although she acted as if she had not heard or understood a word of it and went on to the foot of the trees, where the noisy guinea fowl were now bustling about and running in every direction. Some of them, the most unfriendly ones, made as if to take flight on seeing her, breaking into the high, shrill, nasal call they give to alert their companions to any danger that threatens. But since the voracity of these birds is well known, all that was needed to calm them down and control them were the few grains of corn that Isabel took out of the little basket that she was carrying on her arm and was careful to throw about on the ground at a point close to her. The entire flock flung itself on this scarce bit of feed, their vigilance abandoned, the danger forgotten, occupied only in gobbling down grains of corn or tiny stones. At a sign from her mistress, one of the women slaves took advantage of this circumstance to crawl along the ground and catch two of them, without the others noticing. The meat of these birds is very tasty, as tasty as that of partridges, for which reason Isabel planned to offer her guests a pair of them, roasted, for lunch.

At the sight of the food being thrown about by the handful now, the pigeons came running. These birds, not as unsociable as the guinea fowl, which they were afraid of, and more inclined to be friendly, fluttered about the young lady at first, then alighted on her head, her shoulders, and her arm with the basket, and ended up snatching the corn from her hands and even pecking it from her lips. Such numerous and such tender demonstrations of affection by innocent little birds, despite their being repeated day after day, always touched her, and never, except in unusual cases, did she allow them to be killed somewhere out of her sight. Because of this and other similar acts whereby the influence exercised by Isabel over all the creatures that approached her was revealed, her slaves firmly believed that God had endowed her with a sort of magic charm or secret power impossible to evade or ward off.

Diego Meneses's eyes followed Isabel's footsteps, and even though, as a civilized man, he was not inclined to grant that there was anything supernatural about her, he did believe, as did the others, that she was an extraordinary woman. From his observation post at the window he gave a faithful account of what he was seeing or hearing to Leonardo, who was still lazing in bed and enjoying the wondrously fine-woven sheets trimmed with generous lace edgings and scented with Alexandria rose petals, all the work of Isabel's industrious hands. Meneses said to Gamboa, among other things:

"That's quite a woman, my friend."

"Didn't I tell you?" the latter answered with satisfaction.

"She's worth her weight in gold. There aren't many like her in these parts."

"Do you want to trade? I'll exchange her, even-steven, for Rosa. Come on."

"Don't make fun of me, pal," Diego answered gravely. "My recognizing rare and praiseworthy qualities in Isabel doesn't mean that I like her more than other women, or that I've fallen love with her. But the truth is that as time goes by I'm more and more convinced that you don't deserve her."

"Well I declare! Do you fancy she's better than I am?" Leonardo shot back, hurt by his friend's observation. "You're completely mistaken, my lad. Remember that Isabel is the daughter of a former civil servant, dismissed without a pension, a coffee planter who's lost his fortune, a penniless wretch, in short; whereas my parents own cattle ranches, a coffee plantation, a sugar plantation, are rich landholders and play a different role in Havana. Do you follow me?"

"Yes, I do, only I wasn't referring to any of that when I told you that you didn't deserve that girl. In a nutshell, Leonardo, you don't love her."

"Why do you presume that I don't love her?"

"What! Do you think I don't have eyes? Ever since we arrived here I've been watching what you say and do, and nothing about your behavior persuades me that you love Isabel."

"Good Lord, Diego! I'll tell you frankly what my situation is at present," Gamboa said after a brief silence. "I don't feel for Isabel that blind and burning passion that you feel, for example . . . for Rosa."

"What you mean is," Meneses promptly interrupted him, "that the passion you feel for Ceci . . .'"

"Shut your mouth!" Leonardo exclaimed in alarm, sitting halfway up in bed. "One doesn't speak of rope in the house of a man who's been hanged. Your words can be heard; the walls have ears. That name is forbidden here."

"A name matters little. It's a very common one, and I don't think Isabel has ever heard of this particular person in her life."

"Probably not, but if Isabel starts putting two and two together, she'll soon know the whole story, especially since she's no fool."

"And now that we're on the subject, how did you manage to explain the scene in front of the Gámez's house just as Isabel was leaving?"

"I believe she suspects something and I think her cousins have told her or written her some tall tale about it. It's obvious that Isabel is distrustful of me and apparently feels very resentful of me."

"I don't doubt that her cousins have aroused her jealousy. What happened, however, was too obvious for Isabel to cease to be alarmed and not suspect the very thing that you and I know to be true. What nerve that girl has!"

"What do you expect? She was blinded by jealousy and compromised me in the eyes of Isabel and her cousins. You can't imagine how humiliated I was."

"I'm thinking about it. If I were in your shoes, I'd hide my head a mile deep. But where did Isabel get the idea that she might have been your sister Adela?"

"You'll see some day, Diego. Anyway, if you recall, the two of them look very much alike at first glance."

"I've noticed. How wicked of your father to have had anything to do with someone who looks so much like your sister!"

"Who knows? He's as fond of cinnamon as I am. It wouldn't be surprising if, running around the way he did when he was young, he stumbled on . . . As for C. she drools over him. I'm sure of it."

"Then he can't be her father."

"How could he be! Unthinkable. How absurd!"

"But there's a rumor going around that he is."

"Mere tittletattle, Diego. Do all those gossips imagine that he'd be in love with C . . . if they were that closely related?"

"Maybe he doesn't know they're related, because as you say, he just happened to stumble on her. It's possible too that he's hiding her from you, knowing the relationship between the two of you. Where there's smoke there's fire!"

"In this case there's no smoke, and no fire either. Just because by sheer happenstance C . . . and Adela look very much alike people get an idea in their head and the talk starts . . . What I can tell you is that he's given me more scares that I have hairs on my head. When I least expect it I suddenly run into him. He nearly—or rather, he really—causes me twice as much anxiety as Pimienta the musician does. The only thing that puts my mind at rest on this score is that she disdains elderly men as much as she scorns mulattos."

"Don't put any store by that, though. As everybody knows, the tomcat's son chases mice, and the she-goat leaps where her mother leaps. But to get back to what we were talking about, the result of all this rigmarole is that Isabel isn't on the best of terms with you."

"No. As I was telling you, she suspects something, or someone has prejudiced her against me. Moreover, she stubbornly resists explaining herself frankly, and I'm just a bit less stubborn than she is, so as a result we'll go on this way for heaven only knows how long, or until she lays her pride aside and makes her peace with me."

"That resignation on your part," Meneses remarked, "substantiates my belief that you don't love Isabel."

"Either I haven't succeeded in explaining myself, or else you don't understand me, Diego. Since there are no conceivable points of comparison between the two women, I can't love one of them in the same way that I love the other. The one back in Havana keeps driving me mad; she's made me commit more than one folly and is going to cause me to commit many more still. However, I don't love her, nor will I ever love her the way I do the one who is here. The other one is all passion and fire, she is my temptress, a little devil in the guise of a woman, the Venus of mulat . . . Who is strong enough to resist her? Who can come close to her without getting burned? Who on merely seeing her doesn't feel the blood boil in his veins? Who hears her say 'I love you' without feeling his head reel as if he were downing wine? None of those sensations is easy to experience with Isabel. Beautiful, elegant, kind, educated, stern, she possesses the power of the hedgehog, whose quills prick anyone who dares touch her. A statue, in short, as cold and rigid as marble, she inspires respect, admiration, affection perhaps, but not mad love, not volcanic passion."

"And thinking as you do, Leonardo, will you marry Isabel?"

"Why not? That is precisely the way a man must seek out the woman he chooses to marry. The man who marries Isabel is certain that he won't suffer . . . headaches, even if he's more jealous than a Turk. With women like C. . . . danger is ever-present; a man must always be as wary as a tinder vendor. It has never entered my mind to marry the one in Havana, or any other woman who resembles her, and yet here I am, breaking into a sweat every time I think that she may be flirting at this very minute with some fop or with the mulatto musician."

"Which proves, my friend, that there is no way to serve two masters."

"In love affairs, or flirtations, it's possible to serve up to 20, and serving two is more possible still. The one in Havana will be my Venus of Cythera, the one in Alquízar my guardian angel, my little Ursuline nun, my sister of charity."

"It's not a question then of loving one a great deal and marrying another whom one doesn't love as much."

"I can see that you don't know what you're talking about. To enjoy life to the fullest a man ought not to marry the woman he adores, but the woman he loves. Do you understand now?"

"I understand that you weren't born to be a married man."

As Isabel went on with her morning outing, knowing nothing of the conversation that the two young men from Havana were having about her, she reached the well. There, as everywhere else, her presence commanded respect. The drawer of water stopped working lest in pouring the water into the basin he spatter his mistress's dress, for she had come too close. The Creole carriage driver, on the contrary, who was more or less the same age as his mistress and was on closer terms with her because he had grown up under her very eyes, did not stop bathing the horses, nor did he doff his hat in deference to her. Nor did he bend his knee, as his comrade did, on bidding her good day, a circumstance that we are certain that Isabel did not notice, either because she was accustomed to it, or because subservience, even in a slave, did not accord with with her philanthropic sentiments.

"Blas," she said, addressing the drawer of water, "is there a great deal of water in the well?"

"Aplenty, mistress."

"How do you know?" she asked him.

"Ah, mistress! I always hears glu, glu, glu."

"Then the water can be seen coming in."

"It can, mistress, it can. I watch de boilin'."

"Let me see," Isabel said, drawing still closer to the curb of the well.

"Yo' grace want to see?" the black said in fright. "No, you don' look. Lots deep. Debil push mistress in."

Leocadio laughed at his comrade's melodramatic behavior and suggested that the señorita could satisfy her curiosity with no risk if she held fast to one of the ends of the Y-shaped rope as the two blacks held the other. They did so; but Isabel couldn't see the bottom of the well because it was too deep, because the stone curb of the well was too thick, and because of the innumerable ferns clinging to the inner walls, almost blocking the mouth of the well with their graceful fronds.

Isabel immediately asked the carriage driver whether the horses were ready to begin the next day's journey:

"Mistress Isabelita," he answered in more intelligible language than his comrade's. "Pajarito and Venao need new ho'shoes."

"You wretch! Why didn't you tell me, Leocadio?"

"And when did I have de time? Till las' night I didn't know nothin' 'bout de trip. I was goin' to tell mistress after bathin' de horses."

"Well, you'll have to go to town to have them shod."

"I go after lunch. Mistress gimme de paper fo' de blacksmit'. If he not got hisself drunk, we all right."

"So, then, see to it as soon as you can. Set the horses to galloping hard right now and wearing them them out before it's time to leave."

"Mistress always thinks a person killin' de ho'ses."

"Your name ought to be horse-killer, not Leocadio."

Isabel did not stop at the other outbuildings of the plantation on that side of the *batey*; but on crossing over to the opposite side, she missed one of the field hands and the assistant overseer said that he hadn't shown up in the sick line the night before. She reprimanded Pedro for not having told her sooner and went straight to the infirmary. The slave was sitting on the floor next to the fire with a bandanna tied around his head, looking downcast. The nurse had promptly given him several cups of an orange-peel infusion, sweetened with brown sugar scrapings. Isabel took his pulse, realized that he had a fever and gave instructions that he should rest until the doctor came. On her way back to the manor house, she inspected the stable and the large room where the coffee beans were sorted.

The guests were waiting for her on the porch, together with her sister, her aunt, and her father. It seemed only natural that someone who had so punctually discharged the obligations of administrator of the estate and of the matters appertaining to it should feel pleased with herself and all the more prepared to fulfill her duties as mistress of the household. The cheerful, animated face she turned toward her family was ample proof that the affectionate and gentle mistress of submissive slaves could also be friendly and attentive toward her equals and friends. From that moment on she devoted herself to entertaining them and offering them any pleasure in her power to afford them during their short stay at the plantation.

Since the morning continued to be cool and not very sunny, Isabel proposed to her friends a brief visit to the front garden of the house. That was her Eden. She had little knowledge of the art of gardening, much less of botany; nor had the taste for floriculture yet spread in Cuba, and Pedregal or other French gardeners had yet to import from France the great variety of roses that brought on that flower's invasion of Havana. But Isabel was a florist by instinct and out of sheer love; and since she had planted them with her own hands, she knew by heart the history of all the flowers that grew in her charming pleasure garden. She nonetheless carefully avoided any mention of the rosebush with pale blooms onto which Leonardo, just a year before, had inserted a graft from the rosebush bearing bright red flowers. It was plainly growing vigorously and luxuriantly, showing at each node roses of both colors, a faithful and poetic symbol of two sensitive beings linked by the most human of human passions: love.

Later on Isabel followed up the visit to the gardens with an excursion on horseback by the four young people to nearby plantations. She felt the need to distract herself, and even more to try to forget her troubles by continually keeping on the move. Apart from the fact that her provisional coming to terms with Leonardo the evening before had left her unsatisfied, she regretted that she would soon be taking her leave of her peaceful abode and her loving father and was already suffering from that sort of fever that is an infallible symptom of the painful ailment known as homesickness.

So December 23 passed and the melancholy morning of December 24 came. Long before daylight the postilion had left for Guanajay with the three relay horses. In the saddle, and armed as was the custom with a whip and a long machete with a handle inlaid with tortoise shell and silver, the neatly dressed carriage driver Leocadio awaited his two mistresses about to begin their journey. Several women slaves could be seen nearby and the other servants a little farther away, apparently preparing to begin the new day's tasks, although in reality, as would be seen later, awaiting the sad scene that was about to take place.

Wishing to cut short the painful moment of separation, Isabel hurriedly embraced her father, took the arm Gamboa offered her, and with her eyes misted over with tears, went down the avenue of trees to the east to take the carriage. The ladies were wearing austere travel dress of dark silk and a little straw hat or a French-style bonnet. A general stir was observed as Isabel appeared, followed by a murmur among the slaves standing watching, who broke out as one in the cry or monotonous song of the evening before: "Mistress goin' go 'way, po' slave cry," repeated in solemn chorus in the early morning light of the new day, which faintly illuminated the tops of the tallest trees.

This unexpected greeting was the crowning touch; Isabel was now thoroughly upset. Her handkerchief fluttered in the direction of the slaves as a farewell gesture and she quickened her pace. Then she noticed the assistant overseer.

Standing motionless, silent, his head erect, his plump neck and part of his brawny chest showing through the head opening of his shirt, a Spartacus to judge from his manly musculature, a weak woman to judge from the sensitivity of his uncultivated spirit, he was holding Gamboa's nervous horse by the cheekpiece of its silver bit. Alongside him was his wife, also motionless and silent, with a baby in her arms, deeply distressed, as was shown by the big teardrops rolling down her ebony cheeks. As moved as the wife was, Isabel placed her hand on her shoulder, planted a gentle kiss on the baby's forehead and said to the husband: "Pedro, Pedro! don't forget my instructions."

Without waiting for a reply she took refuge in the carriage.

Once she entered this sanctuary, there began what could be called affectionate importunities from the slaves. The women especially, convinced that their mistress was leaving for good, surrounded the carriage and the most expressive ones pounded on the footboard, poked their head under the back curtain or the folding hood, and as was their custom, gave a great cry of grief: "Farewell, mistress! Come back soon, mistress! Don't stay where you're going, my mistress. God and the Virgin grant mistress a safe journey!" These phrases, which we have translated out of consideration for the reader, were accompanied by extravagant gestures, such as gently squeezing her feet, kissing them a hundred times, as well as kissing the hands with which she was trying to push them back. All this was said and expressed with real feeling, with exquisite tenderness, the slaves never taking their eyes from her angelic face, like that of an idol or a sacred image.

Poor, sensitive, albeit ignorant and simple slaves, they considered their mistress the most beautiful and kindliest of women, a delicate and supernatural being, and demonstrated it in their crude and idolatrous way.

Little by little, now through pleas, now through gentle admonitions, Isabel succeeded in pushing the most petulant of them away, gave the order to leave, and overcome by tears, exclaimed: "I'm no good at such scenes."

As he mounted his horse, Gamboa took a disdainful look at the spectacle around the carriage, and said in a loud voice, so that Pedro, who was holding the stirrup, heard him: "Bah! What's needed here is a good rawhide whip!"

The carriage driver pointed to the reins of the horse on the outside, and by the time Isabel was able to take them in hand the carriage and the travelers had already gone past the facade of the house and almost reached the boundaries, to the east, of La Luz.

I I I

Sweet Cuba! In your bosom there can be seen
to the highest and the lowest degree,
the beauties of the physical world,
the horrors of the moral world.

José María Heredia

On the island of Cuba that region that falls west of the meridian of Havana and begins near Guanajay and ends at Cabo de San Antonio is called Vuelta Abajo or Vuelta Bajo. It is famed for the excellent tobacco that is produced in the fertile valleys of its many rivers, especially on the southern slope of the mountain range of Los Organos. There would appear to be an important factor responsible for its having acquired this reputation, namely the low altitude of this area above sea level, compared to the high elevation of the region already described.

The descent begins a few miles to the west of Guanajay, an abrupt change in the look of the landscape immediately being noticeable. The color of the soil, its component elements, the vegetation, the climate, and the type of crops cultivated are in general entirely different. This steep slope constitutes a descent for those going to Vuelta Abajo and an ascent for those coming from it.

At the edge of this precipitous downward slope an immense, magnificent panorama, which no canvas can embrace nor any pair of human eyes encompass in all its grandeur, unfolds before the traveler. Imagine an apparent plain, bordered on the west by the banks of fog on the distant horizon, on the north by the bare hills that skirt the coast, and on the south by the rugged and lofty mountain ranges that form part of the vast cordillera of Vuelta Abajo. And we have called it an apparent plain because in reality it is a series of uninterrupted transverse valleys, deep and narrow, formed by the same number of small streams, rills, and torrents that flow down the northern sides of the mountains and, after following a gentle and meandering course, disappear in the huge, unhealthy marshy basins of El Mariel and Cabañas.

At the sight of this grandiose panorama, Isabel, who was an artist at heart and loved everything that is good and beautiful in nature, suggested that the riders rein in their mounts at the edge of the steep decline and stepped down out of the carriage without waiting to see whether her proposal would be accepted by her companions. It must have been about eight in the morning. The road widened at that point, describing a Z so as to minimize as much as possible the steep pitch of the descent. For this reason, although both sides were covered with a long stretch of leafy, fully grown trees, their crowns did not top by much the level of the plain on which the travelers were standing, nor did they obstruct to any appreciable degree the panoramic view beyond. The vegetation was amazing. Despite its being late winter, it appeared to have donned its Sunday best and was proudly smiling at the first rays of the life-giving sun. Wherever no foot of man or hoof of beast had ever trod, there grew, in torrents so to speak, modest blades of grass or creeping Bermuda, Spanish Needles, graceful shrubs, serpentine lianas, and sturdy trees. Parasite vegetation of all sorts and shapes hung from the green branches and dry offshoots, like the heads of hair of invisible beings, for such vegetation lives off the dampness with which the atmosphere of the tropics is constantly saturated. The soil of the plain and the woods, thickly carpeted with flowers, now in little clusters, now in festoons of diverse appearance and different hues, formed a whole as elegant as it was picturesque, even for those individuals accustomed to the sight of the immensely fertile fields of Cuba.

As an even greater novelty and delight, life there displayed itself in its most bizarre forms: the nearby woodland materially boiled with almost every species of insect and bird that the fecund Cuban earth engenders.

All of them buzzed, whistled, or trilled as one amid the dark leafy branches or the thick grass, and joined together in a concert so harmonious that humans will never be able to equal it, whether with their voices or with musical instruments. How fortunate those creatures that merely by being tiny and defenseless did not arouse the hunter's greed or fear being interrupted in their innocent forays and flittings as they gathered honey in the calyx of the flowers, or hopping from branch to branch, made the leaves tremble and spilled the dew that covered them, with the drops, on hitting the dry leaves on the ground, imitating a rain in which clouds played no part.

There is no similarity whatever between the appearance of the region as seen from one side of the mountains and the other. From the south side, the plain with its coffee bushes, pasture land, and tobacco plantations stretched almost to the end of the island and is as pretty and pleasant as one can possibly imagine. In contrast, on the side to the north, in the same parallel, it appears so deep, rugged, and gloomy to the traveler's gaze that he is led to believe that he has set foot in another land and another climate. Nor does this bad impression disappear owing to the fact that beyond Bahíahonda the land is now cultivated for the most part. Perhaps because its cultivated areas consist of sugar plantations, because the climate is undoubtedly hotter and more humid, because the soil is black and muddy, because the atmosphere is heavier, because man and beast alike are more oppressed and and more badly treated here than in other parts of the Island, at the mere sight of it the traveler's admiration changes immediately into distastefulness and his joy into sorrow.

This, more or less, was what Isabel felt on coming into contact with that stretch of the famous Vuelta Abajo. Its portals, which in fact were the heights on which the travelers had stopped, could not have been more splendid; they could be described as golden. But what was going on down below? Could peace ever dwell there? Would there be happiness for the white, repose and contentment at any time in his life for the black, in an unhealthful region where heavy and endless labor was imposed as a punishment and not as the duty of a human being in society? To what could so many hard-working beings aspire or for what could they hope once the day was done and night had fallen and they surrendered to the sleep that God, in his holy mercy, grants to even the most miserable of his creatures? Among so many workers did any one of them earn his bread freely and honestly in order to support a virtuous Christian family? Were those huge estates that represented the greatest wealth in the country signs of the contentment and the unalloyed pleasure of their owners? Would there be happiness, peace of mind for those who knowingly crystallized sugarcane juice by shedding the blood of thousands of slaves?

And the thought naturally crossed her mind that if she married Gamboa, sooner or later she would have to live for certain periods of time, whether long or short, at the sugar plantation of La Tinaja, toward which they were heading, presumably on a holiday jaunt. Naturally also, the most important events of her brief existence came rushing to her mind, as in a fantastic procession. She remembered her stay in the convent of the Ursuline nuns in Havana, where amid silence and peace her heart was nourished by the most wholesome principles of virtue and Christian charity. As if in contrast, she remembered the death of her pious mother; the motherless state into which she had been plunged; her desolation and deep grief; the serene and uneventful days which she had later spent at La Luz, that beautiful garden that was a replica of the one our earliest forbears lost forever, caressed by her closest kin and idolized by her slaves as no queen on earth was. She remembered, finally, the distressing situation in which she had left her ailing father, now well along in years, who did not approve of this journey at all, perhaps because it might well be the prelude to an even graver and more prolonged separation.

The silence and the meditation of the young woman were very brief, but her emotion so intense, so deeply felt that she could not keep her eyes from brimming over with tears. Leonardo was at her side, holding his spirited horse by the bridle, and whether in order to divert her from her sad thoughts or in order to act as her *cicerone,* he began to describe the crowning points of the magnificent panorama beneath their eyes. He had passed by those sites a number of times; he knew the terrain that he was about to set foot on like the palm of his hand and wanted to show off his good memory to his lady friends. "The first plantation at our feet," he said, "is Zayas's. The trees on this side of the slope keep us from being able to see the mills, but over there are his most distant sugarcane fields. He must be milling, for the odor of cane syrup rises all the way up here where we are. He is still using a sugar mill driven by mules. We shall have to pass right through the *batey.* Then in the center of this great valley, just a little to our right, next to that silk-cotton tree, the red roof tiles of the boiler house of the very old sugar mill of Escobar or El Mariel can be seen. According to what Mama tells me, it was the first one to be set up in this valley of Vuelta Abajo. They must be milling there too, for I see smoke rising from amid the trees in the *batey.* Then do you not see a white cloud that runs all the way across the valley level with the treetops, meandering back and forth? A poet would say that it is a tulle veil. To me it looks like the skin of a great snake shed by the monster as he fled from the mountains to the sea. But if you look carefully, it is nothing but the mists marking the winding course of the Hondo River, notable for its narrow bed and the great floods it brings on in the rainy season. It is low now and there will be bridges enabling us to cross it with no need for us to get our feet wet. On the other side, there to the right, turning away from the northeast, can you make out a bright green, dense grove of trees out of which several towers that appear to be round loom up? That is the sugar plantation of Valvanera, owned by Don Claudio Martínez de Pinillos, recently granted the title of Count of Villanueva. To the left, at the foot of the mountain known as Rubín or Rubí, the cane fields of La Begoña can be seen, and to the right, not yet within sight, La Tinaja, almost a league away from the town of Quiebrahacha."

The descent down that side of the mountain to the vast valley with the sugarcane plantations was precipitous, and although laid out in a zigzag, the horses toiled hard to keep the carriage at the right level. The carriage driver shortened the driving reins of the horse inside the shafts, fearing that the carriage would skid; and the horse slid down the slope on its rump rather than making its way down standing upright. The leather braces, on which the body of the carriage was rocking back and forth like a top, thereupon started to creak, and the sweat began to pour from the back of the ears and the flanks of the exhausted animals.

"Take it slowly, Leocadio," Isabel said as they arrived at the most disagreeable stretch of the escarpment. "I've never seen a steeper road."

Leonardo was riding alongside the right footboard of the carriage, and said jokingly:

"Is that Isabel speaking? I thought she was braver than that."

"If you fancy I'm afraid, you're altogether mistaken," she shot back promptly. "I'm not the least bit afraid for myself; I'm afraid for the horses. Look at the one inside the shafts; it's a very heavy load and a steep slope; he's bathed in sweat, and I keep waiting for him to fall and roll down. Yes, we'd best alight. Stop, Leocadio."

"No, don't get out, miss," the carriage driver said insistently, risking a clash with his mistresses. "If your grace get outs at this place, she will have to get out on all the hills. Pajarito one very smart horse and he know more than the bibijagua ant. Leave me give him a good hard whipping, and your grace will see how he stop dilly-dallying."

"That's what you'd like, for me to allow you to mistreat the poor horse. Don't you know that he's not used to hills? I'd never in this world consent to your beating him. Stop, I tell you."

"Mistress keep sending animals and people to dere perdition," Leocadio murmured, picking up the reins in order to stop. "When de señora was alive dese horses fly like birds. She one who like to whip hard."

At this point Leonardo intervened, opposing what his friend had announced that she proposed to do, not only because doing it that way the team of horses would start misbehaving as the driver had said, but also because the road was shaded by the grove of trees on the right and therefore the wet, muddy roadbed had not yet dried out. She gave in with notable aversion, and so as not to take part directly in what she called the martyrdom of the horses, she handed over the reins of the one outside the shafts to her sister Rosa and closed her eyes during the remainder of the descent.

Rosa could have wished for nothing better. Young and lively by nature, she loved danger and was dying to drive the carriage, no matter how exhausting it might be for the horses to transport her over those craggy mountain tops, like a baby in his cradle rocked by the wind.

Zayas was indeed milling. The piles of recently dried sugarcane almost closed off the open sides of the building housing the mill, leaving, to be sure, only a fairly wide passageway or path that the travelers were following, along the side of the *batey*. A great uproar and hustle and bustle could be noted, both inside the mill and outside. Inside, the mules powering the sugar mill went round and round as fast as they could in the open space, pitilessly whipped by the black lads who were running alongside them for this sole purpose. Amid that infernal din there could be distinctly heard the creaking of the sheaves of cane that other slaves, naked to the waist, were feeding all at once and without a letup into cylindrical iron drums. On the other side of the mill, although the ruckus or bedlam, so to speak, of confused sounds was even greater, if possible, not a thing could be seen; the view was completely blocked by the dense smoke mixed with steam being given off by the boiling cauldrons in which the very sweet cane juice was boiling and filling the whole interior of the great laboratory with its immense fragrant columns.

Outside, carts in a double file were either heading into the aforementioned building or going away from it empty, making for the sugarcane field or *corte*, as it is called, all the carts drawn by a span of oxen as feeble as they were slow-moving. Immediately next to each pair the driver or carter, a slave armed with a long prod with a sharp iron tip, was keeping pace with them; and all along the double line of carts, the oxherd rode, now in one direction, now in the opposite one, on his ambling mule, he too armed, not with a prod, but with the indispensable rawhide whip, with which every so often he lashed the back of a black whom he found remiss in his use of the iron prod.

The workmanship of the carts was as crude and primitive as can be imagined; the axles were provided with no lubrication, thus making the loaded carts creak continually; while the empty carts, with their outsize wheels and the loose-fitted spindles of their axletree, besides never remaining perpendicular to the ground, whatever its slope, made a most unpleasant clanking noise, the loose washers continually knocking against the fixed iron linchpins, and the planks of the bed of the cart constantly shifting out of place. For a long stretch in either direction, the *batey* and the boundary paths disappeared beneath the straw-colored leaves and even millable stalks of cane that had fallen out of the carts or wagons through negligence or from overloading or because of some material defect of the vehicles used to transport them. The carters contributed the most to this deplorable waste. No sooner had the oxherd left a given spot when the carter immediately seized the chance to pull out of his load the stalk of cane that looked best to him and in so doing pulled out several others that fell on the ground and lay there to be trampled on and squashed by the carts following along behind. This gave him no concern; instead he raised the cane stalk to his mouth and sucked greedily on it, while at the same time continuing to urge the oxen on with deafening shouts and repeated goading to the point of drawing blood, perhaps in retaliation for the blood that the oxherd had drawn from his back with the hard tip or point in the shape of an agave leaf, called the *pita*, of the terrifying lash.

Such scenes or others very much like these were repeated within view of the travelers as they passed through the sugar plantations of Jabaco, Tibotibo, El Mariel or the former Escobar, Ríohondo, and Valvanera.

Between the two plantations last mentioned, they spied, on the edge of the road to the right, only a small *sitiería*, a group of straw huts where a few poor families cultivated a small patch of ground and raised livestock. It could not even be called a village, since there was neither a school nor a church within many miles. The owners of sugar mills generally did not allow these symbols of progress and civilization in their immediate vicinity.

In order to rid herself of her bitter thoughts, Isabel tried to turn her eyes away from the black dirt road, hard and without luster, like unfired iron, and instead gazed out over the light violet flowers or *güines* of the ripe cane, until they fell upon the bluish patch of sky where the horizon met the pitch-dark peaks of the mountains in the distance.

But for more than one powerful reason, the concentration that Isabel's spirit and its torment demanded was not possible for her. The undulations of the terrain were as abrupt as they were frequent; the road admittedly wide, yet necessarily winding; the streams deep and narrow, it being necessary to cross the majority of them via bridges of round logs or planks sawed from palm trunks, built with neither skill nor solidity. It was therefore necessary to walk across them slowly and cautiously, and what was more, Rosa did not know how to control the horse outside the carriage shafts, and thus he was more of a hindrance than a help to the horse inside the shafts, either getting ahead of it or not pulling as hard, or else pulling in the opposite direction from the one in which the carriage was moving. The carriage driver complained more than once of these difficulties, until Isabel, in order to make him hold his tongue and to avoid a serious contretemps, again took over the driving reins of the horse on the outside.

Even if Rosa had known how, she would not have been able to handle the horse outside the shafts better on that happy morning of their journey. Where the width of the road permitted, Diego Meneses rode to the left of the carriage, as elegant on horseback as he was witty and amiable on foot, and for the moment inspired and eloquent, ready more than at other times to look only on the poetic and the bright side of the scenes that they saw on their travels. At each pace he found something to engage the attention of his enthusiastic friend, now pointing out to her the festoons of convolvulus creepers with white blooms or bellflowers hanging from all the bushes on the banks of the streams, now the *güines* of the ripe cane, which brought to mind the panaches of innumerable warriors in martial array, gently swaying in the soft morning breeze; now the flocks of *tomeguines* which with their muffled sound, like wind skimming the ground, followed the travelers in a mad rush for some distance, grazing the grass and then disappearing amid the cane stalks; or the lively but slow-flighted starling who burst out of the thick brush with a great din and alighted with much difficulty on the first cane leaf it came upon in its mad flight; or the aloof white heron that forged a path between the branches of the oak tree on the riverbank, and with its long neck folded over its back and its feet dangling followed in its flight the course of the stream; or the band of chattering magpies that covered the wild orange trees and could be seen only when they clung to the golden fruit to extract the seeds from it; or the sparrow hawk, finally, Cuba's eagle, that flew in circles and let out piercing cries as it hovered above the tallest palms, between heaven and earth.

At last, after ten that morning, the travelers crossed the streams of the Valvanera plantation, within sight of its great mills. Two miles farther on they approached the town of Quiebrahacha. Here the road that they were following divided in two; the fork that turned westward was the road to Vuelta Abajo, and the other, the one to La Angosta, served as the entry point to the sugar plantations, already well established in this region along the coast. Our travelers chose this one. As they went through the town several people recognized Leonardo Gamboa and greeted him with friendly respect.

The territory ahead looked as rugged, uneven, and mountainous as the one they had already traveled through, although the woodland was leafier and more luxuriant, almost primeval, and the soil furrowed with tumultuous streams and clear waters that emptied into the bay of El Mariel and disappeared at the bottom of it, or into the open sea to the north. After half an hour's journey beneath the trees of the woodland, which the sun's rays did not penetrate, they caught sight of the cane fields of a plantation on the steep incline of a hill, marked off by a rustic fence made of tree branches, kept in a horizontal position by split rails or stakes with forked props sunk into the earth and tied together here and there for greater stability with a liana which, when green, was quite flexible and elastic, *Bauchinis heterophyllas*, known in Vuelta Abajo by the common name of *colorado*.

Then, proceeding for a short distance parallel to this crude fence, during which time the travelers reached the top of the hill, there lay before them in all their vastness and grandeur the cane fields, and in the center of the panorama, the various buildings housing its sugar mills, with another hill crowning the even vaster level space at its wider base. This was La Tinaja, and Leonardo Gamboa, serving as guide, showed it to his friends with a certain feeling of pride. There was ample reason for his pride, not only because of the monetary value that the plantation represented and because of the social considerations reserved for its owners, but also because of the beautiful and picturesque panorama of the whole, contemplated from a fair distance away, an effective concealment for the blemishes and stains inherent in almost all handiwork, be it human or divine.

The road the travelers had taken thus far in order to reach that point was the one called La Playa, the road to the beach, because it served to transport the refined sugar to the town of El Mariel, from there to be loaded onto schooners and taken to the market in Havana. It ran across the top of the hill, and a gate or roadblock had been set up on it that was no less rustic than the fence, for it consisted simply of rough-hewn branches, with their ends driven into holes in two parallel beams. Up against the fence, where it met the gate, was a cabin or hut with a gabled roof, thatched with whole palm leaves spread over its sides or slopes, so low-pitched that the tips of the leaves touched the ground.

Leonardo went ahead of the others to see why the black *guardiero* or watchman was not at his post and opening the gate. To this end he left his horse before the only entrance to the hut, and leaning forward, tried to search inside. To no avail: this doorway or entrance was very low and narrow, and human eyes were unable to see two feet past this opening, not so much because of the bright daylight outside as because of the dense cloud of wood smoke from the fire burning inside that had no other outlet than this one opening.

"I can't see anything and I doubt that there's a living soul in the hut," Gamboa said, addressing the ladies in the carriage standing in the middle of the road. "Confounded black!"

"Perhaps he's asleep," Isabel said.

"If he's not sleeping the sleep of the dead," Gamboa replied, "I swear that nobody is going to save him from a flogging."

"What's the difficulty?" Meneses asked. "Getting the gate open? I'll open it without missing out on anything by doing so."

"You won't do any such thing," Leonardo shot back angrily. "I won't allow it."

"Well," Isabel suggested in her sweet silvery voice, "the carriage driver will open it; the horses are much too tired to run away. Dismount, Leocadio."

"No, no, Isabel," Leonardo put in, more and more enraged. "I can't allow that either. I must not. If the *guardiero* is alive he'll open the gate; he's been posted here for that very reason and others besides."

He took out his watch and immediately added:

"It's past 12, the hour when they let the plantation slaves stop work so as to eat. If we had arrived here a little before that we would have heard the bell at the mill. I'd wager that the old uncle who's the *guardiero* has gone into the cane thicket to meet with one of his slave-ship cronies. By God, I swear he'll pay for it. No, he's not anywhere to be found. 'Caimán! Caimán!'" he shouted at the top of his lungs.

The hills around them were all that sent back the echo of his shouts with a continuous tremor, deep and sinister; and then a little bulldog inside the hut began to bark. The *guardiero* is there inside, the young man thought, and he's pretending to be asleep so as not to have to take the trouble to open the gate. "I'll kick him out of there," he added aloud, pounding on the saddle horn. He dismounted without further delay and went inside the hut, keeping hold of his horse by the bridle the while.

These words and those curses echoed most unpleasantly in modest Isabel's ears, even though in order not to embarrass her friend or irritate him more with regard to his poor slave she was careful not to point out to him how absurd and how risky his final intention was if perchance the slave was hiding on purpose because he had a comrade concealed in the hut, or for some other reason. Fortunately, events took an altogether diffferent turn. At that very moment the ladies in the carriage, Meneses, and the coachman mounted on his horse heard a sound of branches rustling nearby in the woods as they were shaken by a person or an animal clearing a path with considerable difficulty, and there then appeared on the edge of the woods a poorly dressed elderly black, with a wool cap on his head and a long knotty stick in his hand on which he was leaning for support, perhaps so as not to kiss the earth with his forehead, for his body was bent almost double from his labors or from many years of living in dwellings with a low ceiling. He spied the travelers the moment he came out of the woods, because he stopped for a moment, hesitating as to what he should do, and dropping amid the tall grass an object that gleamed in the sunlight and appeared to be a bottle or some similar container, he then came straight on to the carriage from the direction opposite the hut.

This chance circumstance saved him from his master's initial fit of fury, for the minute Gamboa came out of the hut he recognized him from a distance and started out after him at full speed. But as he climbed on his horse and covered the distance separating him from his intended victim, he gave the latter time to unconsciously place himself under the protection of the ladies. In all likelihood the unfortunate slave had not been informed that those persons were expected at the plantation, nor that it was his young master who was riding alongside them to guide them there. In all truth he did not recognize him. But on noting that the rider was coming at him at full gallop, shouting: "Ah, you dog! Now you're going to get it!" he could not have failed to recognize him or to fall on his knees at the hoofs of his horse, which, though holding itself back, sent the *guardiero* rolling head over heels merely by bumping him with its chest.

The ladies had a terrible scare. Rosa let out an exclamation of horror; Doña Juana repeated: "Good Lord! Good Lord!" and Isabel sat halfway up in her seat, thrust her arm outside the carriage and said, more indignant than frightened: "Don't kill him, Leonardo!"

"He should be grateful that all of you are there," Leonardo said; "otherwise I think I would have killed him. That's how outraged I am at him."

"Ah! My young masta!" the old man exclaimed, struggling to his feet and then falling to his knees once again, like a humble sinner in the presence of his irate judge.

"Where have you been, you dog, you sorcerer?" the young man asked him, and without waiting for the reply went on asking or saying: "What were you doing in the woods? Why weren't you in your hut? I'll wager you went off to swap sugar scrapings you steal at the mill for brandy with the tavern keeper in town. Yes, yes. I'd swear to it."

"No, no, my young masta, nosir, yo' grace. Caimán not steal sugar scrapins! Caimán not drink brandy!"

"Shut your mouth, you old dog! Off with you, run and open the gate. You aren't running yet? You don't know how to run? I'll have the overseer liven you up a little with the whip. Go on! Be quick about it!" . . . and Gamboa tried to give him a kick in the head from the saddle of his horse (fortunately missing him).

The *guardiero* looked to be a man over 60 years old. At least his hair had turned gray, as had his sparse beard and mustache, a sure sign of old age in men of his race. Along with disproportionately long, bony arms, he had contorted fingers, as though suffering from leprosy; small eyes with a sad, dispirited expression, never sadder than when, after having opened the gate, he cast a look in the direction of the ladies in the carriage and seemed to be begging them to protect him from his master's wrath.

Once his first moment of irritation and blindness had passed, the latter realized that he had shown too much rage and more than a little boorishness in front of ladies who, besides being under his protection, were about to enjoy his hospitality at the plantation. His mount had been more generous than he, since even though it could have done so, it did not trample the slave underfoot when it found him lying prostrate in its path. Gamboa was ashamed of his conduct, but being much too proud to admit the error of his ways and make amends for it with the forthrightness that the episode demanded, he confined himself to relating the principal incidents in the life of the *guardiero*, naturally slandering him in passing.

"Don't imagine, ladies," he said, "that old uncle Caimán here is what he appears to be, a defenseless, mild-mannered elderly man or a loyal and humble slave. I must tell you that he wasn't given his nickname of 'Caimán,' which has the meaning both of 'sly old fox' and of 'alligator,' for no reason: he's the most evil-minded schemer, with streaks of slyness, of anyone alive; nor is he too ignorant to practice certain arts that make him a man of importance among his own people. He has a reputation as a sorcerer and for making himself invisible when it suits him or when he finds himself in danger. He makes idols and chants spells that have magic properties in certain instances. No one would claim that he sees, hears, or understands, and nonetheless, neither by day nor by night is there anything or anybody who escapes his notice; and he knows, like the alligator, how to pretend to be asleep so as to reassure his prey. He spent his youth in the wilds as a fugitive, and in the course of his repeated escapes he has visited all the hideouts in Cuzco and made friends with the most notorious runaway slaves of Vuelta Abajo. He's too old now to trot around like that, and in consideration of his having been one of the builders of La Tinaja, the only one of those who cut the first trees here who is still alive, Mama had the post of *guardiero* given him, and he's been kept in that post despite the opinion of hired hands who know his history and his bad habits. When he wants to or when it suits him no one can beat him as a watchman, not even the most cunning dog. He can be said to be a free man: he raises poultry, fattens one or two pigs each year, which he then sells and buries the money somewhere, and he owns a mare that he's in the habit of taking for a ride at night out to the boundaries of the plantation. But as I say, he's very sly and evil-minded and I'd bet anything that he didn't go a good way away from his shack and his post unless he had some deceitful and reprehensible aim in mind. He meets in the canebrake with his comrades from the plantation; he meets in the wilds with runaways or with tavern keepers from town to trade sugar for tobacco, brandy or something of the sort."

"That's no doubt so, Leonardo," Rosa began saying, "because it seemed to me that he was carrying a . . ."

The aunt and the sister, more prudent than she, did not allow her to finish her sentence; and no one else spoke during the rest of the way.

Between one and two in the afternoon, beneath a searing sun whose rays were reflected by the cane leaves as if they were burnished swords, the travelers dismounted at the manor house of La Tinaja.

*The blackest thing about slavery is not
the slave.*

José de la Luz Caballero

From more than one point of view La Tinaja was a magnificent plantation, an adjective it fully deserved because of its extensive, luxuriant
fields of sugarcane, because of its three hundred or more field hands to
cultivate them, because of its great herd of oxen, its numerous carts and
wagons, its 25-horsepower steam engine, recently imported from the
United States at a cost of over 20,000 pesos, not to mention its horizontal sugar mill, also new, that had been assembled there and had cost half
that sum.

The boiler house or mill house was as sturdy as it was vast: an entirely
open edifice, whose framework was made of round logs of equal size,
resting on flat stone bases supported in turn by forked props, called *hor-
cones* in the region, with no squaring or shaping other than that given
them by the adze of the Basque architect-carpenter who had been hired
at the plantation for such work. The building had the imposing and rustic air that its purpose seemed to require. Its red tile roof protected from
the elements the horizontal mill, the steam engine, and the Jamaican

train or production line for processing the sugar, mounted on top of three furnaces or ashpans. All these pieces of equipment were not on the same level: the boilers were several feet lower; and in order to pass from one section to another it was necessary to go down two wide stone staircases on either side of the level where the horizontal mill and the steam engine were located. Things were arranged in this way so that the fermented sugar cane juice would readily flow downward; after leaving the rollers it ran through a wooden channel to the trough, called a *mansera* in a sugar mill, where it was purified to a certain degree and then went on to the crystallizing vat or evaporator where it went through a preliminary boiling.

Parallel to this building was another one, equally vast and with a lower-pitched roof, closed on the sides by walls of rubblework and with only one entrance, facing the section of boilers previously mentioned. This was the house for purifying and drying the sugar. The carpenter shop, the forge, the infirmary, and what might be called the maternity hospital were located in other separate buildings, along with the dwellings of the overseer, the oxherd, the carpenter, and the steward, as well as one for the master sugar-maker, who also temporarily resided at the plantation. For the machinist, a job held at the time by a young American, temporary quarters had been built with planks of cedar near the steam engine, the only sheltered site in the big, ugly, rambling boiler house. Next came over 200 cabins or straw huts, grouped together with their corresponding animal pens and poultry sheds alongside, to house the 300 slaves or workforce of the plantation. The other open buildings, namely those for the cane pulp, for beating the mud for the purifying of the sugar, and others of lesser importance, were situated in the intervening space between the boiler house and the purification house.

The ground of the manor house, called by antonomasia "the house," was in the form of a trapezoidal parallelogram located on the gentle slope of a hill, whose variation in level the builders had tried to remedy by raising the floor in the front. It was a single building made of heavy, roughly dressed stone, with a roof of red Spanish tiles, a wide porch, a square main room in the middle, flanked on either side by two rows of rooms, corridors leading through the interior, a rectangular courtyard in the center closed off by a high adobe wall with a ridge of glass shards on top, and an entryway in the expanse of wall at the back, which was secured by a bolt and lock and allowed the domestic servants access to the house. Many flowers, several orange and fig trees, and grapevines grew in the courtyard, their verdure and their shade contributing more than a little to the coolness of the rooms, although in order to block the sun's rays around midday, heavy canvas curtains had been placed all along the corridors. The same arrangement could be seen on the porch, which because of its height and spaciousness was more exposed to the onslaughts of the wind and the disagreeable effects of the sunlight reflecting off the vast, desolate *batey*.

From the top of the stairway on the porch the view encompassed, from one end to the other, the boiler house in front, the purification house a little farther to the right, though only along the side with the pans for drying the sugar; then the blacks' quarters or rather the paling fence that enclosed its rustic dwellings, in short, the greater part of the buildings that made up the large plantation village; the cane fields to the west; the straw roofs of the houses on the cattle ranch; and farther in the distance an immense palm grove, a bend in the river, and then the tall virgin forest that formed a sort of dark background for this varied country panorama.

Around noon on December 24, 1830, sitting back in comfortable armchairs upholstered in red calfskin, were the master and mistress of La Tinaja, along with several other persons, protected from the sun by the heavy canvas curtains. Almost all the gentlemen, Don Cándido Valdés, the parish priest of Quiebrahacha, the captain of the district, and the doctor were smoking cigars; Doña Rosa, the wife of the aforementioned captain, the wife and the sister-in-law of the overseer of the cattle ranch, and the young Gamboa sisters were eating sweet sugarcane stalks of a variety not grown for commercial use, called *cañas de la tierra*; others ate Chinese oranges and Peruvian guavas, all products of the plantation farm. Our acquaintances from Havana were also somewhere about: Tirso, Aponte, Dolores, along with another of the black servants who had come by sea, and two or three more from the slave population of the plantation, who because they were native born and better looking had been singled out to be house servants, all of them making themselves useful at the moment.

Of the Gamboa sisters, Carmen and Adela were not sitting down; they were nibbling at a bit of guava or orange and then taking long strolls hand in hand from one end of the porch to the other, with visible signs of impatience because in their opinion their friends Isabel and Rosa from Alquízar were late. Adela in particular raised a corner of the canvas curtain each time she reached the southernmost angle of the porch and cast an anxious glance all along the main boundary path until it ended at the open countryside of La Playa. Finally, shortly after one in the afternoon, the sound of carriage wheels was heard in the distance and the swift gallop of several saddle horses; and Adela, without yet spying anything, joyously exclaimed: "Here they are!"

This time she was not mistaken. Shortly thereafter, the Ilincheta sisters arrived at the foot of the stairway leading to the porch in their carriage, which, along with its occupants, the horses, and their riders, was covered with the dust of the red earth. It would be pointless to linger over a detailed description of the various scenes that took place as the two families met amid the lonely expanses of Vuelta Abajo. There was more than one reason for at least some of those present to view that instant as a truly noteworthy event. It so happens, moreover, that young people, and sometimes adults as well, when they meet in a rural setting with the intention of spending just a few days in informal and cordial company, far from the places where they have been accustomed to live and divert themselves, feel strongly attracted to each other; if they are friends, they give evidence of their friendship more freely; if relatives, they persuade themselves that closer ties unite them; if lovers, ah! their love seems to them eternal, the bliss of loving each other heavenly.

The women heartily embraced each other. Adela wept for joy as she fervently hugged Isabel, for whom she felt extraordinary affection. For her she was the most modest and loving of women. Doña Rosa too singled out the elder of the Ilincheta sisters, and on the occasion of which we are speaking showed her exceptional cordiality. Even Don Cándido, so solemn and unbending, who had not had so much as a smile for his son when the latter came to him to ask him for his blessing, received the Ilincheta sisters with unaccustomed demonstrations of affection and introduced them to the gentlemen guests with the words: "These young ladies are my daughters too." And addressing Isabel, he added: "This house is yours; I hope you enjoy yourself and amuse yourself in it as you do your own charming home in Alquízar."

The welcome on the porch lasted for only a short time. Worn out by their journey, the ladies needed to rest a little, to tidy up, to change clothes before sitting down at the table. Doña Rosa, or the wife of Moya the overseer of the cattle ranch, who acted as housekeeper for that lady so as to save her work, had had lodgings readied for the Ilincheta sisters and for their aunt, immediately adjoining the rooms occupied by the Gamboa family in the corridor to the right, on the far side of the main room.

It was already late afternoon when they sat down at the table in the vast main room of the manor house, some 16 ladies and gentlemen, waited on by half that number of servants. Doña Rosa did the honors. Don Cándido seconded her as much as was compatible with his temperament, although he reserved his compliments for the administrator of the plantation of Valvanera first of all, then second for the parish priest of Quiebrahacha, and third for the doctor for his estate and for the captain of the district. Everyone was to spend the night at the plantation so as to take part in the ceremonies that were to be held on the following day, the first day of Christmas. Except for the wife and the sister-in-law of the overseer of the cattle ranch, none of the plantation employees was invited to eat at the manor house; and Moya himself, the overseer, who had considerable influence with the present owners of La Tinaja, did not take a seat at the table, despite being invited to do so by Don Cándido, on the pretext that he had already eaten.

Joviality and liveliness, tempered by the decent manners characteristic of a good upbringing reigned at the banquet, albeit except for Meneses, young Gamboa and the parish priest, none of those present had received a first-rate education or ever mingled with Cuba's high society. The last named, Don Cándido Valdés, a Creole, had been educated at San Carlos Seminary, in Havana. Concerning religious matters, he was tolerant to the point of indifference; concerning politics he professed liberal opinions that he was in the habit of exalting to the high heavens. Dr. Mateu, from Galicia, had practiced his profession aboard slave ships, and now treated sick slaves for an agreed fee on various plantations in the district. He was considered to be good-looking; but his good looks were on a par with his stupidity and his pedantry. He was persuaded that all women were in love with him, and from his place at the table he cast furtive glances at Rosa Ilincheta, whose graceful figure, vivacity, and ardent nature were more than enough to addle the brain of a man with better judgment than he. The parish priest took an immediate liking to Isabel, who in all her words and deeds revealed the lofty qualities of her spirit. Don Manuel Peña, an Asturian married to a good-looking Creole, had risen in status from the bar counter or tavern of the town to assistant captain of the district, a sort of justice of the peace, the sole circumstance that caused the master and mistress of La Tinaja to seat him at their table. Don José de Cocco was another sort of man; a native of Cádiz, he had delicate features, very white teeth and blue eyes, was of short stature, and was rather witty despite the fact that he had had little schooling.

Don José devoted himself to lavishing attention on the second of the Gamboa sisters, at whose side he was seated at table, with full awareness, however, that under no circumstance would one of the young mistresses of La Tinaja give her heart or her hand to the administrator of Valvanera. As for Adela, the prettiest of the sisters, her extreme youth saved her from the courtly overtures of the men gathered round the table.

The wine cup circulated among the latter freely from the beginning of the meal to the end; once the main courses had been served, the tablecloths were removed so as to serve the desserts on the bare polished mahogany table. Black coffee was brought at once in translucent porcelain cups, along with bubbling champagne, French cognac, and Jamaican rum. Then Don Cándido Gamboa brought out his great fragrant gold-colored bull's bladder and distributed loosely rolled cigars among the captain, the doctor, and the priest, since Cocco did not smoke, nor did Meneses, and Leonardo would not have dared touch a cigar in front of his father.

The banquet ended at sunset. But as the family and the visitors went out onto the vast porch where the servants had already rolled up the canvas curtains, it was plain to see that sufficient light still remained in the surrounding countryside. This was because on the one hand the crescent moon was rising out of the distant woodland and its light obliquely striking the leaves and flowers of the cane and the white trunks of the palms, while high overhead in the blue sky as diaphanous as crystal, countless stars emitted gold and silver sparks.

Depending on the number of steps they took after the banquet, all the individuals gathered together in the manor house spontaneously divided into three groups. Doña Rosa, in the company of Doña Juana; Señora Moya, the captain's wife; and Antonia, the oldest of the Gamboa sisters, sat down once again in the red calfskin armchairs. Don Cándido, along with the priest, the assistant district captain, and the overseer of the cattle ranch, the better to digest the meal and savor their fragrant cigars, took short turns around the porch and conversed at one end of it. Don Cándido in particular seized upon the chance to gather certain information, more impartial than that provided by his overseer, concerning happenings on the estate during the two weeks or more preceding the day of his arrival at La Tinaja. To this end he put, as if in passing, a number of questions to Moya, who, honored by that distinction on the part of the master of the plantation in the presence of the priest and the assistant captain of the district, hastened to answer them with candor and not a little satisfaction. For example, on being asked:

"Is there no news, Moya, of the blacks who ran away last week? The steward told me that there are seven of them, among them a black woman."

"To tell you the verifical truth, Señor Don Cándido, we haven't had a whiff of news of them," he answered, with a great deal of bowing and scraping.

"But have any steps been taken to find them?"

"Yes, of course, Señor Don Cándido! The hills of Santo Tomás and of La Langosta have been searched. Fresh tracks have been found ever'where, but 'cause Don Liborio Sánchez's dogs are guard dogs that bite and not search houns, even though they like to keep good watch on blacks they din't find 'em. An' I got to thinkin' that they hadn't gone past the boundries of the plantation 'cause they hadn't thought things through aforehand and don' know how to make their way in the wilds. With good dogs, they'd of found 'em, that's for sure. Ah! God give me dogs that kin smell a black from a league away . . ."

"I for my part," Captain Peña said, cutting Moya short, "must inform Señor Don Cándido that as a courtesy to him I have done everything within my power. In fact, once I was advised of what had happened, by way of a report that his overseer, Don Liborio Sánchez, gave me, I lost no time in sending on an urgent communiqué, through the courier in Bahíahonda, to Don Lucas Villaverde and Don Máximo Arosarena, the inspectors in San Diego de Núñez, members of the party headed by Don Francisco Estévez which has just been formed by order of the Royal Development Board to hunt down runway blacks in the jurisdictions from the dock at Tablas or El Mariel, Callajabos, Quiebrahacha, and so on up to the western boundaries of Bahíahonda.[40] In my communiqué to the estimable inspectors I included the relationship, age, and description (an approximate one, naturally, since you know that all blacks look alike) of the seven that ran away from you. I hope, then, that should the search party come across them, something quite possible, since I suspect that the fugitives have headed for the nearby mountains of Cuzco, it catches them and . . . Señor Don Cándido ought not to be surprised that seven of his blacks have run away, since in the same period 12 from Santo Tomás, 8 from La Valvanera, 6 from Santa Isabel, 20 from La Begoña, and 40, yes 40, you heard rightly, from La Angosta, the plantation immediately adjoining yours belonging to His Excellency the Count of Fernandina, have rebelled. The list of all of them is already in the hands of the estimable inspectors, and of Captain Estévez as well, I presume."

"It doesn't surprise me that my servants have run away," Don Cándido said thoughtfully. "These aren't the first blacks who have run away on me. But Chilala, José, Sixto, Juan, Lino, Nicolás, Picapica, and others are now back, and they won't give me the lie. When they're not in revolt in the wilds, they suffer, as they are doing now, a more or less long punishment here on the estate, and wear shackles on each leg, or drag about a ball and chain. Goyo, or Caimán, the watchman at the gate on the road to La Playa, is known to have spent his youth up in those mountains that can be seen from here . . . But all of them are Royal, Loango or Musundi Congos, a humble, submissive, loyal race, the one most suited to slavery, which seems like its natural condition. It has only one defect, a grave, capital one: it is the laziest race to come out of Africa. If the Congos could live without eating, no human force could coerce them into bending their backs and working. They'd be capable of spending their lives lying stretched out with their bellies up. . . . And because they won't work they often run away. . . . What does greatly surprise me, what I can't explain to my satisfaction is why Pedro and Pablo, who are Carabalís, Julián an Arará, Andrés a Bibí, Tomasa a Suama, Antonio a Briche, and Cleto a Gangá have followed the example of the Congos. These blacks, industrious, tireless workers, strong, robust, dependable, don't run away without a reason. No, blacks who always have time for their masters and for themselves, who save money and often buy their freedom, don't run away for little cause. They are too proud, that being their one defect, to rebel without a compelling reason. They'd hang themselves rather than take to the hills . . ."

It could be seen from this brief comment that Don Cándido Gamboa had absorbed at least some knowledge of African ethnology. It was only natural that his constant traffic in slaves over many years and the possession of some 200 or 300 of them had taught him that depending on their race, they were more submissive or more rebellious, more or less suited to bearing the heavy yoke of slavery until their dying day. It happened, however, that Moya had learned something else from his long experience in handling his and other people's blacks, and his entire being rebelled when he heard it said that there were good ones and bad, and that some of them never ran away without a compelling reason, and would take their own life first. So Moya, at the risk of crossing swords with the master, said:

"Ever'body knows that Señor Don Cándido has seen blacks and knows the ones that are good fo' this and not good fo' that. Begging Señor Don Cándido's pardon, I say that ever' las' black is the same once they start thinkin' 'bout Guinea. All of 'em pull backwards like mules and you have to give 'em a good lashin' with the whip. Let's see. How come the seven from here ran away? Fo' lack of food? Fo' lack of clothes? Fo' lack of pig? Fo' lack of veg'table ga'den? They don' lack fo' any of that. They got a great plenty of all that. Fo' all the work they got? Fo' all the lashin'? They're not workin' now, strickly speakin', an' to tell you the verifical truth Don Liborio flogs 'em good from Corpus to Saint John's Day."

"If I may be allowed to say what I think," the priest broke in modestly at this point, "my opinion is that people who are as ignorant as blacks are should not be expected to think things through and act as rational creatures. It would be pointless to seek the reason for their rebellions and crimes in their instinctive sense of justice and right. No. The cause may well have been the most chimerical, the most absurd, the least justified imaginable . . . It is nonetheless an odd coincidence that so many blacks, and ones from precisely those plantations that have recently changed their system of milling cane, have all rebelled at the same time. Can it be that those stupid creatures imagined that they would have to work harder because the milling is done with a steam engine instead of milling with oxen or mules? How do we know? It is worth looking into."

"Of course," Don Cándido said, still pensive, following with his eyes half open the columns of ash-colored smoke escaping from his mouth. "My namesake's argument is a good one if it's a question of Congo blacks, a false one if we're talking about blacks from other tribes of Africa. I have closely observed their diverse natures and I know whereof I speak. More than anything else, the slave trade has to do with the conduct of certain blacks. They have all been born to be slaves, for that is their natural condition; in their homeland they are nothing but slaves, either of a few masters or of the devil. Nonetheless, there are some who need to be dealt with severely, very severely, the whip always over their heads so that they'll work; and there are some who willingly allow you to get out of them as much as you like."

"That's the way how it is, like Señor Don Cándido says," Moya remarked, putting his oar in again. "But I say that if there are blacks who cain't complain about the treatment they get, it's Señor Don Cándido's. They're like flowers: well fed, plenty of clothes, ever' las' one with his lil plot of land and his pig, many of 'em married, workin' only from sunup to sundown, and they don't get the whip fo' jus' anythin', like I seen done to 'em on other plantations. They don' have hardly any work, jus' two or three hours, on Sundays, an' when it's not cane-millin' season, almos' all the rest of the time is theirs to play canasta, fatten their pigs, spade their gardens . . . Almos' ev'ry Chrismas they have a day for drummin'. What more do them wicked folks want? Not even the bishop is better off."

"And here we are, back on the same subject again," Don Cándido said in annoyance. "Moya, what you assure us and keep repeating is all well and good; but none of that convinces me, nor does it explain to me the cause, the real and true cause of my Carabalís running away. The worst of it is that I suspect that you know something and don't want to come out with it in front of these other gentlemen, our priest, and our district captain."

"Well, by all these crosses and by the one that Jesus Christ died on," Moya said vehemently as he kissed the five crosses he had formed with the ten fingers of his two hands intertwined, "I swear I don' know anythin' more. An' if I'm leavin' anythin' covered up, may lightnin' strike me right here an' now, and may you all pardon my way of speakin'."

"You mustn't swear to something of so little importance," the priest said.

"Search your memory, Moya," Don Cándido said with a smile on seeing his discomfort.

"The thing is," Moya went on after a brief pause, "that I don't know what cain be the cause and what cain't be the cause of a black runnin' away. Señor Don Cándido says that some blacks hang themselves and don' run away; and then he says that mistreatmen' is the cause of runaways. Very well. Señor Don Cándido also says that the Carabalís be very proud. I say they be very stubborn, more stubborn than all the blacks put together. Pedro the Briche is the ringleader of the blacks on the plantation who came from Africa on the same ship as him. He always speaks their language with 'em, and the overseer is mad at him. I know it; but he's never laid a finger on 'im, an' I don' think that anybody has drawed blood from 'im with the whip since he come from Africa. Well, señor, jus' las' week, Pedro the Briche din't show up in the lineup an' he din't sleep in the slave quarters that night. What would you have Don Liborio do? The nex' day he goes an' catches 'im where he was hidin' out an' gives him some lashes on top of his shirt, and then he clapped 'im in the stocks for two days, took the job of assistant overseer away from 'im, an' sent 'im out to clear land with a machete. He got even more stubborn. I told Don Liborio to give him a good floggin', but he was afraid he'd lead a rebellion of all the blacks on the plantation. And now ever'body's seen what happen. He took to the hills with six of his pals 'cause he wasn't punished enough."

"Didn't I say as much?" Don Cándido said with an air of satisfaction. And he added, before Moya could cut him off: "And what does Goyo, the *guardiero* of the road to La Playa, say about all this? Do you know if they've sounded him out?"

"Of course they did!" Moya answered promptly. "The very firs' one they went to see fo' that. Doesn't Señor Don Cándido see that at the very door of Caimán's cabin they found fresh tracks of blacks what came down from the mountains, from the other side? But he swore by all the saints in heaven that he din't see, hear, or smell nothin' in all this time. Don Liborio got mad at 'im an' tried to give 'im a few lashes so's he'd sing; but I made 'im give up the idea, 'cause I thought Señora Doña Rosa was goin' to get mad once she found out they punish' ole Uncle Caimán."

Don Cándido thereupon stepped up his pace without regard for the guests who were keeping him company, perhaps so that they wouldn't interrupt his train of thought. Then turning suddenly toward Moya, he asked him in a curt and imperious tone of voice where the overseer was.

"When I come from the cattle ranch," Moya answered, "he was with the field hands cuttin' cane, opposite the land that's just been cleared. He won't be long now. Seein' as how there's no need to cut Guinea grass to feed the horses 'cause there's sugar cane tops, he'll let the hands off work earlier. Look, here come the wagons with the las' cane stalks fo' tryin' out the steam engine . . . I can see the oxherd there in the distance on his mule, and still farther on yet, by the other boundry path, I can see Don Liborio now. The canebrake keeps me from seein' his dogs and I cain't say if he's alone or with the field hands. He's comin' on horseback.

V

9. I am clean and without
transgression . . .
10. Yet he invents pretexts against me
and reckons me as his enemy.
11. He puts my feet in the stocks; he
watches all my ways.

Job 34

While the scene already described was taking place at one end of the porch, another very different one was being played out at the other. The Ilincheta sisters along with the two younger Gamboa sisters formed a lively and interesting group there, surrounded by a half-circle of gentlemen courting their favor or admiring them. All of them were standing, the young ladies leaning back against the railing and the gentlemen hanging on the lips of Rosa Ilincheta who, in a few vivid, charming words, was describing the little incidents that had occurred during their trip, her bad handling of the horse for part of the way, and her own impressions.

Leonardo smiled, Cocco applauded, Mateu the doctor pirouetted with pleasure, and Meneses retained his grave demeanor, consumed with jealousy because with Rosa's account the number of admirers of his pretty lady-love was growing. Adela and Isabel, holding hands, stood listening in silence. Suddenly someone tugged on Adela's skirt from outside the porch. She quickly turned about and saw a good-looking black woman, dressed very differently from the other female slaves on the plantation.

"What is it you want?" Adela asked, rather startled.

"I beg your grace's pardon, miss. I was coming to fetch the doctor." (She was unable to see him because of the darkness and the skirts of the ladies standing in the way.)

"And who are you?"

"I am the nurse, and your grace's servant."

"The nurse!"

"Yes, miss, the nurse María Regla. And is your grace not Miss Adelita?"

"I am indeed." Adela answered in surprise.

"Ah!" the slave exclaimed, gently squeezing the girl's feet, since she was unable to reach any other part of her body. "My heart told me so. I saw her grace pass by the *batey* from the window of the infirmary. I had my doubts as to which one was my girl, whether it was Miss Carmen or your grace. How much my daughter has changed! How pretty she has become, Blessed Virgin!"

"My heart told me so, my daughter, pretty," Adela said, repeating her words. "If I'm your daughter, if you love me so much, why didn't you come to see me? I sent you word through Dolores. Why didn't you come out to speak with me? You've made me very angry."

"Ay!" the black woman exclaimed. "Don't tell me that, miss, it will be the death of me . . . Your grace was not by herself."

"No, I wasn't. I was with Mama, Carmen, Moya's wife, and his sister-in-law Panchita. What 's so unusual about that?"

"Say no more, apple of my eye."

"Speak, explain yourself."

"I can't at the moment, my girl."

"What! You don't intend to ask for Mama's blessing?"

"Yes I do, miss. I must, I want to in my heart, I was coming . . . From the moment that the Señorita arrived from Havana, I intended to come running and throw myself at her feet . . ."

"Why didn't you do so? Who kept you from it?"

"Señorita herself."

"Mama? No, that can't be. You're mistaken, you're dreaming, María de Regla."

"I'm not mistaken, nor am I dreaming, Miss Adelita. If only I were! The Señorita has forbidden me to set foot in this house."

"How does it happen that I know nothing about this? Who came to you and told you a tall tale like that?"

"It wasn't a tall tale, Miss Adelita. Dolores told me about a conversation that the Señorita had with the master about me . . ."

"You see? Dolores misunderstood. Mama isn't angry at you. I'm going to go this minute to make sure that she's not."

"Don't do that, Miss Adelita, no, for the love of God," the slave woman replied in terror, holding the young girl back by the hem of her dress. "Whether she's angry or not, it will be better if the Señorita doesn't see me now. Is the doctor here?"

"I wish to see you alone. We'll arrange a way. I'll send you word through Dolores. And what do you want the doctor for?"

"For a black they've brought in from the mountains who's been bitten by the dogs."

"Bitten by the dogs!" Adela repeated. "Oh, my! It must be a very serious case if they're calling the doctor in. What if they've torn him to pieces! It's more than likely. Those dogs are like wild beasts. Good heavens, how horrible! Mateu," she added, raising her voice, "they're looking for you."

In all truth Isabel was beginning to discover very strange things about the family beneath whose roof she was staying and about the plantation of La Tinaja so highly spoken of. She was deeply interested in the lot of the nurse, at one time her affectionate friend's wet nurse, now banished from the manor house, and was moved, horrified by what she had heard about the slave bitten by fierce dogs, things all unimaginable to her. Isabel was unable to hide from Leonardo either her intense displeasure nor her deeply felt feelings.

"What's the matter? What's wrong with you?" he asked her.

"I don't know," she answered. "I feel ill."

"I had the impression," Leonardo went on, "that the story about the black who was hurt upset you. Don't be silly. How much shall we wager that it wasn't anything really serious? That all it amounts to is a few scratches? If you knew the nurse you'd think the same thing I do. Mama can't stand her because she's such a troublemaker. You mustn't believe every word of what blacks tell you. They exaggerate everything and overestimate its importance."

"What's happened, Adela?" Doña Rosa asked from her chair on hearing her call out to the doctor.

331

The nurse disappeared in an instant, and before Adela could answer her mother the overseer appeared on horseback, preceded by his two beautiful wolf hounds, to give an account in a resounding voice of everything that had transpired. He was a tall man, lean but strong-limbed, with a very dark complexion, black eyes, kinky hair, and a thick beard, whose bushy side whiskers covered both sides of his face until they met the corners of his mouth, thus making it look smaller. Despite his broad-brimmed hat that he always wore, both indoors and out, in the open air and beneath a roof since he very often used it for a nightcap, when he removed it to speak with Don Cándido it was plain to see that while the upper part of his forehead looked to be that of a white man, no one would have taken his nose, cheeks, and hands for anything but those of a mulatto; that was how deeply tanned they were. He was armed to the teeth, as the cliché has it, with a machete at his belt and a dagger with a handle made of silver, or so bright it looked as though it were, and carrying a heavy whip with a handle made of a branch from a wild orange tree, a no less terrible weapon for not being lethal yet raising horrible welts.

He began by saying:

"I bid Señor Don Cándido and all the accompaniment present a blessed afternoon. I've comed to info'm you that they've brought Pedro the Brichi in with some dog bites. He resisted and we had to sic the dogs on him."

"Who captured him?" the master answered very calmly.

"Don Francisco Estévez's search party, 'pointed to catch runaway blacks."

"Do you know where he was captured?"

"In the canebrakes of La Begoña, right close up to the mountains."

"Was he alone? What about the men with him?"

"We don' know nothin' 'bout 'em an' Pedro won't say neither. I figure he'll have to be given a floggin' so's he'll sing. Tha's why I be comin' to Señor Don Cándido so's he be tellin' me what I do with Pedro. He stubborn as a mule . . ."

"Where have you put him, Don Liborio?" the master asked after a long pause.

"In the infirmry."

"He's in as bad shape as that?"

"That not why, Señor Don Cándido. I put 'im in the stocks in the infirmry fo' better segurity, and I din't want to put shackles on 'im 'cause of his wouns; and then afterwards I figure he got bad intentions. His eyes look like two ripe tomatoes, and I've notice' that when blacks' eyes turn like that it's 'cause they want to do somethin' that's real bad. I tell the señor: that black be stubborn as a mule. To show the señor if he be pig-headed, when I put 'im in the stocks he said to me: 'a man don't die more than once,' and that 'he was tired of workin' fo' his master.' The señor should know that when blacks take to talkin' that way it's 'cause, as my frien' Moya, here present, says, they get to thinkin' 'bout Guinea. They done swallowed the notion that when they hang theyselves here they go straight back to dere homeland."

"The aberrations of ignorance!" the priest exclaimed.

"Yes, Señor Don Cándido," the overseer went on, "that black is askin' fo' a floggin' the way the dead ask fo' a Mass."

The priest and Don Cándido smiled and the latter said:

"At the right time, Don Liborio; grapes ripen at the right time. For the moment it doesn't appear to me to be the proper time to flog him. He'll get over the bites and there will be time then to punish him for his misdeed, one of the gravest that can be committed on these plantations. For the slave to rebel, to run away, to deprive his master of his services without a compelling and sufficient cause, for more or less time, is un-pardonable; not only in and of itself, but because of the bad example it sets for his fellows. He will be punished, you may be sure of that. There will be no one to defend him. In the case of any other black that same misdeed would appear to be slight. Pedro may hold up under a novena of floggings[41] though. . . . He has strong hams. To change the subject: didn't Estévez's party know that that black belongs to me? Didn't you inform him that I was here?"

"Yes, señor, he knew alla that and I told him he should come to the manor house fo' to hand over the runaway an' get the bounty, which is half a doubloon. But he answers me and says he'd rather sleep in the woods. An' he also said he din't want the sumissive blacks to see him, 'cause they'd pass the word on to the runaways, an' he also said he had to take hisself to La Langosta to see if he could catch the 40 blacks that ranned off on His Escellency the Count of Fernandina from las' week on, and the overseer had sended for him . . ."

At that point the 300 and more slaves of the workforce of the planta-tion passed in review in the *batey* between the manor house and the boiler house, and the overseer, with a "by your leave," went to place him-self at the head of the line to inspect them and give them his final orders of the day through the assistant overseers, who were also slaves. The murmur of the prisoners' conversations and the sound of the irons that they had been placed in had preceded them by a fair distance. Two of them had been put in fetters with a transverse bar and a Y-shaped chain suspended from their waists, and could walk only with great difficulty, for in order to advance they had to do so in half circles, first moving one foot, then the other. One of them was wearing a shackle, from which a chain some six feet long was suspended, the lower end of which was attached to a solid iron ball like the weight of a pendulum clock; as he walked, he was forced to carry the ball and chain over his arm, otherwise the friction of the shackle would grind down his shinbone, though a rag had been wound around it to protect it. This same slave halted from time to time and raised his voice, in a melancholy tone with a silvery timbre that resounded far and wide: "Here come Chilala, a runaway."

Prisoners or not, male or female, all of them were carrying something on their head: sheaves of sugar cane tops, trimmed tree branches that the horses and mules in Cuba were so fond of, bunches of green or ripe bananas, royal palm leaves for the pigs; this one a gourd, that one an armful of firewood. A few of them, 15 or 20, were wearing a canvas shirt and trousers that were new or had been worn only a few months and were still all in one piece; the rest were dressed in rags, through the holes of which their dull black skin could be seen. None of them was wearing shoes, though a few of them were shod in sandals of untanned leather, tied to their feet with cords of *majagua* fiber, or strips of royal palm fiber that are no less sturdy. The females, from 30 to 35 of them in all, mixed in helter-skelter among the men, had little to distinguish them from the males save for the sort of long burlap sack that covered their body from the shoulders to a little below the knees, without sleeves, so that no feature was missing to make of their attire a crude imitation of a Roman tunic.

"Fall in line!" Don Liborio shouted in a thundering voice, riding up and down the straggling ranks like a general ordering a maneuver. Whereupon, without stumbling, out of sheer habit, the majority lined up; but the lazy, the clumsy, those hindered by their irons, by their heavy loads, or by the haste with which the ones in the lead closed ranks, lagged behind, less visible than the others. The overseer's rage at these wretches exploded. He raised his whip and began lashing out to right and left, making no distinction between the innocent and the guilty, until he succeeded in getting them lined up as he wished.

If this is how people have reasoned with the slave in all times and places, was there any hope that the owners of La Tinaja would be an exception? None whatsoever. In their opinion, as in that of the majority of masters, the black was not the "thing" of which Roman law speaks. There was a considerable difference. To them, since they understood by "law" only what did not get in the way of the satisfaction of their passions and caprices, the man-thing of ancient Rome in all likelihood did not think and was nothing but a machine producing work; whereas the modern man-thing, they were utterly convinced, thought of at least three things: of the way of getting out of working, of making their unlawful owner's blood boil, and of laboring at all times in opposition to his intentions, desires, and interests.

For the master in general, the black is a monstrous composite of stupidity, cynicism, hypocrisy, baseness, and wickedness; and the only means of making him fulfill without grumbling, carping, or delay the task that he deigns to impose upon him, are force, violence, the whip. "The black is out to do evil" is a common saying among slave owners. Therefore, to their way of thinking, that overseer who does not cover up or forgive a misdeed, who strikes the delinquent like lightning, who in every circumstance has sufficient firmness and courage to make such perverse and uncontrollable individuals "toe the line" is the most praiseworthy, the most deserving of consideration and respect. The inquisitor who has sent the greatest number of heretics to the stake has always been the one admired most.

This explains why, when the overseer gave the order to let go, they all dropped their load at his feet, no matter whether it was a load of forage or of fruit, as a result of which the latter burst from the fall, giving the overseer an opportunity to use his whip again, and the owners of La Tinaja approved and applauded the "punishment," for it was clear that the guilty parties had acted out of malice and not out of clumsiness and confusion owing to a previous thrashing.

Doña Rosa, a Christian woman who was kind to her equals, who frequently made confession, who gave alms to the poor, who adored her children, who in the abstract at least was inclined to forgive the faults of others so that God in heaven would forgive hers; Doña Rosa, we regret to say, on seeing the contortions of those on whose backs or arms the tip of the overseer's braided rawhide whip opened gashes, smiled, perhaps because she found the spectacle grotesque, or else she exclaimed, echoed in chorus by the persons by whom she was surrounded: "Has anyone ever seen more brutish people!"

The carriage drivers Aponte and Leocadio also smiled, along with two other lads who from the little porch roof of the plantation's huge stable, attracted by the continuous crack of the fearful rawhide whip, witnessed the scene in safety and waited for everyone to clear out of the *batey* so as to go out and collect the forage for the horses and mules that were immediately handed over to them to care for.

If we add that in these circumstances even the overseer's dogs showed in their own way an unusual self-satisfaction, we are not of the opinion that we are saying anything new. As Don Liborio spoke with the masters of the plantation, the dogs continued to lie at the hoofs of his horse; but the moment he addressed the blacks, they positioned themselves at its flanks and never lost sight either of their master's eyes or of the movements of his right arm, no doubt awaiting the order to leap on top of the victim and finish him off.

It must be noted here, however, that not all the ladies present joined in the chorus that has been mentioned previously. Doña Juana, on the contrary, averted her eyes so as not to see, since good manners kept her from retiring to her room and hearing the strokes of the lash and the muffled moans of the victims was unavoidable. The nieces of this lady and the two younger Gamboa daughters found themselves in the same situation, but they at least were free to take refuge in the courtyard. Meneses, Cocco, and Leonardo followed them there, as Don Cándido called out to the latter and ordered him to accompany the doctor to the infirmary and find out all the details of what had happened to the prisoner. Shortly thereafter, in an intimate conversation with the priest and the district captain, he added:

"I wish to accustom him (his son) to such things early on, because I'll be dead and gone one of these days and out of necessity he'll be obliged to manage my holdings in my stead, above all the management of this plantation which belongs to him for more than one reason. This will be the estate he inherits as my firstborn son."

That peremptory order given him by Don Cándido was the reason that Leonardo, disgusted with his father and with the entire visit and given the fact that it was not possible for him to disobey or to excuse himself either, endeavored to get his two friends and his sisters to accompany him. They readily gave in to his pleas, as did Rosa, especially since Meneses and Cocco offered to go with him most willingly. Isabel immediately refused; but when pressed, and reflecting that perhaps there would be a chance to perform on that visit one of the acts of mercy incumbent upon a Christian, gave in as well, and as she left arm in arm with Leonardo, she said to Doña Rosa in passing, in a friendly and cheerful tone of voice: "They're carrying me off."

"Well and good," Doña Rosa replied.

"A fine pair!" said Doña Teresa, Captain Peña's wife, as Leonardo and Isabel went down the porch steps to the *batey*.

"A handsome one!" said Doña Nicolasa, Moya's wife.

"Don't you think, Rosa" (Don Cándido said in an aside to his wife, agreeing mentally with the apposite observation of those two women), "that it is a better and better idea for Leonardo to marry Isabel as soon as possible?"

"Yes," Doña Rosa answered, her mind elsewhere.

"I believe she's a fine match for Leonardo. And it's evident that she's in love with him. And then too, marriage curbs . . ."

Don Liborio did not know how to count up to more than ten or so without having to stop to think. But luckily he had a good memory and a good eye for faces; so that, except for the seven runaway slaves, the eight patients in the infirmary, and the 28 workers assigned to the various outbuildings of the plantation, carpenters, masons, blacksmiths, stable hands, and servants, he hadn't the least doubt that the others, males, females, bachelors, married men, children, and adults, numbering as many as 306, had passed before his eyes, one after the other and entered the slave quarters. Satisfied on this point, he closed the gate, drew the T-shaped bolt, and locked it shut; he hung the key to it, along with the whip, on a nail driven into the door jamb of his house, on the outside, underneath the porch roof.

If he had read the *Quijote*, he would have been able to say along with that knight errant: "Let there none move/ Who dares not with Roldán his valor prove." For come rain, wind, heat or cold the overseer's fierce wolfhounds slept at the foot of these symbols of lordly power in Cuba, and woe unto the poor wretch who dared come near to take down the key or the whip!

After eating alone because the family was visiting the plantation, Don Liborio, with his machete and his dagger at his belt, accompanied by his dogs, went hurriedly on foot to meet the doctor at the infirmary. In order to reach it, there on the far side of the flat area or square around which all the buildings of the sugar mill had been built, he had to go past the corner of a hedge of nut-pines sheltering a cane field in flower. There the dogs separated from their master and in a vain attempt to get past the obstacle, they began to growl or rather to moan, the way the usually did when they smelled their prey close at hand. But we have already said that the overseer was in a hurry, and he went on, calling to his dogs to follow him.

Just as he entered the infirmary, a black on horseback came down the path to the *batey*, rode through it from one side to the other, went up onto the porch of the overseer's house, looked carefully in all directions, saw that there was no light and no one in sight, and without dismounting from his skinny, broken-down mare that he was riding bareback, took the key, drew back the bolt of the lock with it and returned it to its place. This daring feat done, he went on to the manor house and asked to see its masters; since they were still on the porch, receiving him did not embarrass them.

He did not dismount, but rather, slid down the sides of the beast to the ground, not having a stirrup to set his foot on. His first concern was to doff his wool cap, and with his body bent double and trembling all over, he threw himself on his knees before Doña Rosa, and in his bad Spanish said:

"De blessin', my mistress."

"Ah!" the aforementioned señora said, rather startled. "Is that you, Goyo? May God make you a saint. How are you?"

"I be bad off, my mistress."

"Where does it hurt, Goyo?"

He answered, with much beating about the bush and many circumlocutions, most of them unintelligible, that his body was too heavy; that he lacked strength and wanted to go to his rest in the cemetery; that he was very old; that Doña Rosa's father had taken him out of the slave quarters in Havana when the señora hadn't yet been born; that he was one of the slaves who had helped build La Tinaja, one of the first to clear the woods with his ax. All this, which the señora with whom he was speaking knew full well, so as to inform her, amid extravagant gestures and digressions, that he knew where some of the runaway slaves were hiding out, and that they wanted to appear before their master and mistress once they had learned that the latter had arrived from Havana, because they were almost certain that they would not be punished for their misdeed, because it was the first one, especially if the *guardiero*, who had served for such a long time on the plantation, were to ask the señora to forgive them.

"Very well," Doña Rosa said, having cast an inquiring glance at her husband to learn his thought on the matter. "Very well, Goyo. Go. Tell your godsons that they can appear before me without fear; that because of you justice will be done them."

By coming to Doña Rosa to beg her to forgive the runaways, the *guardiero* showed that his brain could at least conceive two quite definite ideas. The first, that he took Doña Rosa's heart to be more apt to be moved by pity, because of the fact that she was a woman, than was Don Cándido's; the second, that even though she was the lawful mistress of the plantation since she had inherited it from her father, she would be more indulgent toward the faults of her slaves than he, for although he was its master in fact, he was not its master by right.

The *guardiero*'s thought set forth in this way seems too abstruse to befit the mind of a black, one become doubly stupid owing to his long years as a slave. But whether or not that was the case, that was how Don Cándido interpreted the slave's discourse, leaving him feeling wounded to the quick, on the one hand, because the latter's mission left him out entirely out of consideration; and on the other, insulted by the odious difference between mistress and master that the *guardiero* had made a special point of. It never rains but it pours, and Don Cándido seized by the scruff of the neck the opportunity to take his revenge for the insult and to mend in the eyes of the persons who had witnessed the scene what he believed to be his diminished dignity as lord and master. In this frame of mind, and as the old man, trembling all over, made every effort to climb back up onto the bare back of his most meek and gentle old mare, Don Cándido said:

"We'd be a fine master and mistress if on account of the first idiot who intervenes we were to pardon not only the gravest misdeeds but even the crimes of our slaves."

Doña Rosa looked at him in astonishment, and then said with apparent calm:

"So you didn't agree with my decision then?"

"That may well be."

"So . . . ?"

"So justice must be done those rogues who dared run away when we needed their services most."

"What do you take doing justice to mean, Gamboa?"

"I take it to mean giving every single one of them what he deserves, to punish anyone who commits an offense as he should be punished," he replied sarcastically.

"But that wouldn't be to do justice."

"Why not? Ask your son who's a law student what doing justice means. Or else remember the way the decrees of the prosecuting attorneys of the permanent military commission that are often published in *El Diario* read: 'I, X, captain in His Majesty's army, etc., by this, my first decree, cite, call upon and summon Y to appear at the public prison of this city within such and such a period of days, which cannot be extended, to acquit himself of the guilt for which he must answer in the case that I am bringing against him for assault and robbery in the wilds or for disloyalty; sure and certain that if he appears within the specified period, full justice will be done him.' . . . Do you hear? Full justice. I know the decree by heart."

"I don't believe that the military commission, or whatever it is called, punishes everyone it summons to appear in order to do him justice."

"You have to believe it, because rightly or wrongly, that's what happens. Why is it that no matter how often they cite, call upon, and summon anyone, nobody ever presents himself *motu proprio*? That's only natural, since this business of 'doing justice' is nothing but empty talk. The person summoned may be as innocent as a newborn babe; nonetheless, if they catch him, it's Mama Jail for sure, for three or four years, and that is a punishment . . . that I'd gladly give all those who wish me ill."

"That's all well and good, Cándido; but the fact is that your interpretation of the term was not what I meant when I spoke. In short, I promised the forgiveness that Goyo came to beg of me on behalf of his comrades."

"Well, that's where you're wrong, Rosa. You didn't promise any such pardon, or any other nonsense of the sort. And even if you had, it wasn't possible to do what you promised. . . ."

"But the fact is that I've given my word."

"And therein lies the whole secret, my dear Rosa. In a word, you didn't promise anything and that was what I tried to prove to you so as to avoid worse troubles. From the mere fact that you said 'justice will be done them,' it cannot be concluded that you promised to pardon them, simply and straightforwardly . . . without conditions."

"Yes, but Goyo is going to believe otherwise; he'll believe I deceived him."

"And what does it matter if you appear in a bad light in the eyes of that black? Nobody has ever remained loyal to those who prove disloyal *a nativitate*."[42]

"Perhaps what Goyo will think doesn't much matter, since when all is said and done he's an old, ignorant black and surely he didn't understand me. But what about my conscience, Cándido? My intention was . . ."

"Your intention was to pardon," Don Cándido interrupted her. "I know that. As for your conscience," he added with exquisite irony, "in this instance it ought to be quieter and more serene than the most peaceful retreat. And if there are any feelings of guilt involved, blame everything on me. You know that the devil shoulders everyone's guilt. Anyone who ever felt scruples of conscience as to what he said or didn't say, what he did or didn't do to blacks, that saintly man, or that saintly woman must never have owned slaves. Scruples of conscience over beasts like that! What a joke!"

At that moment the young ladies and gentlemen returned from the infirmary. The doctor said that the black had received several very bad bites, though not life-endangering ones, on his arms, forearms, and the long bones and carpi of his hands and feet. The epidermis of some of the fingers of his right hand appeared to be torn. "But fortunately," he added in his peculiar jargon, "the incisors of the animal were not so intent on destroying their prey as to break any major blood vessel and there is no danger of hematosis, although there were signs of hemalopsia as a consequence of the exacerbation of the physical and moral pain from which the patient had been suffering for some time. It is necessary to combat this by applications of leeches at his temples; which, it should be said in passing, will have to be brought from town, since there were none in the plantation dispensary. As for tetanus, it is likely that it is present since the black got wet after receiving his wounds. For this reason I have ordered that he be given frequent applications of suet and oil with crushed cloves. I can state, however, that thus far no nerve appears to have been damaged . . ."

Leonardo was more concise. Speaking with his mother, he said in such a way that his father would hear: that Pedro had barely recognized him as the person who was his young master; that he had refused to make a deposition; that he knew nothing about his comrades; that, seemingly to intimidate him and to make him talk Don Liborio had told him that there was now no chance of his escaping being put in the stocks and that he would then be obliged to bow his head in submission, and Pedro had answered with a laugh that any man capable of making him give in against his will had yet to be born anywhere on earth. Filled with indignation, Leonardo had turned his back on him. "And, oddly enough," he added, "as we were leaving, he called to me to tell me that he wanted to see his master, that is to say Papa."

"I was waiting for that," Don Cándido murmured as he went off. "There's time enough tomorrow; I won't be bothered by His Lordship for the moment."

If the young ladies had been questioned about what they had seen in the infirmary, they would have told a very different story from the one related by the doctor and Leonardo. They would have said that the African Hercules lying face up on the hard wooden platform, with both feet in the stocks, with conical holes left by the dogs' teeth still open in his ashen flesh, with his clothes in tatters, with the palms of his hands for the only pillow on which to rest his head, despite the deep and obviously painful teeth marks. An ebony Christ on the Cross, as one of the young ladies remarked, was a sight worthy of commiseration and respect. Their deep regret at having gone to that place was comparable only to the grief they felt, the pious Isabel in particular, when they realized that they could do nothing to relieve the suffering of this further victim of the civil tyranny in their unhappy homeland!

V I

The blacks . . . Oh! my tongue rebels
Against speaking the name of their misery.
D. V. Tejera

In order to show his zeal and industriousness, or else because he had mistaken what time it really was, since he went by the crowing of the cocks, the overseer of La Tinaja aroused people from their beds much earlier than usual on Christmas morning.

With the last solemn toll of the bell, after drinking several cups of coffee, lighting a cigar, and tucking his weapons in his belt, he took down the key, called to his dogs, and went on foot to the slave quarters to open the iron gate at the entrance. He resolutely placed the heavy key in the lock, tried to make it turn in the ward and was unable to: "What the devil!" he said to himself. "Somebody been here. It do seem to me I got more floggin' to do than God on Judgment Day."

He used the glow of his cigar to shed light on the keyhole, gave the key half a turn and distinctly heard the bolt slide and catch in the staple of the lock. "I swear to God!" he exclaimed. "The gate were open and I was so stupid I jus' now lock' it. So I lef' it open las' night then. Was I drunk? or crazy? or upset in de head? Or were there witchery here? What's goin' on, Liborio?"

At that moment the blacks were coming out of their cabins and Don Liborio had to think about what he was going to do with them. Drawing the bolt back, he planted himself alongside the gate to watch them file past one by one as he had ordered. Hence, even though it was still quite dark, he was able to see a black who had hidden herself behind her comrade and was trying to pass unnoticed. Malicious and vigilant, that was all he needed to fling himself on her, grab her by one arm and bring his lighted cigar up to her face. To his surprise mingled with joy he saw that it was Tomasa the Suamo, who had run away exactly two weeks before. As he was holding her fast, Cleto the Gangá appeared, also trying to hide, and behind him Julián the Arará, Andrés the Bibí, and Antonio the Macuá. He stopped them and made them stand to one side.

As all the others filed past and lined up in the middle of the *batey*, he pushed the five that he had caught in front of them and ordered them to halt facing the center of the line, as long as it was ragged. He immediately began the interrogation:

"Come here, Mama Tomasa, and tell me, fo' de life of you, where you come from jus' now?"

"From de wilds," she answered imperturbably.

"Well, I declare! And what were you lookin' for in de wilds, Miss Tomasa?

"Siñó . . . ?"

"Don't tell me. Don't bother, girl; I know: you went there to loaf aroun'. I'm goin' to give you time to loaf aroun'. But how come Doña Tomasa the Suamo has showed up now?"

"She comin' to present herself to the Suamos."[43]

"Good! That the right thing to do. But how did you-all git inside de slave quarters?"

"Through de gate."

"Who open the gate fo' you?"

"Not nobody. De gate were open."

At this point the slave driver's patience gave out.

"So the gate were open, were it? Ah, you piece of . . ."

And without further ado he hit her so hard she landed on the ground in a daze. As she was getting to her feet, he put more or less the same questions to the black woman's four companions and received more or less the same answers.

"Lie down on the ground on your belly!" he said to the slave girl, grabbing her by one shoulder so as to knock her to the ground face down.

But being young, robust, and knowing what was about to happen to her, she stood her ground and said:

"Yo' grace not goin' to punish me, my godmother protec' me."

"Ha! Ha! You makin' me laugh. The Señora your godmother! Well, tell her to get up out of bed and come save you from a floggin'. Look, you black devil, lie down and turn over on your belly or I kill you . . ."

"Go ahead, kill me," she answered arrogantly.

"You there, grab her. You there, knock her down," the overseer shouted to the slave girl's companions, in a paroxysm of rage.

Three of them obeyed instantly. Two took her by one arm and the other by one foot, so that it was easy to make her lose her balance and throw her on the ground face down.

Presumably the same blind obedience with which the three had hastened to carry out the overseer's peremptory order exacerbated his wrath against Julián the Arará, who appeared to be prepared to disobey. Don Liborio looked him over from head to foot with eyes that showed something of the rage that had overcome him, not a little surprise, and a world of fear, because the black's attitude was threatening and because, like the majority of his companions who were present, Julián was armed with a short machete, called a *calabozo*, and a hoe. Don Liborio finally realized then that he had acted a little imprudently, and that he was lost because he had given way at the critical moment. And so, plucking up his courage, he shouted with more apparent fervor than ever:

"And what are you doing, you dog? Why don't you go to it? Bend over . . ." (letting loose one of his usual swear words, for lack of a better expletive).

His words, moreover, were accompanied by such a hard blow to the slave's head with the handle of his whip that it made him stagger and then fall on his knees at Tomasa's feet. Even in that humiliating position, Julián gave no sign that he was about to obey; fearing, rather, that he would recover from the blow and get to his feet, the overseer added:

"Hold down the foot of that big dirty who' . . . Oh! I swear to God I goin' to beat you black an' blue."

And to compel him to obey, he fetched him a second blow, that not because it was harder than the first one but perhaps, rather, because he managed to land it in precisely the spot where Julián's woolly hair did not completely protect his scalp, it parted his hair as though with a knife and a great gout of blood spurted from the wound. Fumbling blindly about, Julián found Tomasa's instep and rested the palm of his hand on it . . . and the flogging began.

Such unusual conduct on the part of that black in such circumstances would have attracted the unbiased attention of individuals less stupid or less blinded by passion than Don Liborio; it would have aroused consideration, if not respect, in any noble and generous soul; it would even have awakened a curiosity to discover the origin of a sentiment that was no less touching for having come from the heart of a half-savage man.

A number of circumstances, moreover, concurred in the case of the black man and woman, serving to explain the conduct of the two of them as they were being so sorely tried. And it is likely that it was because he knew what these circumstances were that Don Liborio dealt so severely with the couple. Julián and Tomasa were more or less the same age: she young, robust, attractive, he athletic and valiant; they both had come from the same region of Africa, aboard the same ship; they therefore considered each other fellow countrymen or *carabelas*, as the slaves said. Why would anyone find it odd that they should love each other?

Because of her youth, her cheerful disposition, and her fine demeanor, Tomasa was the favorite of her comrades and of the white employees on the plantation. Slavery was not as heavy a burden for her, nor did she have any reason to complain of her lot, comparatively speaking. Why had she run away? It seemed obvious: so as to be with Julián, who, led on by Pedro, his godfather at his baptism and the ringleader of the rebellion, had made the fateful decision to run away. Tomasa did something else besides: the moment that Pedro was taken prisoner, in the tragic way that we have recounted, she pleaded with Julián and got him to agree to appear before their master and mistress and seek their pardon through Caimán, who they knew had influence with Doña Rosa.

For better protection, Don Liborio had a cotton bandanna tied over his head, two ends of the knot in it falling down behind, and had pulled his straw sombrero down over it. He was wearing his shirttails outside his trousers, with his dagger tucked into his belt and his machete held in place by a strip of white canvas. He placed his left hand on its hilt, lifted up the skirts of the slave girl's dress past her hips with the end of his whip handle, and unrolled the braided rawhide lash that he had been holding coiled up in the palm of his right hand. All this was done in an orderly, well-planned way, calmly and ceremoniously, like someone who is in no hurry, but instead is intending to savor an exquisite pleasure, to which end events must not be hastened.

The horizon to the east was growing brighter with the wondrously pure light of dawn. Once he had delivered the first whiplash with the aplomb and skill of one who possesses an experienced, iron arm, the overseer was able to assure himself that the *pajuela* or tip of it, made of fine twisted and knotted hemp, with a characteristic crack, had traced an ash-colored furrow in the girl's flesh. He immediately gave her several more lashes and then a whole series of them in rapid succession until bits of her skin went flying and blood came pouring out; through all of this the victim did not give a single moan, or move in any way save to contract her muscles and bite her lips.

Thus the overseer's wrath had a momentary outlet, but the girl's stoicism deprived him in large part of the pleasure that he had promised himself by whipping her. Pain, a horrible sensation to every sentient being, did not reduce her, as he had hoped, to the the extreme of begging her torturer's pardon. For this reason, and because he wanted to finish the job before the sun came up, he entrusted the punishment of Julián and his companions to the two assistant overseers, being content to watch them from close at hand so as to make them "come down harder" whenever he suspected that, out of pity or for some other reason, they weren't going at it with all their might. As soon as they were done with one of them, so as to prevent lockjaw or tetanus Don Liborio had the victim's wound washed out with urine into which some cigar butts had been thrown beforehand, and ordered the blacksmiths to put them in irons, having summoned them for that express purpose from the office of the steward of the plantation. As for Julián, who had fainted two or three times, either from the severity of the punishment or from his loss of blood, Don Liborio deemed it prudent to have him taken to the infirmary to have his head wound cared for. He forced the other prisoners, hindered by the weight of their shackles and the pain of the cruel lashes, to work nonetheless, along with the other blacks, at clearing the boundary lines around the manor house and the outbuildings, the labor that from the beginning it had been Don Liborio's intention to get out of them.

"Do you hear, Cándido?" Doña Rosa said to her husband as they lay in bed. "It seems to me I hear the sound of the whip. Don Liborio is up early today."

Don Cándido was too fast asleep to be awakened by the music of the lashes of his overseer's whip, despite the fact that owing to the vigor with which the latter was dealing them out and the stillness of the natural surroundings, they resounded for miles around. But when the question was repeated in his ears, between one yawn and the next he then answered it with another question:

"What is it I should be hearing, Rosa?"

"The overseer's whip. It's not as if you were deaf."

"You're right. I do seem to hear something. Yes. He's meting out punishment. So what?"

"I admire your coldbloodedness. Apart from other things, does it seem to you a matter of little importance that we were awakened so early? I'm sure to have a raging headache all day today. That confounded man has set my nerves on edge. The worst of it is that I'm more and more persuaded that Don Liborio doesn't have the least bit of consideration for us. I never have liked his face of a brigand."

And what would you like the man to do?"

"What any decent person would have done in his place. Go somewhere else, a long way away from the manor house, to punish the blacks, if in fact they've committed some serious misdeed and punishing them couldn't be put off till later on."

"Perhaps he couldn't help it. Blacks are sometimes determined to get themselves whipped and you must please them or risk having them behave insolently toward you. Moreover, in many cases it is advisable that the punishment follow directly on the heels of the crime in order to have the desired effect."

"But don't you have any better idea than I do of the reason for all this commotion so early in the morning?"

"I presume I know what it is, Rosa, and it's the usual reason. All I need to know is that some blacks escaped from the devil's talons."

"Whether or not blacks in general, and ours in particular, are bad, the truth is that Don Liborio hasn't stayed his hand since yesterday. And if this happens when we're here, what can it be like when we're far away? He's crucifying the blacks."

"Last night you were praising him as an upright man, and . . ."

"What did you expect me to say in front of other people? Inside me I felt as though my vitals were being gnawed away. And the devil hasn't shown all his talons yet either. But he's already gone too far. Doesn't that stupid idiot know that we have visitors? What will Meneses, a well-educated young man, almost a stranger to us, who is not accustomed to these scenes, say? At the very least he'll imagine that this is a prison, an El Vedado, and that you and I are completely cold-hearted . . ."

"Don't worry about the lad," Don Cándido said. "I'd wager anything that he's sleeping like a log, lulled to sleep by the music of the whiplashes. . . ."

"Yes, but now that I think of it, what will Isabelita say if she's been awakened? She must perforce have been awakened. The lashes must have been heard as far away as the wharf at Tablas. They echo in my ears like cannon volleys. Just think how delicate that girl is, how dead set she is against punishments. She may very well break with your son over this, believing that his mother and father are two torturers and that he can't wait to follow their example. I'd regret that on your account, since you're so bent on their marrying . . ."

"Slow down, my dear Rosa," Don Cándido interrupted her, more vehemently than was his habit. "You talk as if you yourself hadn't approved of their planned marriage."

" "Where did you get the idea that I approve of it?"

"Good Lord! We'd even more or less agreed on the wedding date."

"You arranged that; I didn't. If I agree to their marrying it's not that I'm deeply in favor of it or that I'm bent on it. For one thing, I will never be able to approve of my beloved son's leaving my refuge and going off to live in another house. For another thing, I don't know of any woman good enough for my Leonardo. Not even Isabelita, whom I regard as a saint; not even the goddess Venus, should she descend to earth again, would strike me as being worthy of him. If I consent to their marrying (they may still come to regret their decision) it's because of you, it's because you never tire of repeating to me and harping day and night on the fact that the boy is going to ruin his life, that he's going to come to a bad end, that it's necessary to restrain him, that he's very much in love (the poor boy hasn't looked at any girl but Isabel up until now), that he's giving signs of disgraceful inclinations . . . You stuff my head so full of such premonitions that you frighten me and I say to myself: the tailor who is familiar with the cloth is not a bad one; like father, like son; and even though I disapprove, I give my consent. He's still just a boy, he needs my caresses but you're implacable, you want to marry him off and you'll get your way. He'll marry, providing the girl doesn't back out . . . I share your view that marriage is a brake, although if we're to judge from your example, you've committed your greatest follies after you were married, and heaven only knows . . ."

"That's where your obstinacy lands you every time," Don Cándido interrupted his wife once more. "But it's all to the good. By having your say you've distracted yourself and left Don Liborio in peace."

"As far as that rogue is concerned, I won't stop till he's been thrown out . . ."

"It would be a bad policy to dismiss Don Liborio because he's punished the slaves' insolence with a heavy hand. What would happen to the prestige of authority? Here on the plantation the overseer represents the same role as the colonel in command of his regiment or the captain general who commands the vassals of His Majesty in this colony. How, if not, would order, peace, or discipline be preserved on the plantation, in the barracks or in the Captaincy General of the island of Cuba? No, Rosa, the prestige of authority takes precedence."

"So that in order to preserve the prestige of Don Liborio's authority you're going to let him kill off all the blacks?" Doña Rosa replied with the murky logic of women.

" "Kill off all the blacks!" Don Cándido repeated, feigning surprise. "He won't do any such thing, for the simple reason that Africa is full of them."

"There may well be all the blacks in the world there; the thing is that those who are lost on account of the English are becoming more and more difficult to replace."

"That isn't as bad as it sounds either, Rosa. Aside from the fact that no black dies because of a flogging or two, have yourself a good laugh at the idea that the English will ever succeed in putting obstacles in the way of the slave trade to the point that we'll be short of a workforce. You've already seen how we were able to sneak the ones in the last batch aboard the *Veloz* into the country right under their noses, making them believe that they were half-breeds from Puerto Rico."

"The flogging is still going on, Cándido. You must find out what this is all about. Summon the steward. Get up, do something."

"They're calling me there outside. Tell Dolores to ask what's going on out there while I get dressed."

Dolores slept in the room immediately adjacent to that of the Gamboa girls. Hearing the shouts of her mistress she appeared at a window shutter and said:

"Tirso is here, with coffee for the master and for Señorita."

"Ask him what's going on down in the *batey*," the latter said to the slave woman. "What a Christmas day awaits us! And then the sleepless night! . . . and the sultry weather! What prestige of authority and what nonsense! May Don Liborio go straight to hell!"

Tirso, trembling from the cold or with fear, reported that the runaway blacks had come back, that the overseer was punishing them, and that he had killed Julián because he had refused to turn over on his belly for a flogging.

"Didn't I tell you?" Doña Rosa said to her husband. "Don Liborio didn't even respect the fact that I served as their godmother."

"He probably didn't know that."

"They should have told him."

"He wouldn't have taken their word for it. What's more, Tirso is a terrible liar. I'll get up, however, to please you. When you get an idea in your head, things have to happen accordingly."

"I can't tell you how your blissful calm makes me feel. They're killing your blacks and you're not rushing to see what's going on. As if they hadn't cost you money!"

"Well, now you're really talking like a Solomon," Don Cándido said, going out onto the porch.

In all likelihood, the entire family and the visitors in the manor house of La Tinaja were up and about long before their usual hour. The place that offered the most relaxation and shade was the porch, and they all went out there. The sun hit the house from the back, projecting its shadow a long way inside the *batey* where, at eight and nine in the morning, the workforce of slaves on the plantation lay stretched out in their ordinary dirty, tattered attire.

Don Liborio approached the porch on horseback, dismounted, tied the animal up to the porch railing by its halter, and climbed up the staircase as far as the last step. From there, respectfully removing his sombrero, he greeted the company in general, and Doña Rosa in particular, who was seated very solemnly in the most conspicuous armchair, like a queen on her throne, surrounded by her children and her friends, and answered his greeting with an inaudible murmur. The lady in question could not forgive that man the bad time of it she had had, even if Don Cándido had pronounced himself satisfied after hearing the overseer's partial account of what had happened early that morning.

The female house servants witnessed the spectacle from the door of the main room, and through the oldest of them Doña Rosa informed the overseer that he was to summon the two assistant overseers. Once they arrived, they genuflected as usual before their master and mistress, then stood in silence with their arms folded on their chests, like two statues of black stone. The air of proud dignity with which those two men presented themselves was a clear indication that they were not Congos. They were Lucumís, a warrior race in Africa, which says everything.

"How are you?" was the first question that Doña Rosa asked them.

They looked at each other and glanced at Don Liborio out of the corner of their eye, as though encouraging each other to say something, or to relieve their deeply troubled spirit in some measure. Doña Rosa sensed the reason for her slaves' embarrassment: they were dying to speak, but fearful of the consequences, because of the presence of the overseer, deeming it more prudent to keep silent. She needed nothing more to be moved to make them abandon their reserve. She asked a different question.

"Do you have enough to eat?"

"Yes, siñora," they answered as one without hesitation.

"A great deal of work?"

"No, siñora."

"Are you happy?"

The same mimed scene as before was then repeated. After looking at each other, and then glancing out of the corner of their eye at the overseer, who was beginning to show signs of a certain anxiety, the older of the two was perhaps prepared to give an account, as brief as it was heartrending, of his hardships and tribulations, when Don Cándido cut them off by ordering in a loud voice that they be given the *esquifaciones* brought from Havana as a Christmas gift for all the field hands on the plantation.

Each outfit for the men consisted of a shirt of coarse canvas or burlap, a pair of trousers of the same cloth, a cap and a wool blanket; for the women, of a sort of calf-length garment called a tunic, also made of coarse canvas, a colored cotton kerchief and a blanket. These articles constituted what, in a word borrowed from the seafaring language of Cuba, was meant by an *esquifación*.

There was a good proportion of pride in Doña Rosa's temperament, since she was not one of those women whom it is easy to steer away from her avowed ends by means of subterfuges or dialectical subtleties. The mere supposition that Don Cándido, with the excuse that he was protecting the prestige of the authority invested in the overseer, was tending to diminish her rights as the mistress of the plantation, in the presence of people she scarcely knew, sufficed to spur her on in her desire to affirm those rights, and in a noticeable way. To this end, as soon as the assistant overseers withdrew, laden down with the *esquifaciones* for themselves and their companions, she asked, as usual through the overseer, that the black known as Chilala appear before her. He approached slowly and with some difficulty, shouting, as he was under orders to do: "Here comes Chilala, a runaway."

Once he had laid his large iron ball down on the floor of the porch, he knelt before Doña Rosa, folded his arms on his chest, and in his peculiar language, said with great humility:

"De blessin', my misress yo'grace."

"May God make you a saint, Isidoro," Doña Rosa answered in a kindly tone of voice. "Rise to your feet."

"Dat betta, my misress yo' grace."

"Why do you run away, Isidoro?" his mistress asked him in a compassionate voice.

This slave was extraordinarily emaciated. He was almost nothing but bones and nerves. Then too, the reddish color of his hair, the ashen paleness of his face, his wandering, anxious gaze, gave his face an expression of fear like that of a wild animal.

"Ah, my misress yo' grace!" he exclaimed with a sigh. "Work, work; eat little; no piece ob lan'; no pig; no woman: get whip, whip, whip . . ."

"So then," Doña Rosa replied, very calmly and with a certain smile of satisfaction, "if they give you less work and better food and a little plot of land to cultivate and a pig, and a woman to marry and don't punish you so much, you won't run away any more and will behave?"

Yes, sinó, my misress yo' grace. Chilala not run away no mo'; Chilala work; Chilala fine, fine."

"Very well, Isidoro, since you promise me you won't run away any more and will behave like a responsible man, I shall see to it that they don't punish you so much, that they don't make you work so hard, that they give you enough to eat, and a pig, and a piece of land, and a woman for you to marry. Are you satisfied?"

"Yes, siñora, my misress yo' grace; ever'thin' fine, fine for Chilala."

"I would like to do even more for you, being certain that you won't disappoint me. Don Liborio," she added in a loud and imperious tone of voice, "remove this black's shackles this minute."

The long enslavement, the gross ignorance in which he had lived, the very severe treatment he had received on the plantation: none of that had been able to efface the sensibility, the feeling of gratitude in the slave's breast. It cost him effort and imagination to understand what his mistress was saying to him: but as soon as he realized that his shackles were about to be removed, lacking words he called on gestures to express his immense gratitude. He threw himself face down at Doña Rosa's feet, as he would have done before a fetish in his native land, and with extravagant miming and incoherent exclamations of enormous happiness, kissed again and again the floor that her feet had walked upon.

Women of Isabel's sort were an extreme in every way: either they love or they hate; the half-tones of their passions are reserved for rare instances. In the few hours of her stay on the plantation, she had been able to observe things which, although she had heard of them before, she had never believed were real or true. She saw, with her own eyes, that a permanent state of war reigned there, a bloody, cruel, implacable war, of black against white, of master against slave. She saw that the whip always hung over the slave's head as the only argument and the only prod to force him to work and submit to the horrors of slavery. She saw that terrible, unjust punishments were meted out for everything and at all times; that verification of the evidence of a misdeed committed never preceded the application of the punishment; and that often two or three different punishments were dealt out for a single misdeed or crime; that the treatment was iniquitous, with no reason to mitigate it and no restraint to moderate it; that it called out to the slave to flee or to hang himself as the only means to free himself of an evil that had no cure and no letup. That is the synthesis of plantation life, as presented to the eyes of Isabel's soul, in all its nakedness.

But none of this was the worst; the worst, in Isabel's opinion, was the strange apathy, the impassivity, the inhuman indifference with which people, masters or not, looked upon the sufferings, the illnesses, and even the death of slaves. As if their lives didn't matter to anyone from any point of view. As if punishing slaves in order to correct and reform them was never the aim of their masters, but simply a desire for revenge. As if the black were evil because he was a black and not because he was a slave. As if when he was constantly treated like a wild beast, it was surprising that at times he should act like one.

What could be the original cause of a state of affairs so contrary to all sense of justice and morality? Would habit or upbringing prove strong enough to snuff out the sentiment of pity in a person's heart, above all that of a woman? Would the custom of witnessing cruel acts be capable of causing the natural sensibility of the enlightened Christian man and woman to become callous? Did all this have something to do with an instinctive racial antipathy? Was it not in the slaveholder's interest to preserve or to prolong the life of the slave, living capital? Yes it was, beyond the shadow of a doubt; but slavery entailed an element of perversity that gradually and impalpably infused the soul of slaveholders with its poison, turned all their ideas of what was just and what was unjust topsy-turvy, transformed a man into a being who was all wrath and pride, destroying as a consequence the most beautiful part of what was second nature in a woman: charity.

As Isabel went over all these things in her mind, while the others focused their attention on the scenes being played out on the porch and in the *batey* it occurred to her to ask herself: why do I love Leonardo? What do my ideas and his have in common? Will we ever reach the point of agreeing on the way blacks ought to be treated? Supposing that the two of us succeeded in coming to an agreement on this particular, would I resign myself to following him into this inferno? And by following him, would I, like Doña Rosa, impassively witness the horrors and injustices that are committed here with impunity, by day and by night?

At this point of Isabel's soliloquy, Doña Rosa began to show the fine side of her nature, which neither Isabel nor many other persons had yet seen. As has already been said, at her voice the chains of the most unfortunate, because most humble, of her slaves fell away. And once committed to this line of conduct, she pursued it to the very end. The truth was that she was impelled by the sort of fever that brings on the desire to engage in either good or evil acts, and she blindly proceeded to do good. Isidoro was still lying prostrate at her feet when she ordered his six companions to be freed of their shackles, and not content with this most significant measure, she summoned Tomasa and the three blacks who had been flogged early that morning; she listened patiently to their complaints, counseled them, consoled them as best she could in those circumstances and said in conclusion, in a voice seething with anger: "Against my will and express order they have whipped you today. Come, Don Liborio! Remove these blacks' shackles."

Whatever the secret motive that drove Doña Rosa to assume once again, *coram populi*, Dominical authority over La Tinaja, the pious acts with which she gave proof of it made a profound and sincere impression on the minds and hearts of those present. The men approved and applauded; the women, deeply moved, shed tears of joy. In Isabel's eyes Señora Gamboa was transfigured, suddenly rising, there in Isabel's noble heart, from the depths of scorn to the height of admiration. She now saw her as the loveliest and kindliest of women. She would have taken her in her arms and embraced her with the same affection as she once had embraced her own sane and smiling mother on her return after days or hours of absence; she would have adored her on her knees with the same fervor with which the first slave, the object of the compassion of his mistress, had shown her his gratitude. "How sweet it is," she exclaimed, "to forgive the faults of those who depend on us!" And unable to overcome her emotion, she burst into tears.

"What! You are weeping, señorita?" the priest asked her sympathetically.

"It is impossible for me to contemplate generous and charitable acts with dry eyes," she answered, sobbing.

"You would perhaps shed many more tears for contrary reasons were you to stay on here at the plantation."

"I am of the opinion that I would be unable to live here for very long."

"Señorita, I see that you are not made of the same flesh and bones as slaveholders," the priest remarked, amazed at so much sensitivity and discretion.

"No, I am not. If I were to find myself forced to choose between being a mistress and being a slave, I would opt for enslavement, for the simple reason that I believe the life of the victim to be more tolerable than that of the victimizer."

Adela, in her enthusiasm, put her arms around her mother, planted any number of loving kisses on her cheeks and said to her:

"Since today is a day of forgiveness, shall I summon . . ."

She uttered the name almost in a whisper.

"Who?" Doña Rosa asked, frowning.

More timidly than before, Adela repeated in her mother's ear the name that was anathema to the latter.

Doña Rosa's face and attitude suddenly changed, passing from fervent compassion to sternness and to . . . anger.

"No, no. She doesn't deserve to be forgiven . . . Nor has she deigned to ask me for my forgiveness."

"She is here nearby to ask it of you. She is awaiting only a word from me."

"No, no, daughter. Do not let her appear before me. She would make me repent of what I have been doing. No, do not let her appear before me."

Adela, distressed and in tears, left her mother's side.

The latter immediately proceeded to baptize the 27 blacks just arrived from Africa on the brig *Veloz* who had chanced to fall to Don Cándido Gamboa's lot; then to the marriage of three or four female slaves, whose wishes in the matter were not examined, not even for form's sake; and finally, permission was given for drums to be played (for dancing) on the plantation until sunset.

By order of Doña Rosa, the oxherd temporarily took over the marshal's staff, that is to say, the whip, or better put, command of the slaves of La Tinaja.

V I I

15. ... Where is now my hope? ...
16. They shall go down to the bars of the
pit, where our rest together is in
the dust.

Job 17

The afternoon was swiftly drawing to a close. There, off in the most remote corner of the *batey*, the crude drumming with which the blacks accompanied the melancholy singing and wild dancing of their native land could still be heard.

Here, around the sugar mill, there was a great deal of activity and noise. The towers or chimneys of the furnaces for making steam and heating the evaporators of the Jamaican train sent columns of thick blackish smoke into the air.

The black newcomer from Africa, the helper of the mechanic who had recently arrived from Maine, the state of the country to the north known for its granite, went back and forth between the horizontal mill and the steam engine with his oil can with a long curved spout in his hand, lubricating the joints and axles so as to cut down the friction, an inevitable cause of losses of motive force.

The master sugar maker, impatient and anxious, awaited the stream of sugar cane juice that would put to the test his skill at making this sweetener from cane milled by means of a new system. For their part, the blacks in the first processing room watched, fearful and bewildered, the preparations that were being made to confront the problem of making sugar without the need of surly mules or sluggish oxen.

The sun was setting, as round and fiery as a red ball, behind the immense palm grove of the cattle ranch when the plantation owners invaded the boiler house, along with their family, friends, and employees. The priest from Quiebrahachas led the procession, wearing a cassock and a ceremonial bonnet. Two gentlemen walked at his side, each carrying a bundle of cane stalks tied with blue and white silk ribbons, with four young ladies holding the ends of them. When the procession arrived in front of the sugar mill, the priest murmured a brief prayer in Latin, sprinkled the cylinders with holy water, using for this purpose a silver aspergillum, and the gentlemen immediately placed the cane stalks on the feed panel and thus began the first milling with a steam engine at the renowned sugar plantation of La Tinaja.

Later on, or at dusk, the obligatory banquet was served at the manor house. In the pause in the meal as desserts were about to be served, people came to inform the doctor that he was needed at the infirmary. He left and came back after a half hour looking somewhat dejected. Don Cándido went to receive him with unaccustomed solicitude and asked him:

"News, Mateu?"

"Important news, Señor Don Cándido," the doctor answered with equal terseness.

"It never rains but it pours," Don Cándido said. "Out with it."

"You've just lost your best black."

"May all things be as God wills. Which one?"

"Pedro the Carabalí. He's killed himself in the stocks."

"Bah! He's lost more than I have. What weapon did he use?"

"None."

"What! Then he used a length of rope."

"Not even that. In a word, Señor Don Cándido, the black swallowed his tongue."

"What's that you say? I understand even less now."

"You'll understand when I tell you that this is a case of asphyxia owing to a mechanical cause."

"You must be under the impression, doctor, that I speak Greek."

"I'll explain to you, Señor Don Cándido. Whether the black used his fingers or sucked in with all his might, it is evident that, by doubling back the tip of his tongue, he pushed his glottis down over his trachea, thereby blocking the latter and keeping air from entering and leaving his lungs, or in other words stopping him from inhaling and exhaling. This is what is commonly known as swallowing one's tongue, which we call asphyxia owing to a mechanical cause. During my voyages to the coast of Africa I had occasion to observe several cases; but in my long practice on the plantations of the Island, this is the first one I've seen. This sort of death, like that by drowning, must be very painful, worse than strangling on the gallows, because asphyxia does not occur instantly, but by degrees, during which time the man remains in possession of all his senses, and only after a terrible mortal agony. If we were to make an autopsy of the corpse, we would see that very dark, blackish blood has infused the entire venous system, as well as the lungs and brain."

"On my word of honor, I've never in my life heard anything like that," Don Cándido said. "Let's go to the infirmary."

Don Cándido was accompanied on this excursion (that was exactly what it was) by his guests and several employees. The priest and the district captain joined the group simply as a mark of respect, since for the former the opportunity to exercise his holy ministry for the benefit of the suicide had passed, and as for the latter, neither before nor after the death of the slave would he have had an occasion to exercise his own authority, since within the boundaries of his estates or domains Don Cándido Gamboa was *ipso jure*[44] the lord and master of the gallows and the knife.

The latter ordered that the corpse be removed from the stocks. The sight of it was horrifying, with rigor mortis having already set in. Lying on his back on the sleeping platform, his death bed, the dead man was still clutching the edges of it with his clenched fingers. As a result of the dog bites, his arms, legs, and raised chest were swollen; his bloodshot eyes were protruding almost out of their sockets, and his tattered garments were spattered with blood.

The fact that the skin of his forehead had been rolled up from the level of his eyebrows to his hairline and his cheeks slashed vertically from his lower eyelid to the edge of his chin, a tribal custom in his native land, contributed to making him look forbiddingly fierce. Tribal custom also required, as could be seen through his half-open lips, the filing of his upper teeth to a point; they were now locked together with the teeth of his lower jaw: yet another proof of the struggle between life and death. From his face, he did not look to be any more than 27 to 30 years old; so that at that juncture he was at the height of his vigor and development as a young man.

"Poor black!" Cocco said.

"He was worth his weight in gold when it came to work," Don Cándido said, taking the exclamation of the manager of Valvanera in its literal sense.

"That's the true image of an African savage," the priest said. "May God have mercy on his soul."

"That black must have been arrogance itself," Captain Peña said sanctimoniously.

"You can say that again," Moya said with an air of satisfaction because someone present had put his own thought into words at that moment. "A worse cur ain't never come out of Guinea."

"He died as he lived," the Galician steward of La Tinaja said. "May God not take into account his many sins."

"Let's see what María de Regla has to say," Don Cándido remarked without looking the nurse straight in the face.

Without realizing it the persons who had just spoken had all grouped themselves around the corpse, which at that moment was being dimly illuminated from the foot of the platform by a yellow wax candle held by the black woman mentioned by Don Cándido. With her eyes lowered, she said:

"I shall tell my master what happened."

The precision and clarity of the few words she had uttered, along with their silvery, measured intonation, revealing her to be a woman of talent with a certain poise when dealing with her betters, immediately won her the attention of those present. She possessed both these attributes to a notable degree, in view of her lack of schooling and her condition as a slave since the cradle. In addition to her natural perspicacity and her sweet and likable nature, together with a pleasing and refined outward appearance, there was the fact that she had served her first masters as a personal maid; she had thus had the opportunity to be in closer contact with them and with the respectable persons who visited the house than with the ignorant women of her own social status, and to become acquainted not only with the manners of educated whites but also with their way of speaking and behaving in company. She was 36 to 40 years of age or thereabouts, as attested to by her voluptuous and well-rounded contours. Two large gold half moons hung from her earlobes, and to hide her kinky hair, which she abhorred, she covered her head with a kerchief of checkered cotton, called *bayajá*, from the Dominican town where it was made, tied with a good bit of charm and coquetry so as to look like a Turkish turban. At the moment of which we are speaking, her demeanor and tone of voice were indicative of great grief and sadness.

"I shall tell my master what happened beneath my very eyes," she said as if she were speaking with the dead man and not with her master. "From the time they put Pedro in the stocks, he refused to eat or to speak. Only this morning did he drink a little *sambumbia*[45] that I made him swallow, by force as they say. Hunger can be borne, but no one can bear thirst for very long, and he must have felt a raging thirst because of the dog bites. Later, since 24 hours had gone by without his eating a mouthful, and since he had lost a great deal of blood and his wounds had become inflamed despite the ointments that the doctor ordered, he was very feeble and out of sorts and couldn't settle down to sleep. He became a little calmer as soon as his thirst abated. But not a dog barked, not a cock crowed, not a single footfall of people or animals passing by in the *batey* was heard without his moving, his bones creaking on the sleeping platform and his ears pricking up to listen. The first of Don Liborio's floggings early this morning gave him a terrible scare, and he didn't have a moment's rest. At each lash of the whip he trembled from head to foot, just the way a horse does (and may your graces pardon the comparison) when they take off its saddle after a long journey.

"I am certain," the nurse added with a certain timidity, "that the floggings hurt Pedro more than the ones to whom they were given. He became possessed by a sort of fury. He muttered words in his language that I couldn't understand. He seemed to have gone mad. At that moment they brought Julián in, more dead than alive, between four mulattos. Pedro saw him. Julián was his godson and Pedro was convinced that the comrades who had run away with him were being punished. Then he went completely mad. I am persuaded that if he had been able to, he would have smashed the stocks to smithereens. I began to be afraid of him. He was trying to get his feet out of the holes of the stocks; I left off treating Julián and went over as close to Pedro's sleeping platform as I could. I found him sitting there, looking all about, as though expecting that they would be coming for him at any moment to give him a flogging.

"'What's the matter, Pedro?' I asked him. 'What are you feeling? Where does it hurt? What do you want?' He stared at me, heaved a great sigh and said with his throat, not with his tongue: 'Lamo.' 'Call, did you say?' I asked him. 'Who shall I call, the doctor?' He remained silent. 'Tell me, Pedro, do you want me to call the master, *el amo*? He opened his eyes wide, bared his teeth and repeated: 'Lamo . . . his grace'" Maria de Regla concluded, more timidly still, without raising her eyes to look at Don Cándido.

The latter merely smiled faintly and the nurse went on with her graphic account.

"I answered him: 'Not yet, Pedro; everybody in the manor house is asleep; I'll keep watch, and as soon as the master comes out, I'll tell him that you want to see him. Sleep, rest for a while.' Fortunately people were heard leaving the *batey* just then and Pedro heaved a sigh. They weren't coming for him. Later on it seemed useless for me to inform the master. They were busy giving out the *esquifaciones* and baptizing the slaves who had just come off the boat . . . Señorita was taking off everybody's shackles and forgiving them; who would not have believed that the danger had passed? But unfortunately Don Liborio came into the infirmary to look for something he'd left here last night. He was furious. He said that they had taken the job of overseer away from him and Pedro was to blame, but that that spiteful cur wouldn't laugh for long, for Señor Don Cándido had ordered that Pedro be given a novena of lashings as soon as he'd recovered, and that if he himself wasn't going to have the pleasure of giving them to him the other overseer would do the flogging. The master didn't appear and Pedro thought that he was angry and that Don Liborio was telling the truth. That was when he decided to take his life. I peeked out the window to watch the drum dance for a moment, when I heard Pedro moving about; he turned his face toward me and I noticed that he was fumbling around in his mouth with his fingers. I didn't think anything of it, but he suddenly made a motion as though he was becoming nauseated. I hurried to his side . . . He had just taken his fingers out of his mouth and was clenching his teeth and trying to clutch the platform with both hands. Then he began to have convulsions. I was horrified; I sent for the doctor, and without my knowing how or when, Pedro died in my arms. Señor Don José (the doctor) found him just the way he is now. I've seen many die since I've been here, but no dead man has ever horrified me as much."

"The black woman expresses herself well," Cocco said to Don Cándido as they were leaving the infirmary.

"You don't know how bright she is," Don Cándido replied in a muffled voice. "It's been her perdition. If she weren't such a pedant she might be more content with her lot."

"So she's a woman with aspirations?"

"She certainly is! Too much so. Let's step up our pace or else we'll miss out on our after-coffee brandy. Then Rosa will be surprised that we're not back yet and it's best that she not learn of the black's death just yet."

Don Cándido had obviously touched only lightly on the nurse's character, as though he were walking over hot coals. It was not indifference on his part, nor was it disdain, much less contempt: it was fear, sheer fear that the position in which he found himself regarding that humble slave of his might come to light. For we had best repeat yet again that Don Cándido Gamboa y Ruiz, a Spanish gentleman, a rich Cuban landholder, the founder of a distinguished family who would bear his illustrious name for heaven only knew how many generations, a person with pretensions to nobility, well on his way to being granted a title and eager to rub elbows with the elite and aristocratic upper crust of Havana, felt an attachment to the nurse of La Tinaja owing to ties that, albeit invisible, were nonetheless strong and unbreakable. María de Regla was privy to the one secret of his libertine life that he was ashamed of, a secret that made him unhappy amid the grandeur and the ostentatious wealth with which he now found himself surrounded.

On the following day at La Tinaja an amusing excursion on horseback was organized, the party consisting of the Ilincheta sisters and the two youngest Gamboa girls, escorted by Leonardo, Meneses, and Cocco.

The weather was fine, that is to say the lead-colored clouds that cloaked the sky blocked out the full force of the sun's blinding rays, while the dry air from the north, which in its passage across the broad arm of the Gulf had not been able to rid itself of the cold vapors emanating from the nearby continent, delightfully refreshed the atmosphere of this entire stretch of the Cuban coast. Isabel, a skillful horsewoman, proud of her dexterity, loved to ride and fancied that she would rule as she pleased over the countryside from her saddle, would breath purer and freer air, and would widen the horizons of her existence, so cruelly circumscribed at La Tinaja. Her body, her spirit, and her heart demanded as one this unexpected relaxation.

The mad dash of their mounts as they forded the river on the way to the cattle ranch put to flight the noisy *totís* and the shy long-tailed doves that had come down to drink or to bathe at the riverbank, sheltered by the spreading branches of the oak trees.

"What a shady spot!" Isabel exclaimed. "That pool is an invitation to go bathing."

"It's very deep at the foot of the palm on the right bank," Gamboa remarked.

"How deep?" Isabel asked.

"It's over a man's head."

"Then it's easily deep enough to swim in."

"Yes, but it's very dangerous to bathe there because of the caymans that often swim up the mouth of the river. Papa lost a setter he was very fond of in this very pool that Isabel is so keen on swimming in. I was just a youngster at the time and used to go hunting with him. He took a shot at an *agaitacaimán* on the wing and it fell into the middle of the pond; the setter jumped in after it to bring it ashore, but before the dog reached the bird, the setter disappeared underwater as though its strength had suddenly given out. Then a gout of blood gushed to the surface, and that was how Papa knew that a cayman had gotten him."

The rice field in the very bottom of a little valley, lifting up its countless tiny spikes, still green, seeking the heat of the sun, and the fields of maize on the hillsides, with their royal purple flowers and the pale yellow tassels of the ears, were a pretty sight.

In the neighboring banana plantation there was an abundance of yellow bunches of the fruit, whose heavy weight made the trunks of the banana trees bend so far over that the tip of their long broad leaves, like thin sheets of steel, touched the ground.

Riding at random, without stopping anywhere, our ramblers crossed back over the river via a ford farther downstream than the one they had crossed before, leaving behind the plots of land that were part of the Gamboa estate and entering those of the cattle ranch by way of a vast palm grove. Its straight white trunks seemed to be copies of the gigantic columns of an age-old ruined temple. A flock of birds, a species of crow whose song or cry—cao, cao—expresses through onomatopoeia the name by which they are commonly know in Cuba, had made their nests in the grove.

They had gathered in such numbers that they blackened the palm frond or fleshy leaf on which they alighted; and far from frightening them or making them abandon their places, the hoofbeats of the horses or the gleeful voices of their riders seemed instead to intensify the racket they were making and their cheekiness as well, expressed by the sidelong glances they cast from their natural perches, as if they were possessed of intelligence and were trying to make fun of those who did not have wings to fly up to where they were.

"You wouldn't laugh at me if I had my shotgun at hand," Gamboa called to them. "I'd make some of those rascals come down in the blink of an eye."

"What you say is so open to doubt that the saying 'a hare escapes the best hunter,' is apropos here," Cocco said sarcastically.

"How so?" asked Isabel, who considered herself a good shot.

"I'll tell you, señorita," Cocco replied in his twanging voice and with his innate courtesy. "Because with the heat of the day the plumage of the cao, like that of the ring dove, becomes very slippery and the bullet tends to slide off without penetrating the feathers."

The ramblers then changed direction, going around the estate to the north, which was the highest area of the terrain. From one of its slight elevations a bit of the blue sea, apparently calm, could be glimpsed, and farther on the horizon several white sails like so many water birds making ripples in the quiet waters of a lake.

The boundary path that the ramblers were riding along ended at a towering wood that served as the dividing line between La Tinaja and the neighboring plantation of La Angosta. As Leonardo recalled, there should be a path that led through that wood, and by following it they could arrive at the plantation of the Count of Fernandina in half the time it would take if they were to follow the main road or the beach road. The path was naturally very narrow and would prove to be partly obstructed by creepers and low thorny tree branches, which might well catch on the young ladies' dresses and leave them in tatters if they weren't careful. Once this had been explained, he proposed that they undertake the arduous endeavor.

It was a novel proposal, one that involved taking a risk; yet another reason for the young ladies, eager for adventure, to accept it wholeheartedly and enthusiastically. What did one scratch more or less matter if that interval of freedom and expansiveness was prolonged for a time? More than to all the other young ladies, it was to the intrepid Isabel that the fresh air of the countryside and the horseback ride had brought back roses to her cheeks, a sparkle to her eyes, and a smile to her lips, and she now exclaimed: "Who said anything about fear? Onward. Let it never be said that where a man on horseback passed, Isabel was left behind."

They all entered the dark wood, brimful of happiness. But they had gone only a short way, one behind the other, clearing a path for themselves with their hands at times when they were forced to halt. They began to smell a strong stench, like that of a dead body: and immediately thereafter they discovered a vast gathering of turkey buzzards, bending the branches of the trees with their weight so that they served as triumphal arches, so to speak, along the path. Some of these revolting birds, the nearest ones, within sight of the riders, took wing, and making a tremendous din with their broad, heavy wings, flew off and alighted a little farther away. Others, the ones farthest away, not only did not stir from their natural perches, but began to stare about in all directions with a sinister air. The cause of their threatening behavior could be seen then: they were engaged in devouring the dead body of a black, hanging by his neck from the branch of a tree on the edge of the path, and having been interrupted at the height of their feast, they were showing their indignation in the manner that we have described.

Just as the young people drew closer, the body swayed slightly. This circumstance suddenly misled Leonardo, who was riding in front of the others, as to the actual condition of the black; but on reflection the thought that the vultures had caused the body to sway as they abandoned it, a movement that was still visible, promptly made him realize that he was mistaken. The buzzards had plucked out the black's eyes and tongue, and when interrupted they had been eagerly searching for his heart with their curved beaks.

"Look!" Gamboa said to Isabel, who was following close behind him, pointing out to her with his outstretched arm the horrible corpse which he himself had very nearly bumped into.

"Ay, Leonardo!" she exclaimed in horror.

She turned deathly pale and was unable to speak, and would have lost her senses as well and fallen from her saddle to the ground if Leonardo, realizing his imprudence, had not swiftly turned his horse around, grabbed her by the hand, given her the most affectionate dictates, offered her a thousand pardons, and brought her out into the open once again, reversing direction.

As Leonardo sent Caimán the watchman to the wood to identify, if possible, the black who had hanged himself, Meneses went to the nearby brook to fetch some water and had Isabel drink of it out of a crude vessel, in the form of a cone, that he had made from a piece of bark just fallen from the palm tree.

It was determined that the dead man was Pablo, Pedro's comrade, who had stayed behind in the wood when the other five runaways, persuaded by Tomasa and seconded by Caimán, decided to turn themselves over to their masters.

An encounter no less unpleasant than the preceding one lay in store for Isabel in her brief excursion through the outlying countryside of La Tinaja. Returning at a slow pace by way of a boundary path parallel to the one that they had taken before, not with the aim of prolonging their outing but rather with that of distracting Isabel, still not recovered from her shock, they caught sight of an ordinary sized enclosure, with a gate of poorly joined planks and a crude wooden cross nailed to the center of it. This sign of Christian faith seemed to indicate its purpose: but in the total absence of monuments, tombstones, or ridges denoting grave sites, and in view of the luxuriant grass covering the soil, it was difficult to believe that this was the cemetery where slaves who died at La Tinaja were buried. His Reverence Bishop Espada had agreed to the establishment of such cemeteries at rural estates such as La Tinaja because their remoteness from centers of population or from parish churches made it difficult for public welfare services to take the corpses elsewhere.

No doubt because everyone, or almost everyone, knew the purpose of such an enclosure, no one spoke of it. The young riders passed by it and followed the boundary path leading to the plantation. They then descended a long, gentle slope as three blacks on foot ascended it. Two of them were walking in front, each with his grub hoe on his shoulder. The third, a little farther back, was leading from its right a horse with a shabby coat. At a certain distance it was not easy to discern, at least for the young ladies in the cavalcade, the object of the procession or the nature of the load that was being transported.

All that could be seen were two objects that looked like cylinders or the two longitudinal sections of the trunk of a banana tree cut in half, each tied along one side of the usual vehicle for carrying goods in that country: they looked like field cannons being transported by muleback. To Leonardo the entire mystery vanished the moment that he was able to associate with this sight the idea of the three blacks walking in that direction, prepared to dig a grave.

But who was the dead man? Where was he? He was lying on his back, boxed in between the two sections of a banana tree trunk, waging what could be called the battle of the cart. More specifically, his body was jutting out past it and hanging to one side, so that his head, covered with a checkered kerchief, was hitting one side of the horse's neck no matter how slowly the horse walked, while at the same time the heel bones of his naked feet kept knocking against the horse's hind quarters.

The boundary path was very narrow. On either side lay vast, dense canebrakes. The meeting of the two groups was inevitable. In such a fix, Leonardo, anxious to spare his friends, insofar as he could, yet another unpleasant experience that awaited them, ordered them to pick up the pace on the pretext that it was getting late, and he himself tried to position himself on Isabel's right and divert her attention toward the other side of the path. A useless endeavor. All the young ladies, who were now riding behind in pairs, saw and understood perfectly what was going on, this one offering a "poor thing!", this one a silent tear in memory of

Pedro, who, though a black and a slave, was no less worthy of their pity for all that. For although suckled on the milk of slavery, like tender flowers that opened their petals at the first sunbeams of life, they might well have exclaimed with the Latin orator: *homo sum; humani nihil a me alienum puto.*[46]

Doña Rosa welcomed the excursionists with animated demonstrations of affection and rejoicing. She took Isabel by the hand and said, addressing everyone in general:

"Thank heaven you're back. I was beginning to worry. I thought something had happened to you. Then too, I've just been told that this girl (meaning Isabel) loses her good common sense the minute she climbs on horseback. I suppose you all had a fine time."

Isabel merely smiled and went to her room with Adela; but Leonardo, Meneses, and Cocco protested that all the young ladies had behaved very sensibly during the long outing.

"I'm glad, I'm glad," Doña Rosa said. But then, addressing her son in particular, she added, referring to Isabel: "'What is troubling her?'"

"Nothing that I know of," Leonardo replied.

"I thought she looked more downcast when she came back. Did she become ill during your outing? Or did you treat her badly in some way?"

"Who, me, Mama? I've never been nicer or politer to her."

Then Leonardo told his mother all the things that they had seen on their ill-fated excursion: their discovery of the hanged black in the woods and their meeting Pedro's burial party.

"But, in the name of heaven, whose idea was it to take the girls to such out-of-the-way places?"

"How could I have known what would happen, Mama? 'If you're looking for a prophet, choose God,' as the saying goes."

"Didn't I tell you? After what's happened, Isabel won't ever set foot on this plantation again. She'll imagine that it's always like this."

"She hasn't complained."

"Isabel is very wise and too discreet to say what she feels, without rhyme or reason; but anyone can see that this hasn't pleased her one bit. And your father is credulous enough to believe that when you marry her the two of you will often be coming to La Tinaja for long stays. He says that sooner or later you'll be the administrator of it, and it would be most unseemly if your wife were to stay behind in Havana . . ."

"Have you already drawn up the plan for the wedding?"

"What! Are you saying it's not to your liking?"

"The plan or the bride?"

"The bride and the plan, son."

"The bride is very much to my liking; I can't deny it. But is it the right time for me to marry, Mama? Marriage is a serious matter, you know. It shouldn't be entered into on the spur of the moment. As for administering the plantation, do you think I have a duty to shut myself up in this wilderness, when I'm just beginning to enjoy myself?"

"You don't know how pleased I am to hear you talk like that, my son. Solomon would not express himself more wisely. I said as much to your father last night. Why such a rush? But he is very persistent, stubborn, and willful, worse than a Basque. He's taken it into his head that you should marry next year, and that's the way it will be. You, however, have no reason to be worried or distressed. You're the one getting married, not your father; the wedding will take place at the proper time. But if you think everything over carefully, Leonardito, your father is right nonetheless. He shared his thoughts with me, and . . . he has almost, he has very nearly convinced me. For he says: You and I will be dead one of these days. What will become of all this? What about our many landholdings? What about your sisters if they haven't yet married? If you're a bachelor you won't be able to take care of them, give them guidance, protect them. Everything will be careless and slipshod, the properties will go downhill by the day, and above all, the house that has taken us such work to found will be destroyed . . . He believes that in the very next mail from Spain he'll receive the title of Count of La Tinaja or of The House of Gamboa. He's left the choice of the name up to his agent in Madrid. The title will be handed down to you, or rather, you'll have the benefit of it, since it was really for you that it was sought. Then, besides the fact that it would be a shame for you personally to work, the way your father has worked all his life, what need would there be for you to do so? On the contrary, if our death and the district find you married and firmly established, how different your fortunes and your sisters' will be! And who could be better for you to marry than Isabelita, who is so good and so virtuous? That girl pleases me more and more. If I were a man I think I'd win her heart and marry her. Moreover, my son, who could look after La Tinaja better than you who are its master even though that distresses you. Look, it makes me angry at myself every time I remember that it was because of my own weakness . . . no, that 's not so, it was because of your father's stupidities that the one left for so long in the post of overseer of this plantation was Don Liborio, that bandit with the face of a heretic. What was that wretch good for? Only to make the black womenfolk bow low to him and to flay the black men. He delighted in giving floggings, according to what Moya's wife told me. He turned the plantation into a prison. He clapped the best black in irons for no reason at all after flaying his hide. I firmly believe that if I don't throw him out he won't leave me with a single black that's still alive. It was his fault that so many ran away; because of him it's likely that Julián may yet die of lockjaw. He gave Tomasa a flogging, knowing that I had stood as her godmother at her baptism, just as I had with the others who ran away along with her. The cruel brute! We've run out of luck. May it be God's will that the coming year be better for us. To top off all our misfortunes, a letter from Havana has just come, in which Don Melitón sends word that Dionisio has been missing since the twenty-fourth, and that he's heard that he died of a stab wound in the barrio of Jesús María. He broke in through your father's window and took his dress coat, his short wool trousers, his silk hose and his shoes with gold buckles that he used to wear before the Constitution of the year 1812. What did he plan to do with those clothes? Sell them? Nobody would buy them. Do you see what a scoundrel he is? What a wicked man! Can you believe in the honesty and reliability of blacks after that? God forgive me, but the best of them . . . deserves to be burned alive. Such ingratitude toward such a good master and mistress!

VIII

Woe to the lord whose vassals leave it
To heaven to judge their just complaint!

Lope de Vega

The Gamboa family, along with their guests, spent the greater part of the night of the second day of Christmas in the boiler house.

Fires were burning in the sugar mill, lighted by the blacks not so much to shed light in that vast pitch-dark building as to warm themselves, for an unpleasantly chilly breeze could be felt and they lacked warm outer garments save for the wool cap that some of them were wearing. Various noises and a deafening din reigned everywhere. Male and female blacks passed back and forth from the feed panel of the sugar mill to the piles of cane stalks, now with armloads of stalks on their head, now carrying no load, depending on the direction in which they were heading; all of them continually at a run, urged on by the whip of the assistant overseer, who did not allow them a moment's rest or time out for a breath of air. In their goings and comings they passed as close by the fires as they could so as to poke them up with a foot and receive the full heat of them, whereupon the reddish flareup, like a sinister flash of lightning in the middle of a stormy night, illuminated them from head to foot, so that those who were carrying out such heavy work at hours when most of the plantation workers were fast asleep could be seen to be human beings and not phantoms from the infernal realm.

In this part of the boiler house nothing was heard, then, save for the crackling of the green cane stalks and the still-damp waste cane pulp with which the blacks fed the fire, or the grinding sound of the armloads of cane as they passed between the solid, shiny rollers of the mill, or the strange muffled humming of the flywheel of the steam engine in its dizzying revolutions. Thanks to this hectic labor the piles of cane, looking like green walls, which in the beginning were heaped up around almost the entire perimeter of the boiler house disappeared one after the other, so that the flow of cane juice running down the wooden trough produced the same sort of murmur as any other streamlet.

The boiler section properly speaking was dimly lighted by a few ordinary tallow candles hung at intervals from the thick beams, around the laboratory or the Jamaican train. They gave off more smoke than light, emitting every so often drops of grease set afire, which went out as soon as they hit the brick floor. The steam given off by the boiling syrup played its part in making the atmosphere in the place even heavier, dimming at a steady cadence the feeble light shed by the candles. Thus, stepping across the hot and sticky floor around the boilers, those who had just arrived saw the sugar makers for a long time only as if through a thick veil of gauze. Every so often a ray of light penetrated the cloud of smoke and steam and hit the torsos of the blacks and the master sugar maker hard at work around the boilers, whereupon there was reproduced in the flesh one of those paintings representing souls in purgatory.

Chairs were brought and a platform set up in the part of the boiler house opposite the furnaces that was the most uncluttered and the least hot. The gathering grew larger when joined by the white employees, who had come in haste to greet the plantation owners. The master sugar maker had cups brought and boiling hot cane juice with a few drops of brandy in it served to the ladies and gentlemen. He himself, posing as the soul of courtesy, served the cloyingly sweet beverage to Doña Rosa and Doña Juana with his own hand, and would have served the other ladies had Cocco and Meneses, models of politeness, not beat him to it and saved him the trouble. Leonardo and Isabel had not seated themselves; they continued to walk back and forth arm in arm, insofar as the relatively small space and the obstacles on every hand permitted. Nor did Adela and Rosa Ilincheta sit down, preferring to wander about, accompanied by Dolores, looking at the different sections of the boiler house, without venturing, however, into corners that were pitch-dark.

The master sugar maker was not unattractive. He was a bold and alert young man, quite young and fairly good-looking, even though he always dressed in traditional peasant style, which does not contribute, certainly, to the attractiveness of everyone who wears such attire. His name was Isidro Bolmey and he had been born in Guanajay of poor parents who had no education, and since there were no schools in the town, they were unable to leave their son with even the usual meager public schooling. He barely knew how to read and write his name. He professed no religion, although he had been baptized and confirmed in the Apostolic Roman Catholic faith, during the circuit visit made to his native town by His Reverence Bishop Espada y Landa in the year 1818. It is altogether true that at the age of 26 he did not remember ever having entered a church to hear Mass, much less ever having entered one to pray at one time or another, since he did not know even the shortest of Christian prayers: the Our Father. Yet this ignorant lad, too young to have learned his craft through serving as a journeyman, had been, for some time now, the master sugar maker of the famous plantation of La Tinaja, a property that at the time represented a capital asset worth at least half a million *duros*.

The sudden crack of the whip on the opposite side of the boiler house just as Isabel was raising the beverage to her lips made her shudder from head to foot, and in her confusion the cup slipped from her hands.

"The young lady has stained her dress," the master sugar maker said with apparent regret.

"It doesn't matter," Isabel said, shaking her skirt.

"Tell the assistant overseer not to crack his whip like that again," Leonardo said sternly.

"If the young lady would like another cup, the cane juice is still yet drinkable," Bolmey added in a tone of voice which revealed great depths of tender solicitude.

"No, no," Isabel said again. "Don't bother. What would be the use? This beverage is not to my liking, let us say."

The young man from Guanajay was doubtless not pleased by Isabel's refusal, for he murmured in a voice that could readily be heard:

"It would appear that the floggings have kept the young lady from enjoying herself, whereas we go to sleep to that music."

Leonardo took the master sugar maker's remark as an impertinence and turned his back on him in annoyance. Isabel, on the contrary, was aware only of his discernment and gentle manner, and feeling a sort of gratitude toward him, she regretted that her suitor did not share the same noble sentiment. Moreover, she was ingenuous enough to say this to him as an aside. Hence Leonardo, really nettled now, was determined to overwhelm the master sugar maker with definite facts with the aim of making him look ridiculous, examining then and there how good the young man was at the art of making sugar.

To fulfill the function of examiner, Leonardo possessed no qualifications other than those given him for the moment by the resentfulness and cheek of a person who compares his own high social rank and fortuitous superiority with the relatively low status and humbleness of the first rival against whom he happens to pit his moral and intellectual strength. The sort of education that his social status and wealth had brought Leonardo was very far from being a scientific one; it had been purely literary and certainly not at all profound. He had not even looked into any of the natural sciences, since at that time in his country there existed no secular chairs in them. In all truth the only subjects taught were philosophy, jurisprudence and medicine, with none of the other main branches of learning that contribute so much to complementing them. Leonardo Gamboa, like the majority of students of his time, did not know the first thing about agronomy, of course, or about geology or chemistry, much less botany, even though at the time Don Ramón de la Sagra was giving, or was endeavoring to give, lessons in this latter science at the Havana Botanical Garden. Be that as it may, the fact is that the good nature and the supine ignorance of the master sugar maker allowed the future master of La Tinaja to win an easy and noticeable victory this time.

"Where did you learn to make sugar, Don Isidro?" he unexpectedly asked him in a rather arrogant tone of voice.

"At the plantation of Señor Don Rafael de Zayas, the one a person comes upon as he's coming from Guanajay, at the foot of La Yaya hill. My father, may he rest in peace, was the master sugar maker there and I kept him company and helped him to make sugar in a fair number of harvest seasons."

"That is to say, it was your father who taught you the craft of a master sugar maker. Isn't that so?"

"Well, he made sugar as I watched and I learned how for my own pleasure by doing what he did."

"What did your father do? In other words, how did he make sugar? That is what I want you to explain to me." As he said this he squeezed Isabel's arm.

"I shall tell Señor Don Leonardito," Bolmey answered, turning over in his mind how he could find a way to explain the process with words that might be new to his young master. "To tell the truth, it doesn't take *cience* to make sugar; all that is needed is a little practice and a good eye. I saw that once the evaporator in the tower was full of fresh cane juice, my father, may he rest in peace, let it settle a little and rid it of the waste pulp; that he then pumped it from this evaporator to the middle one, and that he then had a beeswax candle put in it. For example, just as I'm going to do today."

As he spoke, two blacks with their pumps and a movable pipe transferred the purified cane juice of the second evaporator on the left to another on the right, and young Bolmey added:

"Does the young master see? I'm now removing the waste pulp and emptying the cane juice out of this evaporator into this other one and putting a little quicklime in it . . ."

"Well, why do you put quicklime in it?" Leonardo interrupted him to ask, secretly rejoicing at having caught him making a ridiculous misstatement.

"I confess I couldn't tell the young master why," the lad said simply and candidly. And as Leonardo gave a smug smile, he added: "I don't know why quicklime is put in it. I only know that if that isn't done, it's not possible to get a good fermentation. God alone knows why. The sugar turns sour and doesn't ferment when no quicklime is added. That was the way my father, may he rest in peace, did it, and I do alikewise, though to tell the truth, I think it depends on luck more than anything else whether or not the cane juice turns to sugar. What I can tell the young master is that it seems that I have luck on my side, that I've already been through five cane harvests on this plantation, and that this will be the fifth, and this is the first time that I've missed getting the cane juice to ferment right. I also know the cane fields of La Tinaja well."

"What difference do you find between one cane field and another? The cane is the same in all of them."

"So it seems to the young master, but that is not true; and I beg his pardon for contradicting him."

"What!" Leonardo exclaimed, surprised and visibly humiliated, for he was not certain that he knew more on this subject than his master sugar maker did. "It's as if you're trying to give me lessons now as to the nature and characteristics of sugar cane! There are a number of varieties of it, and here we grow Otahití cane, ribbon or purple cane, and crystalline cane, which is the most recent variety to be introduced into the country, and also Creole or native cane, which is not used for milling. All of them contain more or less saccharine juice, and that is the only noteworthy difference between them. The toughest and least suitable variety for milling is ribbon or purple cane, because it contains a larger woody part and less saccharine juice. You don't know, of course, what these terms mean, but I am obliged to use them, for lack of others that would be intelligible to you. On my plantation there is much more of the Otahití variety than the others, for it has been proven that it is all saccharine juice, all sweet, and furthermore it is the one that grows best in black soil. Each cartload of this cane makes a sugarloaf and a half, in other words 50 pounds and a half of white sugar, tastier than any made in any other sugar mill in Vuelta Abajo."

"What the young master says is quite true. Señor Don Leonardito is perfectly right . . . but . . . I wasn't talking about the cane; I was talking about the cane fields."

"Better still," the young man said, planted squarely before his master sugar maker with his arms folded, hoping to hear him come out with such egregious nonsense that it would bring a laugh from Isabel, who had remained oddly imperturbable. "Let's hear what difference you find between cane fields."

"The difference that I find," Bolmey replied with great aplomb, "or rather, that my father, may he rest in peace, found between cane fields was this: that those on low and swampy ground are sourer and saltier than those on hillsides, and the sourer the cane field the more quicklime is needed so that the sugar doesn't pick up moisture."

Without further ado, Leonardo turned his back, and as soon as he was a fair distance away from Bolmey, he said:

"He may well be a good tailor, but he's not going to work for me, I swear. What I mean to say is that when I'm in charge here, which will be soon, that dolt isn't the one who'll be making my sugar. The first thing I'm going to do is throw him out on his ear."

In their quick outing Adela, Rosa, and Dolores had had an adventure of their own. The three of them were having a fine time, watching them beat the syrup in one of the cooling rooms, when an unknown black woman approached them from behind and asked them with an air of great mystery:

"Which of these young ladies is Miss Adelita?

"I am," Adela blurted out, more than a little startled.

"Well, your mother is there outside, behind that wooden column, waiting for your grace . . ."

"My mother!" Adela said in surprise. Señorita, you mean . . ."

"No, miss, I mean the nurse."

"Ah! Tell her to come closer, to come inside."

"She doesn't want the master and the mistress to see her. She doesn't dare come in."

"Go to her, Dolores. See what your mother wants. She may be afraid to come inside, but I'm even more afraid to go outside. What! When it's so dark out there? Like a wolf's mouth. I wouldn't dream of it."

When she returned, Dolores said that her mother wanted only to give Miss Adela a big hug and tell her something that she couldn't pass on to her through a third person. Then the girl passed on instructions to her former wet nurse to meet her later that night in her room in the manor house. Dolores was entrusted with the task of waiting for her mother at the false door, unbolting it from inside, and bringing her to her young mistress, whom she had suckled and called her daughter.

In fact, between 11 and 12 on the aforementioned night, the two younger Gamboa girls had gathered with the two Ilincheta sisters and their aunt Doña Juana Bohorques in the room of the manor house assigned to the latter three from the beginning. As the hour for the meeting approached, Adela's uneasiness grew, so that when there was a noise at the door, as if someone's fingertips were being drawn over one of its planks, she leapt to her feet and ran to open it. Dolores looked as startled as her mistress and said: "Here she is."

"Have her come in," the latter replied; and in search of consolation for the misdeed that she was apparently committing, she added, addressing Isabel:

"It's not my fault if I'm taking this step . . . I don't see any other way of finding out why Mama is so angry with the woman who suckled me . . ."

At that moment María de Regla entered the room, led by the hand by her daughter Dolores, and Adela broke off her act of contrition. A single spermaceti candle inside its glass chimney dimly lighted the room, which although spacious, seemed considerably less so because of the various pieces of furniture jammed into it. The ladies, sitting in a half circle, awaited the nurse's entrance with more than a little anxiety. She came into the room dressed in the way that we described the last time, in the infirmary. Passing from darkness into a room that was relatively bright, for a moment she stood stock-still, as if dazzled and confused in the presence of this unplanned female gathering. She scrutinized their faces one by one and suddenly flung herself upon the young lady occupying the middle of the half-circle, Adela, and saying: "This is my daughter," she lifted her up in her strong arms, and as she held her close and whirled about like a madwoman, she smothered her with kisses and said over and over: "My darling! My precious! My lovely girl! My daughter whom I adore!"

Then she placed her back in her chair, knelt at her feet, encircled her waist with her arms, placed her bowed head on her knees and wept and sobbed inconsolably for a long time.

"What are you doing, María de Regla?" Adela said to her, moved at the sight of such feeling so affectionately expressed. "Calm yourself, woman. Don't make noise, because Mama might hear you and then we'll be in for it! Stand up, calm down . . ."

"Oh, my beloved child!" the black woman exclaimed, drying her tears with the palms of her hands. "Let me weep, let me unburden my aching heart at the feet of my adored daughter. I do not believe that if Señorita sees me she'll get angry with me and turn me out of here. Ah! How I've longed for this moment, o just God of heaven and earth! I haven't seen your grace for such a long time and I've endured so many hardships in this exile that has truly been my valley of tears . . . that if they were to kill me now I would let myself die with a smile on my lips! What is life worth amid so many sorrows? This is not living, it is dying every day and at every hour. Your grace does not understand why I am weeping. Your grace is very young, she is white, she is free, she is the pretty girl of the family. If your grace marries and has children, who will dare to dash her delight to pieces or separate her from her husband or from her children? Your grace does not know, and God grant that she may never know, what a slave woman goes through. If she is unmarried, because she is unmarried; if she is married, because she is married; if she is a mother, because she is a mother, with no will of her own. In no instance is she allowed to do as she pleases. Let your grace start from the principle that she will not be allowed to marry the man she likes or loves. Her masters give her her husband and take him from her. Nor is she certain that she will always live at his side, or that she will bring up her children. When she least expects it, her masters will force the two of them to divorce, sell her husband, and her children too, and separate the family so as to keep them from ever getting back together in this world. After that, if the woman is young and is looking for another man and doesn't die of the sorrow of having lost her children, then her masters say that the woman has no feelings, nor does she suffer, nor does she have any affection for anyone. Let your grace think of what has happened to me. For more than 12 years, a lifetime so to speak, I haven't seen my husband, and I have been separated from my children for almost as long a time. Doesn't your grace see the injustice, my girl? It is all well and good that they should punish me if I have sinned, but why should they punish my husband and my children as well? And let them not say that this long separation is not a punishment; it is, my girl, and one of the hardest to bear. I know that the aim was not to take out the punishment for the sin that I may have committed on my husband, or on the children born of my womb. No; my masters are not that evil; but Dionisio is a good cook and was needed in Havana; Tirso and Dolores are good household servants, and they too were needed there. I'm not complaining because they serve their masters; they are slaves and have to serve. What will become of the ox if it won't plow? And if I compare serving in the two households, they're better off there than here. I'm complaining because we're separated. Absence kills. If we're together, there are fewer sorrows to bear. What's more, Dionisio and I loved each other."

"Dionisio, Dionisio," Adela repeated emphatically, cutting her former wet nurse short. "Dionisio is a good sort. He doesn't love you; he's forgotten you. Look at what he's just done. Don Melitón writes to Papa that Dionisio has been gone from the house since Christmas Eve, and there has been no further news of him. People say he got involved in a tragic street fight and ended up badly wounded."

"I know that, my girl," María de Regla said feelingly. "Dolores was there when Señorita read the letter and she told me everything. But who's to blame for that? Why did it seem as if Dionisio no longer loves me and has forgotten me? Because of our separation. Had he been at my side he wouldn't have committed that act of madness. He was always a tender and faithful husband to me. So loving . . . ! I was a most loving wife to him. While we lived together, while we could say that we were married, there was never a cross word between us. Because my young mistress must understand that we married for love. Our wedding was celebrated with a big ball, right in the palace of their graces the Count and Countess of Santa Cruz in Jaruco. They had had the parish priest come to marry us. Her ladyship the countess saw herself in me and was bent on my marrying . . . so as to rescue me in time from the danger that threatened . . . Here, just among ourselves, ladies," the nurse added cunningly, "even though it is wrong of me to say so, when I was a girl, for someone colored, I was good-looking, pretty, and her ladyship the countess suspected that my master his lordship the count had taken a liking to me . . . He was so madly in love with me. He really and truly was! . . . More in love than Cupid . . . Her ladyship the countess did the right thing in marrying me to Dionisio. But what do you the ladies present have to say to me about that nice little count? It appears that he told his father, may he rest in peace: 'Take your leave, I'm here.' He couldn't bring himself to repudiate his caste. The fact was that he was head over heels in love with me. He never let me alone.

"But in the end Dionisio and I married and were the happiest bride and groom in the world. My master died suddenly as he was getting out of his bath; a suit was brought over the inheritance; court costs were levied as a penalty, and in order to pay them a number of slaves were put up at auction, and Dionisio and I were lucky enough to be sold together. From that moment on a shadow was cast over our happiness. If my master his lordship the count hadn't died suddenly, I'm convinced that he would have given Dionisio and me our freedom in his will. We then passed into the hands of my master Señor Don Cándido and Señorita, I to be her personal maid and coif her; Dionisio to serve as the cook. Your grace had not yet been born. All went well until I had a son, who died of the seven-day sickness that kills newborn babies.

"My master Señor Don Cándido hired me out through Dr. Don Tomás Montes de Oca to nurse the baby girl of a person whose identity I was never able to discover, nor her name . . . nothing. And here, my girl, is the source and the beginning of all our troubles, that is to say, mine and Dionisio's.

"I must have been 20 years old at most, and Dionisio 24, when they separated us. We were two young people without good judgment and no experience of the world. However much we loved each other, and bear in mind, my girl, that we loved each other a great deal, if we didn't see each other, if we found ourselves far apart from each other, if our separation seemed to be for time everlasting, if we were fated to die, with me as the nurse on this plantation to pay for my sins, and with him as the cook in Havana; if Dionisio was young and good-looking, according to what women said, and I was young and pretty, according to what men said, what would you have us do? Lie down and die or spend our lives weeping over each other's absence? A person would have had to be a saint, or made of straw, to remain faithful. I suppose that Dionisio, chased after as he was by pretty women, was unable to imitate chaste José. I, as your graces see me standing here before you, an old woman before her time, dealing with the sick and the dead, have been chased after by everyone who wore pants on this infernal plantation.

"The overseer who met me on my arrival from Havana was not Don Liborio Sánchez, but Don Anacleto Puñales. He was tall, thin, very dark-skinned, with long thick side whiskers and a voice like a great bell that made it seem as if it were about to swallow up the world. He was armed with a machete, a dagger, and a whip, leaning back against a column of the porch roof of his house, smoking a cigar, with his sombrero on his head. His dogs were lying all around him, and his wife was sitting in a leather armchair at the door. She struck me as being pretty and refined for a peasant woman. The minute the overseer saw me coming, he straightened up and his eyes shone like a cat's when it smells a mouse. Even his dogs got up from where they were lying. And I let myself down out of the cart, trembling from head to foot, because my heart told me what was going to happen next. 'Come closer, Mammy,' he said to me; and without further ado, he sent my kerchief flying off my head with the end of his stick. 'Pigtails! Pigtails!' he shouted in a fury. 'Ah! You bitch! Let me have them.' He took out his dagger, grabbed my braids, and in one stroke cut them off down to my scalp. Up until that point it hadn't seemed so bad, but then he spied my shoes and stockings and became even more furious. 'Will you look at that!' he shouted, almost unable to speak. 'You're wearing shoes? Who ever saw a black woman with shoes and stockings? You came here to dance, is that it? I'll make you dance all right. The Señorita has told me in no uncertain words that you haven't come here on an outing but in order to straighten you out and make you learn to obey. Come on, take off all that paraphernalia. There's no need to wear shoes to get to dance here. Get a move on.'

"Ay, your graces. I'd rather not remember. I get gooseflesh every time I do. Nobody, none of my masters had laid a hand on me up until then. The overseer gave me a hard cuff in the face that sent me sprawling on the ground, ordered two mulattos to hold me down by the hands and feet, and flogged me till he was worn out, I believe, because after a few lashes I fainted and that was the last thing I remember. I didn't come to until nightfall, on the sleeping platform in the infirmary, where I lay without being able to move for some two weeks. So that your graces understand, that same overseer who had given me such a terrible welcome then took me to his house to be a household servant, and made eyes at me. . . . His wife became jealous and Don Anacleto then sent me to the infirmary to be the nurse there, since the old woman who had been there before me had died. Then he kept pestering me, wanting me to make love to him, but I couldn't. Make love to him, when he'd almost skinned me alive! I was carried away by the devil every time I saw him. I didn't turn him down outright, I eluded him with various pretexts, because I was afraid that he'd get mad and give me another flogging. His wife helped me a great deal in this regard without her knowing it. She dressed him down so severely because of her jealousy of me that the man grew tired of it, asked for his pay, and found a job as overseer on another plantation.

"What a struggle, ladies! It can happen to the best of women. I would have liked to see the most virtuous woman in the world in my place. No man has ever approached me except to talk to me about love. The very first thing each of them said to me was: 'You don't deserve to spend your youth in such solitude; love me and I'll free you.' That's what Sierra, the captain of the schooner that brought me from Havana said to me; that's what the errand boy in rags who drove the horse and cart that brought me here from the dock said; that's what the tile maker, the master sugar maker, the overseer, all of them said to me. It was as if they'd never seen a woman in their life and as if none of them was married or had a family.

"But what do you young ladies have to say to me about Señor Don José, the doctor for the plantation? That one too has courted me and keeps on courting me with a different kind of music. Don't laugh, young ladies, it's the absolute truth. There where your graces see him as innocence itself, always tiptoeing around, confident that he's a handsome fellow and that every woman is dying of love for him . . . , well, the fact is that he drools over me. I've never made love to him. He's such a stingy so-and-so! A tightfisted Don Alejandro. He wouldn't give even the dove of the Holy Spirit a sip of water. Me! I don't want to have anything to do with him."

"So then," Adela said in annoyance, "you love men for their money?"

"No, my dear girl, don't do me that injustice, your grace. I was unable to love; it wasn't in my nature to love anyone. A person only loves once in a lifetime. My heart had dried up. And I didn't want money in order to buy luxuries; I wanted it in order to buy my freedom. I resisted, I resisted; but youth, the desire to better my lot, to get out of this inferno; the devil that puts tinder next to tow and then blows on it . . . How do I know! The fact, my girl, is that . . . I could die of shame. Of all my suitors, I believed the Basque carpenter who was here when I came would keep his word to me to free me; and to my misfortune I was unfaithful to Dionisio with him. Then Tirso was born; that crow that will pluck out my eyes some day."

The ladies listening to her, scandalized by the black woman's brazenness, showed their disapproval with a pronounced general murmur. The nurse, aiming to make amends for her error, added in a rush:

"Your graces will kindly forgive me if I have said something bad. But put yourself in my place for a moment. Let's see: if by some unforeseen misfortune, through a disturbance of the natural order, any one of the young ladies listening to me should become a woman of color, in the days when slavery seems hardest for her to bear, an individual comes along, be he white, mulatto or black, ugly or handsome, and says to her:

'Weep no more, console yourself, lift your spirits, I pity you, I am going to free you.' Would that young lady think of me what she thinks of me now? I'll wager not! How sweet the word would seem to her. How good, how kind, how angelic that person would seem to her! I am going to free you! Ay, your graces! I have never heard those words without trembling, without an inexplicable inner joy, as if I were suddenly going hot and cold all over . . . Freedom! What slave does not desire it? Every time I hear the word I go out of my mind, I dream of it day and night, I build castles in the air, I see myself in Havana surrounded by my husband and my children, going to balls dressed in frills and furbelows, with gold bracelets, coral earrings, satin slippers, and silk stockings; just as I used to do as a young girl in the palace of the Count and Countess of Jaruco!

"But to go on with my story, young ladies, the worst thing of all was that if I smiled at the master sugar maker the oxherd became angry, or the tile maker, or the steward, or the doctor, or the overseer, Don Liborio Sánchez I mean, the one that Señorita has just booted out for his brutality toward the blacks, the one who came when Don Anacleto Puñales left. He was the most fearsome of the ones who sought my love. He wanted to force me to make love to him, and if I refused, it was a lashing for me. Out of fits of jealousy and annoyance he gave me two floggings and crucified my back with his whip. Your graces have no idea how happy I was that Señorita has thrown him out. Feel, my girl, feel here on my shoulders and my shoulder blades. Put your hand there."

Adela slid her hand, with certain misgivings, between the skin and the clothing of the black woman and quickly withdrew it because her pink fingers came upon one huge welt after another, raised in every direction like ridges of soil that has just been plowed, by the tip of the jealous overseer's whip. The young girl then understood something of the torture endured by the woman who had suckled her. Doña Juana and Isabel were horrified and shed more than one tear of compassion for the tortured slave.

"And in spite of all this, your graces," she said, going on with her interesting account, "Don Liborio had the steward write a letter to the master, in which he told him any number of things about me; that I was a so-and-so; that I upset the plantation with my love affairs; that on account of me he had to change workers almost every time he turned around. In fact, he booted out the ones he suspected that I liked. He also said that almost the moment a new worker arrived, I used my evil arts to breathe fumes on him and made him neglect his duties because he'd fallen in love with me. In short, that I seduced men. Me a seductress! What fault of mine was it if white men fell in love with me? If I loved them in return, that was bad; if I rejected them, that was worse still. Just look, my girl, at what a sad situation I was in!

"The replyment to the overseer's letter was, as usual: 'Punish that bitch.' Of course he avenged himself at will for my rebuffing him. Poor me! I had no one to complain to! The master and young master Leonardo came one Christmas holiday, but neither of the two had any desire to hear me out or to see me either. Another time I told Sierra, the captain of the schooner, what was happening to me: he went to Havana and when he came back he told me that he was unable to speak with Señorita or with his grace; he managed only to have a word with Dolores." Adela confirmed every detail of this last incident, giving a brief account of the scene with her mother, described at the end of Part Two, Chapter IX.

I X

To have been deaf and blind
For those brief instants
She would gladly give
Half her miserable days.

El Duque de Rivas

The former wet nurse immediately went on, saying:
"The young lady will now see the real cause of the severity with
which I have been treated. One day . . . I don't remember exactly when,
except that I know it was a long time ago, after the great hurricane of
Santa Teresa, or the year that they hanged Aponte[47] the master called
me to the dining room. He was alone, and he said to me:

"'María de Regla, since you have lost your baby boy and have an
abundance of good milk, I have been thinking that it should be put to
use. With this in mind, I have hired you out through Señor Doctor Don
Tomás Montes de Oca to a friend of his to suckle his newborn daughter.
So then! Be ready to leave after lunch.'

"After lunch, the master went outside and got into the carriage. I followed along after him on foot. But he had me get into the carriage and
sat me down alongside him. I was surprised. The master sitting me

down on the cushions of the carriage, when blacks sit only on the floor! Then he ordered Pío to take off for a street beyond the city walls. Where can we be going? I wondered. We left by the Puerta de Tierra, took straight off down the road to San Luis Gonzaga, and did not stop until we were a few houses away from the corner of Campanario Viejo. The master ordered the driver to stop in front of one of two windows with iron grilles and the *zaguán*, next to another empty calash stationed at the door. I thought that the doctor lived there, or else the father of the baby girl that I was going to suckle. The master alighted and said to me: 'Get out.' He went in through the *zaguán* and I followed along after him. Then I saw that there was a turnbox big enough to put babies into on the wall to the right and that the courtyard was hidden from sight by a tall partition, with a door in the middle.

"The master halted and said to me in a low, very solemn voice: 'María de Regla, you are to knock on that door, ask for Señor Doctor Montes de Oca, and obey everything that he orders you to do to the letter. Listen carefully to what I am going to say to you. Be careful not to breathe a word to a living soul about what you see, hear, or come to know here. And as long as you're still suckling (yes, I said suckling) the little girl, don't even think of seeing Dionisio or anyone else in the household. Above all, no one must hear from your lips who your masters are or who brought you to this house. From this day forward, for everyone—everyone, do you hear?—you are to be deaf and dumb and know nothing about me, about Señorita, about the baby girl you're to nurse, and about the persons who will be around her in this house and in any other house to which they may take her. Did you hear me? Well then! I will say no more. Knock.'

"The master left me there with my head in a whirl. Although he went off in a hurry, he did not get into the calash until he had seen that I tapped on the door with the knocker and someone answered. As if he imagined that I might run away! An elderly black woman opened the door and let me in, and the minute I set foot inside, I knew where I was. I heard many babies crying and screaming on every hand. I was in the Foundling Home. There was everything in there, what I mean to say is white babies and colored, and wet nurses, almost all of them black like me. I did not have to ask to see Señor Montes de Oca, because he was in the dining room examining a sick infant in the arms of her wet nurse, and said to me straight out: 'María de Regla Santa Cruz, right?' Before I could answer either yes, señor or no, señor, he seized me by the wrist, took my pulse, made me stick out my tongue, and opened my eyelids with two fingers to see the color of my eyes. All this without a word or else through signs. Then he took me to the adjoining room. In the middle of it was a mahogany crib covered with a shawl or large veil of white lace, which the doctor raised with one hand, as with the other he pointed out to me a white baby sleeping in swaddling clothes of batiste linen, either embroidered or with wide lace insets. What luxury, your graces, what luxury! I was dumbfounded. Her parents must have been very rich, richer than the Golden Calf. The doctor said to me in his thin, twangy voice: 'This is the baby you are going to nurse. Care for her as if she were your own daughter; you won't regret it. You're young, you're good-looking and healthy, and you must have a great deal of milk. Look at the blue mark she has on her left shoulder. She hasn't been baptized yet.'

"I took charge of the baby girl and intended to nurse her as though she were my own daughter, not so much because of the master's threat as because of the doctor's promise and because she seemed to me to be a divine little creature. She fascinated me. Present company excepted, I had never seen a prettier baby girl in my life. She could only be compared to your grace when she was born. She looked so much like your grace at that time that if she is still alive today and hasn't changed for the worse she's the very picture of your grace. Not even twins would have looked more alike.

"How white she was!" the former wet nurse added, tracing in broad strokes the portrait of the baby girl in the Foundling Home. "As white as coconut meat, your graces: a round face, a pointed chin, a fine-drawn nose, a tiny red rosebud mouth. And her eyes? Marvelous: incomparably lovely; long eyelashes. I never tired of looking at her. The first thing I did as soon as she awoked was to examine her shoulders to see the mark she had. It was a blue half-moon traced with a needle, except for this part here (placing the palm of her hand on her left shoulder blade as she said this). . . .

"In the beginning, the baby didn't want to take my breast; she missed the odor of her mother or of the first woman who nursed her. As long as I was at the Foundling Home they treated me like a princess . . . Ah! What good care they took of me! They didn't allow me to go outside, it's true. The doctor came to see the baby three or four times, and he was the one who brought Father Manjón, the parish priest of La Salud, to baptize her. They named her Cecilia María del Rosario, of unknown parents, and of course gave her the last name of Valdés, as they did all the babies left at the Foundling Home.

"Cecilia Valdés!" Carmen said in astonishment. "That name sounds familiar; it's not the first time I've heard it."

Adela corroborated her sister's opinion, although neither of the two could remember the exact time, occasion, or place they had heard it. At this, the ladies' curiosity and interest were even further aroused.

"For all these reasons," the nurse said, "it crossed my mind more than once that the doctor might be the baby's father. But he was so ugly, your graces, so ugly that I convinced myself that he couldn't have fathered such a darling child, even if the goddess Venus herself had been the mother. A few days after the baby had been baptized, a very luxurious carriage was sent round to fetch her, by order of the doctor. We entered Havana via the Puerta de la Muralla, took many roundabout ways and finally ended up at a little house in the Callejón de San Juan de Dios. As I got out of the calash, I asked the driver whose house it was, and he told me that it belonged to Montes de Oca. But when I asked him who lived in it, he started up at a gallop and said: 'I don't know.'

"A plump mulatto woman, well dressed and very pretty, came to the door. Saying 'Come in, María de Regla' (she knew my name); she snatched the baby out of my arms and nearly devoured her with kisses. This is the baby's mother, I thought. But I realized immediately that I was mistaken, for she went on to the next room with the baby in her arms and showed her to another mulatto woman, younger and prettier than she was, who was lying in bed. 'Charito! Charito!' she said to her. 'Waken up! Cheer up. Look who's here: your Cecilia. Look how pretty she is!'

"Though the woman was a pale as death, almost naked, skinny, with her hair all disheveled, she looked like Cecilia, yes, to me she looked so much like her that I was convinced she was her mother.

"The woman named Charito took a long time to waken up, but it would have been better if she hadn't, because a real ruckus began once she did. She opened her eyes, looked all around as though bewildered and sat up in bed. It seemed to me that she was acting as if she were insane; and she was, your grace, she left me with no doubt in my mind. When the plump mulatto woman, whose name was apparently Chepilla, placed the baby before her eyes, she pushed the two of them away and leapt out of bed in a rage. She seized Cecilita by the neck with her two hands and tried to choke her, and would have if Chepilla hadn't run to the front room with the baby and closed the door of the bedroom. An old, tall black woman who looked like a walking skeleton suddenly came into the bedroom through the kitchen door, and between the two of us we managed to hold the madwoman fast and fling her on top of the bed. Despite being flung down onto the bed and all the rest, she kept fighting with us, using her fingernails and her feet, without saying a word, until the skeletal black woman, bathed in tears, gestured to me to tie her to the bed with a sheet. I did so and . . . o blessed remedy: the mad woman lay there as quiet as a mouse. That's why my master his lordship the count used to say, quite rightly, that if a madman is punished he becomes sane.

"Once all of them had quieted down, I went to get the baby, because I heard her crying, and I found the door bolted from inside with the sort of latch that drops into a catch, and though I knocked several times, *Seña* Chepilla didn't come to open it. I suppose she was too afraid of the madwoman to let me in, and I tried to spy through a hole to see what she was doing. I saw her from the back in fact, leaning out one of the shutters of the window, handing the baby to a gentleman who was outside in the street, but all I managed to see of him was his black broadbrimmed hat with a bell-shaped crown. It was one of those so-called *situayen* hats, which were very much in fashion and I seemed to have seen it somewhere before.

"No doubt *Seña* Chepilla sent word through that gentleman to Doctor Rosaín to come, for all at once he appeared at the house and went straight to the sick woman's room and slowly began to examine her. His prognosis was a dire one. Charito was stark raving mad, he told *Seña* Chepilla straight out, and what was worse, the daughter should be separated from the mother or the mother from the daughter as soon as possible. She had made the baby the fixation of her madness and it was more than likely that she would choke her to death in one of her fits of rage. *Seña* Chepilla, grief stricken, as your graces can imagine, said that although she saw the risk of mother and daughter sleeping under the same roof, she didn't dare make a decision until she had consulted a gentleman whose advice she sought in all her affairs.

"'Can he be the individual by whom you sent word to me to come?'" the doctor asked.

"'The very same one,'" the plump mulatto woman answered.

"'Then he's waiting for me on the corner,'" Doctor Rosaín went on, 'so as to hear from me personally the prognosis with regard to the patient's illness, and since it is an urgent case and there is no time to lose, I shall have him come here so that you may consult him.'

"'No, no, doctor,'" *Seña* Chepilla replied fearfully. 'More time will be lost. He would refuse to come here at this time. It would be better if you would kindly consult him in my stead right there on the corner and then inform me what his decision is.'

"The doctor went to the corner, returned a short while later and began to say: 'Don Cán . . .' 'Don't go on, señor doctor,' *Seña* Chepilla cut him short, more frightened than ever. 'For the life of you, don't go on, say no more, I know his name and that will do.'

"'Very well,' the doctor continued with his usual perfect calm; 'the gentleman on the corner is of the opinion that Charito should be taken to Paula Hospital, and I will arrange immediately for her to be taken there in a litter. Ah! He is also of the opinion that the baby should stay with her wet nurse in this house.'

"'Who was the gentleman on the corner?' Carmen and Adela asked as one.

"'I really don't know, young ladies,' the former wet nurse stammered. 'I couldn't swear that the doctor said Don Cán. He might very well have said Don Juan, Don San, or some other name ending in *an* rather than Don Cán. I was standing at a distance, I was afraid that they would hear me, and then too the baby was still crying. *Seña* Chepilla's wild behavior and the memory of the fashionable man's hat that I saw through the shutter of the window aroused my suspicions, I admit.'"

"Hmmm!" Carmen exclaimed. "According to what you say, you don't know for certain who the gentleman was whose name Rosaín never finished uttering, yet you have your suspicions. What do you believe his name is?"

"I don't have a belief, Miss Carmita," Maria de Regla answered, all upset. "I don't dare say another word."

"What are you afraid of?" Adela asked her in a gentle tone of voice.

"Ay, Miss Adelita! I fear many things, I fear everything. Above all else blacks must watch what they say."

"You have no reason to be afraid. What can happen to you? What you are about to tell us happened so long ago that it's almost forgotten now. Moreover, suspecting something isn't bad; suspicion is sometimes natural."

"But, miss, your grace seems to forget that the slave who is suspicious of his or her owners always comes out the loser."

"What's that you say! What do you mean?" Carmen, visibly angry, interrupted the black woman. "Do you suspect that it was Papa?"

"Not I, my darling girl," the former wet nurse hastened to say. "God save me from suspecting anything bad about my master. I was mistaken, Miss Carmita, I tripped over my own tongue. I didn't mean owners, I meant whites. Slaves mustn't think anything bad about whites. Does Miss Carmita understand now what I meant?"

"No," Carmen replied with marked seriousness. "I don't want to believe what you say now to excuse yourself rather than relating what happened, simply and straightforwardly. You're pretending you don't know a thing when it suits your purposes, and at the same time you believe that you know more than we do. But you're mistaken, and the worst of it is that you clearly contradict yourself. I shall prove it to you. It didn't strike you as bad to recount how Doctor Don José Mateu drooled over you, that more or less the same thing happened with the Count of Jaruco and his son, and that the countess, out of jealousy, made haste to marry you to Dionisio. What could you say about certain white gentlemen that would be worse?"

There was a moment of silence, very painful for the woman recounting the story, and much more so for Isabel, whose vivid imagination went beyond the limits of the present, and beyond those of the place where she was as well; and tying up loose ends, she saw, as through a pane of crystal-clear glass, the not at all spotless or edifying picture of the family with which she was about to enter into ties that can be broken only when life ends. She asked no questions, she did not open her lips to utter an exclamation or breathe a sigh; with what the black woman had recounted she knew enough to guess the rest. Carmen and Adela were not in the same position. They did not possess the talent, the maturity, or the experience of their friend, and it was natural that, far from being alarmed, displeased, or satisfied by María de Regla's account, they should feel a greater curiosity and want to verify the truth of even the most minute incidents of a story that had every appearance of being scandalous, if not highly immoral.

"Let's see," Adela said, returning to the charge in her sweet voice and persuasive manner. "Tell me once and for all, who do you imagine that the gentleman you saw at the shutter of the window was?"

"I am going to tell you because your graces demand it of me, and not because it comes from inside me. May God punish me if I lie, and not count my words against me if I offer false testimony. But I imagined, your graces, that the gentleman I saw at the shutter of the window kissing the baby was . . . the master. He looked very much like him."

"Papa!" Carmen and Adela exclaimed as one, indignant now. "That can't be. Your eyes deceived you. Papa never had anything to do with mulatto women and base people."

"You're lying!" Carmen said emphatically to María de Regla, feeling no sort of consideration for her. "It wasn't Papa. No, no, no. Papa, so responsible, so gentlemanly, noble by birth and by temperament, Papa kissing on the sly, Papa devoted to a vulgar baby girl from the Foundling Home, a little mulatto perhaps! It's unbelievable! I indignantly deny it. If anyone swears to me by all the saints in heaven that it's true, I still don't believe it."

"I was mistaken, your graces," the black woman said with compunction. "Your graces must not credit my words for a moment. I was mistaken, I didn't see clearly. I mistook another gentleman for the master. I was confused. May your graces take into account the fact that I was breathless from the struggle with the madwoman, and moreover I saw what happened at the window in the front room through a tiny hole in the door of the bedroom. It's not my fault that I kept this figment of my imagination to myself for so long a time. What fault of mine was it that the master hired me out to suckle that baby girl? What fault of mine was it that the master took me to the Foundling Home in his carriage? What fault of mine was it that the master ordered me not to say one word about what I was about to see and hear in the Home and everywhere else that the baby was taken? Do your graces not see the mystery involved? Who, then, was Cecilia's real and legitimate father? It wasn't Doctor Montes de Oca; it wasn't Doctor Rosaín; it wasn't the master, because he was married to Señorita. Who was it? Of course: it was the man who often came to see the baby girl, invariably hiding himself from me. What was he hiding from his daughter's wet nurse and not from the mistress of the house? I long pondered this, and it so happened that that man so closely resembled the master that I often took it into my head that the two of them were the same man. But your graces have freed me from doubt."

"Of course," said Carmen, in whom the diplomacy of being a mistress of the household was beginning to exert its control over her passion as a daughter. "Of course you were mistaken. Papa, poor Papa has had nothing whatsoever to do with this mixup other than the well-intentioned desire to help Doctor Montes de Oca fulfill a promise made to a friend of his who needed a black woman to suckle an illegitimate child. It's as clear as day. The odd thing, the very odd thing," she added, addressing her friends, "is that this black woman, the brightest and most vainglorious know-it-all of any of them, didn't try to find out who the women in the little house on the Callejón de San Juan de Dios were, or the name of the gentleman who used to come to see the little girl at the shutter of the window. That's what I find the most incomprehensible."

"Ah!" the shrewd nurse exclaimed. "So that is what your grace believes? Well, let her take into account the trouble I constantly went to in order to find out the least little thing; and I did find out some things and others I never managed to discover. I tried to worm things out of people, believe me! I poked about and scratched around, believe me! More than a hen with chicks. But there was no way to get a word out of them. The two women either pretended to know more than they really did, or else they had instructions from people who knew more than we do. The only thing I managed to find out for certain was that the mulatto woman who looked like a skeleton was named Madalena Morales and was *Seña* Chepilla's mother, that *Seña* Chepilla Alarcón was the mother of *Seña* Charito, and *Seña* Charito was the mother of Cecilia Valdés. That is to say that Madalena, a woman as black as I am, had *Seña* Chepilla, a mulatto, by a white man; that *Seña* Chepilla had *Seña* Charito Alarcón, a light-skinned mulatto, by another white man, and that *Seña* Charito had Cecilia Valdés, a white, by another white man. Now then, who supported those women? Who paid for the house, the food, the doctor, the luxury? Who was the baby's father? I could never find out the truth. I was sly about trying to wheedle things out of them, but to no avail. *Seña* Chepilla was always on the alert. Because if I asked her a question, no matter how innocent a one it might be, she was sure to come back at me with another question: 'How did you come by your way with words?'

"I once asked Madalena how Charito went mad. Unfortunately. She didn't say a word; her expression changed; her face turned ashen; she panted like a frightened animal; she let out many *oufs* and *afs* and took off like a shot and shut herself up in the kitchen. Another time I asked her who put Cecilia in the Foundling Home. Good Lord! She outdid herself: she couldn't even talk. Another time I asked her: 'What is Cecilia's father's name?' It was as if somebody had stuck a candle inside her: she literally gave off sparks all over her body; her little pigtails of kinky hair stood up like snakes; she said 'oh! ah!,' spread out her arms, one this way, the other that way, made two crosses with her fingers as if she'd seen the devil and left me with my mouth hanging open. I can tell your graces that I never dropped the matter.

"The bad part is that from the beginning I believed that the white gentleman, who came almost every week to see the little girl without my knowing it, was the master, and I told Dionisio as much as soon as we saw each other again. Through Pío he found out that the master often got out of the carriage on the Callejón de San Juan de Dios, and that he then got back in it again there, or in the Calle del Empedrado, or in front of Don Juan Gómez's house, where he played ombre every night. Following up on these hints, Dionisio kept looking till he found me. *Seña* Chepilla wouldn't let me go outside even to run errands; but Dionisio and I saw each other, either early in the morning when he went to the market in the square, or late at night when everybody in the house was asleep. Then Dionisio met Cecilia and conceived a . . . mortal hatred of her, because she was the cause of our separation. In order for Dionisio to get out of the house late at night he had old Mamerta steal the key to the street door, which was kept in Señorita's bedroom.

"Finally, *Seña* Chepilla caught Dionisio and me talking in the front room early one morning, and got so angry that she took the baby away from me and kept me from suckling her. Luckily this was after I'd suckled her for some nine or ten months, and by that time she was walking and able to get along on spoon feedings. A few days later *Seña* Chepilla told me that she didn't need me any more and that I could go home. I answered her that I wasn't familiar with the streets of Havana and was afraid I'd get lost. And just imagine, ladies, the next day Pío came for me. Who told him to come? He told me that the master had ordered him to come fetch me. But how did the master find out that I'd been sacked?

"At the Gamboa house Señorita was waiting for me, sword in hand. I wasn't at all afraid though, because I was expecting that the master would defend me. But what reason would he have had to defend me! On the contrary, it seemed to me as though he sided against me and spurred Señorita on to send me to the plantation, without making any attempt to get at the truth of the matter. Dionisio had told me that Señorita and the master had had a good many quarrels because of me, because of the baby girl I was nursing, because the master had taken me to the Foundling Home in the calash, because she didn't believe that Doctor Montes de Oca had hired me out; in a word, because of a thousand other things. The truth is that almost the moment I came in through the door of the *zaguán*, Señorita took me to the study where the master was going over the accounts, and put me through a confession. I don't remember everything she asked me, or what I answered; what I do remember very well is that I told her a pack of lies and that she threatened to send me to the plantation. The master didn't even open his mouth.

"But I was pregnant with Dolores and Señorita was expecting your grace. Being pregnant made her ill, and when your grace was born, since Señorita was in frail health whereas I had come through my delicate condition without any ill effects at all, I was obliged to suckle your grace while old Mamerta fed Dolores on cow's milk and soft bread.

"Just look now, ladies, at what bad luck I had. I, a loving mother, had to suckle my mistress's daughter whereas I was not able to offer the breast to my own beloved daughter, the first one I had had who had lived, or even take her into my arms to kiss her and warm her on my bosom. God knows that I've always loved children; that even though I took good care of Cecilia, I cared for your grace even more affectionately and loved and still love her as though I had given birth to her. But put yourself in my place, Miss Adela, think about how I suffered when I saw your grace healthy, pink, plump, clean, with many lace caps, many em-

394

broidered skirts, many little batiste shirts, short lace skirts, little stockings of fine linen and tiny little silk shoes, sleeping in a mahogany cradle sent to the master from the United States as a gift, always in my arms or in Señorita's, in Miss Antoñica's, and even in the master's, because your grace was greatly pampered by everyone; because if your grace cried, or fussed about something, the house came tumbling down and there were never enough masters, friends, or servants to go fetch the doctor, to go to the apothecary's and to look after the baby, until her little pain was gone and she was better. Most of the time I was to blame, according to Señorita, if your grace cried, because I had pinched her when I swaddled her, because the water in the basin I bathed her in was too cold or too hot, because I was clumsy with a pin when I was dressing her and scratched her, and for a thousand other reasons. And meanwhile what was happening to my daughter Dolores? Imagine, your grace, how heartbroken I was to see her thin, sickly, snot-nosed, dirty, practically bare naked, crawling on the floor, or amid the chickens in the back yard or the feet of the horses in the stable, or alongside the portable stove of the women doing the ironing, or in the kitchen getting spattered with hot lard; sucking from a little rag doll wrapped in a dirty rag that the woman who was taking care of her had made for her, filled with bread or rice moistened with milk to stave off her hunger. If she cried . . . Good Lord! Instead of consoling her, Señorita was the first to say: 'Take that little black baby to the kitchen!' Her screams tormented me. Dionisio didn't know how to handle children, and besides, he couldn't abandon his duties. Mamerta, the one responsible for looking after her, was an elderly old maid who didn't know how to care for children either, who had never had any children of her own in her life and . . . knew nothing of motherly love.

"I spent my days and nights weeping. I was in torment. But I didn't lack milk because of this; on the contrary, as soon as Señorita had me eat more than was usually put on the table before me, my breasts overflowed. I could easily have suckled both baby girls if I had been allowed to. But . . . what chance was there that Señorita would have agreed to that? Not a chance in the world. Seeing my distress and my sadness, Mamerta brought Dolores to me one night, in the room where I slept next to your grace's cradle. Ah! With what joy I nursed her! I have never enjoyed a greater pleasure in my life! The trick worked well that night. After that, Dolores grew fond of me; as if she realized the difference between sucking moist rice from a rag doll and sucking milk from her mother's breast. To be free of Dolores's crying and get some sleep, Mamerta brought her to me on other nights, when she thought that everyone in the house was asleep. But the pitcher goes to the well so often that finally it breaks. One night, when Dolores was with me on the sleeping platform, your grace wakened up, and I had to take her out of the cradle so that Señorita wouldn't hear and catch all three of us together. I put your grace on my right, Dolores on my left, and lay face up between the two. I let both of you suck me, like two little scorpions, till the last drop of my milk was gone. But it so happened, because I soon fell asleep I suppose, that Dolores tired of nursing on one side, tried to suck on the other, and all of a sudden she came across your grace's hands and head, clinging to the breast that I'd given her. The Trojan War broke out then and there. The two of you raised such a fuss that Señorita wakened up, came to the room with a candle in her hand and caught us in the act.

"Mamerta was the one who paid the price, because the steward gave her such a flogging, by order of Señorita, that she had no desire to bring Dolores to me ever again as I lay on the platform. Nothing was said to me; but the next month, or thereabouts, Señorita consulted with the master as to what should be done with me; he gave orders to put me aboard *Seño* Pancho's schooner and they spirited me away to La Tinaja one day when I least expected it, to do penance for my faults and sins."

> *They had reached that point*
> *When her husband came upon the scene.*

Some time after 12 that night, Doña Rosa indistinctly heard voices murmuring somewhere inside the house, and with no other thought in mind save that something untoward was happening among her daughters, she got up out of bed, and pushing open door after door along the entire bedroom passageway, she did not stop until she reached the third room, where the feminine gathering was taking place. Her first impulse was to reprimand her daughters, but she contained herself on catching sight of the Ilincheta sisters and their estimable aunt, Doña Juana Bohorques. She then endeavored to ascertain the reason for this late-night meeting.

None of the ladies, more frightened than not, managed to say one word in explanation of the unusual scene. The one exception was Adela. Far from being upset, she came forward with much laughter to greet her mother, trying to hide the former wet nurse from her with the folds of her skirt, and in a few words explained to her the aim of the meeting and its results. Immediately thereafter she added: "Here is María de Regla. She begs your forgiveness (she had thrown herself at the feet of her mistress) and we all join her in her plea that you allow her to go to Havana to be with Dionisio."

Taken by surprise, Doña Rosa, in her daughter's arms with the slave woman at her feet, did not know what to say in reply; but then she said feelingly:

"Ay, daughter! What a thing you're asking of me! That is more, much more than what I can grant you if I am to fulfill my duty and look after my peace of mind and that of anyone else in the family."

"Mama!" Adela answered, "she has told us her story and we believe her to be innocent of everything that she is accused of. As we listened to her, we wept like babies."

"You innocent, you," Doña Rosa said sarcastically, "being taken in by her tall tales and her crocodile tears. A more hypocritical and wicked black than this one has never been born. She has caused me more troubles that she has kinks in her hair. She has never told me one word that is true; she has always tried to deceive me and has disobeyed me countless times. Yes, here is the place where she deserves to be. They couldn't stand her anywhere else, and I feel pity for you when you intercede on behalf of a black like her. The worst of it is, my girl, that she doesn't love you, because she is incapable of loving anyone."

"But I love her, Mama. She suckled me and keeps weeping and begging me to serve as her protectress with you. I no longer have the strength to resist her tears and her pleas."

"Very well, Adela," Doña Rosa replied after a few brief moments' reflection. "For your sake and for the sake of Isabel (who was unable to hold back her tears) I forgive María de Regla. She may return to Havana, but not to serve me or to live in the house, but rather to hire herself out and work on her own. I shall give her the document necessary for her to do so. The wages she earns with it will be used so that you and Carmen have a little pin money each month.

IV

I

From his rival's lacerated chest
A river of blood is already dancing.

El Duque de Rivas

The wound that Dionisio Jaruco or Gamboa received in the knife fight with the musician José Dolores Pimienta did not prove to be inevitably fatal. The blow was not delivered with the end of the knife but with the edge, and although the weapon separated the muscles of the left side of his chest diagonally, at the height of the nipple, it did not injure any delicate bodily part in its long trajectory. Hence, even though he fell to the ground on his back, it was not in fact because the wound deprived him of all his strength. He stumbled over a paving stone as he dodged the blow, and what laid him low was fear and his loss of blood.

He was lying prostrate and moaning, pressing down on the wound with both hands, in the middle of the Calle Ancha when a man of color with an athletic build happened to pass by. He was barefoot and was wearing a wide untanned leather belt that ran across his left shoulder to his left hip, fastened together by the two loops at the end of it, like a baldric. He was a water vendor or *carretillero*, as they are called in Havana. He came closer on hearing the moans and then hurried on past, murmuring. "He been killed. God save me!"

Another passerby appeared a moment later, he too a man of color, although if we are to judge by his attire more civilized than the one before. He was carrying on his arm something that appeared to be a musical instrument, sheathed in a thick flannel slip case. His attention drawn to the moans of the wounded man, he halted a respectable distance away, and having ascertained what had happened, exclaimed in pity: "Po' man! What a stabbin' he got! He still yet not dead though. But who goin' to get me in trouble? De law . . . May his soul go to heabenly glory."

He hurried on, turning around from time to time to see whether anyone had caught sight of him and was following his trail so as to accuse him of the murder the next day or another.

The third of the passersby, he too a man of color, was a type *sui generis,* unique by virtue of his attire, his actions, and his appearance. The former consisted of what are called bell-shaped trousers, very wide along the lower leg and narrow at the instep, as at the calf and the hips; a white shirt with a wide collar with sawtoothed indents rather than a straight edge; a cotton neckerchief stretching at an angle down his back and tied in front above his chest; shoes with the vamp and the heel so low-cut they barely covered his toes or his heel bone, leaving them showing as if he were wearing house slippers; and a straw hat atop a bramble patch of kinky braided locks, which after making his head look too big assumed in front the form of the twisted horns of a male yearling sheep. From his earlobes hung earrings in the shape of waning moons that appeared to be made of gold, but if tested with a touchstone, the most inexperienced goldsmith, we are certain, would have declared them to be made of ordinary tombac.[48]

We are here tracing with broad brushstrokes a portrait drawn from life of a *curro* from El Manglar, on the outskirts of cultivated Havana, in that memorable era of our history. Our eccentric is not what is usually meant by a *curro,* an emigré from southern Spain who proudly flaunts his flashy Andalusian attire. He is nothing more or less than a black or a young mulatto, a native of the aforementioned barrio or of two or three others in the same city, a good-for-nothing troublemaker, an idler, a brawler by nature or by habit, a petty thief by profession, who grows up on the streets, who lives by plunder, and who seems to be destined from birth to the lash, to irons, or to a violent death.

If it had been in the nature of one born a *curro* to apply himself to anything good or useful, there is no doubt that the one of whom we are now speaking would at least have learned how to read and write; for it is a historical fact that in the era of his early youth there were more grade schools in Havana taught by schoolmasters of color than by whites, and his father, a well-intentioned African, had always been stubbornly determined that his street urchin of a son would receive some education.

Near the Calle de los Corrales, where our *curro* was born and grew up, was the Lorenzo Meléndez School, named after its schoolmaster, a lieutenant of grenadiers in the colored militia, and attended by mulattos, blacks, and whites; the instruction there was practically free, since the pupil's fees were paid in kind and consisted, for the most part, of vegetables, poultry, eggs, and beeswax candles. His father himself took him there on more than one occasion, to no avail; he recommended to the schoolmaster that he not spare the rod with the boy because he was a scatterbrain, to no avail; his father dealt him terrible punishments with his own hand, to no avail; the boy failed to learn even the first letter of the alphabet in the infrequent visits he paid to the school of venerable Master Meléndez.

He always preferred to go fishing for sardines in Tallapiedra, or netting shrimp in the Zanja Real, or flying kites in the vacant lot in Peñalver, or playing *mates* in the little square of San Nicolás, or *picado* against the walls of the church of Jesús María. This, in the vulgar language of the kids at school, was called *fugitivarse*, playing hooky. Not going to school made it necessary to spend whole days in the streets, rain or shine, making a scandal of himself in the eyes of every peace-loving passerby when there was no opportunity to take shelter in such places as the pig slaughterhouse or a tavern, where inevitably there were plenty of chances to swipe something to allay their hunger. But now in one place, now in another, he invariably came out the loser, whether at the hands of the *curro* schoolmate he was playing with, or at those of the tavernkeeper, who never had recourse to a court of law to defend and protect his property.

So he learned the hard way, becoming at an early age an expert at knavery and wrongdoing. And since he was not the only *curro*, inasmuch as the species abounded in the era mentioned, it often happened that he got together with a number of others his age who shared his likings, whereupon his forays took on a more aggressive and malicious nature. In fact, he and the boys in his barrio formed a gang to wage stone fights with the boys in the neighboring one, their mortal enemies; to grab the small coins that godfathers used to throw in the street for them after a baptism; to tie tin cans on the tails of dogs and let them loose in the places most crowded with passersby; to throw stones onto the roofs or into the courtyards of certain houses whose residents they disliked; to use sharp sticks to goad and enrage the pigs and bulls being held in pens on their way to be slaughtered; and finally, to fight with wooden knives until they had scratched each other and drawn blood so as to learn how to wield that treacherous weapon skillfully.

He was nearing adolescence when his father, disillusioned when his son didn't learn in school even though his teacher was not one to spare the rod, placed him as an apprentice with the master shoemaker Gabriel Sosa, a man with a hard heart and a strong hand, and so, by dint of thrashing him with his shoe lasts, of lashing him with his shoemaker's stirrup, and of tying him up with an iron chain like a wild, untamed animal so as to cure him of his propensity to run away, at the end of four years' time he had managed to teach him how to make even women's shoes. After his apprenticeship was over, he used to go regularly two or three times a week to that same shoemaker's shop with the aim of earning his daily bread, as long as no chances came along to earn it by means that, if not honest, were at least easier and more in accord with his innate inclinations.

Master Sosa's shoemaker's shop was at the top of a gully carved out by rainwater. The stream of rainwater came down the Calle de Manrique, and then, after draining off the water from the road to San Luis Gonzaga and that from the roads to La Estrella and La Maloja, it cascaded through the courtyards of the buildings lower down, forming a torrent. There was, consequently, a large difference in level between the floor of the buildings and the street, and therefore access to the buildings was difficult because of the height of their threshold.

On entering the Calle Ancha, our *curro* went round the Campo de Marte. He took big steps, or rather strides, his arms forming an angle of 45 degrees (perhaps to hide their excessive length), like the crank of a whetstone. As soon as he heard the moans and noted the body lying in a heap on the ground, he abruptly ceased trotting. After raising both hands to his ears to make sure the two waning-moon tumbac earrings were still in place, and saying to himself: they not broke, so nothin's 'bout to happen to me, he resolutely addressed the wounded man.

"Well! Who be you, *paisano*?" he asked him in his peculiar jargon and accent.

"I'm Dionisio Jaruco," the man answered in a faint voice as soon as he had made sure that he was dealing with a peaceable person.

"I not hear dat name in all my life."

"That's not to be wondered at, señor, because I'm halfway a stranger in this city. And what is your cognomen, señor?"

"What dat you say?"

"I asked you your name, señor."

"Dey call me Malanga."

"Malanga?" Dionisio repeated, as if he hadn't heard clearly.

"Malanga. But my real name not dat. It be Polanco. My pa's master were a certain Polanco. But Malanga de name dey gib me in El Manglal, 'cause my pa's a African, and my ma too, an' I be Creole. Dey call me dat since I be little."

The rogue was lying. In the barrio of El Manglar they gave him the nickname of Malanga, meaning an awkward good-for-nothing, referring both to his conduct and his character and to his long arms and legs by contrast to his trunk, which was short, and above all to his big, clumsy feet.

"An' what is de señol doin' down dere, lyin' belly up? Did de oil go to his head?"

"I'm not drunk, Malanga; I'm badly wounded."

"Wouned, you say! And who did you dat misservice?"

"A little mulatto who's worth less than a guava. Look here."

"Some woun'! It be easy to see that mulatto fella know his job. But where had de señol been to? To a funeral?"

"I hadn't been at any funeral. I was coming home from a ball when I bumped into the mulatto; we had words and in the fight he treacherously wounded me. But why do you ask me that?"

"Jes' askin'. 'Cause I see you wearin' a undataka's outfit . . ."

"This isn't undertaker's attire; it's court dress."

"I don' know if it be high cou't or low cou't, but seein' as how if it wasn't fo' his boot an' his long coat, el señol get his leg cut off, I mean, he get turned over like a crab. Den it 'pears to me de señol a lil bit too fat to be knife-fightin'. Den it mos' likely dat de señol learn how when he be growed up, and knife-fightin's a art dat mus' be learn' when a body be a young'un. Den you real sho't in de arm and cain't defen' youself 'gainst blows dat come from above. Den . . ."

"Good Lord!" the wounded man interrupted him in a weak voice. "For the love of God and the Blessed Virgin let us say no more about the matter. If you're a charitable person and want to help me, be quick about it, because I can see that I'm drenched in blood."

"I be tyin' scarf roun' you so de blood not come out."

"No, the wound must be washed first."

"Wash de woun'! Is de señol mad? An' if he get a chill? An' if he die? Den the señol goin' to say it happen 'cause of me."

"No, I won't say such a thing, you may be sure of that. If I die, it won't be your fault, but because my hour has come. Come, Señor Malanga, run to the tavern on the corner and bring me a bottle of dry wine and a bottle of brandy."

"Yes, señol, I do that, 'cept that de tabernkeeper be closed. It now good an' late. Den too, dat debbil don' trus' me, 'cause he know me an' he know dat, eben if it be bad fo' me to say it, I done turned over mo' den one of dem crabs like him. I cain't look at a Catalan grocerman widout my blood beginnin' to go up."

"Well, man, go anyway, do this errand. Maybe he'll open up. Knock hard."

"Yes, *paisano*, but don't de señol unnerstan'? I mean dat . . . dat if de señol don't see it fo' hisself, I tellin' him dat I ain't got even a pin in my pocket. I ain't still yet made my firs' lil coin to make de cross on tonight."

"Come on, friend, why didn't you say so from the very start? I have some money. Put your hand in this pocket of my waistcoat. There must be a gold coin in there, two doubloons and a *dobloncito*. Take the smallest of the coins and run, because my mind is going . . . I can't see a thing."

And the wounded man fainted. That didn't stop the *curro*, however. His one concern was to feel about the designated site and pick up in his hand the gold coin of the sort that he had rarely, if ever, in his life possessed with the permission of its owner. He left at once for the tavern which, as he expected, he found closed as tight as a drum; and he began to knock on the door with his knuckles, gently at first, and then repeatedly hammering hard with his fist. Even if the tavernkeeper was perchance as deaf as a post, he would have been bound to hear and hurry to answer the door so as to keep it from being knocked down. It couldn't be a thief who was getting him out of bed like this so late at night. As a precaution, however, he didn't open the little wicket with a grille in the door; he contented himself with sending his voice with its pure Catalan accent through the keyhole, asking:

"Hey, who it is there?"

"It me, *ño* Juan."

"But who you mean by 'me'?"

"Malanga, *ño* Juan. Don' you reconise me? Open de do'."

"Open le porta! Bom Deu, for that you get me out of bed? Go, go your way, Malangue. I'm not about to open le porta. Qué cynic insolence!"

"Open, *ño* Juan, fo' de lob' of yo' ma. Dere be a po' color' man wouned."

"Woundid you say? El diable take me if I open le porta." Mare de Deu! Justicia! I'd lose all I have. All meus dinés! Bona nite, *noy*.

"Lissen, lissen, ño Juan. I not come in. Open de cat hole. I got dough here."

"Aha! That's a dif'rent song. Push lo diné inside."

"Gib an' take, ño Juan. Gib me a bottle ob dry vino. Not wet. You un-nerstan'? An' a glass ob dat stuff what burn."

"Give, give."

"How much?"

"Espanish pese and a half."

"I push in a lil gol' piece."

"Here's la boutelle and here's lo glass. And here's el volte you get back from your gold coin. May these espirits serve you for caridat's sake this time, noy."[49]

With the bottle in one hand and the glass of brandy in the other, which he received through the wicket with a grating in the door, without stopping to count the change that the tavernkeeper had given him, he went back to help the cook. As soon as he washed his wound, that is to say, once he wet it through the cook's shirt, bandaged it the best he knew how and the best he could with two neckerchiefs, had him drink the brandy, and helped him to his feet, he led him by the hand to a room partitioned off with planks inside a *ciudadela* or tenement house at the gate immediately adjoining the Jesús María theater. Fortunately, during this tragicomic scene, not a living soul came by, with the exception of a few cats or dogs that, far from picking a fight with our characters, either fled in terror, or turned tail, barking as they ran.

But what was the source of the unforeseen kindness displayed by that dimwit, the evildoer Malanga, at such a critical juncture? It came from the fact that, having touched the gold coins in the pocket of Dionisio's waistcoat, he rightly calculated that whether Dionisio died of his wound or whether he recovered, he would inevitably become his heir, or else he would use force or deception to become his heir while he was still alive. To this end, of prime importance, Malanga proceeded with his good offices toward a man who was a complete stranger to him. He gave him his bed, consisting of a folding cot, dirty and rickety, with no extra clothes or blanket to cover his "sore spots"; and very early the next morning he went to the intersection of the Calle de la Maloja and Campanario Viejo, where Zarza, a surgeon who didn't speak in Latin lived, awakened him, and took him, willy-nilly, to the wounded man, swearing him to inviolable secrecy. Such services are paid for only in money among honest and upright people. This was Dionisio's understanding, and both out of gratitude and as a precaution, he hastened to pay the debt, giving the new friend that he had acquired the greater part of the money he possessed, just in case a powerful hand charged that much.

During Dionisio's convalescence, Malanga entertained him with the graphic account of his roguish life and his adventures. He hid nothing from him; his labors as a boy; his petty thievery as a young adolescent; dagger thrusts given and received in unfair street fights; and finally, his marvelous escapes from the long arm of the law. He made a special point of telling, naturally with intense satisfaction, keeping count with marks made on his left arm, of the number of "crabs" (as he called tavernkeepers or grocers, most of them Catalans) he had "turned over," as he put it, in his short lifetime, that is to say, murdered in cold blood.

Since in these instances Malanga often addressed him as Dionisio and even Jaruco, the latter warned him not to call him by either of these names, explaining his reasons for this precaution.

"Call me *paisano*, your buddy from the same barrio," he went on. "That was how you addressed me when you found me in the middle of the street more dead than alive. Unfortunately I'm a slave, my friend, and I'm not here with the permission of my master and mistress. I took advantage of their having gone off to the country to pinch from the señora's wardrobe the clothes you took to be an undertaker's outfit. I also made off with the bit of money in the wardrobe that we've been using to get by on. In two days there won't be enough left even to light a candle for the souls in purgatory. You bring in only a little, that you've come by at great risk. So we must think of taking to the streets and seeing how a person goes about making enough to live on."

"De señol not to worry," Malanga said confidently. "I still yet have an alticle we can use to get ourselfs dough."

"Let's see the article," Dionisio replied happily.

The ruffian unsheathed the sharp knife that he always carried with him underneath his shirt, scratched at the floor of beaten earth of the room near one corner hidden by the cot, and took out something heavy, wrapped in a cloth. He immediately added, holding the bundle on high:

"I wanted to say dis to the señol, dat since las' year, 'tween me, a mulatto name' Picapica, an' a lil black name' Cayuco, we stop a white man, a dandy if ever I seen one, ea'ly in the mo'nin', 'longside the lil square of Santa Teresa, an' as soon as I show him de knife he be petlified an' give us ever'thin' he had on 'im. My pals took de dough an' I got dis here alticle. Den I took it to a jewler on de main road to see if he fix it fo' me, but soon's he look at it good he go like: 'Dis be goods what's been stolen an' I ain't givin' a plug a tobacco fo' it.' So, *paisano*, I gets scare', an' since dat day, I keeps it buried. The señol might could maybe sell it."

"Hand me the confounded thing," Dionisio said pompously.

But the moment he had it in his hand, he exclaimed in surprise:

"I recognize this watch, friend Polanco!"

"No foolin'? Now ain't that somethin'!" Malanga said.

It was a gold watch, and from the ring of it, instead of a chain or cord there hung, folded in two, a red and blue moiré ribbon, the ends of which were fastened together with a buckle, also made of gold.

"I recognize this watch," Dionisio said again. "Señorita, my mistress I mean, gave it to young master Leonardo in October of last year. It must have an inscription on it."

Once he had opened the back cover, the cook read: "L. G. S., Oct. 24, 1830: Leonardo Gamboa y Sandoval, who is spending the Christmas holidays with his family in the country."

"And what endeviduals are those?" Malanga asked, all confused.

"My masters," Dionisio answered. "The señora spoils her son badly and gives him a gift every day."

"Well, I begs de señol's pardon," the *curro* hastened to add. "I not know dat those endeviduals be people de señol knew."

"There's no reason to beg my pardon, my friend Malanga. If in order to earn one's daily bread a person had to keep stopping to make fancy apologies, he'd die of hunger. I am sure," Dionisio went on, "that by now my masters are back in Havana, well rested, and that their first concern was to have a notice that I'm missing published in the *Diario*. It's as if I can almost read the part announcing a generous reward for my capture. There will surely be someone trailing me to earn the reward, and I can tell you right now that anyone who tries to lay hands on me had better belt up his trousers good and tight. . . . They won't take me alive; they'll have to make mincemeat of me. Maybe Tondá, who knows me, will have taken on the job . . . I wouldn't like to be in his shoes. But there's no need to go out of my way to get myself in trouble, for as the saying goes, he who avoids the opportunity avoids the danger, and I'm determined to live and be free now that I've run away. I wasn't born to be a slave all my life, Señor Malanga. No. I grew up amid grandeur and abundance, and didn't experience the hardships of slavery while I was with my first masters. They were real nobility, those two, a lord and lady who treated me nobly. Now I'm married and have two children. I misspoke. It's been many years now since they banished my wife to the deepest depths of silence, on a plantation, and she's had a mulatto child with a white man. But I love her and love my daughter with all my heart, and I must work to buy their freedom and mine. So you see, my friend Malanga, why it's best not to call me Dionisio, or Jaruco either, the only two names I'm known by in this city. As long as Tondá doesn't hear my name or see my face, I'm safe."

"'Dat why it not matter to me if people call me Polanco or Malanga," the latter said with a certain resignation. "It all de same to me. Ever'body know me by de two names. I be better knowed in dis city dan de dogs. An' it de same wid me, dey be a notice out fo' me too. I excape Tondá's claws by a miracle. Well, señol, one night las' year, pretty late, I went wid two friends to the tabern on the co'ner of Manrique and La Estreya. We aks fo' a bit of dat stuff what burns, we drink it down an' are sneakin' out, when de tabernkeeper come an' grab me by de shirt so's to make us pay fo' what we drink. An' den de debil made me do it, *paisano*; I grab my knife an' I slash 'im, jes' here (running his index finger across his throat), sparin' his you-know-whats. De slash gush blood like a woun'ed bull, an' den so the señol will see, he leap over de counter an' ran afta us to de co'ner where he had to grab hisself an' den he fall down an' lef' his finger marks on de wall.* Den a while after, Tondá hear dat it was us an' look real hard fo' us till he find us at a party, ober dere by Lo Sitios. I excaped but my two friends fall in de trap. An' dey still yet in de jail. Since den I got no pals, an' Tondá be jubilatin'. You see? I go out only jes' at night an' almos' don't even go by de shop."

"What shop?"

"Masta Sosa's shop."

"What craft is he a master of?"

"Shoes."

"Men's shoes?"

"All kines. I works dere when I cain't make my livin' any other way. I makes shoes fo' women."

"I make them too," Dionisio said, his face brightening. "I learned how to make them from Pío, the carriage driver in my household. I'm not a bungler at shoemaking. And an idea has just occurred to me: if you would be kind enough to speak to Master Sosa, perhaps he'd take me on, in which case we've saved our skins. Tondá will never in the world suspect that I'm hiding out in a shoemaker's shop."

"Well, if de señol wants I take 'im dere one of dese aftanoons, or betta still, ea'ly one mo'nin', 'cause Tondá always go about on ho'seback, an' he neber out on the street at a ea'ly hour."

And that is what happened: as soon as his friend regained his health and was ready to work, Malanga took him to Master Gabriel Sosa and earnestly recommended him, not only as an expert workman at making ladies' shoes, but also as a distinguished person and an honorable man in every respect; he also told him that he had fallen into disgrace and was

---

* Historical. *Author's note.*

resorting to the practice of this craft so as not to die of hunger. Whereby there has been repeated here the somewhat similar story of the wounded lion that a runaway slave in the lonely wilds of Africa took in and cared for, as a consequence of which the animal later on fed the man and protected him against the other wild beasts, when after many years the two of them met at the circus in Rome.

I I

Ille dolet vere qui sine teste dolet.[50]

Martial

Uribe the tailor, Clara his wife, Pimienta, and his sister Nemesia accompanied Cecilia to the door of her little house on the Calle del
Aguacate.

As soon as Cecilia called out in the particular way agreed upon, the
bolt of the door slid back and it opened by itself. This was because her
grandmother, too ill to wait up for her granddaughter, had tied the end
of a slender cord to the end of the bolt, next to the catch that supported
it, and the other end to one of the bedposts, within her reach. Her
friends left without a word being spoken for the moment.

As Cecilia undressed almost gropingly because of the feeble light shed
by the night light in the niche, deep, involuntary sighs escaped her lips.
They were the very bitter aftertaste of the fiesta. She had gone to it so as
to make herself giddy from the movement of the dance, the harmonies
of the music, and the adulation of the men present; so as to suppress in
the tumult of the large heterogeneous gathering the memory of her ab-

sent lover, disdainful and perhaps thankless, to try to avenge herself for his ingratitude; so as to test, finally, whether she could forget him should there be a more serious separation for an indefinite length of time in the offing.

Everything had turned out wrong. She went over in her mind various incidents of the evening's diversion and found that it had dragged on for too long, the music cacophonous and shrill, the women ungainly and ugly, the men arrogant and stupid, the gathering much too vulgar and tasteless to have entertained her and made her feel joyful. She compared this fiesta with the one on September 24 at Mercedes Ayala's, where she had enjoyed herself to the utmost as queen of love and beauty in the arms of her beloved, absent today; it wrung her heart and she was on the verge of being overcome with emotion. She thought of her destiny, deducing as a necessary consequence that the remedy had been worse than the illness, and that vengeance between lovers always ends in the chastisement of one of the contending parties, in the death of happiness, or the end of earthly life.

Cecilia felt so sad and miserable that it was not until she had climbed into bed that she noticed that her grandmother had been stricken by a terrible indisposition. The poor old woman was writhing and moaning almost inaudibly, as though she were at death's door. Cecilia reached out then to feel her forehead, and as soon as she placed her hand on it, she drew it away, exclaiming:

"Ay, Granny! Your grace has a fever."

"Have you come home at last?" the old woman replied in the voice of someone who is dying. "If you had come a few minutes later, you wouldn't have found me alive."

"Your grace wasn't ill when I left for the ball. I wonder what foolish thing she has done in my absence."

"Not one. I spent prime praying to the Virgin; but since daybreak I feel very ill. Something tells me that my end is near. What time is it?"

"It's two in the morning. I just heard the convent clock strike."

"Do you think Padre Aparicio is up?"

"I don't believe so, Granny. He doesn't arrive at the convent until four, which is when matins begin. But why does your grace want to see Padre Aparicio at this hour?"

"To make my confession, dear girl! I feel that my life is ending and I don't want to die like a dog."

"Didn't your grace make confession and take communion yesterday morning?"

"Yes, child. Why do you ask?"

"It's good you did. Because that's enough."

"It's not enough. We're sinners. We sin at every moment and we must be prepared so that when the hour of our death comes our soul appears before His Divine Majesty as clean as the plate for the Eucharist."

"Your grace wasn't seriously ill last night. Had I suspected that she was, would I have gone to that confounded ball? Never. What I fail to understand is why your grace has taken so sick that she's afraid she'll die within hours."

"It's just one step from health to sickness, and as we live so shall we die."

"Could your grace explain what she's feeling now?"

"It's impossible, my darling. The only thing I can tell you is that my soul is being dragged out of me, and that as soon as possible you must go fetch Padre Aparicio . . ."

"The padre is not going to cure you of your fever, and that's all your grace is suffering from. Your grace is very apprehensive. It would be better if I went for the doctor. Yes, I'll go for him at first light. Meanwhile I'll give you a foot bath and put mustard plasters on you so as to make your headache go away. Your grace will surely see how much that relieves her pain, or perhaps even makes her well. Your grace can't be so sick that there's no cure. You grace will bury me yet."

"May our guardian angel San Rafael and the Most Blessed Virgin hear you, my girl. I would regret dying, for your sake, not for mine. You're just beginning to live and I have already finished my life's journey . . . But do as you like and may God's will be done . . . My head is splitting," she added, pressing her forehead with both hands. . . .

Cecilia thereupon hastened to make a fire in the stove, in the patio underneath the roof, using the usual sulfur match and a few lumps of coal. Hence within minutes the bath water was ready and placed in a large basin. She immediately proceeded to bathe her grandmother's feet with no less faith and affectionate humility than the woman who washed the feet of Jesus Christ in Simon's house. As she dried them, she massaged them gently, and every so often planted a warm kiss on them, or brought them up to her cheeks to give them something of the burning heat in her veins.

Her heart touched, the grandmother placed a hand on her granddaughter's head and said: "Poor Cecilia! This means, my beloved girl, that you yourself recognize that my hours are numbered. I say my hours when it may be my minutes, my seconds . . . and you are readying me for the last supper before I undertake . . ."

She did not go on: emotion or pain choked her voice in her throat. Cecilia, for her part, on feeling her grandmother's hand on her head, experienced a sensation very much like the one we feel when we receive an electric shock, and her tears, forcibly contained until that moment, began to stream down her cheeks, adding to the water in the basin.

The old woman noticed this, and mustering all her courage, as people say, she added:

"Don't weep, my dearest one, for you make me suffer more than I already am. Console yourself. You're still a young girl: you have a happy future before you. Although you may never marry, you will have more than enough of everything. There will always be someone to look after you and protect you. And if not, God, who never fails anyone, is there in heaven. I feel a bit better now. Perhaps sickness gives a person time . . . What do we know? Come, my darling girl, calm yourself. Courage. You need some rest. If you go to bed this minute, from now till daylight you'll have two hours of sleep to regain your strength . . . Girls your age are like the miracle flower: one minute it looks dead, and the next it's alive again. Come, give me a kiss, and. . . . until tomorrow. May the guardian angel protect you with his loving wings."

How could Cecilia sleep or rest! No sooner had the gates of the city been opened and the bells with flaking paint of the mule drivers hauling coal begun to be heard in the streets, when she stole out of bed and ran to fetch her dear friend Nemesia to watch over the sick woman while she went for the doctor in the Calle de la Merced. A few days before her grandmother had given her, as a precaution, the directions as to how to get to the physician's house in these words: house with a roof terrace, window with an iron grille, *zaguán* with a red door, in the middle of the block, on the south side of the street. Her granddaughter did not lose her way, but she found the house silent and shut up tight. What to do in those circumstances? It was an urgent case, and she decided to knock. She banged on the door with the knocker and awaited the result in great anxiety.

After a brief interval of dead silence, a window shutter opened and the face of such an extraordinarily pretty, rosy-cheeked woman peeked out that Cecilia was overcome with amazement. Let the reader imagine a pair of black almond eyes, shaded by thick arched eyebrows, a little mouth with fiery red lips, a very expressive aquiline nose, a lovely head with abundant black hair that gave off a bluish cast, the whole framed and set off by a charming batiste cap, "as white as snow," trimmed with a narrow embroidered ruffle edged in lace. Such were the most prominent facial features of Doña Agueda Valdés, the young wife of the renowned surgeon Don Tomás Montes de Oca.

This pen sketch is a copy of the portrait in oil of that lady, done by the painter Vicente Escobar, which when we were young we could contemplate in ecstasy, hanging from the dilapidated walls of the drawing room of her house, in the Calle de la Merced. As for her moral physiognomy, the feature that stood out most, at least the one of which it is our task to speak in these pages, was jealousy. Her own shadow aroused it in her, despite the fact that her husband lacked those physical qualities that make a man attractive in women's eyes. But he was a physician, renowned and rich, and she had a very poor opinion of females, often saying that there was no such thing as an ugly man for an ambitious woman in love.

Driven by her accursed jealousy, she kept constant watch on her husband, on the patients he visited, and on those who came to ask him to share his profound medico-surgical knowledge, especially if such seekers wore skirts. That was why she was up so early; that was why, when she was unable to come by information on her own, she gave in to the weakness of trying to worm information out of her dim-witted and malicious carriage driver, her slave, who, even though on occasion he revealed proven facts to her, almost always filled her head instead with a collection of malevolent old wives' tales.

We may be so bold as to imagine the inner rejoicing of Doña Agueda on discovering that the person who had knocked on the door was a no-account lower-class girl who, since she was hiding beneath a shawl of colored Canton silk, naturally expensive and luxurious, could not be anyone else but one of her husband's lady friends disguised as a patient.

"What is it you want?" the jealous lady asked her, with a certain harshness and haste so that she wouldn't bang on the door again.

"I've come to fetch the señor doctor," Cecilia answered timidly, drawing closer to the window and then raising her eyes to look directly at the unknown lady.

("Now I see!" the latter said to herself, as soon as she noted how good-looking the girl was. "I smell a rat here.") "The doctor," she added aloud, "has had a bad night, and he's sleeping . . ."

"I'm so sorry to hear that!" Cecilia exclaimed, giving a heart-rending sigh.

"What doctor is it you're looking for, my girl?" the lady asked with a wicked smile. "Because . . . it might well be that you've come to the wrong place."

"I've come to fetch Doctor Don Tomás Montes de Oca," Cecilia replied in a loud, albeit trembling voice. "Doesn't that gentleman live here?"

"Yes, Montes de Oca lives here. Do you know him?"

"I've seen him only a very few times."

"Where do you live?"

"On the Calle del Aguacate, next to the convent of Santa Catalina."

"Are you the one who is ill?"

"No, señora, it's my grandmother."

"Is he her doctor?"

"No, señora."

"Then why are you coming to fetch this doctor instead of asking some other one who perhaps lives closer to your house?"

"Because my grandmother knows Senor Don Tomás and Señor Don Tomás knows her."

"Where have they seen each other?"

"At her house and here as well."

"Do you live with your grandmother?"

"Yes, señora."

"Is your grandmother married?"

"She's a widow. She was left a widow long before I was born."

"How many times has Montes de Oca been at your grandmother's?"

"I haven't kept count of them. Not many."

"That neither clarifies things nor confuses them. Do you yourself know Montes de Oca?"

"I don't believe so. By that I mean to say to the señora that I don't believe that he has ever seen me face to face."

"And where were you when he came to visit you and your grandmother?"

"At home, but my grandmother is the one who always received him; I never appeared . . ."

"How very odd! What reason did you have for hiding from him?"

"None, señora. It was only that it so happened that I was never well dressed when he came to see my grandmother."

"Well, I declare! So you were trying to flirt with him then? Don't you know that he's too ugly and too old for you?"

"I didn't try to flirt with the señor doctor."

"What sort of dealings and agreements does Montes de Oca have with your grandmother?"

"I don't know, señora. Nothing that's bad."

"Are you married?"

"No, señora."

"But you probably have a fiancé and will marry soon, isn't that so?"

"I don't have a fiancé and I'm not going to marry soon. In a word, will the señora be so kind as to tell me if the señor doctor . . . ?"

"I've already told you," Doña Agueda interrupted her, "that Montes de Oca has had a sleepless night and gave orders not to be awakened until ten o'clock."

"Woe is me!" Cecilia exclaimed, deeply upset. "How unfortunate!"

Doña Agueda's loving heart having been touched to the quick by this, she deliberately asked:

"Who are you?"

"I'm Cecilia Valdés," the young girl answered through her tears.

"Cecilia Valdés!" Doña Agueda repeated, at once surprised and troubled. Then she added briskly: "Do come in."

Without waiting for an answer or expecting any objection on the girl's part, she herself came to the door to slide back the T-bolt that locked the wicket in it, and gave her free and friendly access to her house.

Amid her deep distress, Cecilia thought she noted something odd about the lovely lady, something that bore a certain resemblance to madness. But that did not arouse the slightest fear in her; on the contrary, she felt strongly attracted to her, not only because of the naturalness of her words, but also because of the grace of her movements and the immeasurable sweetness of her voice. That is to say that, as if controlled by a powerful magnetic force, she silently and submissively allowed herself to be taken to the dining room, into which some light penetrated, thanks to the fact that it was immediately adjacent to the courtyard. Once there, her guide seated herself with her back to a large table of polished mahogany. Holding the young girl (who was standing) by both hands, very close to her knees, she sat contemplating and scrutinizing her from head to foot for quite some time, and as though she were addressing a statue, or someone who did not understand her language, she kept repeating emphatically: "She doesn't look like him! Of course not! Not at all; there's no resemblance. She can't be his daughter. Perhaps she takes after her mother, whose identity is known."

"Do you know who your father is?" she suddenly asked her.

"No, señora," Cecilia answered with the same meekness as before.

"Has your mother never told you?"

"No, señora. I never knew my mother. She died shortly after I was born."

"Who told you that tall tale?"

"What tall tale?"

"The one about your mother dying after you were born."

"What I told you about the death of my mother is not a tall tale, señora. I don't have the least memory of her."

"How old are you now?"

"I was born, according to what my grandmother has told me, in the month of October, 1812. The señora can do the arithmetic."

"And how does it happen that your grandmother hasn't told you who your father is? Doesn't she know? Do you know whether you were put in the Foundling Home?"

"Yes, señora. I was put in the Foundling Home so that I'd be baptized with the surname Valdés."

"Well, I wasn't put in a foundling home and that is also my surname. So your father, even without putting you in the Foundling Home, could easily have had you baptized, putting down 'of unknown parents,' in your baptismal certificate, as is the custom. Apparently he was a callous man. Did your mother suckle you? That is to say, did she give you the breast?"

"I don't believe so. A black woman suckled me."

"Where did she suckle you? In the Foundling Home?"

"No, señora, at my grandmother's."

"What was your wet nurse's name?"

"I believe it was María de Regla Santacruz."

"Is she still alive? Where is she now?"

After hesitating briefly, Cecilia answered, obviously disconcerted:

"I understand that my wet nurse has been banished to the countryside by her master and mistress. At least that is what I was told by a black with whom I exchanged a few words last night at the colored people's ball outside the city walls."

"Here we have another tall tale. A lie. Your wet nurse is not a slave who belongs to the Count and Countess of Jaruco. The one who hired that black woman to suckle you in the Foundling Home and at your grandmother's was your father. There he is! Have a look at him!"

Doña Agueda took advantage of the moment at which Cecilia was looking for the object that she had called to her attention, both by her words and by pointing, to rise to her feet and disappear into the nearest room, pushing open the door that led to the courtyard. Startled and bewildered, the girl turned around and very nearly let out a terror-stricken scream when she noticed that a man with a long pale face, without the least sign of a beard, thus giving him the look of an East Indian, with his head covered down to his ears by a grimy silk cap, was staring at her with little monkey eyes through the iron grille separating the master bedroom and the sitting room.

"What brings you here?" the man asked her in a twanging falsetto voice.

"I've come, señor, to fetch Señor Don Tomás Montes . . ." Cecilia replied hesitantly.

"I am he," he interrupted her. "What can I do for you?"

"Ay! You're that gentleman? Didn't the señora tell me . . . ?"

"Pay no attention. The señora is . . . (and he made a rotary motion with the index finger of his right hand, pointing to his own head). For whom have you come to fetch me?"

"For my grandmother."

"What's the matter with your grandmother?"

"Ay, señor doctor, she is very ill. She's dying. If the señor doctor would be so kind as to come right now . . ."

"Who is your grandmother?"

"I thought the señor doctor had recognized me . . . Josefa Alarcón, the señor doctor's housemaid . . ."

"Ah! The mother of . . . Yes, yes, I understand now, the one supported by Señor Don . . . Well! My head is . . . Ah! and you're her daughter . . . Fancy that! Your name is . . . Cecilia. I'm sure of it. Cecilia, Cecilia Gam . . . Well, all right, Cecilia Valdés. I couldn't possibly have forgotten. Except that since my head's turned into a gourd, things have gotten all mixed up. I have received the highest recommendations with regard to you and your grandmother. But here, between the two of us" (he added, lowering his voice) "pay no attention to what my wife has reeled off concerning me, you, your mother, your father, your wet nurse, and so on, because all these are things she's made up in her head. She's . . ." (and again he drilled his temple with the index finger of his right hand). "You know what I mean. Don't believe any of it. Cecilia Gam . . . I mean Valdés. You look quite a bit alike, a great deal alike . . . Ah! Tell your grandmother that I'll come as soon as the the gig is brought around. The driver must have gone to the wharf at Luz to bathe the horses. . . . If he hasn't taken a swig along the way, he'll be back any minute now; and behind you . . . Go. Tell your grandmother I'm coming. Señor Don, Don, Don . . . what I mean to say is that he pays well for services rendered him. . . . He's generous, lavish . . . Go this minute."

As Cecilia left, indignant and firmly persuaded that that place was a madhouse, in the literal sense of the word, the doctor gave her a piercing, scrutinizing look, and stood clinging to the grille, repeating half under his breath: "She looks quite a bit like him, a great deal, a very great deal! I was about to say that she's his living image. I didn't believe that she was as pretty as people have described her to me as being. An attractive girl! Yes, attractive, very attractive! Look! If we send her to the Jaimanita plantation with her mother, there with the Bethlehem padres. . . . What bedlam that would have turned into! Ha, ha, ha!" And he laughed like a real madman.

Montes de Oca promptly fulfilled the promise made to Cecilia, arriving at her grandmother's at nine that morning; thereby clearly proving, moreover, that he knew how to keep promises made to his friends.

To attend to the sick woman, since neither Cecilia nor Nemesia had any idea of how to do so, *Seña* Clara, Uribe's wife, had installed herself in the little house, and Montes de Oca was not embarrassed to tell her in secret the opinion that he had arrived at concerning the grandmother's illness as a consequence of the brief examination that he had carried out. In a word, an unfavorable prognosis. And although he did not divulge the reasons on which he based his prognosis with his usual frankness and certainty, it was clear that, in view of the advanced years, the misfortunes, and the rigorously ascetic and self-mortifying life of the sick woman, an approaching fatal end should be expected. In such individuals, furthermore, almost any illness, however slight it might be in the beginning, soon becomes a serious one.

The only thing that Montes de Oca spoke of in general terms was the fact that above and before all else, it was necessary to take strong measures to combat the comatose symptom manifested by the illness (it is certain that with the word "comatose" he left his listeners completely in the dark), and as a consequence, following to the letter the antiphlogistic method of treatment, very much in vogue at the time, he prescribed blistering plasters containing a generous proportion of cantharides, to be applied externally, one to the back of the patient's neck and the other two to the calves of her legs; and internally, an opiate to calm her nerves and try to bring on a restorative sleep, and no food until the inflammatory state of her cerebral fever subsided.

Bathed in tears, Cecilia saw the doctor to the front door, no doubt hoping for a word of consolation from him before he went off. But either he did not understand her, or else his mind was absorbed in matters that had nothing whatsoever to do with the grandmother's illness and the granddaughter's grief. The truth is that he merely told her that such distress did not become her, that "her friend" (emphasizing this phrase with a double meaning) had her very much on his mind, and that he would return in the afternoon to see how the sick woman was getting on.

Taking one of her hands, he placed a doubloon in it, without explaining from whom it had come, and as he left he gave her a hug that might be interpreted in several ways. Cecilia's attention was arrested by none of this; but since it was all done with the knowledge and sufferance of the evil-minded carriage driver, although he appeared not to have seen, heard, or understood any of it, one could wager anything that he went with his choice bit of gossip to his mistress Doña Agueda Valdés de Montes de Oca.

The doctor frequently repeated his professional visits. And why not? He had nothing to fear as far as being paid for his work was concerned, nor for the total due him either, which might be a substantial sum; and then too, Cecilia's tears, enhancing her natural charms, were capable of softening stone, all the more so since Montes de Oca's heart had nothing hard or stony about it. But if he really intended to succeed this time and cure the sick woman, he failed, in all likelihood by overtreating her. He remembered countless equally severe illnesses that he had successfully treated in the course of his long career; he searched through all his medical texts, among others the one published recently in Paris by Broussais, the father of the antiphlogistic method, entitled *Irritation and Madness*, which had caused such a stir throughout the world; he tried the infusions most highly approved of, poultices, ointments, cupping glasses, emetics, cathartics, leeches; as a last resort he prescribed the pill invented by Ugarte, thanks to whose heroic remedy he had saved more than one dying patient from death's talons. There is no doubt that if there had been more resistance and vital juices in the emaciated body of poor *Seña* Josefa, Montes de Oca would have subjected it to even more tests and experiments. After 12 or 15 days of fierce and tireless struggle, at least on his part, convinced that her final hour was approaching at a gallop, he handed the sick woman over to the arms of religion and withdrew with his honor intact.

His sudden withdrawal naturally came as a surprise, with all the more reason in that in the early hours of the night of January 12, a cold and cloudy night as it happened, the sick woman had opened her eyes and given other signs of life. However, since *Seña* Josefa had ordered that everything be readied for her death, there was nothing to do but obey her, inasmuch as she had recovered her senses again. To this end, Cecilia asked José Dolores Pimienta, who was keeping watch with her while Nemesia and *Seña* Clara Uribe slept, to go to the church of San Juan de Dios to have the holy oils brought. Meanwhile the young girl, losing neither time nor courage, improvised an altar in the sick woman's bedroom on her own chest of drawers, placing a white handkerchief on the dusty wooden top for lack of a better altar cloth, and a crucifix between two wax candles in their respective copper candle holders.

As the grandmother noticed her granddaughter's preparations, she asked her in an almost inaudible tone of voice:

"What are you doing, my child?"

"Doesn't your grace see?" Cecilia answered, trembling with fear and grief. "I'm making the altar."

"What for?"

"For the padre."

"Has the bell rung for Mass?"

"Not yet. But the padre will be here soon . . ."

"Why didn't you awoken me in time? I'm not dressed."

"Your grace can make her confession the way she is."

"Make my confession!"

"Yes, Granny, make your confession. Doesn't your grace remember that she asked me to go fetch the father confessor?"

"Ah, yes, that's true. I remember now. Well, my child, throw a shawl over me. What time is it?"

"Seven or eight o'clock."

"That late?"

At that moment the characteristic sound of the little bell rung by a young boy, announcing from afar the approach of the holy oils, was heard. Father Llópiz led the way, his joined hands held on high, walking between José Dolores and the church sacristan, each of them with a glowing lantern to show reverence for the Sacrament and light the way. As they walked along the streets, the people in the neighborhood appeared at the door of their houses, knelt on the ground, and also lit the way with a candle in hand. All these sounds and noises reached Cecilia's ears as the procession entered the Calle de O'Reilly, coming by way of the Calle de Compostela. Even the nuns in the convent of Santa Catalina, informed of what was happening in their neighborhood, had the death knell tolled, and in their fervent prayers commended the soul of the dying woman to the mercy of her munificent creator.

It can be said in all truth that *Seña* Josefa was not in her right mind and had not fully come to her senses when she made her confession, took communion, and received extreme unction. Had she lived a few more hours after those solemn and imposing acts, she would have been aware of nothing that had taken place. For her it was all the consequence of an inveterate habit. Otherwise, the sight of the scene that unfolded around her deathbed, as the padre was aiding her to die a good death, would have been so moving it would have hastened her death. Cecilia and Nemesia on one side, *Seña* Clara and José Dolores on the other, a worker from Uribe's tailor shop who arrived during those moments and the sacristan at the foot of the bed, all of them on their knees, murmuring devout prayers and lighting the sad scene with a lantern or a candle, formed an interesting, original tableau, worthy of the paintbrush of an inspired artist.

At the conclusion of the profoundly sad ceremony, all those present felt to some degree a sort of inner relief, since people in general believe that they are prepared for death. Even the dying woman gave every appearance of having come back to life, in view of the fact that she thrust her right arm out from under the sheets and began to grope about in various parts of the bed, as though she were searching for something that she had lost. Cecilia stopped her hand from moving and asked:

"What are you looking for, Granny?"

"You, my darling," her grandmother answered with great effort.

This tender solicitude, this unexpected answer brought a flood of tears from Cecilia, who turned her face away so that her grandmother would not be moved.

"Well, here I am, your grace," she said, squeezing the dying woman's hand.

"I couldn't see you," the grandmother added feelingly. "It's so dark . . . !"

"I put out the lights for your grace."

"Are you alone?" the old woman asked after a long silence.

"Yes, Granny."

She spoke the truth, for on hearing her, the other two women had withdrawn to the front room; and the men had not yet returned from the church, to which they had gone so as to accompany the viaticum.

"I wanted . . . to tell you . . . something," *Seña* Josefa said very slowly, after another long pause.

"Well then, tell me, Granny, tell me. I'm listening."

"Come closer. Why are you moving away from me, my darling?"

"I'm not moving away. Truly not. I'm right here next to your grace."

"Poor Charito! What will become of her? I'm leaving this world first. . . . I'm leaving."

"For the love of heaven, Granny! Don't upset yourself now, thinking about that. It does you harm, a great deal of harm. Calm yourself."

"Poor thing! But you . . . break off . . . relations . . . with the gentleman . . . He's your . . ."

"My what, Granny?" Cecilia, startled, pressed her grandmother for an answer, since she was taking a long time finishing the sentence. "My what, Granny dearest? Speak, tell me; in the name of the Most Blessed Virgin, don't leave me in this terrible uncertainty. Is he my enemy? my torment? my unfaithful lover? My what?"

"He's your . . . your . . . your . . . y . . . ," *Seña* Josefa went on repeating, at longer and longer intervals and in a lower and lower tone of voice, until the sound of the mysterious syllable turned into a lugubrious murmur and the murmur into a mere movement of her lips, which did not last long either. The illness had reached its culmination. She had breathed her last.

Cecilia had never seen anyone die, so that, on convincing herself through her sense of touch that her grandmother was no longer breathing, at the very moment that she had believed her to be most alive, horror rather than grief wrested from her a terrible cry and left her senseless. *Seña* Clara and Nemesia came running, and found her in the bed locked in an embrace with the corpse, from which they had difficulty separating her. Her immense grief was justified. From that moment on, her protectress, her companion, her tender friend, her kinswoman, her adored mother was gone forever; and to her even greater despair, she was now left forever with the remorse of having forgotten in the confusion to place in the hand of the dying woman the candle for her soul, so carefully prepared in advance for just this eventuality.

As long as Josefa Alarcón's illness lasted, the doctor kept giving Cecilia various sums of money, without ever saying a word as to the person from whom they came, money that she received with one hand and with the other passed on to José Dolores Pimienta, who thus became her de facto steward and cashier. During this brief period (very brief for someone who yearned for repeated chances to approach Cecilia and each day lend her new services), José Dolores was responsible, in fact, for paying all the expenses occasioned by the sick woman; and when she died he worked out all the arrangements for the burial with the well-known Barroso, the clerk of a religious brotherhood. Since there was not room enough in the little house on the Calle del Aguacate to receive all the visitors who would be coming to express their condolences to Cecilia, and to hold the wake, Pimienta arranged to have the body taken to the parlor of the house in which he and his sister lived, on the Calle de La Bomba, where it was laid out from ten at night until three in the afternoon of the following day. A catafalque was not erected: the deceased was dressed in her Mercedarian habit, the color of a sulfur match, girded with the usual black leather thong of the Order of La Merced, and placed in her coffin lined with black cloth, which was laid on top of an ordinary portable bier, amid tall wax candles and silverplated candelabra.

Master Uribe, with his workmen and friends along with Pimienta's many friends, kept vigil all night long, and at the burial hour they carried the bier with the coffin on one shoulder, relieving each other by fours till they reached the cemetery, situated in the little suburb of San Lázaro, at the end of the highway of the same name.

The only incident that somewhat marred the solemnity of the ceremony was what we are about to relate in a few brief words. The house in which the wake had been held was over half a league away from the cemetery, and the shortest way was not via the streets of the town, but via winding paths, shaded by the luxuriant trees of the villas and gardens that in that era occupied the entire area of what is today the vast district that goes by the name of Monserrate.

There where the modern church which gives the district its name is situated, there suddenly joined the funeral procession, trying to blend in with it, a mean-looking unknown black, who appeared to be exhausted from having run a long way. Behind him another man appeared shortly thereafter, on horseback, in a military uniform, with a wool jacket, a gold epaulet on each shoulder, and a cavalry saber. He was young, with a peculiar manner about him. With no hemming or hawing, he flung himself on the fugitive, and pointing his sword at his chest, cried out: "Give yourself up, Malanga, or I'll kill you."

"Tondá! Tondá!" came the shout from the men in the funeral procession who knew him by sight or had had dealings with him.

Trapped, then, between the tip of the saber and the bier on which the deceased was being carried, Malanga's only recourse was to deliver himself over to the mercy of his captor; the latter, without dismounting, tied the black's elbows together behind his back, pushed him forward, and with a military salute, his saber held on high, said to the mourners: "I hope you will pardon this disturbance, sirs. I was ordered by His Excellency the Captain General to catch this rogue, dead or alive, and I have carried out his order. Let the burial continue. To your good health, sirs."

The first stop made by the funeral procession was at the great grille of the Public Welfare House that overlooks the blue Atlantic, so that the orphaned inmates of both sexes could recite a prayer for the soul of the deceased, in return for the payment of a gold coin, offered as alms.

The second stop took place in front of the wrought iron gate of the cemetery, beneath the graceful arch at the entrance, so that the chaplain could sprinkle the coffin with holy water before consigning the deceased to her grave. As this final and inevitably sad act was performed, the mourners stood reverently, their heads bared, grouped around the grave.

José Dolores Pimienta, Uribe and several others cast a handful of earth down on the coffin of the one who in life was Josefa Alarcón y Alconado, noted no less for her beauty than for her misfortunes, her ardent motherly love, and the religious practices of her last years. The person first mentioned, who had headed the funeral procession, on thanking his friends and bidding them farewell, could not keep his eyes from growing damp, perhaps because there came to his mind at that moment the image of his idolized Cecilia, overcome with grief, lying in a faint in Nemesia's arms.

I I I

What is life?
I gave it up for lost
When like a wild beast
I shook off
The yoke of the slave.

J. de Espronceda

The Gamboa family returned from the countryside in the middle of January: the servants by sea, the masters by land. Leonardo arrived a few days later.

The first thing that Doña Rosa did in the city was to give María de Regla the document or permit allowing her to seek employment or a master. The paper in question (which is what it is called in Cuba by antonomasia), signed by Don Cándido, read more or less as follows: "This paper is to certify that I grant permission to my slave María de Regla for a period of ten days from this date to seek employment or a master in the city. She is a Creole, rational, intelligent and agile, healthy and strong, has never suffered from a contagious illness, has no known defect, knows how to do simple sewing, has a knowledge of laundering and ironing, and of caring for children and the sick. She is being given a paper because she has asked for one. She has known no other masters save the one in whose household she was born and the one who is now selling her. Havana (etc.)."

When this matter, which Doña Rosa considered to be of great importance, was taken care of, she turned her attention to the runaway black. She attributed all the blame for what had happened to the steward, the reason that at the first opportunity, showing him no respect, she subjected him to the following sarcastic inquisition:

"I presume that you have taken many steps to learn the whereabouts of Dionisio."

"Yes, my esteemed Señora Doña Rosa, many steps," he answered her, in embarrassment, for he was lying like a Turk. "It's just that those blacks . . . In a word, they're the Evil One himself. They know how to duck out of sight . . . there's no doubt about that!"

"Let's hear what you've managed to discover."

"Not much, señora, almost nothing. People have said that he was stabbed to death . . . but don't count on its being true. Because in view of the fact that no witness has been deposed, as far as I know, nor has the malefactor been apprehended or the dead man buried, I presumed, a well-founded presumption in my opinion, that the stabbing episode was a farce, a mere rumor, perhaps spread by Dionisio himself so as to disorient people and keep them from following his trail. I assure you, my esteemed Señora Doña Rosa, that those blacks know a lot, a whole lot . . ."

"I am well aware of that," Doña Rosa said spitefully. She then added: "But that black must be found."

"Yes, he must be found," Don Melitón said, echoing her words.

"He must be somewhere, dead or alive," Doña Rosa added.

"That's what I say too," the steward replied.

"You've said nothing useful," Doña Rosa exclaimed in annoyance. "Why hasn't it occurred to you to place a notice in *El Diario*?"

"It has indeed occurred to me, Señora Doña Rosa," the man replied, happy to be able to vindicate himself. "It has occurred to me more than once, indeed many times. Yes, señora, it has occurred to me."

"Well then, why didn't you have it put in?"

"Well, therein lies the difficulty, my esteemed Señora Doña Rosa. The fact is that I don't know how to write notices like that. I've never seen clumsier attempts than mine. It's understandable; there weren't any newspapers in my town."

"It's the easiest thing in the world. Don't you remember what Dionisio looked like? His build? His bearing? A native-born black, very dark-skinned, chubby, pockmarked, round face, badly receding hairline, large mouth, pug nose, good teeth, bulging eyes, short neck, an aristocratic air, occupation: cook, knows how to read, doubtless considers himself a free man, missing from his masters' house since such and such a date; a generous reward will be given to anyone who captures him and hands him over at such and such a place, responsibility for damages and injuries to be assumed, etc., etc. Everything just like the notices that appear every day in *El Diario*, under the epigraph or whatever its called, of . . . *Slaves and Runaways.*"

"Yes, yes, all that seems to me to be well put, Señora Doña Rosa. It sounds elegant when you say it, but once a person takes pen in hand and puts it all down on paper . . . I'm not ashamed to say, my esteemed señora, that I just don't have a knack for writing for newspapers. Of course, I wasn't born to be a journalist, and as the saying goes, he who wasn't born to be a married man shouldn't go around deceiving women."

"You're making a mountain out of a molehill, Don Melitón. Would you venture to repeat what I've just told you?"

"I believe I can do so. I lack talent but not memory; I have more than enough of that."

"Very well. Just so you don't forget what I told you, go to the print shop of *El Diario* this minute. It's on this same street, past the Rosario Arcades, a building with an entryway and two mirror windows, where at one time they used to play lotto for prizes . . . The print shop is inside. Go in and ask for Don Toribio Arazoza, the editor. You can't mistake him: he's an ordinary-looking man, pudgy, with a beard . . . He almost never shaves, always has a ready laugh on his lips, but not on his face . . . You know what I mean. Then tell him what I told you about Dionisio, because he knows how to write up notices about runaway slaves."

Once Don Melitón left, Doña Rosa raised her eyes, lifted her joined hands heavenward and exclaimed: "Ah! What a stupid steward my husband has! It's a miracle that he can walk upright on two feet."

On the latter's return from the print shop, the master sent him in a rented gig to the Camino del Cerro, to inquire whether Dionisio had been brought in to the detention center for runaway blacks which the Consulate of Agriculture and Commerce of Havana and the Island of Cuba had established, next to the elegant recreation area of the Count and Countess of Fernandina. The fugitive wasn't there, for the simple reason that the only runaway blacks sent to this general detention center were those who had taken to the hills from estates in the country and were caught alive by dogs, and who, out of ignorance or malice, did not immediately reveal the name of their legitimate owners.

Such fruitless inquiries were beginning to make Doña Rosa lose heart, when a black in a military uniform appeared at her house to ask her most politely to grant him a brief hearing. She looked over from head to foot with an inquisitive gaze, and said:

"Tondá?"

"The señora's most humble servant," he answered, bowing from his slender waist.

"What can I do for you?" Doña Rosa asked gravely.

"Does the señora not have a notice out about a runaway black?" Yes."

"What is the colored man's name, begging the señora's pardon . . ."

"Dionisio."

"Dionisio Jaruco?"

"No, Gamboa, since he is my slave. However, since he is a native-born black from the Jaruco family, it is not surprising that he should try to go by that surname."

"Just as I suspected. At the court ball given by colored people outside the city walls the night before Christmas, I met a black who said his name was Dionisio Jaruco. His physical features exactly match the description of him published in *El Diario*, and I believe it wouldn't be hard for me to catch him if the señora would grant me permission to look for him."

"I would give a reward of two doubloons, three, four, any amount of money, to anyone who captures him. He has committed a grave misdeed and I wish to punish him as he deserves. I fear that he will resist being captured. He boasts of how brave he is."

"The señora needn't worry about that. I'm going to bring him in with his elbows tied behind his back."

"My reward is guaranteed."

"Don't give me the money, give me only my rightful due. I am following the orders of my chief, the Most Excellent Señor Don Francisco Dionisio Vives, who, with the approval of His Majesty the King, may God save him for many years, has commissioned me to arrest black miscreants."

María de Regla left her house on the Calle de San Ignacio at an early hour; she knocked on the door of the best-looking house on the street, sent the paper in to the lady of the house, and as she sat on the doorstep resting, the reply came, predictably limited to the statement that the mistress of the house had enough servants and did not need any who were for hire. Among people of color it was considered demeaning to serve any other person save the master, an idiosyncrasy that María de Regla did not even suspect until after many disappointments and disillusionments such as the one that has just been mentioned. In all truth, she did not harbor the hope or nor did she have any intention of finding a master or a man who would hire her: both things were highly repugnant to her, inasmuch as she considered either of the two extremes as the greatest misfortune that could befall her. Had she been a woman capable of showing in her face at a glance her innermost emotions, the most nearsighted individual could have seen how she blushed for shame every time she took the paper out of her bosom to give it to the servant who came to the door when she knocked.

Her intention, her hope, her soul's most passionate desire on asking to return to Havana was to look for Dionisio in order to join him if he was still alive, or to take her own life if he had died. Therefore, far from regretting it, she experienced a sort of secret joy whenever they gave the paper back to her accompanied by a curt and decisive *no*. But the time limit that she had been given was not only short but fixed, and several days had already gone by in vain attempts to find an employer or a master; if it expired and none had turned up, what would her mistress, a woman who by nature dealt with her slaves so harshly and so sternly, do then? In these critical moments María de Regla's daughter Dolores revealed to her the essence of the conversation that Doña Rosa had just had with Tondá, whose name and deeds were on everyone's lips; and spurred on by the fear of losing her beloved Dionisio forever, she resolved to devote the few days she had left before the fateful time limit expired to fulfilling what was now the one purpose of her existence.

After making inquiries, she headed early one morning to the market in the Plaza Vieja, one of the two which in those days existed within the walls of the city. The market was a seething swarm of animals and various goods for sale, of people of every condition and color, blacks being predominant; a very small area, filthy, damp and dark, surrounded by four rows of houses, perhaps the tallest in the city, all of them, or the majority, consisting of two units, the lower one with wide arcades and tall pillars supporting a continuous row of wooden balconies.

María de Regla sat down at the foot of one of these pillars and leaned back against it, contemplating in melancholy silence for some time the multicolored, motley panorama of the market. Everything there was new to her. In the center was a stone fountain, consisting of a broad basin and four dolphins that intermittently poured forth streams of cloudy, turbid water that the black water vendors nonetheless collected eagerly in kegs to sell throughout the city for half a silver *real* each. From this center, radiuses or paths, none of them straight certainly, extended in various directions, marked off by the stalls of the market vendors, flush with the ground, grouped in no apparent order or category, for alongside one where fresh vegetables or garden produce were sold was another with live poultry, or fruit, or game, or edible roots, or caged birds, or legumes, or river or saltwater fish, still in baskets or bag nets just off a fishing boat; or fresh meat set out on ordinary planks mounted on barrels placed at each end or on sawhorses; and everything giving off moisture; the ground strewn with leaves, fruit peels, and husks of fresh corn, feathers and mud; not a roof or an awning, or a decent face; peasants and blacks,[51] some poorly dressed, others almost bare naked; whiffs of this or that everywhere; a strident and unpleasant hubbub; and overhead the blue sky, seen as if through a skylight, in which there appeared an occasional scudding cloud, taking on now the form of a transparent veil, now that of the wings of invisible angels.

Black men and women kept coming in and out of of the plaza; the latter to buy the daily provisions for the households of their masters, the former to buy meat, vegetables, or fruit wholesale to resell at retail prices inside the city or in its barrios outside the walls, this traffic, let it be said in passing, being quite lucrative in a fair number of cases.

There was something about the new Prussian blue cotton dress that María de Regla was wearing; about the way she wore the silk kerchief with which she covered her kinky hair; about the lustrous black color of her face and well-rounded bare arms that showed her to be a woman who was healthy and vigorous; about her overall look of an outsider; about the sadness or shyness that her face and demeanor revealed; there was something, we were saying, about all of this that could not help attracting attention, even of those persons who were indifferent and very much occupied by their own tasks.

But whether curious, sympathetic, or naturally observant, all of them, some entering the square, some leaving, cast a sidelong glance at the former nurse and went on their way. Her seemingly contemplative attitude (and certainly not her attire) made them suspect at first glance that she was suffering from a strange ailment, or that she failed to hold out her hand and ask for alms for the love of God from the passerby because she was too new at begging or too timid. Either of these reasons was enough to temper the compassion and dull the curiosity of the sort of people who came to the market. Only a heavyset black woman with a tendency toward obesity, and with a candid and happy face, who was leaving the market carrying a wooden vendor's box of meat atop her head had sufficient resolve to stop in front of the troubled stranger, asking her in a brusque voice, but with a kindly expression on her face:

"Ah! Po' soul! What you doin' sittin' here? What have you los'?"

"My husband," María de Regla answered straightforwardly.

The unexpectedness of the question had given her no time to hide the thought that was uppermost in her mind.

"Yo' husban'!" the meat peddler replied in astonishment. "Well, go look for 'im."

Her words imitated what children say as they play blindman's buff.

"That's what I've been doing for a long time," the former nurse replied with a sorrowful sigh.

"'Bout how long?"

"Ouf! Some 12 years."

"Oh, my! A body's lifetime. What yo' husban's name?"

"Dionisio."

"Dionisio, Dionisio! I don't 'member any Dionisio. Where he live?"

"I don't know. That's why I'm looking for him."

"You not from de city?"

"No, I'm not from the city. I've lived in the country for more than 12 years."

"Hmmm. You leave yo' husban' behin'?"

"I didn't leave him; my master and mistress separated me from him."

"You a slave, in't dat right?"

"Yes, to my misfortune I'm a slave. They banished me to Vuelta Bajo for as long a time as I've told you, and a few days ago they brought me to the city to look for a master or a person who would hire me. I have the paper here in my bosom. I've kept it with me for so long that it's dirty now. I've gone from pillar to post and haven't found anyone to buy me or hire me. I'm weary and worn out, and now I'm looking for my husband who disappeared from the house of his master and mistress during the Christmas holidays."

"Come wid me," the meat vendor said; and as they went up the Calle del Teniente Rey or Santa Teresa, she asked: "What yo' name?"

"I'm María de Regla Santa Cruz, your humble servant."

"Ah! You de daughta of Dolore Santacrú?"

"No. Dolores and I were slaves of the Count and Countess of Jaruco. On the death of the señor count, in his old age, we were sold at public auction in order to pay his debts and the costs of settling the estate. I had recently been married to Dionisio, and fortunately he and I were both

434

bought by Don Cándido Gamboa, a trader in slaves from Africa. Since then I've had no news of Dolores. Do you know her?"

"I knows her well. Dolore sell meat, sell fruit, sell everthin' and finely she buy her freedom. Den, Dolore get me out ob de slave quarter. I still yet has de mark right here. (On her right shoulder blade the initials G. B., made with a branding iron, could be seen.) Dolore buy a lil house and I sell meat, sell sweets, and sell everthin' fo' her. I works, works and buys my freedom too. De white man bring a suit 'gainst Dolore, Dolore bring a suit 'gainst de white, and de nodary, and de 'torney, and de prosecuta and de judge eat up de money, de lil house, everthin' what Dolore have. Dolore go mad and now she be shut up in San Dionisio."

"Poor thing! I didn't know anything about her sad fate. Mad! What do you mean by San Dionisio?"

"De madhouse what de govermint builded."

"It seems to me that if things go on this way, I'll be keeping Dolores company in the new San Dionisio asylum."

"If you wants work, I give you work to make money."

"I'm ready to do anything so as to earn money and see if I can free myself along with my husband and my children. Where do you live?"

"I lives in de Calle Ancho."

"Where is that?"

"Dere outside de walls. I got a husban'. We not be married by de church. He a peddler what sell water, an' I sell meat, butta, aigs, fruit, everthin' I kin sell."

"What's your name?"

"My name Ginoveve Santa Crú. My husban' Tribusio Polanca. He have a son name' Malanga what turn bad. He kill a white! Tondá catch him de way you catch mouse with cheese, on de Sunday afta de holy day of de Los' Chile, when he happen on de burial ob ña Chepa Alarcó.

"Chepilla Alarcón?" María de Regla repeated as a question.

"Yes, yes," Genoveva added. "De very same. Dat were her name. She losed a good lil house."

"Did she have a granddaughter?"

"Yes, she had one. So beautyful! So purty! I never seen a purtier one in all ob my life."

At this point, following the Calle del Aguacate, the two black women crossed the Calle de O'Reilly, and as they went past, Genoveva pointed out to María de Regla the little house, now closed up, where the old woman about whom they had been talking had passed away. In the very next street, the Calle de La Bomba, the woman leading the way turned to the left and knocked on the third door to the right with the usual street vendor's cry of: "Housewife! You buyin' somethin' today?"

The person who came to the door was none other than Nemesia Pimienta, known to the vendor only as a recent customer, and a total stranger to the former nurse of La Tinaja. As Genoveva handed her the pork, the butter, and the eggs that she asked her for, María de Regla, who had stayed a few steps behind, with her back to the door now closed, inspected at her leisure a fair portion of the parlor. With her back leaning against the wall facing the street, sitting in a rocking chair with her feet resting on the crossbar of the straight chair in front of her, was a young girl whom María de Regla took to be white. That was the color of her dress; but the batiste scarf around her shapely neck was black; also black was her thick hair done up in two braids crowning her well-shaped head; black the color of the fine iridescent wool slippers that imprisoned her tiny feet with a raised arch and a curving instep. This lovely stranger was dressed in mourning, outwardly and in her heart as well, to judge from the profound sadness revealed both by her face and her demeanor. From the garments visible on the floor, on the back of the straight chair and in her lap, it was plain to see that she was sewing, a task from which she did not raise her eyes save for the few moments when her companion, similarly occupied, had risen to her feet to open the front door and helped the street vendor deposit her heavy vendor's box on the threshold.

The occasion could not have been more propitious for fixing the bewitching image of the young woman in mourning in María de Regla's memory; and as a consequence, she immediately repeated in a low voice, following step by step behind her protectress: "Miss Adela! Miss Adela!," comparing in her mind the young woman's face with that of the youngest of her mistresses.

Since the meat vendor had heard those repeated words, she said in a reproving tone of voice:

"Ah! De name of dat girl not Adel. Her name Sesil."

It's best for me to hold my tongue, María de Regla thought, and did not say a word in reply; but she stood firm, unshaken in her belief that there was an extraordinary resemblance between her young mistress and the girl dressed in mourning in this house on the Calle de La Bomba, the features of which she kept well in mind for the first opportunity when such a description might prove useful.

The two black women went on wandering about the streets of the city until two in the afternoon; and in that time the meat vendor managed to turn the merchandise that she was carrying in her vendor's box on her head into money. They went out onto the promenade via the city gate popularly known as the Puerta de La Muralla and sat down on a stone bench, in the shelter of a leafy tree, between the old Café Atenas and the statue of Carlos III.

From a grubby little burlap bag, the mouth of it tied with a string, that Genoveva carried in her bosom, she took out and counted up a total of twelve pesos in Sevillian pesetas, *reales* and silver *medios*; once seven pesos, the approximate cost of the merchandise she had sold, were deducted, this sum represented a net profit of five *duros*. No knowledge of mathematics was required to make the calculation, nor any more convincing argument to prove how remunerative that business was. Convinced of this, María de Regla decided to take it up.

Later on, she spoke of what people were saying about her husband, about the wound he had received in a knife fight in that same barrio, and about his disappearance since the night before Christmas. Then Genoveva remembered having heard Malanga say that around that time he had taken in a badly wounded black he had found at the entrance to the Calle Ancha. The water vendor, who as will be remembered had passed by there moments before his malevolent son and not stopped because he thought the wounded man was dead had corroborated this rumor down to the last detail. When Malanga was put in jail, it was not easy to determine immediately who he was, nor what had happened to the wounded black; but María de Regla was convinced that the latter could be no one else but Dionisio, and she intended to put such precious facts to their fullest use.

At this point in the conversation between the two women, the young black soldier of whom we have spoken several times passed them on horseback and rode across the middle of the Campo de Marte, heading for the road to San Luís Gonzaga.

"Tondá!" Genoveva said, pointing him out to her companion.

The sight of him made María de Regla's heart skip a beat, despite herself. She thought she saw Dionisio in the talons of that intrepid young man carrying a sword, whom the law protected, and whom the prestige of his many heroic acts of courage made well-nigh invulnerable. She stood up, owing to some unknown impulse, and took several steps in the direction in which he was heading when she lost sight of him behind the cloud of dust that the hoofs of his swift horse was raising on the road in the distance, went back to her seat and without a word fell into a faint alongside her astonished friend.

This minor incident was the reason that it was some time before the two women went on their way once again. But the moment they entered the Calle Ancha, they noticed an unusual commotion and an odd movement of the crowd of people. Men, women and children were running wildly in opposite directions. Most of them took refuge in their houses, closed the doors with a bang, and appeared at the shutters of the windows to ask a neighbor or a passerby what the reason had been for those mad dashes, the slamming of the doors, and the outcries. One of them answered: a fire in Jesús del Monte; another: an uprising by blacks in the tannery in Xifré; yet another: a robbery in the Calle de Las Figueras; and then yet another: a dead man.

The last person to speak, the water carrier or vendor Polanco, was the only one who came close to the truth, confirming the news shortly after three in the afternoon, with many extravagant gestures and incoherent words. Since he was well known in the barrio, his appearance in the Calle Ancha was greeted with a running crossfire of questions from one window or another. This effort was pointless, for he had come *motu pro-pio* to announce the death by treachery of Tondá, in front of the shoemaker's shop on the Calle de Manrique at the corner of La Maloja.

Through Malanga, in detention in the public jail, Tondá had learned where Dionisio Gamboa had taken refuge and hastened to seize him with that confidence and carelessness that come from courage carried to the point of recklessness. Called to the door of the shoemaker's workshop by a man as well known as Tondá, Dionisio could not mistake his intentions, and immediately made up his mind what to do. He stood up from the bench at which he worked, and came forward with his hands behind his back, a gesture indicating surrender.

The movement forward on the part of the runaway caused his pursuer to make an opposite move, which proved to be fatal. As we have said, there was a considerable drop from the level of the shop to the street, and furthermore a hired gig had just then halted at the door of the shoemaker's shop and was blocking the way. In order to clear a space, Tondá, already dismounted, moved back a short distance; a careless move that the astute former cook instantly took advantage of to fling himself upon him and slit his belly from one side to the other with the same shoemaker's knife that he had been using to repair shoe soles. Badly wounded though he was, the heroic Tondá pursued the assassin, falling lifeless in the middle of the low street after taking only a few steps.

Almost all of the details of this account are historically true.

I V

What to dream of one's beloved
and what to suffer when he tarries
and what to fear when he arrives
and what to weep for if he goes away?

J. Velardo

On a morning in the following year's benign January, Cecilia's heart skipped a beat, and she said to herself: Aha! He's coming today. And from that moment on, she could think of nothing else or do anything useful. She peered out the window shutter countless times, believing in her anxiety that she would thereby hasten the arrival of the object of her worries; and an equal number of times, her soul and body swooning, she collapsed in the rocking chair leaning against the wall opposite.

She became all eyes and ears, to little avail. On the contrary, her senses were so muddled that when she listened she failed to hear and when she looked intently she failed to see. This explains why several seconds went by before she became aware of her lover's presence, filling the frame of the front door that had been left ajar, his adored image as if seen in a mirror. Then, completely forgetting her plans for revenge, her previous contempt, the supposed affronts she had received owing to his inconstancies and his departure for the country, she ran to meet him with open arms, kissed him, and let herself be kissed by him in the delirium of passion. Beyond all doubt, his brief absence had worked the miracle of turning the two of them into intimate friends, an affectionate brother and sister, the tenderest of lovers.

"Are you alone?" he asked her.

"Yes, I'm alone," she answered with a languid expression on her face.

"Were you waiting for me?" he added tenderly, still holding her about her waist in a close embrace.

"With my life and soul," the young girl replied in her amorous enthusiasm.

"Who told you I was coming today?"

"My heart!"

He kissed her again on her eyes and her mouth, and added:

"I find you pale, and thinner than when I left for the country."

"Do the days and nights that I spent without sleeping a wink watching over Granny strike you as being a mere trifle? Nor have other troubles failed to come my way . . ."

"When was your grandmother taken ill?"

"Granny had not been in good health since last year. But in all likelihood she began to be seriously ill on the night before Christmas. When I came home, around two o'clock in the morning, I found her with a fever that was going up and up . . . She never got out of bed again."

"Where had you been until such a late hour?" the young man asked in surprise.

"Somewhere or other."

"Where exactly?"

"Oh, somewhere or other."

"Will you tell me where?" Leonardo asked her, suddenly serious.

"I'm waiting for you to tell me first where you've been for all this time," she replied, no less seriously, trying to wound him with equally sharp words.

"You know where I've been."

"Yes, in the country; you just said as much. But did you go because I wanted you to?"

"Ah! You're feeling vindictive! Is that what's the matter? If so, you went 'somewhere or other' because you were piqued with me."

"No, I didn't go out of pique. And I'm not at all vindictive. Not the least little bit. What I don't want, what I can't stand is to be taken for a fool. You went off to have a good time with your lady friends in the country; was I supposed to stay shut up at home like a nun? That would be the last straw."

"I went against my will. I would have preferred to stay home, but Mama planned to take me with her . . . Didn't I tell you that?"

"That's what you told me with your tongue."

"I don't tell lies."

"Don't you have a mouth underneath your nose like all other men? Of course you do. Nobody tells lies. Certainly not! That would be a sin. But which of you men, if the opportunity arises, doesn't deceive the nicest woman in the world?"

"What would you know about that?"

"A great deal more than you imagine. The man who deceives me has to be very clever."

"Stop talking nonsense and let's forget about arguments that are groundless. You have an urge to look for reasons to complain. You haven't come up with any to be angry at me. Tell me, where were you on Christmas Eve?"

"Are you going to wring it out of me?"

"No, wheedle it out of you, my darling. I don't want even heavenly bliss from you if I must take it by force."

"All right then. I was coming home from the formal ball that people of color held at Soto's, outside the city walls."

"How did you get there?"

"On foot."

"I don't mean that. Who invited you? With whom did you go to the ball?"

"Uribe the tailor invited me, because he was a member of the committee, and I went to the ball with his wife Clara, with Nemesia, and with her brother José Dolores . . ."

Leonardo frowned and did not know how to or was unable to hide his displeasure.

"If the shoe fits, wear it," Cecilia said with a smile. "What will I say when I remember that you went to the country to chase after a peasant girl?"

"I see that you don't miss a single chance to mock me," Leonardo said, concealing his anxiety. "And it seems to me you'd be capable of loving any man just to make me jealous."

"Not that many, nor any so bald that a person can see their brains. There is any number of men I'd be unable to love no matter how annoyed I was with the favorite of my heart."

"It's a shame that you're so jealous and vengeful by nature."

"Be faithful and steadfast and you'll have nothing to fear from the most vengeful and jealous woman ever born."

"With jealous women the fidelity or steadfastness of the tenderest of lovers isn't worthwhile. They're even less worthwhile if you give entrée to men with whom you ought not to have dealings."

"To what man have I given entrée? Come, explain to me."

"Do you want to hear it from my own lips? Who took you to the ball when I wasn't here? With whom did you dance? Whose house are you living in now?"

"And is that what you call giving men an entrée?"

"At any rate that's the path that leads straight to a woman's heart."

"Not to mine, which is lined and studded with copper. But if there is anyone you shouldn't be jealous of, it's Nene's brother. There has never been anything between us, I believe, nothing more than a sincere and unselfish friendship. We've known each other and been together ever since we were youngsters. We've played blindman's buff and *lunita* together, and we've grown up together without thinking of falling in love with each other, at least speaking for myself. I know that he feels deep affection for me; I know that he's devoted to me; I know that his greatest delight is to be useful to me; I know that he's proud that he can guess my thoughts; I know that if I ask a favor of him he is distressed and blames himself because he hasn't anticipated my desire; I know that he wouldn't let even a fly hurt me; I know that he's capable of doing any sort of crazy thing so as to please me; I know that he thinks I'm the *non plus ultra* of women; I know that he feels so jealous of you that it's eating him alive; but thus far he hasn't made me a declaration of love. He knows, poor thing, because he isn't one bit stupid, that I won't love him or marry him as long as I live. I've often caught him looking at me the way a person looks at saints; I've acted as though I didn't notice or understand and he hasn't dared to declare his love to me. It's gone no farther than that ever since we've known each other. In his dealings with people he's most genteel, very courtly and respectful toward women, well-mannered toward men; all he lacks in order to be treated like a perfect gentleman anywhere is a white face. I am speaking to you about José Dolores with such candor because I fancy that he isn't to your liking, that you don't look favorably on him."

"You're wrong," Leonardo said, alarmed by the handsome portrait of José Dolores Pimienta that Cecilia had just drawn. "I have no bias against your friend. I don't look on him either favorably or unfavorably, for the simple reason that I don't care whether he lives or dies. A little tailor like that can't put me in the shade. I do regret, it's true, that in the present circumstances you've deemed it necessary to explain to me the sort of relations that have existed and continue to exist between the two of you. The matter doesn't interest me in the slightest."

"It's all right for you to talk that way, but it wouldn't be proper of me. I'd be the coldest of women if I were to forget for a moment the many favors I owe to José Dolores. He was my feet and my hands, my all, during Granny's illness; he did the errands; he went for the doctor a number of times; he brought medicines from the pharmacy; he made chicken broth for Granny; he kept watch at her bedside; he went to San Juan de Dios to have the holy oils brought; he took care of the burial arrangements; he wept as much as I did over her death. . . ."

At this point Cecilia's sobs and tears kept her from speaking. Then she went on as though offended by the tone and the scornful words that Leonardo had used in speaking of José Dolores:

"There are favors that cannot be adequately repaid; the woman who forgets them doesn't deserve the daily bread she eats. José Dolores has always esteemed and respected me, and he defended me at the ball, risking his life."

"Why did he defend you?"

"Because a black had offended me."

"Why did he offend you?"

"Because I refused to dance with him."

"You slighted him?"

"No. I didn't know him. He was an intruder . . . What reason would I have had to dance with him? What's more, I had promised to dance the minuet with Brindis. I didn't want to dance with blacks. The two or three pieces I danced with them was because I had promised to."

"What you did wrong was to attend a colored people's ball . . ."

"I know, I admit it, I'll regret having gone to it for the rest of my life. I believe it hastened Granny's death."

Cecilia began to weep once more; and Leonardo, either to put the idea out of her mind or to determine what had happened both inside and outside the ball, asked her:

"What class did the black who offended you belong to?"

"I don't know. I'd never seen him before in my life. He didn't know me either except through hearsay. I think he invited me to dance so as to have the opportunity to insult me and thereby avenge himself for what he took to be an offense to him on someone's part on my account."

"Who offended him?"

"He didn't say. He simply shouted that it was my fault that he'd been separated from his wife."

"He must have been a madman, or else he was drunk."

"No, he wasn't drunk, but he was undoubtedly a madman. He was frightening. He also told me that he'd seen me when I was still crawling on all fours, that he knew who my mother was and that he knew my father as well as he knew his own name."

"He could scarcely have known your father and mother," Leonardo observed sententiously, "inasmuch as you were taken in at the Foundling Home when you were an infant. How absurd!"

"Ah! Listen," Cecilia added, remembering: "he said that his wife was the one who suckled me, that I was a mulatto, and that my mother was still alive and was insane."

"Didn't anyone try to find out the name of that devil of a black?"

"Yes, they finally found out what it was. A worker from Uribe's tailor shop recognized him. He called him by the name of Dionisio Gamboa, though he maintained that that wasn't his real name; it was Dionisio Jaruco."

"Ah! The dog!" Leonardo exclaimed, clenching his fists and his teeth. "What a good novena of lashings he deserves! He's going to get it, as sure as there's a God in heaven, as soon as he's captured. Tondá is already tracking him down. There's no such Dionisio Jaruco; that's nothing but nonsense. His first name is Dionisio, all right, but his surname is surely Gamboa, since he belongs to Mama. The contemptible scoundrel, the ingrate, the vile miscreant, stealing Papa's old clothes and then on top of it running away and leaving Mama without a cook! Such shameless behavior has not been tolerated from any other black in the household. And just look at the result. He'll pay for it. Let him hide underneath six feet of earth, and they'll dig him out. He'll be punished as he deserves, I swear. I'm of the opinion that if they skin him alive it won't pay back what he owes. And then daring to insult you . . . !"

Carried away by his anger, it took some time for Leonardo to realize that he had frightened Cecilia by making such inopportune threats, besides making himself ridiculous in her eyes, for she readily noted that her lover's fury at the black stemmed not so much from his having insulted her as from his having left the Gamboa family without a cook. Backtracking, albeit too late, the young man added:

"All that aside, what did you have to do with Dionisio's separation from his wife anyway? Nothing, absolutely nothing. Even if you had already been born when Mama hid María de Regla, Dionisio's wife, away at La Tinaja because she behaved scandalously and was disobedient. And if you hadn't been born yet, how could she have suckled you? She did suckle my sister Adela. Come on, it was an absurd remark, a mistake on his part, a pretext to take out his anger on you since you couldn't return the insult."

"Be that as it may, it cost him dearly to meddle with me," Cecilia said with satisfaction. "After the ball was over, he waited for José Dolores on the corner of Calle Ancha. They got into a knife fight and the black fell to the ground after the first blows . . ."

"Was he dead?" Leonardo exclaimed, not expecting such a denouement.

"I don't think so. He lay there moaning loudly. Do you regret that he was punished for the error of his ways so soon?"

"No, no," Gamboa said, hastening to correct the error, that of noble-mindedness, that he himself had just committed by showing sympathy for his slave's having been wounded. "I don't regret losing a black. We have a great many of them. I do regret, however, that you found yourself in the middle of the whole thing. It was a scandal. You, involved in a murder! But to turn to another subject, who was the doctor who treated your grandmother during her illness?"

"Montes de Oca."

"How did he happen to be the one who treated her?"

"I went to fetch him."

"Did you know him?"

"By sight."

"Did he know your grandmother?"

"Yes, her he did know. Granny went to see him at his house and he came to see her every month."

"To treat her?"

"No. During her life Granny had almost never been sick enough to consult a doctor."

"What sums of money exchanged hands between them?"

"Granny received a monthly stipend through Montes de Oca."

"A monthly stipend! I remember now that a long time back Montes de Oca hired that same María de Regla, the wife of the cook, to suckle a baby girl, the illegitimate daughter of a friend of his and this explains Dionisio's mistaken impression. Of course: he thought that you were that baby girl. Naturally you weren't, but who was there to disabuse that ignoramus of his error? You hadn't even been born yet. And then after that, you see, María de Regla nursed Adela for nearly two years. What I can tell you is that the other baby that María de Regla suckled made Mama's life miserable. Montes de Oca promised to pay two doubloons to Papa as the price for his hiring her out to him. I suspect that he never kept his promise, because he's bad about paying money he owes. I find it strange, then, incomprehensible even, that Montes de Oca should give you and your Granny a monthly stipend. You don't know where it came from?"

"I don't follow you," Cecilia answered hesitantly.

"I'm asking," Leonardo replied, "whether you know the reason, the motive, or whatever it may be called, behind the monthly stipend that was given to your grandmother."

"I don't know; or rather, I've never tried to find out."

"You know and you don't want to tell me. I can read it in your eyes."

"You're a bad reader then."

"I firmly deny that Montes de Oca handed over the monthly stipend on his own account."

"I too deny that."

"Ah. You see? You knew that and you denied it."

"That wasn't what you asked me. You asked me whether I knew the source of or the reason for the monthly stipend, and I still have no idea. The only thing I know is that Montes de Oca handed it on for a friend . . ."

"A man you know, isn't that so?" Leonardo interrupted her.

"By sight," Cecilia answered, leaving it at that.

"His name."

"Ah. That is left for the curious reader to discover."

"Tell me, tell me," the young man urged, taking her hand. "I don't want to know out of mere curiosity, but for a reason that I'll tell you later."

"You know him as well as you know your own name."

"Who is he, then?"

"Your father."

"My father!" Leonardo exclaimed, stunned at the revelation. "Can it be possible that my father is persistent enough to . . . !" (He contained himself and then added): "Are you certain?"

"Absolutely certain.

"How long have you known him?"

"From the time that I was a little girl."

"How did you recognize him?"

"By seeing him in the streets. I kept running into him all the time. When I least expected it he was there, practically on top of me. He would get angry and say many things to me: that I'd turned into an incorrigible street urchin, badly brought up, and that he was going to have to have the soldiers come and get me."

"Did you know his name at the time?"

"No, I didn't find it out until much later, when I was grown up. He was never friends with me, but he was with Granny. He used to talk to her at the window till the cows came home, always about me."

"What did he say to her?"

"Nothing good, surely. He told her, for instance, to hide me from you, not to let me go to balls with you, because you were madly in love with me; that sooner or later you'd leave me for another girl; and finally, that you were planning to marry a very rich girl and were only waiting till you received your law degree."

"I'm surprised to hear that about my father. I wouldn't believe it if anyone else had told me. What's his real object in this whole affair? His behavior toward you eliminates the idea of love. He's not in love with you; that's not it. Nor has he ever been a man who fell in love because it made him feel happy. I'm losing all my illusions now . . ."

"Granny also was opposed to the relations between you and me. At the hour of her death she ordered me not to love you."

"You aren't thinking of obeying her, are you?" the young man asked in a burst of passion.

"It's too late now," Cecilia answered, blushing. (Then she added in a low voice) "God grant that I not regret having disobeyed Granny."

"You'll never regret having loved me dearly," Gamboa replied ardently. "I swear to it by everything I hold most sacred. I realize, meanwhile, that nothing of what you've told me explains the complicated question of the monthly stipend. Why, in the name of what saint, did my father hand it over to your grandmother? That is what exasperates me and drives me to despair. It may well be that he won't continue to hand it over to you now . . ."

"I think that's how it will be," Cecilia said, thoroughly upset.

"That's not the worst of it," the young man added on reflection, "but, rather, the fact that the doctor will charge you for treating your grandmother. Everyone makes firewood out of a fallen tree."

"My mind is at ease about that. During Granny's entire illness, instead of asking me for money, the doctor kept giving me some for the expenses."

"About how much did he give you?"

"Some fifteen doubloons. I didn't keep count . . . José Dolores . . ."

"Enough of José Dolores. I would like not to hear his name on your lips again."

"What do you have against him?"

The prolonged dialogue of the lovers was perhaps interrupted by the arrival of Nemesia, to the displeasure of all three. To Cecilia's, because she thereby remained submerged in the sea of confusions concerning her future fate into which the sudden death of her grandmother had thrown her. To Leonardo's, because after what he had learned as to Cecilia's position in that house, he realized that he must get her out of there as soon as possible or else lose her forever, and he had not had time to agree with her on a new plan for her life.

Nemesia for her part also experienced a keen displeasure, for on no other grounds nor with any other proof save the presence there of her brother's fearsome rival when she believed him to be farther off and oblivious of Cecilia, she remained convinced that neither the jealousy felt by Cecilia, nor its absence in Leonardo, had wrought the miracle of turning into hatred, or even into indifference, the profound affection for each other which the two of them professed. Poor José Dolores! Nemesia exclaimed to herself. So now you've lost her. What fools we were to have encouraged each other with the hope that he'd stay in the hinterland!

"It is God's will, my boy, that Cecilia is not to be yours," Nemesia said with great feeling to her brother when he returned from the tailor shop.

"What's your reason for giving me such bad news?" her brother asked in alarm.

"My reason is that *he* has come back. I came across the two of them this morning, as close to each other as fingertip and fingernail."

"Where?"

"Right here in this parlor. All by themselves . . ."

"Then *he* didn't go off to the country to get married."

"Get married!! He may well have gotten married and is coming back now to get his mistress."

"What! Do you think he's going to take her away from here any time soon?"

"That at least . . . So as to set her up in her own house."

"Not that at least," José Dolores said, highly annoyed. "No. If he means her to be his mistress, the sooner he takes her away the better, because I'd let someone spit in my face before I'd put up a false front for him. He's not a man to pull the wool over my eyes and make fun of me. He'd better not get in my way. Where is she?"

"Getting dressed there in her room. The fact is that she's expecting him tonight."

"That may be. So it'll be best if I step aside for the time being. A tragedy would cause her more grief than it would him."

"All is not yet lost, José Dolores," Nemesia said thoughtfully. "Where there's life there's hope."

"What hope, sister? It's either him or me. There's not room enough for the two of us. Or would I resign myself to serve as a false front for him? I think not, Nene."

"You're talking nonsense, José Dolores: get from a wolf what you can, even if it's only a hair. What man can truthfully claim that he's first in a woman's heart? You may safely say that she's neither steadfast nor of sterling character. First she says one thing and then later on another. She's as two-faced as the leaf of a star-apple: one side red, one side white. If you had heard her when he left for the country to go chasing after that white girl . . . you'd know what she's really like. As for him, I'll never love him ever again in my life! He'll never see my face again. Even though he kneels before me, even if he kisses my feet, I won't forgive him for what he's done to me. Even the most divine of men doesn't make a fool of me. He wasn't exactly the last one left in the world for me. There is any number of them; I have more than enough. How many, how many young men just as handsome as he wouldn't humbly beat their breasts with a stone if only I would love them? I'm not going to be one of those old maids left with nothing to do but dress saints' images or bring up nephews. I swear that the first man that says hey, hey, hey! to me, I'll say ho, ho, ho! to him. And we'll see who loses most; it won't be him or me."

V

He who spares his rod hates his son;
but he who loves him takes care to chastise him.

Proverbs 13:24

The moment to carry out the plan conceived by Don Cándido before he went off to the country had unexpectedly arrived.

The death of *Seña* Josefa had thrown Cecilia into the arms of Leonardo, who, his father knew, was not so guileless or so virtuous as to allow this opportunity to take her as his mistress to go by, on the pretext that he was protecting her.

Don Cándido looked upon this event as bordering on a catastrophe; the only way of avoiding it, to his way of thinking, was to remove Cecilia from Leonardo's sight and keep her from having any dealings with him, even if in order to do so it would be necessary to use force. But it occurred to him that perhaps he could accomplish the same thing without any commotion and without being held responsible so long as it was given the appearance of being legal. Motivated by this felicitous idea, he decided to consult the attorney and deputy magistrate Don Fernando O'Reilly, a friend and former classmate of Leonardo's, with whom he was on quite friendly terms.

As he walked in the direction of the Calle de los Oficios, he mentally composed a fairly good speech in the form of a dialogue in order to present his case in the best and most plausible light to His Honor the Deputy Magistrate. It so happened, however, that in His Honor's presence, the matters that he wished to discuss with him flew out of his mind like frightened pigeons from a pigeoncote, and all he managed to say was that the young Valdés girl had lured his son Leonardo away, used her wiles to seduce him, and was not allowing him to go on with his law studies, and that he wanted to know how the law could remedy such a scandal.

The magistrate heard him out with a smile of satisfaction and pronounced condescension, and said:

"How happy I am, Señor Don Cándido, to give your complaint a hearing! I am surprised and delighted. How could it fail to attract my attention and please me when you are the first to come to this court with a similar complaint since I have been presiding over it, by order of His Majesty, for over a year now? It is not, certainly, because similar cases do not occur in Havana; they occur by the thousands; it is because ignorance and the relaxation of morals are such that only attempts on people's lives and property, only those acts that are followed by immediate damage to another's person or possessions, are considered crimes. Attacks on morality, uprightness, good manners, religion are not crimes; they are mere misdeeds, venal sins, minor lapses that have no penalty that is laid down in any written code of law. What an error, my friend Don Cándido! What muddled ideas as to what is good and what is bad, what is honest and what is dishonest, what is permissible and what is forbidden, what is praiseworthy and what is reprehensible!

"Saco, in his *Study on Idleness*,[52] which has just been awarded a prize by the Patriotic Society, attributes to gambling—which he calls the den of our idle men, the school of corruption for youth, the tomb of the fortunes of families—the disastrous origin of the majority of the crimes that infest the society in which we live.

"I differ from so authoritative an opinion, and it is my judgment that the evils of which we all complain stem from two principal causes, namely, ignorance and the policy of the Vives government. There are no schools. And what are the consequences? Frequent robberies in broad daylight, murders without cause or provocation, interminable lawsuits, notorious injustices, the prostitution of women, social disorder. The policy of the Vives government is also the cause of endless corruption and malfeasance that are without parallel in the world. Common criminals rot in prison and great criminals go unpunished. And only rarely is the origin of the most atrocious crimes discovered, thanks to the fact that on a few occasions the malefactors are apprehended. Who killed Tondá?"

"What!" Don Cándido exclaimed, interrupting the magistrate. "Has Tondá been killed?"

"His belly was slit open with a knife yesterday afternoon."

"Does Your Honor have knowledge of the details of this regrettable incident?"

"No, señor. I learned of it last night at the theater, extrajudicially. All that is known is that the killer was a runaway black he attempted to arrest."

"I have reason to suspect that the murderer was my cook. A few days ago my wife put Tondá in charge of capturing him . . ."

"That would be nothing unusual," the magistrate went on. "Should he be apprehended, which is unlikely these days, I shall take the liberty of giving you a piece of advice: hand the slave over to noxa . . ."

"To what, Señor Don Fernando?"

"To noxa, I said."

"I understand. But who is that lady?"

"It is only natural that you are not aware of the term, since you haven't studied law. In legal terms handing a slave over to noxa means the act of renouncing ownership of him in favor of a court of law which then assumes direct authority over him and tries him for the crime or the damage that he has committed. You thereby lose a black who is worth at most five hundred pesos at a good sale, but you save the costs and expenses of the trial, which usually amount to twice that sum if the owner makes himself a civil party in the matter. It is a well-known fact that unless the palm of the justice of the peace is greased, he will begin proceedings against the criminal. Then the owner has to do likewise in the case of the court notary who certifies documents, of the judge who tries the case, who sometimes makes rulings as he pleases, of the prosecuting attorney who doesn't want to work for nothing, of the legal advisor, and so forth and so on."

"Me be a party in a lawsuit, Señor Don Fernando? Not on your life. I'd be better off hanging myself from a lamp post."

"You've made the right decision . . . But to return to your complaint . . . You were saying?"

"I was saying, Your Honor," Don Cándido replied as though he were waking from a dream, "that a young girl is driving my son Leonardo mad, is seducing him and casting a spell over him with her cunning stratagems and won't let him finish his law studies . . ."

"Let's take it one thing at a time," O'Reilly said calmly. "What is the name of the seductress?"

"Cecilia Valdés," the plaintiff answered timidly.

"Very well. To what class does she belong?"

"I don't understand."

"What I mean is: is she young or middle-aged? Married or unmarried? Pretty or ugly? White or colored? It is necessary for us to know all this before proceeding to the determination of the degree of blame and the application of the punishment that she deserves by law."

"I will tell Your Honor in all good faith everything I know in this regard," Gamboa said, stammering, his ears bright red with embarrassment. "The girl is young, quite young, I would say that in all likelihood she is barely 18. She has not been married; nor, according to what I hear, can she be described as ugly; rather, she's a pretty, a really handsome girl, I would say. She is poor, yes, poor, quite poor, and colored, though she can readily pass for white wherever her antecedents are not known . . ."

"Very good, perfect," the magistrate replied thoughtfully. "It is evident that you are familiar with the facts of the case. That is how I like to proceed. We can now consider the case with full knowledge . . . There is just one blank space, let us call it a doubt: namely, did you learn the facts that you are setting forth on your own or through a third person?"

"I know some of them from my own experience, others by inference, let us say."

"Let us understand each other. In the first place, tell me if you know with whom the young woman is living."

"At the moment, with some girl friend of hers, I suppose."

"No suppositions, Señor Don Cándido. Do you know that for a fact? Yes or no?"

"No, señor, I do not know it for a fact; I infer it."

"That's more like it. In a matter of this sort frankness is of primary importance. One must speak to a lawyer and a judge as one speaks to a confessor, from the heart. And, with whom did the little mulatto girl live previously?"

"With her grandmother."

"Are her parents alive? Does she have relatives, close friends of her family, protectors, in short, someone who looks after her? Since she is as pretty as you say, it is a good thing to know all that, to find it out in a timely way."

"Her grandmother died not long ago. Her mother (he added, stammering and his face redder than ever), her mother . . . I don't really know if she's dead or alive today. In any event, she would be of no help to her daughter if she were alive. As for her father . . . she has never known him. She was taken in at the Royal Foundling Home. Does Your Honor follow me?"

"Very well. Did you know the grandmother personally?"

"Yes, señor, I knew her, although I never was on intimate terms with her. It would be too long a story and inappropriate for me to go into details in this setting. I am certain, nonetheless, that for a woman of color (she was a mulatto) she led an exemplary life, that she practiced virtue, that she made confession and took communion frequently, that she brought her granddaughter up in the holy fear of God, that she kept close watch on her, and above all, that she would not allow her to go partying, to flirt with boys, or to be courted beneath her window."

"Then the girl we are speaking of is well brought up, leads a decent life, and has as yet caused no gossip."

"All that is true; except that, since she is of mixed race, her virtue is none too reliable. She is a little mulatto and as everyone knows the offspring of a tomcat chases mice, and wherever the kid leaps there leaps the she-goat that nurses her."

"Well put. Let us confess that our proverbs contain great depths of wisdom. Let us also confess that our mulatto girls, generally speaking, are frail by nature and by virtue of the desire, innate in human creatures, to rise in the world or to better their condition. And this is the key for deciphering the reason behind their liking for whites and their disdain for men of their own race. It is a good thing that I am speaking with someone who doubtless understands me. Nobody will have had better opportunities to observe the idiosyncracies of our free colored class than one such as yourself, who, owing to his long residence in this country, has long since adopted its customs. As a general rule, a strong presumption, a theory, however plausible and brilliant it may appear to be, as to the nature or tastes of these people or any others does not constitute a fact, nor does it constitute sufficient grounds for denouncing a crime, even a quasi-crime, which is what laws punish and law courts judge.

"Let us sum up. You appear before me, the municipal deputy magistrate, to bring a complaint against the Valdés girl—whom you accuse of the quasi-crime of seduction and distraction of your firstborn son, who is still under *patria potestas*,[53] you therefore ask that an arrest warrant be issued against the seductress, and that, without a hearing, she be punished by being deprived of her freedom. Agreed. Up to this point there is no apparent irregularity; the matter in question is covered by the law and you have every reason not to allow a harlot to lead your son astray and pervert him, especially when he is pursuing a career as honorable and noble as the one that leads to an attorney's robes. I applaud the vigilance and the severity of the principles to which you adhere."

"Your Honor is embarrassing me!" Don Cándido exclaimed, pleased at the different tack that his complaint was now apparently taking. "I don't deserve such praise. Not at all. I'm a hundred leagues away from deserving it."

"But (the magistrate gravely went on) as a just and conscientious judge, I require proofs of the crime; I hope that the plaintiff justifies his accusation, I conduct an interrogation in order to learn the antecedents and consequents of the accused, and far from calling for an indictment, I pronounce a most brilliant verdict: acquittal. Allow me, Señor Don Cándido, to tell you with my characteristic frankness that it is you yourself, doubtless impelled by the innate love of truth and justice, who have vouched for the conduct of the accused, praised her generously for her character, and defended her from all intimations of misconduct or a bad reputation, thus tying my hands, naturally, should I wish to bring an indictment."

Don Cándido, overwhelmed by the judge's unexpected remark, was unable to say a word for quite some time, merely wringing his hands and bowing his head. Then he said in a timid and confused voice:

"I swear in the name of my mother, Your Honor, that it never entered my mind that the matter was so serious. But indeed it is! So I wasn't wrong! Not completely! And I supposed that it would be a simple matter. Or is it not true that Your Honor is probing the subject where it's most painful, at lance point so to speak? I'm not certain, I merely think as much, Señor Don Fernando."

"Even though it is still a serious matter" (the magistrate said, with his usual equanimity), "issuing an arrest warrant against any individual who is merely suspected of having committed a crime is not what is staying my hand in the present instance; it is the fact that with your frank declaration you yourself have deprived me of the pretext that she could be seized in order to proceed with the appearances of legality. Provide me with the pretext and I will be your most willing servant, despite the fact that I am going to vex my friend Leonardo by playing a role in the abduction of his friend."

Confounded pretext! Don Cándido said to himself. Is it going to fail to appear when most needed? Then he added aloud: "Were it a question of boards without knots or warped spots, Señor Don Fernando, or of bricks without cracks, or of tiles without defects, Your Honor would find me sharper than a tack. But what do I know about judicial pretexts? Not one iota. Why doesn't Your Honor, who knows such a great deal, make short work of this matter and get me out of this quagmire?"

"Because that would not be legal, nor would appearances be saved, at least in the magistrate's heart of hearts. The suggestion must come from you. Meanwhile, I was thinking, Señor Don Cándido: suppose I issue a warrant for the girl's arrest that permits you to seize her and you have her put in prison or manage to hide her for a time; have you thought about the consequences?"

"Consequences!" the plantation owner repeated in surprise. "I give you my word that I haven't given any thought to what they might be. It hasn't crossed my mind that the step might have consequences for me . . . unless there is some fool who comes to her defense."

"Precisely. I say what I'm saying because I believe that she will have more than enough defenders."

"But didn't I tell Your Honor that she's poor, obscure, unknown, an orphan, alone in the world . . . ?"

"You also told me two things about her that are worth more than money, birth, kinship, and good connections: her youth and her beauty. Remember the words of Cervantes; they're perfectly to the point here: ' . . . beauty too has the power to awaken sleeping charity.' With help such as that on her side she will never be alone in the world."

"Running counter to Don Quixote's maxim, there is this other one whose author is unknown to me: 'A saint who is not seen is not adored.' I cite it because if I succeed in catching her, Your Honor may count on my putting her where not even the birds will see her."

"I say to you once again that all this is not as easy as it appears to be at first glance. Where would you put her so that no one would hear her, see her, pity her, and help her? Leonardo, if he is truly in love with her, will be the first to declare himself her champion, will search for her, will find her and rescue her, despite her captors. Would it therefore not be more honest, wiser, and more reasonable to leave the girl at peace at her house and not give rise to contention? Perhaps he is courting her as a pastime, or as a whim or because he hasn't come across anyone he likes more. What do we know about it?"

"What I know by heart, Señor Don Fernando, is that my son is very stubborn, as stubborn as a Basque, and that even though it is purely out of stubbornness, he may yet commit an act of madness and bring disgrace on the family."

"Disgrace!" the magistrate repeated in astonishment. "I cannot imagine such a thing. You say that the girl is well brought up, lives a decent life, is pretty and could pass for a white. What greater disgrace could befall you, your family, Leonardo, in a word, if forgetting himself, blinded by passion, in a moment of madness he takes the Valdés girl as his wife?"

"As his wife, Your Honor says?" Don Cándido exclaimed with a fierce gesture and a determined tone of voice. "Before he does any such thing I swear to God Almighty that I'll break his neck with one blow of a cudgel. No, no, I assure Your Honor, he will not marry the Valdés girl."

"Then what is the disgrace that you so greatly fear?"

"To put it in the plainest possible words, Señor Don Fernando, I do not fear, nor do I even entertain the thought that my son will carry his fatuousness to the point of taking the Valdés girl as his wife; what I fear, what I regard as a great disgrace for the family is the possibility that he may take her as his mistress. Those mulatto girls are devils."

"Isn't the disgrace to which you are alluding something else?" the magistrate asked with a smile. "Look at the subject from whatever point of view you like; either I am so obtuse that I am unable to discover what is so bad about his doing that, or else it is not, and never has been, the primordial cause of disgrace for a family, whatever its social position may be, if one of its bachelor sons takes as his mistress a girl from a class lower than theirs. If this were not so, Señor Don Cándido, what family on this earth would be happy? They would all have this same disgrace to regret or else a worse one. In every country where there are slaves the standard of morality is neither high nor the same for all; mores tend, on the contrary, to be lax, and what is more, strange, distorted, monstrous ideas, as it were, reign with respect to the honor and virtue of women. In particular, those of mixed race are neither believed to be nor are they expected to be capable of acting discreetly, of being decent or of being anyone's legally wedded wife. In the minds of the vulgar, they are predestined by their birth to be the concubines of the men of the superior race. This, in fact, appears to be their destiny. You should thank God, then, that your son, who apparently is obstinate and willful, has not taken it into his head to become involved with a little black girl. That would indeed be a disgrace for the family. Now then, Señor Don Cándido, why don't you forbid Leonardo to visit the Valdés girl? I find this easier and more reasonable, and above all, not as likely to cause scandal. The guilty party is the man who courts and chases after a woman, not the woman who remains quietly at home. And just between the two of us, my friend

Don Cándido, the fact that you are seeking to have the victim punished and the victimizer absolved has all the appearances of an injustice."

"The error stems from Your Honor's presumption that the Valdés girl is innocent."

"What proofs are there for presuming the contrary?"

"There are several. Among others, that of her having been warned to give up this love affair."

"Through whom was this warning given her?"

"Through her grandmother."

"In whose name?"

"In . . . my name."

"And the girl paid no heed?"

"What else would that far too high-spirited girl do? It has made her act even worse since that time."

"She has acted divinely."

"What! Your Honor is siding with her in her wickedness?"

"No indeed, I am not siding with her; I am doing her the justice of believing that she loves greatly and from the heart, and it is my opinion that in affairs of the heart it is not grandmothers or parents of the lovers who are in charge. Not at all: this matter must be brought to an end. Forbid Leonardo to visit the Valdés girl. Aren't you his father? Don't you have authority over him? You do? Then an absolute prohibition; no more visits to the Valdés girl, and the matter is ended."

Don Cándido was stupefied.

"Well then! Let's see what you can say to get out of this," he thought.

"Look; I was expecting exactly those very questions: 'Aren't you his father?' 'Don't you have authority over your son?' And I had a reply all planned. 'He's taken off.' No hope of that. Scatterbrain, scatterbrain, scatterbrain . . ."

"Señor Don Fernando," he added doggedly, hastily cutting his soliloquy short. "I lack words to explain myself with the proper clarity, but I shall try to make myself understood. The prohibition that Your Honor advises. . . . is impossible for me to . . ."

"Would it be an impertinence to ask . . . ?"

"I risk having the boy disobey me."

"Is that possible?"

"Indeed it is. Your Honor knows, doubtless, what Creole mothers are like with their sons, with their firstborn in particular, as is the case in this instance. She adores the boy. She has spoiled him so badly that she has been his undoing. He has become a good-for-nothing, a dolt; he is disrespectful to his elders and refuses to obey me. His mother, however, has been hoodwinked into believing that he is an angel, a meek little lamb; she refuses to believe anything bad about him and will not allow anyone, including me, to lay a finger on him. If it were up to me, he'd be on a warship, getting a taste of the lash. To my embarrassment, he isn't good at any of his studies; and his mother wants him to become an attorney, a university professor, a judge of the Puerto Príncipe Tribunal. And I don't know what else besides! It's of no avail for me to tell her that, what with our fortune and the title of House of Gamboa that I'm expecting to arrive from Madrid any day now, our son doesn't need to rack his brain for nothing over his textbooks. Although he hasn't even learned the first letter of the alphabet, he'll play a role in the world. Yet she's bent on making him a scholar known for his sagacity, and she'll get what she wants or else. . . . she'll explode. I keep telling her: before your son gets to be an attorney, a professor, and a judge, he has to have his bachelor's degree. The examinations are in April, and because the boy spends all his time chasing after that girl, he doesn't open a single law book, he doesn't attend classes. Then after he graduates this year his mother and I would like to marry him to a most virtuous and attractive young lady, the daughter of a countryman of mine and an old friend. Perhaps he'll settle down and devote himself to the administration of our numerous properties. My wife and I are getting on and the two of us will die one of these days; we are all death's children. Who will take the helm then? He, the man in the family, should be the one, not one of his sisters, weak women and as yet unmarried. Does Your Honor understand what a disgrace it would be for us if our firstborn, the son who will bear the family name, the title of nobility, the responsibility for the administration of our estate, and so on and so forth, doesn't study, doesn't receive his degree, doesn't marry the young lady whose hand he has asked for, and instead, infatuated as he is with the Valdés girl, takes her as his mistress? Without Your Honor's help in these distressing circumstances, what will happen to the peace and happiness of my family?"

"So then, Señor Don Cándido, you have spoken up on behalf of the future," the magistrate exclaimed. "Why didn't you put those arguments forward from the beginning? There is no possible rejoinder to your last point in particular; it convinces the coldest and stubbornest mind. I admit defeat, and from this point on I am at your orders. What do you want done with the Valdés girl?"

The magistrate's last words made a strange and profound impression on the rich landowner. He remained stock-still and downcast for a long time, unable to move or to speak. What was happening to him? He had attained the object of his plea. What more could he want? Had he repented of his intention in coming? Was he beginning to feel the weight of the responsibility that he was about to take on? Did he doubt that the measure he had argued for would succeed? Did he regret that he would cause his son great sorrow? That he would be doing a grave injustice to the girl? Was he now afraid of causing a scandal? It is not easy to explain what he was experiencing. He himself, had he been asked, could not have described his feelings.

Since the magistrate had noted his perplexity, he repeated his previous question with greater emphasis.

"I don't know," Don Cándido replied slowly; "I really don't know. As for putting her in prison . . . I would have to give it a great deal of thought. It would be too much for the poor girl. I was considering hiding her away on my cattle ranch at Hoyo Colorado . . . The overseer there is married, with little children, and the place is a fair distance away; yet several great, insuperable difficulties present themselves. No, no, perhaps it would be better to put her on the plantation of a friend of mine who knows the girl and knows the situation . . . Near here: in Jaimanita. He too is married . . . and getting along in years. Incapable of . . . What does Your Honor think?"

"I don't think anything, Señor Don Cándido. You are the one who must give thought to the matter and make up your mind. My responsibility is to issue the arrest warrant as soon as a request for it is presented to me in due and proper form."

"What does Your Honor mean by 'due and proper form'?"

"I mean that I expect the interested party to present me with the complaint in writing."

"But hasn't Your Honor heard my complaint in due and proper form?"

"That is not sufficient; it is necessary to put it in writing."

"And would it have to be signed?"

"Naturally."

"May I be tarred and feathered if it had ever occurred to me that such requirements had to be met . . . Couldn't the matter be taken care of in some other way, extrajudicially? I have a fear of legal formalities."

"This category of misdemeanors cannot be handled *ex oficio*. In order that you may see that I wish to be of service to you, I am going to point out to you how it could be done."

"Let us hear it. Your Honor knows more about such things than I do."

"In what barrio does the Valdés girl reside?"

"In El Angel."

"Do you know the commissioner of that district?"

"Yes, señor. I understand that it's Cantalapiedra."

"He's the one. Now then. Go see him, present the complaint to him and tell him to send me a comprehensive official communiqué regarding the case. He knows how such documents are drawn up."

"Very well, I'll go see him this very day; but is there no way to keep my name from appearing?"

"It doesn't matter, man," O'Reilly answered, close to being annoyed. "The matter won't go beyond the three of us. I'll shelve the communiqué just as soon as I read it; the commissioner can be made to keep his mouth shut and be stimulated to proceed with discretion and zeal by placing a few gold coins in his hand, and you know, just as everyone does, that people who know how to keep quiet are traditionally called Sancho—or perhaps it's Santo."

"I understand. Where do we put the girl?"

"That is my responsibility. It will be in a place where neither her decency nor her person will be in any danger, and at the same time she will be safely confined and no one can get her out without my permission or yours."

"It won't be in jail."

"No, surely not."

"Much less in Paula Hospital."

"Not in Paula either, for obvious reasons. In a word, I'll put her in Las Recogidas, in the district of San Isidro, with a good recommendation to the Mother Superior."[54]

"Very well. Young men are not admitted there, I presume."

"Not that I know of. Perhaps an occasional employee. Now then, for how long do you wish her to be confined?"

"For six months."

"That is the usual period: six months."

"Let's see. I think a year would be better. That's a long time, but my son will not receive his bachelor's degree until April and won't marry until November. Yes, a year."

"Done. As far as I'm concerned," the magistrate concluded solemnly, "what is least important is how long she is to be confined, and what is most important is the injustice, the great haste, the arbitrariness of what is being done to this girl. Please know, Don Cándido, that I am not doing this out of consideration for you, whose friendship does me honor; I am doing it out of respect for the final words of your peroration of a few moments ago: 'for the peace and happiness of the family,' things that I hold sacred."

> *To try to block the path*
> *of two who love each other dearly,*
> *is to throw wood on the fire*
> *and sit down to watch it burn.*

Popular song

On the pretext of having to get a certain friend out of a debt backed by his word of honor, Leonardo managed to convince his wonderfully kind mother to make him an irreclaimable loan of fifty doubloons from her personal coffer.

With this small sum of money the young man hastened to rent a little house on the Calle de las Damas and went about furnishing it with equal haste. He forgot nothing, nor did he neglect to have the things done that he thought necessary in a single central unit with no outbuildings, something that did not exist elsewhere at the time in Havana. In order to take care of all this he visited the secondhand shops in the Plaza Vieja; the hardware shops on the Calle de Mercaderes; the tinsmiths' shops on the Calle de San Ignacio; the china shops on Ricla or Muralla; a secondhand furniture store on San Isidro and others closer to his new house.

It was really strange that this lad, the living incarnation of laziness, fickleness, and selfishness, should at a given moment display the activity, the taste, the dexterity, and the intelligence of an industrious and perfect housekeeper! But he was moved by a boundless passion and was inspired by the bewitching image of the young girl whose ruin he had decided upon in the darkest depths of his prurient heart.

These arrangements having been completed, and highly satisfied with his handiwork, he left the house early one afternoon in the windy month of March, locked the door, placed the heavy iron key to it in the pocket of his tailcoat, and with a light step, his heart beating harder than usual, he went in search of the rare bird whose beautiful plumage was to adorn that cage and turn it into a paradise with her warbles of love.

But instead of the rare bird he was chasing after on the wings of desire, he met up with a species of harpy, with Nemesia, standing motionless and cold in the middle of the parlor of the house in the Callejón de La Bomba, like a statue of a mourner in a cemetery. He repressed his displeasure as best he could and forced himself to be more friendly and polite with Cecilia's companion and friend.

"What does my saintly mulatto say?" he asked her, bowing obsequiously to her.

"This mulatto says nothing because she's not saintly," she answered without moving.

"Then I'll say something," Leonardo retorted cheerfully.

"The gentleman may say whatever he pleases."

"Do you have your head screwed on straight today?" the young man asked, examining her face closely.

"No less so than yesterday or at other times."

"Nene, this is a trick, and it's easy to see through. You have a more serious expression on your face than if you were contemplating the mere pinch of spices that the smallest coin that circulates in Cuba will buy."

"I laud the gentleman's insight."

"That's going too far."

"A person isn't always in the mode for joking." (She meant "mood.")

"Speak or sing clearly, you wretched mulatto," Leonardo added in a loud voice so that Cecilia would hear him if she was in the room next door. "I don't like it when people beat about the bush."

"Nor do I," Nemesio replied.

"In a word, Nene, if I'm the one you're angry at, out with it. The sooner the better, because I fear your anger more than I fear a naked sword."

"The gentleman is unrecognizable when he does what he's doing."

"And what am I doing?"

"You're asking me? Put your hand on your breast."

"I'm thrusting it inside up to my elbow and I don't come up with anything, nothing against you at least."

"Not against me, against God and the Virgin, who are looking down from heaven upon the gentleman."

"Are you speaking in all sincerity? Not that I've committed a grave sin without knowing it."

"So it seems, since once the gentleman has finished doing what he's just done he shows up at this house as cool and collected as though he were as innocent as a newborn babe."

"Am I not being discreet when I come visiting?"

"The gentleman gives little hint of it."

"One of the two of us must have lost our senses. Let's get to the bottom of this once and for all: call Celia."

"I should be the one to call her, is that right?" Nemesia exclaimed with a sarcastic smile. "What courage, the gentleman has!"

"Is courage required to ask you to call your beloved friend?"

"What takes courage, a great deal of courage, is for the person who knows where she is to ask after her."

"And do I know where she is any better than you do? Come, Doña Josefa or Doña Nemesia, don't do this to me. You're making fun of me."

"Anyone who is hopping mad is incapable of making fun of anyone."

"Well, if Celia isn't here, where is she?" Leonardo asked, genuinely alarmed.

"I'm telling the gentleman," Nemesia replied angrily, "that I wasn't born yesterday, nor am I simpleminded."

"For the love of God, Nene, I swear to you that I haven't had any news of Celia for four days now. Have the two of you had a row? Has your brother humiliated her? Ah! Tell me, tell me, for heaven's sake: what has happened between the two of you? What do you know?"

Nemesia began then to believe in the sincerity of the young man's anxious words, and said in tears:

"I wasn't here, and I'm happy now that I wasn't, because I don't know what I would have done to keep them from taking Celia away."

"Taking her away!" Leonardo repeated, fearful and furious. "Who could have taken her away against her will?"

"I fancy she was so afraid that she lost the strength to resist."

"Afraid! Why? Of whom?"

"Of the commissioner."

"What did the commissioner want of Celia?"

"He came to arrest her."

"To arrest her without her having committed a crime? That can't be . . . Ah! There's been a trick, an intrigue, an odious plot afoot to take my Celia from me. Tell me what happened, everything."

"I wasn't here," she repeated, "but a woman who lives in the building who saw what happened told me that yesterday afternoon Cantalapiedra suddenly came in, asked for Celia, and as soon as she appeared, told her that she was under arrest, grabbed her by one arm, and without further ado took her off somewhere."

"What's odd is that Celia would allow herself to be arrested without defending herself, without finding out the reason for her being taken to prison. Not that she would have been sensible and agreed to go along with him! That's something I refuse to believe. Woe to that miserable constable who laid a hand on her! You don't know where she was taken?"

"José Dolores and I haven't been able to find out a thing. The commissar took Celia away in a gig."

"What a plot! As infamous as it is bold. But I'll find out the truth, and whoever is the author of this outrage will pay for it many times over."

Without further ado, Leonardo hurriedly left to go look for Commissioner Cantalapiedra, who, as we have said, lived on the side of Angel Hill that overlooks La Muralla. He was not at home, and his mistress informed the young man that he might be at the Palace of Government receiving orders.

As he headed in that direction, it occurred to Leonardo that if Cecilia had been arrested by means of a warrant issued by the municipal magistrate, they could not have taken her anywhere except the prison (situated at that time in the southeast corner of the Palace of the Captaincy General), and so he stopped before the grille in front of it.

Behind it, or rather, in the cage formed by the two iron grilles, a man, badly dressed and worse looking, was standing. With the aim of obtaining a definite answer, Leonardo confronted him and asked him, with an air and a tone of authority:

"Do you know whether a pretty white girl dressed in mourning was brought to this Royal Prison yesterday . . . ?"

"I don't know," the man answered. "I'm the assistant prison guard and I wasn't on duty yesterday. The señor should look in the magistrate's book."

"The magistrate's office is closed."

"That's because the magistrate has gone home to have supper. The señor will have to wait until tomorrow because I'm just waiting for the clock at La Fuerza to strike to be relieved by the reserve officer and get the hell out of here."

"Who's that black who's having a lively conversation with other prisoners in the middle of the prison yard?"

"Which one does the señor mean? The one in the white jacket?"

"Yes, that's the one."

"They call him Jaruco."

"An assumed name, is it not?

"Well, his real name isn't Jaruco; it's just one that stuck; but it's the one they put down in the book and that's what his name will be while he's in this Royal Prison. He was put in the hoosegow day before yesterday. Does the señor know him?"

"I believe so. Call him over to the grille for me, if you don't mind."

"There's nothing to keep me from it, because even though he's being held incommunicado, there are so many prisoners we no longer have enough cells for 'em. Hey, Jaruco!" the prison guard called from his post.

And once the word had been repeated by other prisoners in the same tone of voice, Jaruco came over, recognizing his young master with no difficulty. The slave was thereupon seized by such a strong convulsive tremor that he had to grip the grille with both hands.

"I beg your grace to give me his blessing," he stammered, bathed in tears.

"Why are you weeping?" Leonardo asked him angrily.

"I am weeping, young master Leonardito, remembering the hard time I've no doubt given the family by being absent."

"By being absent, you cur? You mean by running away."

"I didn't run away, master Leonardito. My reason for leaving the house on the night before Christmas was to attend a ball given by the people of color outside the city. On the way back to the city I had a fateful knife fight with a mulatto. I was wounded in the chest, and an acquaintance picked me up in the street and took me to the room where he lived. While I was recovering thanks to his care time went by. And then after that this misfortune happened to me."

"What misfortune?"

"That of being unjustly imprisoned. All of us men risk being victims of a stroke of bad luck."

"Not of bad luck, but of bad judgment. It's evident, Dionisio, that you blacks don't love people out of goodness but out of wickedness. If Mama had packed you off to the plantation when you pulled the dirty trick in question, you wouldn't find yourself in prison now. What crime are you accused of?"

"I still don't know the reason for my imprisonment, master Leonardito."

"You don't know, eh? Isn't it perhaps for the death of Tondá?"

"It may be that people bear false witness against me concerning his death, master; because anybody who runs out of luck can fall headlong and kill himself. Imagine the situation, master: there I was, sitting very calmly making shoes in a workshop on the Calle de Manrique, when Captain Tondá appeared at the door. As soon as I saw him there, I realized that he was coming to get me, and I tried to slip away. He got off his horse and I went toward him as if I were trying to turn myself in. A gig had stopped at the door of the shop and I sneaked between it and the wall of the building. Tondá took off after me shouting: "Give yourself up, give yourself up! Stop!" He stumbled on a stone, fell on the saber that he was carrying unsheathed and slit his belly open. Was I to blame for his death?"

"Who arrested you?"

"The district captain of La Salud. He caught me as I was leaving for work."

"I presume he told you why he was arresting you."

"Not one word. All he told me was that he had an order to bring me in, alive or dead."

"You've gotten yourself into real trouble, Dionisio. They'll be hard on you and you'll thank God if you manage to save your skin."

"May God's will and the Virgin's be done. I have faith in my innocence. But doesn't master Leonardito believe that the master and Señorita will do something on my behalf?"

"What will they do? Nothing. Don't get your hopes up. You certainly have behaved decently toward your masters! For their sake, for that of the whole family, for your own sake, Dionisio, it'll be best if they garrote you on the barren field of La Punta. Then you'll never again insult white girls."

"Have I insulted a white girl or a colored one, master? No, master Leonardito, I'm not aware of having insulted a one."

"What about the one who was the cause of your fight with the mulatto after the ball let out?"

"I didn't insult her, master. I swear by the bones of my dead mother that I didn't say one bad word to her. I asked her to dance a minuet with me; she said she was tired and then went out on the ballroom floor to dance with José Dolores Pimienta. I complained to her about her slighting me, he came to her defense, we exchanged words and had at each other out in the street."

"If they let you have your say they won't hang you. To change the subject. Do you know if the same young girl who was the cause of your fateful fight with Pimienta has been imprisoned here?"

"I'm certain she's not here. The minute a prisoner sets foot in the prison yard, the news spreads and his or her name is shouted from one to another."

"God protect you, Dionisio."

"Master, have pity on me: one word more. I'm remembering that I should give your grace something that belongs to him."

"What is it? Make it short and tell me quickly, this minute."

"I had been keeping in my pocket, in the hope of giving it back to you some day, the watch that Señorita gave your grace as a present last year; but they took it away from me when I entered this prison. It must be in the magistrate's possession."

Dionisio told, in the fewest words possible, just how and when the watch came into his hands, and as his young master left, he said, deeply moved:

"Could Master Leonardo tell me how María Regla is?"

"Mama brought her back from the plantation. She is now in the city earning a daily wage. Haven't you seen her?"

"No, señor. This is the first news I've had of her return to the city. Why was it not God's will that I should run into her? I wouldn't find myself in this jail today if I had. She would have served as my protectress with Señorita and I'd be cooking in the kitchen."

Night had already fallen when Leonardo went to the commisioner's home and surprised him as he was about to sit down at table to eat supper with his mistress.

"Hello! So good to see you here!" Cantalapiedra exclaimed very cheerfully, coming to the door to meet Leonardo, with his open hand outstretched.

"I'm glad to find you home," the latter said coldly and gravely, pretending not to have noticed the commissioner's show of friendship.

"I was waiting for you," Cantalapiedra added, concealing the bad impression made on him by this slight. "Fermina was just telling me that you had honored this humble refuge with your presence."

"May I have two words with you?"

"And 200 more besides, Señor Don Leonardito. You know that I am your most obedient servant. I regret not having been at the commissariat when you came there at dusk. I had been obliged to rush to the Political Secretariat. So I've no idea how we didn't happen to meet on the way if you were coming from there. 'Bonora!' he shouted, 'a chair for this gentleman.'"

"Spare the polite formalities," Leonardo said haughtily. "There is no need for me to sit down. Let us speak together standing up so that we can be by ourselves."

"Why not right here in front of Fermina? I have no secrets that I keep from her. We're inseparable."

"With what authority did you arrest Cecilia Valdés?" the young man asked imperiously.

"Not with that vested in me by His Majesty King Don Fernando VII, may God save him, but with that of the estimable municipal magistrate who signed the arrest warrant after hearing a complaint from the head of a family."

"What magistrate and what head of a family, if you will be so kind as to tell me?"

"That is asking too much by half, Señor Gamboa," the commissioner answered with a laugh. "It looks to me as though you are rather upset . . . Sit down and calm yourself."

"The girl has committed no crime, hence putting her in prison is improper and illegal, unless the whole thing has been nothing but a farce, or something worse, heaven only knows to what end."

"None of this can be blamed on me, for I have been a mere instrument in this matter."

"If you are not to blame, tell me the name of the complainant."

"You know it better than I do, and if not you will find it out shortly."

"Is it perchance within your power to reveal the name of the magistrate?"

"There is nothing that prevents that: Señor Don Fernando de O'Reilly, a first-class grandee of Spain, the municipal magistrate of the district of San Francisco . . ."

"Where did you take the girl? She's not in the public prison."

"I am not allowed by law to reveal her whereabouts at present. I took her to the place where I was ordered to take her."

"Then you are hiding her with dishonest intentions."

"Such an offensive deduction does not follow from my refusal to satisfy your curiosity. Logic, logic, señor philosophy student."

"It matters little that you wish to appear to be secretive and mysterious with me. I shall find out the truth, and it may still weigh heavily on the author and the instrument of this gross and indecent intrigue."

This said, Leonardo left for home in a rage. The family had a caller in the drawing room. Without entering it, he ordered the carriage to be readied for him and changed clothes, and when his mother gestured to him at the grille of the *zaguán* to ask him the reason for his haste, he answered curtly:

"I'm going to the opera."

Rossini's *Ricardo e Zoraida* was being staged as a benefit performance for the Santa Marta Women's House of Correction, in the handsome

Teatro Principal. The manager of the company at that time was Don Eugenio Arriaza, and the orchestra conductor Don Manuel Cocco, the brother of Don José, whom we have already met at La Tinaja. The orchestra and the boxes were only half filled with an audience that was not at all keen on opera at the time. Leonardo entered the theater a little after the curtain rose. Naturally he did not hear the overture to *Tancredo*, which preceded the opera being performed that night.

He was looking for a man whose seat in the theater was known to him beforehand, for as deputy municipal magistrate he was to preside over the performance from the main box, on the second floor. He was seated in it alongside his wife from Madrid, absorbed in the music and the singing, as his mulatto page, acting as his guard, in full livery, embroidered with castles and lions in gold, stood next to the door. Leonardo observed all this through the bull's-eye window of the door to the box that closed it off from the corridor. He could have called to him, certain of being admitted to the box and of a friendly reception, but he preferred to wait on the balcony of the refreshment room that overlooked the Paula promenade.

According to Leonardo's calculations, it was shortly before the first act was over that he heard measured steps crossing the room, then felt a hand on his shoulder and immediately thereafter heard a dramatic voice declaim: "What says the friend of the valiant Othello?"

"Ah! Is that you, Fernando? The farthest thing from my mind."

"What are you doing out here all alone and so deeply absorbed in thought?"

"I've just arrived."

"I didn't see you in any of the orchestra seats. Why didn't you come straight to my box?"

"I presumed that there wasn't a place for me."

"For you there is always a place right next to me."

"Thank you."

"Are you in the midst of being seized by inspiration? The oracular tripod of the priestess of Apollo at Delphi? I'm glad. I would regret interrupting you."

"Me inspired! Perhaps: by the devil."

"There would be nothing strange about your being inspired by the urbano-marine scene unfolding beneath this balcony. I'll wager that you were composing in your mind an article describing it, am I right? Without a doubt. In fact, who is there who harbors within himself the soul of a poet who is not inspired by the sight of that line of houses of different levels on our right, on which the tall balconies of the ancestral home of the Count of Peñalver stand out? Or of that of this treeless promenade that ends at the Cafe de Paula, now dark and deserted? Or of that of the hospital of the same name in the background that looks like an Egyptian pyramid, from whose summit plunged in darkness, as Bonaparte said, the centuries look down upon us? Or on the opposite side, the sight of the pitch-black bulk of the ship *Soberano*, riveted, so to speak, to the serene waters of the bay? Do you not see how it stands out from the sky, where the stars are twinkling? Who would not say that instead of light they are shedding tears for the imminent disappearance of the last remains of our naval glories?"

"Fernando, that scene, so poetic to you, has no meaning whatsoever to me. Perhaps because I know it like the palm of my hand, or because I'm in a bad mood."

"To me, my boy, nature always holds me spellbound. In the presence of it I forget all my troubles. And by the way, have you read "A Sketch of My Visit to Mount Etna" in *El Diario*? Arazoza came to my house the other day in search of something original. He was persistent and I gave him my rough draft of it."

"I almost never see *El Diario*."

"Well, look it up and read it. It's a short article. It was published three or four days ago. I wrote it in Palermo. I didn't want to sign my name to it because it speaks badly of a certain municipal magistrate. You know the one I mean. It came out signed with only my initials, and can you believe that more than 20 friends have already come to congratulate me? It's true. Pedro José Morillas embraced me and praised the article to the skies. I want to hear your opinion."

"You may have asked me for it too late, Fernando. My head is on fire and I'm more inclined to shoot myself, or to shoot somebody else, than I am to read anything."

"I say! That surprises me. I don't recognize you. Are you the same student who attended philosophy class at the Colegio de San Carlos, or someone who has taken on your appearance? What has become of that good humor and that contagious happiness with which you earned the affection of all your classmates? Stop acting foolishly and childishly. Are you in love? That might lead to such inanities even after your 20 Aprils and more and all your experience . . ."

"It isn't the passion of love that is devouring my breast at present. It's the anger, the grief, the despair that stems from one's first disillusionment as regards the world, men, and friendship."

"Come, come. Why deny it? You're in love and it's unrequited. Your symptoms all indicate love. What is the real origin of your troubles? Share them with me. You know that I'm your friend."

"My friend!" the young man exclaimed with a sarcastic smile. "I thought you were, but I've been disillusioned and realize that you're my worst enemy."

"When does your disillusionment date from?"

"The same date as the underhanded trick you played on me. I don't know how you can keep the memory of it from gnawing at your vitals."

"Have you gone out of your mind? Come on, man! I get it now. All your rage stems from . . . Ha, Ha!"

"Don't laugh," Leonardo said gravely. "It's no laughing matter."

"What is it then?" the magistrate insisted. "For the first time since we've known each other, I've seen you being serious and . . . stupid."

"Don't call what borders on rage seriousness or stupidity."

"Stop acting childish at this late date. I appear to be the principal cause of your annoyance, and if you weren't so exasperated you'd see that, far from hating me, you should be grateful to me."

"That would be the last straw, if after having wounded me where it hurts me the most, you expect me to be grateful to you. How cheeky of you! Did you know that Cecilia Valdés was my mistress?"

"I learned it on the same day that, according to what you tell me, I played the underhanded trick of . . ."

"But before that, did you even know that she existed? Were you familiar with her character and background?"

"What would I have known about her! Not one thing."

"Then how, without knowing the facts, without a preliminary hearing, did you come to issue an arrest warrant?"

"Because there was someone who asked for it without my meeting such requisites."

"And you call such a procedure an act of friendship toward me?"

"You'll see."

"What crime is the girl accused of to justify such an outrage?"

"No other crime, as I understand it, save that of loving you too much."

"So you knowingly committed an injustice; let us say it straight out, an arbitrary procedure."

"I confess that I am guilty of that sin."

"Sin, you say? It's more than that. In our laws it is known as a quasi-crime, and it may blow up in your face. If certain people imagined that the sad orphan has no one to defend her, they're completely mistaken. I'm here, and I'll raise questions."

"You'll be making a mistake," the magistrate replied, his manner calm and dignified. "You'll be making a mistake, I repeat. As for me, your lance thrusts will do me no damage whatsoever; they will bounce off the coat of mail of my high position, my titles of nobility, and my favor here and at court. I for my part am immune. But you, by taking the path you speak of (I am speaking to you as a comrade and a friend), would succeed in doing nothing but cause a bit of scandal and place your father in a ridiculous position, since what you call my arbitrary procedure was based on his formal written complaint. Your father, your good and esteemed father, came to my tribunal and brought a complaint, in due and proper form, against that girl, for seducing a minor, the son of a rich and decent family, with her charms and wiles. In the discussion we had, he mourned, almost with tears in his eyes, the fact that you had become a wastrel, a gambler, a womanchaser; that you didn't study and wouldn't be able to receive your degree in April as he and your mother had been hoping, so as to take on the administration of the family properties next year, that is to say, after marrying the beautiful and virtuous young lady from Alquízar to whom you were engaged, all on account of that scatter-brained young girl, whose amorous relations are doubtless tarnishing the reputation of a young man who is to be a count before long."

"So that's the sum and substance of the story my father told you? Listen, or rather, look now at the reverse of the coin. There is no such seduction, deception, or anything like that involved in this affair. The girl is extremely pretty and adores me. Why would I not love her in return? But it turns out that ever since she was a little girl, Papa has been following her footsteps, keeping her, dressing her, buying her shoes, keeping a sharp eye on her, hovering over her, looking after her much more and much better than he has ever kept, dressed, shod, hovered over, and looked after any of his daughters. What for? To what end you will ask. Only he and God know. I don't want to think badly of him yet; but the fact that he abducted her at the very moment when her grandmother had just died, the only person who could place a serious obstacle in the way of his realizing perverted desires, makes me suspect that my father does not harbor the best of intentions . . . It puts my mind at rest and gratifies me, however, that no matter how much gold he rains down at the feet of the girl, he will not gain in return anything more than what he has already gained: her bitter hatred. But you, my friend, snatch her away from me for my own good and deliver her over, tied hand and foot, to my father's power. Should I forgive you for this foul trick? Never."

"You are being unjust, very unjust to your father and to me. To him, because I gave in to his pleas only when I had fully convinced myself that his intentions with regard to you, the family, and the Valdés girl herself were hallowed and honorable. You do me an injustice, because when I saw that your father was determined to cut off your clandestine relations with the girl, in any way he could, whatever the cost, I decided to have her confined to the Women's House of Correction for a brief period of time, let us say until you receive your bachelor's degree and marry as God wills and as befits your class and your family fortune. Then later on, if you care to, you can take up . . . your earlier love affair again."

Leonardo remained silent and thoughtful, and then he said lukewarmly: "Farewell, Fernando."

The latter held him back by the arm and replied: "You mustn't go off like that, as though we had quarreled. Come to my box: you'll say good evening to my wife and hear the second act of the opera at my side. To relieve certain pains there is no balm comparable to some good music."

VII

Jealousy, the greatest monster.

Calderón

How are you involved with a girl from the outskirts of the city?" Doña Rosa asked her husband while they were still in bed. "Tell me," she added, poking her elbow into his back because she thought he was playing dumb or pretending to be asleep.

"I don't have any involvement with anyone, Rosa," Don Cándido answered, half asleep.

"Yes you do, yes you do. I've been told as much; I have it from a reliable source."

"Who told you that tall tale?"

"It's not a tall tale; it's the truth. A few days ago you removed a young girl from her house . . . Who the person is who told me so is beside the point."

"No it isn't. There's someone who has a powerful influence over you."

"Then let's clear up that point. Nobody can keep me from believing that you've gone back to your old ways . . .

"You see what I was saying? They've prejudiced you against me. Your son . . ."

"Go ahead and blame my son."

"Your son, I'm saying," Don Cándido went on imperturbably, "was on the point of committing the worst of all the many reckless acts he's committed thus far. I stepped in, because I'm his father after all, and kept him from it . . . You don't allow anyone to lay a finger on *him*, so what other recourse did I have save to go after *her*? That, in short, is what my 'old ways' amount to."

"That's all I needed to hear! So in order to keep his son from doing something utterly stupid, his father goes and creates a scandal?"

"In this instance there wasn't a breath of scandal."

"What! So the matter was taken care of in secret then? So much the worse. Let's talk about what interest you had in it."

"No other interest, on my word, than that of keeping a really infamous act from being committed by a person as close to us as our own son is."

"What infamous act? You use certain blasphemous words . . ."

"Leonardo has been chasing after a girl of color for some time now."

"And how do you know that?"

"I know it for the same reason that you don't."

"That doesn't tell me anything. It's natural for Leonardito, a good-looking young man, to chase after girls, as you say. What doesn't seem natural is for you, who are old and ugly now, to be so well informed about the boy's skirt-chasing. Are you envious of him? Would you want him to become a monk? Why are you jealous of him?"

"Because I'm responsible for his conduct in the eyes of God and the world."

"Such virtue! Didn't you do the same thing and even worse when you were his age?"

"Perhaps I did the same thing as he's doing when I was a lad, but nothing worse; at least I have no pangs of conscience for having corrupted any decent young girl or one with close ties to the family."

"Good for you: forgive yourself. But it seems to me you're going to a great deal of trouble for nothing . . . I'll always believe that when it comes to women, Leonardito is as innocent as a suckling babe compared to you."

"Let's leave recriminations aside, Rosa, and get straight to the point, to what concerns us most as the boy's parents . . . It's no laughing matter; it's very serious . . . I found out . . . how or where or when doesn't matter one iota. I found out that he made large purchases of furniture and household odds and ends. He must have spent a fortune. Where did he get it from? Has he gone into debt? Has he made it by gambling?

Or . . . was it you, as easygoing as ever, who provided him with the means?"

Don Cándido had hit the nail on the head. Would Doña Rosa deny having lent her son the money because she had done so without her husband's knowledge? If she confessed, it would amount to discrediting the son in the eyes of his father, invariably inclined to look at his failings from the darkest possible side. Therefore, despite being convinced of and humiliated by the deceit of which she had been the victim, she preferred to tell the truth and take the blame for her favorite child's dissipation.

"Do you now see the evils that result from the blind affection of certain mothers for their sons, Rosa?" Don Cándido said without bitterness. "Don't you realize that in certain cases it is better to sin by being too hard on them rather than by being too complacent? Leonardo asks you for money and you lend it to him, because you can't say no to him, and because you imagine that if you refuse to lend it to him he'll die of grief. And he takes the money, buys furniture, rents a house . . . What the devil for? It's clear, perfectly clear: in order to take his mistress to it. It doesn't take great insight. And the result, if I'm not getting ahead of myself, is good-bye studies! Good-bye bachelor's degree! Good-bye marriage in November!, as you and I had agreed, with his consent."

"Everything you say is all well and good, but I'm hoping you'll say where you've hidden the girl away."

"In the Women's House of Correction . . . It seems to me," he added hastily, seeing that his wife had fallen silent and was tossing about in the bed, "it seems to me that this was the best and least risky course of action that could have been chosen to save the boy from the abyss and the girl from her ruin . . ."

"So you imagine then that because you've put the girl in the Women's House of Correction everything is now settled and over and done with?" Doña Rosa said. "I want you to know that you've accomplished nothing. The boy has taken the matter very much to heart. He's madly in love."

"Nonsense!" Don Cándido exclaimed in a scornful voice. "Love, love! Not the least little drop of it. What that lad feels is his blood seething, fever on the brain. His heart has nothing to do with it. Don't worry, he'll get over it."

"He'll get over it, will he? Perhaps. But the boy isn't eating or sleeping, he's suffering, he's grieving, he's upset, he keeps weeping. I fear that the price he'll pay for his feelings will be an illness. It's because you don't see all that, or hear it, or understand it that you speak the way you do."

"Put some of the blame on your own shoulders. It's up to you, who have more influence over him than I do, to console him and make him toe the line. I'll wager that you haven't told him that I'm waiting for the arrival of the next mail from Spain, bringing the title of Count of Casa Gamboa that our august sovereign has seen fit to grant me, have you? How much do you care to wager? The news may cheer him up."

"Cheer him up! How little you know your son! I did tell him. And do you know what his answer was? That nobility bought with the blood of blacks that you and the other Spaniards kidnapped in Africa so as to condemn them to eternal slavery was not nobility but infamy, and that he looked upon the title as the greatest shame . . ."

"Ah! The rogue, the rebel, the abject wretch!" Don Cándido burst out in a paroxysm of indignation. "His Creole blood really boils in his veins. The wicked scoundrel would be capable of starting a mass murder on account of his father, just as the utter disorder of the motherland was plotted in this Island. And they want freedom because the yoke is too heavy for them to bear! because they can't tolerate tyranny! Let the lazy loafers work and they won't have the time or the opportunity to complain about the best of governments. I would willingly beat them between the ears like mules . . ."

"Enough of your stupid remarks and vituperations," Doña Rosa cut him off angrily. "You run down Creoles as though my sons and I were from your country. Do you hate natives of Havana because it hurts your feelings that they pay you back in the same coin? Leonardito is partly right. You deprive him of everything he likes and takes pleasure in . . . I don't know how he manages not to give in to despair. He's counting on the fact that he'll do whatever is in his power to get the girl out of that place where she's confined . . ."

"As long as you don't give him money for bribes," Don Cándido said, giving a start, "I doubt very much that his attempt will succeed. Don't give him money, don't give it to him helter-skelter. But inasmuch as your affection consists of choking gifts down his throat, let us give him one of such quality that it will fill him with pride and make him feel ashamed of the abyss of baseness into which he was planning to descend."

"What gift is it that you hope will work that miracle . . . ?"

"The Soler house that Abreu won in a raffle is for sale. Let's buy it and furnish it for Leonardo when he marries Isabel. It's being sold for sixty thousand *duros*."

"Nearly the price of a plantation."

"The house is worth that much money. It's a palace; there's not another one like it in Havana. You mustn't worry about trifles: what's at stake is the salvation of your beloved son. The purchase and the furnishing of this splendid cage are my responsibility, and yours the domestication of the bird who is to occupy it."

Taking care of the planning and the paperwork, Don Cándido carried out his share of the responsibility without delay or difficulty. From the first steps on, however, as a consequence of her peculiar nature, Doña Rosa placed an insurmountable obstacle in the way of the implementation of the plan.

Hauteur and mistrust were components of Doña Rosa's character that played too great a role in her behavior for her to cease being frequently unjust and imprudent in her domestic relations . . . No one was more familiar with this weakness of his mother's than Leonardo. Once she announced to him the conditions that would apply with regard to the domestication project, all of them based on the understanding that he would give up Cecilia, he resolved to prejudice his mother against her husband by arousing to the utmost her jealousy as a wife. To do so, all that was necessary was to tell her, without naming his source, everything that he had heard from Cecilia regarding Don Cándido's suspicious clandestine dealings, beginning many years back, with the young girl and the old woman of the barrio of El Angel: the sums of money that he had continually spent on them with the largess or the prodigality of an elderly man in love; the strange interest that he had always taken in the support and the well-being of the two women; the vigilance that he had exercised over the girl and his concern for the health of the old woman; and finally, the constant efficacious services rendered him by Montes de Oca in these matters of questionable morality.

Each and every one of these revelations, together with others already mentioned, had reached Doña Rosa's ears at different periods and through various channels. Her son's belated and cleverly altered account merely served as a complement and a confirmation of what she already either knew only too well or merely suspected.

It seems pointless to add that in this case, as in all those of this sort, Leonardo's nefarious stratagem had the desired effect. For as vengeance or in retaliation, his mother, infuriated at his father because of his supposed persistent violation of his marriage vows plotted in secret with her son the planting of the mine that was intended to blow up the barricades erected by Don Cándido in defense of Cecilia Valdés's honor. Doña Rosa committed her money and her influence to the execution of their plot.

To aid her in the arduous undertaking, she laid down only three conditions: first, that her son continue his studies until he received his law degree; second, that he marry Isabel Ilincheta at the end of the year; and third, that he accept without grumbling the palace which, with that precise objective in mind, his father was giving him as a gift. Leonardo promised outright to fulfill all three.

The first step taken was to seek the services of María de Regla, the erstwhile nurse at La Tinaja, whose cleverness and talent both mother and son recognized by common accord, despite the ill will with which they regarded her. She consented most willingly to lend her services, as much because the role of conspirator was innate in her nature as because she promised herself to repay with good the many evils suffered at the hands of the two of them. The work of sapping began without delay.

Cecilia's admission to the Women's House of Correction brought on a veritable revolution. Her youth, her beauty, her laments, her tears, the reasons themselves for her imprisonment, supposed spells used to seduce a young white man from a family in Havana worth millions, all worked together to arouse the curiosity, the sympathy, or the admiration of the women of different colors and conditions who were serving periods of confinement of varying length.

However vulgar they might have been, however muted in their hearts the feeling of personal dignity, it was impossible for them to escape the influence of circumstances whose magic would exert its power in this sublunary world as it reflects the light of the sun. To all appearances, their sympathies and fits of admiration were of little avail to Cecilia; nonetheless, they were powerful enough to create around her that atmosphere of respect and consideration that contributed so much to alleviating her sorrows while she was confined in the Women's House of Correction, and which in the end opened its doors and enabled her to leave.

The keeper of these sheep gone astray was a lustful bachelor, a sort of lay brother in whom neither the passing of the years nor penance had tamed his human passions. To date, only women of low estate, old, ugly, and wasted away by their vices, had entered the institution of which he was in charge. Cecilia arrived, thereby increasing the number of inmates, under very different circumstances. Perhaps she had sinned; but surely not out of vice or evil inclinations. Her scant years, her decent, modest demeanor, her elegant air, and the mother-of-pearl of her smooth cheeks vouched for this. The sorrow, the shame of finding herself confined and thrown together with women known to be badly behaved, was doubtless what made her constantly burst into tears and lamentations. Such frequent and such great extremes of genuine grief were incompatible with crime.

So the keeper of the Women's House of Correction reasoned, and without further reflection declared himself Cecilia's champion and friend. It was his pleasure to go very late at night to the window of the cell that had been assigned her so as to contemplate her, in secret, in the course of her displays of emotion, fall even more madly in love with her and fly into fits of burning rage at her persecutors. He sometimes came upon her in her chair with her head and arms resting on the table, as she left to her abundant undone locks the task of covering those parts of her back that her loose-fitting garment was unable to hide from profane glances. At other times she suddenly raised her eyes and her joined hands heavenward and exclaimed in the greatest anguish:

"Dear God! Dear God! For what faults have I deserved this dreadful punishment?"

In each of these instances the keeper withdrew to his caretaker's lodge in a fury.

In one of these moments of generous indignation on his part, María de Regla appeared out of nowhere, on the pretext of selling fruits in season and preserves, a business in which she was engaged at the time. The man did not want to buy anything or get involved in a conversation that might distract him from his bittersweet thoughts. But this did not deter the peddler. She had been expecting, on the contrary, an even more definite rejection. She asked him in her usual honeyed voice:

"Does the señor have a headache or a toothache?" (She did not address him as "your grace".)

"I don't have any aches," he growled.

"I'm glad, because those two are the worst aches of all. Will the señor see if the inmates would like some fruit or sweets in syrup?

"We have no craving for fruit or sweets at present. Besides, there's no money anywhere in the place."

"I sell on credit."

"Go with God and leave me in peace."

"At other times they've bought fruit and sweets from me here."

"Not when I'm on duty. It must have been when the dolt who relieves me was here."

"Perhaps."

"I don't allow anyone to peddle things to the inmates. The rules prohibit any deals cooked up through the keeper."

"I've been told that the señor was goodness itself when it came to looking after the poor inmates."

"You've been misled. I'm bad, very bad."

"The señor isn't a bad man. Nothing of the sort! I can tell by his face that he's not."

"Enough. I'm not in the mood to chat with you."

"Very well. The one who's in charge gives the orders. I'll be off; but first will the señor be kind enough to hear the message that a young gentleman has just given me for him?"

"What's the message? Out with it," the keeper replied after looking long and hard at the peddler.

"Does the señor have a white girl imprisoned here?"

"I don't have anybody imprisoned. I'm not a jailer; I'm just a caretaker of the inmates, appointed by His Excellency the most illustrious Bishop Espada y Landa."

"I beg the señor's pardon. I meant to ask if there wasn't a white girl who has been admitted here."

"Yes, one that looks to be white at any rate. So?"

"Well, the young gentleman I'm talking about is very interested in that girl."

"What does his interest matter to me? It won't put food on my table."

"Don't be too sure of that! Because the young gentleman I'm talking about is very rich and very much in love with the girl. And the señor knows what a rich young gentleman is capable of when he's madly in love and is kept from seeking and speaking to his adored torment."

"We understand each other," the keeper said, a little more sympathetically. "What is it that the aforementioned young gentleman wants?"

"Very little. He wants the señor to give the girl these oranges he's sending her (choosing six from among the finest in her vendor's box), and to tell her that he is making every effort and spending a great deal of money to get her out of her confinement here as soon as possible."

"Good heavens!" the keeper stammered. "I've never played the role of go-between before."

"Come, señor, you won't regret it. Rest assured: the young gentleman is very rich, very much obliged to you, and very much in love."

The keeper, fearful, all atremble, hesitant, stood there for a long time, looking now at the black woman, now at the oranges. Finally he asked in a voice hoarse from fear or embarrassment:

"What is the young gentleman's name?"

"The girl knows what it is," María de Regla replied, and abruptly walked off.

The keeper stood there lost in thought, as though riveted to the grille just outside the caretaker's lodge. Shortly thereafter he barred the gate, locked it, and with three oranges in each hand entered the spacious courtyard of the Women's House of Correction.

There was everything that can fill a man in love with dreams, and a sorrowful woman with hope, in the brief conversation that the keeper had with Cecilia. There were the words: "You are my savior. What angel brought you to this poor persecuted woman? I am innocent. My only crime is dearly loving a young man who is dying of love for me. The father of the young gentleman of whom you are speaking to me has put me in here. All his wrath toward me is because I don't love him and instead love his son. Have pity on an unjustly persecuted woman."

The keeper left the courtyard a changed man. "To whom would it ever occur to bring a girl like that here?" he asked himself. "To the devil, only to the Evil One, so as to tempt peaceable people and bring them out of their shell. He would like to see strong men, the saints themselves in here. Would they resist? They would turn soft, they would melt, they would deliver themselves over to Satan's talons on their knees. Is there anyone who would have the courage to see her weep, to hear her moan and beg, and not stand up for her? She can do whatever she pleases with me. That's clear. And I will be in trouble with His Excellency the bishop, my protector; I will fall from his good graces; I will lose the post I have in this place. But what can I do? She is so pretty, she weeps, and I'm not made of wood. Confounded fruit peddler!"

The latter returned two or three days later, and the keeper of the House of Correction did not receive her rudely. She had a new objective: speaking alone with the inmate inside the prison. Visits inside the House of Correction were forbidden; it was possible to speak with the inmates only in the presence of the keeper, at the grille outside his lodge. But María de Regla cleverly argued the point, saying, among other things, that there was little likelihood that the keeper would let an innocent girl die of grief and thus be a party to the greatest of injustices ever committed thus far in Havana. She also said that the young gentleman, the girl's lover, had already carried out many of the necessary steps to get her out of confinement, and naturally he would not extend his gratitude to all those who had oppressed his adored torment. She then added immediately thereafter, as though she had suddenly remembered:

"The young gentleman gave me this half dozen doubloons for the señor, in case the girl needs something to eat, or to wear, or has some sudden craving . . ."

This last argument put an end to what was left of the keeper's virtue or his embarrassment. He allowed her to come inside. We shall now describe in a few words the scene that followed the meeting of the messenger and the prisoner.

María de Regla found Cecilia in the same position in which we have said previously that the keeper had surprised her a few days before; except that this time her hair hanging loose did not cover that part of her back facing the entrance to her cell. The former nurse noticed something there, which drew her concentrated attention.

"Heavens above!" she exclaimed. "What do I see? Can it be possible that this girl is the same one I suspected she was? The things that happen in this world!"

On hearing that voice and those incoherent exclamations, Cecilia raised her head and asked in a dejected, sorrowful voice:

"What is it you want?"

"I want your grace to tell me her baptismal name."

"Cecilia Valdés."

"Heavens above!" the black woman exclaimed once more. "Exactly the girl I thought she was. It's like a dream. Does your grace know who drew that half moon on her?"

"What half moon?"

"The one that your grace has on this shoulder" (touching the girl's left one with her index finger).

"It's not drawn on, it's a beauty spot, or rather, a mark I still have there from a blow I received in my childhood."

"No, if your grace is truly the Cecilia Valdés that I know, that is not a beauty spot, nor is it the mark of a blow: it's the half moon that your grace's grandmother drew on her with a needle and indigo dye before putting her in the Royal Foundling Home."

"Oh! Granny never told me about any such thing."

"I know about it because that was the sign they gave me so I could recognize your grace among the other babies in the Royal Foundling Home."

"Who are you to know so much about me?"

"Is it possible that your grace still doesn't recognize me? She should remember me."

"No, I truly don't."

"Well, I suckled your grace, first in the Royal Foundling Home and then later, for nearly a year, at the home of your grace's grandmother, when she lived in the Callejón de San Juan de Dios. Your grace had already taken her first steps and could say a few words in the days when they took her from my arms, and I will tell you no more. Ay! Your grace has no idea of the tears and sorrows it cost me to nurse you; not only me but my husband too. Yes, your grace has been the primary and principal cause of our misfortunes."

"What happened to the two of you?"

"I was sent away from Havana about 12 years ago, and my husband is in prison. They hold him responsible for the death of Captain Tondá."

"So it's as you say! And I am the unhappiest woman who treads this earth! Woe is me that without my having done harm to anyone, all of them fling themselves upon me!"

"Do not weep, do not grieve, my girl. Although your grace was the cause of our misfortunes, she is innocent; she is in no way to blame."

"Why wouldn't I weep and grieve, if after finding myself unjustly persecuted, then made a cause for scandal among the women confined in this house, who harass me with their questions and absurd remarks, you come along to top it all off, saying that you were my wet nurse, and throwing your misfortunes and your husband's in my face? Can there be any greater unhappiness than mine?"

"When I tell you my story, interwoven with your grace's, you will be convinced that I am quite right."

"But who are you?"

"My name is María de Regla, your grace's humble servant, and master Leonardo Gamboa's slave."

"Ah!" Cecilia exclaimed, rising to her feet and embracing the woman with whom she was speaking.

"Listen!" the latter said, with feeling. "Your grace recognizes me and embraces me as the slave of young master Leonardo, not as your grace's wet nurse, who I also am."

"No, I embrace you for both reasons, above all because your coming is the harbinger of my salvation."

The black woman folded her arms and began to contemplate Cecilia face to face. Every so often she murmured in a low voice: "Just look at you! The same forehead! The same nose! The same mouth! The same eyes! Even the same dimple in your chin. Yes, her air, her body, her demeanor, her very own charm! Imagine! The living portrait of her!"

"Portrait of whom?" Cecilia asked.

"Of my mistress Adela."

"And who is she?"

"My other suckling daughter, a sister of master Leonardo's, born of the same mother and father."

"So do I resemble her that closely? Some friends of mine who know her by sight have told me the same thing."

"And indeed there's a close resemblance between you. Twins wouldn't look more alike. Can that be why master Leonardo is so deeply in love with your grace? But he suffers and your grace sins by loving each other as you do. If you loved each other as friends or as brother and sister, that would be permissible; if you love each other as man and wife it's a sin. The two of you are in a state of mortal sin."

"Why do you tell me that?" Cecilia asked in surprise. "I don't know that it's a sin if a man and a woman love each other dearly."

"Yes, my girl, it's a sin; sometimes it can go as far as to be a black sin. On the one hand, he's white; but soon he'll be blue-blooded, because his father is Count of Casa Gamboa. And he has a palace to live in with the woman who will be his lawfully wedded wife. And your grace . . . I beg your pardon, my girl, for being so frank. Your grace is poor, lacks even one drop of blue blood and is the daughter . . . of the Foundling Home. There is no possibility that master Leonardo will be allowed to marry your grace."

"May he do whatever he's of a mind to do. Since he's a man and does what he pleases. And even if he doesn't, I'm sure he'll keep the promise he made me."

"He isn't able to keep it, my girl. Open your eyes. He won't be able to keep his promise even if he wants to."

"Why not?"

"Because he can't. When the time comes, your grace will know why. His marrying you is a dream; it won't come true . . ."

"So you're opposed to it. I don't understand the reason why."

"I'm not opposed to it, my girl. I'm not the one who's opposed, it's something else, it is nature, it is divine and human laws. It would be a sacrilege . . . But what am I saying? In any event it's too late. Tell me, my girl, what do you have in your eyes?"

"I don't have anything in my eyes," Cecilia replied, rubbing them innocently.

"Yes, I see something in them that's a bad sign. It looks to me as if your eyeballs have a yellow tinge. There's no doubt of it. Those circles under your eyes, that paleness, that sickly-looking face . . . Poor thing! Your grace is ill."

"Me ill! No, no," she said, very embarrassed.

"Your grace is already master Leonardo's wife."

"I don't understand what you're saying."

"Has your grace felt nauseated? Feeling as though she wanted to vomit?"

"Yes, several times. More often since I've been in this place. I attribute it to the fears and sorrows brought on by my unjust confinement here."

"I see! It's as plain as day. Didn't I tell you? The cause of your grace's illness is something else. I know what it is, I sense it. Doesn't your grace know that I've been a nurse for many years? That I'm married? There's nothing to be done about it. Nothing . . . Poor girl! Innocent! Unfortunate! That pretty little face that God has given you has done your grace a great deal of harm. If your grace had been born ugly, perhaps what is happening to her now wouldn't have happened. She'd be free and happy. But . . . what can't be helped is best forgotten. In a word, I'll tell master Leonardo about the state that your grace is in, and it's quite certain that he'll make haste to get your grace out of this accursed place."

Leonardo Gamboa was deeply affected by the latest news of Cecilia that the slave woman brought him. Losing no time, as the latter had foreseen, he met with his former classmate and friend, the municipal magistrate who had issued the arbitrary detention order, pointedly reminding him of their ties of friendship and of the present state of affairs. He likewise revealed to him in confidence the girl's delicate condition. He handed out money liberally on every hand and had the indescribable satisfaction of seeing his efforts crowned with total success around the last days of the month of April.

Cecilia was finally his, despite his father's stubborn opposition. Leonardo took her from the Women's House of Correction to the house that they had rented in the Calle de las Damas, giving her the same María de Regla as always to be her cook, trusted servant, and duenna. It seemed as though there was no happier man on the face of the earth. Even though all this was carried out without Don Cándido's knowledge, Leonardo had hidden nothing from Doña Rosa. From first to last he kept her informed of the steps that he was taking as each of them was taken. And, we regret to say, we do not know which of the two was more overjoyed by the denouement of the drama, the son or the mother. In this way an insuperable barrier was erected, she sincerely believed, between the girl and her husband's imprudent objectives.

In the midst of these scenes, Leonardo displayed unexampled good sense and willpower, taking the greatest care to fulfill the conditions of the secret agreement negotiated with his mother. He attended his law classes regularly, and as graduation day neared, he visited the professors who were to be his examiners, in particular Don Diego de la Torre, who had a reputation for strictness among the candidates for a degree: he buttered up Fray Ambrosio Herrera, the secretary of the university, whom he told in secret that instead of the usual three-*duro* tip he was planning to place three doubloons in each of the paper rolls of coins to be given him. He thus smoothed his path to receiving a degree; he thus managed to jam the traditional hood over his head, mount to the academic chair, place the red biretta on the crown of his head, pronounce an unintelligible discourse in Latin, and obtain the degree of bachelor of law, *nemine dissentiente*, on April 12, 1831.

Having fulfilled his obligations in this regard, he still had time to take formal possession of the palace that his father had given him as a gift. Immediately thereafter, with the intention of lulling the latter's vigilance, he hastened to go give a "little caress" to Isabel in her paradise at Alquízar, and try to arrange with her, if possible, the date and the details of their wedding.

He found her rather cold and downhearted. She was deeply repelled by the idea of witnessing, for the second time, the horrifying scenes at La Tinaja. Neither as a visitor, since both the opportunity and the desire would be lacking, nor as the mistress, since if as Leonardo's beloved she had been unable to put a stop to the terrible punishments dealt out to the blacks there, owing to a fateful necessity of the institution of slavery, she could hardly promise herself that as his lawfully wedded wife she could do away with them. And Leonardo, now taking these reasons of his friend to be mere nunlike scruples, now persuading himself that they might perhaps free him of a promise which was no longer heartfelt, he returned to Havana without having tried to overcome this unexpected difficulty.

Time had flown by with unbelievable swiftness. At the end of August Cecilia gave birth to a pretty baby girl, an event that, far from bringing joy to Leonardo, seemed only to make him feel the full weight of the grave responsibility that he had taken on in a moment of amorous ecstasy. That woman was not his wife, much less his equal. Could he introduce her anywhere without embarrassment, despite her being as pretty as a picture? As yet he had not descended so far down the gentle slope of vice as to wear the sackcloth of the penitent as though it were festive dress.

The dream of the easy possession of the coveted object that consisted only of the perishable quality previously mentioned was doubtless vanishing. Shame soon took the place of love. On its heels repentance was bound to make its appearance, and it did so at a gallop, long before it was to be expected, given the coldheartedness and moral laxity of which young Gamboa had given proof.

It did not take Cecilia long to painfully discover the first symptoms of the change; to complicate the situation, endless fits of jealousy then ensued. After three or four months of illicit union, Leonardo's visits to the house on the Calle de las Damas became less frequent and less prolonged. Of what use was it for him to shower gifts on his mistress, to anticipate all her likings and whims, if he was increasingly cold and reserved toward her, if he showed no pride or joy in his daughter, if he was never able to manage to exchange for even one night the house of his parents for his own house?

Leonardo's extreme behavior toward Cecilia can be explained by the great influence that his energetic mother exerted over him. Because even if it was certain that all the virtues had fled from the lad at the early age of 22, as timid doves flee from a dovecote struck by lightning, it was no less certain that her heart, as hard as marble, was still warmed by his tender filial love.

Doña Rosa, moreover, had learned during those days the true story of the birth, baptism, wet nursing, and paternity of Cecilia Valdés, now told to her by María de Regla with the aim of obtaining full pardon for her sins and a certain amount of help for Dionisio, who was still being held in close confinement. Horrified at the abyss into which she had plunged her son, the aforementioned lady said to him one day in a seemingly calm manner:

"I've been thinking, Leonardito, that the time has come to abandon that stupid, common girl . . . What do you think?"

"Good heavens, Mama!" the young man replied, shocked by the suggestion. "That would be a terrible thing to do."

"Nonetheless, it must be done," his mother added in a determined tone of voice. "Now, on to marrying Isabel."

"That too? Isabel no longer loves me. You've read her recent letters. In them she doesn't speak of love, only of taking the veil."

"Sheer nonsense! Don't pay any attention. I'll fix that in the wink of an eye. Things have changed. It's best that the first born son marry early, if only in order to ensure the legitimate inheritance of the title. On to marrying Isabel, I say."

By way of a letter from Don Cándido to Don Tomás Ilincheta, Doña Rosa asked for Isabel's hand for her son Leonardo, the presumptive heir to the title of Count of Casa Gamboa.

In reply, the presumed bride-to-be, accompanied by her father, sister, and aunt, came in due course to Havana and put up with Isabel's cousins, the Gámez sisters. Plans were then made to hold the wedding in early November, in the picturesque church of El Angel, since it was the most appropriate one, if not the one closest to the Gámez's own parish. The first of the three regular banns was published on the last Sunday of the month of October, after the San Rafael holiday.

There was naturally someone who told Cecilia the news of the coming marriage of her lover with Isabel Ilincheta. We abandon the task of depicting the tumult of passions that the news gave rise to in the breast of the proud and vengeful mulatto. Suffice it to say that in point of fact the lamb turned into a lion.

As night was falling on November 10, an old friend of Cecilia's whom she had not seen since becoming Leonardo's mistress, knocked at her door.

"José Dolores!" she exclaimed, bathed in tears as she threw her arms about his neck. "What good angel has sent you to me?"

"I've come," he replied, his tone of voice frightening and his face gloomy, "because my heart told me that Celia might need me."

"José Dolores! José Dolores my dearest! That marriage must not take place."

"No?"

"No."

"Then my Celia may count on its not taking place."

Without further ado, he freed himself from her arms and left the house. A few moments later Cecilia, with her hair hanging down limply and her dress unbuttoned, ran to the door and shouted once more: "José! José Dolores! *Her*, not *him*!"

A useless admonition. The musician had already rounded the corner of the Calle de Las Damas.

Numerous candles and tapers were burning on the high altar of the church of Santo Angel Custodio. Several people could be seen leaning on the parapet of the wide landing at the top of the two stone staircases. A large group of ladies and gentlemen whose carriages were waiting down below was mounting the staircase overlooking the Calle de Compostela. The bride and groom were just setting foot on the top stair when a man who had come up the other stairway, with his hat pulled down to his eyebrows, crossed the landing diagonally and met up with Leonardo in his effort to reach the south side of the church before the latter, finally disappearing from sight on that side.

Leonardo raised his hand to his left side, gave a muffled moan, tried to lean on Isabel's arm, and collapsed at her feet, spattering her gleaming white silk wedding gown with blood.

Grazing his arm at the height of his nipple, the tip of the knife had penetrated straight to his heart.

Conclusion

Far from her being placated by the conviction that Cecilia Valdés was her husband's illegitimate daughter and therefore the half sister of her unfortunate son, that very fact seemed to kindle Doña Rosa's wrath and arouse her violent desire for vengeance. Hence she pursued the girl with veritable bloodthirstiness, and it was not difficult for her to have the young woman brought to trial for Leonardo's murder and sentenced as an accomplice to a year's confinement in Paula Hospital. These were the paths whereby mother and daughter met at last, recognized each other and embraced, the mother having recovered her sanity, as those who are mad generally do, only moments before her spirit abandoned its wretched human envelope.

As for Isabel Ilincheta, disabused of the illusion that she would find happiness or peace of soul in the society within which it was her destiny to have been born, she withdrew to the convent of the Teresian or Carmelite nuns, and there took her final vows at the end of a year's novitiate.

After Rosa married Diego Meneses, she tried her best to replace her elder sister in the affections of her father and her aunt, going to live with them in the Eden of Alquízar.

The criminal charge brought against Dionisio for the murder of Tondá did not come up for trial until five years after the events here related. The tribunal sentenced him to ten years' imprisonment at hard labor, and the renowned Don Miguel Tacón[55] sent him to the penal colony of Havana to be put to work at paving streets.

The End

Notes

1. The titles of the works cited here by Villaverde translate as follows: *The Girl with the Golden Arrow; The Blind Man and His Dog; The Excursion to Vuelta (A)Bajo; The Fretwork Ornamental Comb; The Cuban Peasant; Two Loves; The Missionary of El Caroni; The Penitent*.

2. References are to *Paul et Virginie* (1788) by Bernadin de Saint Pierre; and to *Atala* (1801) and *René* (1802) by François-René Chateaubriand.

3. This dialogue, like many others in the novel, represents the vernacular spoken by Cubans (often people of color) with little formal education. One of its characteristics was the use of hypercorrections that are almost impossible to render into English.

4. *Señá* (or *seña*) is a shortened form of *señora* (as *señó* is of *señor*). According to Rodríguez Herrera, it was commonly used in Cuba to address older, respectable women of color and needs to be distinguished from *ñá*, which was used to address women of color of a lower station, including slaves. Elsewhere the woman who is here addressed as *Señá Josefa* is called *ñá Chepilla*, Chepilla being a affectionate version of Chepa, short for Josefa.

5. Normally, children born outside of marriage were given the mother's name, which in this case would have been Alarcón. Gamboa's decision to make the child pass through the Orphanage named after Bishop Gerónimo Valdés—which meant that she would be given the last name Valdés—thus might seem capricious and unnecessary (Rodriguez Herrera). One possible explanation is that according to Spanish law foundlings were to be registered as "seemingly white" (Martínez-Alier 72 and 84). This is documented for the late eighteenth century, and it would seem likely that the practice was still in place in 1812. It

would explain why Gamboa associates the name Valdés with the possibility of an advantageous (meaning, in all likelihood, white) marriage, although later on her identity as a *mulata* is never a real question.

6. The first constitutional period was 1812–1814; the second constitutional period began in 1820 and was effectively over in 1823. Francisco Dionisio Vives took over as Captain General of Cuba on May 2, 1823; his rule lasted until 1832.

7. According to Rodríguez Herrera, "lunitas" was a children's game that involved jumping up and down a lot and reciting a nonsensical nursery rhyme that began with "Lunita, Lunera. . . ."

8. Bishop Espada y Landa was born and educated in Spain under the influence of leading figures of the Spanish Enlightenment; he introduced important educational and architectural reforms in Cuba.

9. The *pesote columnario* was a silver coin that was introduced in the Spanish American colonies in the eighteenth century. It owed its name to the picture of two crowned columns on the back.

10. *Bailes de cuna* were balls organized by lower class people of color, often in conjunction with *ferias*. Usually they were small, informal events.

11. El Angel Hill (in Spanish "La loma del Angel") was a small hill in the north of the old center of Havana. It was considered particularly picturesque. Located at the highest point of the hill was the church Santo Angel Custodio. Most of the events in the novel take place in the area surrounding this hill, hence the subtitle. Today the hill is almost imperceptible because of urban development.

12. In Spanish, the term of endearment used here is *china*, which denotes some racial mixture (therefore rendered as "halfbreed" here), but is also used, whatever the color of the interlocutors may be, to express familiarity and fondness.

13. The *décima* is the 10-line stanza of classical Spanish verse.

14. Vicente Escobar (1757–1834) was Cuba's most popular portraitist in the early nineteenth century. He enjoyed cordial relations with the colonial administration and the local aristocracy. He accumulated some wealth and had several slaves. While Escobar's birth was listed in the register for people of color, his death appeared in the register for whites. He was sent to Spain to perfect his skills by Captain General Vives; there he was awarded the title *Painter of the Royal Chamber*. In Cuba, however, he was never admitted as a teacher to the Academy San Alejandro, which was founded in 1818, as part of the Creoles' attempt to wrest the pictorial arts from the artisans of color. In fact, his style, which did not conform to the conventions of academic painting, fell out of fashion with the liberal Creoles when European painters were brought to Cuba to teach their artistic techniques.

15. Roman as well as old Spanish law distinguished between those who were born free and those who were given freedom or were descendents of the latter (Rodríguez Herrera).

16. "Cinnamon" and "coal" were terms characteristic of male language use in Cuba, referring to *mulatas* and black women, respectively.

17. All the names listed are historical: Eduardo Facciolo y Alba was executed in 1852 for his collaboration in the publication of the revolutionary newspaper *La voz del pueblo cubano*; General Narciso López, the annexationist whose cause Villaverde joined in the 1840s, was executed in 1850 after a failed invasion of Cuba; Ramón Pintó was from Catalonia and was executed in 1855 for conspiring for Cuban independence; Francisco Estrampes was one of Pintó's co-conspirators and was executed the same day as Pintó. The reference to "innocent students" is to November 27, 1871, when eight Cuban students were executed by the Spanish authorities for what appeared to be a minor infraction.

18. Félix Varela was born in 1778 in Havana. As a priest and professor of philosophy of relatively progressive orientation, he exercised considerable influence over young Cuban intellectuals at the time. He died in exile in the United States in 1853.

19. José Antonio Saco (1797–1879) was one of Cuba's most prominent writers and intellectuals. An ardent supporter of Cuban independence, he was forced into exile by the Captain General Tacón in 1834. Although Saco is usually counted among Cuban abolitionists, he was more concerned with the slave trade and the dangers of a race revolution on the model of Haiti than racial slavery itself. Among Saco's most important works are *Historia de la esclavitud desde la antigüedad hasta nuestros días* and *Historia de la esclavitud de la raza africana en el Nuevo mundo y en especial en los países américo-hispanos*. He died in exile in Madrid.

20. The famous poet José María Heredia (1803–1839) was born in Santiago de Cuba. His family, of Dominican origin, had fled ahead of Toussaint Louverture's invasion of Santo Domingo in 1801. For most of his life he lived in exile in Florida, Venezuela, and Mexico.

21. Celia is a familial short form of Cecilia.

22. The titles mentioned here translate as follows: "The Star of Cuba," "To Emilia," "Hymn of the Exile."

23. José Antonio Aponte was a free black man of considerable standing in the Afro-Cuban community. In 1812 he was accused of being the head of a vast conspiracy whose goal it was to overthrow the slaveholding regime and transform Cuba into a black state on the model of Haiti. He and his co-conspirators, which included both slaves and free people of color, were executed; their heads were exhibited in public places around town. The transcripts of the Aponte trials have been published and are among the most fascinating accounts of the ideology of revolutionary antislavery and Afro-Cuban culture in the early nineteenth century (see José Luciano Franco, *Las conspiraciones de 1810 y 1812*. Habana: Ciencias Sociales, 1977).

24. In 1817 Spain and England had signed a treaty banning the slave trade.

This treaty came into effect in 1820. This meant that after 1820, the slave trade was illegal, and therefore both more risky and potentially more lucrative.

25. This is a reference to the Battle of Tampico of 1829, in which the Mexicans defeated an attempt by Barrada's troops to retake Mexico for Spain, years after the former had declared independence.

26. While Cándido Gamboa is a fictional character, Pedro Blanco, who appears several times in this novel, is a historical figure. He became known as one of the most successful and ruthless slave traders of the nineteenth century (see William Luis 163–184).

27. The *totí* is a Caribbean bird with black plummage and a curved beak.

28. Plácido (1809–1844) was the pseudonym of Gabriel de la Concepción Valdés, a mulatto poet who was executed during the repression that followed the Escalera Conspiracy (see Introduction). He was quite popular with the colonial aristocracy, while the liberal elite tended to consider his poetic production vacuous and incorrect. Rodríguez Herrera points out that Plácido would have been ten at the time of the event described here; he may therefore not be the actual author of the poem.

29. Jean Baptiste Vermay was a student of the French painter Jacques-Louis David. After Napoleon's fall, Vermay fled and settled in Louisiana. Bishop Espada invited him to Cuba to carry out his architectural reforms (see note 8). Vermay was also the founder of Cuba's first art academy, San Alejandro, in 1818.

30. "The Fifteenth of August."

31. The poet is Ramón de Palma. The stanza quoted here comes from his poem "Quince de Agosto," which is mentioned earlier in the present chapter (Rodríguez Herrera).

32. The church Nemesia here refers to is Santa Catalina, not Santa Catarina. Villaverde is marking Nemesia's speech as popular and slightly incorrect by having her confuse the *l* and the *r*.

33. "Scenes in sight of El Moro, Havana."

34. Salvador Muro y Salazar, Count of Someruelos, govenor of Cuba 1799–1812.

35. A verse form that consists of octets of verses with 11 or 12 syllables and is based on a rhythmic rather than a syllabic pattern. It was first used by court poets in the fourteenth and fifteenth century.

36. The 1817 treaty between Spain and Britain provided for the complete cessation of the slave trade by 1820. It gave Britain the right to search suspected Spanish slave ships and impound vessel and cargo if slaves were found. Special tribunals were set up in Havana and Sierra Leone to resolve disputes (the so-called Mixed Commission that is mentioned several times in this novel).

37. See note 23.

38. The Spanish term here translated as "throwback" is *saltoatrás*, literally "leap back." It can only be understood within an ideology in which human value

and social progress is measured by whiteness, an ideology that is of course operating in the society depicted in *Cecilia Valdés*. Here is the definition Esteban Pichardo gives in his *Diccionario provincial de voces cubanas* (Matanzas: Impr. de la Real marina, 1836): "a person who instead of further refining his or her African origin which is by birth already almost white, regresses by mixing with the black race." Rodríguez Herrera gives a slightly different definition: "a *mestizo* with the atavistic characteristics of only one race" and adds a remarkable, almost two-page long footnote of racialist speculations about inheritance and attempts to assess whether or not Cecilia's worries and hopes are justified by biological reality.

39. On the Escalera Conspiracy, see Introduction and, for more details and an account of the political conflicts of the 1830s and 1840s, Paquette, *Sugar Is Made with Blood*. Juan Francisco Manzano, too, was imprisoned several times during the repression of the Escalera Conspiracy. Two minor errors in Villaverde's otherwise correct account: Plácido's given name was Gabriel (not José) de la Concepción Valdés; and Dodge was a dentist, not a carpenter.

40. Like many of the other secondary characters in *Cecilia Valdés*, the slave hunter Francisco Estévez is a historical figure. In fact, Cirilo Villaverde was in possession of Estévez's diary, which had come into his hands through his father, who had been member of a committee in Pinar del Río that oversaw the activities of local slave hunters. Villaverde transcribed and amended the text and wrote a preface for it that was published separately at the time. The text of the diary is now available under the title *Diario del rancheador*, usually listed with Francisco Estévez as the author, sometimes without a mention of Villaverde's role in the production of the text.

41. A *Novena* is a nine-day prayer cycle in the Roman Catholic church; it is here applied to nine consecutive days of punishment.

42. *A nativitate* (lat.) from birth, by nature.

43. This appears to be a pun. Tomasa is, we are told, an African-born Suamo; in Spanish, however, the term that designates her ethnic origin could be read as "su amo," which means "her master."

44. *Ipso iure* (lat.) by law.

45. A Cuban beverage made of molasses, water, and hot pepper. *Translator's note.*

46. Terence: "I am a man; nothing human is alien to me." *Translator's note.*

47. See note 23.

48. An alloy consisting of a very small proportion of gold, adulterated with copper, zinc, or other metals; often used to make cheap jewelry. *Translator's note.*

49. This dialogue between the Catalan tavernkeeper and the *curro* Malanga mixes Catalonian words and expressions, corrupt Spanish, and the sociolect of the *curros*. Like some of the other popular characters in this novel, the curro tends to say *l* for *r*. As to the untranslated Catalan words: *Porta* door, *bom deu*

good God, *diable* devil, *mare de deu* mother of God, *meus dines* my money, *boutelle* bottle, *volte* change, *caridat* charity.

50. (*Lat.*) The pain of the man who weeps without witnesses is real. *Translator's note.*

51. Villaverde appears to be making a distinction here that would imply that there are no black peasants in Cuba. As a matter of fact, this is false. However, there is a racially inflected ideology attached to the figure of the "guajiro"—the Cuban peasant—which makes him out to be of purely European descent.

52. The *Study on Idleness* (*Memoria sobre la vagancia*, 1832) is one of Saco's best-known texts. In it, Saco pillories gambling and various other forms of socially unproductive behavior (typical for a slaveholding society where labor is the domain of slaves) and discusses ways the white population could be encouraged to take up useful professions.

53. *Patria potestas* is a term used in Roman law to signify the power a father has over his children, grandchildren, and other descendants, and generally all the rights he has by virtue of his paternity.

54. Originally, the *Casa de las Recogidas* (Women's House of Correction) took in poor, abandoned, or divorced women as well as female delinquents; at the time of this novel, the institution had been ceded to Ursuline nuns and the female prisoners had been moved elsewhere.

55. Miguel Tacón, Captain-General of Cuba 1834–1838.

Bibliography

1. SELECTED WORKS BY CIRILO VILLAVERDE

Narratives:

La cueva de Taganana; La peña blanca; El ave muerta; El Perjurio (brief stories, 1837)

El espetón de oro (short romantic novel, 1838)

Engañar con la verdad (description of Cuban Carnival, 1838)

A Don Quitín Suzarte desde las Sierras del Aguacate (description of region of Aguacate, in letter format, 1838)

Excursión a la Vuelta Abajo, part I (travel narrative and description of local customs, 1838–39)

La cruz negra; Amoríos y contratiempos de un guajiro; Lola y su periquito (brief stories, 1839)

Teresa (sketch for a novel, 1839)

Cecilia Valdés (brief narrative, 1839)

Cecilia Valdés o La loma del Angel, vol. 1 (expanded version of the brief narrative of 1839, also 1839)

La joven de la flecha de oro (Historia habanera) (short romantic novel, 1840)

Amor fraternal; Equivocación de nombres (brief narrative, 1840)

El guajiro (description of local culture; written 1842, published 1890)

Dos amores (novel of customs, 1843)

La tejedora de sombreros de yarey (narrative sketch for a novel, 1843)

Excursión a la Vuelta Abajo, part II (travel narrative, 1843)

El penitente (historical novel set in Havana in the eighteenth century, 1844)

La peineta calada (brief narrative, 1845)
Comunidad de nombres y apellidos (first and only volume of a novel, 1845)
El librito de cuentos y las conversaciones (children's literature, 1847)
Cecilia Valdés o La Loma del Angel (novel, 1882)

Politics and Geography:

Compendio geográfico de la Isla de Cuba (geography pamphlet, 1845)
To the Public (General López, the Cuban Patriot) (short pamphlet in defense of
    Narciso López, 1851)
El señor Saco con respecto a la revolución de Cuba (attack on José Antonio Saco's
    pro-Independence stance, defense of the annexation of Cuba to the
    United States, 1852)
La revolución de Cuba vista desde Nueva York (pro-Independence pamphlet, writ-
    ten in New York, 1869)
*Apuntes biográficos de Emilia Casanova de Villaverde, con parte de su larga corre-
    spondencia política* (a brief biography of Villaverde's wife, a political ac-
    tivist, and extensive collection of her letters on matters of politics; New
    York, 1874).

Edition:

Transcription and introduction of *Diario del rancheador* [Diary of the Slave
    Hunter] by Francisco Estévez. Original diary 1837–42. First publication
    of Villaverde's edition unclear. Reprinted in Roberto Friol (ed.), *Diario
    del rancheador*. Havana: Letras Cubanas, 1982.

Translations:

Dickens, Charles. *Autobiografía de David Copperfield*. 3 vols. 1857.
Pollard, Edward Albert. *Historia del primer año de la guerra del Sur* (a history of
    the U.S. Civil War, 1863)
Mühlbach, Luisa. *María Antonieta y su hijo. Novela histórica* (historical novel,
    1878)

For more titles, publication details, and reprints, see Imeldo Álvarez
(ed.), *Acerca de Cirilo Villaverde*, 419–25, or the Spanish language editions
of *Cecilia Valdés* listed below. None of the bibliographies of Villaverde's
works claims to be complete.

2. CRITICAL EDITIONS OF
CECILIA VALDÉS O LA LOMA DEL ANGEL

Ed. Esteban Rodríguez Herrera. Havana: Ed. Lex, 1953.
Ed. Olga Blondet Tudisco and Antony Tudisco. New York: Las Américas Pub-
    lishing, 1964.

Ed. Raimundo Lazo. México City: Porrúa, 1972.
Ed. Noel Navarro. Havana: Letras Cubanas, 1977.
Ed. Imeldo Álvarez García. Havana: Letras Cubanas, 1979.
Ed. Iván Schulman. Caracas, Venezuela: Biblioteca Ayacucho, 1981.
Ed. Jean Lamore. Madrid: Cátedra, 1992.

3. FURTHER READINGS

Álvarez, Imeldo (ed.), *Acerca de Cirilo Villaverde*. Ciudad de La Habana, Cuba: Editorial Letras Cubanas, 1982.

Bueno, Salvador. *Temas y personajes de la literatura cubana*. Havana: Ediciones Union, 1964.

Carpentier, Alejo. *Music in Cuba*. Ed. Timothy Brennan. Trans. Alan West-Durán. Minneapolis: University of Minnesota Press, 2001.

Deschamps Chapeaux, Pedro, and Juan Pérez de la Riva. *Contribución a la historia de la gente sin historia*. Havana: Ed. Ciencias Sociales, 1974.

Foner, Philip Sheldon. *A History of Cuba and Its Relations with the United States*. 2 vols. New York: International Publishers, 1962–63.

Fornet, Ambrosio. *El libro en Cuba: siglos XVIII y XIX*. Havana: Editorial Letras Cubanas, 1994.

Friol, Roberto. "La novela cubana en el siglo XIX." *Unión* 6, no. 4 (1968), 179–207.

González, Reynaldo. *Contradanzas y latigazos*, Havana: Letras Cubanas, 1983.

Henríquez Ureña, Max. *Panorama histórico de la literatura cubana*. New York: Las Americas Publishing, 1963.

Martínez-Alier, Verena. *Marriage, Class, and Colour in Nineteenth-Century Cuba: A Study of Racial Attitudes and Sexual Values in a Slave Society*, 2nd. ed. Ann Arbor: University of Michigan Press, 1989.

Moreno Fraginals, Manuel. *The Sugarmill: The Socioeconomic Complex of Sugar in Cuba, 1760–1860*. Trans. Cedric Belfrage. New York: Monthly Review Press, 1976.

Ortiz, Fernando. *Cuban Counterpoint: Tobacco and Sugar*. Trans. Harriet de Onís. New intro. Fernando Coronil. Durham: Duke University Press, 1995.

Paquette, Robert, L. *Sugar Is Made with Blood: The Conspiracy of La Escalera and the Conflict between Empires over Slavery in Cuba*. Middletown: Wesleyan University Press, 1988.

Thomas, Hugh. *Cuba or The Pursuit of Freedom*. New York: Harper & Row, 1971.